of love & life

ISBN 978-0-276-44222-3

www.readersdigest.co.uk

The Reader's Digest Association Limited, 11 Westferry Circus, Canary Wharf, London E14 4HE

# of love & life

Three novels selected and condensed
by Reader's Digest

The Reader's Digest Association Limited, London

CONTENTS

glamour
louise bagshawe

Three beautiful, powerful women—
all-American Texas honey, Sally Lassiter;
bookish English rose, Jane Morgan;
and shy, serene Jordanian, Helen Yanna.
Once best friends . . . now deadly rivals.

Prologue

GLAMOUR

The name was written in brass letters, each one sixteen feet high, polished like a mirror. They glittered on the front of the store like solid gold, sparkling in the California sun, like a permanent firework.

What a store! In Hollywood, the city of the stars, GLAMOUR said it all. A landmark attraction since the day it first opened, the new building was a must-see on every tourist itinerary, a monument to luxury, money and power. At GLAMOUR, shopping was an exquisite pleasure. Once you entered its doors, the cares of the day fell away. You were in another world; soft carpeting underfoot, exquisite fresh flowers at every corner, assistants to wait on your every need. Every shopping trip was a vacation, and around the world, women with money just couldn't get enough. If you bought so much as a hairband in GLAMOUR, somebody would wrap it in the iconic triple-G tissue paper, tie it with mint-green ribbons, and carry it to your car—should you so desire.

They loved it. And the women who had founded it were set to become among the richest in the world. Everybody knew their story.

Three women. Beautiful, powerful and rich.

And, it seemed, absolutely ruthless.

Once they had been the closest of friends. Once, they had all suffered. And, together, they had triumphed.

So how had it gone so wrong?

'It's the Princess!' The little girl tugged on her mother's coat sleeve. 'Look, Momma! It's her. There she is!'

Her mother, Coco, leaned over the velvet rope that flanked the red carpet. Keisha's childish enthusiasm was infectious. She hoisted her daughter up on her shoulders, so the girl could get a better look.

Across the street was a gaggle of media reporters, cameramen and boom mike holders. Two TV news choppers whirred overhead. These three young women were legendary. America—and the world—was watching this meeting. Coco turned towards the limo as the LAPD shouted, motioning for everybody to get back. The security men swarmed around the gleaming black vehicle. There were olive-skinned soldiers, the palm tree of Ghada emblazoned on the chest of their uniforms. Mingling with them, brawny Americans—the Secret Service.

A man stepped forward and opened the back door of the limo.

A slippered foot emerged, swathed in embroidered gold thread. It was followed by the swish of a floor-length robe in butterscotch silk, modest, self-assured and beautiful. The woman stood up; she wore a simple veil across her hair, secured with a solid semicircle of polished gold; her aquiline face was calm and confident.

'She's so beautiful,' Keisha gasped.

The crowd recovered from its fit of awe. 'Princess Haya!'

'Haya, over here! Highness!'

The gold-robed vision waved; to the dismay of her handlers, she strode up to the barriers, shaking hands and greeting the crowd.

Keisha clapped her hands. 'You're a real live princess!' she shouted.

And as Coco watched, Princess Haya laughed, reached forward, and gave the little girl a big hug.

'And so are you,' she replied. Then she turned smartly, and walked up the red carpet, silken robe fluttering in the light breeze.

'Miz Nelson.'

'Yes?' Sally shouted back. She had to shout—the whirring of the chopper blades was just too loud.

'If you look to your left, ma'am,' the pilot bellowed, 'you can see the store. We'll be landing in just a second.'

'Great!'

Sally shook her long blonde hair smoothly down her back. It was a shimmering curtain of platinum, expertly coiffed on Fifth Avenue. She snapped open her Hermès Kelly bag and removed a compact mirror. Too fabulous for words! No wonder it had been the hit of spring's accessory line. Customers couldn't get enough of that Sally, GLAMOUR

magic. And whatever the other two said, *she* was the one who knew
how to give it to them.

Sally examined her face critically, looking for flaws. But there were
none. Her body was lithe—a personal trainer worked it out daily—and
her dress was French Riviera chic—a Pucci print with a white silk jacket
over the top, designed just for Sally. Sassy, cool and irreverent, she carried
it with her Kelly bag and trademark Manolos. Throw in a large pair of tortoiseshell glasses and she was the living spirit of summer.

Sally knew she looked like a star. But then again, she *was* one. She
leaned across the soft leather seats of her personal helicopter and
looked down on the crowd milling outside the GLAMOUR red carpet.
They were her fans—the fans of the dream. The other two girls, well,
they'd just helped with the mechanics.

Sally Nelson was the star here. The all-American icon, blonde hair,
tanned skin, healthy California lifestyle, and oh, yes, the small matter
of a billion dollars or two. GLAMOUR. That was her, wasn't it? Not
bookish Jane, or regal Haya—who, let's face it, had taken herself out of
the game. It was her store, her dream. They had named it after Sally!

Of *course* GLAMOUR should be hers.

'**P**lease remain seated until the airplane has ground to a complete halt,'
said the steward.

Jane Morgan had already unbuckled her belt and jumped to her feet.

'Ma'am, please take your seat,' he said uncomfortably.

'Please get out of my way.' She turned to him, her famous emerald
eyes cool. 'This flight was delayed for four hours.'

She snapped open the overhead locker and retrieved her laptop bag,
oblivious of the other first-class passengers' stares.

'You're defying FAA regulations.'

'Correct. I don't pay ten thousand dollars for a first-class ticket in
order to be prevented from doing my job. I have a meeting. And I'm
late.' She made it sound like a terminal condition.

He heard himself almost pleading. 'It'll just be a minute . . .'

There was a small shudder, and the plane docked with the exit
tunnel. Jane Morgan was already standing by the door. First in line.

The steward smiled weakly at the passengers shoving past him. He
sure wouldn't like to be on the opposite side of the table at that lady's
meeting. She should come with a government safety warning.

'**H**ighness, I must advise against it.'

Ahmed al-Jamir, the Embassy's special adviser, leaned across the table, his dark eyes intent on Haya's. 'Your position—'

'I am a member of the board,' Haya said mildly.

'I meant your *royal* position. This business stuff can be left to others. You should simply sell your stake. What is the point?'

'The point is that GLAMOUR is *my* company. It's *my* store. And I haven't forgotten that.' Even if the others had.

He was ready to weep. The Princess would be Queen one day, maybe one day soon. Her husband controlled countless billions, a major army. Haya had her pick of no less than sixteen separate palaces, more jewels than she could wear. For all its high-profile branding, this company was nothing. Nothing!

He lowered his voice and said as much. They both knew what he really meant. It was unseemly for a princess of Ghada to be playing around in American business! It demeaned Prince Jaber. It lowered the royal house!

'When I married His Highness, I told him I had no intention of surrendering my past life. I founded this company. I began its spirit. Something Sally and Jane apparently want eliminated. You need not fear; today will be the very last day I spend in the world of business. I know my duty.'

She tugged her silken robes a little tighter round her shoulders, and the diplomat was impressed. Whatever her origins, Haya al-Jaber bore herself as though the crown were on her head already.

'But you and everyone else needs to understand something. *I will not let them destroy this place.* Today is the last meeting. And I'm going to make it count.'

Sally blew one last kiss to the crowds, waving just the tips of her manicured fingers at them. 'Thank you all *so much!*'

She crossed the red carpet to where the media were waiting. Flashbulbs popped like fireworks; a forest of boom mikes jostled towards Sally's face. The Arabian princess had cut them dead, but so what? Sally was the real golden girl! The reporters shoved forwards.

'Sally! Is it time to get your revenge?'

'Are you here to take control?'

'What do you have to say to the fans?'

That last one was a perfect softball. Sally turned to camera. 'I want to thank them for their love and support! I couldn't do it without you guys!' she purred.

'What're your plans, Sally?'

'You know how much I love GLAMOUR! So don't y'all worry,

because I'm here to see everything works out *just fine.*'

'But Princess Haya! Jane Morgan!'

'I love those ladies,' Sally said. 'But everyone knows that GLAMOUR is Sally Nelson! Now, if you'll excuse me, I have to get to work.'

She blew another kiss, pirouetted on her Manolos, and sashayed up the red carpet while the doormen saluted.

'It's coming up ahead, Miz Morgan.'

'I know where the store is,' Jane said shortly. She examined the letters from her bankers.

'Shall I take you out front?' Her driver peered ahead. 'There sure is a big crowd.'

'No. Make a left here.'

'A left?'

Was he deaf? 'Yes,' she snapped.

'But GLAMOUR—'

'We're not going to GLAMOUR. We're going to the storage warehouse. There's a closed parking lot between the warehouse and the offices.'

'You don't want anybody to see you,' he said, slowly clocking on. In the rearview mirror he watched the chestnut hair, a neat bob, as tight as she was. He'd seen porcupines with less prickles.

But Jane Morgan paid real good, and at Christmas his bonus could run into thousands of dollars. He swallowed and shut up. So she didn't fraternise. That was OK. Everybody that worked for Morgana, Inc. knew who the boss was.

'Yes, ma'am, you got it,' he said.

Two minutes later he had dropped America's toughest new business-woman, queen of the Dow Jones, at the back of the warehouse. He watched as she marched off, between the enormous trucks full of GLAMOUR goodies, through the parking lot.

Most thought this was her last stand. That it was all over. Not him. He'd never bet against Jane Morgan.

The boardroom crackled with energy. The long mahogany table was packed. Rows of men and women in dark suits, high-priced lawyers, investment bankers and Mergers & Acquisitions sharks, all toying with their pads and Montblanc pens, or pretending to read their figures. Round the head of the table, on the left, sat Princess Haya, her security men hanging back behind her chair, cradling their guns.

Directly opposite her, Sally Nelson, those baby-blue eyes steely and hard, revealing the businesswoman behind the star. She was more than a figurehead, and she was here to let them know it.

And, insisting on her right to sit in the chairman's seat, Jane Morgan, all in black. Dressed for her own funeral?

Three powerful women. Once best friends. Now deadly rivals. Each of them determined to control the world's most famous store. Its fate, and theirs, would be determined today.

Jane Morgan stared down the length of the table; she nodded coldly at Haya and Sally. Her voice, that famously cool English voice, betrayed no fear. 'The meeting will come to order.'

Chapter One

'YOU GOTTA FIGHT for your RIGHT to PAAAARRRTTYYY . . .'

The boombox in the corner of the playground was pumping out into the still air of a muggy fall day in Beverly Hills. It was the start of term, and already the overprivileged girls of Miss Milton's Academy were settling back into their tight little cliques. Julie Manners, the queen of eighth grade, was showing off. Julie and her friends wore their white socks round their ankles, hitched up their skirts, pinned their hair back with Ray-Bans and wore badges proclaiming heavy-metal bands. They banged their heads, long hair flying, to show just how tough they were.

The teachers pretended to be deep in conversation, ignoring Julie and her clique. Her dad was a movie director, and that made her powerful. This was the eighties; fame and celebrity counted for a lot. They shut their ears to the deafening music, pretending it was no big deal. Heavy metal and rap were *in*. So was Julie. And everybody wanted to be just like her.

Well—almost everybody.

A dark, slender girl sat in the opposite corner of the playground, reading a book, her neat leather satchel beside her.

'Limey,' hissed Melissa Smith, kicking at her as she passed.

'Do sod off, Melissa,' the girl replied. She wasn't much to look at but there was a certain resilience to her.

Melissa Smith was one of Julie's cronies. 'The bookworm's at it again. What's this? *Ariel* by Sylvia Plath. Studying up on laundry detergent?'

Melissa sniggered. Jane Morgan didn't suck up. And she didn't fear bullying. Two reasons to hate her.

'It's poetry. Course, you'd have to actually be able to read to know that. How was summer school?' Jane asked coolly.

Melissa flushed; she had been forced to take summer school to catch up on her grades.

'Great,' she lied. 'And you know, there were *boys* there. Not something you'd know a lot about.'

'Not interested,' Jane replied.

'That's right. They aren't.' A rather smart insult from Melissa. 'You never sent Julie a birthday card, weirdo. People notice these things.'

'That's because I can't stand Julie.'

Melissa bridled. 'You'd better watch yourself. We can make life very hard for you in this school. If you want to be picked for any teams, or get a part in the play, or go to parties . . .'

'Yeah, well, I don't.' Jane Morgan snapped the book shut.

'Watch yourself, weirdo,' Melissa repeated, and stalked off. Damn! That ugly Brit. She should have been hounded out of Miss Milton's by now. Of course Melissa, Julie and everybody else knew why it hadn't happened. One word. Sally.

Sally. The dumb blonde with a stupid Texas twang, Barbie's hair, and illegal curves. There was nothing hip about Sally, nothing cool. She didn't listen to the Beastie Boys or Mötley Crüe. She didn't wear the right clothes—no black leather jackets and metal studs.

But Sally had two things in her favour. First, she was rich. And not just film-biz, common-or-garden rich like most of them. No, Sally's family was Money with a capital M. Her pa, Paulie Lassiter, was in the oil business, and one thing was definite. Her daddy could buy all their daddies ten times over and still have plenty to spare.

And second—even worse—Sally was *gorgeous*. You could sneer— and they did. Dumb blonde. Bimbo. Cheerleader. Yet, as their brothers' admiring stares confirmed, Sally Lassiter's looks were devastating. She had coltish legs, large, bright blue eyes, and over the whole package, a white-toothed, milky, all-American wholesomeness. She was always smiling, and when she laughed, she lit up the entire room.

So she wasn't a brainiac. So what? She was an only child, heir to a vast fortune. She knew she was untouchable, knew she was better than all of them. It was so unfair!

And of course, if she wasn't smart, she had a friend who was. Jane Morgan.

They made such an unlikely duo. Best friends as long as anybody could remember, yet totally different. Jane was, in Miss Milton terms, a bum. Her folks had no cash; her fees were all paid by the British Embassy. She wasn't pretty, either, no style whatsoever. Jane was a real little bookworm.

Jane Morgan didn't have Sally's weapons. Status, sure; Daddy was practically royal, and the cars that picked her up sometimes had little fluttering flags on the front, which was cool. But this was LA, not Washington. It didn't count for a whole lot. Yet they could not touch her. Sally protected her. And as long as they stayed friends, those two girls, together, were so much more than the sum of their parts. They made no sense on their own, but together they were unstoppable. Jane had the brains. Sally had the looks. Jane had that smart mouth. Sally was loaded. Melissa had to admit they made a hell of a team.

Jane watched as Melissa's tense back receded into the distance, joining the throng round Julie. It wasn't till Melissa was safely out of reach that she could breathe a sigh of relief. Not that she would let it show. Jane Morgan had no truck with weakness. But she *was* unhappy, even depressed.

Another bloody term. Stuck in this shithole. With no decent teachers. How the hell would she get into Oxford or Cambridge after studying at this dump? But that wasn't why she was unhappy.

Jane looked wistfully at the crowd surrounding Julie Manners and wished she was the other girl. What would *that* be like? To be popular, to have people fighting for your attention.

She looked at the front gate. She had never wanted to see Sal as much as she did right now. As long as she had Sally, it wasn't all black.

But Sally wasn't here yet. And as she sat by herself in the playground, Jane Morgan felt a wave of loneliness crash over her. It was a wretched feeling, and she lifted her head; jutted her chin up, as though she were in danger of drowning.

Jane thought of her dad. His Excellency the Hon. Thomas Morgan, smiling that politician's smile at her, as she tried to persuade him to want her close . . . to love her the way she loved him.

'But, Daddy . . . I really hate that school.'

She'd been hovering at the top of the stairs, her suitcases packed, in the limo already.

'We all hate school, darling.' He gave her an absent-minded kiss.

'I want to be with you.' Jane's words tumbled out, although she'd promised herself she wouldn't beg. 'I want to stay here—in Washington.'

'The political hothouse?' He waved his hands vaguely. 'Not good for teenagers. And I'm so busy, you'd never see me. Boarding school is best.'

'But . . . Dad.' Her voice, already pleading, whiny. 'If I were here, you could see me more. And you'd like that, wouldn't you?'

'Of course I would.' His voice softened, just a fraction, and he kissed her on the forehead; a brief touch, but manna to Jane. She wanted desperately to hug him, but he pulled back, and his clear grey eyes regained their professional detachment. 'And I'll see you this summer, sweetheart.'

Sweetheart. Darling. If only that were true.

But Jane Morgan squared her slim shoulders and pasted on a smile, as brisk and impersonal as Daddy's always were.

'OK. See you then,' she said, and gave him a hug; he patted her stiffly on the back. 'Love you, Daddy.'

'Love you too, Jane.'

As she walked down the stairs, she heard him turn and go back to his office. He didn't even wait to wave goodbye.

The memory was bitter. And she had chewed on it, like a foul herb, all the way to the airport, and then all the way to the smart, lonely, rented house she lived in when she was at school. Her life sometimes seemed like one long story of rejection. And yet, that bright spot, her best friend; Sally, who was the closest thing, Jane sometimes thought, that she had to real family; Sally, who was almost a sister.

There was a sound. Yes—that was Sally's car, straight out of Texas, a large, gleaming white monster. Her blues temporarily banished, Jane scrambled to her feet.

The car parked; the driver, dressed in an immaculate uniform, got out and held the door open for his passenger. Jane hovered. Behind her, she was aware of the general drop in the hum of voices—everybody was waiting for Sally.

'I'm so glad to see you,' Sally cried, flinging her arms round Jane. 'It's been so boring while you were in DC.'

'Me too.'

'What's going on?' Sally waved to her chauffeur, who tipped his cap. 'Is that Melissa talking to Julie? Horrible haircut. She looks like a boy.'

'Tough is in this year,' Jane answered wrily. 'Have you seen Julie's black leather jacket? She's all over Whitesnake. And she had platinum highlights put into her perm, and it's gone all crispy.'

'No!' Sally squealed with delight. 'I gotta see. That girl has no style.'

'Knows a lot of movie stars, though,' Jane observed.

'Whoop-de-do,' Sally said. 'They're ten cents to the pound around here.'

Her pretty face reflected such total unconcern that Jane instantly felt lightened. How could she have let Melissa Smith get to her?

'Can you help me with my vacation project?' Sally asked, lowering her voice. 'I think I got the Tudors muddled up. I could use an A, Daddy's kind of bothered about my SATs.'

'Sure.' Jane was on her own ground now.

'Thanks.' Sally blushed. 'I know I should have gotten it right by now.'

'Don't worry about it. I'm always here.'

Sal squeezed her arm, and they walked off into the playground, chattering away like starlings.

'**W**hich concludes the assembly for this morning.' Miss Milton herself, her doughy body encased in a couture Dior tweed suit, surveyed the room. 'Orientation for the new girls we welcome into the school this year will continue at first period.'

Jane glanced at the gaggle of new chicks that were standing off to one side like sheep waiting to be herded into a pen. She didn't see anybody interesting. Most of them, with an unerring sense of social accuracy, had tried to glom on to the crowd surrounding Julie.

There was one latecomer. Dark-haired, average height, slim without being skinny. Rather shy-looking. Unlike Jane, she seemed to make an effort with her appearance; whitened teeth, plucked eyebrows, neatly brushed hair worn loose instead of scraped into a ponytail. She looked uncomfortable, and twisted her fingers around. Very tanned, though, and pretty enough not to be an obvious target for bullies.

'We will now stand for the Pledge of Allegiance. Foreign citizens are excused.'

There was a rustle of cotton as the room got to its feet; Sally stood, her blue eyes fixed patriotically on the Stars and Stripes displayed at the front of the room. She always meant it, whereas some of the other girls sneered and rolled their eyes; another reason to love her.

'I pledge allegiance to the flag of the United States of America . . .'

Jane, from her chair, cast her eyes around the room, picking out the other diplomats' daughters. Wait. The new girl wasn't standing either. One lone chair had been provided for her, and she was sitting in it, sticking out. The other new girls were casting sidelong glances, sneering at her. Jane looked closer; that wasn't a tan, she was from the Middle East. Large dark eyes, an aristocratic nose. Israeli?

'. . . liberty and justice for all.'

The bell rang, and Miss Milton left the stage.

'I got art history first period. You?'

'Maths,' Jane responded, still looking at the new chick. She was being jostled. Almost exactly the same had happened to her when she first got here—before she'd found Sally. 'Hey, Sal. See that new girl over there? They're picking on her.'

'They always do.'

'Let's go and say hi,' Jane urged. 'Come on, it'll be your good deed for the day.'

Sally sighed. 'Sure, why not?' she said.

She walked towards the new girl. Jane was her conscience; Sally knew there was a streak of iron in Jane, something she respected, even feared at times. Jane would have gone over to that chick whether she had come or not.

She scrutinised the object of her friend's attentions. Modest, shy, disturbingly pretty. Sally felt a moment of misgiving. This new girl was looking threateningly gorgeous, and also had a sharp light in her eyes that Sally recognised from a long association with her English friend.

Would that work? What if the new girl wanted to be real friends? She might be clever enough to rival Jane and pretty enough to steal her own thunder, too. Then she blushed. Those were mean thoughts, worthy of Julie or Melissa, not her. The new girl needed help. And Sally Lassiter, even though she schemed and gossiped and loved her own reflection almost as much as everybody else did, was fundamentally kind.

'Hey!' she called out, waving brightly to the new girl, who was heading towards the door. 'Hold up, hon! We want to talk to you.'

The other girl hesitated and nodded.

'I'm Sally, Sally Lassiter.'

The new girl's dark eyes swept over the blonde, drinking her in. Sally was a million miles away from her own long hem and high socks. Her shirt had an extra button undone, revealing a glimpse of bountiful, all-natural breasts. 'Helen,' the new girl muttered. 'Helen Yanna.'

'I'm Jane.' Jane moved forward, adjusting her glasses up the bridge of her nose. They were thick, and made her eyes disappear behind them. Helen pegged her as English at once.

'How do you do?' Helen replied formally. Warily. Were they about to start teasing her like the other girls had done?

'You're new,' Sally observed. 'We figured maybe you'd want somebody to show you round? Help you fit in.'

The olive-skinned girl nodded shyly. 'That would be very kind.'

'Where are you from, Helen? Israel?' Jane guessed.

The girl didn't take offence. 'Jordan. It is nearby.'

'You're an Arab!' Sally said, blue eyes widening.

Helen nodded, and Jane noticed her stiffen. 'Does that upset you?'

'Of course not,' Jane said quickly. 'We have people in the school from all over. I'm English, my dad works in Washington.'

Helen made a face. 'How sad, to be separated from your father.'

'Not particularly.' Jane tried to harden her heart to match her words. 'My father's a diplomat. He mostly thinks of politics. I don't think he'll be winning father of the year any time soon.'

'Your mother, then.'

'She died, when I was three. Car crash.'

Helen looked horrified. 'I'm sorry.'

Jane shrugged. She sometimes wondered about that night. Her father had been driving, had emerged almost unscathed, apart from one long scar on his back. Who knew the truth? Maybe he had been drunk.

'I can handle it,' she said shortly. 'I'm a daygirl here. And I have a nanny in our place by the beach.'

'I'm day too. Daddy has a house in Bel Air,' Sally said artlessly. 'Right next to Aaron Spelling, but twice as big. We're in oil.'

'My father is a businessman.'

'What business?' Sally zeroed in.

Helen spread her hands. 'Many.' It was true, her father had his fingers in many different pies. 'He arranges contracts, meetings, for Americans who want to work in the Middle East. They build roads, apartment buildings, water facilities . . .'

'That's swell,' Sally said, losing interest. 'He's not in oil?'

'Jordan has no oil.'

'So he's not a sheik or a king?'

Helen smiled. 'I'm afraid not. Just a businessman.'

'Oh well, never mind.' Sally was too bubbly to be put out for more than a few seconds. 'Come with Jane and me and see the school. We'll introduce you *way* better than orientation.'

Helen looked behind her; a bossy-looking matron with white hair in a stiff bob was taking the rest of the new intake towards the labs. Rebellion was not her strong suit, but the enthusiasm of the American and the friendliness of the English girl intrigued her.

'Why not?' She tried out her practised English vocabulary. 'That sounds like . . . fun!'

The three of them went round the school grounds. Jane watched Helen as she drank it in. It was nice, she realised, to have somebody else there. Good to have more back-up.

And of course Helen Yanna was a foreigner, too. That made her even more of a target. It was something they'd have in common. Plus, Jane could tell at once that the girl was clever, brighter than Sally. It might be nice to have somebody around she could chat with about the stuff that didn't interest Sal. Like her exams.

'That's the fountain.' Sally beamed. 'Impressive, no?'

'No,' replied Helen, thinking the question was serious. 'We have much better in our garden in Amman.'

Jane bit back a smile.

'And the statue, it's old. *Real* old. Victorian, imported from San Francisco. Almost *two hundred years*.' Sally was determined to show off.

'I think she's seen older.' Jane smiled at their new friend. 'Have you ever been to Petra?' she asked, with a touch of envy.

'Yes, of course.' Helen returned the smile.

'And here's the pool.' Sally wasn't interested in archaeology or ancient sites. 'Olympic size. The gym is fully equipped. Rock-climbing walls, TVs on stands while you work out, treadmills. Even kick-boxing.'

That did it. Helen's eyes roamed excitedly over the massive pool. Yes, this was fun. Kick-boxing! Why not? This was an all-girls school. She'd *love* to do that.

'And here,' Sally went on, 'are the classrooms.' Her pretty mouth made a moue of dislike. 'Gotta say, I still hate class. Learning about General Custer, and stuff. When are you gonna use that in real life?'

'History teaches us about the future, too,' Jane said.

'Deep.' Sally winked at her friend. Helen looked at her enviously. She wished she had that American confidence.

'And this is the chapel,' Sally continued, gesturing at a long room with benches, an altar and a crucifix. 'Want to go inside?'

Helen shook her head. 'No, thanks. I'm a Muslim.'

Sally stopped walking. 'Huh?' she asked, really amazed.

'Of course she is,' Jane swooped in quickly. 'She's from Jordan.'

Helen was amused at the blonde girl's discomfiture. Didn't they understand not everybody was like them? 'Actually there are lots of Christians in Jordan. More than five per cent. But my family is Muslim.'

Sally made a good recovery. 'That's cool. And here's where we eat lunch. Do you want to sit with us and eat lunch?'

Jane looked at her best friend, and felt a rush of warmth. Really, Sal was a kind, good girl. Asking somebody to sit with you at lunch was a big deal. She was offering to support Helen Yanna, in public, in the full view of all the nasty, cliquey, bullying teenage girls that otherwise could make this shy young Arab's life a perfect misery.

'I'd love to sit with you.' Helen felt nervous for the first time that day; she peered in to see the refectory full of loud, noisy, American girls, already bonded into their little groups. 'But . . . I can't eat the food. It isn't halal. My father made an arrangement. They will bring me my food especially.' She hesitated. Was that too weird for them? If they left her, she would be the new, strange Muslim chick, and the brash American students would bully her.

'I *dig* that!' Sally sensed the fear, and hastened to reassure her. 'See? You're special. Like waiter service, right in hall!'

'Thank you. *Shokran*.' The Arabic slipped out, from habit. 'Do you two have other friends?'

'Sure! Plenty. But we're *best* friends,' Sally said confidently, squeezing Jane's arm. 'We're our own group.'

'And can I be in your group?' Helen asked artlessly.

Jane smiled warmly at her. 'Absolutely! We'd be delighted.'

'Thank you,' Helen said again, with a grateful smile. The ache that had been in her heart since her family had left Amman started to dull, just a little. It was so great to have friends.

Chapter Two

'WHAT YOU DOING, FREAK?'

Helen touched the mat in front of her with her forehead and tried to concentrate on her prayer.

'I *said*, what you doing, Towel-head?'

There was a sharp kick in her ribs. Helen flooded with anger and fear. She knew that voice. That was Julie Manners, first-class bitch.

'I don't like Ay-rabs,' Julie announced.

'*Allahu Akbar*,' Helen whispered. She prayed, towards Mecca and the holy shrine.

'Look, girls. Little Miss Sand Nigger here thinks she can act all hoity-toity in the U S of A—*oof!*'

There was a gasp and Helen, her eyes closed, heard shouting. She continued to pray. There was the sound of a slap and a howl of rage.

'Y'all better back off *our* buddy.' That was Sally, Helen thought, with a rush of gratitude. 'You're a fat ugly waste of skin, Julie. They ain't made the surgeon yet who can turn you into a babe.'

'Leave me alone!'

'Let her *go!*' Julie's groupies chiming in.

'I suggest you leave Helen be. Permanently. Otherwise I will go directly to Miss Milton and report what I saw. You'll be expelled.' Jane Morgan, speaking with that British accent. Daring them to continue.

'Screw you, you limey bitch! And *you*, you redneck slut!' Julie shrieked, but Helen could hear it was from further away.

'*Allahu Akbar,*' she whispered again, and stood up, finished. She opened her eyes and saw Julie and half her gang skulking off to the other end of the playground.

'Don't mind about her. She's ignorant,' Sally said, as Helen rolled the prayer mat up.

'Did she hurt you?' Jane touched her friend's ribs through her jumper. Helen winced. 'No,' she lied.

It would make a pretty fair bruise, that was for sure. But the insults kept ringing through her head. *Sand nigger. Towel-head. Ay-rab.* 'Why do they talk like that?'

The irony was that as the months ticked by, Helen felt she was losing some of her identity. Her Arabic was disappearing. She couldn't follow her parents when they slipped back into the mother tongue. She was trying to keep rooted in her culture. But of course the bullies didn't see her becoming more westernised. Helen was merely an *Ay-rab* to them.

'They're just showing off. They think you're strange because you never have any boyfriends.'

'Nor does Jane.'

'Ouch,' Jane objected. 'You don't understand tact, do you, Helen?'

'What does it mean, "tact"?'

'Never mind.' Sally was full of beans. 'You want to be accepted, don't you?'

'She has us,' Jane retorted, still mildly stung.

'But the other girls . . .' Helen had an outsider's longing to fit in. 'The rest of them. You know.'

Jane glanced at Sally. 'I agree. They never let up.'

'Then we should do something about that.' Underneath her milk-and-honey Southern tones, Jane heard real anger. There was a streak of steel to Sally. And right now she was furious.

'Let's throw a party,' Sally said, after a pause.

'A party?' Helen asked.

'Yes. A real party. Like, party of the year. Must-attend, social death if you don't show up. Crack the whip a little bit over these girls. Prove to them y'all really *are* my friends.' There was a dangerous light in Sally's eyes. 'And there are consequences if they mess with you.'

Helen's dark gaze flickered over the loud gaggle of girls at the other corner of the playground.

'But they won't come to our party,' she said. 'I don't understand.'

Sally smiled at her friend. 'Oh, they'll come,' she said coolly. 'We just make the party hot enough and they'll be begging me for invitations.'

She reached out and patted Jane and Helen on the shoulder. 'You need to understand. Glamour is a weapon.' And she winked.

Jane turned the pages of her calculus textbook, trying to absorb the maths. It was a glorious October day, and she couldn't concentrate. She wondered, with a pang, what her father was doing right now. Last time he had called, Thomas Morgan had sounded even more stressed than usual. She shouldn't care, but she did. The hope that he would love her one day never really went away.

'Jane!' Her nanny, Consuela, was calling. 'Your friends are here.'

Jane jumped up, pushing the book away. What? Sally never came out here. There was nothing in her cottage that Sal didn't have ten times better at home—they always hung out on the estate. But sure enough, her white limo was pulling in at the front gate, or trying to.

'Hey, get in.' Sally flung open the door. 'We're going to a beauty salon. And an optician's.'

'What for?' Jane asked suspiciously, pushing her glasses up the bridge of her nose.

'Don't argue with me, honey. We're going to fix you right up.'

Helen poked out her head, smiling. 'I'm going too.'

'You both are. I won't take no for an answer,' Sally said firmly. 'Get in.'

'Try these.' The optician leaned forward and handed her another pair of lenses. 'Don't worry, you'll get it; everybody drops them at first.'

'Sorry . . .' Jane was embarrassed. She hated clumsiness.

'On the tip of your finger . . . *there* you go.'

'Ah.' Jane gasped. But she could see! She blinked.

'Now the other one.'

Her vision swam, then settled.

'What do you think?' the optician said.

'She looks hot!' Sally approved.

'You're very beautiful,' Helen agreed. '*Very.*'

'Don't be silly,' Jane said gruffly. But she couldn't suppress a smile. Without glasses, her face was so different. Almost beautiful, in its way.

'Thanks, Doc. Messenger her lenses to our house, OK?'

'Sure thing, Sally.' Dr Madrid smiled benignly. The billionaire's daughter would get whatever she wanted. 'A pleasure . . .'

'Come on.' Sally was tugging Jane along by the hand. 'We haven't even started with you yet.'

'I don't know . . .'

Jane shifted uneasily in her seat; the hairdresser was holding a large lump of her hair.

'Of *course* you don't know. If you did, would you look like *that*?' Maurice snapped his fingers. 'Nuh-uh! I'm the artist, baby, you're the canvas. Let's leave it to the experts. You got it?'

Jane swallowed her pride. 'Right.'

It wouldn't do much good to go to the party of the year as guest of honour if she was also wallflower of the year. 'Go for it,' she said shortly. 'Give me the works.'

No pain, no gain. It took hours, boring hours. There was washing, combing, cutting, dyeing and blow-drying. 'Does it always take this long?' she complained, as Maurice wrapped the millionth piece of foil round her newly shorn head.

'You have to suffer for beauty. Head back,' Maurice commanded. 'This is going to sting . . . a little.'

'What's that?'

'Hot wax. You're way too cute for that unibrow.'

'Aaaargh!'

'I'm giving you French. Manicure and pedicure. No colours, though.'

'If you don't use colours, what's the point?' Jane asked, staring at her hands. The other two had gone off for a coffee in the diner across the street. She was *still* stuck here.

'You'll see,' he said mysteriously.

Finally, it was over. Ten minutes after Helen and Sally sauntered back in, Maurice flicked the switch off on his sleek steel dryer. He beckoned them forward, spun the chair round, and whisked away the black silk drape he'd placed over the mirror.

'Holy Toledo!' Sally shrieked.

Helen gasped.

'Oh my goodness.' Jane was reduced to childishness. She placed one hand over her mouth. 'Oh my goodness . . .' Her hair, cut to just above the shoulders, was streaked with subtle lights of bronze. It was full of bounce and fullness, the lack of weight giving it a lift it had never had. Jane felt as light as air. Her beetling eyebrows had vanished in favour of high arches that opened up her face. And the hand clasped across her mouth boasted neat, shiny nails with attractive white cuticles.

'Wait till we get some make-up on her.' Maurice preened. 'I am magician, no?'

'No—you had great stuff to work with,' Sally said, smiling. 'But you *are* good.' She pressed forward and gave the outraged stylist a kiss on the cheek—and put five hundred dollars into his hand.

Maurice smirked back. '*Merci, chérie.* It was *un plaisir.*'

'**N**ow we get you a dress,' Sally announced briskly.

'You'll look fantastic,' Helen said delightedly. Her friend was transformed, prettier than she was. It wasn't in Helen's nature to be resentful, she was happy for Jane. She had some beauty after all, a consolation in what Helen instinctively understood was a tough life. Poor Jane. For all Baba annoyed her, at least she had family. What did Jane have? A useless father, not worthy of the name. And Jane Morgan was so walled-off all the time. Angry at the world.

'Not just her—*you.*' Sally's Southern tones interrupted Helen's reverie.

'You can't get me a dress!' Helen was half flattered, half offended. Unlike Jane, her family had their own cash.

'I want to style you,' Sally wheedled. 'Like Jane.'

Helen shook her head. 'I don't do low-cut, Sally. I'm not like you.'

'What? Are you calling me trashy?' Sally's eyes flashed.

'Of course not,' Helen prevaricated. Her eyes slipped to Sally's tight white dress. 'I just don't think we have the same style.'

'Relax. I know that, I know what'll suit both of y'all.' Sally nodded. 'I'm throwing this party *for you.* Trust me.'

'For us,' Jane said, nudging her. 'Come on!' Sally loved being the leader of the gang of three. The party was hers, it would only underline her untouchable star status, her truly limitless wealth.

'OK, then. For us. The three musketeers!'

'Excuse me?' asked Helen.

'Never mind,' Sally said. Impatiently, she tugged at the two girls. Making them over was like playing with grown-up Barbies. She adored her friends, and wanted them to look as hot as she knew they could. 'Neiman Marcus. Now. I got a personal shopper waiting!'

'**Y**ou ladies look wonderful.' The manager was gushing as hard as he could. Of course it meant sales for him, but Jane could see the light in his eyes; he really did seem enthused.

'What do you think, ladies?' Sally didn't trouble to keep the triumph out of her voice. 'We make a pretty cute trio, don't you think?' The reflection in the mirrored wall opposite confirmed that diagnosis.

Sally—blonde, tanned, stunning in a knockout dress of golden sequins, with a scalloped neckline, tiny fluted sleeves and a fishtail. She looked like a mermaid from a fairy story.

Jane—newly beautiful, now made up by the counter assistant from Chanel, her hair bouncing with life, her delicate features enhanced with a natural, glossy make-up that emphasised her youth. She was wearing a sheath of dark green velvet that picked out her emerald eyes and honey-highlighted hair.

Helen—exotic and aristocratic. Playing to her heritage, Sally had chosen for her a long-sleeved gown with a dramatic sweeping train, a satin and lace confection of pewter and grey, with a matching cape of lambswool. A collar of seed pearls was knotted round her neck.

Her friends had protested they couldn't accept anything so expensive.

'Screw that,' Sally said forthrightly. 'My daddy don't count his money, girls, he weighs it. And if he wants to spoil me, I want to spoil *you*. We're friends, so don't be stupid.'

Lots of people sucked up to her. But she knew these two really liked her; would do, in fact, if she had nothing. That meant everything.

'If you say so. Thank you.' Helen kissed her on the cheek, thrilled. It was an exquisite gown, modest as well as stylish, and her parents would have no objection.

'Thanks, hon.' Jane gave Sally a bear hug. Anything more, and her voice would have started to crack. She could hardly believe how Sally had transformed her. She barely recognised herself. And the nasty bitches who tried to make her life a misery weren't going to either. Jane was big on brains. Not so much on self-confidence. After this party, that was going to change.

Paulie Lassiter glanced around his home, and tried to forget the troubles he was going through at the office.

The big mansion soothed him. A man who lived in a house like this couldn't have any real problems at work, could he?

His home. Green Gables. The most fabulous estate in Bel Air. Paulie loved it. It was his home, his castle, and the definition of his status.

LA ran on star power, the electricity that supplied the city grid. And Paulie had none of it—nothing but the thick black ooze that poured out of his desert wells in the Lone Star State. He'd grown up poor, and he wanted only the best for his little girl. In America, Hollywood was the best, and Paulie Lassiter was determined to be a big fish.

That meant one thing. Conspicuous consumption. The buzz word of the eighties. So what if his name was never mentioned in *Variety*? Mona, his wife, would be at all the right parties. So what if he had nothing breaking out at the box office? He would have the biggest pad in LA and a fleet of luxury cars. Ferrari Testarossa, Rolls-Royce, Aston Martin . . .

Paulie glanced out of the window, down his manicured lawns to the glassy surface of his private boating lake. Yes, Green Gables was his. What they were telling him about the pension fund just had to be wrong. You couldn't afford a place like this unless you had really made it. He had come from the roughest part of Texas, and he was never going back.

'I'm having second thoughts about this party,' Baba suddenly announced.

They were preparing dinner and Helen was chopping the coriander. As her father spoke, her knuckles whitened on the knife.

'But I would never do anything wrong.' Helen burned with resentment. Her father was such a hypocrite! He wore Western clothes, gave them Anglicised names and drank like a fish. She hardly ever saw him attend prayers, or go to the mosque. 'There are going to be chaperones,' she reminded him.

'If it's so innocent what do they need them for?' asked her father. 'Anyway, Helen, there's no need for you to mix with Western boys.'

'No need?'

'You tell her,' Baba said to her mama.

'We found a nice man for you.' Aisha stirred the sauce, not looking at her daughter. 'He's family . . . my cousin Lallah. Her nephew. Ahmed is his name. He's twenty-four . . .'

Ugh. An old man.

'He's a merchant, in Cairo. Has a very nice house, like our old house in Amman. You'll like it. You'll like him.' Aisha's back stiffened. 'Baba and I are all agreed.'

'Well, isn't that nice.' Helen was surprised to hear the bitterness in her voice. 'But you forgot to ask me. I'm not agreed.'

'You've always been a good girl,' her father grunted. 'You knew this had to be.'

'Not now. Not any more.' Helen stood firm. '*I'm* going to decide who I marry, Baba.'

'You will obey me on this, Helen, I am your father,' Baba reminded her stiffly. 'Our family has reputation to think of. Maybe I should pull you out of that school. And not let you go to that party.'

Leave Sally and Jane? Like hell! 'I tell you what, Baba.' It suddenly occurred to Helen that her father was a businessman. They could do a little horse-trading. 'It's going to be a major social event, you know.

Paulie Lassiter is a billionaire, all from oil. There are going to be movie stars, diplomats, bankers. You should let me go, it'll be a feather in your cap. You already said yes. Just stick to that.'

His eyes narrowed. 'And if I do? You'll marry Ahmed?'

'I'll consider it. Certainly, why not?'

'You're in no position to bargain!' said her father, crossly. He marched to the dresser and took out his bottle of whisky.

Helen knew that look. She just waited.

'I suppose you can go. We want you to fit in. Ahmed will like it if you have friends here . . . he can expand his business . . .'

'What business is he in?'

'Carpets.'

Helen looked away so Baba would not see her roll her eyes. Carpets, what a cliché. Did he have any flying ones? she wanted to ask.

'*Very expensive* carpets,' Aisha announced. 'Priceless works of art, some of them.'

'That's great!' Helen lied. It didn't hurt to give them a bit of flannel. Agree to meet this spotty youth—anything, as long as she could go to the party. Helen looked at her father. She could meet Ahmed, be nice to him, try to manage a few sentences in Arabic. Who cared, really?

'You're a good girl,' Ali pronounced smugly. He watched his daughter, dark head bowed, turn back to the coriander. She was ready for marriage. If they waited, like Western girls did, it would be a disaster. Let her complain, Ali thought; she will enjoy her life, once she has a husband, some babies and a fine house. Yes; he knew what was best for her.

Sally had played it carefully, stacking the party with rides and beauty treatments until it sounded like paradise—manicure tents, masseuses, firework displays, flight simulators, camel rides—then she added cool little gifts, like necklaces designed at Frederick's of Hollywood, and lastly, the killer ingredient—boys, and stars.

The sixth forms of the *most* exclusive LA boys' schools were all invited before *any* invites went to the girls of Miss Milton's. And Paulie Lassiter knew actors. Mona was able to get several of the younger, hotter Hollywood set. Molly Ringwald was an acceptance. There were producers there, aching for some of Paulie's cash for financing. Actors followed producers, and the girls of Miss Milton's followed the men. Nobody tried to play it cool.

'We'll put Julie at the *worst* table—I'm talking Siberia!' Sally decided.

'Out by the tennis court?'

'Yeah, with the guy who comes to teach Dad French.'

Helen laughed. Yes, Julie would *hate* that. Plus, it would be the talk of the school.

'And Melissa . . .'

'She ain't coming. Baby, I gotta have me some standards.'

'I can't wait,' Helen said truthfully. She would be at the centre of things for once, right at the epicentre. The idea gave her a buzz.

Do you think we're doing the right thing?' Aisha asked nervously.

'Of course.' Ali gave her a quick peck on the cheek.

'But to force her. We brought her up here. Sent her to that school . . .'

Ali's face darkened. He wasn't sure if that had been the right move. Helen was growing too rebellious.

'The old ways are the best ones. We're not doing this *to* Helen, we're doing it *for* her. Think of that—her happiness. Why should young ones make their own choices? Who says they have any idea how to do it? All these American marriages ending in divorce—how many ex-wives do you know, stuck with babies?'

Too many. Aisha nodded.

'In the end, it is the solemn bond, the friendship that wins through. We are doing what's best for our little Haya.'

Aisha smiled. He hadn't called Helen by her original name since they'd arrived in America, six years ago.

'Ahmed lands tomorrow,' she said, reassured by her husband.

'Good. That is the day of her big party.'

'He can take her to it!' Aisha suggested brightly.

'I don't think that's the best idea.' Ali had no intention of letting Ahmed see his daughter in any light other than as a suitable bride.

'But he can be here, waiting, the next morning. As soon as she wakes up. We will organise the meeting in the morning, and in the afternoon, the *nikkah*. What do you think?'

The engagement ceremony. Under Islamic law, they would be as good as married. All the rest, just so much paperwork.

'She might refuse,' Aisha fretted. 'You know her, Ali!'

'She won't understand what she is getting into. Her Arabic is rusty. Once she realises . . .' He shrugged. 'We'll have her in Cairo, and she will accept it—and be happy. Once she's pregnant and has taken to him, in her heart, they can come here, and we will all be a family again.'

Aisha nodded, but wept a little into his chest. Ali stroked her hair fondly. His own marriage had been the most solid thing in his life, and he loved his strong-willed child enough to do right by her. Of course, at first she would feel betrayed, but soon she would be accepting.

Chapter Three

THE DAY OF THE PARTY dawned bright and clear. All over town, girls were getting ready. Everybody who was anybody.

By the evening, Green Gables was on fire. Helen ran excitedly to the window of Sally's enormous bedroom. It had a walk-in closet bigger than Helen's lounge, its own bathroom complete with Jacuzzi and stand-alone power shower, a separate dressing room *and* a private kitchenette!

Helen wondered what it'd be like to have this much money. Her dad was comfortable but compared to Sally they were paupers. She wanted this kind of success.

'Look at that!' Another rocket arched into the sky and exploded, a fiery rain of stars and whistling comets descending on an awestruck crowd. 'Come on, Sal! We *have* to go down!'

The party had been raging for two hours already. Mona kept popping her head in to report this movie star or that supermodel had arrived.

'Yes, let's go.' Jane was surprised at her own eagerness. Dressed in the gown Sally had picked out for her, carefully made up by a pro, spritzed with a little rosewater, she looked astonishingly lovely, and she knew it.

'Five more minutes. We want to make an *entrance*.' Sally smirked. 'This is our *moment*, ladies.'

'**D**amn.' Julie Manners seethed. She was gyrating on the dance floor, but it was having no effect.

'That preppy kid from Beverly Hills High was checking you out,' Emma Lightfoot suggested helpfully.

'Screw him!' Julie pushed her fringe out of her eyes. He was probably some dentist's kid . . .

She was frustrated. All the girls from school were watching her and Emma like hawks. It was a battle for supremacy. The party was awesomely great, so now all that remained was to see who was the most beautiful. The music suddenly stopped, leaving Julie in mid-grind. Emma sniggered. Julie scowled at her.

'Ladies and gentlemen,' the voice of the Lassiters' English butler came over the tannoy. 'Please welcome Sally Lassiter, and her best friends Miss Jane Morgan and Miss Helen Yanna!'

The glittering crowd, gathered round the dance floor, buzzed in anticipation. Everybody's eyes were fixed on the top of the stairs. Julie Manners had a sinking feeling in her stomach. And there they were.

'Oh—my—*gosh*,' said Emma. 'Oh my gosh!'

There was a collective gasp.

Sally—in the middle. Long blonde hair, illegal curves, in her glittering gold sheath, scalloped neckline, looking like a Greek goddess— Aphrodite, the queen of love.

Helen Yanna. Flowing robes, statuesque as a model, a diamanté circlet in her hair, her Arabian features exquisitely calm and confident, was holding her left hand.

And holding her right hand, glasses vanished, hair light and gorgeous, high cheekbones glowing under radiant skin, emerald-eyed Jane—perhaps the loveliest of all.

The crowd froze for a moment. Sick with jealousy, Julie glanced around. She saw the men's eyes narrowing with interest and admiration; the girls from school staring as if star-struck. Then the applause broke out—and the cheering. The three girls started to walk downstairs, holding hands. Three best friends. Unbreakable. Perfect.

Flashbulbs popped as the official photographers captured the moment. Julie knew just how that picture would look: a glorious capture of youth and a beauty that neither she, nor any of her friends, would ever be able to match.

Julie saw that hot new movie star with all the Oscars go up to Jane Morgan—and ask *her* to dance! It was just horrible.

Julie turned to Emma. 'I'm leaving,' she said.

But Emma was gone. She was pushing through the crowd, shouting to get some attention. 'Helen! Hey, Helen!' Julie heard her calling. 'That's a great dress. Who's the designer?'

Furious, Julie stalked off to the cloakroom.

'I want my bag!' she yelled. 'Like, pronto!' Time to split. Seething, she stewed in her failure. Damn it all to hell. Would anything ever go wrong for these bitches? Well, when it did, she, Julie Manners, would be right there waiting. She had no idea just how soon it was going to be.

The house on Washington Avenue. He loved it. It had been the scene of so many of his triumphs. The intimate party for the Princess of Monaco. The negotiations—bugged by both sides—between the UK and Russia over the Ukraine . . .

And more. The scene of his personal rise—and he did mean rise. The

Hon. Thomas Morgan took a last, unsteady walk through his house. Ah yes . . . the billiard room, scene of so many great screws. Two of the sexy young nannies, right there on that table. A couple of Washington housewives, longing to climb that social ladder. What a room! It was there that he had his power. Nobody more charming. Nobody more brilliant . . . The grip of the drugs subsided in his mind, and for a second melancholia swept in. What the hell . . . what the hell did it all mean?

The unwelcome thought arose that maybe he should have paid more attention to his daughter. Maybe he shouldn't have gambled. Maybe he shouldn't have neglected his job . . .

Thomas Morgan let out a loud, wretched sob. The maudlin wash of regret peaked on another chemical dip and turned into anger. Morgan strode up to the bedroom, sat at his antique William and Mary dressing table, and snorted the next of the thick, fat lines he'd chopped out earlier this evening. Instant rush. His dismissal, hand-delivered from his boss, lay ignored on the bed. Morgan was flying, riding a fresh wave of self-confidence and pride. He looked at himself in the mirror, a tall, handsome man. The white tie, Washington's most formal style of attire, looked *fabulous* on His Excellency. As ever.

Swap it for an economy ticket home and a cheap pension? Live in a semidetached somewhere cheap? He thought not.

His Excellency the Hon. Thomas Morgan walked over to the Victorian sash windows, threw them open with one arm and swung his legs over the edge. Fuck them, fuck them all! They'd never catch him.

His daughter, Jane, briefly floated back into his mind. But he didn't want to think of her now. Wasn't the moment. She was *his* daughter. She'd be OK, and besides, her mother was waiting, expecting him . . .

He tossed himself over the edge, high as a kite. Falling, his arms spread out, as though he were flying, offering himself to the elements.

But he wasn't flying. He was dying. In that long second before death, Thomas Morgan knew it. His mind threw up a vision of Jane, all grown up—she was happy, he thought.

He blew her a kiss as the ground swallowed him up.

'So, how did it go?'

Helen's father helped her into the car. He had to admit she looked marvellous, modestly gowned but at the same time splendidly beautiful. He was pleased—young Ahmed would be an amenable bridegroom.

'It was so much fun.' Helen sighed with contentment. In all her young life, she had never had such an evening. The girls had all adored her outfit, and she'd felt simply beautiful—not different, just the centre of attention. The solid friendship of Sally and Jane had buoyed her up. And if young men had asked her to dance, asked for her number—well, she didn't have to say yes—that was nice, too.

'Excellent. I trusted you,' he reminded her.

'I know, Baba.' Helen gave him a reassuring hug. 'It was all fine.'

'Tomorrow morning Ahmed is coming.'

She sighed, but a bargain was a bargain. 'I'll be there.'

The sun was streaming through the window of her bedroom when Jane woke up. It was a glorious winter's day in LA; sunny, but not too hot. The Malibu ocean was crashing against their private beach, and as Jane tossed in bed, she smelled the welcoming aroma of Consuela's bacon sizzling in the pan. Jane pushed a hand through her tousled hair and smiled.

For the first time in a long time—maybe for ever—she woke up happy. Last night had been truly wonderful. She'd been asked to dance by no less than three film stars, one soap actor, and a rock star—and asked for her number by countless studs. And the girls had fluttered about her, offering compliments—wow, it felt fantastic!

She was overwhelmed with gratitude to Sally. Call it superficial all you want—as bookworm supreme, Jane certainly had—but being pretty made *all* the difference. She felt confident, feminine, as if the missing piece had been added to her life. Maybe she'd never have Sally's brazen, starry glow, but Jane Morgan felt good about herself.

She swung her slim legs out of bed and padded over to the mirror. Even without make-up, the beauty was still there; the great hair, ruffled by sleep; her pretty face, without the glasses; a little mascara on her lashes that hadn't come off with the cursory wipe she'd given her face last night.

She wandered into the shower and was revelling in the sensation of the powerful jets, when Consuela hammered on the door.

'Mees Morgan—phone—for you.'

'Take a message,' Jane yelled. 'I'll call them back.'

'They say ees important. Ees Washington.'

'I'll get dressed, call them right back,' Jane snapped. Damn! Couldn't she at least put her clothes on?

Still, it wasn't like Daddy to call her and insist on talking. Reluctantly, Jane dried off fast and selected black jeans and a matching T-shirt, then went to find Consuela.

Consuela passed her a scrap of paper and Jane dialled back. 'This is Jane Morgan,' she said confidently. 'I believe my father called me?'

There was a long pause at the end of the line.

'Hold please, Miss Morgan.'

A couple of beeps, and Jane found herself talking to Cyril—Sir Cyril Clark, her father's senior attaché. 'Jane?' he said.

She knew instantly, from his tone, something was wrong. 'What is it? Let me speak to my father, please.'

'Now listen, Jane,' he said heavily, and her stomach curled into a knot. 'You're going to have to be very brave.'

'And this is my daughter, Helen.' Baba was speaking in Arabic; Helen's was rusty, she was ashamed of that.

'*Wa-es salaam*,' she said politely.

He nodded back and said something too fast for Helen to understand. Ahmed was a young man of reasonable height, and a pleasant enough face. He looked about as enthusiastic over the whole exercise as she did herself. Helen smiled at him—he, too, probably had parents to placate.

'Ahmed's father is also visiting town. He'll be here this afternoon for the ceremony.'

'What ceremony is that?' Helen asked, confused.

'The friendship ceremony.' Ali spoke in English, and Ahmed looked on uncomprehendingly. 'Traditional in Egypt. You will go through with it, Helen?'

'Course I will.' She nodded. Fair's fair—they'd let her go to the party, the greatest night of her life. At the very least, she could show willing. 'It will be good to meet your father,' she added to Ahmed, haltingly.

'Thank you.' He added, 'I am very happy.'

He didn't look it.

'And I have a surprise for you,' Ali added. 'Tonight we are all going on a family trip—to Cairo. Your mother is visiting her cousins. Afterwards we'll go back to Amman.'

'Really?' Helen asked, thrilled. Back to Jordan? She hadn't seen her childhood home for years. It was all a bit hazy, a bit confusing, and she was very tired. But Helen loved the idea, and if it meant being polite to this distant cousin for a little while, she would go along with that.

'Will you excuse me?' she asked Ahmed. 'I want to go and see my friend Sally. Thank her for that amazing party. I'll be back this afternoon, for the ceremony.'

'No later than noon—your mother has a special dress for you to wear,' Ali told her.

Helen kissed him on the cheek. 'I promise.'

The cab dropped Helen out front. Green Gables was already immaculately clean—she could hardly believe it. An army of servants had descended on the place in the night; after only a few hours, you'd never know there had been a party there at all.

She rang the bell, eager to see Sally. A moment later and the door swung open. Richard, the second butler, greeted her.

'Good morning, Miss Yanna.' All the staff here knew Helen by name. 'Please come in. Miss Lassiter is in her bedroom.'

Helen half ran up the stairs, feeling as light as thistledown. She knew the way, third on the left at the top of the sweeping marble stairs. She hammered on the door. 'Sally! You sleeping? It's Helen. Let me in!'

'Just a moment.'

Helen blinked; she could hear that Sally was crying. Why? Last night had been perfect. 'What's up?'

Sally opened the door, red-eyed, tear tracks streaked down her face. 'It's Jane. There's been . . . an accident.'

Helen's stomach turned over. 'What kind of an accident? Is she *dead*?'

'Not her. Her father. He fell out of a top-floor window in his house in Washington . . .'

'Oh my God.'

'The British Secret Service came . . . took her away to Washington. She called me before she left.'

Sally would never forget the bleakness, the desolation in Jane's voice.

'Does she have family there?'

'Nobody. Her father never got on with them.'

'Then who's going to look after Jane?'

Both girls flopped down on Sally's huge bed with its silken sheets.

'I guess I am,' Sally said finally. 'I told her she can come live here, like in one of the guest cottages. We can afford it . . .'

'Won't she inherit—'

'No, that's the thing. It was all government stuff—dependent on her dad's job. Now that's gone, so's everything else. She has no house . . . nothing. Helen, her dad didn't really fall. It was suicide.' Sally dabbed at her red eyes. 'He got caught . . . drinking on the job, taking drugs. They fired him, dismissed him. And he had a gambling problem, apparently. There was no money there at all.'

'Oh God!' Helen cried out. 'Poor Jane. But the British have to look after her. She's still a child legally.'

Sally mulled that over. 'She didn't sound like she wanted anything to do with them. Jane told me the Brits are going to cover it up. They're just calling it a suicide.' Sally sighed. 'But she's not coming back to Miss Milton's.' Sally rubbed her eyes; the thought of losing Jane was dreadful. 'She says she never wants to see that school again. I think she means it.'

'Well, whatever she decides, we'll be here.' Helen knew it sounded lame. She looked at Sally. 'My family's taking a short trip too, but I'll be back very soon. Look after Jane for me.'

Back home, there were ribbons tied to the gate, and balloons. Oh, man. Baba's party for Ahmed!

Aisha hurried out of the kitchen door.

'Come with me upstairs. I have your betrothal dress.'

Helen allowed herself to be pushed upstairs. 'What do you mean, betrothal?'

'The ceremony, the friendship ceremony,' her mother said hurriedly.

Helen quickly got changed; her mother had got her a beautiful Jordanian robe, traditional and, she thought, antique. She admired her reflection as Aisha fastened a flowing silk headscarf round her hair.

'Can I keep this? It's beautiful.'

'Of course you can. Now run downstairs, Baba is waiting for you.'

'Mama, you know I'm not actually going to marry Ahmed.'

'Just do this for your father,' Aisha said vaguely. 'Hurry! His father is there waiting for you.'

Helen sighed and walked downstairs. Her father was waiting with an ornate-looking document. Ahmed was there, looking as embarrassed as she was, in traditional Islamic trousers and hat.

Baba put Helen's hand into his. Feeling every sympathy for Ahmed, she gave him a surreptitious wink. He looked at her properly for the first time; his eyes widened, and he gave her a very small smile.

Baba was speaking in Arabic now. She didn't follow what he was saying. He told her he would lead her, she should repeat after him.

Helen willingly agreed. She wanted to ease the tension for poor Ahmed, and to forget today's troubles. Get to the airport, get on the plane. Do some thinking. When she returned from Egypt, Jane would have worked out what she wanted to do. *Inshallah*, she would be back at school, with Helen and Sally protecting her.

Her father was placing a golden pen in her hand.

'Sign here,' he said. 'Darling. My little daughter.'

He kissed her on the forehead and Helen pressed her head against his. She adored her parents. Their ceremony was over now, and they seemed happy with her. Tired, confused, she signed the papers.

'**D**o you like it? We'll sit here.'

Ahmed smiled at her—his English was as rusty as her Arabic.

'Yes, brilliant.' Helen laughed, she loved flying business class. She wasn't Sally Lassiter—for her this was an adventure. Helen was tired, but running to make the plane had given her a surge of adrenaline. It had been chaotic at the airport, with her parents running and shouting and waving boarding passes. Helen was handed hers separately and asked to sit with Ahmed by Baba. They had barely made it onto the plane, Baba stopping to sort out their cases and waving Helen and Ahmed ahead. She hadn't seen her parents in the departure area, they were probably already seated. Helen spun round in her seat. She couldn't see her parents. Where were the others?

'Ahmed,' Helen said urgently, summoning her Arabic as best she could. The plane groaned, shuddered and started to accelerate as the pilot eased it onto the runway. 'Where are Mama and Baba? Where is your father?'

'I do not understand,' he said heavily, dark eyes fixed on her. 'What are you asking me?'

Helen tried again. 'Where are our parents?'

He blinked. 'In America. The airport, they said goodbye. Why are you asking me this?'

She felt sick. 'I don't understand. Isn't this a family trip to Cairo?'

'Of course,' he said, and for a second her stomach unknotted. 'It is a family trip—a honeymoon trip. Yours and mine.'

Helen repeated dully, 'Honeymoon?'

Ahmed showed the first signs of impatience. 'We are married, are we not? You and I. Married. *Mashallah!*'

'Married?' she repeated. 'Who said we were married?'

Ahmed stared at her anxiously. 'Helen,' he said slowly and, she noticed, gently, as one addressing a frightened child. 'You and I signed the *nikkah*, did we not? We are married now, in the sight of the Most Compassionate.' He offered her a tentative smile.

Stunned, she was silent.

He took her hand. 'I did not want this either. But if we surrender our selfish desires, we will find true peace, *inshallah.*'

The puzzle pieces fell into place with slow, terrible clarity. That 'friendship ceremony' had been her *nikkah*. The binding engagement ceremony between Muslims—in the eyes of God, she was already married. Helen's head spun. Yes, Mama had said it—friendship ceremony. When Baba read from the sacred Qur'an, God forgive her, she had not been paying attention. But she had happily gone through with it. Ahmed had no idea she was not consenting to be his wife.

'In truth, I had already lost my one true love. I could have lived for ever by myself. But you and I can be friends, I think? Is it not so?'

Helen understood, in a second. She had underestimated her father, her mother too. And even now, she did not blame them. Her father and mother had arranged a marriage for her after the old ways. And she had to admit she had gone through the *nikkah* of her own free will.

Helen looked at Ahmed, older than her, his own face drawn from duty to his parents and indeed to God. He was, she knew instinctively, a good man. Helen was mature enough to believe that what her parents had done had been from sheer love of her. She knew their own had been an arranged marriage, and she knew, too, they had been extremely happy.

Ahmed had his hand in hers. Helen had no wish to humiliate him. After all, her American passport was in her pocket. Whatever her parents' schemes, she was a free woman. But she would not hurt this man. Or her parents. There could be a divorce—after a decent interval, of course.

'Yes. We can be very good friends,' she agreed, with a generous smile.

'That is well.' He beamed at her.

'And friends should be honest,' Helen ploughed on. 'So tell me, why didn't you want to go through with the *nikkah*?'

Ahmed blew out his cheeks and sighed. 'I don't want to offend you.'

'You won't.'

'Her name was Firyal,' he said eventually. 'I thought . . . well. I thought we were destined for each other. She was not from a good family, but I saw her, in the mosque, each day. She was an exceptional woman. She had a job working for the Department of Antiquities. Firyal was beautiful, modest, and brilliant.' He looked across at Helen. 'She died,' he added simply. 'A car accident. Cairo traffic. So mundane.'

'And you did not want to marry again?'

'I was never betrothed to her.' He fell silent, and stared out of the tiny window at the sky below them.

And you're not really betrothed to me. Helen picked up her headphones and plugged them into the seat. She would stay in Ahmed's house for a week or so, then, once the divorce was concluded, come home. Her father meant well, but she would arrange her own marriage—to a man who actually *wanted* to be her husband.

'Sally. It's Jane.'

Sally gripped the receiver. 'How are you? Where are you?'

'At LAX,' Jane said. Her voice sounded tense and miserable. 'Can you come and pick me up?'

Sally bounded down the stairs. Jonathan, their English butler, was polishing a statue in the hallway.

'Any of the cars ready?'

'The Aston Martin is around, Miss Lassiter.'

She snatched the keys from the rail and made to rush out the door. Paulie waddled out of his study and almost crashed into her.

'Hey, where's my princess going?'

'I got to pick Jane up at the airport.' Sally stopped for a second; her dad was all red-faced.

'You should go easy on that bacon at breakfast, Dad,' she said.

'You're as bad as your mom. I drink OJ, I'll live for a thousand years.' Paulie patted his rotund stomach. 'You'll never get rid of me.'

Sally flung her arms round him and gave him a hug; poor, poor Jane.

'I might not be back till late. I'm gonna pick up Jane, we might spend some time together.'

'That's fine.' Her dad looked distracted. 'Something came up at the office. I'll be late too.'

'Mom'll be stuck with *Jeopardy* and a TV dinner,' Sally joked. 'See you later, Pop.' She kissed him on the cheek and ran out the door.

'See you later,' Paulie said to her departing back.

But he would never see her again.

Jane was standing with her suitcases, a forlorn little figure on the kerb.

Sally screeched to a halt and jumped out. She crushed Jane in a big bear hug. 'Tell me everything,' she said as they got into the car.

'Nothing to tell.' Jane laid her head back against the headrest as Sally pulled smoothly out into traffic. 'A diplomatic funeral. Just me, his secretary and the pastor. Then the lawyers told me what my options were.'

'So . . . it wasn't good?'

Jane shook her head.

Sally glanced across at her. 'He left you nothing, hon?'

'Some personal effects. I can't bear to keep them, so I asked they be donated to charity.' Jane's voice had a cold determination to it that tore at Sally's heart. 'He had debts up to the eyeballs, but the Embassy got a lawyer and they won't attach to me, as I'm a minor.'

'Which means they have to look after you . . . You should really consider coming back to school.'

'They refuse to pay for Miss Milton's.'

'That's bull,' Sally exclaimed. 'If they won't pay for you, we will. Daddy will, I promise you that.'

Jane reached over and squeezed her hand. 'Sally, I love you for that.' Tears started to prickle in both their eyes. 'But I can't go back there, don't you see?'

'Oh, Jane.'

'They offered me a small place in Washington in a not great area, and a local private school. I said no way.'

'So what are you going to do?'

'Stay right where I am. I guess I'll get a job. And an apartment.'

'But you're not a legal adult. And what kind of job can you get?'

'I'll work something out.'

Sally could hear the tears lurking just under the bravado. 'Y'all can come and live with us,' Sally suggested. 'The maid and you. We'll pay her wages . . . you can have a guest bungalow. Daddy won't mind.'

'Thanks, honey.' Jane smiled at her gratefully. 'But I want to rely on myself. Does that make sense?'

'You always were ornery,' Sally said, but she did understand. Jane had always had that fierce pride, as long as she'd known her. 'We'll go see Helen, go get a long lunch somewhere.'

'Sounds good,' Jane said.

They pulled up outside the Yannas' compact little house. 'You stay here,' Jane suggested tactfully. 'I'll ring the bell.'

Sally was wearing one of her typical short skirts, just off the knee. Somehow Jane assumed that her own plain black trouser-suit would be more reassuring to their friend's parents.

She climbed out and pressed the buzzer. Helen's father came to the door, a stocky, bearded man, gazing at her very coolly.

'Mr Yanna, I'm Jane, Helen's schoolfriend. Is she about?'

'No. My daughter is not here any more. She has got married.'

'I—I don't quite understand—'

'She got married to the nephew of her mother's cousin, Ahmed, and they have gone back to Cairo to set up house,' Helen's father replied flatly. 'She may not be back here for many years.'

'But she didn't say anything to us.'

'A wedding is a private family matter,' Ali Yanna said. 'If she wishes to call you, she can.'

Jane digested this. 'If she speaks to you, will you tell her Sally and I would like to talk to her?' Jane asked.

He shrugged. 'Goodbye then.' The door closed.

Sally and poked her head out of the car window. 'What happened?'

Jane got back in the car and motioned for Sally to drive off. 'He said she got married to some distant relation and left for Cairo.'

Sally's face was a picture of dismay. 'That can't be true. She never said a damned thing to us.'

'Mr Yanna told me it was a private family matter.' Jane chewed on her lip. 'I know Helen, I don't think she would do that.'

'Guess we'll just have to wait for her to call. Oh, man,' Sally breathed. 'It just hit me. I'll be all alone at school now. No you and no Helen. I don't want to go back.'

They both contemplated Julie Manners and Melissa Smith.

'Don't,' Jane said boldly. 'Sal, just don't. Get your dad to pay for a private tutor, or go to a different school.'

'Maybe you're right,' Sally said wearily. 'I should think about it.' She grinned at Jane. 'We still got each other. Let's go get some coffee.'

'**S**o.' Paulie Lassiter shook his head. He was getting worked up. He was in the Century City offices of his extremely high-priced corporate lawyers, surrounded by suits, and not one of them was coming up with any damn solutions!

'What do we do? We gotta fix this.' His stare said, *you* gotta fix this.

'Paulie, these accounts . . . they're fiction.'

He snorted. 'Three accounting firms signed 'em.'

'Yeah, but your CFO was cooking the books.'

'I told you, I fired the son of a bitch.'

'That won't do it.' Lionel Javits, head of the lawyers, pushed horn-rimmed spectacles up his nose. 'You have to notify the Feds, the Dow, the regulatory authorities. The stock is going to go through the floor. Jack Lessing is going to jail.'

'Damn right he is,' Paulie snapped. 'My concern now is to save the stock. Nobody's selling, not while this is going on.' He mopped his brow, struggling with his breath.

'Paulie, they already did. Most of your board, even the non-execs. They've been quietly dumping stock for the last eighteen months.' Javits paused; it was clear to him that Lassiter had no grasp of what was happening. 'And if you haven't been selling, then it doesn't look good for you either.'

'But at least it proves you're honest,' a junior suit piped up brightly. '*You* won't be going to jail!'

Javits glared at him.

Paulie glanced outside at the bright, blue sky. It seemed such a normal day in LA. How could everything look normal when his world was coming apart!

'That *can't* be right,' he said patiently. 'We're not some paper company. We got *assets*. Oil fields.'

'Your executives have been living pretty high on the hog, Paulie.'

Well, he knew *that*.

'But the money was there,' he said weakly. His heart started thumping. A picture of his wife, chattering about Sally's party, floated into his vision. How the hell would he explain this to Mona?

'No, it wasn't, Paulie,' Lionel Javits said gently. His client was such a big, lumbering bear of a man. A *good* man, an oilman, not into business. And far too trusting.

'It's corruption.' The junior suit was piping up again.

'Corruption?' That was something he *did* understand. 'You mean my workers . . . the pension fund . . .'

'It's bankrupt, Paulie. It's looking to me like the entire company is going belly up. We'll need to show you are an innocent party. I'll contact the authorities myself. You say, on the advice of counsel I assert my Fifth Amendment rights not to incriminate myself . . .'

Paulie Lassiter felt needles in his left arm, then a huge stabbing pain in his chest. He couldn't breathe. 'Ugggh,' he groaned, and struggled to his feet. A glass-topped coffee table crashed to the ground.

'Paulie!' Lionel Javits shrieked. 'My God! Call 911!'

Paulie, clutching ineffectually at his chest, gasped and tumbled forward, the blocked blood rushing to his face. Two lawyers dived on him and attempted to start CPR.

'Leave it,' Javits said. He found he had tears in his eyes. This was a massive coronary; you didn't need to be a doc to see it. Paulie Lassiter was very dead. And Lionel Javits knew what was coming, for Lassiter Corp and for Paulie's family. Ruin—lawsuits—total humiliation—ostracism. He liked Paulie. Paulie was dead now. And Javits thought he was better off that way.

Chapter Four

'WHO IS IT?' Jane had the door on the chain.

'Repo!' The man's voice was gruff.

Jane swallowed hard and opened the door. 'Hi there! Come on in. You guys want coffee?'

The guy entered with three other men. 'No, thanks.' He couldn't meet her eye. 'Which way is the living room?'

'Right in there. I unplugged everything. It was mostly too big to move by myself, though, I'm sorry.'

'That's fine. Let's start with the TV.'

The men moved fast. Her big-screen TV, the stereo system, the furniture, the antiques—they took everything. Efficient as ants at a picnic.

Jane withdrew into the kitchen and put the kettle on; they had already removed the cappuccino machine.

'Sure you won't take that coffee?'

'No, thanks. We got to get to West Hollywood. The bed . . .' He looked back into her room. 'That's not on my sheet—the inflatable bed. We can leave that, I guess. And you can keep that kettle! They won't notice a sixteen-buck kettle in my office.'

'Thanks. You guys have a great day.' Jane saw them to the door. She shut it, leaned her head against the wood, and listened as the truck drove away. She glanced around her empty house—not hers, any more; the Embassy had made it clear that the lease was up at the end of the month. It was stripped of everything down to the last framed print. She went over to the inflatable bed and flopped down. And finally, she allowed the tears to come.

When she was done, she took a shower—at least the hot water was still on, and she had a towel and clothes in a suitcase. Sure, the Embassy wanted to 'look after' her—on *their* terms. Jane was not into that. Stuck in some hideous Washington two-bit school, where everybody would know who she was? Laugh at her? Humiliate her?

Hell no. Jane Morgan had no room in her heart for further bruising. She finished with the shower, carefully brushed her teeth, and got dressed. Then she let herself out of the back door with the key Consuela had left for her when she was fired. Jane glanced at the driveway; empty now, like the house. She was only seventeen, and everything in her world had fallen apart.

Her father—useless; unloving; selfish. But *hers*. Deep down, she had hoped that one day they could forge a relationship. That chance had gone. For ever. And her lifestyle. The money—she felt she could have managed without that. Because at least there had been the girls. Her best friends—no, her *family*. But, like her father, like the money, her friends had gone. Just like that. One week, and they'd evaporated.

Helen. Vanished from school, gone back to Egypt to get married. How could Helen not tell them?

And Sally, her older friend? Far different, and far worse. For Sally, life had exploded, in almost the same way it had done for her. Paulie

Lassiter's heart attack had been Monday morning's big news. But the afternoon's big news was the collapse of the company. Jane had watched, horrified, on her TV, as the squad cars proceeded to Green Gables; as a black-clad, half-fainting Mona was taken into police custody; as Sally, a blanket thrown over her head to protect her from the paparazzi, joined her.

She'd called, of course. But the phone had been disconnected. Sally eventually called Jane, too distraught to speak much. There was no doubt her best friend was facing trouble. Very serious trouble.

'The Feds are taking everything,' Sally confessed to her, once she'd stopped sobbing. 'We're bankrupt. They froze Dad's accounts . . . Mom's still under investigation, but they think she'll likely get off with innocent spouse defence.'

'You sound angry.'

'Innocent spouse? Makes my dad seem guilty. And he wasn't no crook.' Sally sobbed.

'I decided to move to Washington after all,' Jane said. It wasn't true, but she didn't want Sally to worry about her. And she had to figure out her future. Jane had to deal with this, on her own.

'Yeah.' Sally sounded so dull, so depressed. 'We're going away, too. Mom's friends—they've all vanished. I told her she needs to get out of Bel Air. We have family in Texas we can go to.'

'You'll like Texas, right? That's home.'

'Was once.' Sally sighed. There was a long, wretched pause. 'Take care of yourself, hon.'

'And you, Sally.' Jane was unused to the emotion that washed through her now. 'Be kind to yourself,' she said. Her voice cracked a little, and she hurriedly replaced the receiver.

Now Jane sat in her still-neat garden, on the iron bench they hadn't bothered to remove, and looked at the sea. The ocean was clear, blue, and immense. It crashed, and crashed, eternally, on the beach below.

She had come out here to think. The disasters, one on top of the other. No friends, now. No money. No contacts. At the end of this month, no house. She was entirely on her own.

A sleazeball lawyer was the right start. Emancipation—Jane had read about that in the library. A teen petitioning to be designated a legal adult. Once she had the important pieces of paper, she'd be two things. An adult; and an American. She could do whatever she wanted. Jane had learned a hard lesson, and learned it fast. Money counted in this world. When she'd had privileged access to it, she had despised money.

Now, she wanted revenge. And that meant cash. The kind that could help get her own back on Julie, and all those snobby bitches at school. The kind that could help Sally deal with the rich friends who'd seen fit to dump a devastated and grieving widow. Money was protection. Money was control. Money was something *women* didn't have. Jane watched the ocean and let that thought sink in. Plenty of rich girls . . . except it was always somebody else's money. Sally had nothing of her own, it was all in Daddy's accounts. When they were cut off, so was she. Helen Yanna, daughter of a wealthy, middle-class man, now married, apparently, to another wealthy, middle-class man. Jane worried about her. What happened if she fell out with her husband? The world didn't prepare people like Helen—or Sally—for the moment the Jericho walls crashed into rubble. What would Sally do now? Marry somebody? She still had those blonde Barbie looks, and right now it seemed she'd be reduced to trading on them.

Jane didn't want that for herself. No way. She still had assets. Brains—thank God, for everything stemmed from that. Beauty—not like Sally's, but she would never go back to her dowdy self. Sally had once told her glamour was a weapon. It got you through the front door. After that, your brains had to take over. It was time to grow up. Jane saw things much more clearly now. She went inside, picked up the phone book lying on the dusty floor of the living room, and made a call.

'Then there's the matter of my fee.' The lawyer looked at Jane down his nose, expectantly.

She sighed. The office was filthy; the windows were dusty, and he had papers all across his desk.

'Two hundred,' she said.

'Two hundred!' He snorted. '*Fifteen* hundred, *and* that's a discount because you're a minor.' He leaned across his desk and leered at Jane. 'In *one* sense. In another, of course, you're legal . . .'

She knew exactly what he meant.

'Maybe we could work something out.' His gaze travelled slowly up her legs.

'Look, Mr Richards, can I speak frankly to you?'

'You can be as frank as you want to, honey.'

'You're a loser,' Jane said.

That brought him up short. 'Excuse me?' He was outraged.

'You're a loser,' Jane repeated. 'Going nowhere fast. It's why I picked you. I can't afford a decent lawyer, and you desperately need some work.'

'Two hundred ain't work.'

'I mean real work. Cases. You need your name in the papers. Nobody's going to hire you if you slob around like this.' Disdainfully, she lifted one of last week's papers, the sports section. 'You got to get yourself a neat office, a secretary, a decent suit, and some real clients.'

Richards wanted to tell the schoolgirl to take a hike. But it was true, he did need work. He was already behind on the rent here. 'All that takes cash. And I got clients like you who don't want to pay it.'

'I bring more than cash. I bring you a *chance*. Represent me, and I can guarantee you press coverage. In fact, forget the two hundred. You'll do it *pro bono*—much better PR that way. And once it's taken care of, I'll give you a fabulous quote.'

'A quote?'

'Yes. Let me see.' Jane composed herself and looked at him; her eyes were suddenly brimming. 'After my father died the Brits abandoned me,' she said, her voice breaking. 'Nobody cared, nobody would help me. Except Josh Richards . . . I know what they say about lawyers but he's one who *really cares*. You can trust Josh Richards. I owe this all to him.'

'Wow,' he said, impressed. He had the uncomfortable feeling he was being railroaded. On the other hand, she did sound like she knew exactly what she was doing.

'I take you on—for free. And you organise some publicity?'

'Hey, you read the papers. My father was a high-ranking British diplomat who gambled away his money and took lots of drugs. He was going to be fired.' As she recounted this tale, Jane Morgan seemed almost totally devoid of emotion. Josh flinched—the chick was a robot. 'I want to be a legal adult. And I want US citizenship. I've been here almost all my childhood. I'm naturalised. You take care of the emancipation and get me a pass from the INS. I'll get you great PR for your *pro bono* work for the Ambassador's orphaned daughter. Deal?'

She offered him her manicured hand. 'No time-wasting—you file those papers this morning. Or else I'll walk down the street and find myself another hungry lawyer.'

'Don't do that,' Richards said hastily. 'I'm on it, I'll file this afternoon.'

'Good.'

So what do you think?'

Think? Jane thought the place was a dump. Studio apartment on Sunset Strip. Tiny, filthy bathroom, with cracked shower tiles, mildew and a stain in the loo.

'It has a separate kitchen.' The fat landlady puffed her cheeks out.

What a joke. A tiny alcove, one cupboard and an electric socket.

'Fridge is broke,' the landlady said succinctly.

Jane watched as a fat black cockroach scuttled up the kitchen wall. She shuddered.

'Five hundred a month and the same as deposit, minimum one-year lease.'

'Forget it. Two hundred and no deposit.'

'You forget it.' She was outraged. 'Get out, you're wasting my time.'

Jane stood firm. 'Think about it, lady. You won't get anyone in here but section 8. And they'll just trash the property. Now what *I* am is an English lady down on her luck. You rent to me, and I'll clean up this shithole. It'll look good. I'll make it bohemian and funky, and when I'm gone you can rent to a student at a thousand. I pay cash—no contracts—meaning no taxes for *you*. And you get to kick me out whenever you feel like it.'

The fat woman hummed and hawed. 'Two hundred ain't enough.'

'It's all I got, so it'll have to do.' Jane reached into her handbag and pulled out two hundred-dollar bills. She waved the portraits of Benjamin Franklin temptingly in front of the owner. 'By rights, you ought to be paying *me*. Two hundred, I'll only be here three months, and there'll be something rentable when I've gone.'

'What's gonna happen after three months?'

Jane tossed her head. 'By then, I'll have a real job.'

'*Suuure* you will.' But she snatched up the money. 'Three months, girlie, then the price goes up to five hundred. You get free electric—no heat. Here's the keys.'

Jane stood by the window, watching until the landlady drove away. Then she turned round and went through her handbag. A grand total of three hundred and twenty-two dollars. All she had in the world.

Carefully Jane hid the money under a squeaking floorboard, after she had extracted thirty bucks. She needed to invest in some sponges, some serious disinfectant, and the cheapest new bedding she could find. She stripped the bed, emptied the stinking fridge and the garbage pail, nearly gagging, and hauled the black bin liner downstairs. Then she came back up, threw the window open and locked the door. For a second, despair overcame her, but only for a second. This was independence, she told herself. The start of a brand-new life. And she was going to make a go of it.

That night, she worked her tail off. While the drunks and hookers fought and screamed below her, Jane cleaned. She wore out three scrubbing brushes and got her hands raw. The stinking refrigerator she emptied of bugs and droppings, closed tight and then switched off. There'd be no way to get rid of roaches other than keeping zero food in the apartment.

When the place was done, she unpacked her other purchases. Amazing what you could get for a dollar or two in the bargain bins. A mattress protector for the single bed—who the hell knew who'd last slept on it. A shade for the light bulb transformed the bleak glare into a pretty, peach-coloured light. Fresh sheets on the bed—not exactly matching, but all basically white or cream; a pillow and a quilted bedcover. A snap-up wardrobe made of fabric and plastic, with a zipper, and hangers for her clothes. A cheap Mexican rug, for a splash of colour. A shower curtain, decorated with suns and moons. Finally, Jane had blown a whole $2.50 on a cheerful yellow plastic vase and a bunch of carnations.

On her kitchen table lay an application form. Shop Smart, always looking for helpers—'greeters', they called them. Paid minimum wage. That was fine by Jane. All she was asking for was someplace to start. Tomorrow she would be legal. Jane knew quite a bit about Shop Smart, a large company with lots of potential. She had no qualms about getting in on the ground floor. Jane didn't plan to stay there long.

'Jane! Jane!'

'Babe! Over here!'

She emerged from the courthouse to find a small knot of reporters, and two local TV cameras. Dressed in her best suit and carefully made up—cosmetics, clothes and shoes were about all the bailiffs had left her—Jane walked out onto the courthouse steps, one arm threaded through her lawyer's. Josh Richards was wearing a suit, too. He beamed—he looked almost presentable.

'Do you blame the Brits?'

She held up a hand. 'Thank you, ladies and gentlemen. No, I don't blame anybody. I have a very good lawyer, who worked on this case for free. And I'm grateful to be recognised as both an adult, and an American.'

'How does it feel to lose all that cash?'

'I never expected to have anything handed to me.' She smiled dead at the camera. 'Tomorrow I'll be going for a job at Shop Smart. I want to work my way up, and that's an all-American company.'

They snapped and took pictures, and eventually drifted away. Richards was ecstatic. 'Hey, thanks, babe. I think one of those guys was from the *Times*. You want to get lunch?' he asked hopefully. Hell, she *was* an adult now, totally legal in every way. 'I'm buying . . .'

'No, thank you. I have work to do.'

'Thought you didn't have a job,' he sulked.

'That's the work—finding one.'

He had a brainwave. 'Hey, I'll give you a job. Come be my assistant.'

'No, thanks. I don't want to be anybody's assistant.'

'In Shop Smart you get minimum wage. It's menial work.'

'Yes, but they have a management programme,' Jane said.

Mrs Doherty saw Jane coming, and smiled.

'Good morning. I was wondering if any vacancies had opened up?'

The English girl was well groomed. Good accent, too—the customers would love those classy limey tones.

'Saw you on TV. You said nice things about Shop Smart. My boss said if you came back to give you a job.'

'Great.' Jane felt a wash of relief surge through her. 'If you've got a uniform, I can get changed right away?'

'You need to fill in a form first.'

Jane opened her bag, took out the neatly completed form and handed it to the recruiter. Disbelievingly, the woman scanned it.

'Damn, girl. You in a hurry?'

Jane didn't reply.

'There are uniforms in back. Put one on and clock in. You're going to be a greeter. Seven-day trial, be here at seven a.m. tomorrow. If you're late, you're fired. Got it?'

'Yes, ma'am,' Jane said.

'**G**ood morning! Welcome to Shop Smart. I hope you have a lovely day.'

Janice Esposito, personnel manager, sourly watched the new girl at the front door. Ticking off performance stats. Looking for a fault. Janice couldn't believe the new girl really *wanted* a shitty job like this. Celebrity orphan? Right, like she was really poor. Why the hell would she want a minimum wage job that was strictly for the unqualified? Janice instantly disliked Jane Morgan. But she had a job to do. And it involved ticking off little boxes.

Friendliness—check.

Neatness—check. Not a hair out of place.

Smile—check. Crocodiles had smaller smiles than this chick.

Janice's pen hovered as she watched Jane Morgan quickly glance at her watch. Finally, a no-no—she was *supposed* to be looking out for new customers, one hundred per cent of the time.

'Good *afternoon*.' Jane Morgan beamed. 'Welcome to Shop Smart!'

'Well, would ya look at that, Dick,' the portly matron said to her husband as they waddled in past Janice and her clipboard. 'Bang on twelve noon and she switches to "afternoon". Ain't that a kick!'

Janice sighed. Unfortunately, in a job where there was no such thing as taking the initiative, this girl had just found a way to do it.

There was a box at the base of her form. 'Consider for promotion?' Reluctantly, she ticked it.

Jane didn't do a lot of crying. Mostly, she was too tired. The cheque at the end of the week was tiny—man, she resented those taxes and social security payments—yet she still had to save from it. Needed a deposit on a car. Never mind how much of a wreck, she had to have *something*.

Now her citizenship had come through, she had to queue to get herself a social security number, a driver's licence, a bank account. Credit was the worst. If you didn't have any, it was hard to get any.

She managed it somehow; a starter card at an exorbitant rate. Daylight robbery, but Jane started an account, and set it up with her bank so that payments were made automatically, on time.

It was amazing what you could get, for free, if you were persistent. Most every day, Jane ate in the staff cafeteria, where food was plentiful and cheap. There was no private gym in her life, but Jane ran daily, every morning at 6 a.m.; a golden hour, when the junkies had finally crawled home to bed, and the regular joes hadn't yet surfaced. She ran up and down the Sunset Strip, ignoring needles and bottles, keeping her eyes fixed on the horizon. And when she got back to the apartment, Jane forced herself to do forty pushups before her stretch routine.

Punishing. But energetic. When she got into work, there were free bagels and orange juice and she had the energy she needed to push herself through the day.

When she finished greeting, there was lunch—ten minutes flat, and a bathroom break. Next, Jane swapped uniforms and went to the checkout till, where she worked two sessions. She got home nights at 9 p.m., showered, and tumbled into bed.

It was a disciplined routine. After a while, it became automatic. And with the free stuff she got from the store—spoilt items, frayed T-shirts you could sleep in—Jane spent next to nothing. She worked seven days, and actually watched her savings start to mount.

One day blended into another. It was mindless. And that suited her fine. Jane Morgan didn't want to do too much thinking.

'Let's go see her.' Julie Manners stretched out on her lilo in the pool.

'What do you mean? She's gone.' Emma Lightfoot laughed meanly.

The girls extended their legs and applied a little oil.

'Did I tell you guys? Momma got me a birthday present,' said Melissa Smith, tossing her silky black hair.

'We know. A yellow Maserati. You told us already,' Emma complained.

'Not that one, another one. Season tickets to the Dodgers. A *box*.'

'Oooh,' Julie said, instantly seeing the possibilities. 'Great for invites, let's have a party there.' What dude could resist tickets to the Dodgers?

'Right. And we'll drive some of them in your Maserati. And my Jeep. It'll be way cool,' Emma said.

Not exactly Sally Lassiter-style cool, but what the hell? Sally was gone. All three witches were gone.

Julie returned to her theme.

'It'll be even cooler if we go to Shop Smart to pick up the party gear—invitations and stuff.'

'Shop Smart?' Emma looked at Julie like she was mad. 'My mom knows this great woman on La Cienega who will do invites, like, with calligraphy and pressed flowers.'

'Yes, but *Jane Morgan* doesn't work for her.' Julie gave her friends a silky smile. 'Hoity-toity Miss Jane is a *greeter* on minimum wage! Right on Sunset!' Julie sniggered at the delicious thought. 'We should go see her,' she repeated cruelly. 'It'll be fun. Let's have her wrap our purchases, call us "ma'am" . . . bow and scrape like a little shopgirl. Which she is. And if she acts up, we can report her to her bosses. The customer is always right, you know.' Julie cackled.

'Oooh.' Melissa's eyes widened. 'You are *evil*.'

'Come on, you know she deserves it. Don't you remember how *mean* she was to all of us? She stopped you getting invited to that party.'

'Yeah, it's true,' Melissa said angrily. That still burned. 'Let's go there and show her who's boss!'

The girls laughed.

'I got the new car parked outside,' Melissa said, eager to curry favour.

Julie rewarded her with a smile. 'Let's have her walk our groceries to your Maserati, and if she does a *real* good job, maybe she'll get a tip.'

Rhodri Evans, Shop Smart's Senior Vice-President of Marketing, West Coast, looked over the store carefully. Hollywood—an important location. They were expanding from the Midwest, moving into the cities. He wanted to keep the prices rock-bottom but soften the image, away from vast concrete warehouses in the middle of nowhere.

He walked through the front doors. 'Good morning, welcome to Shop Smart.' A young African-American college kid shook his hand with a perfunctory smile. Evans was not impressed, but it was a perennial problem. They didn't pay enough to attract the best staff.

'Good morning! Welcome to Shop Smart. Great to see you!'

He turned his head, distracted. A young woman with a foreign accent, beautiful enough to be a model, was standing at the opposite door. She was smiling like she'd just won the lottery, and her uniform looked like it had come from the dry-cleaner's.

'Who *is* that?' he asked the greeter.

'Jane. Y'all can't have her number, though,' the kid said wearily.

'Do lots of people ask?'

'Lots of *men*,' he said with contempt. 'She's all about work, though. Wants to get noticed. What the hell she's doing here I don't know.'

Rhodri Evans walked into the store and pretended to browse. He never began an evaluation without actually doing some shopping.

He stood in front of a rack of DVD players, looking confused. Nobody came to help him. One black mark. The beautiful girl was still there, smiling and shaking hands like the customers were long-lost relatives.

Rhodri was fascinated. He edged back to the front of the store and pretended to be interested in a pile of discount khaki trousers.

'Good morning! Welcome.'

'It's great to have you at Shop Smart today!'

'Welcome, what a beautiful day for shopping!'

Wow! She was always beaming, always performing. He was impressed.

'Well, well, well, look who it is.'

There was a pause. He looked up from the polyester trousers to see a small knot of beautifully dressed teenagers—girls far too rich to be shopping in *this* store.

'Good morning, Jane,' said the lead girl cattily. The others sniggered. 'Nice to see you've landed on your feet.'

'Good morning, Julie,' Jane said stiffly. 'Do you need some help?'

'Actually yes,' said Melissa Smith, smirking. 'We're having a little party. My dad bought me box seats at the Dodgers. We want napkins and party items.'

'They're in aisle three.' Jane gritted her teeth, but her face was flushing from the humiliation. 'I'll get somebody to help you.'

'Noooo,' Julie purred. '*You* help us. Then you can carry it all out to Melissa's new Maserati. What are you driving these days, Janey? Or do you take the bus?'

'The name's Jane, and I'm afraid I can't leave my post.'

As Evans watched, a podgy woman bustled over to see what the fuss was about. What was her name? Oh yeah—Eileen something. Doherty. A recruiter. And a Personnel woman. Janice Esposito.

She had an unpleasant look on her face.

'Hello, ladies,' cried Mrs Doherty heartily. 'Are you getting good service here today?'

'I'm afraid this young woman was saying she was too busy to help us.' Julie pouted. 'Which is a shame because we were going to spend a *lot* of money in this store. Oh well, guess you don't want our business.'

'Jane, is that true?' snapped Janice.

Evans didn't like the way this was going. He moved towards the knot of women. Other customers had started to stare.

'You know,' the girl called Melissa said nastily to Jane, 'if you had been willing to help, we'd have given you a tip. I'm sure you could have used it.'

'Ma'am, I'm so sorry you've had this trouble today,' Janice said triumphantly. Finally! An end to all those positive evaluations. She couldn't stand little Miss Perfect making everybody else look bad.

'That wasn't the case,' Jane said calmly. She struggled to keep her voice under control. 'I told these young ladies where their goods were located and I was going to fetch an assistant to help them, since I'm a greeter this morning . . .'

'We don't *argue* with the customers!' Janice snapped. 'Get back into the staffroom immediately, Ms Morgan!'

'That's right.' Julie triumphed with a little snigger. Her eyes danced over Jane with contempt. 'Get back inside immediately, *Jane*, so I can be sure you're fired from your crappy little job. Go on, get!'

Jane stood there, and he watched her tense shoulders slump, and painful tears of humiliation fill her eyes. Why weren't his staff standing up for their young colleague?

'Didn't you hear me? You move,' spat Janice Esposito. 'What do you think you're doing?'

That was it. He strode towards them and addressed his personnel manager.

'What do you think *you're* doing?' Rhodri Evans stood in front of the group, angry. 'You did not observe the situation,' he said coldly to Janice Esposito, 'and you are making a scene in front of the customers.'

'Who the hell are you? Security!' said Janice, flushing scarlet and snapping her fingers. Two guards wandered over. Rhodri withdrew his wallet and handed one of the guards his business card. 'My name is Rhodri Evans, I'm Senior Vice-President, Marketing, West Coast. You're fired,' he said to Janice. 'Human Resources will be in touch.'

'You can't do that,' she hissed. 'I *am* Human Resources.'

'Not any more.'

Janice went bright red. 'I'll sue you!'

'Try it.' Evans shrugged. 'The whole thing's on camera.' He turned to the security guards. 'And these young *women*'—the term was deliberately insulting—'are also leaving. They attempted to harass a member of our staff. They aren't welcome here.'

Julie Manners went bright pink in the face. 'My father will—'

'Save it. There's a video. The contents of which I very much doubt any of your fathers would wish released to the press. You know, bullying is very unattractive.'

He turned to Mrs Doherty as security hustled the shamefaced girls away. 'Who is this young lady?' he asked gently.

'Her name's Jane Morgan, Mr Evans,' she said eagerly. 'I hired her myself, one of our best workers. I fully supported you just then, Jane, I was just about to step in . . .'

Evans turned to Jane. 'You handled that well.'

'Thank you,' she said. He realised she was struggling not to cry.

'You come with me. I want a word—privately.'

Jane fought her tears all the way to the office. It was hard, so hard. Somehow it was easier to be strong when she was being attacked. No damn way she'd let those girls see her crumble. But when this stranger defended her, the emotional walls she'd erected tumbled down. The hard work, the exhaustion, the low pay—and then, pure humiliation. Why hadn't she assumed they'd come looking for her? Maybe she should apply for something in the comfort zone—librarian, or schoolteacher. It would pay higher out of the gate, but it would be a dead end after that; no career prospects, no advancement. She had come here with a purpose. For the first time in her life, Jane Morgan was gambling.

Was she about to win? This manager, he'd stood up for her, yeah. But he *was* a guy. She had become adept at brushing aside advances. Did Rhodri Evans have a motive? If so, this could be the end. Because she *wasn't* going to sleep with anybody.

He opened the door. 'Take a seat.'

'Thanks,' she muttered.

Jane drew her legs together and tried to tug down the hem of her Shop Smart uniform's skirt.

'Don't worry.' Evans was looking at her sympathetically. 'I'm gay.'

'Oh.' She smiled weakly. 'That's great! I mean . . .'

'I know what you mean.' He studied a file on his desk. 'There's a note of how you came to us.'

Jane didn't say anything; she waited for him to speak. Evans smiled; that was clever.

'You must have known Shop Smart would take advantage of the free publicity and hire you.'

'Yes, I did.' She started to feel more confident. 'Publicity has value; you can trade it for many things. I traded it for free legal advice, and then this job.'

Evans decided he was enjoying himself hugely. When did moments like this ever happen in his tightly wrapped corporate life? She was a most unusual girl. Obviously keenly intelligent.

'Why were you looking at Shop Smart? We pay low wages. With your qualifications . . .'

'Firstly, I have no qualifications.'

'You could have been a nanny. There are many families in this city would pay highly for a girl with an English accent, from a good school.'

'Nannies aren't Senior Vice-Presidents, West Coast.'

'Ah.' He grinned. 'You wanted to get into the management programme?'

'I wanted to get into *management*,' she corrected him. 'Get noticed— and promoted.'

'You always knew this day would come?' Evans teased her.

But her reply was deadly serious.

'Yes. Because if you do something brilliantly, you'll get noticed. And promoted.'

'And you think you were brilliant, at the door?'

'I know I was,' she said confidently.

'So I should make you a manager, huh? Just like that.'

'I've worked in this building seven days a week for three months. There's nothing I don't know about this store—and nothing your management programme can teach me.'

'What do you know about business?'

'Try me. I read *The Economist* and *The Wall Street Journal* at the library.'

He believed her.

'OK, rookie,' Evans said. 'Tell me. I put you in charge of women's merchandising. What happens next?'

'I say I want a bigger job.'

'What?'

'It's part of the problem. Managers for every section of the store, all fighting for their patch. It's one store. It needs integration, not turf wars.'

'Example.'

'Electronics are in aisle six. But telephones are in aisle two. You need to store similar goods together. Food needs dedicated checkout lines. The layout needs to be thought through—they shouldn't be able to walk right out. You need tempting quick-purchase items by the tills, not the same old magazines . . .'

Jane went on, sketching a vision for the store. He listened attentively. The girl made a lot of sense.

'You realise this would mean slashing jobs.'

'Slashing a wasted layer of management jobs. For a company so concerned about wages, you waste a ton of money on pencil pushers.'

'And how do you know that?'

'I've *watched* them,' she said simply. 'With the savings, you announce an incentive scheme. Bonuses to staff who get special commendations. And an invitation to study for the management programme once they reach a level of excellence. You really need to improve morale. Get some family picnics going, events. Better food—the canteen can do a lot better on the same budget.'

He nodded. 'I'm not going to make you a manager.'

Jane sighed, disappointed.

'It's too much of a risk. I take a seventeen-year-old girl and put her in charge of a multimillion-dollar store? If you fail, I become a laughing stock. And get fired.'

'I see.' She did.

'So what I'm going to do is test you. I'm promoting you to junior manager in charge of staff.'

'Reporting to Mrs Doherty?'

'Only technically. She will be instructed to let you have your head, but on paper you will report to her. It covers my back.'

She grinned back at him.

'Your brief is to get this lacklustre bunch of employees into a team that could be Disney World cast members. You talk a good game—I expect you to deliver. You have six months.'

Jane flushed with pleasure. 'Yes, sir.'

'And that's not all. I want you to continue your observations of the store. Logistics, and cost-cutting. Write daily reports, collate them into a monthly assessment, and send it to me at central office. When you have six months of cost-based analysis, maybe I can see about a promotion. What is your current weekly salary?'

'Two hundred and fifty a week.'

'From now on your salary is forty thousand dollars a year basic. There will be incentives—I'll send you a contract. The signing bonus is five thousand dollars—you can pick that cheque up today—and you'll get use of a company car. Junior management gets a Ford. Any colour as long as it's black.'

Jane sat quietly. 'Thank you, Mr Evans,' she said eventually. 'Thank you very much.'

'You didn't tell me you can't believe it,' he observed.

'But I can believe it,' she said coolly. 'It's why I came here.'

Chapter Five

'SO HERE WE ARE,' Ahmed said. '*Mashallah!*'

They were in a crowded Cairo street, and Helen was tired, and hot. It had been a long flight, and the city seemed overpowering—the flood of traffic, workers on bicycles, a choking sense of dust.

Helen felt lost—and slightly ashamed. She had been foreign in LA—too Arab, only protected by her girlfriends. And now she felt foreign here. Her native tongue had atrophied. The garish billboards with their smiling photos embarrassed her; she could not read the Arabic inscriptions. Helen felt herself between two cultures—and not fitting either one.

'*Mashallah!*' she repeated, bowing her head.

The doorway was hidden, almost secret, set anonymously into a wall of the city street. While Helen waited with their suitcases, Ahmed pulled out a small brass key. He inserted it into the lock; she heard the clicks and tumbles, like a puzzle solving, and the little door swung open on its hinges. She had to stoop to enter, and then they were inside. He stopped to pray when they entered the courtyard.

She looked around. The place was magical. She was standing in a high, ancient courtyard, where the walls were many feet thick, strong enough to drown out the traffic. The height offered a pool of natural shade. The garden was green; shady palms placed strategically around gravel paths. Tiny bricks, painted blue, fenced off flowerbeds, dotted with azaleas, blossoming cactuses and thick beds of lilies. In the corners of the garden, low-level fountains bubbled with water; it spilled, burbling, into square pools, giving the air a moist feel, a sense of a true oasis. She felt her soul thrill with unexpected pleasure.

'This is our house.' For the first time, Ahmed smiled warmly at her. 'I worked on it, many years. The garden, especially. I hope you like it—since that is your name.'

She nodded. Helen Yanna—al-Yanna, the garden. She'd always liked that. She glanced around, drinking it in.

'This is beautiful.'

'It isn't rich, not a big house,' he said apologetically. 'My business is not as good as it should be, not yet. But you will like it, I hope so.'

'We can try in Arabic,' Helen said, switching, awkwardly.

'You've forgotten?' Ahmed spoke softly, and looked into her eyes, with a new confidence. 'I will remind you,' he said. 'I will teach you.'

To Helen's amazement, her stomach started to churn. She blushed and lowered her eyes. A tendril of something—desire, she realised—was trawling over her belly.

To cover her confusion, she said, 'I would like to bathe . . .'

'Of course. How tired are you? Can you manage dinner?'

She was rocky with exhaustion, but she nodded, still blushing.

'And then . . . bed.'

Helen's head snapped up. As she opened her mouth, wondering what to say, Ahmed lifted his hand and traced a fingertip across her mouth, softly and possessively.

'No, not tonight. I do not want you tired. I want you fully awake.'

'The bathroom . . .' she said, dry-mouthed. 'Please?'

He grinned, and extended his arm, opening the house to her. And as Helen walked inside, she was aware of Ahmed watching her. Wanting her. She didn't know what she was feeling.

The house was not as spectacular as the little garden; she thought it was beautiful, modest and comfortable. Three large bedrooms, a master suite with a bathroom and two dressing rooms; a kitchen, servants' quarters; a living room, and a dining room, and a small ornate room set aside for prayer, with the mats and a window facing Mecca.

But the decoration! Every room carpeted with a priceless antique— Persian silks, rough kilims, each gorgeous, lining the house with beauty. There were mosaics, brass lamps that cast intricate shadows, scrollwork on the walls, glass vases, sculpture. Small pieces, but carefully collected. The servants greeted her kindly and seemed genuinely happy that Ahmed was home. He introduced Helen, and she was polite.

'I will bathe, also.' Ahmed stood back from the master bedroom. 'When you are ready, come downstairs; they have made supper.'

'OK. Thank you.' She turned aside, towards the large copper tub with the modern, rain-like shower attachment . . .

. . . and then his hand was on her shoulder, firmly turning her towards him, and a strong arm lowered her down into the crook of his shoulder, and his lips pressed onto her mouth, teasingly, lightly brushing over hers, his tongue flickering against hers, probing, owning her.

Helen shuddered, taken utterly by surprise, and feeling his strength; she had never been kissed, and he knew what he was doing. She could feel the strength of his muscles under his shirt . . .

And then, as she was in turmoil, he let her go. Stunned, Helen stood there, her thumb on her mouth, her lips half open, staring at him.

'Later,' he said. His dark eyes swept across her again. And then he suddenly turned, and went down the stairs.

She chose, deliberately, a Western dress for dinner: a long-skirted Armani. It was modest but chic and simple.

The kitchen was full; servants, cooks, had materialised out of nowhere. Helen greeted them, shyly, and went through to the dining room. Red silks hung from the walls. Antique glass and brass lamps were lit, casting detailed shadows. Perfumed candles, scented with attar of roses, were dotted about, floating in powder-blue ceramic bowls. Ahmed had changed, too. He was now in traditional dress. Long black trousers and an open-necked shirt revealed to her that he was slim, but strong. He was sprawled comfortably against the Moroccan cushions piled on the divan, master of his own domain.

'Good evening,' he said.

'Hello.' Helen blushed. After that kiss, she did not know how to look him in the eyes.

'Will you start with a drink?'

'Thank you,' she said.

'They have spent a month deciding on the menu,' he told her. He lowered his voice. 'So I hope you eat something.'

There was coconut-scented rice, and small roasted birds; Moroccan tabbouleh salad and delicious local pastries. Helen nervously picked a little at everything; it was all delicious. For drinks, they offered freshly squeezed orange juice, pure, icy water, or hot mint tea, heavily sugared and served in frosted glasses.

Slowly, she began to relax. After all, he had said he wouldn't come to her tonight. So why worry?

'This is wonderful. Thank you.'

'You don't need to thank me,' Ahmed said, dark eyes on her. 'This is your house.'

Helen bit her lip. Should she tell him?

But no, this was not the time. She made polite conversation instead.

'How long have you lived here?'

'Four years. My business has done well. It is also four years since Firyal died,' he added, unembarrassed.

'And you loved her?' Helen was curious.

'Infinitely.'

She was conscious of a stab of jealousy.

'Then why agree to this?'

'Because I want to have children, *inshallah!* And what better for that than a young girl, intelligent, a believer, of good family? I saw it as my duty. What was the point of looking for love?'

'And now?' she demanded. Her pride, stung. It was *she*, Helen, who was doing her duty here. Ahmed should be *desperate* to marry her.

'And now I find you interest me,' he said. 'You stir me . . . you are different. I want to train you.' His eyes bored into hers.

'I am not an animal,' Helen managed.

'You are. We both are. Human animals.' Ahmed smiled, confident. 'Tomorrow . . . in our marriage bed . . . I will show you, little American.'

'I'm going to want to talk to you.'

'Talk all you want.' He grinned, not allowing her to drop her eyes. 'After tomorrow, you will be mine.'

'You're very sure of yourself,' Helen said.

He smiled. 'That's right. I am.'

She had no idea how she made it to bed. Ahmed, soon afterwards, clicked his finger for the ayah, and the woman came, and helped Helen away from the table to the master bedroom.

'Thank you. *Shokran.*' Helen bowed, and eventually the woman went away. Drained, she brushed her teeth and passed the flannel over her face. She did not have any energy left to hunt around for a nightdress. As soon as her ablutions were done, Helen flopped onto the bed, and she was asleep almost before she had closed her eyes.

'What time is it?'

Helen rolled over, onto her side, to find Ahmed lying next to her, dressed in white, his eyes closed. Groggily, she rubbed her eyes.

'Ah.' He sat up. 'I thought you would never surface. I was about to call the doctors.'

'It can't be that late . . .'

'Try three p.m. You've been asleep for almost eighteen hours.'

Helen groaned. 'It'll take me days to get over the jet lag.'

'I would not worry. You have years.' Ahmed smiled down at her. 'I have taken a nap myself. So I will be full of energy tonight, also.'

Helen sat up. She was thirsty. As though reading her thoughts, Ahmed clapped his hands, and a woman materialised, bearing a pitcher of freshly squeezed orange juice and two enormous glasses.

'Better than water,' he said. 'It will also replenish your body salts.'

Helen thirstily gulped down the golden nectar, as the servant melted away as quietly as she had come.

'Talk,' he said, in English.

'Excuse me?'

'Talk. We will not be disturbed. Whatever you have to say, now is the time.' He grinned. 'And then I am going to begin training you, Haya.'

She was outraged. 'What did you call me?'

'Haya,' Ahmed said. 'It is your name. What you were given at birth. It means modesty, and it suits you. I asked your father. He put "Helen" on you when you went to the United States, so that you would fit in. But you are not Greek; you are Arab. And your name is special, as you are. You are my Haya. I will never call you by that fake name again.'

His speech stopped her anger dead. But she felt obliged to add, 'You can't train me, Ahmed. I told you that last night.'

'Let us see if you are telling me the same thing three hours from now.'

'I won't be telling you anything,' she said, feeling out the name 'Haya' in her mind. It was, in truth, very beautiful, much better than boring Helen. 'I'm not yours, Ahmed. I'm mine.'

'What is the contradiction?' he asked, dark eyes on her.

'I . . . didn't understand what I was doing. When I signed the *nikkah*.'

For the first time, he registered shock.

'What?' he said. 'Do you not understand the purpose of the *nikkah*?'

'I do,' she said. 'Of course . . . but I did not realise I was signing a *nikkah*. They spoke so fast . . . My Arabic is poor.' She blushed. 'As you know. And my father told me it was a friendship ceremony.'

He considered this for a second. He looked at her calmly; and with that same assessing stare that had disturbed her yesterday.

'Then tell me, Haya,' Ahmed said. 'Were they wrong when they informed me you were intelligent, and a believer?'

She flushed. 'No. Of course not.'

'Then you know the faith. What "friendship ceremony" did you think this was . . . exactly?'

She had no answer.

'And was marriage never mentioned to you?'

'It was,' she admitted. 'But I said that I would choose my own husband.'

'Yet of your own free will went through this ceremony?'

She blushed. 'Yes.'

'So on some level you knew what was going on.'

It was true. She knew it in the depth of her soul. 'I have the right to choose my own husband!' she said.

'That is so. I will not force you.' He leaned across the bed, his face inches from hers; a young man, but older than her, confident. 'In fact, my Haya, I would make you come to me, and beg for it.'

Her eyes widened. 'You are so arrogant!'

Ahmed inclined his head. 'And you want me. Do you not think I know my own?'

'How could you tell I am your own?'

'I tasted your lips,' he said to her. 'And you will yield to me.'

Ahmed stood up, gave her a little bow, and withdrew.

She woke up in the middle of the night, sweating, unsure where she was. The hum of traffic and the splashing of the fountains seemed strange and wrong; as she came to, Helen longed for the reassuring quiet of her compact, American bedroom . . . her parents. She felt so alone.

She twisted her dark hands, confusion springing up in her. Ahmed had all the power in this situation, all the money, all the knowledge. He spoke the language . . . she was his, in his house.

And it scared her even more that she was starting to feel for him. A longing, in the belly of her, when he was close; wanting him to reach out, to kiss her, even . . . She was disturbed. She hated her own power-lessness. She had herself to blame for this, for her modest obedience to her parents, for always wanting an easy life, to avoid confrontation. Yes, she still loved them. But how had she given the impression that this would be acceptable? That they could ship her off to Egypt, and choose the man to whom she would belong?

No, she thought. She would not bow to this. She would not submit to Ahmed's rule of her body. She wanted to go home, now.

A night breeze came in through the arched window, fluttering the thin cotton of her nightdress. Helen shuddered and ran to her suitcase. Frantically she tugged on her underwear, her socks, a pair of jeans and a shirt. Frightened, she worked quietly, grabbing whatever she could. She had about thirty bucks, she'd assumed Baba would bring the cash for the holiday. No airline ticket, but she had a credit card. And her passport, *Mashallah!*

She put on her sneakers and quietly opened her bedroom door. Helen's heart thumped wildly in her chest. What if he heard her? Would he be angry? Hit her . . . beat her? Worse, drag her back to her room and rape her? She did not know this man at all.

Delicately, she tiptoed down the stone stairs, their ancient surfaces pocked and pitted. The clock in the hallway said half past midnight. She reached the door to the kitchen, then the door to the garden. Helen ran across the courtyard, quietly in her sneakers, unlatched the gate, and made it out into the street. She had no idea where she was. She ran, blindly, towards the sound of traffic.

Helen, terrified, thudded through the streets, her sneakers pounding the pavement. There were few lights; she thought she must be off the centre, somewhere. The storefronts were all shuttered. A man rode by on a donkey, pulling a cart full of trash; he scowled at her. She turned left into a major street, her breath ragged, and slowed to a walk.

OK, OK. Don't panic. She looked around, hoping for a taxi, a bus— did they run at night? Anything. A way to get to the centre.

A group of men walked past her and laughed raucously. She heard them say something, it didn't sound pleasant. Helen hesitated, desperate to ask for directions, but one of the group, a thin man with a scarred face, whistled at her. Hurriedly, she crossed the street and raced off down a narrow alleyway.

She needed a landmark. Look for a crescent, she told herself, look for a crescent rising above the modern apartment blocks and ancient tumble-down houses. She would find a mosque . . . it would have directions near it, and she would be safer. There—towards the north-west, a crescent glinting against a street lamp. She walked towards the north, down another alley, and then into an open street.

There was a squeal of tyres and a beat-up red Ford Fiesta screeched to a halt beside her. The window wound down; the driver stared at her calmly. 'How much?'

That, she understood. And realised he thought she was a prostitute. 'Leave me alone,' she said, in English. He flashed her a sick grin.

'Taxi,' he said. 'Pretty lady want taxi to airport?'

'Go away,' Helen hissed. She started to pick up speed, but he pressed his foot on the gas.

'What you doing out here at night? Ladies don't come here. Give me money, I take you hotel. Airport.' He cackled. 'Pyramids!'

Helen squealed; he thrust his arm out of the window and took a swipe at her handbag, wrenching the bag away. Helen grabbed, but it was too late, and now his scrawny hand had closed round her wrist.

'You get in car,' he said. 'Now!'

In her blind terror, Helen remembered a self-defence move from kick-boxing class. She bent her hand backwards, naturally breaking his grip. He shouted in rage and slammed on the accelerator. Helen pivoted and ran the other way, leaving him to execute a sharp turn in the street.

And then she blinked, thrust her hand in front of her eyes, as headlights, full on, dazzled her and lit up the whole street. Another car had turned into the road, at speed, a shiny Mercedes, its horn blaring. It rammed the Fiesta, hard, then pulled back and rammed it again. The red car lurched and skidded from the impact, but the thief slammed his foot down and it moved off, fast, down an alley.

The silver car was now sideways across the street, blocking her exit. Helen breathed in, shuddering, looking around her wildly for any escape. Oh God!

The door was opening. A man was getting out. Helen struggled against the scream that rose, choking, in her throat.

'Don't be afraid, Helen,' he said, in English. 'I won't hurt you.'

She stared. It was Ahmed. He rushed across to her, his eyes searching her body, her lips bluish with cold.

'I heard you leave . . . when I got up you had gone.' His words tumbled out. 'I followed, I asked men on the street where you were headed. In the end, I found you. Did he hurt you?'

Numbly, she shook her head. 'He tried.' Her teeth were chattering, she could barely speak.

Ahmed looked her over. 'You didn't have to run. You were always free to go. It's your decision.'

'If it was my decision, I wouldn't be here,' she said wildly. And then she burst into tears.

He got her into the car. As she buckled up, Helen thanked God for the soft leather, the clean seats, the warmth coming from the heater.

'I went too fast with you.' Ahmed shrugged. 'I would never force any woman. Do not worry, I will drive you to a hotel.'

Helen's eyes swam. 'I only have thirty dollars.'

'I'll pay,' he said easily. 'All you will need is your passport. And I'll arrange for a ticket back to Los Angeles.'

She shook her head, plunged back into misery even as her body started to thaw. 'He stole my passport,' she wailed. 'It was in my bag.'

Ahmed was silent.

'Hotels here will not register a foreign guest without one.' He sighed. 'It would appear you are stuck in my house, at least for a day or so. I promise you, I will not bother you. A woman servant, my cook, will take you to the Embassy tomorrow so you can start on the paperwork.'

'Thank you,' she whispered. 'I owe you.'

'I think of you as a guest in my house, under my protection.'

'I'm sorry,' Helen muttered. 'I just didn't ask to be here.'

Ahmed drove back in silence to the house. When they got there Helen went to her room, feeling stupid, but safe. She undressed, put her nightdress back on—it had remained, crumpled, on the terracotta tiles—and crawled into bed. Within seconds, she found herself drifting off. Emotionally exhausted, as she slipped into sleep, she thought of Ahmed, his dark eyes ranging over her body.

When Helen came down to breakfast, he had already gone. There was a short note on the table, and a pile of Egyptian dinars. Ahmed wrote that the cook, Fahdah, had only a few words of English, but she would drive Helen to the American Embassy and bring her back. He included a list of telephone numbers just in case she got lost.

It was very thoughtful but very brisk. Helen felt a pang of loss. She figured it would have been good to get to know him better, the handsome merchant with the probing eyes. But her world was an ocean away. There was no point in pining over him now.

At the Embassy, it was hot and crowded. It took Helen forty minutes to get through the gatehouse without ID. She queued for over two hours, and finally explained her plight to a bored young man who hardly looked at her. 'We gotta backlog. We'll take your prints and details, but likely you won't get a passport for two weeks.'

'But it's an emergency,' Helen spluttered. 'Can't you help me?'

He looked up. 'Are you in physical danger, miss?'

She shook her head.

'Leave a number. We'll call when your passport becomes available. 'Next,' he called, beckoning a fat woman in a niqab up to the counter.

Helen rode home dejected. How humiliating. She would have to explain, and then presume on Ahmed's hospitality. For two whole weeks. That is, if he let her stay.

Helen waited in her room for Ahmed to come home, but lunchtime bled into afternoon, and he still did not come.

She washed her hair, carefully blow-dried it, and plucked her eyebrows. And then, for want of anything better to do, she made herself up, beautifully and carefully, just neutral, natural shades, the way Sally had taught her, and picked out her prettiest shalwar kameez, something she had packed for the sun, a delicate white and yellow chiffon layered thing, shot through with gold.

She was playing with an armful of thin bronze bangles when the knock on her door finally came. 'The master is here,' Fahdah said, smiling. 'He's waiting in the kitchen.'

Helen jumped up. 'Thank you.'

Ahmed was standing in the kitchen, reading some papers. He looked at her, just once, and Helen saw his eyes flash with interest.

'Fahdah explained what happened at the Embassy. You are welcome to stay here, under the same rules as before. I can also make some calls. Perhaps we can speed matters up.'

'You're very kind.' She wanted him to look at her, to compliment her.

'Or you can call your parents, and they can arrange for a hotel.'

Helen thought about that. She really didn't want to speak to them right now. 'I'd rather not do that. I have some issues with my parents.'

'Some issues? How very American of you. Then your friends, perhaps. Did you not tell me you had rich friends?'

'Well—one. To be honest with you, Ahmed, I—I don't want her to know.' She blushed at the thought of Sally's incredulous stare when she found out what Mama and Baba had done. 'If I can stay with you for this time, I will send you some money when I get home.'

Ahmed's head snapped up, and the dark eyes bored into hers. 'You insult me,' he said. 'Did I not tell you you are a guest in my house? Even now, you do not think me an honourable man.'

'Forgive me,' Helen said, speaking in Arabic the best she could. 'You have been a good friend and cousin. I would like to stay under . . . under your generous roof. If you will permit it.'

He was silent, and when she looked up, he was still glowering. 'And you will regard me as your host, trust me not to force myself upon you, and not speak again of money?'

'No. As my host.' Helen bit her lip. 'My kind host,' she said. She half wanted to stay, half to run. Feeling him so near was disturbing. His anger at her dishonouring him made him all the more attractive.

'Very well, then. I'll call the Embassy tomorrow. Will you eat supper?'

'Yes, please. And you can tell me all about your work.'

Ahmed's eyebrow lifted. 'I was going to arrange for your meal to be sent to your room.'

Helen started. 'Oh no, please don't. I want to talk to you. It's been so dull. I've nothing to read, and I don't dare go outside and get lost.'

Now he looked at her with a flicker of amusement. 'But we are not staying married. Do you think it is proper?'

Helen had the strong feeling he was teasing her. She felt a rush of desire across her skin, her knees weakening.

'I am your guest. And we are relatives,' she reminded him. 'So I think it's OK.'

'Very well then.' He clapped his hands, and one of the serving men ran in. 'Bring us some supper,' he said. 'My cousin and I will eat.'

Helen lifted her face and smiled radiantly at Ahmed. She was so grateful. And she was longing for his company.

He chatted lightly and pleasantly enough, as the servant bustled about them, bringing spiced kebabs with tomato paste and cumin, vine leaves wrapped around goat's cheese, figs and honey, and wine. The flavours of the Middle East blended against her tongue, everything natural, nothing processed. Ahmed ate lying sideways, lounging against his silk divan, and Helen, nervously at first, imitated him.

She could hardly look straight at him. Ahmed was so confident; so tough, upright, uncompromising. The thought of how he had driven in the dead of night, saved her, danced in Helen's head. His eyes, just now and again, sweeping across her, and finding her beautiful. And she found she desperately wanted him to find her beautiful.

The evening stretched on, and Helen ate, slowly, trying to draw it out. When he finally washed his fingertips in the small bowls of rose-water, she did the same.

'We could have coffee in the garden,' she suggested. 'Talk some more.'

Ahmed grinned. 'Dinner is over . . . *cousin*. And I am sure you know you are far too delectable for me to linger over. Already you tempt me. You should go to bed. We can dine together tomorrow.'

Helen blushed. 'I like to be with you.'

His eyes darkened. 'I am not the sort of man to be teased. You have signed the *nikkah*, but you say you want to leave. And yet now you want to be with me. Which is it?'

The longing to kiss him raged in her. Or rather, to be kissed; to have Ahmed reach out and pull her to him. But he wouldn't make it that easy. He would force her to make the choice.

Ahmed stood up. 'You know you are free to leave any time,' he said. 'Go back to the West, go and find some surfer who will call you Helen, or some lawyer who will want you to dye your hair blonde.'

She watched in dismay as he walked towards his own bedroom; but then he halted at the door.

'I will be sleeping in the guest bedroom,' Ahmed said, once again answering her unspoken question. 'If you want me, come to me. But come as Haya. And come prepared to be my wife. In all things.'

Her heart pounded, and her palms broke out in a sweat.

'Ahmed . . .' she began. But he had left her. In turmoil she rose and went to the window. He was arrogant! But a good man. She could see Ahmed was a believer, that he knew her rights, would not attempt to deprive her of her natural liberty. And yet, if she chose, freely, to go to him, it would be on his terms. Come as Haya, he had said.

She tried out the name again in her mind, and it felt right. Her birth name, her Islamic name. Haya. That Ahmed had given it back to her, that she was here, in Egypt, learning her native tongue, felt now as if she were crossing into another, ancient, more fitting world.

Haya wanted Ahmed. Her body was in turmoil now. Was it because he was the first, the only one to have kissed her, to have made her squirm? She didn't think so. The boys she'd seen in America, at Sally's party—none of them had ever made her feel this way.

A few days here, and Haya already felt her childhood slipping off her like a snakeskin. She had passed into womanhood. And the thought of Miss Milton's and schoolyard politics was ridiculous. Of course she would see her friends again. But what was to stop her doing that as a married woman?

Haya realised she had no desire to go home. She knew that if she did go, she would never see Ahmed again. Then what was her choice? To go to him, and let Ahmed touch her . . .

Her lip trembled. She was afraid but she climbed the stairs to the guest bedroom suite.

Ahmed was sitting in a carved wooden chair, facing a western window, watching the sun set.

'You have come to me, Haya?' he asked, without looking round.

'I don't know,' she said, and her voice wobbled.

Ahmed stood up, came over to her, and enfolded her in his arms, gently this time. Haya started to cry. She didn't know why, not exactly. But she was here, in Egypt, and it was strange, and her parents had sent her here. And she wasn't sure if she had fallen in love.

'Come on,' Ahmed said, when she had finished. He kissed her lightly on the top of the head. 'Do you want to be a tourist?'

'What?' she said, dabbing at her eyes.

'Let's go out to the pyramids,' he said. 'See the *son et lumière*. It's . . . what do you Americans say?'

'Cheesy?'

'Exactly. But it's fun.' He stood up and reached for a lambswool cloak, a soft pure grey. 'The desert gets cold at night.'

'Thank you,' she said. 'And . . . I like it that you call me Haya.'

He was right; the desert was freezing. Ahmed got them chairs at the back, and they sat together, the cloak thrown over them, watching the eerie green light over the pyramids. The head of the Sphinx reared, massive, in the spotlight. Haya gasped.

'Do you like it?'

'Like—that's not the word. I mean, I've seen pictures. But they are so inadequate.'

'This is your heritage,' he said. 'Not a sports car, or a hamburger. Tomorrow we will go and see it, in the day. And maybe next week we can see the Valley of the Kings. But I won't overwhelm you. The tourists try to see all Egypt in seven days, and see nothing. It blurs into one.'

'We'll take our time,' Haya said. She looked up at him; his profile was strong, his jaw set against the red and green lights on the sand. He was handsome; he cared for her. Already, home seemed distant.

'*We* will?' Ahmed turned his face to her, his dark eyes above hers. And Haya wanted, longed for him to bend down and kiss her. Her lips moistened, parted . . .

'No,' he said, softly. 'You did not sign the *nikkah*.'

'I did,' she said. 'I did . . .'

He lowered his mouth, close to her, not touching her.

'Then who are you?'

'Haya,' she said, her voice thick with desire. 'Haya . . . your wife . . .'

Still, he did not kiss her.

'Please, Ahmed,' she whispered.

He laughed, softly, and pressed his lips on hers; he kissed her, hard, this time, no teasing, his mouth almost crushing hers, his teeth on her lips, the hard muscles of his chest against her breasts.

Haya gasped; she felt lust flood through her.

Silently he rose and offered her his hand. Haya stumbled to her feet, blushing. Ahmed flung the cloak round her shoulders, and led her to the car, while the ghostly lights of the show danced over the ancient monuments behind them.

'*Tisbah ala-kheir*,' Ahmed said quietly to her, when the moon was starting its descent over the palm trees in the garden, and Haya lay, drained and sore, and deeply in love, in his arms. She loved the scent of him, and did not want to let him go. 'Good night.'

'Good night,' she said, copying his Arabic. 'My darling.'

The next day, when she awoke, Ahmed had ordered that breakfast be brought up to their room. He handed her an iced glass of juice, and watched her as she drank it. He put a finger under her chin and tilted up her head, forcing her to stare into his eyes. Haya flushed; her breathing seemed to be coming raggedly. Ahmed put a hand to his wife, and she gasped.

'So eager,' he said, with a grin. 'I'm not going to work today. It's our honeymoon. And I want to show you what pleasure means.'

Their first month together passed in a daze. Love of Ahmed, and desire for him, consumed Haya. And yet there was anger, which simmered into rage, against her father. On the plane, what Baba and Mama had done hadn't seemed that important. But happy though she was now, Haya had grown furious that she had never had the chance to decide for herself to come here.

Her period came and went, and came again. It seemed so wrong that she did not conceive, right away. She could hardly stay away from her husband. Her passion excited him; her naked desire, visible to him even when she was fully robed, made Ahmed want her more; he was on her, all the time, locking the doors of their study, coming home from work at lunchtime, burning for his wife.

And still there was no child. And as Haya stayed in the house, barely improving her Arabic, she became restless.

'I need to do something,' she said, after they had finished a sticky session of lovemaking one afternoon. 'I was not made to sit in a house, and I have no friends, nobody but you.' She missed her girlfriends, Sally and Helen, dreadfully.

He thought about it. 'Why don't you come with me? Into work. Do you object to wearing the hijab?'

'Not at all.'

'The women in our workshops are very traditional. It would save some questions . . .' He grinned. 'And anyway, your hair is so beautiful, I want it all to myself.'

She rolled to him, eagerly.

Maybe it was better he take Haya to work, Ahmed thought. When he was away from her, he spent every moment looking for excuses to get out of the office. And he did not want her to get bored, or restless. Until the children came along, *inshallah*, could it hurt?

'And this is the workshop.' Ahmed greeted the women sitting there, weaving; they smiled and nodded at Haya. 'They make some carpets here. Mostly, I deal with importers, or find goods myself. It is all in the eye.'

She smiled at his workers and followed him up the wooden stairs. Every inch of the place was hung with beautiful carpets, and the store-room smelt a little fusty.

'Mothballs,' he said, in answer to her question. 'Nothing works better. And this is the showroom.'

'Amazing.' It was. A long room, full of windows, but they had muslin drapes across them all. She understood; daylight would bleach out the precious fibres. Instead, even in the day, the room was gently lit with candles. Piles of gorgeous silk and woollen rugs lay on the floor, they hung from the walls, they were suspended from the ceiling. To counter the mothballs, he had placed scented oil burners in strategic places; there was a strong smell of frankincense.

'Do you want some tea, pastries?'

Haya was hungry; she nodded shyly.

Her husband nodded at an employee; the man disappeared and returned with a silver tray holding a teapot, glasses, and a delicate selection of tiny cakes.

'We keep a kettle boiling for customers,' Ahmed explained. 'It is a way of forcing them to stay, to take time, and then the beauty of the goods . . .' He shrugged. 'They sell themselves.'

She leaned across, put her lips up to him and kissed him. 'Your carpets are magnificent.'

'Thank you, darling.'

Haya ran her hand possessively over his sleeve. 'Do you think I could help you? With the business. I have better English . . . I know America. My father could get some contacts. Maybe you could export.'

Ahmed smiled back at her. 'I'd like you to take an interest.'

Haya was excited at the prospect and the last of her doubts lifted with it. Now she would go to America, too, see her family and her old friends. She had been lost in Ahmed to the exclusion of all else. But the other girls would understand, wouldn't they?

Haya took it slowly, at first. A week or two meeting the staff, getting to know Ahmed's stock, his prices, his carpets. Brushing up on her written Arabic, learning how he kept his books; the old-fashioned way, in leather-bound volumes. Haya's first move was to buy a computer, enter all his data onto spreadsheets, and start filing on his customer base. Ahmed didn't like it much, but she kept plugging away. And within a few days he was staring, amazed, at the easy system she had set up, and then trying to use it himself.

Haya called her father. They had a long, stilted conversation. She decided to avoid talking about the marriage. What was the use? Instead, Haya demanded her father's assistance. That was the price of forgiveness. She didn't say it openly, but they both understood it.

Baba promised he would help. He could talk to some people who knew people. There were exhibitions, trade fairs. Retailers, although many of them already had suppliers . . .

'We will undercut their suppliers,' Haya said, ruthlessly.

Ahmed grinned. 'And once they're hooked, the price goes up.'

He kissed his wife on the forehead. She was a true help to him and he liked it. It was his business, of course; he was in charge. But Haya argued her case, and Ahmed listened to her.

'We need to find more customers like the hotels,' Haya said, one evening, after a fine sale. Ahmed had won an order from an Egyptian hotel chain in Sharm el Sheikh worth forty thousand dollars.

Ahmed was listening, she saw. 'You need to sell these beautiful carpets individually. They should be given space. Why should you not be like the owner of a gallery?' Her Arabic was rough, but she continued. 'They give stories to their artwork. Provenance . . . catalogues. You can sell your carpets that way. They are all unique.'

He looked intrigued. 'And how would you propose to do this?'

'We must export,' she said, confidently. 'To America. To the quality stores. Perhaps first to a gallery. Somewhere very expensive. I can help, I speak perfect English. I also know what sells to them. Let me be your export director. Let me work for you.'

Ahmed's arm stole round her waist. 'You *do* work for me.'

'That's not work.'

'I don't want you leaving me for the States. Even for a week.'

'Then come with me,' she said persuasively.

He thought about it. 'You really think I could sell these better?'

'No question,' she said confidently.

Ahmed leaned down and kissed her, hard, on the lips. 'Then let us try it,' he said.

He believed in his wife. There was that core in her that a man could rely on. They could be partners in business, as well as in life.

Chapter Six

IT WAS AMAZING how fast Sally's world collapsed.

Paulie Lassiter's death was on the radio and hit the television before anybody placed a call to Green Gables. Mona had been in the beauty parlour. Her chauffeur had hustled her out and driven her home, chased by paparazzi.

Sally had refused to believe it. As long as she lived, Sally would never forget the howling rage of her loss, the sick feeling in the pit of her stomach. The photographers, like locusts, camped outside the gates of her house; news helicopters chopping loudly overhead, their spotlights beaming down into their lawns. Hugging her wailing, disintegrating mother, turning off the TV that showed her father's ample body being loaded onto a gurney.

'They called me the merry widow,' Mona choked out.

Even in her grief, Sally had felt the rage rising, blocking the air from her throat so that she could hardly breathe. Bastards! For the first time in her golden, charmed life, Sally Lassiter experienced grief and loss. The devastation almost overwhelmed her. Every moment, thinking how she'd never speak to her father again. He'd never walk her down the aisle, never hold her children.

It was bad. The pain was a hurricane, battering at the hatches of her heart and dignity. And it was all going to get much, much worse.

The next months were a haze of pain and fear. First the funeral. Sally, throwing dirt and a rose onto Daddy's coffin. Walking away from that graveside. Trying to support her mother, who was falling apart.

The lawyers—first her own, then the government's. And the companies. The executors, and the insurers. Her father was accused. Fraud and embezzlement on a massive scale. Thousands of workers had lost their pensions, ordinary families bankrupt. Her mother—who could hardly sleep, who had stopped washing, or brushing her teeth, or combing her hair—Sally took care of her as though she were a child. Her mother offered nothing but a blank, Valium-induced stare.

And so the police and the investigators talked to Sally, roamed through her house like burglars, looking for documents. Took away every computer. Impounded her parents' cars.

She dropped out of school, and hired her own lawyer. Not for long, though; the federal government froze their bank accounts. And the worst thing was that Sally couldn't blame them. Sick with dismay, she was forced to confront the idea that her father might have been a crook, that the luxury they lived in might have been built on the suffering of others. Her father's lawyer, Lionel Javits, promised her privately it was not that way, and Sally clung to that.

'There were thieves in that company, Sally, but your dad wasn't one of 'em.'

'And this house?'

He flinched away from her cool gaze and stared at his hands.

'Your father didn't realise, but the oil profits that paid for this estate were built on paper. What my office is hearing is that the government is about to repossess.'

'Can we fight that?'

'Not in my judgment. No lawyer can make a case that this,' he waved a hand inadequately around the vastness of their kitchen, 'that this is necessary as a dwelling.'

Sally drew herself up. 'And what will they leave us with?'

'Nigel Farrar is the prosecutor. He looks slick on TV, wants to run for Congress . . .'

'Wants to look tough on criminals?'

Javits nodded. 'He gets good press if you and your mother are left with nothing.' He sighed. 'Like all the other Lassiter Oil families.'

'Nothing? No settlement?'

'He has an excellent case. Your mother can try innocent spouse relief, but they'll never let you keep above a token amount.'

Sally stood up. 'When are they going to do this to us?'

'Maybe next week. Is there somewhere else you can go? I think you should do your best to get out of here. Go stay with friends.'

Friends. Where were they? Helen had run off to get married, and Jane was dealing with her own troubles. Sally felt the abandonment almost physically.

'I tell you what,' she said slowly. 'Can you negotiate with them for me? My mom's got some jewellery . . .'

'Anything Mr Lassiter gave her is forfeit.'

'No. Her own. She was a society belle back home. Brought some into the marriage. I have a diamond brooch I can give you for a fee. You go to the prosecutor and get us free and clear on my mother's personal savings account—that was frozen too. It was a dowry, she never touched it. There's fifty thousand dollars in there.' Fifty thousand—that used to be the wage of their live-in chef. All of a sudden, it looked like it was all she had left in the world.

'I can do that. Where will you go?' he asked wretchedly.

'My mom has a niece in Texas. We'll go live near her. It's a small town, very quiet.' Cheap too, Sally didn't say. 'I'll get that diamond pin for you, Mr Javits, and you get that account unlocked.'

Well, now.' Emily Harris glanced from Sally to Mona, and Sally squirmed inwardly.

They were sitting uncomfortably on her cousin Emily's velvet sofa, in a small, soulless guest parlour. Sally's cousin was stiffly dressed in a blouse and long cotton skirt, but Mona was a wreck. Sally had done her best to clean Mom up this morning, before they checked out of the final hotel; forcing her to brush her teeth and swig with mouthwash, although she suspected Mona was swallowing the minty stuff just to get the alcohol. Washing her hair was a no-go—Sally wasn't strong enough to physically wrestle her mother, so she had to make do with pulling a brush through it, tying it into a ponytail and dousing it with hairspray.

In truth, Sally was frightened. Depression had turned Mona into a helpless, sick person, listless and lifeless. The speed and shock of loss was too much for her mother to deal with. As the money vanished, so did Mona's support network. Half of them dropped her before the funeral, the other half vanished as the lawyers and federal government closed down their accounts.

The Lassiters, once kings of Beverly Hills, were pariahs. And Sally could see the same disgusted look in the eyes of her cousin Emily.

'Well,' she repeated, and her smile was cold. 'It certainly is a surprise to see y'all here. What can I do for you?'

'We've left LA for good,' Sally said, taking the lead. 'We're going to settle back home. In Texas. Near family.'

Family. What a joke. The only family Sally had was sitting next to her, staring into space.

'I don't know if that's such a good idea,' Cousin Emily said, smiling all the brighter. 'You're hardly Texans any more.'

'I was born here,' Sally countered. 'Spent my childhood here. I'm as Texan as you are. And of course you're one of our nearest relations.'

There it was. She waited to see what her cousin would say. Emily was a rich woman, not oil rich, but plantation rich; her dead husband had left her plenty of land and some big condo developments. She was in a position to turn their lives around, if she chose to. A grace-and-favour apartment. A nice car.

'I think we better get some things straight,' the older woman responded. 'When Uncle Paulie left for California, some of us thought that was best. We were never very close. Y'all never visited me here, and I never came to you. We're not really family in that sense. And I have to tell you, Mona,' she turned and addressed her remarks, coldly, to the glassy-eyed woman, 'that I'm really highly disappointed in you and my uncle. You stole from hard-working families—'

Sally jumped up. 'Daddy did no such thing!'

A long sigh. 'That's not what the federal government says. And now y'all turn up here, disgraced . . . I declare, Mona, if I don't smell liquor on your breath at ten o'clock in the morning.'

'I see. Thank you for your hospitality.' Sally tossed her golden hair, defiantly. 'Come on, Momma. We're leaving.'

'I'm sorry, but I have a position in society . . .'

'Yes.' Sally gave a mighty heave and hauled her mother to her feet. 'It's better to know where we stand. And yes, you are sorry. A sorry excuse for a Christian woman.' The tears were threatening now. She was exhausted. Her back hurt from days of driving, she had nowhere to go, and her last hope was looking at her with total contempt.

'Please leave,' said Emily Harris, flushing with anger.

'Don't worry. We won't bother you again.' Sally thrust up her chin.

Sally pushed her mother out of the gracious porch that had looked so welcoming when they first arrived, all whitewashed wood, cane sofas and heaped cushions.

'Now what?' Mona asked, as Sally angrily spun the rented van round.

'Don't worry, Momma.' Sally refused to give in. 'We'll be OK. We have some money, enough to rent a place. Look.' She turned left, into Hartford, the nearest town, and slowed as they reached main street. 'This place has everything.' Sally gestured. 'A drugstore . . . banks . . . a post office.' It was small, a place for the working middle classes, Sally assessed instantly. Just what they were, as of now. An anonymous American town. It even had a high school. Perfect.

'Let's get a local paper,' Sally decided. 'I'll have a house legally rented by the end of the day. This is home.' She glanced at her mother, who was watching the dashboard, betraying no interest.

'We'll be happy here,' Sally insisted, bravely. But even she didn't believe it.

That afternoon, Sally trooped round apartments—mostly run-down. In the end, forced to raise her price, she found a two-bedroom estate house on the edge of Hartford's main road. Poor location, but all the basics; neat, clean. Sally put down three months' rent to avoid a credit check, and breathed a sigh of relief. The utilities were connected. There were no roaches. It was respectable. And she could afford to rent there for a couple of years, at least.

Mona was making noises about going to the local bar, so although Sally hated herself, she went out and bought cheap gut-rot vodka, in the forlorn hope it would turn her mother's stomach. And not at the liquor store, either; she could just imagine what gossip would do in a one-horse joint like this. Instead, Sally went to the grocery store and shopped, for almost the first time in her life. Meat was expensive, so she bought spaghetti and mince for bolognese.

She came home to find Momma passed out on the couch. That was a relief. Sally quietly unpacked and took a long, relaxing shower. Then she left a note on the table and drove out of town to a Shop Smart they'd passed on the way in, paradise for shoppers down on their luck. For an hour or so Sally forgot her troubles; she scoured the aisles, looking for bargains—a five-dollar rug, a white wicker wastepaper basket, fluffy towels for the bathroom, oversized and underpriced.

When she got back, Mona was still snoring. Her limbs drained, Sally nonetheless managed to unpack, to make the beds, fluff the cushions, lay out the towels, put the toothbrushes in the holder. On less than seventy dollars, she'd made the place look normal; it was cheerful and clean. Quite an achievement. When her mother woke, hung over, it would be in a proper house for a family to live in. Not what they were used to, but miles away from skid row.

She undressed and tumbled into bed, enjoying the feel of the brand-new sheets. Tomorrow was the start of a new, tough life, but she knew she could handle it. She slipped into a deep sleep.

'**M**om . . .' She hated the way her voice sounded, all whining and pleading. 'You don't need that.'

'Hey.' Mona gripped the vodka bottle, swayed in her slippers. 'Don't lecture me, missy. I can't stand it when you get all uppity.'

'You've already had too much.'

A tear of self-pity rolled down her mother's cheek. 'Why can' you leave me alone?' she slurred. 'Can' I have a lil bit of pleasure left in this world . . . He's gone . . . he's gone.'

'I know.' Sally fought back her own tears. 'He's gone, Mom. And he'd hate to see you like this.'

Mona reached out to steady herself, missed, and fell over; the vodka bottle smashed on the floor. She burst into loud, drunken tears.

'We gotta go out,' she whined. 'Gotta go out and get some more. I don't have no more here.'

Thank God, thought Sally. She went over to her mother, picking her way through the broken glass. 'Never mind, Momma. You come with me. Just take a little lie-down . . .'

'Yeah . . . lie down. I don' feel so good . . .'

Sally got her into bed. She pulled down the blinds. Their house was now permanently shuttered but Sally had learned to cope with just the cracks of sunlight that beamed through the dusty windows. No way did she want any of the neighbours to see her mom looking like this. Worse still, the press . . .

They had come crawling around here, those vultures. Sally had learned to manage them. When they doorstepped her on her way to her new public school, Sally would smile and say that she was settling in, and her mother was still in mourning. That it was a beautiful neighbourhood. That her daddy always taught her to take the lemons of life and make herself some lemonade. And then she would remind the snapper that she was still a minor. Could they please back off?

That always worked. Whether it was from fear of legal action or shame, they left her alone.

The tabloid articles were out there. 'Brave Sally, starting over.' 'Sally Lassiter, staying strong for Mom.' At least it was better than castigating her and her mother for living off the backs of the poor.

There was some of that too, of course; the shrieking phone calls, late at night, the hate mail, notes from people swearing her mother was a greedy bitch, that they had money stashed away in Switzerland or the Caymans. Sally tried to remember that these folk had lost everything.

She dealt with grief. She had to. There was only room for one invalid in the family, and Momma had taken that slot, had dived into the clear, numbing depths of her vodka bottle, and she wasn't coming out any time soon. But Sally had discovered within herself a core of stone. A parting gift from her dad, perhaps.

Sally knew she was not brilliant but she had something. Something more than long blonde hair and a tan. She knew how to sell herself, and how to sell situations. She had managed—still was managing—to change the story from 'embezzler's widow' to 'brave survivors'. She had negotiated a settlement with the IRS that left them without any more creditors. And she learned how to shop on a budget. Sally took care of school enrolment, and signing Mom up for benefits and Medicaid.

The most important thing was to look after Momma. Sally didn't mind the press stalking her; but she couldn't bear them to see the wreck of her mom. No. Although no reporters had been round for months now, Sally always drew the blinds.

She went upstairs, to her own room. To think. Sally's room was her haven. A tiny box, sure, but she had decorated it as best she could with cheap touches from Wal-Mart, little pink cushions and swatches of gauze; her clothes hung neatly in the wardrobe, and she had candles to give the place a soft glow at night. It smelt good and looked fresh, and Sally hung a framed photo of Laguna Beach, California, right over her desk. There was a calendar underneath that picture, and she noticed the next day was ringed. Oh. Right. Her birthday.

Yeah, she thought, morosely. Happy birthday. To me.

Tomorrow she was seventeen. She could *leave* school. Leave being ogled by the boys and teased by the girls at a little hick school, where pupils were content to make low grades and scrape by. Knowing she was friendless, the boys hit on her. Leave school? Why not? It didn't offer her anything. Mediocre SATs, and no money for university.

Sally felt like pacing her room, only there was no space. So what *did* she have? Well, beauty, of course. But Texas had lots of pretty girls. Still, there was something else. Even after she'd had to sell all her designer outfits, Sally realised she still managed to look good. For all the 'Barbie' taunts, girls in the playground copied her style. Style. That's what Sally Lassiter had. And if there was one thing Hartford needed, it was style.

Style had kept her sane, had helped her fight her mother's descent into the pit. She made sure that, like it or not, Mona was washed and dressed every day. Once a week, Sally insisted on giving her a manicure. And Sally Lassiter never left the house without her eyebrows styled, mascara, and a slick of lipstick—at the very least. What did style mean to her? Bravery and beauty. Glamour, as a weapon . . .

That thought made her wince. A reminder of past history. When she, and Jane, and Helen, had come walking down those stairs. Sally wondered if her friends ever tried to find her. Of course, she had intentionally disappeared. Put that down to style too, if you like—the shame that lurked round the edges of the brave face Sally put on things. She could not bear for Jane to know how small her life was, or for Helen.

Style was Sally's way out. She had it. Hartford needed it. Sally came to a decision. It was time to get a job.

The next morning, Sally carefully selected her outfit. Sexy, but demure. A dark blue pair of boot-cut jeans. Next, a crisp white shirt, a cute silver cuff to show off her carefully manicured French nails. Next, high-heeled cowboy boots. Next, make-up. That was easy; she was going for healthy and young. Mascara, good and thick, a sexy smudged black liner. A good rust-coloured blush, half blusher, half bronzer—real 'rose of Texas' stuff. Gold eye shadow. Natural lip gloss, no liner. A spritz of perfume, and she was done.

She pirouetted in the mirror, loving what she saw. Yeah. She looked like a cheerleader for the Dallas Cowboys; every boy would want to be with her, and every girl would want to be her.

'But I don't understand.' Mr Rogers, the principal, looked dismayed. 'You were doing very well in your studies, Sally.'

This was shocking news. Rogers liked and admired the young girl, a ray of sunshine, determined and fierce. He personally knew folk who had lost their life savings in the Lassiter Oil collapse, and he had been almost determined to loathe the billionaire princess who had turned up out of nowhere. But it had soon become clear that there were no billions left. And gossip soon discovered the mom had serious problems.

'You could make college.'

'I have other talents. I want to go get a job, and then maybe start my own business. Doing what I'm good at.'

'And what's that?'

'Glamour,' she said. 'Style.'

Undeniably, Sally Lassiter was a born expert there. 'And where are you going to get a job?'

'At Fisk's Beauty Parlor.'

Her principal blinked. He thought that Sally Lassiter got on badly with young Leo Fisk; she'd refused his advances, and he amused himself making sexual cracks about her whenever she came within earshot.

'I wish you the best of luck, young lady.' There was no point arguing. 'And if it doesn't work out, come back to school . . .'

'Same to you, Mr Rogers.' She shook his hand, and was gone, leaving nothing behind but the faint scent of jasmine.

We-e-ell,' Leo said, giving a long, low whistle. His eyes flickered hungrily up and down Sally Lassiter's knockout body. 'Damn, baby. You look about as pretty as a peach. What's up?'

Leo wasn't too smart. He'd hated being humiliated by the leggy blonde from California who'd refused to go out with him. She was supposed to be grateful for his attentions.

But at least she'd come to him now. And out of uniform. Sally could make a pair of jeans look like it should come with a triple-X certificate.

His buddies stood behind him, book bags over their shoulders, murmuring and ogling. There would be an especial pleasure in laying her now they'd all seen what a grade-A piece of ass she was.

'Leo,' Sally said, straightening her back. 'I'm fixin' to leave school and get a job. And I'm hoping you won't stand in my way.'

'Why would I want to do that?'

'We haven't always seen eye to eye. You know that.'

Her voice was soft as melted butter, and there was something strong about how she carried herself. He started to think that maybe she'd make a good date, as well as a good lay.

'I'd love to let bygones be bygones,' he said, his gaze travelling the entire length of her delicious body.

'That's mighty good of you, Leo. Because I'd like to go work in Mrs Fisk's beauty parlor.'

He couldn't stop a broad grin from spreading across his face. Perfect! The sassy little minx would be in Mom's shop every day, and she'd be real beholden to him. He could have her fired any time he liked.

'You go right ahead,' he said. 'I'll put in a good word for you, too.'

'That'd be real nice of you.'

'And maybe you'd consider stepping out with me Friday night.'

'Why, that's a very sweet offer,' Sally said, smiling at him. 'But I never mix business with pleasure.'

He opened his mouth for a sharp retort, but just couldn't do it. The girl was too blindingly hot. Better to just put his time in—it'd be all the sweeter when she tumbled into his bed.

'I understand that,' he said slowly. 'So I'll call Mom for you. Maybe see you around.'

'Sure thing. And thank you again,' Sally said, and this time gave him a real smile, one that reached all the way to those clear blue eyes.

She knew the store well, passed it every day. Fisk's, the only beauty place in town, drab and underused. It seemed to be well stocked but with old cosmetics, since only Elaine Fisk's friends actually used the store. The ladies of Hartford preferred Catfield, closer to Dallas and with a bunch of Korean-run manicure places. Mrs Elaine Fisk, a fat woman into velours trouser-suits and diamonds at all times, knew as much about style as she did about advanced calculus.

Which was why this was such an attractive prospect.

'My son speaks highly of you,' Elaine Fisk said. Her stern eye danced over Sally's breathtaking outfit. Just looking at Sally made Mrs Fisk wish she hadn't eaten that second muffin for breakfast.

'Leo's been so kind to me,' Sally said sweetly. 'He's a credit to you and Mr Fisk, ma'am. Y'all have raised a real gentleman. Everybody says so.'

That did it; Elaine liked nothing better than to hear Sally Lassiter talk that way about her baby. And maybe Sally could shake things up, she thought. Not that Elaine cared about making money, nothing so vulgar!

'Well, I could certainly use somebody to sweep the floor, maybe wash hair in the basins,' Elaine conceded.

'Actually, I want to be your beauty therapist.' Sally stood firm. 'What I'd like to do is work with you on a new vision for Fisk's. Your beauty parlour will be *the* place in town, Mrs Fisk. You'll have all the ladies, all your friends *begging* for appointments . . .'

Elaine looked sceptical. 'And what do I use to attract all this attention?'

'Me,' Sally said proudly.

'Honey, what could you know about fancy cosmetics?'

Sally didn't flinch. 'Mrs Fisk, I was in LA, and we mixed with the top Hollywood celebrities. I can tell you all the style secrets.'

'Hollywood Dazzle!' Elaine cried. 'That's the new name for the store!'

Sally bit back a smile. Hell, at least the woman was getting enthusiastic. 'Nobody'll buy that down here. At least, not yet,' she added, diplomatically. 'This is your place so it should reflect *you*, Mrs Fisk. How about this—Rodeo Girl. It's down-home, it's sassy, it's us.'

'I like it,' Elaine said excitedly.

'We'll need a little money. Some paint, some new lights, letters for the storefront . . .'

'My husband will give me that.' Elaine waved her fingers dismissively, lost in the dream. Then her eyes narrowed. 'But just because *you've* got style, how can I tell if you'll be good in the store? We don't make a lot of money here, I don't think I can give you more than minimum wage. We're taking losses . . .'

'I want a thousand dollars a month.'

Elaine Fisk's eyes widened, and she laughed. 'Young lady, you are plumb crazy talking like that. We don't even take a thousand dollars in a month. Not even half.'

'But we will. Look, Mrs Fisk, when was the last time you had a real romantic date with Mr Fisk? Tell you what. Why don't you let me style you? I'll show you just how good I am. You'll look ten years younger. He'll think he's romancing your little sister!'

'He better not,' Elaine Fisk said darkly. But it was a tempting pitch. 'OK . . . I'll try it.'

Well. This would be a challenge. But Sally gritted her teeth. She could certainly make Elaine look, if not good, at least better.

'We'll start with hair and make-up,' she said. 'No cutting—just styling. And then we'll go shopping for a new outfit. I'll do your nails and brows. Why don't you come on over here, and we'll start with washing your hair.'

Elaine waddled over to the washbasin and sat down. 'I've no idea why I'm agreeing to this. You certainly are a sweet-talker . . .'

Sally hastily ran the warm water into the basin and wet down her new boss's hair. She didn't want to give Elaine a chance to change her mind.

'**M**y stars,' Elaine Fisk murmured. 'Oh my goodness.'

She gaped at her reflection.

Her heavily sprayed, stiffly backcombed hair was softly washed, blow-dried, and styled into a long bob round her face. The layers of thick mascara that only a young woman could get away with had gone; Sally allowed her one coat of brown mascara to pick out the blue in her eyes. The rouge and the face powder that caked every wrinkle were replaced with a sheer anti-ageing formula and a neutral blush that Sally cleverly used to design cheekbones that really weren't there.

The vile trouser-suit had been replaced by a well-cut dress in a heavy fabric, which made Elaine look stately rather than fat. The flashy diamonds Sally had swapped for some luminous freshwater pearls, and she'd picked out a lace shawl to complete the effect; and finally, the masterstroke, a pair of sturdy, stacked heels, which forced Elaine to stand differently. She looked younger, thinner—*better*.

Elaine couldn't contain her delight. 'Oh, Sally, you're a genius.'

'Just wait until you send your friends out looking like that,' Sally prompted. 'I want to offer make-overs, hairdressing, and a styling service if they pay enough—for the elite customers, two hundred dollars a session. I'll go shopping with them and show them what to get.'

'Oh yes—yes, certainly,' Elaine said, dreamily staring at her reflection.

'Ask Mr Fisk for a budget to renovate the store? And I want to throw an open day. Free make-overs. Believe me, that'll get them talking.' Sally was almost high on her plans and dreams. She *could* make it happen.

'I wrote up a contract. A thousand dollars a month plus basic health-care benefits . . .' Sally produced a neatly typed document from her handbag. Elaine signed it without even a murmur, went to her desk, took out her chequebook and scribbled in it.

'Delighted, dear,' she said. 'Say, could you look after the store for me this afternoon? I want to go and surprise Mark.'

'Of course. You go on home, Mrs Fisk. I'll look after things here.'

Elaine drifted out and Sally looked around the store. Dingy and underused. She could change all that. It was the first bit of real optimism she'd felt in ages.

Things changed. Not overnight; Mark Fisk moaned over the fifty thousand dollars—Elaine's place had never been more than a drag on his finances. The two current employees, jealous of Sally, tried to rebel, until Elaine laid down the law. The builders and decorators were lazy, and it was a constant struggle. But Sally persevered. She had a job and a purpose. She worked like a demon, painting, decorating, sourcing cool artwork, fancy mirrors, bronze letters three feet high, designing the ad for the local paper. And if the renovations took three months, well, that was plenty of time for Hartford to get good and curious.

When the grand opening happened, all Elaine's friends were there, as well as several curious teens from the high school. Sally had trained the other two girls in beauty basics, properly, and left them doing pedicures and neck massages while she flitted from chair to chair, flash-styling the small-town girls in ten minutes each, showing housewives addicted to plaits and buns what natural styling looked like. The oohs and aahs from the mirrors didn't put any cash in the coffers, but Sally had faith. There was no business as sound as beauty. If you could show women you made a difference . . .

The older ladies booked the place up almost immediately, and their daughters scrambled for appointments. Sally was busy, nine to five, every day, and sometimes at weekends as well. It was exhausting, but it was a rush.

For the first six months Sally's life moved into a routine. She spent her spare time at home, looking after Mona as best she could. Sally felt guilty, at times, that she couldn't turn her mom around the way she was shaping up Elaine Fisk's business. Fighting Mona's alcoholism would need Sally to be there full time, and she had to make choices. Sally tried not to think too much. She let her days fill up, her savings account slowly increase. It was easier to cope that way. She didn't know exactly where she was going yet, but she was not going to stay here.

'**L**ook at her,' Leo Fisk said.

His Porsche was parked across the street, with three of his buddies sitting inside. The top was down, and they stared at Sally as she sauntered out of Rodeo Girl's front door.

Leo had been watching Sally Lassiter coming in and going out of his mom's store for months and months. The original plan was to drop by, watch her doing menial tasks like sweeping the floor and have Sally flirt with him, begging him to notice her. Only it hadn't worked out that way. Since day one, Sally was surrounded, first by workmen, then by customers. And obviously she was key to Rodeo Girl, whatever his mother told people. Leo had no power over her any more. All the eager, desperate schoolgirls he'd fumbled with or taken to bed paled into nothingness compared with Sally. And the further away he got from her, the more he wanted her.

'Pity you didn't bang her when you had the chance,' Simon Bernardillo said.

'He never *had* the chance. Remember? Chick turned him down flat,' piped up Keith Brand, from the back, and his annoying friends fell about laughing.

'Can it,' Leo said shortly. 'She's just another piece of tail, fellas. Let's go play ball.' Aggravated, he put the Porsche into gear and slammed his foot down. Leo hated it when his friends laughed at him. He was going to have to teach that girl some manners. She damn well *would* go out with him, and in public. Or else.

He left after practice, so as not to be obvious, and went over to his dad's garage, where they had a liquor concession and nobody asked questions. Leo took a little supply, some crates of beer and a pint of vodka. He liked that best because it didn't leave a smell on your breath. And it was a man's drink, something to get riled up on before he confronted Sally. She had a snappy, cool way about her when she put you down, and Leo wanted to stand up to her. He packed the beer into the trunk, then unscrewed the vodka and took a good, fiery swig. He felt himself gearing up. Carefully, not wanting to attract the cops, he turned the car back to main street and the way Sally walked home.

Sally was tired, but glowing. Saturday night, and a great week for tips. Mrs Ellis, the wife of the local realtor, had been so thrilled with her personal shopping session that she'd pressed five hundred-dollar bills into her hands. And there had been over four hundred from the rest of the clientele, which meant she'd got almost a month's worth in a single week. With what was left over from LA, Sally now had thirty-two thousand saved, with the promise of more to come.

It would be almost a year soon, and then she'd ask for a big rise. Rodeo Girl was a huge success. Sally thought she might walk Elaine through share structure and get her to give her a slice. Once they'd done that, she could maybe start a new store, even one in Dallas. Maybe, Sally suddenly thought, she could even go home . . .

But no; not yet. Not till she'd accumulated at least, what, eighty? That way she and Momma could get a little apartment. And she'd need working capital to set up a beauty parlour in LA. How much did rehab cost? More than she had. No, not ready yet, not ready to go back. Perhaps in a few years, when she was twenty-one.

A car honked; she jumped out of her skin, spun round, her hand flung up against the dazzling light.

'What the . . . Oh, hey, Leo.' She dropped her hand and drew aside as his big Porsche slowed down. 'You startled me.'

Leo Fisk was smiling at her, with that lascivious look in his eyes. 'You're far too cute to be tramping home in the mud, Sally. Let me give you a lift.'

'It ain't muddy,' she replied. 'I like the exercise.'

'I know, but you should relax once in a while. Go home early.'

She didn't want to be rude to Leo, he was Elaine's son, after all. 'OK, why not.' She opened the door and climbed in. 'Thanks.'

'So,' he said, pulling out into the road again. 'You never did give me that date. You owe me a dinner, at least.'

Sally sighed. She was surprised it had taken him this long to get round to it. 'Leo, look. You're a real good-looking boy'—hell, he hated that, he wasn't a goddamn boy—'and I know all the girls are wild to go out with you, but I'm not ready for a romantic relationship. I'm focusing on work right now. I want to get a place of my own.'

'All work and no play makes Sally a dull girl,' Leo said. He slurred the s's, and she realised that he was more than a little drunk.

'Make a left right here, Leo,' she said. But he missed the turning and shot past the intersection.

'Oh, you missed our street. Never mind. Just pull over and I'll walk.'

He didn't look at her; his eyes were fixed straight ahead, and he pressed his foot down on the gas.

'Just pull over,' Sally repeated uneasily.

Leo drove on. They were going fast now, very fast. The car was wobbling. The lights of Hartford disappeared in the distance.

'Please stop,' she begged.

The car pulled to a halt.

Sally glanced wildly around. They were in the middle of nowhere, a cornfield to the left. Quiet road, no traffic.

'Leo, you're drunk. I'm walking back and we're gonna forget this ever happened.' Sally tried for confident, but her voice cracked with fear.

He reached for her, one hand brushing against her breasts. 'Come on, baby, you'll like it. All the girls do.'

'Get away from me!' Sally shouted. She tried desperately to twist away, but he was strong. 'Leo, you're better than this . . . What would your mom think? Don't, don't touch me!'

Angrily, he backhanded her across the face. Sally gasped in pain and shock. She tried to clamber out of the door.

'You're trying to ruin it,' he hissed, grunting. 'Bringing my mom into it. You're just an uppity bitch.'

'You're a bully and a coward,' Sally sobbed. 'I'll scream . . .'

The light in his eyes was manic. 'You do, and I'll kill you,' he snarled. 'And dump you in that damn corn field and you can rot away in the fall.'

Sheer terror froze her to her seat.

'Now,' he said, fumbling at her shirt. 'Yeah . . . yeah, you sure are well-built, baby, and I'm gonna be your first . . .' His hand was on her. She was tight, dry as a bone. He didn't care. Sally sobbed and leaned her head back. She didn't want to die, so she said nothing. And Leo Fisk raped her.

He dropped her home afterwards. She said nothing.

'Don't worry, I'll see you again,' Leo said. 'Take you out to the movies tomorrow. It'll be better next time, baby, you got it in you.'

She climbed out of the car, and he was gone. Sally had seen true-crime shows about rape victims. How they would scrub themselves till they bled. Or go to the police. Sally did neither. Instead, she ignored her mother, snoring upstairs on the bed, and went to grab her suitcases.

The police would not believe her. She knew that deep down in her bones. And she didn't want the publicity, all that prurient interest in the rape of a teenage blonde. They'd find Mona, too, in her personal hell.

Forget this shithole of a town. Sally was gone. She had thirty-two thousand in the bank. They could rent in LA. And she could start her own store. Buy a lease—get it done. She was angry in the very depths of her soul. She was going to go the hell home, show all of them. The bastards who'd dropped them when her dad died. The snooty friends who never called. All the bullies, all those snooping vultures in the press.

Sally needed money. If she had money again, she'd have protection. If she wasn't poor, Leo could never have got away with raping her.

Never again. She knew how to make it. First, she was going to change their lives, again. Next, she was going to cure her momma and get rich. And last, she was going to take revenge. Not just on Leo Fisk. On the whole damn world.

Chapter Seven

'You can't fire me.'

He was older than Jane. Thirty at least, in his fancy Armani suit, with a Princeton degree and an arrogant air.

'I can and I am. The San Diego store is failing to attract customers and growth.'

'A rise of nine per cent. Read the report,' he replied with contempt.

'That is insufficient. The Sunset Boulevard store is making between twelve and fifteen per cent.'

'That's a special case,' he said.

'Of course it is.' She smiled thinly. 'I run it. And now staff have been trained to follow my principles. Which is why I'm here in head office, and you're being sacked. There's a severance package on the table, but it won't be there for long.'

He jumped to his feet, puce with rage. 'What the hell do you know? No college degree, no MBA. Everybody knows why you're here, *Miz* Morgan. You're the best little whore in the company. Fucking half the board of directors, no doubt. And I bet you're *real* good at it.'

'Security can be up here in thirty seconds. And they really are good at it,' Jane replied coolly. 'And by the way, the severance package just evaporated.'

He snarled at her, cheeks mottled with rage, but he left.

She walked to the window. The office was her favourite part of this job. The Manhattan skyscrapers jabbed into the hazy blue of the sky; the traffic crawled, in miniature, at ground level, yellow cabs crawling along like beetles. Her office. Vice-President in charge of Personnel. And she deserved it, damn it.

She tried to brush off what Michael Tiersky had said as the rantings of a failure. But it bothered her. She heard it far too often. From any man, and half the women. Sex toy. Bimbo. That she might be here on her merits—impossible. She was twenty years old. And, Jane was starting to understand, too beautiful.

It aggravated her. She'd proven herself out there in LA. In six months, she had transformed the whole store's productivity. Under her regime, merit was rewarded. With Jane Morgan watching, slacking was impossible. But if you were a worker, Jane made life good. Even for the lowest levels. She ordered the canteen redecorated, new coffee machines installed, and the food improved. Sexual harassment was no longer tolerated. For the college kids, she offered daily internships in the management offices, so that the stint packing groceries would look better on their résumés. For the working moms, Jane brought in a crèche. For the families, she negotiated discounts at Universal Studios and the museums. There were reward schemes, bonuses, and a better staff area. People were motivated. Jane revolutionised the store.

They promoted her three times, and then the call to New York. A vice-presidency of Shop Smart. Translate your methods across the country.

Jane had moved into a smart two-bedroom flat on the Upper East

Side. Her Ford had long ago become a Lincoln town car. In Manhattan, they offered her a driver. Jane demurred. She'd take the subway. It was cheaper and quicker into midtown.

Her bosses loved it, and they loved her. Before she knew where she was, Jane was appearing on the Shop Smart corporate website. Along with a note on her tragic story.

She wanted to object, but didn't. It was all an irrelevance. And if the company looked good for having a woman at a senior level, then fine. But now—now she was getting sick of it. Jane's trouble was that she did this *too well*. Shop Smart just wanted more of the same. But she wasn't a Personnel drone. What interested her was *selling*. It was the store, itself. But the board had other ideas. They told her they liked her where she was. Why mess with success?

Jane stared down at Manhattan. She sensed danger. This was a trap—a very comfortable trap, but a trap, all the same. She had trained herself to be a *businesswoman*, not an overpaid nanny. Five months in New York, and she was done.

She made up her mind. Go to Rhodri and ask him for a transfer. Marketing would be a start. And if they refused, she would quit.

'I'll take it to them.' Rhodri Evans sighed, and polished his glasses. 'Really, Jane, you're only twenty and already a vice-president.'

Jane leaned across his desk. 'You know what I tell my juniors, Rhodri? Up or out. If they're not promotion material within a certain time, they are gone. Why should the rules be different for me? You put me in as VP in charge of staff. OK, I've delivered. The dead wood is gone. The motivation programmes are there . . .'

'So you should see it through.'

'Like hell.' She stood and ran a hand through her long hair, and he admired her, dispassionately. 'I'm not into that. I want a real job. Supply, management, marketing—there are lots of possibilities.'

Rhodri stood firm. 'You are a kid. Whatever the numbers say, shareholders and, more importantly, analysts are going to bitch at seeing you promoted to board level.'

'Then explain why.'

'We did OK for many years before you got here,' he said calmly. 'And we would do OK after you left.'

'But this is so dumb. You gave me a brief, and I delivered. I could be so much more. Shop Smart—'

'Time for an object lesson,' Rhodri said. 'This store is at a peak of performance and sales. No director is going to give a crap if you come or go. At twenty years old, you can expect at least—at *minimum*—five years in this slot. You're good, and relatively cheap—'

'And if I quit?'

Rhodri rolled his eyes. 'At twenty you're on two hundred k. If you quit, you're a moron. In *this* company you have a track record. Anyplace else, you're just another college dropout—because they won't be giving you a glowing reference.'

Jane snarled. 'Damn it!'

'You're an analyst.' He treated her with the same dispassion she treated everyone else. 'You figure it out. The fact you're so beautiful makes a difference.'

'You have a boyfriend. I don't,' she lashed out.

'Sweetie, if you want, I can fix that in five minutes.'

Jane grudgingly offered him a smile. 'Thank you, no.' He was a smart cookie, Rhodri Evans, and a good friend.

'Seriously.' He stood up, and walked over to her. 'You're frustrated, but maybe that's not because of work. You need a relationship.'

'Yeah, sure,' she said.

'How did it work out with Peter Ralston?' Rhodri had introduced her to this banker from Chase, newly divorced, considered handsome.

'We had a couple of dates,' Jane said. 'I just don't think we clicked.'

'Why?' Rhodri was upset. 'Are you really making an effort?'

'What, are you going to complain you'll never have grandchildren?' Jane chuckled, and Rhodri smiled back. It was good to see the girl laugh. He worried about her. Sometimes he wondered if he had done the right thing, giving her that first promotion. She was so absorbed in business.

'But he was perfect for you.'

'Evidently not,' Jane said wrily.

'Then I have somebody else you should meet.' Rhodri nodded, determinedly. 'Somebody different to anyone you've seen before.'

'Another damn banker or lawyer. I don't think I can deal with that. Face it, Rhodri, I'm just not ready to date.'

'He's none of those things. He's English.'

That brought Jane up short. 'English?'

'Yes. From Sussex. Some place called Rye.'

'I know Rye,' Jane said. Instantly, she wanted to meet this man.

'He went to Eton. No title but lots of cash. He's in town buying a place in the Hamptons. Just broke up with the daughter of some earl or something. I met him at a party last night. And he wants to meet you.'

Her response surprised him. 'Yes, that'd be great,' Jane said. 'Give him my direct line. Thank you, Rhodri, he sounds interesting.'

Finally, then, he had solved it, cracked the puzzle. What she needed was a guy from her own culture. As soon as she had left his office, Rhodri telephoned his new protégé to give him the good news.

Jane floated through the day.

Jude Ferrers was going to pick her up tonight at eight, and take her to a concert. Carnegie Hall, a candlelit dinner; his voice on the phone had sounded gentlemanly and urbane. She was intrigued, impatient.

She dressed with exquisite care: her favourite Azzedine Alaia dress, black and tight, bands of brilliantly cut black silk tapering around her body, ending just over the knee; high Manolo Blahnik heels, with crystal-cut buckles; Wolford tights; Hermès 24 Rue Faubourg as her scent. She chose to make up with a daring plum lipstick and charcoal liner, emerald-green shadow on her lids. A bold look, but the mirror told her, without a doubt, she had pulled it off.

Jane paced up and down her apartment, trying to contain her excitement. Come on, she told herself. He might be ugly, he might be short, he might be far too skinny, or fat as a house. But it didn't work. Jude had sounded so different, so cultured. Miles removed from all the investment bankers who always gave the impression of wanting to check their phone messages.

The doorbell rang and she raced to answer it.

He stood on the doorstep with a large, expensive-looking bunch of roses, dark red, set with berries and twigs and glossy foliage. He was a tall man, light brown hair, hazel eyes, a handsome enough face, and wearing a good suit that looked a bit rumpled.

Jane felt her heart flip over as Jude casually gave her the once-over; she suddenly, ardently, wanted to be found pleasing.

'My goodness. You might just be the prettiest girl I've ever seen.'

'. . . is the right answer,' Jane said, and they laughed.

He was absolutely smooth. He held open car doors for her, walked on the outside of the pavement, offered her his arm as they climbed the stairs in Carnegie Hall to the box he had hired.

Jane sat, fascinated, at dinner while he told her all about his parents' interests in land and property, his own desire to do 'something in art history'. Jude didn't want to work. He told her he had no desire to join the rat race, and Jane envied him, and thought it amazing he could be so detached.

'But you're buying a place in the Hamptons? They cost a fortune.'

'I have a trust fund.' He shrugged. 'You know, the idea we all absolutely have to spend our lives working our fingers down to the knuckle is very recent. Did you ever read any Jane Austen?'

'Of course; all of it.'

'Well, Darcy never went and toiled in an office, did he? And nor did Elizabeth. So why should I, when I don't have to?'

'I think that's wonderful,' Jane said, a little starry-eyed. Gosh. Wasn't he urbane. So charismatic, so confident!

'Tomorrow's Saturday,' he reminded her. 'Maybe you could come out to the Hamptons with me. I'm going round a few places.'

She beamed back at him, and wondered if this was what love felt like; her whole soul was bathed in sunlight.

The next day she went for smart-casual, as English as she could: tailored corduroy trousers, green Wellington boots, and a cashmere T-shirt.

'You look delicious,' he said, kissing her boldly on the cheek. And then, when she responded, lightly on the lips.

Jane blushed.

They took a helicopter ride to the Hamptons, and Jude showed her round: a modern, glossy house on the seashore; a cute four-bedroom white clapboard cottage, old by American standards; a red-brick Victorian in the centre of town. Jane loved each one. They were two million bucks apiece. Jude bought her lunch at a clam shack in the Vineyard, where they drank a delicious, rough Italian white and ate deep-fried soft-shell crabs, whole.

Jane sat, absorbed, as Jude told her all about Rye—a medieval town, she remembered now, full of buildings from history, Queen Anne, Tudor, earlier, and the flat fields and rolling downs of Sussex.

And she started to fantasise about what might happen. If he liked her . . . what if she gave up work, what if she just got married, maybe started a family?

He said he wasn't interested in buying anything on the spot. Jane waxed lyrical about the white clapboard cottage, but Jude's eyes glazed over. After a few minutes he interrupted her.

'There's the Old Shipping Inn in the centre of town. I thought maybe we could stay over. Steal a night. Like honeymooners.'

She nodded her head, briskly, her throat dry, and he whisked her away to the hotel and up to a suite.

'Ever since I saw you in that tight little dress, I wanted to unwrap you, all shiny and new, like a Christmas present.'

Ever since? It had only been last night.

But Jane didn't care. She nodded, half eager, half terrified, as they tumbled onto the bed.

'**A** virgin.' He smiled afterwards, as though he'd won a prize. 'I can't believe you were actually a virgin.'

'Everybody has to start somewhere,' Jane joked, although she was afraid it sounded lame.

'But you're twenty years old. I thought virgins that survived their teens were myths. Like unicorns.' He ran a hand across her thigh, touching the drying blood that lay there. 'You can be my pet unicorn.'

'I'll take a shower,' Jane said, feeling embarrassed.

'How was it?' He yawned. 'What you expected?'

'Fantastic,' she lied. In fact, she'd been dry and tense, he had started too soon. But she blamed herself. She hadn't told him she was a virgin . . .

'Well, I'll soon have you trained up to be an expert.' He rolled over on the bed. As an afterthought, he added, 'You better get on the pill, darling, we don't want any complications. I just hate those, don't you?'

'Oh—of course,' Jane said. She went into the shower; he had already closed his eyes.

She washed herself for a long time, scrubbing the embarrassing blood from her legs. It felt as though the world should seem different now, as if the sky should have a different colour. But it didn't; everything was normal.

Except, she told herself hopefully, for Jude. He had taken her virginity, and she was glad. As she dried herself and dressed, Jane snuck a look at him, sleeping on the bed. Rhodri had said all the women were flinging themselves at him. No wonder, she thought, and I've got him! It was a brilliant feeling.

When Jude woke, he suggested they check out. 'I hate wearing the same clothes two days in a row. I'll pick you up tomorrow for brunch.'

'OK,' Jane said, happily enough. She had been looking forward to spending the night with him, but tomorrow would do.

He dropped her off at her door with a little pat on her ass, and Jane spun round to kiss him, deeply, romantically. But Jude laughed, and said, 'You're a lot of fun.'

She didn't like that. Something profound had just happened—surely he must feel the chemistry. She went to sleep in her own bed, alone, and not wholly happy.

He picked her up at eleven. The brunch spot was crowded and hip, and Jane nervously picked at waffles with strawberries, while Jude polished off bacon and eggs and a mug of cinnamon coffee.

'So after this we'll go back to my hotel,' he suggested, throwing down a hundred-dollar bill carelessly. 'If you want to. And tonight . . . that book launch at the Metropolitan, and back afterwards for more?'

'Perfect,' Jane said, reassured. He was still interested. Yes, there was some reserve there, but she found it all the sexier, all the more exciting. For once, she was the pursuer. And every time he looked at her, Jane thrilled with happiness. The sex wasn't great, but she didn't care. She went along, easily enough. It was the price of being with someone so charming. And that was what a relationship was . . .

Over the next week, at work, she floated through her days, waiting for him to call. They met at odd hours; at lunchtime, often, and then she would duck out of meetings at three or four. Nobody complained. She knew they could see she was in love. So what? Some day she'd be announcing an engagement . . .

And then he rang, and her world crashed in.

'Baby.' That soft, familiar tone at the end of the workday. How she loved to hear it. 'You have to come over to the hotel.'

Jane glanced at the clock: 4.45. Good enough.

'On my way,' she said, grabbing her bag. And hung up. All Jude had to do was call, and she came running.

'So.' He rolled off her, stretched out for a minute, then jumped up from the bed. 'I'm going to miss you,' he said, grabbing his dressing gown and pulling it on, casually.

Jane felt the tiny hairs prickle on her arms, and jumped out of bed herself, reaching for her clothes.

'Miss me? Are you going somewhere?'

'Well, the summer's over,' he said lightly. 'Time to push on home.'

'You're going back to England? I have a major project, re-staffing in Arizona. I can't get leave for a while.'

'Leave? To come with me? I don't think that's a great idea, darling.'

She shivered. 'What do you mean?'

He started to pace around the room, then said, quickly, as though wanting to get the words out, 'This was a holiday romance, great while it lasted, but I don't think we've got a future. You've got your career . . .'

Jane was seized with blind panic. He was leaving her, abandoning her . . . 'Is there someone else?' she whispered.

'Yes,' Jude said brutally. 'Actually, more than one. I just don't want to be tied down. You're beautiful, but you're just too . . . clingy.'

Numbly, Jane pulled on her panties and bra, and reached for her skirt.

'And there's your father . . . well, it wouldn't be right. Not in England, anyway. Not after what he did. I'm sure you can see that, Jane. You'll be better off here, with a Yank—somebody who won't ask too many awkward questions . . .' Deliberately not looking at her, he walked into the bathroom, and she heard him switch on the shower.

Jane dressed as quickly as she could, her heart thumping and her mind racing. Clingy . . . better off here . . . *your father* . . . Abandoned. Again. First her father, and then Sally and Helen, the only two real friends she'd ever had. As she stood, humiliated, in Jude's hotel bedroom, the pain of the loss of those two girls was worse for Jane than what had just happened. Perhaps because Sally and Helen actually *cared* about her. Those girls were the only *real* family Jane had ever had. And everybody needs a family.

Even as the tears were rolling down her cheeks, Jane suddenly, in a flash of light, understood why she'd felt so attracted, why she'd jumped on him desperately, even when the sex was lousy and the conversation strained . . . *Her father.* Jude was English. In some weird way he'd reminded her of Thomas, and he had wanted her. Praised her. Spent time with her. Lavished attention on her . . .

She steadied herself, one hand pressed against her heart, looking out over Central Park, the leaves just starting to redden and brown. It was so revelatory. Jude was nothing. She had lost her virginity to nothing.

Calm now, Jane reached for her coat. That was all over. She would go on, and succeed, despite what Thomas Morgan had done to her. If love came, it would come. But Jane Morgan was not about to go looking for it. She would not use romance to heal a childhood wound.

Jude's clothes and his packed suitcase lay on the bed. Jane glanced out of the window; below them was a terrace. Casually, Jane tossed everything Jude owned out of the window and walked out of his suite, leaving the door wide open.

In her apartment, Jane found the answering machine blinking. She pressed it. 'You bloody *bitch*! I've got to call housekeeping, they might blab. This could make the gossip columns . . . I'll be a laughing stock . . .'

She pressed delete.

She needed a change. It was no longer any fun in Human Resources. Jane wanted ownership. She wanted it to be *her* helicopter, *her* house in the Hamptons. She was getting lazy. Middle management was not in her game plan. And she was overwhelmed with a desire to recapture some of what she had lost. Find Sally Lassiter, even if Sally had disappeared—find Helen, even if Helen was babied up in a Cairo suburb. They had private investigators these days that were as good as the FBI. This was America; money opened every door.

Jane smiled. Shop Smart and she would play a game of chicken, and Jane was not going to be the one who blinked.

Chapter Eight

THEIR FIRST TRIP to America was a big success. Baba and Mama met them at the airport; they hugged and cried, obviously so sincerely overjoyed to see Haya that she could forgive the smug look in her father's eyes. 'I was right,' he kept saying, on the drive back from the airport. 'You see, darling? We *did* know best.'

Haya wanted to explode, but Ahmed kept pressing her hand, his eyes lit up with amusement. And then he switched to tracing an A with his fingers, slowly, in the small of her back. A for Ahmed. Telling Haya she was his. It turned her on, and her rage evaporated.

Ahmed looked at LA with open eyes. Yes, it was brash, and Western, and vulgar in lots of ways, but it was also exciting, big, and rich. His wife's enthusiasm was infectious. He loved that about her—that she made life an adventure. His father-in-law had kept his word. There was a meeting at Neiman Marcus, at Saks and at the Beverly Hills Hotel. All three agreed to buy a carpet or two. Before the month was out, he had a small client base.

'We could do more,' Haya suggested. 'Sell in department stores, regularly. Of course, such things take time . . .' She looked up at Ahmed under her lashes. 'And also presence.'

And I could try to find Jane and Sally, Helen thought to herself, too. She adored Ahmed, but she missed her girlfriends.

'You mean move here?' he said slowly.

'Talal could run the Egyptian store.'

'I don't know. It's a big step.' Ahmed looked down at her sternly.

'We should do it,' she said, her stomach flipping over in that sexy, slow way it did when he held her eyes. 'Please . . .'

He ran a finger down her cheek. 'Persuade me.'

In the end it was seamless. Haya trained Talal, his manager, on the computer; they organised insurance, and wages for his staff; a cousin from Aswan came with his wife to stay in the Cairo house. And Haya took her dowry, which Baba paid to Ahmed, and some of the profits from their last year's trading, and purchased a property; Ahmed approved of the third place she showed him, a modern villa in mock

Spanish style at the foot of the Hollywood Hills. The garden was verdant, and Ahmed enjoyed the large television, the power showers with multiple jets, the soft mattresses and air conditioning.

They moved in, storing a pile of their best carpets in a guest room. Haya helped to set up the new American company, and Ahmed closed the deals. Business was not quite so simple. The famous stores had their suppliers already, and the larger orders were slow in coming.

But the orders were there, and they kept their heads above water.

Yet Ahmed was disturbed by one thing: the months came and went, and still the wife of his heart was not pregnant.

Haya leaned on the balcony of the kitchen window; it looked out into their little garden, one of her favourite spots. She might sunbathe later, under an umbrella, sipping a chilled fruit juice. But despite trying to relax, Haya was anxious. There were things missing from her life.

Haya couldn't find her friends. When she first got back to the States she plunged into the search, but it had all led to a dead end. She gave up for the time being. Ahmed was happy, and so was she, but they had not spread their wings the way Haya had hoped. She wanted more.

When Ahmed came back that night—he had made five thousand on the placement of a beautiful Afghan in the beach-house of a famous actor—Haya asked him if she could come along the next day.

'Your meeting tomorrow. With Richard Drayson.' The sales director of Broderick Stores. Ahmed was going to try, yet again, to get a department store to place a major ongoing order. It would be the sixth pitch meeting he'd had this year. Something was going wrong—they were failing, somehow. And Haya wanted to see why.

'If you'd like to,' Ahmed agreed. He too was unhappy. There was no progress, they were stuck in middle-class comfort. 'Sure. Why not?'

We think you have good pieces, Mr al-Amin.' The buyer's eyes were flat. 'And we'll happily take two rugs.'

'We were hoping for a larger order,' Ahmed said. 'We are a reliable supplier and cannot be beaten on price.'

Drayson shook his head. 'I can't take the risk.'

'What do you mean by that?' Haya protested.

'Our traders deal with thousands of rugs per year. They have a constant supply of product. They get exclusive, or near it, presence in the stores because we rely on them. I can't offend them. You have good carpets, Mr al-Amin, but you're strictly nickel and dime.'

Ahmed's eyes darkened, and he opened his mouth to speak, but

Haya laid a gentle hand on his shoulder. 'Thank you, Mr Drayson,' she said. The buyer was only being honest. No point getting mad.

Drayson looked satisfied. 'So you'll sell us the two carpets,' he said briskly. 'Good.'

'No,' Ahmed said, suddenly, looking at Haya. 'I'm afraid not. We're going to go into business for ourselves, and from now on the line will be exclusive.'

She beamed back. Her thought exactly. She was so proud of Ahmed—they were hand in glove.

That very afternoon, they got to work. They found a site at a dusty road intersection; applied for planning permission, sought out an architect. Baba knew builders.

Haya suggested the name. Sekhmet. The ancient Egyptian goddess of vengeance and war, lioness-headed, beautiful and fierce—like they were going to be with the competition. Ahmed worked with the architect—huge windows, lots of light, UV protection built in.

It was their vision, and they worked to make it happen. A gallery. The carpets stretched out, displayed like paintings. Each as individual as a jewel. Baba contacted his network; Ahmed his sales prospects. On opening weekend they sold ten carpets. Not brilliant, but solid.

Haya brought in flowers and Moroccan mint tea. Ahmed placed a small advertisement in the *LA Times*. The second week, they sold another twelve carpets.

The gallery was profitable. It was hard work, but Haya enjoyed it; staying up late with Ahmed, making love in the bathroom, at home, on the back seat of their car, like teenagers. They increased the trips back home, and she got used to dealing with suppliers, talking to customs men. Haya's Arabic became perfect, and she was happy; they were crafting a future. Haya had everything, except her friends. And, *inshallah*, a child.

'It's so good to meet you.' Marcus Hardie, the sales director, looked at Haya and gave her a perfunctory smile. 'Your husband has quite the business model; you must be very proud.'

Ahmed's eyes danced as Haya's flashed with annoyance. 'Actually, my wife had a good deal to do with this.'

'Of course. We all need the support at home.'

Support! The gallery had been *her* idea. Haya stiffened with anger. Now everybody—well, not Ahmed—was trying to take the credit away from her. Baba insisted success came because of *his* contacts. The press ran stories about Ahmed, the backstreet carpet seller turned gallery owner. Now the Hollywood Mall marketing man was ignoring her too.

'Mr Hardie. The first consignment will be no more than fifty carpets,' Haya said firmly.

'Per store? We'll want more than that.'

His chain of luxury goods stores was important, but not vital. 'You should have no more than one or two per store, at any one time.'

'That's not going to happen,' Marcus said patronisingly. He switched his attention back to Ahmed. 'What numbers did *you* have in mind?'

'You heard my wife.'

'Our customers want product.'

'And they'll get it,' Haya said, 'eventually. After the carpets become impossible to obtain. When you have orders in hand for fifty, we ship another ten. It will create a feeding frenzy,' Haya said.

Marcus parried. 'You can't run a business on hype.'

'Actually, you can. But in this case it isn't hype. Our goods are exquisite. We merely add to the joy of the purchase.' Haya warmed to her theme. 'Shopping is like a love affair, Mr Hardie, if it's done correctly. Prolonging the courtship is no bad thing.'

He barely refrained from rolling his eyes. 'I'll think about it.' He got to his feet. 'Ahmed, come and see me in the office, OK? And you, little lady, nice to meet you.'

Haya exploded once he was out of the door.

'Did you hear that? He wants to do business with *you*.'

'You can't let it get to you.' Ahmed stood up and walked across to her, standing behind her, his hands on her shoulders, tracing a line down them to her rib cage. Haya gasped. 'Let's go home,' she said.

'You go,' he said. 'Wait for me. I have to finish some tax stuff.'

'Don't be long.' She was trying to get control of her breathing.

'Did you see the doctor?'

That broke the spell; Haya calmed down. 'Results this afternoon.'

That was it; the one cloud in their happiness. No children. She had not wanted to make the appointment. To lay her womb open to medicine seemed intrusive. Like slapping nature in the face for the gift they had received—burning love, and a passion as hot now as it was the first night he had taken her. Surely such a love could not be barren?

But Ahmed had insisted. Children mattered so much to him. It was why he'd agreed to marry her, before he fell in love with her.

Haya had submitted herself to Dr Felicia Nevins, one of Bel Air's leading obstetricians. The woman had prodded and poked her briskly, drawn blood and taken tests. Haya felt like a laboratory animal.

The results were due at 5 p.m. And she was nervous about them. What if, God forbid, she was infertile? Ahmed was hers for ever, of that

Haya had no doubt. But that would mean the end of this long period of perfect happiness. Their lives would never again be free of sorrow.

'Then hurry home and I'll help you pass the time,' Ahmed said. She ran to his arms, and he kissed her.

'*You* hurry,' Haya said.

She paced in their bedroom. Where the hell was he? Haya was still aroused, her body holding the memory of his touch, not wanting to let it go. This was not like him. Haya picked up the phone and called their assistant. 'Claire? Haya.'

'Hi. What time are you guys getting back in? I have a ton of messages.'

'Getting back in? Did Ahmed leave already?'

'An hour ago.' Claire was confused. 'I thought he was going back home for lunch with you, sorry.'

'He was.' Haya wondered what on earth had happened. 'Maybe he stopped off for something. I'll call when he gets here.'

An hour later, she called the police. Uninterested, they told her she couldn't report a missing person for twenty-four hours. An hour after that, she started ringing round the hospitals . . .

'**I**t can't have happened. He was with me a few hours ago.' She felt stupid, just kept repeating it. 'He was fine.'

Ahmed lay there—she could hardly believe it really was him. Bandaged and trussed, with drips and feeders running from his arm. Around her, there was chaos—an overwhelmed A & E.

'Move him,' Haya said sharply. 'Get him into a private room.'

'Mrs al-Amin.' The doctor was trying to be kind. 'There's no point. It was a very bad accident—the other driver died at the scene . . .'

'My husband is still alive,' she snapped. '*Mashallah*. And I want him to get the best care.'

'He is not still alive,' the doctor said, flatly. 'Ma'am, I'm extremely sorry, your husband is dead. The stem of his brain is dead.'

'Then why . . .' Haya's voice broke on a sob. 'Why is that machine sounding? I can hear his heartbeats. I can see them!'

'Artificial respiration. We kept him alive in the hope you'd be willing to donate his organs. All that means is his heart is pumping. It's up to you, ma'am.' For the millionth time that day, Dr Kim tried for patience. 'But I have a very sick father of two who needs a liver and a lady waiting for a heart, with no other options.' Haya looked stricken. 'I'm sorry there's no time for you to decide. If the answer is no, we unplug him immediately and the Medical Examiner will take over.'

At these hurried, harassed words, a strange feeling of calm enveloped Haya. He was gone, gone to Paradise, and she was here alone. And Allah is the Most Compassionate, she said to herself.

'Yes. I'll sign the form. Take what you need,' she said. 'And then return him to me, this day. He must be buried at once. He is a Muslim. We cannot delay the burial.'

Dr Kim couldn't believe it. 'Thank you. I'll get you a consent form. Tell me where you want . . .' Her voice trailed off. '. . . him sent.'

Haya went into automatic mode. She called Egypt, and Ahmed's parents. Called Baba and Mama. Ahmed was lying in the funeral home, and she was here, in Hollywood, alone again, a widow at twenty. Ahmed was her life, her love, the sun and moon to her. Without him, life seemed utterly pointless.

The telephone rang. Haya answered automatically.

'Hello, Mrs al-Amin. This is Dr Nevins. I have the results of your tests. And in fact I have some very good news!'

No, you don't, she thought, there is no good news any more.

'You're not barren. These things just happen sometimes. It takes a little longer than planned. You see, you're in fact pregnant. Congratulations!'

Haya shuddered. 'What?'

'You're pregnant.'

Haya was swaying on her feet. 'I have to go,' she said, and hung up. Oh God! Pregnant!

For the first two months, Haya did not tell anybody. She could not deal with that, on top of everything else. It was enough to have to fly back to Egypt, be plunged into a world she could hardly cope with: instructing lawyers, enduring the anger of his parents, who blamed her for Ahmed's death. After all, she had dragged him to America, that godless, decadent land, and there, he had died.

Then there was everything else. The dismissal of all the staff, with compensation, paid from the sale of the Cairo house. Yet she could not bear to rid herself of the carpets, the evidence of that eye for beauty that had assessed Haya herself, and found her pleasing.

Haya wasn't rich, but there was enough money to see her through the birth of her child. His son or daughter. A small piece of her love that would come back to her. Right now, that was all she cared about.

On the other hand, it wouldn't last. One way or another she was going to have to make a living. She had to give his child all he would have dreamed of. Anything less would be a betrayal.

Chapter Nine

'WE'RE HERE. MOMMA.' Sally reached across the passenger seat and shook her mother. 'Wake up. We're here.'

Back in LA. This was her home, not Texas, this was the place where she had shone. With Jane and Helen, they were the three musketeers. Sally had tried to forget about her friends when her life was falling apart. Now she wanted more than anything else to find them again.

Mona opened her eyes. She rubbed the lids. 'I want a drink,' she said groggily. 'A little champagne, huh? To celebrate. We're back.'

'Let's see.' Sally tried every trick in the book to keep alcohol away from Mona. Sally made the decision to try rehab as soon as she'd saved enough money. That was her goal, why she needed a good job. In her heart, her momma didn't want to be this way. Plus, they were back in LA. That gave Sally a chance for some prime emotional blackmail.

'You know, people might report us to the papers, Mom. You don't want Lucille and Kimberley,' Mona's ex-friends, 'to read in the society columns that you were drunk in a cheap apartment?'

Her mom's eyes flashed with a spark of her old spirit. 'Hell, no,' she said. Mona clutched at her daughter as Sally fumbled with the keys. 'D'you think they'll find out we're living here?'

Sally shrugged. 'It's a decent place. It's got security and underground parking.' She pushed her mother inside the apartment. 'See? Not so bad.'

It was plainly furnished with the basic essentials. All the charm of a roadside motel.

"We won't be here too long, Momma. You'll see.' Brave words. She wondered how she could make them come true.

Sally got a job the first week. Beehive was a cute little place on Sunset with a customer base of hip West Hollywood teens. Sally agreed to work on commission in exchange for being off the books. She didn't want to be found in her own city. Not till they were truly on the up.

Of course, what applied to the press didn't apply to Helen or Jane Morgan. Sally made a few calls, even went to the public library to comb through old newspapers on the microfiche. But she found nothing.

She did make-overs, styled hair, and kept the place clean. Nothing exciting, but they could afford to live.

After a month Sally splashed out on a car, a respectable Ford Fiesta, her only indulgence. Sally worked seven days a week, till late, and kept herself booked up to the eyeballs. She wanted to do something better, but the first step was to fatten up their bank account until she had three or four months' reserve. Sally Lassiter was tired of being an employee. She wanted to start her own business. And that required cash.

At night, when she got home, Sally would go to her room and practise sketching. She wanted to design clothes—easy, wearable, hip. Style was more than make-up. Sally had it planned—her own designs, hand-sewn at first. Sold into stores. A boutique line, then more, rolled out across the city. Maybe the country. She knew she had talent, and she certainly had glamour.

She sewed up some clothes, put them on to work. Compliments flowed. Girls asked where they could buy the skirts and her favourite one-shoulder T-shirts. The reaction told her she was ready.

One sunny Monday morning, Sally shook hands with the beauty parlour owner and told her she was quitting. Fiona Bryce's face was a picture of dismay. 'You're my best girl, Sally, people come here just because of you.'

'That's mighty sweet of you, Fi, but I want to do my own thing, make some real money. You only do that by owning your own joint. Sorry.'

The older woman pouted. 'It's tough, making it on your own.'

'I'm used to tough.'

'Well, good luck to you, honey. And if it doesn't work out, you always got a job here.' But Sally knew, as she walked out of the door, that she would never return. She'd waited years, and finally, Sally Lassiter, tempered by tragedy, and poverty, and abuse, was ready for the big time.

The next step was the easiest. Sally booked Mona into a downtown rehab place.

'I don't need this, Sally. I can cut down. It's just the stress.'

Sally kept her eyes on the road. 'I can't face coming home every day, not knowing if you've choked on your own vomit. Your face is all red, you look like you're sixty years old. That ain't us, Momma. Daddy would hate it. We're back in LA . . .'

'We'll never be back,' Mona wailed, her voice full of the booze she'd chugged before Sally manhandled her into the Ford. 'We lived in Beverly Hills.'

'And we will do again.' Sally's knuckles whitened on the wheel.

Mona's teary, drunken tones turned aggressive. 'Stop the car! You can't make me do rehab! I won't check in . . . I'll look after you, Sal.'

Sally pulled over to the side of the road and looked at her mother, all swollen-faced and drowning in self-pity. 'These past years, I've been looking after you. Paying all the bills. Running the house.'

'I've been fine looking out for you, Sally . . .'

Mona was delusional. Sally would not allow that to continue; not one more minute. 'Do you know why we left Texas, Momma? Because I was raped. By Leo Fisk. One night when I was walking home after slaving all day to support us.' Her mother's mouth opened in a round O of shock. 'And when I came inside, you were passed out drunk. Again.'

Her mother started to sob now, in earnest.

'That's how I lost my virginity,' Sally said coldly. 'To a rapist. And I couldn't even tell you. That all ends now, Momma. Today. You're going to rehab, and you're not going to lose your life inside a vodka bottle.'

'I'll go,' Mona whispered. 'Sally . . .'

She put the car in gear. 'Don't you worry. I won't let some no-account piece of trash ruin my life.' Sally raised her chin, proudly. 'Like I said, we're starting over. And today is day one.'

'So you can see the movement.' Sally smiled and turned the skirt round, letting the hem flute out in the breeze. 'And these stones— they're designed to be sold individually, with a chain. You can make your own message. It's like jewellery-as-pizza, you pay for each topping. They're like candy, no girl will resist.'

DeMarco's top buyer, Ollie Foster, moistened his lips. Sally noticed his eyes roaming across her ample breasts and steeled herself not to stiffen. 'You got anything else to show me, baby? It's hard to break into sales in this town—real *hard*.'

'I have these sketches . . .'

'I'm not talking 'bout sketches. Why don't you slip into the changing rooms with me and model that skirt? You know, show me something. Got a cute little ass on you, girl. If you want a deal here, you know what you got to do. . . .'

Sally snatched her necklace back and turned on her heel. She thought of Leo Fisk, and her eyes filled with tears.

'Where the hell do you think you're going?' he shouted. 'You gotta learn to play nice if you want to be in the game . . .' But she was gone.

Sally didn't go home. She couldn't bear to. She was back here on her own turf, she had to make something happen.

Screw it, she thought, with uncharacteristic passion. Screw them all. So nobody was going to help her? Fine. She'd do it herself. It was just cutting out the middleman. I have ten thousand dollars to rent a store, Sally thought, fiercely. Why the hell not?

Wiping the tears away, she walked from DeMarco's down Melrose. It was a long walk, but she didn't care. Here was the epicentre of LA hip. All little biker bars, leather clothing stores, Gothic fashion, witchcraft and palm-tellers.

The first four stores Sally tried turned her down flat. Their businesses were doing OK. Moving was too much hassle. It took her three days before Sally found a candidate. FINE FASHIONS. An optimistic name. Run-down and seedy, it was flogging racks of discount T-shirts at five bucks a throw, plastic earrings and elasticated bracelets. But it was a decent location, halfway up Melrose with an empty parking lot across the street. She marched inside. Behind the counter was a little Korean woman, looking bored and reading a magazine.

'Hi,' said Sally. 'This your place?'

The woman was instantly defensive. 'We paid that fine, if you from City Hall.'

'I'm not. I need a shop. How long is your lease?'

'Six months.'

'I'll buy it out. Fifteen hundred a month. Another three grand for the fixtures and the stock.'

'I want five.'

'Don't push it,' Sally said. 'I'm saving y'all from foreclosure.'

'When you bring money?'

'You call your lawyer. I'll be back here tomorrow with a cashier's cheque and a contract.' Sally had another idea. 'You know any seamstresses? I need to hire some ladies to cut and sew patterns.'

'Of course. Plenty.'

'I need four women. You could bring them with you, tomorrow.'

'So this is what we're going to do.' Sally smiled at her employees. 'Cut one shoulder off every shirt. Neckline diagonal. And slash the hem like so.' She showed them her design. 'Then sew it back up. You see the pattern? I pay minimum wage plus a dollar. Once this stock is sold out, we'll get health coverage.'

An older lady spoke up. 'Health?' she asked. 'For real?'

'For real. And there's an hour for lunch; I'll get us sandwiches and coffee. We're in this together, ladies.' Sally's warm Texan drawl encouraged them. 'Do you think you can handle it?'

'Yes,' the woman said, smiling weakly.

'Yes, miss,' another of them said, looking hopeful. 'Here—' and she took a large raspberry T-shirt, applied Sally's pattern, and started to cut.

'*LA Citizen*. Editorial.'

'Can I speak to Mike Reardon?' Sally gripped the phone. Hiring the staff, buying the lease—the money she'd saved had almost gone. Sally had the stock. Now it was all about sales. It was do-or-die time.

'Editor's office. Janice speaking. Who's calling?'

'This is Sally Lassiter. I'm the daughter of Paulie Lassiter—the oilman whose company went bust and he died of a heart attack? Big story.'

'OK . . .'

'Mom and I fled to Texas in disgrace.' That stung, but the paper would see her as a human interest story or not at all. 'Now I'm back in LA and I want to give an exclusive interview. Tell our side of the story.' She gave her their number. 'Have him call me if he's interested in doing a feature. Goodbye.'

Sally hung up, her heart thumping with adrenaline, and headed to the kitchen to make coffee. She was opening the jar when the phone rang.

'Is this really Sally Lassiter?' A man's voice. Sceptical.

'It sure is.' She tried to sound confident. 'I'm prepared to offer you a deal, Mr Reardon.'

'We don't pay for interviews, Sally, company policy.'

'Not what I'm looking for. I've started a little store. It's called Wave. I need the publicity. You come and do a feature on me, you include mention of the store and shots of my T-shirts.' He started to say something, but Sally cut him off. 'I'll give you plenty of emotional stuff about Dad and being poor. All I want in exchange is the PR.'

Reardon chuckled. 'You've got guts, young lady. I'll take that deal. But beware, if your clothes suck, my journalist is gonna say so.'

'Fine with me.' Sally was elated. 'Let's do it.'

Sally made them take the photos first. She knew after she'd been speaking to the journalist her eyes would be red. She posed, sexy but demure, in her little blue skirt and a white cut-off T-shirt; long blonde hair flowing loose round her waist.

The interviewer was bespectacled and serious. Sally poured her heart out; she sobbed, she railed at Miss Milton's lack of support, she castigated her mother's friends. Explosive stuff. She needed it to be; this had to make the paper.

'I'm filing it this afternoon.' The journalist clicked the off button on her tape recorder, clearly impressed. 'And Sally, I think your T-shirts are *so* sexy. Plus, I adore those beads.'

'Here.' Sally jumped to her feet, collected a handful, and strung her a necklace. 'It says Annalise.' Her name. 'If you like it, maybe you'll wear it, tell your friends.'

'Maybe.' The journalist smiled. 'This piece runs on Sunday. If I were you I'd stay open that day.'

The next morning was Thursday. Sally came to work to find her store already full; Koko, her Algerian counter girl, had opened early. 'There was a crowd outside.'

The journalist from the day before was back. And she'd brought her friends. As the chic young women shopped, Sally reflected that you could be big in this town if you were hip and you were first. At the end of the day she was already showing a tidy profit. Sally gave the girls a small bonus: fifty bucks apiece, all she could afford.

'There'll be more later,' she promised.

They laughed and hugged her, eyes bright with tears.

On Sunday, the piece came out. Sally didn't read it; she had no desire to relive that harrowing shit all over again. She just looked at the pictures; herself, golden, laughing and beautiful, with her kicky little skirt and innate confidence.

Annalise, the journo, had pegged it. Sally's shop was swarming. They sold almost every T-shirt, and the jewellery was gone in three hours.

After that, she started taking orders. Payment up-front, delivery in two weeks. Sally Lassiter was still small-time. But she was also a success.

Chapter Ten

'You can't play chicken with me, Ms Morgan.' Turnbull Scott, the chief executive of Shop Smart, narrowed his eyes at his young vice-president. 'Your story reads well in the reports. But you're far too young for this sort of promotion. Think what it'll look like if we take a risk on a kid who can't even legally drink the wine we sell.'

'My track record proves I'm risk-free.' Jane felt strangely detached.

'We are *not* going to put you into a front-line division. You got an offer on the table.' The board had instructed him to keep her. 'It's a *huge* offer,' he insisted, frustrated.

'It is.' Jane smiled. Their offer was nearly double her salary. Three hundred and fifty thousand dollars. The top young stars in investment banking, plucked straight from the Ivy League, didn't make as much.

'I don't want it,' Jane explained.

'You'll make *more* than if you ran a sales division.'

'I don't care. I want the training.'

'Training?' He blinked. 'For what?'

'For when I own this company.'

Turnbull Scott laughed. Jane didn't.

'Are you going to switch me into a front-line job?' she demanded.

'No!' he almost shouted.

'Then I quit.' Jane reached into her jacket and took out her letter of resignation. 'It's been nice working with you.'

Scott stared incredulously at her. 'You arrogant *bitch!*' he snarled. But she had already turned on her high heels and was out of the door.

'I want a ticket to Los Angeles, please.'

'Certainly, ma'am.' The ticket agent looked curiously at the young woman standing in front of her. She sounded intelligent—probably a student. 'Let me see what comes up for you on the standby tracker . . .'

'No. First class.'

Her eyebrow lifted, but the girl produced a Prada wallet and coolly handed over a gold Amex.

'And when will you be returning?'

'I won't. One way.'

'That's three thousand dollars,' the older woman said tentatively.

'That's fine. Ring it up, please.'

The ticket agent did as she was told, even more curious than before. 'The first-class lounge is upstairs.'

Jane gave a little mental shrug as she walked into the first-class lounge. Let them stare. She knew how people thought about her, and she really didn't care.

Turnbull Scott thought she was insane. Junking her comfortable corporate life in favour of the wild blue yonder. But that was only because he didn't understand. She wanted serious rich, Paulie Lassiter rich. And you didn't get that from a pay cheque. You got it from ownership.

She felt a little fear as she strode over to the bar and ordered a mineral water, choked with ice. This was new territory.

'Can I buy you a drink?' It was a relaxed, confident masculine voice. American—certainly nothing like Jude.

'No.' Jane didn't look round.

'That's correct. Well done.'

Now, she looked at him—annoyed. 'Excuse me?'

The speaker inclined his head. Fifteen years older than her, around thirty-five, she guessed. Dark eyes with thick black lashes. A rather arrogant, cruel mouth; a strong jaw, and a tan.

'I can't *buy* you a drink—because they're free. But we could still have one together.'

'I'm already having one. By myself.' Jane turned back to it. This game was for losers, and she wasn't playing. She had been hurt. Too recently.

'A great idea.' The man was unfazed. 'I'll have one by myself too. Right next to you. And then we can both get on our respective planes and we'll never see each other again.'

She relented. 'Sorry if I was a little cold.'

'Cold? I don't think you need the ice with that drink.'

Jane's eyes sparked again. He was *laughing* at her, this arrogant bastard. His body language was completely relaxed and confident. He was at ease with himself. Another man would have slunk away.

'Does that often work for you?' she asked.

'What?' He grinned, dark eyes holding hers.

'Insulting girls.'

The bar girl sauntered up to them and made goo-goo eyes at him. 'Mr Levin. What a *pleasure* to see you again, sir.'

Jane's mental Rolodex did a quick check. 'Craig Levin?'

His eyes danced again, with pleasure. 'Yes, ma'am.'

Craig Levin! To Jane, dedicated reader of *Fortune* magazine, a girl who idolised billionaires and entrepreneurs, the name was magic. He was the king of them all. She flushed, and adrenaline sent the tiny hairs prickling on the back of her arms.

'What can I get for you, sir? Your usual?' purred the bar girl.

'That's fine, and please call me Craig, Iris.'

'Coming right up,' she promised, in a breathy Marilyn Monroe voice.

Craig Levin was rich. Craig Levin. Wall Street wonder, except not on Wall Street. A genius investor, Jane had seen him described as the 'next Warren Buffet' more times than she cared to count. He had influence enough to swing a stock. And Levin had a myth about him. He never gave interviews. No cosy little chats with *Fortune*—which is why she'd never seen his picture. Levin was young, independent and loaded. No wonder he was arrogant.

Jane shuddered a little at the thought of being so close to him. And Levin clearly realised the effect he was having.

'Does knowing my name mean you'll be nicer to me?'

She stiffened. 'It certainly doesn't. I'm not for sale.' Jane couldn't help herself; she nodded at the bar girl who was fixing Levin a Scotch on the rocks. 'Maybe she is, though. You might get lucky after all.'

His smile abruptly vanished. 'You're sitting here in the first-class lounge because you've got a first-class ticket. I don't know anything else about you, but I know you're a woman of means. She's a waitress. Probably on a bit more than minimum wage. So you sitting here in that elegant suit and calling her a whore isn't cool.'

Jane flushed purple. 'I'm sorry,' she said, wrong-footed and ashamed of herself.

He replied coolly, 'Enjoy your drink,' and walked away to the other end of the bar, retrieving his whisky from the waitress as he passed her.

Jane winced. She should have been better than that. And he'd immediately lost interest in her.

'Can I get you anything else, ma'am?' The waitress was back, oblivious to anything that had happened.

'No. That's OK. Thank you,' Jane added guiltily.

'That Craig Levin—he's hot. So funny, too.'

'Is he in here a lot?' Curiosity filled her.

'All the time. He has more air miles than Santa Claus. And remembers people's names.' She sighed. 'And so handsome. Don't you think?'

Jane shrugged. 'If you like that sort of thing.'

'Man! I would in a heartbeat. But the girls I see with him are mostly models. Socialites . . . you know. None of them last too long.'

'Rich playboy,' Jane said, glad to be able to dismiss Levin. But she still wished he hadn't walked away.

'Flight 961 to LAX is now boarding at Gate 33.'

Jane thought about Craig Levin as she walked through the corridors of the airport. She had actually studied his portfolio. Levin was a hero to her, one of the people she most admired. And now he'd asked her for a drink, and she'd told him to go to hell! She was annoyed with herself for regretting it. Jane tried to wrestle her mind back to the business at hand. Finding Helen and Sally. Starting her own Shop Smart.

'Good morning . . . second on the left . . .'

The air hostess was repeating her inane instructions. Why did they do that? How tough would it be to find seat 2B? She took her heavy holdall and struggled to lift it up to the hand baggage compartment. A strong pair of hands whisked it away from her and tucked it inside.

'Thank you.' Jane glanced round. It was Levin. She gasped in shock.

'We're sitting together.' He smiled easily at her. 'Hope you don't mind.'

'I—no.' Her mind raced, and she thought about apologising for earlier. But the moment had passed, what could she say? 'That's fine.'

Jane slid into her seat. He was extremely attractive. There was an air of complete command to him. She tried to cover her confusion. She busied herself with the pocket of the seat in front of her and took refuge in the free magazine, pretending to read it.

'Yes,' Levin said. 'That article on the strawberry growers of the Midwest is fascinating stuff. I heard the journalist is up for a Pulitzer.'

Jane's eyes glittered. 'So the billionaire is laughing at the impoverished writer, is he?'

He grinned. 'Touché.'

Jane felt an unreasonable elation that she had scored with him.

'Ms Morgan, can I get you some champagne, or freshly squeezed orange juice?'

'Orange juice. Thank you.'

'I'll have the same.' Levin passed Jane her glass. 'Are you teetotal, Ms Morgan?'

'For another three months. I'm not yet twenty-one.'

'Don't I feel old,' he said, with a grin that said he didn't. 'So let me see. Morgan—female, twenty, British. That makes you Jane Morgan. Senior Vice-President of Human Resources, Shop Smart Corporation.'

She blinked. 'How the hell did you know that?'

'I have a photographic memory. So I'm right?'

'All except the last part. I quit Shop Smart yesterday.'

'Excuse me a second.' Levin turned from her, and swiped a black Amex through his Skyphone, punching in the numbers.

'Anna? Craig. Dump Shop Smart. Everything, the whole half-million. Tell the brokers to feed it out slow. See ya, babe.' He turned back to Jane. 'Tell me the rest of your story.'

She struggled with the unexpected wave of desire that rocked through her body. On two words from her, he'd just sold over ten million dollars' worth of Shop Smart stock. The power. The decisiveness. The unutterably sexy, casual way he did it, and then turned back to her, as though he'd done nothing more important than check his watch.

'Why did you sell those shares?' she almost whispered.

'Jane Morgan,' he replied. 'Junior VP. Promoted from the shop floor. In her first year, cut costs in one store by thirty per cent and increased productivity twenty-seven per cent, all through personnel changes. Promoted to central management, applied techniques across the United

States; immediate savings of fifteen per cent on salaries, management redundancies saving another eight per cent. Productivity data increase not yet in. You see, in such a low-cost store, staffing costs are about half the overhead. You had something. If they've let you go, they're nuts.'

He knew all about her. Jane struggled against her arousal. She was used to being smarter, more driven, and higher achieving than every man she ever met. Not this time.

'I'm not interested in being a VP of Personnel,' she said. 'I'm interested in being a CEO. Of my own wholly-owned business.'

'Why?'

Jane hadn't expected that question. 'I don't like being dependent.'

'I could help you.'

'You could buy me Saks and give it to me for a birthday present.' Jane spoke strongly, on more certain ground now. 'But I'm not interested in being a kept woman. I want to make it on my own.'

His smile deepened. 'Impressive.'

'And you should know a couple of things, Mr Levin,' Jane said, challenging him. 'The first is that I admire you. Like everybody else working in business, I guess. The second is that I am *not* going to be one of your trophy girlfriends. Your throwaway identikit supermodel arm candy.'

'My *what*?'

'Remember Iris the waitress? She and I had a good talk.' Jane smiled triumphantly. 'And I'm not really interested in taking a number from any man, no matter how rich and . . . powerful.' Saying it sent little trawls of electricity across her stomach; Jane ignored them. 'So I hope we'll have a pleasant flight, but you should know that all this flirtation is just a waste of time. I'm not interested.'

He lifted an eyebrow, and grinned at her. 'Intriguing,' he said. 'You have a right to express all these things, and I have a right not to accept them. But don't worry, I've never had to pester a girl yet. When you decide you'd like to date me it'll be entirely of your own volition.'

'You're very cocksure.'

'I've earned that right.'

'Not with women,' she said, outraged.

'Certainly with women. Ask any of my ex-girlfriends.'

'*Ex*,' Jane retorted, with emphasis.

'I'm afraid so. They weren't enough of a challenge.'

'You date beauties, and yet you want to be challenged?'

'That's about it. I want everything in a woman. Brains, beauty, strength, humour—a certain style.' He shrugged. 'If we're expected to spend the rest of our lives with only one person, then I think we should be allowed as long a shopping list as we like. I start with beauty, yes.'

'Why?'

'It's the only quality that can be instantly assessed,' he replied calmly. 'So what do you require in a man?' he asked.

Jane was silent. She didn't want to be psychoanalysed by Craig Levin. 'So what are you doing in LA? Business?' She changed the subject.

'Yes, but I can't tell you what.'

She understood. The market watched Craig Levin's every move.

'Well, I'm going to start my business there. Buy a house. And find some old schoolfriends.'

He grinned. 'You make that sound easy.'

'Why shouldn't it be?' Jane said. 'People overcomplicate life.'

As they touched down, she turned to him and briskly offered her hand.

'It's been nice to meet you, Mr Levin.'

'Craig,' he said, eyes dancing.

'I don't think we should use first names. We might do business in the future.'

'Oh, we never will,' he said, at once.

'How do you know?'

'I'm attracted to you. And you're attracted to me. That's two complications too many for any kind of financial dealings.'

The plane halted and shuddered to a stop. Levin was up, instantly, retrieving his briefcase and handing her the holdall.

'You have no idea whether I'm attracted to you or not,' she hissed in a low voice.

Levin leaned down, in to her, where she was sitting in her seat. He placed his mouth to her ear, so none of the businessmen milling around them could hear. 'Of course I do. There are certain physiological signs; you only need a basic understanding of biology.'

Jane bit her lip. She had never come across a man like Levin. She knitted her hands in her lap.

'Here.' He offered her a business card. 'Goodbye, Jane Morgan.'

She took the card. Of course, she ought to have shredded it to confetti in front of him. But instead she slipped it into a jacket pocket. Levin's hand reached out, and a fingertip casually, secretively, traced a line across the back of her neck to the top of her spine.

It was electric. Her body shuddered, and she had to grip the sides of her seat to prevent anybody else from seeing her reaction. She blushed, hot with shame, and waited it out. In a few seconds he was gone. Jane had returned to Los Angeles the way she had left it. On her own.

Chapter Eleven

HAYA STOOD UP gingerly. She was only two months gone, but her feet were swelling. She walked into her garden, the *LA Citizen* clutched in her fingers. Her stomach was churning—and it wasn't the baby. That was Sally, her Sally, in the papers!

She was in turmoil. First, the simple shock. After all this time, Sally's face. Older, calmer somehow, but unmistakably the golden girl. Haya had almost forgotten what simple happiness was. And seeing Sally, alive, well, thriving—that gave her joy.

But then she read the article. And Haya was flooded with guilt; when Sally needed her, Haya hadn't been there; she was half a world away, in the grip of Ahmed's arms.

What had Jane and Sally thought? When they found her gone? They must have felt it as a betrayal. And in a way it was. She hadn't tried hard enough to find them, even when she got back to America.

And now—here was Sally. The clothes looked good on her body. There was a bit of sassiness that squeezed at Haya's heart—big-hearted, optimistic, golden Sally. And she hadn't given up, she was just clawing her way back in. The *Citizen* gave her designs a rave review.

Haya's heart beat a little faster, with pure nerves. But she steeled herself. She would go to see Sally. If her old friend damned her to hell for not being there, Haya would understand. She picked up the paper again, and committed the address to her memory.

'I'll take twenty in each colour. Just mail them to my billing address.'

'I will, ma'am, thank you.' Sally gave her the patented smile.

She sighed with relief. That was it; the society wife was the last customer. Not that she minded sales, but her heels, dizzy five-inch Manolos, were *painful*. With the first little bit of money, Sally had bought herself a killer wardrobe. That was even more important than a new house, because it was business. They'd all read the *Citizen* article. Half of her customers were rubberneckers—come to see *her*. Paulie Lassiter's daughter, starting over. If they came to see her, then *she* was the product. And that meant being one hundred per cent glamorous, at all times.

She added platinum highlights to her butterscotch hair. She deepened her tan with lotions. She wore Manolos on her feet—nothing else. She wore only her own line of jewellery—her necklace read: SURVIVOR—and her own designer clothes. Glamour, she reminded herself, was a state of mind.

She nodded to Koko to lock up and gratefully slid her stocking feet out of her narrow-toed shoes. There was a knock on the door. And Sally heard a familiar voice.

'Are you still open?'

'Sorry, missy. No. Tomorrow, nine a.m.,' Koko said.

'I wanted to see Sally Lassiter.'

'Wait—Koko, wait.' Sally froze. 'Helen? Is that you?'

'Yes . . .'

'My God! Koko, let her in.'

Sally jumped up as Haya walked in. She was lovely, wearing a long blue dress, with gold embroidery; her hair curled softly to her shoulders, and her skin was luminous.

Sally was so happy, she actually squealed. 'Helen, oh, oh my God! I never thought I'd see you again. Is it really you?'

Haya's eyes brimmed with tears, and she smiled. 'It's me.'

'Wait just a second. Koko, can you shut up the store and bank the cash for me? I'm going to take my friend to dinner.' Sally grabbed her shoes in her hand and raced over to Haya, enveloping her in a crushing bear hug. 'Look at you. You're amazing. Come out the back.' She wanted Helen all to herself. 'Can you eat dinner?' Sally found herself nervous, hurried. 'There's a great Thai place round the corner.'

'Sounds good. Thanks.'

Sally ushered her out and into the packed, noisy restaurant. They sat in a dark corner booth lit dimly by a red lamp. It was a kind light, but Sally could see Helen was crying—and that she had a ring on her left hand. A ring! Then that marriage story was true.

Sally didn't know where to start. She plunged in. 'Helen! God, girl, I missed you.' There were tears in her eyes. 'You and Jane.' She grabbed Helen's hand. 'So. Tell me all about you. You disappeared so fast . . .'

Haya shook her head. 'I'm sorry I didn't call right away.' She couldn't bear to tell Sally the truth, not yet. 'When I first got to Egypt, I—I was sorting some things out. I just assumed you'd both be there when I got back.' She blushed. 'And after that, I couldn't find you.'

'Same here. Well, you're back now.' Sally smiled. 'Thank God.'

'Definitely. Do you know where Jane is?'

Sally shook her head. 'No. My mom and I went to Texas, and it was hard. I didn't want to call, I guess I was embarrassed.'

'We have to find her.'

'Oh, we do,' Sally said. 'We do and we will. Now you're back I feel like I could do anything. We'll hire detectives if we have to. Oh, it's so *good* to see you again, Helen!' She reached across the table and squeezed her friend's hand till it hurt.

'It is! Oh, *Mashallah!*' Haya exclaimed. 'But I warn you, I tried detectives already. Didn't get anywhere. And Sally—I changed my first name.' Haya sighed. 'It's Haya—Haya is my birth name, and my husband preferred it to the American version, so Haya, if you don't mind.'

'Not at all. It's beautiful. Haya,' Sally said, rolling it around with her tongue. 'It suits you. Now, tell me everything. And I mean everything.'

'I don't know where to start,' Haya said honestly. 'Well, basic facts. I'm pregnant, and I'm widowed . . .'

'Oh, Hel—Haya.' Sally pressed her hand again.

'I was in Egypt.' Haya blinked back tears and now, putting away her pride, she told her friend the story. It was so good to talk to somebody at last who would understand her. 'And you,' she said, at the end, as Sally was dabbing away tears. 'I had no idea what happened—when we came back here you were gone.'

Sally told Haya everything, almost everything, stuff she had never confessed to another human soul: Mona's drunken binges, the pit of poverty and public disgrace. And how she'd climbed over it all.

'Anyway.' Sally wiped away more tears; it felt good to let the tears flow. 'It seems to have paid off. The customers are here . . . and they're buying. They want a little glamour in their lives.'

'I can understand it.'

'And the baby? What about that?'

'At least Ahmed left me something,' Haya said blankly.

'And now you have a friend, too.'

'Yes,' Haya said, and they smiled at each other, gladly.

Jane glanced round the bungalow. It was warm, and different to her last place. A view over the Malibu ocean in the distance. Clean modern lines, all in sands, greys, greens and whites; a decent little pool in the back. 'How much for the furniture?'

'That's not included.'

'If you negotiate right, everything's included,' Jane said.

LA was all about the new and the shiny. She was sure that the vendors would be happy to dump used sofas and last year's TV for newer models, and everybody would be happy.

Within fifteen minutes she had her house. Fully furnished.

Yes, she thought, with a blissful sense of triumph. She *owned* a house in Malibu. Very like the one the bailiffs had hustled her out of. Jane Morgan was back!

She took care of the basics first. It meant she didn't have to face her major problem—how the hell to start. Also, she didn't think about Craig as much when she was busy. She called a cab into Beverly Hills and bought herself a car. A small silver Porsche, chic and flashy; Ray-Ban shades on top of her head, and a bright red leather briefcase by Coach. When all *that* was done, she stocked the fridge.

And when that was done, it was time to go clothes shopping. Jane had donated her New York wardrobe to charity. When she was raising finance with banks, she needed to look like she understood the hip LA scene. Designer jeans, an eye-poppingly expensive Chanel jacket, and a hot little T-shirt underneath it. Something that said rich *and* trendy. A maverick entrepreneur on a mission.

The rich girl jackets and coats were easy to pick up. A quick trip to Rodeo and she was done. The stylish, newest T-shirts and jeans were harder. You needed to prove your sense of style. She asked around; not the snooty sales assistants in the expensive boutiques, but young girls, stylish Latinas and African-Americans. One name kept coming up— Wave, on Melrose, the hot new place in town for low-end glamour.

Jane thanked them and got the address. Perfect. A Wave shirt under a Chanel jacket. That would impress her investors. And she'd also look good in it; something that was starting to matter to her, despite herself.

There it was. Jane parked across the street and slid her sunglasses down her nose, watching the place for a couple of minutes. Damn, it was packed. The storefront stood out in a row of dingy shops; painted bright white, with a pale blue wave design all over it—unmissable. It was brightly lit and covered in seagrass matting. A little slice of the beach, right here on the boulevard.

And the women were almost fighting to get inside. Jane noted shoppers from every price bracket, skinny girls and heavy ones. She hated to think what the changing rooms were like. She'd just buy up some basics, the Wave brand easily visible, and get out of the scrum.

Jane wondered about the owners of the store. Could she make them an offer? Could they produce designs for her? Once she had the financing for a superstore . . . why not? She crossed the street, clutching her new Prada handbag.

The store was beautiful. It was just as bright inside, with mirrors on two walls and a sand-and-sea motif. The signature T-shirts were brilliantly laid out. Instead of racking by style, Wave had laid out the racks by size—6 through 14. Brilliant! Even she hadn't thought of that.

She pushed her way up to the size six and took ten T-shirts up to the counter. It was a long queue; the sales staff were smiling despite the press, all dressed in pale blue trousers and sandy-coloured tops of various kinds. They looked good; busy but exhilarated. It was how she wanted her staff to look.

The queue moved up a little, giving Jane a sight of the counter. She gasped with shock. Standing behind it, ringing up purchases, chatting and smiling, was Sally Lassiter.

'Oh my God,' Sally said. 'Jane, it's really you. It's you!'

All Jane's thoughts of business evaporated like morning mist. She managed to say, 'Sally . . . Oh God, Sally . . .' And then there were spots in front of her eyes, and she fainted.

Jane came round a few moments later, in Sally's back office; her friend was splashing water on her face.

'OK!' Jane laughed. 'Enough. I'm back.' She stared at Sal as if she'd seen a ghost. 'I can't believe it, I thought you were gone for good.' She grabbed at Sally's arm. 'Do you have a clue as to where Helen went?'

'I found her!' Sally said, bubbling up like a hot spring. 'Last week. She came into the store too—it's the best damn thing I ever did!'

Jane grinned foolishly. 'Incredible. How is she?'

'She's called Haya now.'

'What?'

'Let her tell you.' Sally ran to open the door. 'Li-Soon, I'm taking the rest of the day off.'

'I have a car parked out front. Oh, Sal!' Jane hugged her dearest friend. 'You have no idea what this means to me! I missed you, so much. Can we call Helen? Where is she?'

'This way.' Sally showed her out back. 'Let's drive out there right now. She has a place near the Hollywood Hills.'

'That's my car,' Jane said, nodding to where she had parked her car across the street from the shop.

'Wow.' Sally's blue eyes widened. 'I guess you've done pretty damn well for yourself.'

'Money isn't everything. Without you two, it hasn't been much fun.'

Sally smiled, a touch of the old fire back in her eyes. 'Honey, that is about to *change*.'

'**A**aaaaah!' Haya squealed for joy, and the plate she was scrubbing smashed in the sink. She ran out to her yard and flung her arms round Jane as she stepped from the car. 'It can't be!'

'You're pregnant?' Jane kissed her, and patted her round belly. She grabbed Haya's left hand. 'I heard about Ahmed. I'm so sorry.'

'Yes—but this helps,' Haya said, full of an overwhelming gladness. 'It helps so much. Sally told me about your father—I'm sorry too.'

Jane shrugged. 'You two were always my real family.'

They stood in Haya's driveway, each reluctant to break the spell.

'Do you have a back yard?' Jane asked eventually. 'A pregnant woman shouldn't stand out in the sun . . .'

'Yes! Come inside. I'll fix some lemonade.' Haya could hardly stop herself from jumping up and down. 'I am so happy to see you, Jane. It's been far too long. It's been horrible,' she said simply, and Sally laughed.

'Amen to that.'

They ate a picnic on the lawn, with tall glasses of lemonade, and Jane thought no fancy restaurant dinner had ever tasted quite so good.

'And so what happened to you?' Sally demanded.

'I lied about going to Washington,' Jane admitted. 'I didn't want you stressed over me. I had to pull myself out of the pit, you know.' She described her life, briefly; the scuzzy walk-up flat, the roaches, the sixteen-hour days, the bitchy girls from school . . . then a brief sketch of her rise to the top. Glancing round, she could see instantly that Haya, and to a lesser extent Sally, had managed to do OK; everybody was comfortable, and Sally had a thriving little store, but only she was now rich. She didn't want to rub that success in their faces.

'And you? Tell me, Sal. How was Texas? Tell me everything.'

Sally hesitated. Even with Haya, she hadn't wanted to mention the rape. But the girls were her closest friends, and friends shared everything, even the ugliest, bleakest wounds. Perhaps especially that.

'I was shunned by the extended family and Mom's friends dropped her. Worked in a beauty salon, made a little money. Mom was—is—an alcoholic. But it was worse then. Sometimes you felt you were running as fast as you could just to stay still.

'And then there was this jerk. I went to high school with him before I dropped out. He was the son of the owner of the store, and he drove me out of town one night and raped me. That's how I lost my virginity.'

Jane shuddered. 'My God. Sally, I am so, so sorry.'

'I couldn't tell you before,' Sally said to Haya. 'Couldn't find the words.' She stuck up her chin. 'But I'm telling y'all now because I'm not ashamed of it. It was his to be ashamed of, not me.'

'But are you OK? Have you had counselling?' Haya asked.

'Haven't had time. Somebody had to fix Momma.'

Haya took a deep breath. 'I also was too embarrassed to say, but the reason I went to Egypt was my parents tricked me. They shoved me into an arranged marriage with Ahmed. I ran,' Haya said simply. 'But I knew nothing of Cairo, couldn't speak the language. I was mugged . . . Ahmed followed me, saved me. He was the perfect gentleman, showed more respect for me than my own parents. I fell in love with him. And thus it became a true marriage.'

'I don't have anything that bad to tell you,' Jane said.

'Thankfully.' Sally grinned wryly. 'It ain't a competition.'

'I did lose my virginity to a total asshole, but that pales in comparison.' She told them anyway. 'I'm good at money.' Jane shrugged. 'Not so good at men.'

Haya lifted her glass of lemonade. 'We found each other, and we're never going to be split up again.'

'Amen!' Sally said.

'To the future,' Haya proposed. 'To us.'

'To us,' the other two agreed, and they chinked their glasses and drank.

'I got to get back to the store,' Sally said, with a sigh.

'Come to my place tonight,' Jane suggested immediately. 'We've got so much to talk about. We only just started.'

The three of them met for dinner in Jane's back yard. Jane allowed herself to revel in the moment; now she had her friends, she had everything. After all the sorrow, and the struggle, they were back together. And at this moment, Jane thought, she was with the closest family she'd ever had. She vowed she'd never let them go again. No matter what.

'Do you like it?' Jane asked. She'd finished giving the girls the tour.

'I'll give you a carpet—a housewarming gift,' Haya suggested. 'I have a silk Kashmiri rug that would go perfectly in your bedroom.'

'I couldn't accept something like that.'

'I want you to have it. Ahmed would have hated to see his things gathering dust in some warehouse in Laguna Beach.'

'You should sell them . . .'

'I can't. I have no store,' Haya said. 'And I won't dump them wholesale on some dealer. They are precious and deserve better.' She sighed. 'Maybe after my baby's born, I can deal with it. I'd like to find all his things good homes—the way Ahmed wanted them sold. With respect.'

'My crowd is only into fashion,' Sally said.

'How is that going?' Jane asked, curious.

Sally smiled. 'It's wild. Can't keep up with the demand. All the local press want to talk to me, and I have to say yes to everyone. You know,' she blushed, 'give them a little razzmatazz. So what about you? Why did you quit that cushy number back East?'

Jane told them. 'So now I want to start a store. Tomorrow I'm going to the banks. I have thirteen appointments.' She shrugged. 'It'll be a tough sell, but I think I could follow the Wal-Mart/Shop Smart model and find some savings. At least I do have a record there. I'll need money to lease out the warehouse and buy the stock lines, computers, staff. It's a major amount of cash.' She tried to look confident.

Haya carefully sliced into a ripe nectarine. 'Why don't you *not* do that? Why don't you do it another way? All of us have problems. Sally needs space for her stock and a manufacturer—she can't rely on house-wives sewing in back rooms for ever. I don't want to run a shop by myself but I know about the business, and I have stock—beautiful stock. And you have training in the mechanics of selling.'

Sally blinked. 'You're suggesting we form a company?'

'A store. Yes. Why not?' Haya warmed to her theme. 'You said you were good with money, Jane. Well, I'd like some of my own. Not my father's or husband's, but *mine*.'

'Me too,' Sally exclaimed. 'I feel like I'm stuck at the starting gate.'

'So we all have talents. What would it be like if we combined them?' Haya suggested. 'Start our own store. A *great* store. Like Harrods or Saks.' She turned to Jane. 'I know you were thinking of mass volume and deep discount but that field is packed. Why not turn it on its head? Designer goods. Low volume, high price. Each one sold like a jewel. Like art. We had the right idea with the gallery; we just didn't know the mechanics.'

Jane shivered with excitement. Man! Why not? Instead of trying to clamber up the mountainside all by herself, why not harness these two? Sally knew glitz like nobody else—she'd seen that. And from what she had heard of Haya, the woman had grown up, through her tragedy. Why not start a store that sold treasures for the discerning—glorious Eastern carpets, objets d'art, hot fashion, the best make-up? There were so many rich women in LA. And it had worked as a concept all over the world. The *superstore itself* as star. In Los Angeles, as Jane well knew, the up-market stores were just big, soulless malls where you rode escalators and walked down corridors of luxury shops. Do it this way, and Jane could provide those women with a single destination.

'I can design a range of cosmetics,' Sally said.

'And I can go to Jordan. Source your moisturisers from the Dead Sea.

Those muds have properties all the laboratories in Paris can't replicate.'

'What about a location?' Jane chewed on that. 'It will be our biggest capital expense.'

'But I already own a gallery,' Haya cried. 'It's about ten thousand square feet. And it has a good-sized parking lot.'

'We'll need a lawyer.' Jane couldn't hear a perfect idea and sit still. 'Form a company. What do you say, ladies, a third each way?'

Sally was nervous. 'Look, you girls both got money. I'm just starting to sell, I don't have any yet.'

'The company will loan you what you need.' Jane waved that aside. 'Sal, you have style we never will. That's what we need from you, interior design, fashion purchasing. Not just clothes. Haya can take care of the exotic stuff, but you need to find us the bread and butter—fabulous handbags, accessories, electronic gadgets, beauty therapists. It needs to be full of juicy, perfect little things. Toys for girls. The store has to be talked about—half of good retail is promotion. It has to be packed from the word go. Just like your little store on Melrose.'

'We need a name. Something that sells what the store is all about. Something that sells what *we're* all about.' Sally thought for a moment, then smiled. 'Glamour,' she said.

'**N**o.'

'I'm sorry—not for us.'

'I don't think so.'

'You have to be kidding me—you chicks are barely legal.'

It was the same story wherever they went. Only the degree of rudeness varied.

'I wish Ahmed was here. They wouldn't treat men like this.'

'Well, they wouldn't ogle them, I guess,' Sally said wisely. 'But they might kick them out. We have some experience, but it's not a lot.'

Jane frowned. 'You guys go on home—Sally, you get back to Wave, sell some skirts. We need the cash.'

'And what are you going to do?' Haya asked.

'I'm going to get our capital.' Jane shrugged. 'From another source.'

'Hope you're not gambling your house on a racehorse,' Sally said.

'No.' Jane grimaced. 'This is nothing that sensible.'

When the others had gone, Jane got back into her car, and shut the door. She was exhausted, but focused on what she had to do. *Had* to do—not what she wanted to do. She took out her cellphone and dialled.

'Levin Corporation. Craig Levin's office.'

Jane blushed. 'May I speak to Mr Levin, please?'

'He's not in the office today, ma'am.' Jane couldn't believe how disappointed she felt. 'May I tell him who called?'

'Certainly. This is Jane Morgan.'

'From which company?'

'From GLAMOUR Stores.' It was sort of true. She gave her number.

'I'll pass on the message,' the assistant said. 'Thank you for calling.'

Jane hung up, and gently rested her head on the steering wheel. Why had she done that? He wasn't going to call her back. Craig Levin had bigger fish to fry. No, she was just going to have to start over. Find some independent banks. Some venture capitalists—

Her phone rang. She jumped out of her skin.

'Jane Morgan.'

'Craig Levin,' he said, and she felt the warmth spread from her face all through her chest down into her belly. 'I'm disappointed, Jane.'

'Why?'

'You didn't call me at home. Or on my cell. Which means you want to talk business, or at least that's the excuse you're giving to yourself.'

Since he couldn't see her, she smiled. 'You got me.'

'Then come see me. At home. Hollywood Hills.' He gave her the address. 'I'm free right now.'

'Do you promise not to hit on me?' Jane demanded, fighting for some control. She could hear his grin down her phone.

'I certainly do not. On the contrary, I promise to hit on you hard. Come see me—at your own risk.'

Levin hung up. Jane immediately started the car and pulled into the traffic. What choice did she have? She had to go. So it shouldn't matter that she also wanted to.

'Good afternoon. Miss Morgan?' The butler smiled at her. 'Please follow me, miss.'

Jane's father had taken her into quite a few grand mansions, but never in her life had she seen anything like this. The house was huge. Interior designed, with modern art and old masters jostling side by side; internal fountains and lush greenery. As she followed the servant, Jane was led through peristyles and garden squares, caught a glimpse of a vast library, a home cinema, an indoor swimming pool complex. It was a staggering display of wealth. Levin made Sally's dad's estate look like a cottage in Virginia.

'Jane.' Craig Levin was sitting on a lounger by an Olympic-sized pool carved out of the hillside; smooth and glassy, it perched on the edge of the estate, so that you appeared to be swimming into the sky. 'Good to see you.' He got up and came over, kissing her on both cheeks, as his butler melted away. 'I took the liberty of fixing you a Bellini—fresh peach juice.'

Jane took the cocktail. It seemed the safest thing to do. That way she could concentrate on sipping the drink and not have to stare at his body. His chest was thickly muscled and oiled with sunscreen.

She had a visceral reaction to that kind of strength. She was, she realised, already turned on. 'Thank you for seeing me . . .'

'If you say "Mr Levin" I'll throw you out.'

'Craig.' She surrendered.

'You want finance, and the banks won't help.'

Jane blinked. 'How the hell do you know that?'

'If that weren't the case, you would not be here.' He grinned lazily. 'You wanted to start a discount chain; no commercial lender's gonna fund you. And you could have taken a few more weeks, exhausted all the bankers and venture houses. But I know you. You're impatient. You want the world, yesterday.' His eyes fixed upon her. 'So you came to me, because I can give it to you. Correct?'

Her throat was dry. 'Correct.' She took a sip of her Bellini.

'I told you I would not do business with you.'

Jane's confusion deepened. 'I see.' She tried to gather the shreds of her dignity. 'Well, thank you for seeing me.'

'But I'll *give* you the money. A gift. No strings. A million dollars.'

She didn't ask if he meant it; that much was obvious. 'I can't.'

'You can do whatever you want.'

'I can't. If you give me a million dollars, I'll be like Marie Antoinette playing at being a shepherdess. Mr Levin—Craig. Give me the million, not as a gift but as a commercial loan. You won't be doing business with *me*. You'll be doing it with GLAMOUR—and that's a company. Not just me. There's Sally Lassiter. She's our fashion buyer.'

He nodded. 'Hot shop on Melrose. I was considering making her a finance offer in exchange for a stake.'

'And Haya al-Amin. My friend from school. She has an eye, I've seen her stock. Haya brings us the physical building with a great lot, and some glorious Islamic art and antique rugs. And she will source other stuff for us too, exclusive cosmetics you can't get in the United States.' Jane wanted to be the evangelist. He would give her the money anyway; now she wanted to convince him.

'Haya and I had a talk last night. Haya wants something special for GLAMOUR. She wants us to be at the forefront of ethical business— and I want to do it because it sells. Like Anita Roddick. Haya will set up a worldwide operation for us sourcing handmade goods from indigent women, in Jordan, in the Middle East, where she has contacts—Egypt, everywhere. Later on in Africa and Asia too, once we have the money for scouts.' Jane rushed on, aware she was gabbling. 'Women will like it, the press will cover it. And Haya is determined. It's the way she is— if you could meet her, you'd know.'

'Perhaps I would.' His eyes danced over her, amused.

'So. Consider us as an investor. You know my track record with staff and costs. You said you might have approached Sally anyway. And as for Haya, OK, that is my say-so. But you can't deny that she brings us the store and the parking. So our company has physical assets.'

Levin inclined his head. 'Good pitch. Done.'

'No.' Jane stood strong. 'I want *two* million. For this store to work we need the best. Staff, uniforms, valet parking, stock. I need it to be *rich*, Craig. We're selling the all-American dream, with a little exotic flavour thrown in. And that has to be good.'

'Three million,' he said. 'And I take ten per cent of the company.'

'I have to run it by my partners.' Jane smiled. 'But I'm pretty sure they'll be OK with it.'

'Good.' He walked up to her, his face above hers, his mouth close, too close. 'That's done. Can we move on?'

She struggled, fought with herself. Jane longed for him to kiss her, so much it made her weak.

'I'm not for sale,' she whispered.

Levin's eyes bore down on her, his mouth inched closer to hers; Jane's lips, moistened, parted. Just before the kiss, he pulled back.

Jane swallowed a gasp; she was left aching for him, frustrated.

'I don't want a girl I can buy.' His eyes flickered across her face, assessingly. 'I'm going to have those papers signed and the money in your corporate account by tomorrow. Once my lawyers have reviewed the share agreement. After that, you'll have what you needed from me, and I won't be able to take it back.' He reached out, and ran a fingertip down the side of her face; Jane shivered at his touch.

'After that, I'll come to you. And we'll see what happens.'

She forced herself to take a step back. 'My lawyers will be in touch.' She had to add, 'Thank you.'

'Tomorrow,' he said, with soft intent. 'See you, Jane Morgan.'

She turned on her heels and fled.

'I don't wanna go,' Mona whined.

'You have to.' Sally was firm. 'Mom, you have to. Here are your sneakers. You want me to lace them up for you?'

'I can dress myself,' Mona snapped.

Sally was glad to hear it; lately, she'd been wondering. 'Here. I got you a new track suit. Nike—the best. We'll jog along Venice, next to the beach.' Because none of Mona's old friends would be there. 'After that I'm giving you a make-over, and you can come and see our new store.'

'What store?'

'GLAMOUR,' Sally said. 'You'll love it.' If she could change style in LA, she could change her mom. Couldn't she?

Mona was an addict. Sally had faced that, as calmly as she could. You couldn't get an addict to just stop the addiction. It had to be replaced by something else. A positive addiction. Sally decided on fitness. Mom would become a fitness freak. If that meant Sal had to jog an unnecessary three miles a day, then so be it.

Mona was sitting sullenly in her oversize pink track suit, and Sal, her long blonde hair swept back in a neat ponytail, was wearing the same, only half the size, painfully aware how pretty she looked and how wrecked her mother was. But Mona could change. Everybody could. Sal had—she was a company director now.

She *believed* in the GLAMOUR philosophy. Beauty was more than skin deep, it was a matter of pride. Not everybody could fit the golden girl ideal like she could, but everybody could look their best. And Momma's best was better than this.

'Come on.' She forcibly grabbed her mother by the elbow.

Every morning and evening, for a week, Sally forced Mona to jog. At first it was little more than walking pace, and her mother could only manage a mile. The second day, Mona occasionally broke into a trot before slipping back to walking. Sally didn't care. It was progress.

She tried to make her mom feel proud. Day one was the best: forcing her into a long shower, making her shave her legs, and get her hair styled. On day two, after the post-jog shower, Sally took time off work to give Mona a make-over. On day three, she took her to the shell of GLAMOUR and helped her pick out a couple of dresses—forgiving, beautifully worked Arab gowns from Ghada, flown in the day before.

And it was working. Sally could see the glimmer of interest that came back to her mother's face, the basic stirrings of self-esteem. At the end of the first week, Sally came back from the store to find her mom had been shopping—all by herself. She'd bought some cushions, and she had rearranged the decor in their apartment.

At the end of the first month Mona fitted back into her old jeans. She hadn't touched a drop of alcohol for almost half a year. And there were other encouraging signs. She asked Sally if she could go to the dentist and get her teeth whitened. Sally signed her up to a yoga class, where for the first time since Paulie died, Mona started to make friends.

Sally had tears in her eyes the first day she waved her mom off for coffee with a girlfriend. Fitness had done that, and self-esteem, and feeling good about life. Sometimes lipstick and a good dress really mattered. It wasn't an exaggeration to say that style had saved her momma.

While Jane did her wheeler-dealing and Haya took her pregnant body off on weekly flights to the Middle East, Sally instructed her team of designers. She drew sketches, placed orders, did deals with unknown talents. Anything to get GLAMOUR the hottest new styles and the simplest classic pieces. Nothing cheap; nothing skimpy. Sally designed flaws away, she didn't want clothes that required a perfect body. All skirts and dresses were lined. There was a working woman's corner, too. Sally paid for rich fabrics, silks, satins, velvet and heavy cotton—no linen, it wrinkled—and worked exclusively in black, white, sand and navy; every piece went with every other piece. The blouses had cuffs and little shell buttons, but they were tapered at the waist; the skirts swung to the bias and hovered on the knee; the trouser-suits had narrower waists but wider thighs, a little help where most women needed it. Add a pair of Sally's stacked heels and you got height, comfort, style—immediate weight loss of five pounds.

But Sally knew GLAMOUR had to be more than that. It needed to be an experience. Sally understood why women shopped. It was for a sense of being surrounded by gorgeous things. She started work on the smaller stock: independent cosmetic houses, brands that didn't do business with the bigger stores. And she only went for gorgeous. Lipsticks with jewel-studded cases, perfume spritzers in dazzling cut glass. Little eye shadows from a joint in Venice that packed them cleverly into seashells.

And so, slowly, the stock took shape. Floris bath oils from Europe. Charbonnel & Walker chocolates. Scottish cashmere and Irish linens. Austrian silver coffeepots. The store would be like a vacation for rich Americans who didn't feel like grabbing their passports. It was paradise.

She worked like an obsessive, like Jane or Haya. All Jane thought about was getting that Levin guy his money back. Haya was into finding a legacy for her kid and helping poorer women who had been dependent on a man; profit meant little to her. Sally, on the other hand, thought about her mom, her dad, style and pride. She wasn't selfless. She wasn't Mother Teresa. Her sense of style had got her this far. If she could help other women, then *she* would get rich. She would get her whole life back. While Mona worked out, sinking herself into her new fitness craze, Sally Lassiter got lost at the office, never thought about anything except her new job and keeping an eye on Mom. There was no time for anything else. Certainly not for men.

'**A**nd here's the ocean, on the left.'

Sally nodded, conserving her breath. Great. Mom was fitter than she was, now. 'We'll cut through here, through the woods.' Mona was turning left, and Sally saw her legs moving efficiently down the sandy path. Damn, that woman had got some musculature going . . . 'Aaah!' Her mother slipped. It was so quick, Sally barely saw it coming. She heard her mother groan, heard the nasty thud as she dropped to the ground—and she plummeted off the cliff-top path, slicing through the scrubby plants and crumbling earth, down the side of the rock.

Sally screamed, and rushed to the side of the rock face. Mona fell awkwardly onto an outcrop of rock; she didn't move, clearly unconscious. Sally felt a wash of dizziness surge through her body, but she could not afford to black out now. 'Oh God! Help me!' she screamed.

'You need help?' It was the voice of a man, further down the path.

'Yes! Please come! It's my mom.'

'I'm coming,' he shouted. 'Hold on.'

There was the sound of running feet and he appeared on the path, a strong-looking man with mirrored shades and a Dodgers baseball cap.

'What's the problem?'

She grabbed his arm, babbling. 'Oh, thank God. My mom—she slipped. She went over. She's down there . . .'

He took one look and straightened up. 'Stay right there. I have a car-phone, I'll call 911.' He ran back down the path. Sally looked over; her mother did not stir. The seconds dragged on horribly. Eventually he came back. 'Highway Patrol is sending a cruiser. I argued with them, looks like you need the coastguard and a chopper. They said it shouldn't be long . . .'

There was a shiver in the rocks; some stones, dislodged by Mona's fall, tumbled onto her prostrate body. One of them struck her ankle. She shifted, and hung further off the edge of the lip of stone, a dead weight pointing down.

Sally sobbed. 'Mom, oh God, Mom. She's gonna fall. She's gonna die.' She clutched at the stranger. Ever since Leo, Sally had avoided men. She had never wanted to touch them. But now she clung to this man.

'Wait there,' he said.

Sally inched closer to the edge. Her mom was all she had in this world. Had she saved her from addiction just to watch her plunge into the sea? But she saw no way she could climb down.

The man was back. He had a length of rope round his waist and a pair of spiked shoes on. He ran up to the nearest tree, looped the rope round, and hastily knotted it; then he tied another loop, and another, round himself.

'What are you doing?' Sally asked hesitantly.

'No harness. I'm gonna get her.'

Sally crammed her knuckles into her mouth. The tree did not have a wide trunk. It bent forward, leaning with his weight. He was tall, a strong guy, lean but bulky with muscle. She could see the muscles of his back working as he moved, with purpose, down the rock face; stones and plants gave way under his footing, but he just shifted his weight.

Sally saw Mona slipping a little further. 'Hurry, please,' she shouted.

The man kept abseiling; lower, lower . . . There was a loud crack; the small stone ledge shifted, tilted. Mona Lassiter slid forward . . . And his thick, weightlifter's arm reached out and grabbed her by the elbow.

Sally watched in horror as the tree buckled and doubled over, the rope fraying. The man gasped and grunted, his feet losing their grip, scrabbling to get it back as he heaved, with brute strength, her mother's unconscious form over his back.

Sally looked over the cliff. He was climbing, slowly, agonisingly. She could hear the grunts of pain; her mother's weight was being supported by a single hand as he used the other one to climb. Oh God! She was not a religious woman, but she prayed. Please let him not drop her . . .

After an eternity he was at the top, his face puce with effort, sweat pouring down his forehead. 'Take her,' he gasped.

Crying and laughing, half hysterical, Sally tugged and pulled at Mona's arms. Her mother slipped off her rescuer's shoulders and flopped forward onto the grass. She was bleeding, cut in several places, obviously concussed, but still breathing. As Sally examined her, trying to wake her, the man hauled himself onto the grass and fell onto his back, struggling to regain his breath.

Sally looked at him with pathetic gratitude and then winced. His palms were raw, bleeding from the rope burns. His barrel of a chest was heaving, trying to get his breath, to recover from the monstrous effort.

'You saved her life,' she said. 'Thank you—thank you so much.'

There was a wail of a siren in the distance, getting closer.

'Thank God for that.' Sally was in tears from the relief. 'The police are coming. They'll get you both to a hospital—you need the paramedics.'

He looked at her for the first time. She couldn't see the eyes behind the sunglasses, but she did register how his gaze flickered over her body. He seemed like man who had looked at a lot of women.

She detested being ogled. But this was different. She sensed that his look had desire in it, but not contempt. And Sally, to her amazement, found her own body answering. She dropped her gaze. An instinctive reaction, Sally told herself. The guy had just saved Mom. But all the same, she suddenly wished she didn't look quite such a mess.

'I'm not staying.' He stood up. 'Your mom will be OK.'

'Are you a doctor?'

'No. But I see a lot of sports injuries.' Finally, he took off the shades; and Sally blushed scarlet.

'Now you recognise me,' he said, without false modesty.

'I—yes.' Sally tried to cover her confusion. 'You—on the cover of that magazine.' Why was it coming out so stuttery? She felt moronic.

'*Sports Illustrated*.' He grinned. 'You really had no idea, did you?'

'I didn't. You're Chris Nelson. The baseball player.' Sally wasn't a fan, but she knew about Chris Nelson, the shortstop for the Dodgers. Single-handedly turning the team around. A megastar, in this city.

'Yeah, well, do me a favour. Don't tell anybody about this. The press will hound me for weeks.'

'I won't. Thank you, again.' Sally bit her lip. 'And . . . you know, you're a hero—Mr Nelson.'

'That's cute.' He winked at her. 'Long time since I've seen a girl blush.'

'Your hands are all messed up.'

'Yeah, well. My shoulder's practically dislocated.'

'I think your physio is going to put a hit on me,' Sally joked.

'John Tepes will, if I miss the series against the Yankees,' he said. Tepes was their manager. 'But don't worry. I'll come round and save you. Your name is Sally Lassiter, right?'

She jumped out of her skin. 'How the hell do you know that?'

He was amused by her saltiness. 'Papers. My girlfriend showed me a picture. She bought some T-shirts in your store; looked hot on her.'

Girlfriend. Right. Of course. 'Thanks, Mr Nelson.'

'I think it's Chris, after all that. Goodbye, sugar.'

Sally was still staring down the hill when the troopers arrived. She told the story, leaving out Nelson's name.

'Some story,' one said. 'Some guy.'

Yeah, Sally thought, regretfully. Some guy.

Mona had suffered little more than concussion, a broken arm and some bad bruising; it was almost a guilty relief for Sally to have her tucked away in hospital for a few days.

Sally tried to forget Chris Nelson. But now that she was aware of him, she was reminded of him everywhere—on the news, whenever she saw a fan in a Dodgers shirt. And a few days later, the news came through. An undisclosed 'injury' had put him on the disabled list for a month's recuperation. Sally waited fearfully for the story to break; if the cops had traced his cell call or something . . . Half the sports fans in LA would be picketing their new store. It didn't happen. He went into physiotherapy (the radio told her) and the rescue remained a secret.

So Sally got on with her job. Making GLAMOUR a statement, a sumptuous experience from the second a buyer put their car in the lot. She had a vision. GLAMOUR. The name said it all. Every shopping trip would be a vacation. Maybe Letty Berry would come and shop here, Sally thought. Chris Nelson's girlfriend. Tall, slim, African-American, with flawless ebony skin. She shopped at only the best stores, drove a Ferrari and, as Sally was finding out, had been dating Chris Nelson for about a year. The gossip rags said they were getting married. Sally tried to be happy for Letty. And Chris. It didn't work.

Chris Nelson had warmed her blood, stirred something in her she thought she might never feel. Desire. After the rape, she had closed herself off, become almost like Jane; a robot, obsessed with her career, saving her mother, climbing out of poverty. When a man ogled her, she felt contempt, sometimes fear. Never desire. Chris Nelson had risked his life to save a stranger's. He used his strength for protection, not for bullying. And Sally responded.

Luckily, she was busy. The store was rolling towards the grand opening. Now she had a PR campaign to organise. She got the hell on with it.

Chapter Twelve

HAYA STEPPED INTO the limo with relief. It was air-conditioned, a blessed change after the baking heat. She'd thought she could handle this weather, but the further along her pregnancy got, the less she liked it. 'Take me to Bar-al-Yanni, please,' she said to the driver.

'Of course, ma'am.'

Haya really wanted to get this trip over with. There would be no more sourcing from the Middle East after this. Haya needed enough goods to last in the stockroom for a good while; she wasn't getting on a plane until her child was six months old and weaned.

Choosing the precious objects had been a big deal for Haya. Sourcing art, jewellery, fabric, lamps and rugs from the Islamic world, and not from dealers; from the collectives that had sprung up—widows or unmarried women, whose meagre income from the glorious things they worked was keeping flesh on the bones of their children. Haya had big ambitions. She wanted to transform lives.

Haya wanted GLAMOUR to make money for her own independence, and for Ahmed's child. Profit and principles. If she could combine them, Haya thought, she could salvage something from her husband's death, make a difference in the world.

The remote kingdom of Ghada was her last stop on the tour. The desert tribeswomen crafted elegant necklaces and bracelets dripping with small metal discs, a variant on the coin jewellery in other Arab countries. The intricate pieces would be the centre of the opening GLAMOUR jewellery collection. The traditional metal was silver; Haya wanted a commune of women to work them for her in copper. Americans didn't like silver, it tarnished.

'We have some delays on the road north of the city,' her driver said.

Haya sighed. 'Why is that?'

'There is a visit there from one of the sheikas. Sheika Aisha, the daughter of the King's half-uncle. They will have security.'

'Of course.' Haya chewed on her lip. The royal family of Ghada was large and well-funded. There was the King, old and tired, an absolute ruler. His many brothers and sons, sisters and daughters, all princes and princesses. A few degrees removed from that, the royalty had lesser titles like Sheik and Sheika. 'Why is she going there? Is there a function?'

'The royal women often patronise the bazaars there. They support the traditional crafts.'

Haya smiled. Perhaps she could get something out of this. If they could market the Ghadan necklaces 'as worn by royalty', they would sell even better. Would the Sheika agree to be photographed in a necklace? She got excited, she could see the advertising campaign now.

'If you can get me close to where this visit is happening, I will pay you a bonus,' she said.

It was a triumph. Firstly, Haya had the pleasure of having the work presented to her by Begum Ghida al-Ali, the widow of a former chief. She had organised this group of poor women, many of them widows or former street children, who lived in grinding poverty. They worked the tiny metal discs into the most exquisite pieces. They deserved to be treated as works of art, and Haya saw no problem in selling them as such. She signed a deal, the women toasted it with mint tea, and she left money behind, as down payment. The joy with which it was received made her day.

And secondly, with great determination, Haya had approached a woman in the Sheika's retinue, an efficient-looking sort in a Western suit. The lady would not see her now, she was told, but she took a number, and said somebody from the palace would be in touch.

Haya left a card and returned to the hotel. There she took a long bath, washed her hair, and went to lie down on the bed, wrapped in a soft robe. All she wanted to do was sleep well, then get on the plane. The phone rang. Sighing deeply, she rolled on her side to answer it.

'Hello?'

'May I speak to Haya al-Amin, please?' Arab with an English accent, she thought, educated abroad.

'Speaking.'

'Ms al-Amin, my name is Jaber Ibn Mohammed. I work for the palace and the government of Ghada.'

Haya closed her eyes briefly. 'It's good of you to call,' she lied.

'I understand you are to fly back to the States tomorrow. Do you have time for a meeting this evening? I can come to the Radisson.'

'Of course, I'd be delighted.'

'If the palace is going to approve any project like this, involving a sherifa, we have to vet it.'

'I quite understand,' Haya said. 'Is six o'clock convenient? We could meet in the lobby, or have dinner.'

'Wonderful. See you then.'

He was waiting in the lobby. Haya was surprised to see he was a young man, tall, with aristocratic, searching eyes. Olive-skinned, with a tan, and a beautifully cut suit; a strong body, she thought, not bulky.

'Ms al-Amin. Thank you for seeing me.' His eyes swept over her, appreciatively, she thought, and then blinked; his gaze had come to rest on her belly. 'You're pregnant,' he blurted out.

She smiled. 'Yes, *Mashallah!*'

'Excuse me, I was just surprised. Is your husband with you?'

'I'm a widow,' she replied coolly.

He flushed, embarrassed. 'I'm sorry.'

'You weren't to know.'

'Shall we eat?' He'd been confident initially, but Haya could see he'd been thoroughly fazed.

'That sounds good.'

'Then come this way.' And to her surprise, he offered her his arm.

Beautiful manners, she thought. And a handsome face. And then felt instantly disloyal to Ahmed. She was seven months pregnant. What was she doing thinking about another man?

They ordered some local specialities, vine leaves wrapped round spiced meats, tiny roasted birds, a Ghadan version of tabbouleh, and a lemony whole goat's cheese in oils and herbs. She discovered Jaber had been educated at Cambridge and had served a military apprenticeship in the US, at West Point. Haya told him some of her story. Just a little.

'And your store?' he asked eventually, getting down to business.

'It's going to be prestigious and luxurious, and will charge high prices. We have backing from a senior financier—Craig Levin.'

'Levin,' he responded, clearly impressed.

'I am a full partner; the site is my husband's former gallery. My further role is to source art, jewels and cosmetics from the Middle East. We are hoping to engage in ethical commerce, to buy from women, and to pay fair prices.'

'And to make a profit.'

Haya was unabashed. 'Yes, this is a for-profit enterprise. These women don't need handouts, they need long-term commercial partners. That can only be sustained if the buyers are making a profit.'

He smiled. 'You sound like a woman who knows her own mind.'

'I am. And we must be perfectly honest with you, since we want the participation of a sheika or a princess. The photograph of that lady in the jewellery will help our cause; it will make our company richer— come to that, it will make *me* richer. Although I have no doubt these pieces are of sufficient quality to sell without it.' Haya smiled. 'So you see, Mr Ibn Mohammed, I'm trying to be honest; it's a business proposition, though, in the end.'

'And a sound one.' He paused, his eyes travelling across her. 'As long as you can prove you will be paying a fair price to the Ghadan women who are supplying you.'

'As soon as I get home, I'll fax the documents to the palace.'

'Then we may be able to do business. I suppose you will not be back here for some time.'

'Not until after the birth of my child.'

'Of course.' He paused, and looked at her again. 'If I may say so, Ms al-Amin, you're a very unusual woman.'

'Is that a compliment?'

'It is. I like to see a fellow Arab succeeding in the United States.'

'You're pretty unusual yourself. I would expect a diplomat to be stuffy.'

'Thank you.' He inclined his aristocratic head to her, then returned to business. 'I can see Sheika Aisha consenting to the photographs.'

'Wonderful news, Mr Ibn Mohammed,' Haya said, thrilled.

'Please call me Jaber.'

'Then Haya.' She smiled.

'And . . .' He hesitated. 'Not that it matters, but when you communicate with the palace, it isn't Mr . . . as it happens. I take a close interest in the affairs of Sheika Aisha, you see, because she's my mother.'

Haya's water went down the wrong way; she spluttered in surprise. 'I'm sorry, Highness,' Haya said, wanting to run off and hide.

'Nothing to be sorry for. I led you to believe otherwise. I should apologise. It's just that I hold a government position, and I'd rather be dealt with that way than as a member of the family.'

Haya saw he hadn't said *royal* family—he hadn't had to.

'I understand. Highness,' she added, again.

'I'd much prefer Jaber.' He signalled for the waiter, and spoke to him in the Ghadan dialect, too fast for Haya to follow. 'I should be leaving. I hope you have a pleasant flight, Haya. We'll be in touch.'

He bowed briefly to her, turned and left.

Jane! What does it feel like for the store to be this mobbed?'

'Sally! Are you taking the offer from Chanel?'

'No,' she shouted, trying to be heard.

Behind them, in the store, it was pandemonium.

'Haya! When is the baby due? Boy or girl?'

The flashbulbs popped around them. It resembled a movie premiere.

'GLAMOUR by name, glamour by nature,' Sally whispered

Haya squeezed Jane's hand. 'I don't feel so good. It's crowded in here.'

'I'll get rid of them,' Jane whispered back. Her friend looked bad, her face pale, her breathing laboured.

Jane stood up. 'Ladies and gentlemen, we're so glad you could come. GLAMOUR was a dream of three friends. Today it's a reality. I won't bore you with a long speech, since this store speaks for itself.' Jane smiled; at the back she saw Craig Levin. And she looked right into his eyes; today was her triumph, but he had made it possible. Her lips parted, she paid tribute to him.

'Please,' Jane said, softly. 'Enjoy.'

The flashbulbs popped, and Levin, unobserved, winked at her.

Jane shivered with pleasure, and admitted to herself how much she wanted him.

Haya squeezed her hand; Jane glanced down and saw her friend wincing. She sat down and put her head near Haya's.

'What's up?'

'I think I'm in labour,' Haya whispered. 'Can we get out of here?'

'Right,' Sally said. She stood up, subtly lifting Haya to her feet.

'Thanks very much, y'all,' Sally said brightly, her Texan drawl like melted honey. 'Have fun!'

The two girls took Haya out, smiling and waving so nobody noticed her grimacing in pain, and a second forest of light bulbs popped and flashed as they passed.

'**M**s al-Amin, your mother is here,' said the midwife. 'Shall I send her in?'

Haya screamed.

'Send her in!' Jane said.

The baby was close now, very close. Jane could see the head crowning. She gripped Haya's hand, sweaty and hot.

'Here it comes,' Haya gasped. The door swung open and her mother bustled in, saying something rapid in Arabic. Jane let go of Haya's hand.

'No!' Haya said. 'Stay! All of you stay!'

The older woman grabbed her other hand, leaned over and whispered something to her daughter; Haya screamed again, and the baby popped out in a wet, slithery rush, into the waiting arms of the doctor, who took the child, rubbed a towel all over it, and cut the cord.

'Let me see!' Haya cried.

The doctor brought the baby across, wrapped in a striped cotton blanket. 'Here, Ms al-Amin, a beautiful daughter.'

'A girl,' Haya said wonderingly.

Sally cooed, 'How precious—she's so tiny.'

Haya's face was a picture of joy, and Jane did not need to ask if she was disappointed. She bent down and kissed the baby on the forehead. 'Praise be to God,' she said. 'I love her. Her name is Noor. Light. Because she's the light of my life.'

Mrs al-Yanna leaned over and kissed her daughter and granddaughter.

'She's adorable. We'll see you later,' Sally said. But Haya was already lost in her baby.

'Come on, Sal.' Jane wiped away a little tear from her eye; she thought briefly of the mother she barely remembered. 'It's been a long day. Let's go get some dinner.'

They sat in the front of Jane's Porsche, the top rolled up, at a discreet distance from the store, eating thin-cut roast beef sandwiches and drinking iced Diet Cokes, watching the parking lot.

'I can't quite believe it,' Jane said wonderingly. 'When you think what happened to us.'

Sally sighed with sheer pleasure. 'I know. We did it. We made it.'

The girls hugged. 'And Haya's a mom.'

'Right.' Sally glanced across at her friend. 'You know what makes this better than before? I mean—if I could, I'd have Daddy back. But better than being at Green Gables? It's that this store, it's *mine*.'

'Ours,' Jane said, laughing.

'Sure.' Sally grinned. 'Good job you got that loan from Mr Moneybags.'

'It was, wasn't it?' Jane said, thinking of Craig. 'I know what you mean. Not long ago I was cleaning dead roaches out of my refrigerator.'

'And I was buying my groceries late at night to get discounts. We did good. Real good.' She offered her best friend one manicured hand, and they smiled at each other, and shook.

There was a constant queue to get in and out; women swarmed, weighed down with GLAMOUR's signature glossy navy and gold bags. Several times every few minutes, male attendants in crisp navy uniforms appeared carrying rolled-up carpets, or heavy items of furniture, and transported them to waiting SUVs.

'I guess those articles last week really helped,' Sally observed.

Jane licked a spot of mustard off her lower lip. 'It's only the first day. We have to see if it's sustained.'

'But this is good,' Sally insisted.

'Yeah.' Jane could not deny it. 'It's good.' Her brow furrowed a little. 'I hope we have enough stock . . .'

Sally hit her. 'Cheer up.'

They grinned at each other, companionably.

'I'm going back to the office. Do a debrief of the staff at the end of the day, call our bankers.'

'You mean Craig Levin,' Sally suggested slyly.

Jane blushed. 'Last time I looked, he was our banker.'

'You won't be able to hold him off for ever,' Sally said. 'I'm going into the store. I'm gonna serve behind the counter, like at Wave.'

'You'll be mobbed. You know you're turning into a star.'

'Honey, please.' Sally opened the door of the Porsche and tossed her long, blonde hair. 'I have *always* been a star.'

It was only half a joke. In reality, Sally was starting to think of herself that way. The press adored how she combined all-American good looks with design savvy. Maybe she wasn't brilliant, but in Jane Morgan, Sally had found a woman who was; and Haya added soul to their project that got them ten times the coverage. Together they were way more than three times what they could have been singly. And Sally was the star in the middle. The fashion was designed by her—it was her.

She was it. She was back. She was GLAMOUR. Maybe she wasn't as smart as the other two, but Sally was starting to believe in herself. She glanced back at Jane's car as she went inside. By the end of this week, Sally promised herself, she'd have a sports car too. A better one—a Ferrari. And a home in the Hollywood Hills.

'**H**i,' Sally said, for the fiftieth time.

'Hi! You're Sally Lassiter. Oh, I just love your stuff.'

'Why, thank you, ma'am.'

'And those fabulous moisturisers from the Dead Sea. I tried one on my hand, and it was so soft and luxurious . . . And the gift wrap was great.'

'Satisfaction guaranteed,' Sally said, smiling broadly. 'It's been an honour serving you, ma'am.'

The fat woman clutched her husband. 'Isn't she amazing?'

'Amazing,' he said, in a bored voice.

'You know, sir,' Sally said, deftly wrapping the woman's Ghadan disc bracelet, 'we have an electronics area on the third floor. It sells gadgets and the TV screens are permanently tuned to sports. We also provide armchairs and couches to sit in, if you'd like to wait while the lady shops . . . And there are waiters serving pretzels and ice-cold beer.'

'Kitty,' he said, 'you enjoy yourself, honey, charge whatever you like. This is a hell of a store.' He lumbered upstairs.

'You see, ma'am,' Sally stage-whispered, 'that area—it's like a crèche for husbands.'

The fat wife giggled. 'Wonderful! I shall tell all my friends.'

'Please do. And keep shopping.' Sally winked at her, and the customer waddled away satisfied.

'So tell me,' said a low voice, one she recognised. 'Do those TV screens show baseball?'

Chris Nelson was standing in front of her.

'I—yes, sir. They do,' Sally murmured. She rested herself on the counter, so he couldn't see her knees buckle. He leaned in a little closer, his eyes moving across her body. Sally felt acutely aware of the button that was open at the top of her blouse; her lips moistened, and parted.

'Don't call me sir,' he said, his voice low. 'Got that, sugar?'

'Yes . . .' she wanted to say 'Mr Nelson' but dared not give him away. '. . . Chris.'

'Better.' He gave her a lazy smile. 'Pretty busy place you got here.'

'It's just the first day.' Oh God! He was so handsome. Sally stiffened her back and lifted her head. She had to fight this. 'Maybe you could get Letty to come here and shop.'

'How's your mom doing?' he asked, ignoring her response.

Sally blushed. 'Well. Thank you.' She lowered her head. 'Sorry, that was uncalled for, I—I know you didn't mean to hit on me, or anything.'

'Sure I did.'

Her head lifted. 'What? I don't fool around with other women's men.'

'Even me?'

Arrogant bastard! 'Yes, even you,' she snapped. 'But I'll send Letty an engagement gift to your office, no charge.'

'It wouldn't reach her.' He looked at her, amused. 'We're not engaged. So send any gifts to her own office. We've split up.'

'Why?'

'We just drifted apart,' he said. 'So what time do you get off work?'

'Whenever I want to. It's my store.'

'Then maybe you can buy me a cup of coffee,' he suggested.

'You want me to ask you on a date?'

'What's the matter? Not a modern woman?'

Sally tossed her hair. 'I don't beg.'

'We'll see about that,' he said softly, and she felt her stomach turn inside out. 'But for now . . . coffee?'

Sally's throat went dry. She came out from behind the counter, 'How come you haven't been mobbed?'

'In here? You got to be kidding, this is oestrogen central. Maybe if I went upstairs. To the husbands' crèche.' He grinned. 'Come on, I know a great place we can get something.'

Sally followed him, meekly, her head down; she didn't want to be stopped either. Not right now. The store, her success, none of it seemed to matter. He was all she could think about. She hoped it didn't show.

'You might want to be quick in the parking lot, though. More men out there.' As they left the store, he slipped his shades back on, and put one arm possessively round her shoulders; as a couple maybe they'd attract less attention.

'Hey!' They were almost at his car. 'Aren't you Chris? Chris Nelson?'

'Not today, pal.'

'Oh my God!' a woman squealed. 'I love him!'

'What now?' Sally asked, dismayed.

He chuckled. 'Run!'

They made it to the car with moments to spare. Nelson opened the passenger door, Sally jumped in, and he wound up her tinted window. She watched as he wound down his own window, where a thick little knot of fans was banging on the glass, and smiled broadly.

'Hey, it's good to see you folks.' They cheered wildly. 'Enjoy shopping at GLAMOUR?' He reached out his hand and brushed at various grasping fingertips. 'See you guys here again, maybe. It's a great store.' Then he put the Jeep into gear. The crowd scattered, obediently, waving, and he deftly took the Jeep into the anonymity of the LA traffic.

'You're very good at that,' she said.

He smiled. 'I've had quite a bit of practice.'

'So where is this place?'

'Malibu. Out on the coast, not too far. Nobody bothers you, plus they have an open-air terrace overlooking the ocean.'

Sally laughed. 'OK, then.'

Suddenly he turned the car and pulled into a lay-by. 'You made a wrong turning?'

'No.' He looked across at her, dark eyes hot. 'I just want to introduce myself properly.'

Sally blushed, her skin tensing, and Nelson reached across the car, put one hand behind the soft skin of her neck, and tugged her to him. His mouth crushed hers, his tongue probing deeply across her teeth, the roof of her mouth. His left hand brushed lightly, teasing, across her breasts. Sally felt desire rock through her; she kissed him back with helpless passion. Then hated herself for it. Why? What girl didn't melt in the arms of the big superstar? She fought, and reluctantly broke away from him. 'Why did you do that?'

'I had to,' he said simply. 'Been thinking about you for weeks. Even when I was still with Letty. Once we broke up . . .' He shrugged. 'Your picture's been in the paper an awful lot. I said to myself I'd come find you, check you out. For sure, you wouldn't be as cute as I remembered—not the big entrepreneur that you are. Except when I saw you behind that counter, you looked hotter than hell. And there's no way to test a woman out without kissing her.' He grinned, then started up the car again, put his shades back on, and concentrated on the road.

Sally turned her head aside and looked out of the window. Hoping he could not see her smile. Hoping he could not smell her desire. Oh God! She had to be careful now. Going out with somebody like Nelson could never last. Too many girls, everywhere, too much competition. She had to be careful not to fall in love.

'Good to see you again, Mr Nelson. And Miss Lassiter, welcome.' Sally's eyes widened; she slipped her hand into Chris's nervously. 'I've got everything ready, sir. This way, please.'

The maître d' conducted them through the expensive-looking restaurant—Sally recognised two movie stars and a senator—out to a terrace. There was a single table, directly overlooking the ocean, set with a white cloth and candles in silver holders. A silver bucket on a stand held a chilled magnum of vintage Pol Roger champagne. There was a bowl of crushed ice, filled with fruit—nectarines, plums, crisp-looking grapes; and a series of small dishes set out across the table.

'Tapas,' Sally said, surprised. 'I love tapas.'

Nelson grinned. 'I know.'

The maître d' showed them to their table, uncorked and served the champagne, and then melted discreetly away.

'Here's to the start of something,' he suggested. And she drank, thankfully, in the hope that the wine would make her feel less nervous.

'How did you know I liked tapas? And how does he know my name?'

'After that day I did some research on you.' He smiled. 'Read that article again. Asked around.'

'You researched me?' she asked, outraged.

'That's right,' he said easily. 'And I bet you researched me, too. Went and looked up my stats on ESPN. Didn't you?'

Sally blushed scarlet. She had. And more. 'But that waiter?'

'I told him I was coming here with you, as my date. No questions about Letty, we'd broken up.'

'You used to bring her here?'

'Of course. It's my favourite restaurant. Have one of those spiced ham slices and you'll see why.'

'But . . . that means you knew I'd say yes.'

He gave her a lazy grin. 'Sally, I've known a lot of women. You were interested, that day. I knew once I'd finished with Letty you'd see me.'

'Good job you were right, or you'd have lost your girlfriend for nothing,' Sally said acidly.

'It was.' He picked up a plate of vine leaves stuffed with rice. 'Try one. I ordered them specially for you.'

She bit into one. The herbed oils drizzled a little across her lips. She licked it away, and blushed again. Everything she did, here, seemed to be charged with sex.

'I don't have sex,' she blurted out.

His eyebrows lifted.

'I had a bad experience,' Sally whispered.

His eyes clouded. 'How bad? Do you want to talk about it?'

Sally shook her head. 'No. I'm not—not going to sleep with you,' she said abruptly.

'And what's wrong with me?' Chris was leaning forward now, eating, but not concentrating; his eyes never seemed to leave her body.

'You're too much,' she said. 'You're too good-looking, and strong, and you saved my mom . . .'

'I hope that's not going to be a strike against me.'

'You're famous. And rich. And you date supermodels.'

'One. Singular. Ever.' Chris was protesting, but gently. His eyes fixed on Sally's. He was serious, and she couldn't fault him.

'You're so . . .' She flailed. She wished she could be as cool as Jane or Haya, find some fancy words to finesse it, instead of saying what she meant. 'You're so damn hot.'

He grinned. 'So far, this doesn't sound like a list of crimes.'

'Stop playing with me!' Sally said, passionately. 'You know what I mean. So I sleep with you, you get what you wanted, you dump me and I'm left pining after you.'

Nelson's face softened. 'I'm not that way,' he said. 'Really.'

'I was raped,' Sally blurted out.

There. It was out. She felt a weight slip from her shoulders.

Chris reached out and took her hand. 'I'm real sorry some bastard did that to you,' he said, gently. 'Are you past it, do you think?'

Sally nodded. 'But I'm not a virgin. And I wanted . . .'

'Saving it up for marriage?'

She blushed defensively. 'Maybe. Somebody special, anyway.'

He sighed, defeated. 'OK, then,' he replied, and gave her a warm smile. 'You want to accuse me of having laid a lot of girls. I'll tell you right now, guilty as charged. I started in school as the best batter in the team. Went up the minors. Got drafted in college. All the way through, I got the prettiest girls throwing themselves at me. You do the maths.'

She nodded, smiling slightly. At least Chris Nelson was honest.

'Same time I hit the bigs, it starts to get old. Can't tell you why—just did. I looked down on the girls, started to look down on myself. Waking up in strange rooms with some random broad who might start crying, or stalking me. It was a headache.' He paused. 'And this may sound dumb, but I started thinking about my aunt Esme, she raised me since my mom died when I was two. She's like a mom to me. Anyway, she's been married to Uncle Jake for twenty years and they have three kids apart from me. Didn't used to have much money but they were always happy. I wanted that.'

'They didn't *used* to have money?' Sally raised a brow.

He shrugged, admitting it. 'I bought them a house and gave them a bank account. My cousins too. They're all millionaires now. Anyway, I decided to cut out the one-night stands, grow up and pick a girl. She had to be especially beautiful—like you, say. There's a lot of temptation. And also strong, because I don't want to be bored. When I met Letty, she seemed like a good fit. Also she was as rich as hell, so I knew she wasn't a gold-digger.'

'Makes sense,' Sally said, hating Letty Berry.

'It was never great, but it was pretty good. I never cheated on her.'

'So what happened?'

'Told you, baby. We drifted apart. It happens. And right when the wheels were coming off, I went jogging. Like I say, you intrigued me. You were brave. Polite and reserved. You carried yourself different from most girls when you knew who I was.' He shrugged. 'Even though I could see you wanted me. Of course I told myself it was only an intense moment, nothing to get worked up about.' Sally smiled; she had thought the same. 'But then I started looking you up. Your guts. Your talent. How you looked after your mother, not just that day at the cliff. You and your two gutsy friends. They're cute, too.'

Sally felt a stab of jealousy.

'Nothing like you, though, Sal. I started to think about you all the time. And one night, I was with Letty, we'd already had a fight and I started thinking about you. Closest I ever came to cheating on her.' Sally blushed. 'I broke up with her the next day.'

'Was she upset?'

'Yes. But if I loved her for real, I wouldn't have been thinking about you.' Nelson paused. 'I'm not going to say I love you, I hardly know you. But if you want to wait to find out how serious we are before you slide into bed with me, that's cool. I can wait.' He paused. 'A little.'

Sally smiled. 'Thank you.'

Nelson stood up, leaned across the table, and kissed her on the lips, his mouth just brushing hers; a more modest kiss than the first but still Sally was on fire. She couldn't help herself; a tiny moan escaped her lips.

'Good,' he said, pulling back. 'At least I won't be the only one to suffer. Want some mineral water?'

'So where have you been?' Mona was sulking; her arm still in a cast, she was fussing at not having heard from Sally all night.

'Sorry, Mom. I'll call next time.'

'Sally! What man were you with?'

Sally started guiltily. 'How do you know I was with a man?'

'That look on your face.'

'Just . . . a nice man. We're going out again tomorrow. He's the man that saved you, Mom.'

'Oh—well. I suppose it's OK, if you don't do anything stupid. Remember Daddy is watching over you.'

'I will,' said Sally.

'And Jane and Haya called. Haya said to tell you thanks and you can come by the hospital at two tomorrow.'

'OK.'

'There isn't going to be a problem with those two, is there, honey?'

'What do you mean?'

'I don't know.' Mona shrugged. 'That Jane, I know you always liked her but she has a bit of a hoity-toity way about her.'

'Mom, that's just her accent. Jane's been my best friend for ever.'

'Well, honey, I hope it lasts,' Mona said doubtfully. 'But I'm so proud of you, all this work you've put into the store. And I know it's nice to have some lotions from the Middle East and stuff—'

'Haya does a lot more than that, Mom.'

'And Jane runs the accounts for you, but that's not the main part of the job, is it? You're the one with all the glamour and style, baby, you're the one picking what they sell.'

'I know that. So do they.'

'It's *your store*,' Mona said protectively. 'I don't want any stuck-up foreigners taking it away from you just because you hung out at school.' Her mother's face was pink. 'I think you're going to be very rich, honey, and Daddy lost it all once. I'd just *die* if anybody tried to take it from you again.'

'Mom! I love those girls. They both know I'm GLAMOUR and they don't mind.' Sally patted Mona on the shoulder. 'We've been through so much together. We're not rivals.'

'Well, if you're sure,' Mona said slowly. 'Anyway, Jane wanted you to know that the store opening broke some sort of record. She says you have a problem with enough stock and can you bring in anything extra from Wave? And then lots of journalists called and asked if you were going out with a baseball player.'

She froze. 'What did you say?'

'I hung up on them.'

'Good job, Mom.'

'So are you?'

Sally surrendered. 'Yes. The man who saved you plays a little ball.'

'He's an All-Star shortstop? For the Dodgers?'

'I don't know why you're asking if you already know,' Sally sulked.

'I didn't. The journalists told me.' Mona smiled. 'It was somebody famous who saved me and I reckon he must be a good man. Those celebrities are usually pampered brats. He took a risk.'

Sally remembered the welts on his hands. 'He certainly did.'

'Just remember, honey, you only have one heart.'

Chapter Thirteen

JANE WAS TRYING to keep her feet on the ground. It was only one week. There had been factors: curiosity, well-managed press. Additional coverage after that, from stuff you could never script: Haya in labour, Sally starting to date some famous athlete—boy, they'd loved that. But if the shoppers came back, it would be because of their excellent service, first-rate staff, and the whole experience she was selling. Maybe she would wait and see if they did come back. But damn, these numbers. She was now fielding new calls. From Wall Street analysts.

She turned off her computer and flopped down on the bed, exhausted. With Haya gone, and Sally's eyes dazzled by Chris Nelson, all the stock rearrangement had fallen on Jane, as well as staff evals, billing, and the rest of it. They needed to hire management, she thought. Vice-presidents. And that wasn't all. The brand now had critical mass, and their foundations of quality were there. It was an out-of-the-gate success. Well, at this rate of money, they'd have to expand. New York. Chicago. DC. Seattle. After that, they'd be looking for major new investment and places abroad: Paris, London and, to be different, perhaps a boutique in Mauritius.

The store was going to be a major success. Perhaps she should push to formalise her leadership of the company. Just to avoid any misunderstandings, later. Wouldn't everybody be happier if the roles were more clearly defined? But there was so much to do. Maybe later.

Jane sensed exhaustion creeping up on her, and she couldn't have that. Burnout was what happened to other people. She had to be able to cover Haya for a couple of months. Resolutely, she peeled off her clothes and put on her swimsuit. The pool in the yard would do fine.

Tomorrow this house would go on the market. Part of GLAMOUR was the fantasy; the owners had to live well. They were the brand.

She plunged into the pool. Man, she loved exercise. It was the one time when she could totally focus on herself. Jane swam twenty lengths, revelling in the movement of the water against her body, then propelled herself lazily up to the steps and slowly walked out of the pool, reaching for her towel—

'Good evening.' She gave a little shriek. Craig Levin was sitting on her sun lounger, dressed in a lightweight summer suit. His gaze ran quickly across her body before she wrapped it in a towel.

'What the hell are you doing here?' Jane snapped.

'I called, I faxed, I emailed. No reply.' He grinned. 'Started to think you were ducking me, Miss Morgan.'

She had been. 'I was busy,' Jane extemporised. 'Opening week . . .'

'I noticed.' He inclined his head. 'I do have three million dollars in your store. Ten per cent of the company. And it appears I'll be getting a nice return on that ten per cent.'

'I'll buy your shares,' she said. 'Six million dollars, and you doubled your money in six months.'

'Now why would I sell something for six that's worth seven now and, I strongly suspect, twenty or thirty in a couple of years?' Levin asked coolly. 'If you were me, would you sell?'

Jane had to shake her head. 'No.'

'Then don't ask foolish questions.'

She stood there, dripping, water from her hair streaming down her back, her feet naked on the hot tiles.

'I have to get dressed,' she muttered.

He spread his hands. 'Please don't bother on my account.'

Jane fled into her bedroom and whisked the curtains closed. Five minutes later she was back out there, wet hair combed through, her feet in stacked mules, wearing the closest thing to hand—one of Sally's new summer dresses; spaghetti straps and a close-fitting bodice, with a light skirt that fluted prettily round her knees.

'Nice,' Levin said, making her wish she'd added a shawl.

'Can I get you some iced tea?' Jane was flustered.

'Thank you,' he said, to her discomfiture. It meant that he was going to stay. And that she would have to fetch him the tea.

'Delicious,' he said. 'Unsweetened.'

'I'm watching my figure,' Jane confessed.

Levin shook his head. 'No need. Believe me.'

'So what can I do for you?' she asked, as briskly as she could.

'I want daily accounts sent to my office.'

'You can't have them.'

'I own ten per cent. I want a seat on the board.'

'Can't have it. Talk to your lawyer.'

'If you want my money for expansion, you'll cooperate.'

Jane shrugged. 'I think the banks will be ready to talk to me, now.'

He grinned. 'I think so, too. But you won't be able to do the mom-and-pop thing for ever, you know. Even Branson went public. And when you do, I'll be there with my chequebook.'

'And until that time, I'll send you a once-monthly summary,' Jane said. 'And we'll be repaying your loan early.'

Levin was still looking at her in that disturbing way. 'You do understand that I could take anything I wanted from you. I could buy out the contracts with your suppliers. I could hire away your staff by doubling their salaries and send them on fact-finding missions to Cancún.'

Jane squared her shoulders. 'We'd sue.'

'Whatever resources you have, throwing them at me would be like dropping a pebble into the ocean,' he replied matter-of-factly.

'I will *not* let you sit on the board. I'd rather go under.'

'Don't worry,' he said, smiling at her. 'I wouldn't force you. But I want you to know that I can.'

'Does that usually work? Puffing out your chest like a pigeon in mating season?'

'You respect work. And success.' His eyes lingered on hers. 'I want to remind you of mine, so you stop fighting me so hard. I've been treated better by companies that were my takeover targets. No matter how much you came on to me in that press conference.'

Guilty. She knew it. He knew it.

'I know you, Jane Morgan,' Levin said suddenly. 'You're one of the most driven women I have ever met. And you don't have time to waste on the wrong guy. But I'm not the wrong guy. I'm not Jude Ferrers.'

Jane stiffened. 'How the hell do you know about that?'

'It's nothing sinister. You didn't exactly have a lot of boyfriends in New York. When you went out with Jude, people noticed. Mostly to wonder if you'd totally lost your head.' Craig's eyes narrowed. 'The guy wasn't good enough to fetch your coffee, let alone date you. But yeah, I asked. And I know you got burned.'

Jane didn't reply. He wasn't mocking her. He was sympathetic.

'You need somebody stronger than you, not weaker than you. Why do you think you fascinate me? We are so alike.'

'There's nobody stronger than me,' Jane said, dry-mouthed.

'You're not as tough as you think you are,' Craig said. 'And I want to prove that to you. I want to be the part of your life that you've been ignoring. I see a very feminine woman. You're soft and responsive. And, of course, extremely lovely. So tell me,' he said, drawing the sentence out. 'Do you treat all your benefactors this way?'

'I apologise,' Jane said, blushing. 'I should have been more responsive.'

'My question is why you weren't.'

She tried, 'I've been so busy . . .'

'Tell the truth,' he said, grinning. 'Admit it. You'll feel better.'

Jane shook her head. He was too close to her, too strong. 'I—I find you attractive.' There. She had said it aloud. Jane lowered her head.

'Better,' he said. 'And I think that's still legal in all fifty states.'

'And it's best not to get involved with a colleague!' she added, in a burst of inspiration.

'Now, Jane. You were doing so well. And then you relapsed.' Jane could hardly look at him. She stared at her sandals. 'Shall I help you out? You're frightened of me, of my past girlfriends, of being one of a list. Slightly ashamed of yourself for having used my attraction to you to get this deal. Determined that you'll return my money and never see me again. Scared of any romance, any man, maybe. Thinking that one day perhaps you'll marry a house-husband, a nice, unthreatening guy who can give you a baby or two and then run a farm somewhere, while you bring home the bacon; somebody who'll never challenge you . . .'

Jane's eyes flashed. 'Cut that out!'

Levin put his face close to hers. 'Pretty near the knuckle, am I, baby?'

'I'll tell you this. I'm never going to be used by any man.'

'But you used your beauty to get to me, didn't you?'

'No.'

'Oh yes, you did,' he said softly. 'Oh yes, Jane, and you know it.'

She ran her tongue over her lips. Wanting to kiss him. Or run.

'You're hard,' Levin said. 'The hardest woman I've ever met. I have no idea why I'm chasing you like this. And no idea why you're running.'

'I just—'

'And now I'm going to kiss you,' he said, and came forward, and she froze, couldn't move a single muscle, and then his lips were on hers, just brushing lightly against the skin; she could smell the scent of him, feel the strength of his torso right in front of her . . .

Jane was unable to help herself. He was daring her to resist. Or ask for more. Her body, so focused and tensed, melted and warmed and she moaned under her breath and surrendered, her lips pressing against him, pleadingly. He chuckled deep in his throat. Underneath her dress her body was leaping against him as he ran a hand slowly across it. Jane fell into his arms, feeling his jacket, his belt, the buttons of his shirt. She wanted him so much. A voice in her head was telling her not to, to leave him alone. They hadn't even dated. But she would not listen. His strength, his assured touch, all over her, like he owned her . . . she wanted it, at that moment, more than anything.

Levin kissed her again, triumphantly, and swung her into his arms; her weight was nothing to him. Jane buried her hot face in his chest, pressed her breasts against him. As he carried her into the coolness of her bedroom, Levin was already unbuttoning the top of her dress.

She lay, naked, drained, against him. It was night now; they were both covered in sweat; Jane's body was relaxed, as though orgasm had unknotted every muscle under her skin.

'Craig . . .'

He dropped a slow kiss on the top of her shoulder. 'At least we've got rid of Mr Levin.'

Jane hung her head. 'What have I done?'

'I could remind you,' he said. 'If you have short-term memory loss.'

'Stop it,' she protested, smiling. Was it possible he could have her again? Three times, in rapid succession; he had the vitality of a teenager.

'I'm done,' he said, sighing. 'You're dangerous. It's a good job I keep in shape.' He pulled away from her. 'Let's shower. Together.'

But Jane looked down, knotting her fingers together in the bed linen. 'Am I going to see you again?'

She was miserable, now; her body felt good, but her heart was sick. This was it, exactly what she had feared. She'd wanted him, craved him, for months, and as soon as he touched her, she'd fallen into his hand like a ripe peach. But the chase was over. Now she was just another conquest.

'Do you think I'm that kind of man?'

'I don't know,' she said. 'That's the point. I hardly know anything about you.'

'Let's get in that shower,' Levin said, his eyes flickering across her naked body, dappled by the moonlight, warm and blotchy from his touch. 'I won't promise not to molest you, though. And then get dressed. And come with me.'

'What do you mean?' Jane asked.

'You want to see me again?'

She nodded; he knew her intimately; there was no point trying to hide anything now.

'Then why wait? See me again now. Come home with me. Spend the night at my place.'

'We didn't even date,' Jane said.

'So this will be our first. Dinner. I could eat. Couldn't you? Then breakfast. And I'll pick you up for lunch. That makes three dates in what, eighteen hours?' He winked at her. 'I know how to play catch-up.'

She slid her long legs off the bed. Even now, when she was trying not to hope, he was leaving her no choice. Jane tried to come to terms with it; where there were two people, she could not have total control; and she was afraid of how much she liked that. Levin stood up and stretched his hand out. 'Come on, Jane. Let me earn your trust.'

It was strange how shy she was. After all that passion. Yet sitting in his dining room—or one of his dining rooms—Jane felt as nervous as a teenager.

'Come on. Eat something.' Levin gestured at the slices of roast partridge, delicately fanned out in front of her, next to buttery parsnips and spinach.

'I'm embarrassed,' she murmured, and lowered her head. Levin watched her, and to his amazement found himself stirring again. What a woman. Why was she like this? So reserved, and so beautiful?

'Because you don't know me? Other than in the Biblical sense?'

'And the pages of *Fortune*,' Jane admitted.

'Ah, yes. I recall you saying you admired me.' He grinned. 'I hear that a lot. From you, it was a turnon, though. Tell you what, I'll make a deal.'

'A deal?'

'Eat your food. Drink some water, some juice. A glass of champagne. You eat, and I'll talk. The unofficial version of my life. Then you'll know me. Anything to get you to relax.'

'All right,' Jane said softly. Levin was unlike any man she'd ever known; he didn't crumple in the face of her coldness. He stood firm against her. And he directed things. She took a bite of the partridge and she found she wanted to eat it. To please him.

'I don't have a rags-to-riches story. I grew up an only child, and that's about all the bad things you can say of my early life. Dad worked in the Sanitation Department as an administrator, Mom was a court reporter. We had an estate house in a decent part of Queens, back in New York, a nice car, took a vacation to the Jersey shore most summers. A big extended Jewish family; we weren't religious, but there were still plenty of weddings and bar mitzvahs. Most of my friends were Jews, too.' He grinned. 'I hated my life. Does that sound awful? Loved my folks, hated my life. I felt so trapped. And at school, I was the weeny little Jew. There were bigger kids there who used to kick my ass on a regular basis. Dad wouldn't let me quit, said I had to be tough. Good girl—now drink some wine.'

Jane took a sip. Warmth started to spread through her again, and she didn't think it was just the alcohol.

'There had to be more. I knew it. Every time I took a subway into the city it was so exciting. Those skyscrapers—electric. Wall Street. The big theatres, Times Square, Fifth Avenue. Manhattan was life and Queens was nothing. They wanted me to get into real estate or become a school principal. I was brighter than most kids they knew. Partly because of my memory, with a photographic memory you ace most multi-choice tests. But mainly because I was good at maths.'

'So what did you do?'

Now she had started eating, she was ravenous; Jane helped herself to a slice of the raspberry cheesecake set on a silver platter in front of her.

'First, I started lifting weights, till I was big enough to kick a little ass myself. Next I sat down and figured if I wanted to get into Wall Street, I'd need to be a broker. So I started buying the *Wall Street Journal* with my allowance. Next I started figuring out the numbers. Seeing patterns. Looking at stocks. I quit school early and my parents cut me off, but by that time I had a job as a gofer in a brokerage house. I used to give them tips—and they worked. They thought I had insider info.' He smiled. 'Nothing they couldn't have figured out if they were paying attention. But at eighteen I was a trader. Before I could drink, I owned my own apartment. Sound familiar?'

'So far,' Jane said. 'But I'll never be as successful as you.'

'That's true,' he said, cool as you like, and she thrilled to it.

'Your parents forgave you?'

'Soon as they knew I'd be OK. I was a senior broker at twenty, VP at twenty-one. Had a nice little brownstone in the Village at twenty-three, drove a Spider. At twenty-four I quit. Started to put together a fund. You know most of the rest.'

'I heard you were a workaholic.'

'I don't see it as work.' His eyes lit up, and she responded to his passion. 'I love business, I love numbers. I *see* stocks. I don't know how else to explain it. For me, trading is like a computer game. Winning is fun. Money is fun. I always wanted this, I wanted to live like my house was a hotel. Got lots of staff and I pay them outrageous wages. Give lots to charity. My parents are in Florida, in a mansion with a private beach. I keep my head down, I don't talk to the press, I just play the game. And I win, nineteen times out of twenty.'

'So.' She spooned up the last of the cheesecake. 'Tell me about your personal life.'

'I thought I just did. Oh—you mean women?' Levin smiled. 'I like beautiful women. I never promised any of them anything serious, unless I meant it. I've had three proper girlfriends—one for six months, one for two years, another for a year.'

'And me?'

'You're different. Incredibly so.'

'Tell me why.'

Levin grinned. 'Very well. You are more intelligent and more independent. I never dated fluff—maybe when I was younger there were a couple of trophy dates. Later on models, but always smart ones. One of my long-term girlfriends was a lecturer at Vassar.' His eyes flickered across her. 'None of them were like you. A self-made woman. One who came back from a tragedy—an orphan. What you did with Shop Smart was amazing. And leaving your job was pretty great, too. Maybe I saw something of myself in you. You didn't want that comfort trap. A house in the suburbs or a vice-president's salary, it's all bull if you know you can do better. And of course there just aren't that many women who do well in business.'

'Sexist pig.'

'It's the truth, and you know it. You and your girlfriends have something here. But I warn you, I don't think it's gonna work long term.'

Jane froze. She had been worrying about the same thing. But it stung to hear him say it.

'Power-sharing never works, honey, just ask the United Nations. Somebody has to be the boss. And you'll want that somebody to be you.'

Jane shrugged. 'I take all the business decisions, Sally does the styling and Haya adds the ethics. No reason for us to tread on each other's toes. And anyway, we're *friends*.'

'You are now. But for how long?'

'You don't know us.'

'We'll see. You're like me. You're in this game. You're . . .' He paused, then smiled. 'Not a civilian.'

She smiled back, stood up from the table and held out her hands to him. She sensed she was in great danger, that he already had her heart, and she had surrendered every part of herself. She wanted to be his girl, his only girl. Yes, it was a womanly desire as old as the hills, and Jane knew already that she wished for marriage. But her body was a traitor; it wanted him. Now.

Craig came over to her, leaving the rest of his food untouched. 'I thought you just wanted to sleep,' he murmured, whispering into her neck, kissing it, his tongue tracing the line of the caress.

'That was then,' Jane said. 'And at least now we've had the first date.'

'You can trust me.' Mrs Doughty was firm. 'She'll be fine.'

Noor waved her little clenched fist happily. She gave a gummy smile to her mother and her nanny.

'Do you know about warming the bottle? And don't use those commercial wipes. Just tissues in warm water, or she gets a rash . . .'

'Ma'am, I've brought up four of my own.' The Irishwoman shook her head. 'Now get in the cab. The sooner you go and do your trading, or whatever it is, the sooner you can come back to her.' She gave Haya a shove. 'It's been four months. They need you at work, too. Now go.'

Noor scrunched up her face. She started to wail, and Haya wanted to as well.

'Go,' Emily Doughty insisted.

Haya did as she was told, and as the limo door shut behind her, she watched the nanny put her baby comfortingly over her shoulder.

'LAX?'

'Just drive,' Haya snapped. She turned her face to the window, so that he would not see her tears. She knew she had to do this, of course. Haya couldn't stay home for ever. Not with the way GLAMOUR was going. They had queues at the store daily, just to get in. Jane was negotiating with some defunct American chains, trying to buy up real estate, looking for a good lease on Fifth or Avenue of the Americas, jetting off to Paris and London. Sally, when she took an evening off from the ballpark, was turning into a bona fide star; her days were spent designing, her nights at glittering premieres, jetting off to talk shows, or giving interviews for magazines. They called her 'fashion's Martha Stewart' and, more cruelly, 'Business Barbie'. But Sally rode it all like a pro, and every item she wore in public was sourced from the GLAMOUR store.

Their next opening was to be New York, and Jane and Sally had begged Haya to come back. Ethical business was a money-spinner—the women's magazines loved what they were doing with local craftswomen, and when had Sally posed in *Women's Wear Daily* wearing her own new trademark, a floor-length red velvet sheath, with one of the Ghadan necklaces draped round her long neck, orders had gone wild.

'Haya,' Jane insisted. 'You can't just go on buying trips, what you have to do is find staff—buyers—people you trust. They can purchase the ethical trade in bulk as long as it's up to standard. We can't jeopardise the brand.'

'I suppose you're right. There's just no way I can fulfil the number of orders.' Haya was excited. 'Is it really that busy?'

Sally groaned. 'Please come back.'

Of course she adored Noor, her little sunshine, but Haya had missed her friends, missed her business. She was too driven to spend every day in the nursery.

Haya agreed to recruit buyers. Frankly, she didn't want to lose her position. GLAMOUR was her idea, she had been the one to suggest it, that night at Jane's new house. Without her putting some soul into the company, they would be nothing to write home about. Women's magazines and TV channels were eager to cover them because of the good they did in the developing world. This store was in her soul now. It was her own thing, and she would fight like a tigress to protect it. And to protect herself at its heart. And so now she was on her way back, to Amman, Jordan. Leaving Noor behind for four whole, brutal days. It had to be done; but she didn't have to like it.

Jaber shook his head and tried to concentrate. The computer screen before him was thick with facts and figures. Important stuff; costings for the schools and the hospitals he had persuaded the King to invest in. He knew he should focus. His star was rising in the kingdom. There were plenty of advisers, from bankers to generals, and an assorted gaggle of princelings and relatives clustered round the King. But he had never been one of them. He had merely excelled at his job, quietly and methodically, and the ruler of Ghada had noticed. He was formally promoted, and the King raised his mother and himself in rank. Jaber was on his way. There was a chance, a real chance he might make the inner circle, and have a say in how the kingdom was governed.

Surely it was time to consolidate his position; to marry a suitable woman from inside the royal family, play his part in the social life of the court, as well as the government offices.

But then he had met Haya al-Amin. And everything changed.

What was he thinking? Surely she was *completely* unsuitable. A Muslim, yes, but that was about it. An American citizen, educated in Los Angeles. No virgin—a widow with a child, and a knowing sensuality about her that he found utterly intoxicating. He would be raising another man's daughter, and a merchant's daughter at that, in the villas and gardens of the Royal Palace enclosure. And she was the antithesis of the women his cousins married: of aristocratic family, with no ambitions other than to give the right parties and win the favour of the queen of the day. Maybe shop a little in Dubai or Paris.

Haya al-Amin was different. She was a combatant on the great stage of life, like him. A child bride who had succeeded in two businesses, a single mother, a champion of the underclass. But not in the usual way of moneyed women, throwing charity parties and writing cheques. Haya got out there and empowered poor communities, and the knock-on effects were huge.

Although he had told himself, repeatedly, that this fixation was nuts, he had never stopped thinking about Haya since the day she had left Ghada. And now she was coming back. And Jaber was going to see her. He had no idea what was going to happen.

'Welcome, Ms al-Amin.' The desk clerk was all smiles. 'It's good to have you back, ma'am. I hope you enjoy your stay in Ghada.'

'Thank you.'

'Your meetings have been arranged in the Roosevelt Conference Room for nine a.m. tomorrow.'

'Great. If I could just get my room key . . .' Haya was very tired; it had been a long day.

'Here you are. The Presidential Suite. Take the penthouse elevator, second on the left.'

'I didn't book that suite,' Haya said wearily.

'No, ma'am. It is a complimentary upgrade. And we have a message to deliver to you,' the receptionist said with a coy smile, 'from His Highness Sheik Jaber.'

Haya blinked with shock. He remembered her? They had negotiated with the Ghadan palace through the office. She had never expected to hear from Jaber again.

'Here.' The receptionist handed her an envelope; thick vellum, with a small gold crest, a stylised palm tree, on the back. 'Shall I have a bell-hop show you to the suite?'

'No, I'll manage.'

Haya walked into the elevator, barely noticing her surroundings; her case was compact, neatly packed with lightweight, long dresses. She rode up to the Presidential Suite; it was incredibly luxurious, with tinted windows on four sides looking out over Ghada City. Haya ripped open the note.

Dear Ms al-Amin,

Congratulations on the birth of your daughter. The Office of Protocol has kept me up to date with developments with your company; His Majesty's Government is quite satisfied with the funds that have flowed in to our citizens thus far. We are willing to consider further involvement of the royal family in exchange for more significant orders worldwide.

I would, however, prefer to discuss such matters with you personally. Could you call the palace and confirm if you are free for lunch on Saturday at one o'clock?

Wa-es salaam,

Jaber

Stop it, Haya told herself. You're reading way too much into this. He is a young sherif, not a man to be tempted by a widowed single mother. And anyway, what if he was? She was a partner at GLAMOUR Inc. and he worked for the government here. It would never work.

But it was no good; she had thought of him often and her heart pounded as she dialled the number on the stationery. Well, hell, it *was* exciting. She'd been stuck in a nursery for the last four months. She should just see it as a business success. Haya gave herself permission to enjoy that. She thought of Ahmed, her love. He was in Paradise—he would not mind if anything was to happen.

'Good afternoon,' said a voice in Arabic.

'Hello. My name is Haya al-Amin—'

'Oh yes, thank you for calling, madam. Will you be able to join His Highness for lunch?'

'Yes, I will,' Haya said, taken aback that the operator knew so fast.

'That's wonderful news. We will send a car to your hotel at twenty to one, if convenient. If you could bring your passport for identification.'

'Thank you,' Haya said.

She hung up and went into the suite's sumptuous bathroom; a stand-alone tub made of pure copper that you could almost swim in. Tomorrow morning she had interviews, eighteen candidates for six positions, and they would have to be done by twelve forty. Those with a love of beauty and Ghada would stand out. The important thing was to get them hired, fast, and then come back here. Whether she was right about Jaber's interest or not, she had to look fabulous. If she could get a true princess of this country involved . . . Forget it. GLAMOUR's PR and marketing would explode just as Jane was opening the new stores. Haya had been out of commission for a while. She wanted to con-tribute, to be as much a part of this as Sally and Jane.

'Here we are, ma'am. Passport, please.'

Haya meekly handed it over. She leaned forward, out of the window, and looked down the drive to the palace complex. It was exquisitely beautiful. Vast, covered with blue and gold tiles, like the decoration on a Pharaoh's headdress. It glittered in the sun like jewellery, and the gardens stretched ahead of her, lush and beautifully stocked. There was something of the Alhambra about this place. She shivered with tension. Did she look good enough? She had selected a traditional Jordanian caftan, red silk, embroidered with gold thread, antique, flowing beautifully about the body. Round her neck she wore a jangling, original Ghadan coin necklace from GLAMOUR's own stock; it was disturbingly sensual, she thought, like bells on her when she moved.

'Thank you.' Her passport was returned to her, and the limo pulled through the ornate carved gates, covered in Moroccan-style mosaic work. Haya tried not to stare as the driver took her round the left wing of the palace, into a small courtyard, and parked in a spot they were waved to by a saluting guard, who came round to open the door. 'Greetings, madam,' he said, in thick accented English.

'Thank you,' Haya responded in Arabic. The soldier smiled, and lapsed into his native tongue.

'*Sidi* Jaber is waiting in his office. If you'll come this way.'

Haya nodded, and was led through marble corridors to a modern room where Jaber was sitting. He jumped to his feet. 'Haya.' He came forward, and clasped her shoulders warmly, kissing her on both cheeks in the Arab fashion; Haya, feeling awkward, clumsily dropped a low curtsy.

Jaber raised an eyebrow. 'You do not have to curtsy to me. Although your manners are as beautiful as your face.'

Haya blushed deeply. 'I was delighted to get your letter, sir,' she began, formally.

'Good. And it's Jaber. I won't have to spend the afternoon calling you Ms al-Amin, will I?'

She shook her head. 'Haya.'

'Then come.' He extended a hand.

Jaber took his time. He made small talk, about the store, the candidates Haya had interviewed, the GLAMOUR expansion programme. 'And you?' he asked, at length, when she was picking through a delicate pastry of roasted chicken and raisins. 'You are taking a full part in this?'

'This is my first major contribution since Noor was born.'

'And it will be major,' he said, with calm assurance. 'I wonder, have you been following events here in Ghada?'

Haya was embarrassed. 'I haven't—I have hardly listened to any news since she was born. I was nursing . . .' Her voice trailed off. Was that too intimate a detail to have shared with him? Why was she starting to think of him as a friend, rather than who he was? 'Please excuse my ignorance, High—' She caught sight of his face. 'Jaber.'

'Much better,' he said. 'Anyway, His Majesty has decided to honour my mother, his cousin, who is widowed, and has raised her to the rank of a princess here, with the title Royal Highness.'

'That's wonderful,' Haya responded automatically, trying to work out what that meant for her company. She already had photos of the sherifa—now princess—wearing GLAMOUR jewels. They could start a whole new ad campaign on that.

'And me,' he said, matter-of-factly. 'I have been involved in government, as you know. I am now Foreign Minister.' He shrugged. 'And my rank has been raised to emir, prince.'

'The King promoting your family must have been a great joy.'

'I'd be lying if I said Mama wasn't thrilled,' Jaber admitted frankly. 'Not so much at the rank, although that's nice. But over what it meant for me. King Nazir trusts me.'

'And I suppose the King will select a princess for you?' Haya asked.

He looked so deeply into her eyes, she could not hold his gaze.

'I'm old-fashioned. I don't believe in divorce. I don't want a succession of wives. The woman must be perfect. I have made it clear I will not accept an arranged marriage.'

'I understand.' Haya would not look at him.

'I think you're beautiful. You're modest, and a lady, but you have something else. A steel spine. You started this business, you found a way to make money and to help others. I admire how you work with your friends from the West. Yet you are a believer. Your daughter has a Muslim name.'

Haya smiled. 'Her father insisted I change my own.'

'And you're not afraid to talk of your husband to me. I would not have admired a woman who could abandon his memory.'

'I loved him.'

'That is clear.' Jaber put it to her with that directness she liked. 'Tell me now. Could you ever love again?'

'It is possible,' Haya said. 'I only loved Ahmed when I got to know him . . . I don't want to rush into marriage again, Jaber.'

'No. Of course.' He was eager. 'And you have a child. And an enterprise of your own. I see that you are not about to be mine for the asking, Haya. So I have a proposal. Not of marriage,' he added, with a grin, and she smiled. 'Yet. Why do you not establish yourself in Ghada for six months? You could set up a department here, a buying division. That would consolidate your position in the stores more than a few one-off purchasing jaunts. Meanwhile, your child can grow here, where she will hear Arabic spoken every day.'

'And I can see you?'

'I never said I had no ulterior motives.' Jaber smiled. 'Let us see if we like each other. Whether or not you do, you will have my protection. In the end, if you can't stand me, what have you lost? Nothing. Your career will be advanced.' His eyes searched hers. 'I have thought often about you. Tell me the truth. Did you ever think about me?'

'I did. I just didn't believe . . .'

'Believe it,' he said. 'So. Will you come?'

She thought about it. She would be breaking up the trio, for the second time. But GLAMOUR was big now. Bigger than all of them. It could no longer be run by three friends making it up as they went along. 'It is a brilliant idea,' she said. 'Of course I will have to discuss it with my friends.'

'And if they say no?'

She looked at him. 'I will still come,' Haya said. She smiled. 'I have got used to making my own decisions.'

They discussed it over dinner, two days after she got back. She found Noor thriving and not particularly overwhelmed to see her; the baby was engrossed in banging a tin drum Emily Doughty had bought her.

Emily cluck-clucked over the baby, who gurgled and buried her chubby cheeks in Haya's skirt. 'You have a bath and go to your meeting. You can see she survived.'

They'd dressed up for the meal. Nobody suggested it; all three women knew they had to. At this point, they were minor celebrities, and Sally was turning into a major one. Haya chose a sweeping gown of Egyptian cotton in bright yellow, embroidered with green thread; a Chanel handbag, and one of the jangling Ghadan bracelets, her feet encased in buttercup-yellow leather Manolo strappy sandals with a high heel. Sally wore her own red dress, with a GLAMOUR necklace of rubies by Montfort Jewels; Jane chose a cream silk suit, with pearls, Wolford tights and Christian Louboutin shoes in dove grey. They met at the Ivy and posed for pictures outside, arms around each other, smiling and laughing. The business press loved the shot. They were as glamorous as their company. Three sexy friends; three powerful women. Nobody knew the tensions behind the smiles.

Work had become strained. Jane was exasperated when the other two could not follow her financing. Sally took offence when Haya and Jane didn't dig a new line of hers. And Haya resented being pushed to the side; she loved her friends, but they weren't showing an interest in what she'd sourced or the ethics programmes she set up. They were a team, but increasingly each girl did her own thing. And each of them was convinced she did most of the work. This dinner had an inevitability to it.

'I know what this is about,' Sally said glumly, as soon as the waiter had departed. 'It's Noor, isn't it, Haya? You've hired those buyers, and you're quitting. You want to stay home.'

'I'm not quitting.' Haya was a little annoyed Sally would even suggest such a thing. 'But I am leaving. I need to be in the Middle East.'

She explained, leaving out the part with Jaber; that was too fragile a thing to talk about.

Jane listened in silence and then looked over at Sally.

'You can't leave!' Sally was saying. 'We'll never manage—'

'But we will,' Jane said. 'And actually; I think I should go, too.'

Sally blinked. 'What?'

'To New York.'

'I don't get it.' Sally was angry. 'I can't manage the store by myself.'

'We have to delegate. Even you, Sal.'

'Salads, ladies!' The waiter put down their salads with the fried soft-shell crabs, and vanished.

'We're too big,' Jane said simply. 'You guys have to decide what you want. The company can't go on like this, with us in LA. I need to be in New York. I'll do the banking, the real estate, the distribution deals. All the major work.'

'That's not the major work, now is it?' Sally said reasonably. But Jane ploughed on.

'Sally, you're the public face; you *are* GLAMOUR—what every little girl wants to be,' she said, mollifying her friend. 'We don't need you stuck in a back office in LA, we need you out there, on magazine covers. And if you're the face, Haya is the soul. So, yes, she can do that properly in the region, not here. She's wasted in LA. So am I. But it's where you should be—you're the *star*.'

Haya told them about Jaber's mother.

'I love it!' Sally momentarily forgot her anger. 'Get a princess to a photo shoot? I'll do it with her. That'll make *Elle*. Maybe *Vanity Fair*, if we do it right.'

'You're the glitz, Sal; now we have some royal gravitas.' Jane grinned. 'My goodness, girls, this is really going to be big.'

'And it means we can't stay together?' Sally asked glumly.

'It's not like we won't be friends,' Haya replied. 'This time you'll have my phone number.' She smiled.

'I know it has to happen.' Sally sounded heartbroken. 'I just . . . I didn't think it would be this soon.'

Haya examined Jane. 'There's a man, isn't there? Your Craig Levin. *He* lives in New York.'

'He has a house here,' Jane said defensively.

'But he mainly lives there.'

She couldn't deny it. 'It may have something to do with this, yes.'

Sally clapped her hands. 'The ice maiden melts?'

Jane blushed. 'God help me, I love him,' she said; and her girlfriends thought she sounded a little despairing. 'No man I've ever met understands me the way he does. And nobody else is strong enough for me. But that's why you can stay here, Sally, isn't it? You're practically living with Chris Nelson.'

Sally blushed. 'Actually, I moved in yesterday.'

'What about your mom?'

'She's in a guest cottage at his estate in Malibu, but she's talking about getting her own apartment. She doesn't need me any more.'

Haya felt a pang of loss—Mona might not, but she wasn't sure she didn't. Sally had been her first protector. And now she was going to be all on her own.

'And you?' Sally flicked her fountain of glossy blonde hair. 'Haya, you've been very quiet on the subject. But I know you. There's something in your eyes. Is there a man?'

'Possibly.' She wouldn't say any more. 'In Ghada . . . But I don't know; we haven't really started going out yet . . .'

'Well, you'll need to be back here in six months,' Sally said firmly. 'We weren't going to announce it, but since you two are skipping town . . .' Sally lowered her voice. 'Chris and I are getting married.'

Chris whistled a little, as soon as the pushy realtor had left them to themselves. 'This is quite a house,' he said. 'Are you sure we need this much space?'

'Think of the fun you'll have christening every room.'

He kissed her, one of those slow kisses that got her squirming.

'But, baby, ten mil. I'm not *that* rich. Sorry.'

'We'll bid five,' Sally said. 'They'll take it. I have to have this house.'

'There are lots of other good ones—'

'You're not that rich, but I am,' she interrupted, kissing him back, stretching up on her toes to do it. 'GLAMOUR . . . it's doing well. More than well.' She summarised for him.

'Man.' He blew out his cheeks. 'When I met you, you were living in a scummy walkup apartment.'

'Hey, at least I know you're not marrying me for my money!'

Chris slapped her playfully on the behind. 'Just for that, when I get you home, I'm gonna make you work out naked.'

'Promises, promises,' Sally teased back.

Chris took her hand. 'Let's go. I want to see you on that exercise bike.' He whistled loudly, and the realtor came running back in, like a well-trained puppy.

'Seven and a half mil. Not a cent over,' he said firmly. 'Call me back if you have a signed contract. Come on, sweetness.' And he ushered her out, back to the car.

They hadn't driven more than half a mile before the carphone rang.

'Chris? It's Jemma. They've accepted!' she trilled. 'I'm having a signed contract messengered over to Malibu. Congratulations! I'm sure you'll enjoy Beverly Hills.'

'Good. You'll get the money wired by tomorrow.' He punched the button and hung up. 'Looks like you got it, baby.' Nelson shook his head. 'Man, that house is so big, it's like owning my own country. So why did that place appeal to you so much?'

'That was my home. My dad's place.' Sally's face was bright with a fierce pride. 'And now it's mine again. Mom can live in the guest cottage. Maybe one day I'll give her the whole house.'

He was shocked. 'Seven point five million?'

'The way things are going, we'll soon be able to afford six of them,' Sally told him.

'Man, what am I doing in practice all day?'

'Getting ready to win the World Series?'

'There is that, I guess. You're still gonna be working out naked. Somebody has to keep you under control.'

Chapter Fourteen

'HAVE YOU SEEN the latest consignment?' Haya was angry. 'I expect quality control, Suri. You can't assume honesty. When I made a surprise inspection at the Cairo docks I found four machine-woven carpets. Machine woven! Do you know the scandal that would cause if we misrepresented them? Do you understand what that means?'

The older woman hung her head. 'That the suppliers did not buy them from the artisans?'

'Exactly. So not only are we being cheated, some poor woman who depends on us for her survival is too.'

'It won't happen again, *Siti* Haya.'

'It had better not. Or you're fired. And don't call me *Siti*,' Haya snapped.

They were always doing that. She hated the assumption that Jaber would marry her in due course. The more she was seen at the palace, the more they said it was a done deal. Only Haya knew differently. She knew she was falling for him. Yet in the last month, he had withdrawn from her. They had met for dinner only twice, and he had been moody and distracted. The only time he seemed like his old self was when he played with Noor, ten months old and delicately taking her first steps.

There was some other woman, Haya was sure of it. And her heart ached at the thought. She loved Ghada now with a passion, but she couldn't stay here; couldn't turn on the TV, read the local papers and see the Emir, the favoured Foreign Minister, accompanied by a new princess, his chosen bride.

So she would have to move. And Haya had already decided she would go back to Amman, live in a villa, somewhere secluded and safe for Noor to grow up in; the country her own father had left for America. With her, it would come full circle.

'I understand,' Suri said, chastened. 'I'll check them all personally, Ms al-Amin.'

There was a hard rap on the door.

'Come in,' Haya called.

A soldier opened the door; he wore the epaulettes of the royal house and had a gun at his belt. Suri shrank back.

'What do you want?' Haya asked, fighting to stay calm.

'Madam, you must come with me,' he said, in guttural English. 'It is His Royal Highness who orders it.'

'I'm not going anywhere.'

He looked at her, expressionless. 'I have orders to take you by force if necessary. It is for your own protection.' He lifted the gun.

Haya was terrified; her palms started to sweat. 'What's going on?' she cried. 'Where is Noor? *Where is Noor?*'

'There is trouble at the palace. Your baby and her nanny have already been collected—they are at His Highness's compound.' He moved forward, to grab her, but Haya was already ahead of him.

'Take me to my daughter,' she said firmly. 'Do you hear me?'

Startled, the soldier gave a small bow.

'Yes, *Siti*,' he said. This time, she did not object.

Jaber walked over to her, and kissed her on both cheeks. '*Mashallah!* You are safe.'

'And Noor?' They were in his private apartments, and Haya was still shaking; during the ride through the streets, her car, armoured and flanked by riders with guns, had taken fire; screaming, she had dropped to the floor. The centre of Ghada City was on fire. People in the streets were running, yelling, throwing rocks. Even inside the royal compound, it was all different; rows of the palace guard, no longer ceremonial, AK-47s at their side.

'She is upstairs. We have supplies, baby formula. You are too well-known as my companion—they would have come for you.'

'What's going on?'

'The sons of the Crown Prince have prepared a revolt. Mercenaries intend to kill the King. I am to fight them. If I fail, take this.' He withdrew some papers and money from a cabinet. 'Passports in a false name for you and the child, money to take you across the border. My personal bodyguard will see you out of the palace.'

Haya wept—she wanted to hold him, to kiss him. 'Be careful,' she blurted out. 'Come back to me, safe. I pray you will come home!'

'It will be quick,' he said grimly, and then, to her astonishment, leaned forward and kissed her lightly on the lips.

'Haya, I love you. Maybe this is not the time, but I have no choice. If we survive this, will you marry me?' She opened her mouth to consent, but Jaber stopped her. 'I knew this was coming. It is why I did not ask you. But, Haya, know this. If you are my wife, you cannot be directly involved in GLAMOUR any more. You will be a princess. You will have to perform duties with me.' He pressed her hand. 'And they *are* duties, Haya, and there is no time off. So choose.'

There was gunfire in the distance. She looked at him; now her heart was on the line, there was no choice. Not really, not when he might die.

'I accept,' she said, and kissed his hand. 'Go with God!'

He looked back at her, briefly, then picked up his gun and rushed from the room.

Haya's heart was full. Oh God! She loved him now, loved him so completely. She had no idea what the night would bring. She clutched the papers to her. If she had to flee, she would flee. Noor's safety came first. But she didn't want to go. She never wanted to leave Jaber.

The baby was crawling round the bedroom, with a frightened Emily Doughty still trying to play with her; she laughed with delight at seeing Haya. There was a burst of gunfire outside the windows.

Haya picked Noor up and covered her with kisses.

The older woman wrung her hands. 'Oh God! What shall we do?'

'It's fine if you want to leave, Emily, but I believe if there's unrest here, they'll be at the airport too. Prince Jaber has an armed force to protect us. I'm staying here,' Haya said.

Mrs Doughty looked at her friend and employer, Haya's shoulders squared, the caftan swirling round her feet. 'If you think we should stay, we'll stay,' she replied. 'You've a smart head on your shoulders for a woman who's not even Scottish.'

Haya took control. She arranged calls for Emily Doughty and herself to their worried families on a secure line. She tried to distract the staff by organising the cooking of a meal on the single working gas ring in Jaber's kitchen. When the violence was close, so close you could hear the shots outside the gardens, Haya sang nursery rhymes to Noor, loudly, so that the crashes would not frighten her.

By the time the baby was sleeping soundly—Haya had had her cot moved into the centre of the villa, into Jaber's bathroom—the fighting had died down. Into the night there were occasional bursts of gunfire, or a flare arcing overhead. Haya remained awake, with her papers at her side. Her bags for Noor packed, by her feet.

At half past three Jaber finally returned; there was blood on his shirt, and more that had dried in his beard. Exhausted, he slumped on a couch in the reception hall; his servants gathered round, and he muttered a few words in the Ghadan dialect. They smiled and clapped.

Haya leaned forward anxiously. 'It's OK? What happened?'

'They put down the coup attempt. The ringleaders are in custody. Nobody liked them coming here with a foreign force. In the end the men of the city took to the streets. Then it was over.'

'*Mashallah!* Are you injured?'

'A knife wound. Don't worry,' he said, as she darted forward. 'A doctor has dressed it. There was hand-to-hand fighting at one point. They came within feet of the King.'

'The man who wounded you?'

His eyes darkened. 'I killed him.' Jaber looked away. 'I didn't want to tell you of this, when I had my suspicions. But I should have spoken up, warned you. Is the baby OK?'

'Fast asleep.'

'I have to sleep,' he said, apologetically. 'But call your parents, have them fly out here, first class, and anybody else you wish to be here. We will sign the *nikkah* the day after tomorrow.' He squeezed her hands. 'That is, if you still wish it?'

'I do,' Haya said, her heart full.

'And you will even give up your enterprise?'

'I will still own it,' she said, with a touch of stubbornness. 'But otherwise, yes, I can see that I must give up the day-to-day business.'

'Good.' Jaber sighed. 'That will certainly make things a little easier. He'll be pleased I persuaded you to do that.'

'He?'

'The King. He did not want me to marry you.'

Despite the desperate circumstances, Haya felt a moment of annoyance. 'Why not?'

'You are an American. And not a virgin—and there is already a child.'

Haya frowned. 'That's backward thinking, Jaber.'

'I know it.' He shrugged. 'But it is protocol. I have been trying to persuade the King for some months. It wasn't good to be seen with you.'

'And if you had not been able to persuade him?'

'Then we would have left Ghada.' Jaber looked into her eyes.

Haya was bold; she leaned forward and kissed him on the lips.

'You sleep,' she said, 'my love. I will make some calls.'

Jane Morgan tossed on her bed. It was blisteringly hot and muggy. Her apartment was a ten-million-dollar penthouse on Fifth, overlooking the museum, a real palace; triplex, with eight bedrooms and four bathrooms. All her own. And the air conditioning had broken down. She bet the air con was working just fine at Craig's place, in the Village.

Her body ached for him. Levin was like an addiction. She was struggling with her feelings. Trying, and failing, to give him up.

Craig wouldn't marry her. They had been together now for six months. Well, if you could call it together. Dating, and sleeping together, minus the sleep. Sex that was hotter than hell. His touch was certain, and inexorable. Levin turned her inside out. Jane would get aroused now, whenever she so much as read his name in the papers. She loved every moment she spent talking with him. They spoke the same language. Craig Levin made her laugh; he fascinated her, he was her mirror.

They were two halves, she sometimes thought. They could finish each other's sentences. He was as much her best friend as Sally or Haya had ever been.

Craig could always surprise her; he was thoughtful, imaginative; life with him was the perfect adventure. All Jane wanted in this world was for their love to go on for ever.

And yet. Craig would not marry her. He had not asked. Jane had followed him to New York—but GLAMOUR needed her. Proud, she had purchased her own, fabulous apartment. Levin shrugged, and kept his own town house in the Village, 4,000 square feet of Victorian brownstone. He would have this relationship on his own terms. Jane wanted it on hers. Not that she said anything explicit; she would not beg to be loved.

They both continued with their business. Jane worked like she never had before. Haya was sending excellent articles, and generating lots of goodwill; Jane traded on it expertly. Sally Lassiter was a superstar. Jane did not mind every time she saw Sally's golden prettiness beaming out at her from the cover of *In Style* or *Women's Wear Daily*. Jane had a different following: smaller articles, fewer pictures, but ones that mattered to her; her peers knew all about her. For the broker reading the *Wall Street Journal*, GLAMOUR was Jane Morgan. At a ridiculously young age, shaping up to be one of America's most notable businesswomen. There were others ahead of her, but Jane wanted to change all that. She didn't see her competition as Sally. She saw it as Craig Levin.

All her rage, all her frustration, she poured into her business. Expand. Invest. Supervise. As the GLAMOUR empire spread, Jane's plans got bigger. Turn it into the Wal-Mart of luxe. Own the sector. Maybe one day she could compete with Craig, on his own terms . . .

Sally was getting married. And her blithe, bubbly love of Chris Nelson grated on Jane. Whenever she saw Nelson on TV she had the opposite reaction to when she saw Craig. Anger. Because Chris was *marrying* Sally. He'd asked, she'd accepted, and it was to be like the old days—a party at Sally's former house, with 800 guests. Jane couldn't bear Craig to come with her. Couldn't bear 'So when is it *your* turn?'

She was rich, beautiful and a self-made woman, and yet she was a slave to love. Shamed to be so much Levin's, and know that he was not hers. And all Jane wanted to do was to cry out why—to ask him why he would not marry her. But there could only be one answer.

He didn't love her.

Craig liked her, cared for her, was best friends with her, desired her. Saw himself in her, as he told her again and again. But it must be that he did not *love* her. Not the way she loved him. That was it. Wasn't it?

Jane felt tears, private tears, wetting her cheeks, and let them fall; nobody could see her here. She was completely alone. Her cellphone rang. Jane blinked. It was three in the morning.

'Jane Morgan.'

A brief pause. 'I've woken you—I wanted to leave you a message. I'm sorry, I thought the phone would be off.'

'Hey, Haya. It's never off. But don't worry about that, I was awake anyway.' Jane dashed the tears off her face. 'What's up?'

'I know it's short notice, but could you get a flight to Ghada City tomorrow?'

Her stomach squeezed. 'Are you OK?'

A laugh. 'I'm fine. Actually . . . I'm getting married.'

Jane blinked again. 'Huh?'

'Well, it's the *nikkah* ceremony, there will be another formal wedding later, but once the *nikkah* happens, you are married. Just my parents, you and Craig, and Sally and Chris. If you can come.'

'Who is he?'

'Jaber. I think I might have mentioned him to you.'

'A little.' Jane shook her head disbelievingly. 'You mean *Prince* Jaber?'

'Yes. I didn't want to talk about it until I was certain.' Haya paused. 'There was some political stuff here.'

Jane ran the details through her mental processor. 'But Prince Jaber is the Foreign Minister of Ghada. How can you—'

'Jane, I can't,' Haya said, knowing what Jane was about to say. 'I can't. I have to retire—just from active management, of course,' she added hastily. 'But I've trained up some excellent people and the systems are in place . . . I've got to be a sleeping partner now. Devote myself to charity works and do-gooding,' she said self-deprecatingly.

Jane thought she might pass out. Emotions washed through her, one after the other, so strongly she could hardly believe it. Haya! A damn *princess*. Sally, in her way, American royalty. And she, Jane, rejected by the only man she would ever love.

'Sally and Chris will be there,' Haya went on, oblivious to Jane's torment. 'Can you and Craig make it?'

'I—no.' Her and Craig? He had a meeting in Stockholm tomorrow, the chances of cancelling it for a social trip to the Middle East were nil. And to go by herself? No way. 'We can't. I'm sorry, it's too short notice.' Her tone was cool, that practised formality she used against all pain. 'I'll come to the real wedding.'

'This is the real wedding.' Haya was a little distant now herself. 'But of course it is hugely short notice . . . we just want to be married.'

'I understand.' What woman in love didn't?

Jane thought for a few moments. 'If you are retiring from business, Haya, will you sell me your shares? I'll happily give you market price, or a premium, even.' There was silence. 'Haya? Are you still there?'

'Yes; no, thank you, Jane, I won't be selling. The business of GLAMOUR is key to Ghada and the region. I'll just be leaving day-to-day management to you and Sally.' Her tone now was as crisp as Jane's.

'I see—that's fine,' Jane lied. She was angry, now, though she couldn't immediately fathom why. But this was out of her control, the whole thing. Her business. Her life. She wondered if Haya would sell to Sally—those two had always been closer.

'Congratulations on your wedding, Haya, I'm sure you'll be extremely happy, and I'll come to the next ceremony. Can I send a gift to you?'

'Just donations to the Red Crescent,' Haya said.

How impersonal. Jane felt it as a rebuff. Was her friend already acting like a princess?

'I'll be glad to make a donation. A hundred thousand, first thing tomorrow.'

'That's very generous, Jane. Thank you. Good night, then.'

'Good night, Haya,' Jane replied, hanging up.

She crawled back into her bed, tears welling up again. Tomorrow she would go to see Craig, and once and for all she would finish it.

'I can't believe I'm doing this two days before the World Series.' Chris was still pissed off. 'It's as hot as balls out here.'

'Ssh,' Sally hissed angrily. 'You're here now. How many other royal weddings are you going to get invited to?'

He squeezed her arm. 'True, but you'll always be my princess.'

In front of them, Haya was bending over the scroll; she lowered her head and signed it.

Sally stared at her friend with something close to awe. She felt loss, too; envy, a touch of anger. With that signature, Haya, as she knew her, had gone. Vanished from the company. Surely vanished from their friendship. There she stood, robed head to toe in fluttering golden silks, a long caftan-like dress, studded with seed pearls and embroidered with crystals; there was some kind of headdress on her head, like a storybook princess, square, with delicate chiffon scarves of pale gold floating behind it. Haya did not look real to Sally. Her husband wore a traditional, embroidered coat, white satin, encrusted with diamonds.

The imam said something in Arabic. The assembled guards presented their guns in a salute, pointed them out at an angle, and fired. Chris instinctively moved to cover Sally, with his body.

'It's OK. It's ceremonial.' She was watching her friend. There were women in the same sort of robes, just less ornate. Sally guessed they were maids of honour. They moved forward, leaned closer and removed the square headdress from Haya and a round white cap from Jaber. Then the couple were led to two ornate chairs. As they passed the King, Chris bowed and Sally curtsied. The King said something to them, then they sat down in the chairs. Two soldiers stepped forward bearing white silk cushions.

'What's that?' Sally whispered.

Chris put his mouth next to her ear. 'Crowns,' he said. 'Little crowns.'

Open-mouthed, Sally watched as they placed the glittering circlets first on Jaber's head, then on Haya's; her tiara, all gold and icy white diamonds, glittered in the sun.

There was a burst of trumpets from the military guard; then Jaber and Haya stood, and processed back down the red carpet; Sally watched as everybody curtsied or bowed as Haya walked past them. Her parents' faces were a picture of ecstatic joy; as her daughter walked past, Mrs al-Yanna sank into a curtsy so low her knees practically scraped the ground.

The royal couple were approaching them now. Chris stood up straight; he smiled at Haya as she walked past. Sally, aware she was Haya's only invited friend, dipped into an awkward bob. Chris stared at her, amazed, annoyed.

'You're a damn American,' he said, taking care to keep his voice low. 'What the hell did you do that for?'

'We're the only Western guests without some kind of title, I wanted to show respect. Not let her down.'

He shrugged. 'I don't bend the knee to no man. Never thought to see you do it, either.'

'Another reason why I love you,' Sally said honestly.

She was jealous; it couldn't be denied. What all-American little girl didn't grow up wanting to be a princess? And Haya was a real one; nothing metaphorical about it.

The band struck up a Debussy waltz, and the ceremony was over. A uniformed officer from the palace approached them.

'Mr Nelson, Miss Lassiter? Her Royal Highness, Princess Haya al-Jaber, asks me to conduct you to the top table. May I take you to the Emira?'

'Why, certainly,' Sally said. What a moment. If her mom could see her now. If her *dad* could see her. Then it struck her, like lightning, that Haya would definitely not be coming back to GLAMOUR. What if she could take her shares?

'I would love to sit next to the Princess,' she said confidently.

The guards ushered Chris and Sally to their places, opposite Haya and Jaber. Jaber, deep in conversation with an emir to his right, nodded and smiled at them, but said nothing. Chris, in an attempt at good manners, introduced himself to his other neighbour, a plump woman with her hair in a bun set with jewels. She shrugged and responded to him in Arabic.

Chris exchanged annoyed glances with Sally. The thoughtlessness stung her; her fiancé couldn't have been found a place next to somebody who spoke English?

Desperately, Sally addressed Haya. Trying to get her onto a subject they both knew. 'So, Haya. You're quitting the company?'

'Day to day, yes. I'll be a sleeping partner. So, how are your wedding preparations coming?' Haya tried to change the subject—she didn't want all Jaber's relatives listening to her talk business on the day of her *nikkah*. His mother, Princess Aisha, was already looking her over with a narrowed glance of disapproval. Mentally she tried to signal to Sally.

'Just fine. Y'all will enjoy it,' Sally promised, smiling broadly at Jaber. 'It's going to be a lot like this, but different food. Hope you don't mind American!'

'Not in the least,' he said, with a broad smile.

'We'll get you cooking on the barbecue,' Chris Nelson promised the Prince. 'I make my own marinade. It's famous in the locker room.'

Haya died a thousand deaths.

'Haya.' Sally came right to the point. 'If you're going to do the Princess thing full time, you should let me buy you out.'

This was too much, really. On her wedding day.

'Funny, Jane asked me the same thing. I'm not selling. I'm surprised she didn't tell you that, Sally.'

Sally recoiled, shocked. *Jane* had asked to buy the shares? Didn't she already have enough, with all her stock deals on the side and her billionaire date? GLAMOUR was Sally's baby, all she had. Jane hadn't told her. Was she trying to force her out? Take the whole thing?

'But why? You know you don't need that company now.'

'Because it's mine,' Haya said.

Sally's eyes flashed. If Haya's thoughtless unconcern for her friends was bad enough, this was different. This selfishness was extending to Sally's life now. Haya was being a real dog in the manger about it. Didn't she *see* that pretty gold crown sitting on top of her head?

'And we won't talk business on my wedding day, if you don't mind.' Haya decided hinting was no good. 'That's not the custom here.'

Sally was angry; she'd moved heaven and earth to be there, taken Chris away on his two days' rest in the middle of the biggest event of his life, the World Series. And Haya—get a title, and suddenly her friend had turned into some kind of mega-snob.

Chris sensed her anger. 'Wanna split?' he whispered.

She shook her head. Haya, with a frown, had turned aside to speak to her father. 'I need Ghada for the company,' she whispered back.

There would be no scene. Sally made small talk with Chris, and sat through the first course of tabbouleh and the second of spiced beef. After that she gave her fiancé the smallest look; he cleared his throat.

'Haya, it's been great. But Sally and I are feeling kind of beat, and we have to get back to the airport—I can't skip practice tomorrow. Jaber, many congratulations. We wish you guys all the best.' He offered his arm to Sally, and she took it, thankful that she had a man who wasn't fazed by anyone or anything.

'Haya, congratulations to you both. It was a wonderful wedding,' Sally said, forcing herself to draw on her reserves of Southern politeness. 'Enjoy the rest of your special day.'

Haya blinked—they were actually *walking out* of her wedding, leaving two empty places at the top table, where the whole of the royal family were sitting.

'Have a safe flight,' she said, icy cold.

Sally nodded, gave her a brisk smile and left.

Tears of embarrassment and anger were prickling the eyes of both women.

Jaber leaned over, kissed his wife on the cheek.

'Not your fault,' he said. He turned aside and beckoned sharply, murmuring softly to one of his bodyguards; the man nodded, and within moments a sherif from the protocol office, and his wife, overjoyed at the honour, had been shown to the empty seats.

Chris waited while Sally packed her case—she was done in about five minutes—and arranged with the hotel for a limo to take them to the airport. He took charge, as Sally fumed; pulled out his credit card, and had them safely ensconced in a first-class seat on Royal Jordanian, winging their way home to New York. He was the first to speak. 'Don't let the Princess bother you, honey.'

Sally shook her blonde head. 'Ever since she first went out to Ghada she's been drifting away from us. So serious about her damn carpets and lamps. Made me feel bad about having a little fun.'

'But that's not it, is it?' Chris, like Sally, was sharp. He respected his girlfriend's mind. Sally had proved her intelligence to him a thousand times over. And right now he could see the wheels ticking.

'No.' Sally chewed her lip. 'She wouldn't sell me her shares. And she told me Jane already asked. Jane didn't tell me.'

'Did you tell Jane?'

'I only just decided to ask. Anyway, I would have done.' Sally wasn't a hundred per cent sure that was true; she glossed over it in her mind. 'The *point* is that neither of them are being fair. Haya's a princess now. What the hell does she need to hang on to GLAMOUR for? GLAMOUR is my deal.'

'And Jane?'

'Same thing. She doesn't care about the store, to her it's just a business deal. To her GLAMOUR could be a baked bean factory. She just wants the money. Why can't she get it trading shares? I *live* GLAMOUR, Chris. I do worldwide press for it twelve hours a day. I've got *fans*.'

'Starting with me,' he said.

'You know, those girls will always be my friends—I hope.' He didn't think she sounded certain. 'But I have to make sure that GLAMOUR is mine. When we get home I'm gonna find a way to take control.'

Jane checked herself out in the mirror. She looked good. She wanted to look good every time she dated Craig. For breaking up with him, though, she wanted to look perfect.

She switched on the TV. It was Sunday morning, no need to rush to his place before the morning coffee had brewed.

'Thanks, John. And now for a little light relief.' The co-anchor turned her head to the man on the couch. 'Did you hear this one, Ken. America has a new princess!' Jane stared as the TV cut to footage of a sumptuous marquee, in the desert; there in the middle, sitting on a damned throne, next to a handsome man in white, wearing a real crown, was Haya. 'That's Haya al-Amin, better known to America's women as one of the fashionable trio of ladies who run the GLAMOUR superstores. And now she's Her *Royal* Highness, Princess Haya of Ghada! Princess Haya grew up in LA and was the daughter of a local auto trader.'

'Hey, GLAMOUR by name, GLAMOUR by nature, I guess,' said the male anchor, turning a bland white smile to camera.

'Sally Lassiter, America's sweetheart, the *hottest* designer coast to coast, who founded the stores with the Princess, was in attendance with superstar fiancé Chris Nelson.' The screen flashed to a shot of Sally sitting next to Chris; he had her hand in his.

'Definitely the royal wedding of the year. Two amazing couples there. I expect this will bring even more shoppers through the GLAMOUR doors.' Jane waited for them to mention her. 'And now we jump to

Richard for the traffic. Rich? What you got for us?'

Bitter, Jane flicked her remote at the TV. It wasn't just the States; everywhere was like that. Part of a couple, glamorous, then you got attention. She was not as beautiful as her friends. She had no princely coronet, she didn't muck around with dress designs. Hers was the business of business. She was the one whose brain had come up with this store. She had financed it, single-handedly. At the cost of her heart. Who had found sites for twenty more stores? Who had bought the ad buys that Sally's pretty face featured in, in billboards across America?

Jane Morgan. De facto CEO—but on paper, sharing that title. Multimillionairess, sure, but sharing it with two friends who had ridden to the top on her coattails. She had done fine by her friends, she'd given them wealth and position beyond dreaming. It was time to take control for herself. Something to focus on. Something to get her mind off her inner pain.

She went into the kitchen and, mechanically, made herself a pot of coffee and toasted half a bagel. When she was done, she brushed her teeth again to lose the coffee breath, spritzed on a little scent, and headed for Craig Levin's house.

'Jane? That you?'

There were no staff at his place on Sunday mornings—Craig gave them the day off. And Jane had the code to his keypad entry gates. Another excellent reason to do this today.

'Take all your clothes off except your jacket,' he called from the bedroom, 'and your high heels, and come upstairs.'

Man. She loved that thick-throated, sexy voice. And she loved how he knew she was wearing a jacket.

'I'll be right there,' she shouted out, and went to the refrigerator. Craig's five chefs had prepared various things for breakfast. Jane selected the large, ice-cold jug of freshly squeezed orange and peach juice, poured out two tumblers, and took them up with her. He was lying sprawled under the Pratesi sheets on his designer Swedish sleigh bed; the sheets cut off, very sexily, at the thick line of hair right above the flat of his groin.

Jane wanted him instantly. She wished to hell she didn't have to do this. They could spend a normal day together, making love, eating a leisurely brunch somewhere, laughing together, having one of those talks that could last for five hours at a stretch and you always wanted more. Craig got under her skin and into her head, so many more ways than sexually. Man, how she loved him.

Jane took refuge in a long pull on the juice. 'Here's yours.' She handed him the tumbler.

'You're not naked,' he observed, taking it in. 'That's not good, honey.'

'Here,' she said abruptly. She opened her Chanel handbag and handed him two sets of keys. 'The spares to your place in Hollywood. And the flat in Rome.'

'I don't want to know what this is about, do I?'

Jane shook her head; she was already fighting down the tears. 'I'm finishing it. I love you, and you don't love me.' She forced a smile. 'Not a good position to make a trade.'

'I do love you,' Levin insisted. The 'but' hung in the air.

'You have what you want. Sex and friendship, no strings, no commitment. Why should you change that?'

Levin winced, just slightly; perhaps she was too near the knuckle, after all. 'I've never cheated on you, Jane. I gave them all up for you.'

'Your trouble is you want a gold medal for doing the right thing. You're an amazing man, Craig. You're brilliant; you're funny; you're driven; you're a dominant male.'

'Exactly what you're looking for,' he said, quite serious. 'Jane, if you make the perfect the enemy of the good, just because I'm not ready—'

'I told you,' she said. 'I love you. I can't give myself to you when you hold yourself apart from me. There's no reason not to get married, not to have kids. On some level, you're keeping your options open.'

'I'm just not ready,' he repeated.

'Unfortunately I am. So. This is it. I'm going to take over GLAMOUR. I want your ten per cent. Please give it to me.'

'Jane—'

'Don't. Just don't,' she said, crying in earnest now. 'I never tried to force you into anything, and I'm not now. Either you choose me or you choose your freedom.'

'I've never felt about anybody the way I feel about you.'

She flinched; the soft words hit her heart with a physical stab of loss. 'It isn't enough,' Jane said. 'Will you sell me your stock?'

'My broker will call tomorrow and sell them to you at market,' he said, a touch bitterly.

'Thank you.' She paused. 'Goodbye, Craig Levin. I love you.'

'I love you too,' he responded. Her heels were already clattering down the stairs.

Levin flopped back onto his bed; it was a sunny day, but his world had gone dark. Was she the kind of woman a man married? Everything that drew him to her shouted no. So hot, so strong, so driven.

Passionate and independent. Would she settle with him? Mother his children, look after them? He could not tell if Jane would ever stop looking, ever stop being hungry.

She said she wanted to be married. Levin thought that would ruin it. What if she did stop? Would he want her if she was there all the time, available, not having to be chased? Would he want her after a morning of picking out drapes or talking to some boring interior designer? He loved his freedom. And Jane was freedom. But he did not want to let her go.

Ruefully he stared at the ceiling. It was so, so like her. To confess her pain and love so matter-of-factly and then ask for his shares. At the one time he could not deny her.

She was moving on. She was tremendously impressive. Burying herself in work was exactly what he would do himself. God, how he loved her; they were partners.

Levin, a man's man, never cried. He tried to ignore the fact that as he rolled over onto his pillow, his eyes were wet.

Sally breathed in deeply. She couldn't take the tension. It was a bitterly cold autumn night in Boston, but nobody felt that. The electricity in this stadium could have powered the national grid.

Game seven. The World Series. Tie-breaker. This was it—win, or go home. Baseball's biggest prize. Every player on the field had been dreaming of this moment since he was knee high. For half of them, that lifelong dream was about to turn into a nightmare. Just to up the pressure, the game was in overtime.

It hadn't been Chris Nelson's finest hour. He'd scored a useless single in the third, got a walk in the seventh, apart from that he was oh-for-eight. This from a guy with a post-season average of .376.

Sally didn't need to have a radio with her to imagine what the commentators were telling America.

'He's exhausted.'

'What was Nelson thinking, spending two days off in the air?'

The guilt boiled up inside her. What the hell had she been thinking? Lost Chris his dream so that he could get snubbed in the desert, thousands of miles from here. The World Series was more than just one match. It was life. It was the ring you wore for ever. Lose it, and you might sink into despair. Would their relationship even survive?

She bit her knuckles. Every inning he failed to connect was a new chance the manager would pull him.

Leo Olsen—first up. Single. Thank God. Sally clapped wildly. Even if Chris couldn't do it, it wouldn't matter as long as the Dodgers won. His performance thus far would make him man of the series—even with a terrible last game.

Next, Rick Angelo. Swing and a miss. Ball. The crack of the bat, connecting—she could hardly look. No—no good! He popped it up, and the Boston shortstop caught it with ease.

Another Dodger came up to the plate—hit a flyout, just shy of that magic wall that would have added two runs to their total. That meant Chris was next.

Sally shut her eyes tight. Then she opened them. She couldn't miss this, she had to share his pain. That was her punishment.

And she thanked God she did, because a second later the in-ground cameraman found her and flashed her face up on the jumbotron screen, next to a still shot of Chris's face. The crowd booed. Sally wanted to shrink in her seat. As far as the fans were concerned, she was public enemy number one.

Then the cameraman found Chris, at the mound. He was listening to them booing Sally. His handsome, square-jawed face looked monumentally angry. The Dodgers fans shut the hell up. The Red Sox fans cheered even louder.

Holding his hand up to the pitcher, Chris turned round, looked up in Sally's general direction, and blew her a kiss. The knot in her stomach melted; his protection, his salute, was like a shot of hot buttered rum against the cold.

The umpire shouted something. The pitcher, eyes cold, wound up and swung forth with a deadly fastball—and Chris connected, not off pitch like the other two, dead in the middle of the bat. She could hear the crack in the stands. The ball was soaring, higher, deeper; Chris's bat had shattered, he flung it from him and raced to first base, Olsen was already at second . . .

But the ball wasn't stopping . . . It arced high, long, and into the stands at left field. Home run!

Sally blinked, hyperventilating. Home run! Two run home run! Olsen and Nelson raced round the bases. The Dodgers fans went nuts.

The jumbotron had fixed on Sally again. She waved, she smiled—she blew a kiss back down to Chris. The crowd went wild.

The fight trailed out of Boston. They gave up another run off a double and single before striking out the side. When the Dodgers closer, Ramiro Sanchez, came up to the plate, it was a foregone conclusion. Two strikeouts. And just to add a little sugar to the cake, Chris unerringly caught the final out; a pop-up direct to the shortstop. The Dodgers fans went completely crazy; Sally could not stop shrieking.

She raced down the stairs, down through the tunnels reserved for the players, and out onto the field; Chris was just being lowered to the grass by his teammates who had hoisted him around; he caught sight of her, ignored the forest of microphones shoved in his face, put his arms round the small of her back, and bent her into a slow, powerful kiss that had every housewife in America fanning herself.

'Don't you think you should sleep?' Sally asked, as they settled into the private jet, parked on the tarmac at Logan Airport.

They had just come from a riotous post-game dinner, yet Chris had refused more than a single glass of champagne, and had told Sally not to have anything either.

'I don't want you listed as my girlfriend for one more minute. This has been the most spectacular day of my life and I don't want it to end.'

'But going back to LA now—'

'We're not going to LA. We're going to Vegas. We're getting married. At the Bellagio. I have it all arranged.' He bent forward, kissed her lightly on the lips. 'I decided that in the seventh inning stretch, win or lose. Called the owner on my cell; this is his jet. Screw the party, we can do that too, but I want to elope. Just you and me. No damn guests. No protocol. It's the fairy-tale night, baby. Anything's possible.'

'Oh God!' Sally burst into tears. 'I love you, Chris!'

'Glad to hear that,' he said. 'I love you too, honey. And it's a good thing, because I have nothing else to do with myself now except make love to you and bring up the rugrats.'

She blinked. 'Why?'

'I'm quitting baseball. I'm at the top of the game.' He grinned. 'World Champ. Hit the winning homer. Caught the final out. You know what every last athlete does? They hang on, one more season. They wind up watching their stats slip, being booed off the field and playing in the minors.' He shook his head. 'Not for me. You be the star now, 'cause I'm looking forward to a long, anonymous retirement, as rich as Midas and getting laid every day.'

Sally wiped away the tears and started to laugh.

'Not gonna try to talk me out of it?'

'Hell no. I want to be Sally Nelson. And I want you there, not halfway round the country.'

She moved closer to him, feeling his warmth, slipping one hand inside his shirt; he was aroused, she could tell just by looking at him.

'No,' he growled, batting her away. 'Insatiable little minx. If I can wait, so can you.'

He'd done it perfectly: the honeymoon suite, an enormous bed covered with rose petals, white, her favourites; no tacky Elvis chapel, just a black-robed Justice of the Peace, with an off-duty cop as a witness.

After they were wed, Chris shook hands with the judge and the cop, then half shoved Sally into the nearest elevator. He rode it in silence to their suite and unlocked the door. Then in one strong motion, he swept her into his arms and hoisted her unceremoniously over his shoulder, head down, long hair streaming. He flung her down on the bed. 'Evening, Mrs Nelson,' Chris said, straddling her and pinning her down with a kiss.

Sally moaned; it was four in the morning, but she had never felt so alive. She reached down, fumbling, for the buttons of her shirt.

'No time,' he said, yanking down her jeans.

Eventually, three hours later, sweating in each other's arms, they surrendered to sleep as the sun came up over the desert.

They stayed in the honeymoon suite for three days, ordering room service, leaving only for a dip in the rooftop pool. Sally sent orders via the bellhop, and fresh clothes were delivered to the suite; they had packed nothing. It was pure bliss. Mona, once told, didn't even mind; Chris's uncle and aunt were mad, but managed to swallow it, especially when he reassured them the big wedding party was still on.

Finally, even Chris wanted to go home; it was fun being cheered every time he set foot outside his rooms, but even poolside they wanted his autograph. 'That eighty-acre plot in Beverly Hills is starting to look real good.'

'Told you,' Sally said smugly. 'And I want to get back to work. Jane Morgan's flying down for a meeting.' Sally looked at him out of the corner of her eye to check if he was annoyed, but Chris just shrugged.

'Like I said, knock yourself out. I'll be the one taking lengths in the pool. And lying on the couch with the remote.'

Sally beamed. He was the *perfect* man!

The GLAMOUR boardroom was a beautiful thing. Architect designed, in the new extension, it said that the company was owned by women. Sally had been meticulous. A long table and chairs, Scandinavian blond woods. Some of Haya's finest tapestries framed on the walls; a few select magazine covers—Sally on the cover of *Time*, Jane on the cover of *Fortune*. Fresh flowers, daily, just in case. Soft Aubusson carpets. The latest in audio/visual. And a terrific view of the Pacific from the huge windows, tinted against the sun.

Not that they needed all that space. Jane had insisted that nobody be there except Sally and herself. Sally wondered what Jane had to prove.

'I want to take the company public,' Jane said.

Damn, Sally thought. No chitchat. Jane meant business.

'Why? Financing?'

Jane nodded. 'We can go global. And we can still retain enough shares to have a controlling interest.'

Sally held her gaze. 'You asked Haya if you could buy her shares.'

Jane flushed. She had underestimated Sally, perhaps. But it didn't make any difference. What she was doing was just.

'She wouldn't sell them to me.'

'But why didn't you tell me?'

Jane's eyes narrowed. 'Did you ask her the same thing, Sally?'

Sally nodded slowly.

'For the same reason you didn't tell me, I suppose.' Jane gave a great sigh; she was glad, cards on the table. 'I know both of you have made a huge contribution, and I'd never force you out, and you're both rich. But GLAMOUR is mine. I'm at the stage where I want to control it. I think it would be best for me and the company, and you guys too. Haya can get on with being a princess, you can be a star. I'll take care of the dollars and cents.'

Sally was furious. What blatant contempt! 'Um, excuse me, Jane, but GLAMOUR is mine. *My* designs, *my* image. Being a star, as you put it, is what sells this store. I could get anybody to do the financials, any damn firm in New York. That's back-room stuff.'

There was a long pause. 'Don't let's fight over this.'

'I think that ship has sailed,' Sally responded.

Jane twisted her fingers. 'Do you have the other shares, then? Did Haya give them to you?'

'No. And I think she's being a total dog in the manger about it. She doesn't even want to stay involved. At least you and me both live it.'

Jane nodded, hugely relieved. There was still a chance, then. 'We can force her to go public. You and I, together, can vote for that with two-thirds of the shares. That way things are on the open market. If you can get control, good for you. You know I'm going to try to. I value our friendship, Sally, you know I do. But this is my life. You've got Chris, Haya's got a whole new life . . .'

'So what's Craig Levin? Chopped liver?'

Jane had to smile at the New York expression. 'My ex-boyfriend,' she said, simply. 'He sold me his shares.'

'Go*damn* you!' Sally shouted. 'You never even told me!'

'Same way you never told me after asking Haya. We both think our way is best. Let's not make this personal.'

'It's always been personal. GLAMOUR is me. Not some random brand.'

'If we go public, you have a chance to compete for those shares. So do I. I want to form my own company now, aimed at taking over GLAMOUR. Morgana, Inc.'

'I want to make Nelson a company, too,' Sally admitted to Jane. 'My own-brand cosmetics.'

'If we don't go public, it'll be eternal stalemate. You and I on each other's nerves. Both of us resenting Haya.'

Sally nodded. 'I'll call our lawyers and vote my stock with yours. So long as we have seats on the board and a controlling stake.'

'Of course. You want to tell Haya?'

Sally thought of the wedding, of Haya's haughty attitude. 'You do it.'

'You two fallen out?'

'We seem to have drifted apart a little.' Sally felt a pang; anger, relief, regret, she wasn't sure. 'Same as you and me. Same as all three of us.'

Jane was silent then, her dark head bowed. 'I'll make you a very generous offer for your shares, Sal. I can get the money. Then this wouldn't come between us.'

Sally stood up. 'At the end of the day we are friends, not sisters. Things happen. Life happens. I want GLAMOUR, Jane. I hope you get even richer any which way, but I want this store.'

Jane nodded sadly. 'I'll call Haya. And I'll be in touch. We should do it fast. I'm looking to float in six months. In the meantime, I can still work with you?'

Sally laughed. 'You kidding? I'll be tripling the promo. We want this to be the biggest launch ever. When GLAMOUR floats, I want it to be a global chain.'

Jane offered Sally her hand; after a second's hesitation, the blonde girl shook it. She gave Jane a knowing smile. 'I think you Brits might say, "May the best girl win".'

'It's beautiful,' Haya said. 'Thank you.'

She gave the little Moroccan girl a hug and a kiss. Her parents looked on, beaming, called down God's blessings on Her Royal Highness. Haya lifted up the picture, clumsily drawn in bright felt-tip pen, showing Haya standing beside a GLAMOUR store that resembled a large bazaar. Appropriate really, since that's what it was.

Salma was twelve but had Down's; the drawing was as garish as a five-year-old's. Salma grinned toothily, pleased with her hug and kiss. The special school was a new one in Casablanca. Haya was making a whistlestop tour of charitable schools in the region; she'd planned out a full schedule with Jaber, and started on it the day after their honeymoon.

'But you've got an event every day.' He shook his head.

'I can't sit on my hands,' Haya told him. 'If I'm going to do the charity thing, I want to *do* it. Full time. Use the title, use the position. Noor will come with me. And they're mostly in Ghada, I'll only be apart from you a couple of weeks a year, at most.'

'And when our children come, *inshallah*?'

'Then I'll stick to Ghada. But hey, princesses here travel in style,' Haya teased him. She wondered if she'd ever get used to it, the enormous limos, the outriders, the crazy jewels and exquisite robes. 'Up until the end of the pregnancy, it shouldn't be a problem at all.'

'If it happens, you'll travel with the royal physician.'

'Well, yes, sir.' Haya kissed him on the lips.

Haya grinned, remembering. Today was her last day in North Africa and the royal flight would be taking her home tomorrow. She hated to be away from Jaber.

Her aide, a Miss Aisha al-Akhtam, was giving her that discreet wave. Haya stood up, gave an enthusiastic little speech about the wonderful work being done at the school, shook hands with the bowing and curtsying staff, and allowed herself to be escorted out by her bodyguards.

'Ma'am. We must get you to a secure place.'

'There's trouble?' Haya demanded, instantly alert. She beckoned to Emily to come over with Noor, who was already half asleep.

'Yes—no—please get into the car, *Siti* Haya.'

She obeyed. But as soon as they were safely heading to the airport, Haya demanded Aisha tell her what the problem was.

'His Majesty is gravely ill.'

'The King? Poor man, God spare him! Where is my husband?'

'The Prince asks you to come home at once. He says things are happening and you must be there. Your appointments for this afternoon have been cancelled.'

'Is there any danger?'

'No, Highness.'

'Then let's get going,' Haya said.

'And one more thing, your friend rang from the United States. Miss Morgan. She said it was important.'

'That can wait.'

Aisha nodded. 'She said if you said that, to tell you they are selling the company.'

Adrenaline poured through Haya; she felt the soft hairs on the back of her neck start to prickle and rise. 'Get me on that airplane!' she said to her driver.

Chapter Fifteen

WHILE NOOR WAS SETTLED, eating her lunch of puréed fruit and soft cheese, Haya retreated into her private cabin to call from the Skyphone. They had in-flight TV, and although the national station was censored, she could pick up what was going on; the King, suddenly ill with a stroke, and now recovered, was tinkering with the succession. His eldest son had long been exiled; the younger brother was a playboy, and was apparently being removed. That meant it was wide open. He had five other boys, a half-brother and a vast array of cousins.

Would the new Crown Prince favour Jaber? Would he be finished as Foreign Minister? Almost certainly. A new administration would put its own man in . . .

She wanted to get back there, to be with her husband. When she got through to him, he was calm. Talked about the King's health and said it was all in God's hands; Haya thought the palace lines might be bugged; if he was anxious, he wouldn't discuss things over the phone.

That left Jane. Haya wanted this nonsense out of the way, and fast. She dialled the number Jane had left.

'Morgana, Inc. How may I direct your call?'

'I'm sorry, I was looking for GLAMOUR,' Haya said, confused.

'Were you looking for Miz Morgan, ma'am? This is her new company. Any queries about the stores can go directly to her office. Who shall I say is calling?'

Haya felt an icy chill. What the *hell*? 'This is Haya al-Jaber,' she said, angrily. 'Put me through to her at once.'

'Yes, certainly, Your Royal Highness.' Haya was impressed; typical Jane to hire the best staff. Even the operators were capable of putting two and two together. 'One moment, ma'am.'

There was a pause, and Jane came on directly. Haya supposed she should be grateful for not being put on hold.

'Haya?'

'I got some crazy message, and believe me, Jane, this isn't the time,' Haya said crisply. 'We're not doing anything dramatic with GLAMOUR right now. My husband—'

'Yes, it's on the news. I know you'll want to focus on him, Haya.'

'If that's another pitch for my shares . . .'

'Not directly. Look, I've known you too long to soft-soap it, and I can see you have your hands full, so here goes. Sally and I are determined to take GLAMOUR public. We're holding a board meeting on Monday, and this is your notification. You don't need to be there, because we form a quorum without you, and we are going to instruct banks to put the company on the market.'

Haya gasped. 'You wouldn't.'

'It has to be, Haya. We all have different visions.' Jane sounded slightly wistful, but she was ploughing on. 'Both Sally and I want to own the company, and the only way out of the stalemate is to float the shares. We'll be holding back enough of a personal stake to make sure the three of us still sit on the board—if you want to.'

'Damn right I do!' Haya was shouting, and she didn't care who heard her. 'Are you two using this crisis to shove me out of the picture? I'm the *soul* of our store. I provide half the stock and ninety per cent of the vision. Without me you wouldn't bother with one ethical sale—'

'When you're a public company, ethical is making money for the pension funds who own your shares.'

'But we're not public!'

'We're going to be.' Jane was clearly amused by Haya's claim, and that drove her to a white-hot fury. 'It seems all three of us think we made the biggest contribution here.'

'So much for friendship.'

'We could argue that since you are now a royal with no intention of working again, you would have been a friend to sell your shares to Sally and me. It's a bit selfish, Haya.'

'I could never trust anybody else with my regional operation. You know how much sweat I put into that thing?'

'Haya, face it.' Jane was blunt. 'You're done. You're finished. You could at least let your co-founders run with the ball.'

'We'll see if I'm finished,' Haya shouted. 'I don't want to be just somebody's wife. Ahmed had his business and Jaber has his politics, but GLAMOUR was my thing. My store, my stock, my damn business model!' She was enraged. 'Have you forgotten who suggested the idea of this store in the first place? It was me! I'll be there on Monday, Jane Morgan. And if you start that meeting without me I'll sue your asses off!'

She slammed down the phone and jumped to her feet, seething.

There was an urgent knock on the door, and Aisha, her face shiny with excitement, poked her head inside. 'Highness!'

'Did I say come in?' Haya was simmering with rage, and her unfortunate aide was in the line of fire.

'Excuse me, Highness!' Aisha said. She bowed her head low, and sank into a very deep curtsy, which brought Haya up short. Except in public, Aisha never curtsied. 'But you must come in here, you must come and see the television!'

Haya hurried out into the main cabin. Everybody was staring at the TV, which was tuned in to CNN via satellite; as she entered, they all turned to look at her. The screen showed her husband, dressed in a dark Western suit, sunglasses on, surrounded by soldiers, exiting from the Queen Fizouleh hospital in Ghada City; Haya's mouth dropped open as she saw the caption scrolling across the bottom of the screen.

'And regional sources confirm, I repeat, we have confirmation,' the red-headed anchor was saying, 'that King Nazir has appointed Prince Jaber Ibn Mohammed, as the new Crown Prince of Ghada. Prince Jaber's wife is Princess Haya'—her own face, an old PR shot, flashed up—'an American citizen and a founder of the wildly successful GLAMOUR chain of luxury stores. So we could wind up with two American queens in the Middle East, Jack!'

'Prince Jaber is known for his moderate attitude towards the West and a strong commitment to social justice and democracy,' the co-anchor said. 'But Ghadan officials were keen to stress that the King's health remains good . . .'

Haya steadied herself against a seat.

'Turn it off,' she said quietly.

A soldier leapt to obey her.

'We will all pray for the health of the King,' she added. And as they were staring at her, she covered her face and turned towards Mecca. Oh God . . . please spare him!

If her life was to shift again, in this cataclysmic way, the palace would definitely want her to stay the hell out of the boardroom. Haya did not care. Jane and Sally would be counting on that. But the one thing Haya was damn sure of was that she was going to save her company. She hoped Jaber would understand why it mattered. But come hell or high water, Sunday night she was getting on a plane to LA.

'Great doing business with you.' Rose Rothstein of J.R. Realty shook hands briskly with Jane. 'I think you'll be very happy. If we can assist you with anything more, get in touch.'

'I will. Thanks.'

Jane walked round her new offices. Great views of lower Broadway, looking up to the World Trade Center; perfect for a Wall Street new-comer. Jane would employ fifteen brokers, two analysts and fifteen assistants. As she expanded, she hoped it'd be more.

Maybe she could never be another Craig Levin, but she was sure as hell going to try. Until GLAMOUR was hers, that meant trading in cur-rencies and stocks; Jane intended to take buy-and-hold positions, maybe start a retail hedge fund. Plus, she thought she might dabble in real estate. Buying and leasing sites for the stores had taught her about commercial property. To persuade stockholders to sell their GLAMOUR shares to her, she needed to be playing in the mixed divisions.

The thought of Haya, shouting and raging, crossed her mind; of Sally, telling her any broker could handle the finances. And of Craig, lying there, not stopping her, not holding her. Her father; the last time she had seen him, clutching ineffectually at him as he got into his diplomatic car. Friends. Lovers. Family. In the end, you could trust only yourself.

Let Monday come. When she sat down in that boardroom, her offices would be trading. Time to get her hair and nails done. The press would be there, Monday. Haya was an almost-queen, and Sally was a star. She, the single girl, didn't want to look bad.

Sally glanced down at the little stick. She'd had the pregnancy test included in her grocery deliveries; that way it could be anonymous. The little blue flush crept up to the window. Sally held her breath . . . No; there was only the one line. She waited. Nothing. Not pregnant. She sighed. It wasn't gonna happen right away. She was just gonna have to be patient. And practise a lot.

Before, it had been good. Now they were married, it was perfect. Every time she looked down at the thick band of white diamonds, Sally felt a rush of profound pleasure. He was hers—signed, sealed, deliv-ered. She relaxed in bed in a way she hadn't thought possible. All she wanted now was to have his babies . . .

And to run her company.

Hey. This wasn't a once-and-for-all thing, she consoled herself as she looked at the single, lonely little line. They got an infinite number of attempts. With GLAMOUR, not so much. Sally went downstairs to call her lawyers again. She might not be the world's biggest brain, but she was smart. And there were brains around for hire. She was her daddy's daughter to this day. Let Haya and Jane pit their bookish minds against her street smarts. Sally knew who was going to win.

Jaber sighed with pleasure and rolled off Haya, panting; drained, he lay on the bed and stared at the mosaics in the ceiling.

She was exhausted herself. But man, was he good. Patient, exacting, knowledgeable . . . Jaber applied all his considerable intelligence to manipulating her body.

'I couldn't handle this without you. None of it.'

'You couldn't have refused?' Haya asked timidly.

'Refused?' Jaber propped himself up on his elbows and stared down at her, her dark hair pooled out over the white Egyptian cotton sheets. 'You can't refuse your destiny when it calls. That way lies eternal regret.'

She nuzzled kisses into his ear and throat. 'Which is exactly why I have to go.'

'Haya.' He sighed. 'The King could die while you're out there. You would be the Queen of Ghada, and sitting in some boardroom in Los Angeles! How would it look?'

'Like you aren't a man who compromises his principles,' she said. 'You took a risk when you married me, Jaber. You know what I am—a businesswoman. Yes, I set it aside. But not so that they can destroy everything I've built up. Let me save the company. One day. It's all I ask.'

He shook his head. 'Haya, I cannot deny you. But make it as quick as you can, and be back on the jet the second you get out of there.' Jaber shrugged. 'I should have married that distant cousin.' He reached for his wife, kissing her lightly, deliberately. 'I'm going to give you a chance to make it up to me.'

'The press is coming,' Sally told Jane, bluntly. 'They got word of what we're doing—and the fight.'

'You told them?'

'No,' Sally replied coldly. 'There are three sets of lawyers' offices involved now, Jane.'

Jane pursed her lips. Damnation. 'Then I suppose the answer is dress well and act civilly. If the analysts think we're at each other's throats, the Initial Public Offering will be disappointing. They need to understand we remain a team—you and I, at least.'

'Agreed. See you Monday,' Sally said crisply, and hung up.

Jane slowly replaced the receiver. She had no doubt that Monday afternoon, she would be making the deals with institutions that would give her control. So why did she feel so down? Her phone rang again, and Jane jumped. The concierge was calling. 'Miz Morgan, we got a delivery here. Boy, do we ever.' The fat old man was chuckling. 'Flowers, from Mr Levin.'

She shivered. Hadn't she been clear? She wanted a clean break.

'You can bring them up.'

'No, ma'am, I can't. But the delivery men will.'

'What do you mean?'

'He sent you flowers—like, a *truck*load. There has to be about a hundred arrangements. In pots. There's even a flowering orange tree. Smells pretty good down here, ma'am.'

'Is the truck still there?'

'Unloading now.'

'Ortiz, refuse delivery, OK? I don't want them. Tell the men to take them back.'

There was a pause, but he knew not to argue with her. 'Yes, ma'am. Any message?'

She thought about it. 'Yes. Tell him "All or nothing".'

She replaced the receiver again and fled into her rooftop garden. Somewhere with no phone, where she could lie on a recliner, by her Japanese fountain, look at the sky and have a little peace.

My heart can't take this, Jane thought. I know they all think I'm made of stone. But it hurts to love him so deeply.

She decided she would check into a hotel, the Victrix on Central Park. Nice and anonymous, no incoming calls. She'd stay there until the flight left on Monday. Craig would get the message. And perhaps her rebellious heart would get the message, too. Grief is there so you can move on.

Craig Levin sat in front of his desk and tried to concentrate. Last night he'd dated a model. Very smart girl, Israeli, dark and doe-eyed, a pre-med student before she quit for the catwalk. Just a date; just dinner. Even though she was obviously willing, he'd stopped at dinner; feeling sick, feeling like he was cheating on Jane. Dumb. They'd broken up.

He spent a poor night thinking of his ex. Angry with her. Why had she taken the hottest thing in his life, the best thing, and messed with it? Stupid, conventional notions of love. He *did* love her—passionately. What the hell difference did a ring make?

Lots of folks had told Levin it was their way or the highway. He'd never failed to take the highway, and it had worked out well enough.

Not this time. He knew Jane, though. He knew every inch of her, just how she was pining for him.

What was he thinking? He had got Jane in the first place with patient months of waiting, letting her longing do the work. Now he had to get her back. He lifted the phone and called the all-night florist, delivery first thing in the morning.

Just now, his chief assistant had called with the news. And Jane's message. So classy. She was everything the model hadn't been. Levin felt himself start to surrender. For once in their relationship, he thought, she was going to triumph. He called her building.

'She's gone, Mr Levin,' Ortiz told him, with, Craig thought, a touch of pride. 'She said to tell you to stop chasing her. She won't be back until after her meeting, and she doesn't want you to call even then.'

He hung up as his assistant buzzed. 'Craig, your nine a.m. from Bank of America's in the outer lobby and the nine twenty from KKR are waiting in reception . . .'

'Emily, apologise to them, cancel all my appointments. For the week.'

'Are you feeling OK, Craig?'

'No. I'm sick. And I'm going home. Tell Peter to deal with everything.' His deputy in the firm. 'And don't call me.'

He called one of his personal PAs, back at the house. 'Claudette, send the limo to the office. We're going to JFK. I want to be on the first flight to LA. Call the people at the Hollywood house and get it ready.'

He had no idea what he was going to say to Jane, but he was going to see her. She'd be in LA on Monday, going to attend that meeting at GLAMOUR. And Craig Levin was gonna be waiting.

By Thursday, the story had broken. It was ugly; a blood bath. The *Wall Street Journal* said it all: the single-word headline was CATFIGHT.

Haya—the Yank princess. Anita Roddick, or an obsessive putting her cash before her country?

Jane—a workaholic boss from hell. Loner, antisocial, not a feminine bone in her body. A fluky career, too young, no real track record . . .

Sally—business Barbie, or brainless bimbo? The dull grey suits in the business press had been waiting to tear her down. Good to design clothes and get her picture taken—hardly the stuff of corporate governance.

Put together, the news hacks reluctantly concluded, these women had something. But after explosive growth and more cash than most male CEOs made in a lifetime, they were at each other's throats. When GLAMOUR went public, it would be a great opportunity for some *true* retailers to come swooping in. On Monday, the shares were out there for the grabbing. It was time, the consensus said, for the market to clean up the mess. There was a little speculation as to which shark could mop up most of Jane Morgan's shares first. Surely she'd be most easily elbowed aside. Her expertise could be replicated.

But what about Haya? Ethical business? Even The Body Shop sold out to L'Oréal, they sneered. On the other hand, what if Crown Prince Jaber used his personal fortune to hoover up the shares before US brokers could get to him? Nobody could compete with that kind of firepower.

And Sally? That was different. America loved her. Brand gold. The male writers agreed she'd have to be placated. The new corporate owners should pay her a very handsome premium, give her a non-exec directorship, anything to keep her there.

Whatever, it would be interesting. The shares went on sale right after the meeting; 10 a.m., Pacific time. Of course, they'd all be rich: but one, or all, of these women would find their dream had been ruined.

'The Embassy is on the phone, Your Royal Highness.'

Jaber frowned. He did not need to ask which embassy. This was the third call this morning. His Excellency began with the usual formalities, then got down to business.

'The Princess cannot come, sir.'

'Haven't we had this conversation, Ambassador Rashman?'

'Yes, but Your Royal Highness has not seen the press.'

'Indeed I have,' he said heavily. 'Her Royal Highness has decided to make the trip. That's all there is to it. You may send along a special adviser to accompany her.'

'But—'

'If I find the Princess has been interfered with, you will be replaced within twenty-four hours. While His Majesty is sick, I am regent. Not to put too fine a point on it,' Jaber smiled thinly, 'my word is law. Do I make myself clear?'

He heard the official swallowing. 'The Princess's wish stands. Please do forgive my—'

'Goodbye, Excellency,' Jaber said firmly. He hung up.

Haya was standing there, in the archway to his private apartments.

'Excuse me—I heard most of that.'

'I hope you know what you're doing,' he said heavily.

'When I go, I will go as a princess. I will wear the circlet. They will see a modern woman of Ghada who bears herself with dignity.'

'Hurry back,' he said.

Jane wanted to be sick. Her hands shook when she read those papers. They were saying Sally was right. That anybody could manage the finances. That once they went public, she would be replaced.

She had to perform at that meeting, to give the performance of her life. The only way to survive was to get her hands on one of the other girls' shares.

She wondered how Craig Levin, financial genius, would handle it, and then hated herself for her need. No, damn it. There was no white knight ready to ride and save her this time. Craig had been there at the start. At the end, it was going to be up to her.

Sally stepped out of the shower and reached for a robe. She had these brought in from GLAMOUR, and they were the fluffiest things this side of the Regent Beverly Wilshire hotel. Perfect, in fact, for moments like this, when she barely had the energy to towel herself off.

Chris was out at the ballpark, playing catch with a bunch of disabled kids. She was so proud of him; the only work he did these days was for charity. She hadn't complained to Chris. This fight was her deal, no need to involve her husband. Pay her off? Bribe her with a salary? Those male writers thought she was the bimbo, but they'd somehow failed to see that when GLAMOUR went public, forget it, she'd be able to buy her own country. She didn't want money. Didn't they get that? It was all about control, self-esteem.

Right now, she was gonna take care of herself. Go sit on the terrace, and watch the sun set over that big lawn where the tents had been pitched for her party, all those years ago. Jane Morgan's social debut. Sally found herself sighing, with nostalgia, and regret.

She glanced behind her at the long, spiralling staircase. The three of them had walked down that staircase, together, beautiful, sixteen years old and with the world at their feet. At Sally's feet, anyway; she had spread the blanket of her popularity across them for protection; that dazzling night, it had worked. Maybe those things didn't count for much now. Maybe it was time to put the past behind her. Jane and Haya evidently had.

She was walking out of the door when something caught her eye. There, in the bathroom bin. The little stick she had tossed. No *way*. But yes—there was something different about it, something half covered with a tissue, that had caught her peripheral vision. Sally picked it up. She hadn't waited the full three minutes. There was a second line. Faint, but distinct. She reached out and steadied herself against the wall of her walk-in marble wet room. She was pregnant.

Chapter Sixteen

THERE WAS NO SOCIALISING. No small talk. They shook hands; their lawyers shook hands. Nobody curtsied to Haya; she had not been expecting it.

'The meeting will come to order,' Jane said loudly. The lawyers shut up. When Jane Morgan spoke, people listened. 'We're here to sign off on the exact terms of the IPO. I take it you all have the documents?'

Haya raised her hand. 'Madam Chairman, if I may?'

Jane sat down immediately.

'Of course, Your Royal Highness,' she said, with studied politeness.

'The company has aggressively pursued ethical commerce, my focus as a director. What guarantees can you give me this will continue?'

'I can't. A public company can make no such arrangements.'

'That's unacceptable,' Haya said instantly. 'We made commitments, and I intend to honour your word.'

That stung.

'May I say something?'

'Mrs Nelson has the floor,' Jane said crisply.

'My lawyers have discovered that Lassiter make-up and Lassiter designed clothes accounted for twenty-five per cent of total merchandise sales. Further to this, we estimate that at least a third of the goodwill value of the chain comes from my personal image.'

Jane inclined her head. 'I think you'll find that my figures for the total real estate, staffing, distribution, funding, inventory management, analyst presentations and general costs come to over fifty per cent of the total value of this company.'

There was a long silence. The three women round the table glared at each other.

'Well, ladies.' Kent Green, the head of Sally's lawyers, spoke up. 'Perhaps it's time to let the professionals take over, otherwise this meeting could go on all day. And we *do* have a deadline.'

'Just a second.' Sally spoke up. 'I'd like y'all to give us the room, please. I want to speak to my partners alone.'

'I don't think that's wise, Sally,' Kent said paternalistically.

'I can't allow Her Royal Highness to be unrepresented in the room,' piped up Ahmed al-Jamir, the special adviser.

'I won't let my client go to bat by herself.' Jane's lawyer, Rachel Frohman, spoke authoritatively. 'Sorry, Miz Nelson, but we're staying.'

Jane was looking over at Sally; then she glanced at Haya. 'No, you're not. Give me the room, please, Rachel.'

'But Miz Morgan—'

'Now, please.'

'Mr al-Jamir, you too.' Haya nodded at the diplomat.

There was a creak and a shift, and with great reluctance the small army of lawyers, advisers and accountants left the room. As soon as the door shut, Sally smiled. 'Girls, what the hell are we doing?' she said.

'What we have to,' Jane replied, with a heavy heart.

'Bull*shit*, girlfriend. We're doing what we think we have to. Nobody wants to be here.' Sally looked at her two friends—determined they would stay that way. 'Y'all want to know what happened to me today? I found out I was pregnant.'

Haya beamed. 'Get out of here, Sally!'

'Really.' She shook her head, tears in her eyes. 'You guys remember that day in the playground, the first day Haya turned up? I figured we'd look out for her. Why? Because I was pretty and Jane was smart. We filled the gaps with each other. Don't see why we still can't do that.'

'But GLAMOUR is everything we've worked for,' Jane said. 'It's everything I am.'

'The hell it is. You were doing just fine before we started. And you'll do great after this. I want the company. We all do.' Sally passed one hand over her belly. 'I've started *Sally* make-up. Jane's got Morgana now. Haya, looks like that crown you're wearing's gonna get a bit bigger, no? *This is just a store.*'

Jane jumped up from the table and went to the window; not before they saw the tears streaming down her face. She had lost Craig. And now she would lose these two? 'You're a hundred per cent right.' She turned round. 'But we have different ideas. This store is special. Let's not let men chew it up. Let's just decide who's going to run it.'

Haya said, 'I owe you both an apology. I haven't talked enough to you.' She blushed richly. 'Sally, I dumped you at my wedding without bothering to explain a damn thing. I'm sorry.'

'Me too, Haya.' Sally came over and gave her a hug. Haya stood up and went and rubbed Jane's back.

'You guys will guarantee the livelihoods of all the poor women supplying us, right?'

Sally and Jane both nodded.

'Then you can have my shares. Fifty-fifty. I'll give the money to charity.' As soon as she said it, a smile broke out on her face; something lifted, almost physically, from her heart. 'What a relief,' she said. 'It's been great, you know? But nobody needs this kind of pressure.' Haya cocked her head, looked at Sally. 'If you want my two cents, let Jane have it. She's been the most driven of all of us.'

Sally exhaled, then shrugged. 'Yes. All right, then. Jane.'

'No.' Jane rubbed the tears away. Like Haya, she was smiling. 'All these years, I've been fighting the fact I had nobody to love me. No father, no mother. But that was wrong. I had you two. I just couldn't see it.' She paused. 'I have succeeded in everything I've done. Why does it have to be the thing I started out in? Maybe I'll go into real estate. It hardly matters. But GLAMOUR is special. There can only be one choice. It's you, Sally. You who looked after both of us. You who taught us how to use being beautiful. There are a lot of sceptics out there, a lot of analysts sneering. But street smarts count for a lot in this world. You take it, and you show them all that being a woman isn't some kind of choice between beauty and brains.' She grinned. 'Besides, I want to trade stocks. I could use all that liquid cash.'

Sally could hardly believe it. She clapped her hands, like a kid at a birthday party. 'Really? It's mine?'

'It's all yours,' Jane replied, and shook her hand.

The three girls came together and gave each other a hug.

'Shall we let them back in?' Haya asked, with a wink. 'There are gonna be some pretty sad lawyers. All those billable hours, down the drain.'

'Let's.' Jane chuckled. 'Can't wait to see the press when we announce this. What are they going to say now?'

Sally nodded, and Jane flung open the doors. The large knot of eavesdroppers raced back in and sat round the table.

'Don't get comfortable,' Jane said. 'The deal's off. No public stock.'

There was uproar.

'We have arranged a private sale. Ladies and gentlemen, I give you the new Chairman and CEO of GLAMOUR. Ms Sally Nelson.'

Jane got up from the head of the table and surrendered her position to her friend; as she went and sat at Sally's seat, she felt no pain; just an open sense of joy and possibility. The future was hers; no limits, no ties. She looked across at Haya, and saw that she felt the same way.

Sally shook out her hair in a shimmer of gold, leaned back in her chair, and glanced over the table full of dumbstruck advisers.

'I'm in charge, gentlemen,' she said. 'So let's get to work.'

Epilogue

KING NAZIR DIED a day after Haya touched down in Ghada City. Jaber led the mourning, and Haya found herself Queen, mingling with royalty and heads of state at the funeral. A week later, just before the coronation, she discovered she, too, was pregnant. Haya never let a day go past without visiting some charity, and the people loved her. She founded girls' schools across the kingdom, and worked with Jaber as a full partner on drawing up new laws to promote democracy. She and Noor were often seen dropping in to the new GLAMOUR being built in Ghada City, the hottest store in the country.

Sally continued work up until one day before her wedding party, the social event of the year, and two days before she gave birth. Queen Haya attended the wedding, and was Sally's matron of honour; Jane preferred to sit quietly in the front row. But at the birth, Jane was there, holding Sally's hand as Chris Junior came shrieking into the world. His dad, the toughest guy in sports, had refused to come in and watch Sally moaning in pain he could do nothing to spare her from. Sally took two months off. When she came back, she instituted flexible working and staffed crèches at every GLAMOUR store around the world. Women loved it, and the global sales soared.

'See? It's always the good guys who finish first,' Haya told her friend.

Jane Morgan had believed that. She left the meeting at GLAMOUR smiling. She posed for pictures with Haya and Sally, Sally in the middle, the boss, the winner, and Jane didn't mind at all. She had other things to think about. Like starting over. And mending her heart. When the press finally melted away, Jane headed back to her limo and sighed a deep sigh of release.

'LAX, please.'

The driver tipped his cap. 'Yes, ma'am.'

She checked in, in no particular hurry. First class meant you could take the first flight that became available.

'I'm afraid we only have seat 1B available, miss. Is that OK for you?'

'That's fine,' said Jane, even though she usually chose her own seat.

'Great,' said the flight attendant, glancing at her colleague. 'Then you're all set. Have a great flight.'

When she boarded, Jane looked around the first-class cabin; it was empty. 'I was told there was only seat 1B.'

'Yes, ma'am, all these seats are booked. Can I show you to your . . .'

But Jane was already marching up the cabin. They were going to be really late, all these last-minute boarders. But she wouldn't let something like that spoil her mood. At least there was one passenger—the back of a man's head in seat 1A. So much for a peaceful flight. Jane grabbed her case and lifted it.

'Let me get that,' he said, standing and walking into the aisle.

Jane gasped; it was Craig Levin. He took it from her, just like that first day, and hoisted it easily into the overhead rack. 'I'm not sitting here,' she said, looking wildly around for the stewardess. But the woman had melted away, smiling discreetly.

'You are if you want to fly in this cabin. There are no more seats. I bought all of them.'

Jane blinked. 'What? You bought an entire first-class cabin?'

'Just so you had to sit next to me. I think you'll agree that a gesture like that is worthy of respect, at least. Sit down.'

She sat. He leaned over and kissed her softly on the lips.

'I saw what you did today. That was brave, Jane. That was good.'

'She's right for it.'

'And you're right for me,' he said. 'I want to see if I can soften you up a little more.' Jane stared as he reached into his pocket and drew out a ring case. He flipped it open, showed her the small circlet of gold, set with emeralds. 'It was my mother's.' He took her trembling hand, and gently slipped the ring onto it. 'It's a simple fact; you were made to be my woman. I can't sleep without you. And the thought of another man so much as touching you is more than I can bear. So there's only one way to get you to myself. Pre-emptive strike.' Levin kissed her again, much harder, wanting her urgently, hating that they had to wait five hours.

'That's a hell of a proposal.'

'I'm not asking you. I'm claiming you. You're my woman. My wife.'

'Yes,' she said, melting with happiness, and lust, and the sheer exhilaration of it. 'Your wife.'

They kissed, hard; then slower; then his arms snaked around her.

'Damn,' Jane said, grinning, when she came up for air. 'This is going to be fun.'

Louise Bagshawe

For many women, being a wife and mother is all that they wish for in life. Very few wives and mothers also become best-selling authors. Louise Bagshawe is both wife, mother to two children under four and expecting her third child in July, best-selling novelist *and* is now also a prospective Conservative Party candidate.

So what makes Louise so ambitious, so driven? 'I want to change things. I'm tired of sitting around and talking about it. I believe that I can make a positive difference to people's lives and I am absolutely delighted to have been chosen to stand for Corby and East Northamptonshire in the next General Election—as long as there's time to have this baby first. Motherhood, politics and writing are three very important elements in my life.'

If anyone can make a difference, Louise can. She may be only thirty-five years old but she has a wealth of experience behind her. Educated at Oxford University, she was the Young Poet of the Year in 1989 and a former President of the Oxford University Rock Society. Her love of music drew her into the record business, but at only twenty-three she decided that it was not the industry she wanted to be in and so she quit to write her first novel, *Career Girls*, and, eleven best-selling novels later, has never looked back. Her writing took her to live in America, where she met and married her husband, Anthony. 'I lived in Los Angeles and New York, but it never felt like home, even though I was there for nearly six years. England was always home; my family was here and I always wanted to come back when the time was right.' Eventually Louise persuaded her husband to move to England and they bought a house in East Sussex.

Louise had joined the Conservative Party at the age of fourteen, becoming an activist in 1997, and once she had settled the family in Sussex, she began the lengthy, rigorous process to be adopted as a prospective Conservative candidate.

'Since being elected to stand for Corby, I have been commuting to Northamptonshire a couple of times a week. I'm very lucky that Anthony works from home—he rents out properties in the States—and we can share childcare. But the travelling is very tiring and I am getting fed up with British Rail food!' In fact, Louise spent much of her commuting time writing *Glamour*. 'When I first started writing novels I could finish a book in six weeks. Now, owing to the children and politics, it takes about a year. But it's great to be able to switch from Mum to author to Conservative candidate.'

'Motherhood, politics and writing are three very important elements in my life.'

Many prospective candidates do not move into the area they hope to represent until they are elected but that situation does not feel right to Louise. 'I need to live in the constituency to fully understand the local problems and the people's priorities and I firmly believe that moving to the area is essential. I don't drive—I passed my driving test but don't feel confident behind the wheel—so it will give me a chance to use the local transport network and, with young children, I'm sure I'll come into contact with the local hospital!' As I listened to her talking about what she and the Conservative Party hope to achieve in the future, there was no doubt in my mind about Louise's dedication and passion.

I wondered, too, whether she has yet been interviewed by Jeremy Paxman? 'Oh yes, I've felt the full weight of that sardonic sneer! I was running late, the traffic was awful and I was still stuck in the taxi when the debate began. I arrived all in a rush and didn't have much time to think about anything—I was just thrown into the discussion. Luckily, in the editing, they focused on my face and not on his look of disdain, which is all that I saw!'

Even with her busy political workload, Louise is currently writing another blockbuster. 'I think that reading should be relaxing and I want my novels to give the reader a holiday from everyday life. At the same time I want to help to fire business and personal ambition in today's woman. Women can do anything if they set their minds to it.'

Jane Eastgate

Love out of Season

Ray Connolly

For romantic fiction writer Amy
Miller, life has become horribly
complicated as the press are
hounding her, trying to get a shot
of her with the famous married man
who is her lover. She needs to run
and hide, but where?
Fate leads Amy to a north Devon
hotel, where her education in the
true nature of love begins.

Chapter One

Given the choice, which would you prefer: that the person you love is making love to you and thinking about someone else, or that he, or she, is making love to someone else and thinking about you?

Amy considered the words on her screen. Was that an original thought or had she overheard it somewhere? She couldn't be sure. She hesitated for a moment, weighing up the risks of unintended plagiarism, and then continued anyway.

Why can't he, or she, be thinking about me as well as making love to me? you might ask. But you never do. You don't dare.

She stopped writing. Was this getting personal? Her finger dawdled on the *delete* button. Of course it was personal. Whatever else love was, a bunch of red roses, a metaphysical excuse for sex, a passing moment in human evolution, a confidence trick designed by nature, an accident, a song, a game, a poem or a pain, it was always personal. The telephone broke into her musings: a welcome distraction. 'Amy!'

Her work frown dissolved at the voice. 'Oh, *hello*! Nice surprise. I was just thinking about you! You were very good this morning with that . . .' she searched for the right words, 'that pre-Raphaelite loony. What are you doing? Can you get away, come over—?'

'Amy, they're on to us.' The famously mellifluent tones interrupted.

'*What*? This is a joke! Right?'

'They may already be watching.'

She wanted to laugh. That morning on television he'd been the epitome of the urbane, metropolitan man gently ribbing an over-dramatic, tumbling-haired actress whose view of the world ended at her mirror. Now his voice was as hushed as a conspirator. 'Come on! That's just paranoia,' she scolded. 'No one's watching us. I'd have noticed.' And swivelling round on her typing chair she rolled on casters across the wooden floor to her study window and looked down through the black winter trees that lined the drive below. 'There you are, noth—' she began, then stopped and stood up to get a better view. 'Oh, my God!'

Two figures had emerged from the shadows of the bushes and were standing on the pavement, gazing up at her window. Seeing her, one of them indicated her. Immediately a camera bearing a very large and long lens was pointed upwards.

She didn't need to hear the shutter. As she dropped to the carpet she knew what the pictures would show—a fair-haired, pretty-ish woman in her early thirties in a pale blue working shirt and jeans, staring in dismay as the most exciting part of her life came to an abrupt end.

'Amy?'

She was on the floor, dragging the curtains across the window. 'How did they find out? How did they *know*?' she gabbled into the phone. 'We've been so careful.'

'God knows! But don't worry. We'll sort it out.'

'*Don't worry*! They'll roast us. You'll be skewered.'

'Not if we do the right thing.'

'But we've been doing the *wrong* thing!' She regretted saying that instantly. It wasn't supposed to sound like a wail, either. She didn't wail. She wasn't the type. But she knew that in that moment her life had changed. What she'd most dreaded, yet always half expected, had happened. 'It's my fault,' she said, lifting the hem of the curtains and trying to peep outside. But, as the camera was raised again, she pulled back. 'We're being punished.'

In truth, she wasn't sure she meant that either. In fact, she probably didn't, not being at all certain that she believed in a God who dealt so arbitrarily in rewards and punishments. But this wasn't the moment for reflections on the nature of divinity.

'Don't be silly. We've done nothing to be punished for. Don't panic,' he calmed.

'I'm not panicking,' she lied.

At the other end of the phone there was now a silence.

'Teddy?' she enquired at last. She recognised the sudden quiet. It worried her. He used it very effectively as a technique in his television interviews before asking outrageous questions.

'I was just thinking . . .' he began. 'Perhaps if you were to, you know, disappear . . .?' It came as a vague suggestion and question combined, but there was an emollient persuasion to the tone.

She was surprised. 'You want me to go away?'

'Just for a few days. A holiday. You know, lie low. Go to ground.'

'You mean, go into hiding? Like a criminal? On the run?'

'Amy!'

'But I'm working . . .'

'You can work anywhere.'

This irritated. It wasn't true, but he wouldn't understand. He never did, and she'd given up trying to explain to him that writers work best at the same desk in the same room day after day. She'd been pathetic about that. Now she was giving in again. 'Where would I go?' she heard herself ask, and realised she'd already agreed.

'Anywhere.' He was coaxing now, cooing almost. 'Somewhere anonymous and quiet until I can—' He stopped and corrected himself. 'Until *we* can, you know, sort things out.'

He's getting rid of me, she thought. I'm in the way. And, still on the floor, she gazed around her study walls at the silver-framed posters of the novels she'd written, the trophies that charted the somehow largely vicarious life she'd been living until she met him. Finally, her eyes came to rest on the blinking cursor of her computer, still waiting for her to finish her paragraph. She wouldn't be doing that tonight. Would she ever finish it? When it comes down to it, she thought, he's just a married man, a very famously, happily married man. And for a single woman, particularly one with a well-known name, to be in love with such a man had become an inconvenience he could do without.

Will Abbott contemplated the top-floor window of the apartment block. An expensive place, but then she was a successful girl. Pity she'd spotted them so soon.

At his side, the photographer, cocooned in wet-weather gear, sniffed. He'd be complaining soon. Photographers always complained. But stake-outs weren't fun for anyone on a cold and wet February evening. Famous adulterers would be doing everybody a favour if they only let themselves be outed in the summer. Their pictures would come out better then, too.

Rubber brakes squeaked quietly behind them as a bicycle bumped onto the kerb and came to rest. A gawky girl in a school raincoat stood astride the pedals, watching them. 'Her name's Amy Miller,' the girl volunteered at last. 'She writes romantic fiction.'

We're so obvious, thought Abbott, the policemen of celebrity morals.

The girl indicated Amy's window. 'I read one once. It wasn't bad. But the sex was a bit on the tepid side.'

Abbott chose to ignore that observation. She was all of thirteen. 'Have you . . . er . . . have you ever seen anyone visit her?' he asked. 'Anyone famous, I mean.'

The girl considered him without expression.

Reaching inside his overcoat he withdrew a ten-pound note.

'More famous than that,' she said scornfully. But now she smiled.

They settled at twenty, which he could later inflate to forty for his expenses. The girl's name was Polly.

'Yes, I've seen someone,' she confided with quiet glee. 'Teddy Farrow from *The Teddy Farrow Show*. He usually comes at night when I'm finishing my homework. He parks his car round the corner. It's a black BMW. Then he sneaks in . . . and . . . sneaks out again . . . much later!'

Abbott looked again at the sixth-floor window. There was now no sign of activity behind the curtains. 'Do you live here?' he asked.

Polly nodded.

He smiled at the girl, as though taking her into his confidence, flirting really, if one could flirt with a child. 'You know, Polly, this may be really important. I don't know. But it might help if you could invite us into the building so that we could talk to the lady,' he said.

Legally it would, he knew, still count as trespass, but it was no use standing in the porch speaking into an intercom that could be slammed down at any moment. Until you actually knocked on the door and confronted your quarry you never knew what reaction you might get.

She was dashing from bathroom to bedroom, quickly filling a large canvas bag with jeans, shirts, underclothes, shoes and sweaters. In her study she copied her work onto a disc and slid it into her laptop case. Then, turning off all the lights, she grabbed her coat and car keys, and, opening her front door, stepped out onto the landing.

Even before she'd finished locking the door she realised that the chase had entered the building. She could hear the hunters murmuring to each other as they came up the stairs. Tiptoeing along the landing she reached the lift. A red light read 'Occupied'. She winced. Her plan had been to take the lift down to the garage, and then drive out at speed, taking her tormentors by surprise. That was no longer an option.

'Next floor,' she heard a man's voice echo in the stairwell.

She glanced at her door. It was too late. She would be spotted now if she tried to get back.

Taking off her shoes, she shoved them into her coat pockets and crept silently up the stairs to the top landing. There was only one door. Pushing down the bar of the fire lock, she opened it and stepped out onto the flat roof of the apartment block.

He knew she hadn't gone down because Polly, the neighbourhood snitch, was earning an extra fiver in the lobby blocking the lift door with her bike. But she wasn't answering her door either.

Kneeling down, the photographer tried to see through the letterbox, then shook his head.

She could, of course, have been sitting inside the flat with the lights turned off, waiting for them to give up and leave. On the other hand . . . Abbott looked up the stairs to the top floor.

Holding the handrail, the other hand gripping her bag and laptop, she felt her way down the iron steps of the fire escape. Soon she was passing the lighted, curtained windows of flats lower down the block. She was already regretting her decision to leave, wondering what on earth she was doing, hating herself for being so easily persuaded. But to turn round now and face her pursuers was out of the question. People with nothing to hide didn't run, they'd say, and they'd be right.

From above she could hear footsteps and voices on the roof, instinctively she tried to make herself smaller. Pressing close against the wall, she realised she was peering into a sitting room. A couple of teenagers were lolling on an island of large cushions, the girl watching a rock video on television round the side of the boy's hooded head while he snogged her, one hand up the back of her sweater trying to unfasten her bra.

Amy looked quickly away. This would be all she needed: a conviction as a peeping Tom.

Disregarding the hounds above, she hurried on down the iron staircase.

Amy didn't even think about going back for her car. As her feet hit the garden she was already running towards the drive, the road and the yellow for-hire light of an approaching taxi. She just had to get away before this night got any worse.

Abbott watched her from the roof. When he'd received the tip from the television researcher about Amy Miller and Teddy Farrow he'd been disinclined to believe it. Farrow had built his daytime-TV career on an unblemished image as a family man, now with sensible, grown-up children and a clever, attractive wife. Amy Miller was the pretty bookworm who led a quiet, unreported life, didn't give interviews and sold, it was said, mountain ranges of books.

But now Abbott had no doubts. He smiled to himself. The cute run-away author and the goody-goody TV star making the beast with two backs. It was going to be an interesting chase.

'I'm sorry, sir, I'm getting no reply from 1507.' The hotel operator was a middle-aged, homely woman.

Tim Fairweather considered the rain splashing off his gutterless attic roof and running down his window pane, and wondered whether his home could take much more. February in London was a terrible, dismal month, and he could see a patch of damp plaster beginning to bubble and flake around the edge of the skylight above his head. 'I see,' he said. 'By the way, what time is it in Denver now?'

'A quarter after two . . . in the morning.' The operator stressed the last part. 'Would you care to leave a message?'

'Well, perhaps you could just tell her that . . . Tim rang.'

'I'll do that, sir. "Tim rang . . . *again!*" Good night now.'

The connection went dead. Night in Denver, Colorado; morning in London. It was a pity the operator had added the 'again' bit. If only Amanda would switch on her mobile. A text would do.

Putting the phone down, he considered a sequence of musical notes on the laptop screen attached to the Yamaha keyboard that dominated his small living room. One-handed, he played a short sequence, then stopped, unhappy.

He was a tall man of thirty-five, and his hair was dark, long, wavy and unkempt. This wasn't a shaving day. Not many were. He wore jeans and a navy blue shirt, and the room around him suggested the comfort-able if frugal chaos of a musician who lived alone. Records and CDs rose in stacks like miniature housing projects where music by Gershwin and Chopin inhabited the same neighbourhood as the Blind Boys of Alabama, the Red Hot Chili Peppers, Dylan, favourite movie composers and hundreds of others. Sheets of discarded music manuscript lay abandoned across the furniture, while on the mantelpiece, along with the old letters and various bills, was a partially obscured photograph showing an attractive, dark-haired, slim, determined-looking woman in a black mandarin outfit standing beside a battery of chimes.

Beside the photograph was a clock. Glancing at it, Tim swore quietly to himself. He was going to be late for his lesson. Pulling on his over-coat, he began to look quickly through a box of CDs. 'Pie-Eyed Posse,' he muttered to himself as he searched. 'Where are you, Pie-Eyed . . .?' His fingers stopped as five young men stared accusingly at him from a plastic box. 'Got you!' And pushing the CD into his pocket he ran from his flat, down the echoing, uncarpeted stairs and out into the busy cacophony of a North Kensington street.

The school wasn't far away, a stern Victorian building where, as he arrived, pupils were mobbing their way from one lesson to the next. Pushing through, he made his way to the staff room, retrieved a portable CD player from his locker, and hurried to his classroom.

He would reflect later that 3M looked unusually pleased to see him as he entered. But, having told them at their last music lesson to expect something interesting today, he put it down to enthusiasm.

'Good morning. Sorry I'm late,' he said as he stepped up onto the rostrum at the front of the room.

The thirty-strong class of fourteen-year-old boys and girls, who, for various reasons, few likely to be educational, had ticked the 'music appreciation' box as their cultural activity choice, grinned back.

'As I said last week, I thought we'd listen to something new today to see if we can hear connections between different kinds of music,' he went on. 'So, I've brought along a record I know some of you at least will like—Pie-Eyed Posse . . .' As he'd been speaking he'd been taking the CD he'd brought out of its box and slipping it into the player.

'Oohh!' the class murmured sarcastically, mock impressed.

Tim smiled. He'd done the same when he'd been at school and young teachers had tried to earn some street cred. 'Yes, even I've heard of Pie-Eyed Posse! And, despite their appearance,' he said, happy to play for the ridicule he knew he'd get, 'they're a clever group . . . interesting rhythms, a bit of techno, hip-hop . . .' At their desks the pupils exchanged exaggeratedly pained glances, humouring him. 'Anyway, let's give them a listen, shall we?' And, pressing the PLAY button, he settled into a chair by the teacher's desk and looked around the class as he waited for the disc to engage. Form 3M were almost attentive now. Perhaps they weren't as bad as their reputation suggested after all.

They were. There was a sudden explosion of derision. The music had started, but it was not the drum and bass of Pie-Eyed Posse. It was the swell of a full symphony orchestra. Tim groaned. 'I'm sorry,' he said above the music and the laughter. 'Tchaikovsky seems to have sneaked into the wrong box.' There was more guffawing. 'All right, calm down.'

Eventually they did.

But what should he do now? Best to brazen it out, he decided. 'Well, as we can't really discuss the merits of Pie-Eyed Posse without hearing them, what do we know about Tchaikovsky? He was one of the great classical Russian composers. Just listen to this. Does anybody recognise it?' And turning the music louder he leaned back in his chair as he always did.

Perhaps, he would also think later, he should have suspected something when he noticed the quiet boy from Mogadishu, the one they called Jay-Jay, staring fixedly at the legs of his chair, but he didn't. The music had taken his attention, and he was wondering exactly how he was going to explain it to them. 'Well, we're listening to Tchaikovsky's music for the ballet *Romeo and Juliet*,' he began, 'and—'

He didn't finish. There was a sudden jolt as though a minor earthquake had occurred right under him. Then a shudder. And then with a crack he felt the back legs of his chair bend and snap sharply. There was nothing to grab hold of as he and the broken chair tumbled backwards off the rostrum and the back of his head crashed onto the floor.

And as the class roared in triumph and hilarity at the success of their practical joke, he lost consciousness.

'**R**omeo and Juliet, you say. That was lucky.' The young Egyptian doctor stared at the X-ray of Tim's skull on the light box.

'It was?' Tim put a hand gingerly to the lump on the back of his head.

'Oh, yes. Think what they'd have done to the *1812 Overture*. Ingenious buggers. Sawed through your chair legs, just for the fun of it?'

'I don't think they meant to injure me.'

'Well, luckily, you haven't fractured your skull or damaged your brain, so that's good news, just a deep cut and a coconut of a lump.' He wrote out a prescription. 'Get these from the pharmacy on the way out. Concussion can be tricky. You'll probably need a few days to get over it. Is there anyone at home who can keep an eye on you?'

'No. I live alone. And my girlfriend's in America. But I'll be all right.'

'If I were you I'd go and stay with relations for a few days.'

Tim shook his head, then immediately regretted it. It felt heavy, and made his neck ache. 'I can't do that,' he said.

The doctor looked at him over his glasses, one of those professional expressions that conveys authority. 'Well, you can't go back to school. And certainly not *that* school. The noise alone would probably kill you.'

'Yes, but you see . . . I'm writing something . . . composing, I mean. Well, trying to . . .' Tim realised he was stammering, embarrassed, as he always was, by the word 'composing'. It sounded so pretentious. He tried again. 'I mean, the teaching bit is only part time. I play in a bar as well, actually several bars, but I write music, too. And as I've entered a competition for new works I'm really very busy at the moment.'

'What about a hotel? Go and spoil yourself.'

Tim grimaced again.

The young doctor gave up. 'Well, it's up to you.' He handed over a list of instructions. 'Read this. Any headaches, blackouts, dizziness or nausea, come back here or call a doctor. You'll probably feel tired and a bit shaken at first. But that'll pass. Otherwise, a few days' peace and quiet and you should be as right as rain.' And with that he hurried from the consulting cubicle.

A nurse holding a roll of elastic bandage, entered and peered at Tim's head. 'Right,' she said in a flat Glaswegian accent, 'if you've ever fancied yourself as Che Guevara this is your day.'

Amy hadn't slept well, not at all, until after four, the previous evening's events and her abrupt change of plans having tormented her.

She'd intended, in her first moments of panic, to seek sanctuary with one of her friends, but had quickly realised that that would have called for explanations which she just hadn't wanted to give. The affair had been that secret. So when she'd spotted a blue neon vacancy light over the door of a small hotel near Paddington Station, its anonymity had beckoned. She'd needed time to think of a better idea.

Unfortunately, she hadn't been able to. Woken by the racket of passing traffic she'd found herself in a narrow, cream room under a framed photograph of Princess Diana at the Taj Mahal, feeling locked out of her own life. Going without breakfast, because she really hadn't wanted to face anyone, she'd watched *The Teddy Farrow Show* on the television in her room, wagging her head admiringly at his skill in encouraging his guests to betray themselves so unwittingly. Sometimes when she'd watched the show at home she'd wondered whether he might send her a little message in code, and that had crossed her mind this morning, too. But when he hadn't she'd told herself she hadn't expected him to, anyway. He was, after all, renowned for his professionalism.

After the show had gone off the air, she'd taken a long bath, killing time. Only at eleven, and with some trepidation, did she put in a call to Teddy's mobile phone. It was switched off. Leaving a carefully worded message that would have meant nothing to anyone else, she'd then waited, afraid to leave the hotel because in her haste the previous night she'd left her own mobile on her desk.

Teddy hadn't returned the call, but then he'd obviously have to schmooze with the guests after the programme, after which there was always a production meeting to discuss the next show's line-up.

So she'd waited even longer, desperate for a word from him, yet, with every passing hour, hating herself more for being so bloody pathetic. How could she be behaving like this? No leading character in the novels she wrote would have put up with it. Her women were independent, witty creatures who knew exactly how to put a man in his place, the sort of girls whom reviewers in friendly newspapers described as 'feisty'. Yet here *she* was, totally *feistless*, if there were such a word. She was a fraud. And she remembered with some shame the intolerance she'd had to hide as she'd seen friends unroll themselves like doormats for men they loved.

A noon check-out time finally forced her to make a decision and, carrying her belongings, she made her way through the rain down the street, still unsure of what to do next. If she were to return home now, she wondered, would the Press leave her in peace?

A photograph staring out at her from a rack of newspapers on a corner news-stand answered her question. It was of her, caught the previous night, her fair hair looking as though it had become electrified in shock as she'd spotted the photographer's telephoto lens. A headline under the picture teased coyly: **ROMANCE FOR AMY—BUT WHO'S HER MYSTERY MAN? (Turn to page 5 . . .)**

In despair she turned to page 5.

'**S**horter,' she said.

'"Shorter"?' the young hairdresser with the ring and silver chain hanging from her belly button repeated. 'Your friends won't recognise you.'

'Promise me,' Amy replied. This girl certainly didn't recognise her, but then Economy Cutz didn't look the sort of place where the reading of books, not even the books she wrote, would have been a priority.

With a raising of her shoulders, which Amy interpreted as a 'suit yourself' surrender, the girl continued to chop at Amy's hair. Already it lay around her like the jettisoned frills of a former, happy life.

Cautiously, as the stylist moved from one side of her to the other, Amy glanced at her newspaper, which was lying folded on a shelf below the mirror. The article on page five hadn't named the 'mystery man'. It couldn't. Get that wrong and it could mean a serious and expensive libel. Instead, knowing hints about a new friendship with a 'television family favourite' came free of risk.

'Something special in today, is there?' the girl asked as she noticed Amy's attention stray to the paper.

'What?' Amy quickly looked away. 'Oh, no.' But as the stylist went off to find a fresh pair of scissors she sighed and looked again at her newspaper. She hadn't noticed when she'd first read it, but at the bottom of the page about her was a travel advertisement, an engraving of a large rambling house with balconies, ivy and a palm tree on the edge of a range of cliffs.

When you really want to get away from it all . . . the advertisement beckoned. *The North Devon Riviera Hotel.*

He'd fully intended to stay at home, work at his music and shiver in his mansard flat. But then the head teacher had called, and, relieved that Tim wasn't more seriously injured, had offered, on the school's behalf, to pay for a week's recuperation at a resort of his choice, 'provided it's reasonably priced, of course'.

The stain around the skylight decided him. If he stayed at home, watching it grow bigger by the day, he'd probably have to do something about it, which would inevitably turn into a displacement activity when the music became even more difficult, which in turn would defeat the whole object of staying at home. Besides, there was still no word from Amanda in Denver. So he accepted the offer.

As it happened, it turned out to be a resort of Valerie the school secretary's choice. She'd been there on holiday three years earlier with her mother and they'd had 'a lovely time', she said when she called him with the details. 'It was very quiet, with very nice people.' It was called the North Devon Riviera Hotel.

So Valerie made the booking, and, after calling Razza, the manager of the Settle Bar in Muswell Hill and Harry at Ballantine's in Victoria, to explain why he wouldn't be able to play for a week, Tim quickly packed and set off for Victoria Coach Station.

They were all stiff with embarrassment. Standing on the Swindon station platform, waiting for the Intercity express, they could have been taken for a funeral party as much as a wedding celebration. Even Michael's new suit was dark grey. At his side, Eleanor, his wife of just three hours, her iron-coloured hair freshly cut, gazed away across the tracks, avoiding all eyes.

They should have just slipped away and done it in secret, Michael told himself. What could have possessed them to think they could share their moment with others, when they could scarcely share it with each other? Was it guilt? Was it loyalty to those with whom they'd each lived their lives for so long? Or was it hope that they might finally find understanding and a blessing from these two unbending slabstones of the Church parochial, who, like warders seeing off prisoners at the end of their stretch, stood waiting with them equally lost for words? Only Sister Catherine, hardly more than a novice, and foolishly amused at the incongruity of the situation, seemed to be enjoying herself. She won't stay locked in holy orders, Michael thought. Not as long as Eleanor. Please God, not as long as he had done.

At last he heard the electric rattle and hum of their approaching train. Eleanor peered down the line, suddenly animated as above them the station announcer echoed his message of blessed relief. 'The train approaching platform three is for Bristol and Taunton only.'

'All aboard for the train of love,' laughed Sister Catherine as the roar reached the platform, and then giggled at her own naughtiness.

The elderly nun pursed her lips. The old priest next to Michael pretended not to hear.

They'll take anybody these days, Michael thought, though not uncharitably because he liked Catherine. She'd been a constant source of amusement, if not exactly a confidante, for Eleanor in the convent. Turning to the priest at his side, he said, 'Thanks for everything, Dermot, and for being, you know, so . . . so understanding.'

'Isn't that all we priests ever do . . . understand?' Dermot growled back. 'Though, God knows, it isn't always easy.'

Michael didn't answer.

The elder nun was looking at Eleanor now. 'All the sisters will be praying for you, Eleanor,' she said. 'Every night at bedtime.'

Eleanor looked at her feet and the new sensible, clunky, navy-blue shoes she'd bought to match her wedding outfit. 'Thank you, Mother,' she said meekly.

'No need to call me Mother now,' corrected the nun.

Eleanor tried a wan little nod of agreement, but all Michael could see was a timid, middle-aged woman cowed by an authority greater than any of them, a centuries' old discipline. It's been harder for her than for me, he thought, and he loved her more than ever.

The train doors unfolded in front of them. It was a first-class carriage, the cost of the tickets being part of a wedding gift from the doctors and nurses in the hospital where he and Eleanor had met. He'd gone to administer the last rites to an elderly parishioner; Eleanor was pushing the library on wheels. Falling into conversation she'd allowed him to borrow a biography of Nelson Mandela, although as a non-patient that had, strictly speaking, been against the rules. After that, he'd made sure he borrowed a different book every week.

'Well, then,' Michael said, picking up both suitcases. Beaming, he indicated that Eleanor climb the train steps ahead of him.

Without warning, the older nun suddenly softened: 'Good luck. Both of you!' she called. Michael looked back at her. Behind her little round glasses her eyes were wet. 'God bless you both.'

'Thank you, Sister,' he said.

'Don't do anything I wouldn't do,' the young nun, Sister Catherine, hooted. She tossed the last of the confetti over them.

That girl really wouldn't last long in the convent.

Quickly, amid a benediction of thanks and goodbyes, Michael shepherded Eleanor onto the train. With a *clunk*! the carriage door closed behind them, sealing, it seemed, their break with their pasts.

Cautious with each other, feeling as though they were on display for the world to watch, they searched for their seats. As Eleanor sat down, Michael lifted their suitcases onto the luggage rack.

Facing them was a young woman in her early thirties, her head covered in a hood, a laptop computer open on the table in front of her. With a polite smile, the young woman pulled the laptop closer to herself to make room for Eleanor's handbag.

Discreetly, Michael picked a piece of confetti from the shoulders of his wife's new coat as Eleanor looked around the carriage.

'I've never travelled first class before,' Eleanor whispered.

Michael smiled. 'There's a first time for everything,' he said, then wondering if that might, in the circumstances, be misconstrued, he hurried on as the train began to slide away. 'It was good of Dermot to come. I never expected to see him in a register office.'

Eleanor was silent, thoughtful for a moment. 'No.' Then she added, 'I don't suppose he ever expected to see you in one, either.'

It had been a serious observation, but Michael smiled. 'Well, no. But, what I meant is, the world's changing, and Dermot has difficulty with that. Old habits, you know . . .'

'I gave mine to Sister Catherine.' Eleanor was looking down.

'I'm sorry?'

Eleanor looked up, smiling now. 'My old habit.'

'Oh, yes, I see.' And Michael laughed rather too loudly as belatedly he got the joke. Eleanor liked her little jokes.

She blushed with pleasure. Then she took the carnation he was wearing in his buttonhole and put it into her handbag for a keepsafe.

She's such a kind and lovely woman, he thought. And she's given up so much for me. Please God, don't let me disappoint her.

Sitting across from them Amy studied her laptop. It wasn't her intention to eavesdrop the couple's conversation, but it was difficult not to overhear. She'd never seen such an anxious pair, the man, thin and grey and mid-fifties, and the woman probably a couple of years younger.

And as the two talked quietly together, short, stilted sentences about the weather or the scenery, Amy's eyes wandered to the label on one of the suitcases stacked above them. *The North Devon Riviera Hotel*, it read in a neat, woman's handwriting.

Eventually, as the couple's conversation lapsed into silence, neither seeming to know what to say next, Amy typed a note to herself into her laptop: *Blessed are the lovers*. And she remembered the story of Abelard and Héloïse. He'd come to a very sticky end.

He felt like a beach boy out of season as, with the bandage tied round his now throbbing head like a bandanna and carrying his keyboard in its case over his shoulder like a surfboard, Tim made his way with his suitcase and laptop the few steps from the bus-stop to the lifeboat station on the sea wall. This was where the hotel collected its guests, Valerie had told him: 'I imagine they'll be waiting for you when you get there.'

They weren't. Instead, a tall, solid girl of about eighteen sat huddled on a bench, her face turned against the wind and rain, her hair frizzy and rather too red and gripped by two large tortoiseshell butterfly clips. Wearing jeans ripped at the knees and scissored into slices at the hems, and an ancient angora coat tied round her waist with an old school tie as a belt, she was reading, by the light of the street lamp, a book on hotel management, while eating something from a plastic container. At her feet lay a suitcase and a large cardboard box bearing a *Handle With Care* sticker.

'Excuse me.'

The girl looked up with wide, pale, nonchalant eyes and carried on eating. She wasn't exactly pretty, her mouth was too wide, and her face looked slightly cock-eyed. But she was certainly striking.

'Are you waiting for the hotel car?'

She nodded, but again didn't answer.

Tim nodded in return. Teenage cool was something teachers understood well. 'Right. Thank you,' he said, and, turning away, made a point of considering a poster for a St Valentine's Ball stuck to the sea wall. *Music, romance and dancing at the North Devon Riviera Hotel from Lorna and the Doones*, beckoned the message. Valerie hadn't said anything about romance. But then she'd been with her mother.

Eventually glancing back towards the girl, Tim was just in time to see her take another morsel of food from her container. But this time, instead of eating it she slipped it inside her slightly open coat. Intrigued, he watched, only to realise that she was staring at him.

Quickly he looked away again and stared out to sea. There was nothing to be seen, but he didn't want her to think he'd been admiring her bosom. For God's sake, she wasn't much older than his pupils! That would amuse Amanda no end.

'This looks like our lift,' the girl suddenly said, and stood up as a pale green-and-blue people carrier headed towards them. 'On the other hand, it could be a very large budgerigar. What d'you think?'

It had been very kind of the young lady to offer to give them a lift in her taxi, Eleanor told herself, as the car dropped down from the blackness of the moors towards the cliffs. It made sense if they were going to the same hotel, but the presence of a third party in their new life was unnerving. Michael, for his part, had been instantly jolly and enquiring, the way she'd seen him with patients on the wards when she knew he didn't really know what to say. He was actually a shy man, especially in the company of women.

'So, you're down here on . . . business . . . holiday?' he'd asked as the train had come to another of the many unscheduled stops along the way. Rainwater on the tracks was playing havoc with the timetable. The conductor had frequently apologised.

'Just a break,' the young woman had replied, then, probably not wanting to appear unfriendly, had added, 'And you're on your . . . honeymoon?' She'd smiled congratulations.

Eleanor had felt her mouth tighten with embarrassment as it had that morning at the register office. 'We were hoping to keep it quiet,' she'd almost whispered back. The very word 'honeymoon' suggested something fleshy and improper; the register office had been quite godless.

The young woman had backed off immediately. 'Oh, yes, of course. It was just that I couldn't help but see you get on the train and . . .' Her voice had faded away.

'They say February can be very clement in these parts,' Michael had joined in, anxious to change the subject. 'We're hoping to get some nice cliff walks in, if we ever get there!' He looked at his watch. 'At this rate we're going to be very late arriving.'

They were. Now, hours late, the taxi slipped off the road and between pine woods, and, as the lights of the hotel came into view, Eleanor felt the palms of her hands dampen. Michael was all smiles. 'At last!' he gushed nervously as the taxi came to a halt alongside a brightly coloured hotel people carrier. For a second, Eleanor looked at her husband as he held the door for her. He was such a well-meaning man.

Amy could see that in the summer it might be a pretty hotel, a white wedge of faded, late-nineteenth-century stucco caught between trees. But in the dark, in a February gale that sent rain and sleet scything up the Bristol Channel and swayed the lanterns that hung on the trees around the car park, it hardly promised the warmest welcome. I should have stayed in London, she reproached herself yet again as she followed the honeymooners up a couple of steps to the entrance. Would she have chosen this place for a honeymoon? Never. But then another thought interrupted. Would she ever have a honeymoon? And with this in mind, she stepped into the hotel.

She was immediately surprised. From the outside the building had suggested a traditional English conservatism, all dark woods and heavy varnish. Inside, however, it was a cavalcade of seaside colours, few matching but all jolly, as though anticipating disappointment in the weather and already compensating for it.

Making her way across the lobby she joined a short queue at the reception desk where a tall man with a bandage round his head was checking in before a boy of about eighteen in an old-fashioned maroon porter's uniform. To one side of the man a tall, red-headed, bizarre-looking girl waited by a very large box.

'Fairweather,' Amy heard the man say.

'You should see it in June,' the boy porter replied, puzzled yet proud, his Devon accent undulating.

'No, I mean my name's Fairweather. I have a reservation.'

The boy looked at him, then flustered. 'Oh, yes, of course. Here we are. Fairweather, Timothy. A late booking. Sorry, Mr Fairweather.'

The waiting girl listened, and almost giggled. The boy porter noticed and was embarrassed.

Suddenly a door at the back of the reception area opened and, with an excited yelping, a large black Labrador bounded into the lobby, closely followed by a stout, large-breasted, woman in her late-forties, her thin, mousy hair pulled back off a pink, pale, oval face. 'Yes?' She smiled to the red-headed girl.

'I'm Shona. For the student placement. Work experience.' The girl grinned, as now the dog dashed round the counter and began jumping up at her, sniffing her clothes excitedly. She tried to push it away.

'Staff?' the woman asked, her voice seeming to curl in derision.

'Yes!' The girl nodded, laughing, still trying to escape the attentions of the dog. 'Hey, get down, that's rude.' She giggled as the dog tried to push its wet snout under her coat and between the tops of her thighs.

'Darrell!' the older woman hissed, her large face twitching. 'Put Giles outside.' And, moving to one side, she abandoned the girl and took the boy porter's place as he pulled the dog away. In an instant, her features softened and her brow cleared for the guest with the bandage. 'Ah, Mr Fairweather,' she gushed, lifting her eyes sympathetically. 'I'm so sorry Darrell was late picking you up. We're so pleased you chose the North Devon Riviera Hotel for your . . . convalescence?'

The man looked embarrassed and touched his bandage lightly. 'It's nothing, really. Just a bump.'

The manager purred. 'Brave soldier,' she murmured, and with what looked to Amy like the slightest flutter of over-lacquered eyelashes, reached for a key. 'Darrell, the Exmoor Suite for Mr Fairweather,' she ordered the returning boy, and passed him a key.

Dragging his eyes from the girl, the porter grabbed the man's bag and put it on to a trolley. Peripherally, Amy was aware that the man was turning to pick up a large oblong object propped against the desk, but as she did so her attention was drawn to a morning newspaper on the reception desk. Once again her own shocked face looked back at her: **ROMANCE FOR AMY—BUT WHO'S HER MYSTERY MAN?**

For a second she froze, then, afraid that someone would notice and she'd be recognised, she swung away, back towards the man just as he was passing the oblong object to the porter. She gasped as her head collided with it. 'Ouch!' she exclaimed, more in surprise than injury.

'Oh, I'm so sorry!' the man with the bandage apologised.

'It's all right.' She wasn't hurt. 'My fault.'

'No, I was careless. It's my keyboard and . . . Are you sure . . .?'

'Certain. It's nothing.' Amy was smiling now, anxious to divert attention from the newspaper.

'That's a relief . . .' he began.

But at that moment Eleanor the honeymooner, who was waiting behind them and unwrapping her scarf, accidentally sent a shower of confetti over them both. Embarrassment crowded the lobby.

'Oh dear.' Eleanor blushed.

Amy felt for her. If the couple's marriage had been a semi-secret when they'd arrived, that was no longer the case. 'Don't worry,' she consoled. 'It looks like apple blossom.'

The man with the bandage smiled and picked up a few pieces.

'I'd better take that, if you don't mind,' the young porter said, taking the keyboard from him and carefully sliding it onto a trolley alongside the bags and the large box.

Now it was the turn of the girl with red hair. 'You'll be very careful with that box, won't you?' she insisted.

Amy watched. It was obvious already. The boy was smitten.

'I thought I'd take it up to your room for you,' he said. 'Something special in there, is there?'

'There might be. I'm not sure.' The girl looked mysterious. 'I was told it was Hitler's missing testicle, but it looks a bit swollen to me.'

At her side Amy felt the keyboard man contain a chuckle. But the poor porter just stared at the girl, blood surging to his face.

'I'll show you to the Exmoor Suite, Mr Fairweather,' he managed at last and, putting his head down, hurried away towards the lift.

The girl, meanwhile, looked around with a merry, triumphant glint.

At the desk, the manager glowered at her. Then, in another triumph of muscle control, she transformed her face once more into a brilliant welcoming corporate smile as the honeymooners stepped forward. 'Mr and . . . Mrs Nichols?' she teased.

The couple nodded, glum-faced now.

'Congratulations and welcome! I have some very good news for you. You've qualified for our complimentary North Devon Riviera Valentine's Weekend upgrading . . . to our Passion of the West Country honeymoon suite! What do you think about that?'

There was a stunned silence from the couple. At last Michael found the words. 'Thank you very much,' he said quietly.

It's going wrong for them already, Amy thought, watching Michael sign the hotel registration form, and remembering their quiet, shared excitement as she'd seen them get on the train at Swindon. Then as the manager slid a key across the desk, seeming to wonder why they were not more grateful, Amy looked away as, insisting they didn't need help with their luggage, the honeymooners trudged unhappily up the wide staircase to find their room.

'And what name would it be?' The manager's voice, now a little sharper, redirected Amy's thoughts. She took out her credit card.

'**A**re you in a band?' Darrell asked, as, recovering from his embarrassment, he leaned the keyboard against a wall in the Exmoor Suite.

'No, but I know someone who is,' Tim said, and smiled to himself, as he did whenever he teased Amanda by referring to her orchestra rehearsals as band practice.

'Anyone famous?' The boy porter looked hopeful.

Tim didn't have to hesitate. 'Sorry,' he said. Not even Amanda would think that being a late replacement percussionist with a touring symphony orchestra made her famous. 'Do you play an instrument?'

'Oh, no.' Darrell almost laughed at the question. 'I've no time for that sort of thing. My mum always says playing music's all right for those with nothing else to do with their hands. But there's a chap down the village got a keyboard like yours. A Yamaha. He's in a band. His mate's the singer. He doesn't play anything, but he gets all the girls.'

Tim nodded. 'That sounds about right. The players play the tunes but the bloke who can't play gets the girls. That's life.'

'He's got a rotten voice, too. All croaky, like a crow squawking.'

Despite the headache, which was now returning, Tim was amused.

Darrell had a winning lack of guile. He was a thin, fair young man with a pudding-basin hair cut that was just growing out, giving him a step all round his head. It was probably the boy's single teenage attempt at being different, and it hadn't come off.

'Anyway, better be getting on . . .' Darrell made for the door, adding, 'Oh, thank you very much,' as Tim pushed a tip into his hand.

Alone, Tim crossed to the window and looked out at a small, pink-tiled balcony on which a large puddle had formed. Suddenly, he felt the sag of loneliness. Hotel rooms could do that. Irritation followed as he unpacked. Having detached the legs of his keyboard in order to carry them, he realised he'd left them behind in his flat.

All the same, a bashed skull wasn't the sort of thing to put a composer in a creative mood, he reflected, as he unzipped the plastic case, took out the keyboard and placed it across a small writing table. Then stopping, he immediately erased the word 'composer' from his mind. Whatever Amanda might like to tell herself and her friends, he was really, so far, just a part-time music teacher and occasional bar pianist. At college he'd played with a rock band, and had even mastered the organ to play at his friends' weddings. And there were, of course, his dreams, always unspoken. But whatever happened in the competition he was about to enter, should he ever finish his piece, that wouldn't make him a composer. Not in his mind, anyway.

But as he set to work plugging in his wires and headphones, he couldn't help but imagine a cross-faced Amanda shaking her head at his lack of ambition. He almost felt guilty.

Michael had never been in a hotel bedroom with a woman before. He and Eleanor had entered the room in silence. Now he didn't know what to do. For months he'd anticipated this moment, and thought about how happy they would be—alone, together, married and close, in short, everything he'd wanted. But he'd never been able to imagine it in pictures, to see the expression on Eleanor's face, to guess what she might say. And all he saw now was fear. Even in the mirror.

Putting their suitcases down, they closed the door behind them and looked around. A white four-poster bed draped with lace dominated the room. Together they crossed to the window, looked out at the balcony, tried all the lights with their romantic dimmers and then peeped into the bathroom. The bath was unlike any either had ever encountered.

'It looks very clean,' Michael said at last, considering the heart-shaped whirlpool for two in the centre of the room.

'I'll make some tea,' Eleanor murmured, and, quickly returning to the bedroom, she plugged in a kettle, hesitated, then added, 'The tea's PG Tips. Is that all right?'

'Perfect!' Michael said, and wondered why it might not be.

Eleanor nodded to herself. Unable to think of what to say next, Michael began to re-examine the room. It was all voluptuously, expensively suggestive. 'Yes, well, it's a very big room,' he said at last, and snapped open his suitcase. 'What do you think? Would you like to take the left or the right?' And he indicated the wardrobes on either side of the bed.

'Either is fine for me, Michael,' Eleanor said. 'You choose.' Their politeness with each other was stifling.

'Right then, I'll take this side,' he said and began to unpack. Behind him, he was aware that Eleanor was already discreetly slipping her underclothes into the dressing-table drawers, as though hiding a secret. This isn't how it should be, a voice inside him shouted.

'Eleanor.' He put a hand out to her. It fell on her elbow. 'Thank you for marrying me. You've made me very happy.'

She tried to smile, she really did. He could see that. But then she bit her bottom lip. She was close to tears.

Putting an arm round her shoulders he tried to turn her towards him, but her body was stiff and awkward. For a moment they stood together, close yet hardly touching.

A knock on the door made them both part, guiltily. Michael hurried to open it.

Darrell was standing with a silver tray bearing a bottle of champagne, two glasses and a single red rose in a fluted glass. 'Compliments of the management,' he said with a smile as he entered. 'Shall I open it now?'

'Er . . .' Michael looked to Eleanor for guidance. He got none. 'Perhaps we'll have it later. Thank you very much.'

Eleanor put two tea bags in the teapot. 'The kettle's boiled,' she said.

In the next room Amy, still wearing her coat and hood, sat on her bed as she called the voicemail on her home number.

Amy . . . what's all this in the paper? You didn't tell me!

She listened for a little while and then deleted the message.

It's Dill, Amy. What 'Mystery Man'? Have you been holding out on us?

Again she deleted.

Amy . . . Helen! What did you mean 'Speak later'? Call me!

In the end she deleted all the messages. Why was there never the voice you most desperately wanted? she asked herself, then answered her own question: because if life and love were so predictable no one would ever be desperate for anything. Then, although all the way down on the train she'd sworn to herself she wouldn't do it, she called Teddy again. He still wasn't answering. She left another message.

'Hello, it's me, the fugitive,' she spoke into his message service. 'Just to say, I'm here in North Devon's equivalent of Devil's Island . . .' She could hear the whining in her voice and hated it. 'I saw what they wrote. And what a photograph! They've made me look like a mad wraith.' She hesitated. 'Not any more, though. I've disguised myself . . . as a . . .' And for the first time since she left Economy Cutz that morning she examined herself in a mirror. ' . . .Crikey, a platypus!'

She meant it. She scarcely recognised herself. She'd been fifteen and a Goth when she'd last had short hair. It had been black then. Now it was a strange shade of khaki and terrible, cropped at the back of her neck and longer at the sides. It just wasn't her at all.

'Anyway,' she finished, 'if you get a minute . . . well, this is where you can find me.' And, apologising for having left her mobile at home, she read out the hotel name and phone number. Finally, as almost a postscript she whispered, 'Love you.' Then hung up.

She immediately hated herself for that, for phoning him at all, in fact. She was hopeless, a desperate-to-please other woman, grateful for any scraps of attention that might be tossed casually from her lover's bed. And every day that it went on she demeaned herself further.

She stopped herself there, and, picking up a ballpoint pen from the bedroom desk, made a note on a postcard of Exeter Cathedral.

Love isn't just blind. It's mad. It's a mental illness which leads to irrational acts being committed by otherwise sensible and intelligent people. Love isn't strange, like it says in the song, it's insane.

'Amy Miller, yes that one.' As he spoke into his phone, Will Abbott's free hand rested on a small stack of Amy Miller paperbacks sitting on his desk. Behind them was a computer screen showing a faintly glamourised publicity photograph of the author.

He'd bought the books that morning on his way into the office, noticed the uniform, joky branding of their covers, all easily identifiable as Amy Miller novels, then casually dipped into them during the day, looking for lines and characters he thought might heighten or season his story with a little irony. Because when 'one of the country's most popular romantic novelists', which was how Amy Miller's publishers described her, was having a secret, adulterous affair with the nation's favourite television Mr Clean, irony didn't come much sweeter—not in tabloid newspaper terms, anyway. Teddy Farrow was the main target, he was the hypocrite. But the titbit that the author was said to be currently writing a nonfiction book on the very nature of love was a detail the bitchy columnists in the up-market papers would happily smirk over for days. This story had angles for everybody.

There was, however, one flaw. Abbott couldn't yet *prove* the affair with Farrow, and without at least the semblance of an admission, there was no story to write. And now the bloody woman had disappeared.

Increasingly he blamed himself for that, since a day working the internet and the phones, calling publishers, her bitch of an agent, neighbours and the Society of Authors had provided no clue as to where she might have run. Nor had the cuttings library been much use. Most authors begged to be interviewed when their books were published. Not so Amy Miller. From the beginning of her career, five best-selling books ago, she'd kept her privacy.

'So, who's she been doing it with then?' the voice on the other end of the phone line asked, not unexpectedly.

'Who said she's been under the sheets with anyone?' Abbott blocked. He was trying to buy information, not give it away. 'All we want to know is when she last used her credit cards and where. Can you help?'

'I don't think so.' The reply was cautious, whispered.

'We'll see you right if you can.' The bribe extended its fingers.

There was a pause, then: 'I can't promise anything. It's bloody difficult these days. Just about impossible.'

'Yes, I know. But there are ways, aren't there, Jerry?'

Another silence followed, and then: 'I'll let you know.'

'Thanks, Jerry.' Wearily, Abbott hung up. Wondering what to do next, he looked around the editorial floor. A freelance photographer he'd taken for a drink a few nights earlier, a pretty, lippy, pug-faced, streaky-blonde girl called Suzy Tallis in the tightest of jeans was hanging around the picture desk flirting with the guys.

After a moment or two she noticed him and sauntered across. 'Are you watching me?' she asked.

'Yes.'

'That's all right then.' She smiled at him.

'I think so,' he said.

'I dreamed about you the other night,' she said after a moment.

'That's nice.'

She laughed quietly. 'It was for me.'

'Yes?'

'Not half. I nearly fell out of the bloody bed.' And she raised her eyebrows as she watched him interpret what she'd just said. 'Anyway, see you again!' And with that, she walked on and out of the office.

Abbott looked after her. Well, well, he thought.

Silently a shirtsleeved man appeared at his side and stared at the photograph of Amy Miller on the computer screen. It was McKenzie, an assistant editor. 'So where is she then, Will? What cosy little hideaway love nest is cheating the great British public of its right to know?'

'I'll find her,' Will Abbott promised.

The trouble with love is that it's obviously governed by the same laws of physics as the seesaw, in that neither love nor seesaws are ever in total balance for more than a few moments. Put another way, no two people are ever in love with each other to the same degree of intensity at the same time . . . not after the first weeks of passion, anyway. And since that's usually just oxytocin-fuelled sex in two momentarily chemically clotted brains it hardly counts.

In the real world, the one everyone has to live in after those first few weeks, either he's on the up side of the seesaw and she's down, or vice versa. All of which can make things at the wrong end of the love plank . . . a bit like sitting on an emotional spike. Painful! No. Worse. Desperate!

Now, it seems to me that since this unfairness in the nature of love is a universally observed design fault, evident over millennia among all ages and at all stages of love, it needs a name. So let's call it the Lovers' Law of the Eternal Seesaw.

Amy, crosslegged on her hotel bed, her computer in her lap, stopped typing. *The Lovers' Law of the Eternal Seesaw!* Was that a book title, or just a chapter heading? She didn't know. Her name was famous for spiky modern love stories. She enjoyed writing them. But this wasn't fiction and it made her uncertain.

'I want to write about the very *why* of love,' she'd told her editor, Dill, some weeks earlier.

'Yes?' Dill sounded pained.

'I want to write about where it comes from, what it's for, what sex has to do with it and why it can hurt so much,' she'd hurried on.

Dill had, she said, thought they were meeting to discuss a new novel, which was what Amy's readers expected from her, not some misty-eyed cornucopia of dubious science and back-of-an-envelope psychology. Actually, she hadn't put it as bluntly as that, but that had been her drift.

Amy hadn't been put off. 'I want to find out what love is.'

'God, Amy!' Dill had laughed. 'Don't tell me some appalling man's finally got to you.'

'As if . . .' Amy had fibbed. 'No. I just want to think about love in the abstract for once and wonder why it runs so much of our lives, why I write about it and you publish it.'

Naturally, Dill had argued her publisher's point of view, that what the world really needed now was another Amy Miller romantic novel. But seeing that Amy wouldn't be moved she'd finally shrugged grudgingly. 'Well, OK, if you must, but I wouldn't waste too much time on it if I were you,' she warned. 'The world and his goldfish have been asking what love is for the past five thousand years, but they never find out.'

Amy now scratched her leg unhappily as she remembered the conversation. Dill had been right, of course. Teddy's entrance into her life had thrown her so much off balance she didn't want to make up love stories for the time being. She was living one . . . sometimes. The rest of the time she was waiting to live one.

There'd been other men, of course, and before them other boys. And some had seemed wonderful at the time, at school, at college and afterwards when she worked in the bookshop. But there'd been no one as remotely overwhelming for her as Teddy, no one who'd left her so completely on the wrong end of the seesaw.

The sound of a gong echoed around the hotel, summoning the hungry to dinner. Her fingers stabbed a final thought into her keyboard:

And if you don't believe in the Lovers' Law of the Eternal Seesaw, just take a look at any couple you know.

'That's a table for one, isn't it?' Darrell said, greeting Amy at the dining-room door. 'This way, please.' And the boy porter led her swiftly past islands of empty tables to a corner close to a large open fireplace where the few winter guests were collected.

Picking up the menu, Amy glanced around, mentally shivering. An English seaside hotel in February had its own damp chill, as though staff and guests were afloat somewhere, cut off from the rest of the world.

A couple of tables from her a red-faced, sandy-haired man in a brown suit and an orange floral tie was eyeing her. He smiled when he saw that she'd noticed him. Nodding politely, she looked quickly away, past the tall, slightly scruffy man with the bandage, who'd bumped into her in the lobby, and Michael and Eleanor, who were now sitting tensely at the next table, both dressed smartly for dinner. Only in an alcove by the window did there appear to be any joy. There an old lady was cheerfully ladling tomato soup into the mouth of a very old, disabled man in a wheelchair, occasionally wiping his chin with a napkin as he dribbled.

Pulling on her glasses, Amy was beginning to consider the short menu when she suddenly found herself thinking about Teddy. Would he be having dinner, sitting with his colleagues discussing the next day's show? No. He hated the executives' dining room. Perhaps he was sitting unhappily at home in Richmond making small talk with his wife, Gillian? Yes. That was where he would be. But *would* they be making small talk? Surely not now. He'd be confronting the situation, asking for the divorce he'd so often nearly talked about with her. But then the question that had been pursuing her all day finally caught up: why hadn't he called?

She stopped herself. Such thoughts lead to paranoia.

She looked again around the dining room. Shona, the college placement, now wearing a tight, short, black waitress's dress with a white pinafore, evidently cut for someone shorter and slimmer, was serving the elderly couple, chatting, apparently amusingly, to the old lady. Behind her, Darrell watched her as he manoeuvred his way across the floor with a tray of drinks. But as Shona passed him on her way back to the kitchen and his eyes met hers her smile withdrew into an expression of infinite indifference. Meekly Darrell lowered his glance.

'It must be good having someone new to help out,' Amy said, indicating Shona, as he arrived at her table.

Darrell shook his head. 'To be honest, I don't think she'll like it much here. She keeps calling it Carbuncle-on-Sea.'

Amy smothered a smile. 'Oh dear.'

'And it's not fair. There's nowhere nicer in England.' The local boy was puffed with indignation.

Amy considered the rain-lashed windows. 'I'm sure,' she said, and, addressing her menu, she made her choice.

Darrell hurried back to the kitchen.

Again Amy looked around the room, her eyes fixing now on a wiry-looking, middle-aged, Scottish-sounding couple who had entered the dining room after her and who were now poring over maps and guides. Suddenly she envied them their companionship.

A murmur reached her from the next table: ' . . . and for that which we are about to receive, may the Lord make us truly thankful. Amen.'

'Amen,' responded Eleanor to Michael's grace.

Amy wished she couldn't hear, but every breath carried in this almost silent room.

'I'm feeling quite hungry now, aren't you?' she heard Michael say.

There was no answer.

'Is everything all right, Eleanor?'

Perhaps there wouldn't be an answer.

There was. 'Everyone knows, Michael.' It was almost a sob. 'We're a spectacle.'

'Now that isn't true.'

Now Eleanor's voice cracked unhappily. 'But what *is* true? Are we true . . . the priest and the nun who renounced their vows, and for what, Michael? For what?'

This time there was no reply from Michael, just the leaking wound of hurt and confusion.

'I'm sorry . . .' Eleanor was now whispering. 'I didn't mean that.'

Amy stared hard at the embroidered pattern that ran round the edge of her tablecloth. She really wished she hadn't heard.

And how are we this evening? Head feeling better now?'

Across the room Tim looked up from a sheet of music manuscript he'd been considering. Immediately the musicians in his brain stopped playing. The large-breasted manager of the hotel was holding a bottle of red wine and glowing down on him. 'Yes, thank you.'

'Excellent! We'll soon have you as right as rain again.' It sounded more like a command than an encouragement. The woman uncorked the bottle. 'I expect you'll be looking forward to our Valentine's Ball,' she said, slipping an invitation onto the table. 'Free to our guests, of course.'

'Actually, I'm not much of a dancer.' Tim indicated that he wouldn't bother to taste the wine and that she could fill the glass. She did.

'No? Well . . .!' She feigned surprise, then added, 'Let's just see how the sap rises, shall we!' And putting the bottle down she set off across the room to nag at the new work-experience girl.

Tim considered the invitation to the ball. It was festooned with garish pink transfers of a woman's very full lips. Well, that would be one way he wouldn't be spending his Friday evening.

A few tables away a mobile phone rang an electronic opening to the *William Tell Overture*. The woman he'd bumped with his keyboard started for her bag, then stopped just as quickly as she realised the phone wasn't hers. Tim was glad about that. She didn't look like a *William Tell Overture* ringtone sort of person.

He could see who was. It was the chap with the brown suit and orange tie near her who was telling his caller in a jovial voice, much to the obvious annoyance of the manager, that he was 'ready, willing and able' for whatever was required.

Tim returned his gaze to the woman sitting alone. She was about his age, maybe a few years younger, with a copper-coloured bob of hair, and had now taken out a book to read while she waited for her dinner.

Slowly he sipped his wine, checked his watch and thought about Amanda in Denver, always a whirl of energy, her forehead permanently furrowed behind her black, sculpted fringe. Would she now be at a morning orchestra rehearsal? He imagined her at her cymbals and kettle drum. Then, as an unwelcome picture began to emerge, Amanda laughing and flirting, enjoying being the centre of attention, he turned away from it to watch the other guests, two late-comers, elderly women who were probably sisters, the brown-suited man, the robust Scottish couple and the old people by the window. Dinner in an English hotel in a seaside resort in the off-season could be a pretty muted business.

Once again his eyes found the attractive woman with the copper hair, the one without the *William Tell Overture* on her mobile phone. Why would a woman like that be sitting alone?

Shona! What kind of name was Shona, anyway? Darrell fretted as together he and the new girl stacked the large, industrial dishwasher in the kitchen. *Shona!* It sounded sort of exotic. Posh, too. Despite the clothes she'd arrived in, which made her look like a bag lady, Shona was the sort of girl who'd been to a private school and who could say whatever she wanted because she was confident, clever and spoke nicely. He wished he spoke nicely. If he did he wouldn't have said the things Shona said, though. She shouldn't have called the North Devon Riviera a Carbuncle-on-Sea. That wasn't very clever. It was just mean and snobbish. And untrue. But he couldn't stop looking over at her.

When he'd first taken her into the kitchen he'd noticed how Domingos, the handsome black Brazilian chef had looked at her, not leering or anything like that, because Domingos was actually a very polite man, but with a kind of joky twinkle. Agnieszka, the triangular-faced Polish sous chef, had noticed the twinkle, too, and frowned. She and Domingos just didn't get on. In fact, most of the time they didn't even bother to speak the same language to each other: Domingos always moaning at Agnieszka in Portuguese and Agnieszka snapping back in Polish. And that was just silly because they both spoke English perfectly well. But, as Darrell folded the last of the napkins and reflected on that twinkle, he offered a silent prayer that Domingos wouldn't forget about annoying Agnieszka and start getting on with Shona instead.

'Is that it for the night?' Shona asked after Darrell had checked the dining room for the last time. 'Am I finished?'

Darrell nodded. 'We start at seven,' he said. 'If you like, I'll knock on your door when I get up. Make sure you're awake.'

Shona raised her eyebrows. 'You're such a gentleman, Darrell. Yes, please.' And opening the fridge, she took a large slice of lamb.

'Actually, we're not supposed to . . .' Darrell began to say. But Shona, her face illuminated into an eerie kookiness by the fridge light, fixed him with such a smile that the words died on his lips.

'Just in case I get peckish in the night,' she explained. 'Do you ever get peckish in the night, Darrell? I bet you do. I bet you get peckerish, too, sometimes, don't you?' Again the smile shone.

Darrell felt himself blushing.

'Anyway, good night,' she pouted. 'God bless!' And away she marched back through the dining room, her too-tight waitress's skirt clutched across her bottom, her bright, dyed, scarlet hair bouncing.

Darrell didn't know what to think. Usually he didn't like girls who talked dirty or were suggestive, but tonight, well, he just couldn't wait for the following day.

She changed into her buttoned-to-the-neck cotton nightdress and her powder-blue dressing gown in the bathroom, taking as long as possible to clean her teeth. She wanted to cry, but she was too strong for that. Besides, she didn't rightly know what she wanted to cry about. Opening the bathroom door she returned to the bedroom.

Michael was already in his pyjamas, also new, the Marks & Spencer cardboard-and-cellophane packing folded tidily in the bin by the mini-bar. He turned and smiled when she entered the room.

Together now they knelt on opposite sides of the bed to say their prayers, Eleanor hiding her face in a fold of the lace drapes. But no prayers came. Instead, she found herself thinking of the year she'd spent working in the hospice when she'd left the convent, after she'd fallen in love with Michael. She'd had her own room there, her freedom for the first time since she'd been a teenager, and the only discipline that of her own making. Sometimes she'd longed to ask Michael back to her room, just for a cup of tea and a biscuit, to show him how cosy she'd made her home, and how happy and agreeable she would make their life together. But she never had done. And he'd never suggested it. He wouldn't. He wasn't just a priest who had struggled with and then lost his vocation because of her. He was a shy, courteous sort of man.

Sex. The word approached her slyly through her prayers. Yes, she'd thought about sex, often, and fought it, every time putting such thoughts and images aside for some future moment when they would be appropriate. She'd been told when she was young that impurity of thought was as grave a sin as an impure act if it was purposely entertained. And although she didn't quite believe that any more, the manacles of the life denied still gripped.

So, sex, yes, she'd thought about it, as some distant event when she would be a different person, a confident married woman, instead of the frightened foolish soul now missing the comfort of God's certainties.

Yes, sex, yes, she'd thought about it. And thought about it. But now, here in this honeymoon room, she didn't want to think about it.

Michael was waiting. She crossed herself and stood up. He was wearing the kindest of smiles. Taking off her dressing gown she folded it carefully over a chair and turned back towards the bed. He was watching her. She stopped as her fingers reached the sheets. She couldn't.

'It's all right, Eleanor,' Michael said quietly. 'There's no hurry. We have the rest of our lives. Let's just go to sleep, shall we? We've had a busy day.'

'I'm sorry, Michael.'

'Don't be. Thank you for becoming my wife.'

They slept together, but they didn't lie together. The bed was broad and they were slight, two lonely people clutching the outer edges of the mattress, leaving uninhabited the conjugal space between. And finally prayers came easily to Eleanor. She prayed for help.

Along the corridor, Amy watched a late-night movie starring Meg Ryan. She'd watched a lot of movies on TV since she'd met Teddy Farrow.

In the Exmoor Suite, Tim stared at his keyboard and calculated once again the time in Denver, Colorado.

Chapter Two

LOOKING DOWN on the little port from her attic window, even Shona had to admit that as carbuncles went this was the prettiest she'd seen. Her view of the bay wasn't the best, rooms with that view being reserved for the guests. But standing on a chair in her bedroom above the hotel's old stables, now the staff quarters, she could see the merrily coloured fishing boats moored along the harbour wall, the sandy beach rinsed clean by last night's rain, and above the town the distorting shimmer of steam rising off the slate roofs of white- and buttercup-painted cottages. Even a winter sun as low as that in February made a world of difference.

She'd been awake for an hour, dressed and ready for work. She looked at her watch. A couple of minutes passed, then there was a knock on her door. She didn't answer. Then another knock, louder. She yawned, as though struggling out of the deepest sleep. 'What . . .?'

'It's seven o'clock.' Darrell sounded nervous.

'Oh God,' she groaned theatrically. Then: 'All right, thanks . . .'

She looked out at the day again. In the distance she could faintly hear a waterfall as the river dropped down from the moors and raced through wooded gorges to the sea. She'd listened to it half the night when, still crying, she couldn't sleep. 'You've always been a disappointment to us, Shona. Your mother and I have done everything we can for you, but you just disappoint. Why you can't be more like your sisters, I don't know.' Her father's words had pursued her, as so often, through a lonely night.

Climbing down from her chair she considered herself in the mirror over her washbasin, for which she had to stoop to see herself.

'What do you think, Monty?' she said at last, her eyes smarting as she fitted her new contact lenses, which did so much to magnify her eyes, directing her voice at the large, closed box tucked underneath her bed. 'Am I the cleverest and the most beguilingly beautiful girl you've ever seen? Or am I just brilliant and stunning?' Then blinking her lenses into place, she hoisted her already despised maid's uniform up at the waist, thus making the skirt even shorter, and set off for the day.

It didn't matter how well you knew someone, you rarely really recognised that person when they appeared on television, Amy reminded herself as she watched *The Teddy Farrow Show*. It wasn't just the pancake make-up, or the lights that seemed to rinse his grey hair a tint of blue. It was something to do with the way Teddy sat, artificially more upright, patronising the studio audience with his one-way friendliness, and that easy, pally sincerity with today's guest. But most of all, it was the fact that she knew she was watching a performance. Teddy wasn't like this in real life. He was nothing like so glib.

Before she'd got to know him, which had happened seven months earlier at a charity auction, she'd rarely seen the show, but when she had occasionally happened on it she'd marvelled at how promiscuous his guests were with their secrets. How did he get people to tell him this stuff? she'd wondered. Then she'd met him, and, casually invited to dinner as the auction ended, had quickly found herself laying bare the admittedly unremarkable details of her own life.

On reflection, what surprised her most was that she'd told him any-thing at all. Having, to her great surprise, found success with her first novel she'd made the immediate decision that she wouldn't live her life in a media spotlight. Giving up her job in the bookshop, and not with-out some regret, so that she could write more, she'd remained a private, secretive person, behind a famous name—now a successful brand. But at dinner that night all she'd been aware of was the way he listened so very carefully, and how he made her feel good about herself. *So* good. She wouldn't go on his show, she insisted, laughing, absolutely no way, but when an invitation had come for her to join him for lunch a couple of weeks later she'd been pleased. Then there'd been another lunch and more requests for a TV interview. Then another dinner, always some-where small and out of the way. And soon, somewhere between one invitation and the next, the suggestion that she should appear on *The Teddy Farrow Show* had stopped, and she'd realised she'd fallen in love.

She'd known from the beginning he was married. And happily. He'd made sure the entire nation knew. His was the perfect, long-distance, celebrity marriage, Teddy the star, Gillian the beautiful, gracious home-maker, wife and mother. But as Amy had never expected to find herself in an affair, it had never seemed to matter that he was married. Then suddenly it was too late. They were in bed together, again and again.

With the affair her life had changed. Now with guilt a factor they'd begun to go out together less, for fear of being spotted. He'd worried that his children might find out about her, explaining that he had to go slowly and prepare the ground. It couldn't be rushed, he'd said. She'd understood. And when he'd fretted that his public image was in peril she'd understood about that, too. She was in love.

And because she was in love and wanted only to be with him, she became used to staying in alone more than ever, waiting until he came to her and never missing his programmes. Sometimes she even watched the late-night repeats of his old shows on the satellite channels. That's the kind of cringing wreck I've become, she would tell herself. But she still watched, sensing her self-esteem sinking ever lower. She'd known why it was happening, but there'd been nothing she could do to prevent it that wouldn't have made her more unhappy.

Sitting up in bed on this Devon morning, she watched now as Teddy joked with a football manager about the difficulties of keeping the late-night activities of young footballers out of the Sunday newspapers.

'My life would be a lot easier if more girls would just learn to say "no",' laughed the manager to a round of applause. 'And if the papers were less hypocritical.'

Teddy shook his head sagely. 'Come on, now, Billy,' he jibed. 'Let's not blame the messenger when we don't like the message. The newspapers are only printing what we like to read, isn't that a fact, now?'

The newspapers are only printing what we like to read! Amy was puzzled. Was he deliberately mocking their pursuers?

A knock on the door broke into her ruminations. It was Darrell with the continental breakfast she'd requested the previous night.

'Sorry I'm a bit late.' The boy beamed as she let him in. 'Breakfast in Paradise.' And putting down the tray he drew back the curtains.

About to admire the view Darrell thought so heavenly, she stopped. There was a complimentary newspaper on the tray, and yet another photograph of her, this time in the contents box that ran down the side of the front page. **SO WHERE IS AMY? Page 7**, prompted a teaser.

Quickly she put the newspaper on the dressing table and joined Darrell at the window.

'It's a beautiful day.' He seemed almost to be boasting, and she noticed that he'd washed his hair and shaved the dark floss from his top lip since the previous night. The scent of aftershave lotion lay on the air. Then, with a polite nod, he was gone again.

She returned to the newspaper, and, flicking to page seven, read a short gossipy piece about herself alongside an old photograph. *So who's the big secret, Amy?* it ended.

It was froth, nothing more. No revealing facts, no naming of Teddy, nothing libellous, nothing new at all, in fact, just a reminder that they were onto her. All the same, she hated it. It was *her* froth.

'**G**od! You look like—' Shona blurted and then stopped.

Tim waited at his open door. 'Like what?'

Suddenly Shona dropped, not accidentally, a napkin from the breakfast tray she was holding and bent down to pick it up. 'I know what you're looking at,' she snapped.

'I'm sorry?' Tim asked.

'No, not you,' came back the girl, and, looking round, indicated Darrell who was passing and had glanced at her show of thigh. The boy hurried away as though bitten.

'So, what do I look like?' Tim continued, amused.

'Well, like, er, tired,' Shona replied, less abrasive now.

'Is that all?' Tim pressed. She was a contradictory girl.

Shona set the tray down on a table. 'I meant, you look as though you didn't sleep very well,' she said.

'Fair enough.' Tim touched his bandage. It was beginning to itch behind his ears. 'But that wasn't what you were going to say, was it?'

Shona looked him in the eye, defiant now. 'No. If you want to know, I was going to say you look like Death with a sick note.' And she poured his coffee.

Tim didn't react. The girl puzzled him. 'Why didn't you?'

She shrugged. 'It seemed a bit unkind to say it to someone with a bandage round his head.'

'And a bit rude? Not really the sort of thing you should say to a guest, eh?' The teacher in Tim was emerging. He didn't like that.

Shona looked surprised. 'If you like I'll apologise. But as I didn't actually say it, not until you asked me to, anyway, and wouldn't have done, I don't really think I've got anything to apologise for, do you? It was only a thought. We can't help our thoughts.' Now she smiled, a wide-mouthed, crooked, slightly zany smile.

For a moment she seemed very young. Eighteen going on fifteen, in turns outrageous and then sweet, desperate to get a reaction and test how far she could go. Actually, Tim didn't care what she said or what she thought. He was used to much worse at school.

'Perhaps not.' He grinned and took his coffee. Who knew why some kids tried to be chippy and draw attention to themselves? 'Maybe you're not cut out for the Samaritans after all, though,' he teased as Shona went to the door.

'Thank God,' she said, and left.

Sipping his coffee, Tim sat down at his keyboard and wearily considered what he'd written. She'd been right. He'd hardly slept. Putting on his headphones he played a few lines and then stopped, irritated. During the night his legless keyboard had developed a wobble on the table where he'd placed it. It was worse now.

An unrequested newspaper had arrived with the tray. Carefully folding it into two he wedged it between the keyboard and the table. The newspaper disappeared: the wobble ceased. Brilliant. Once more he began to play, but again not for long. Bored, he logged on to the internet and, eating a croissant, waited for his overnight email messages.

There were four, but the email he'd hoped for, the one from Amanda, wasn't there. That was disappointing. So he wrote her one, a casual, chatty one, intended to show that he wasn't disappointed at all at not having heard from her.

Hi, I've called once or twice, but Denver's obviously got you very busy. Good for you, I hope. Let me know what's happening. The head doesn't hurt much any more, but I'm a bit tired today because I worked all night on my new piece for the competition.

He hesitated, then:

To be honest, I really don't know about it. Give me a call if you have a minute. Miss you. Love you, Tim

Then pressing SEND, he got up, opened the French windows and stepped out onto his balcony.

It was mild for February, with great calico clouds drifting across a blue sky. Going to the rail, he looked down across the hotel gardens where a tangle of rhododendrons, pines and creepers pushed upwards competing for light and life. The sound of a door opening prompted him to look farther along the side of the hotel. The woman he'd bumped with his keyboard was coming out onto the next balcony but one. Politely, he smiled a 'good morning'. She nodded back.

Tim turned back to look at the sea. The music wouldn't come. Not in London, not here. Not anywhere. It just wasn't working. Perhaps if Amanda were here she might offer some inspiration. Then he dismissed the idea. She wouldn't.

God loves a tryer, he told himself, and going back inside he reached once more for the headphones, accidentally catching the lead sharply on the corner of his bed as he did. 'Oops.' He frowned as he unhooked them. A wire had broken away at the headphones end. 'Bugger!' he said.

What To Do and Where To Go on The North Devon Riviera!!!

Pulling the flyer from the rack in the hotel lobby, Amy added it to her collection. She already had information on moor and cliff walking, riding, cycling and sailing, and where to book for Lorna Doone tours. None of these activities appealed, but now an advertisement caught her eye. *Madame Cora*, it read, showing a spidery outline of an upturned hand. *Available daily for palm reading. First floor, Victoria Arcade.* Amy didn't believe in palmistry, but on an empty, lonely day in February it couldn't hurt to hear what the lady had to say. She could ask her about love lines. At the very least it might make an amusing paragraph.

As she turned to leave, the man in the brown suit she'd seen at dinner the previous night approached, smiling like a Sunday. Today he was wearing a camel-coloured short overcoat, the kind people used to call car coats. 'Morning,' he cackled.

'Good morning.' She forced a smile.

He looked at her brochures. 'Thinking of seeing the sights, then?'

'Well . . . I thought I'd . . .'

'I could show you a few sights.' He laughed, then quickly continued. 'Devon's littered with them.'

'Well, perhaps another day.' Politely she tried to put him off.

It didn't work. 'Right! You're on!' he relished. 'Now, I'm sorry, but I have to dash. I'll see you later. All right!'

And before she could unscramble the misunderstanding, he was off towards the car park, samples of floor covering poking out from under the arm of his coat. At reception the manager scowled after him.

Amy shut him quickly from her mind as a fool, and, making for a side door, stepped out into the hotel garden. It was too good a day to stay in and work, but she needed to buy a new mobile phone if she was ever to escape her hotel room.

A steep, zigzagged path, hewn out of the cliffs, made a short cut down to the sea. Sheltered by wind-broken Scots pines, and decorated by patches of early daffodils, it was a pretty walk. In other circumstances this could, after all, have been the right place for a romantic break, she reflected. Unfortunately, romance wasn't something to be enjoyed alone.

She set off across the ribbed, damp sand, the only person on the beach. She wanted to think about Teddy, to bask in reveries of a future different from the present, one in which she was permanently with him. But all thoughts of Teddy now came with worry lines.

For a while she walked slowly, pondering the waves breaking on the sand, wiping away the footprints she'd just made, as though continually deleting the past. Then, finally beginning to head towards the little port, she took a micro-recorder from her pocket.

So, where was I? The Lovers' Law of the Eternal Seesaw, Part Two, she began, and, stopping again, drew a cartoon outline of a seesaw in the sand with her shoe. *Yes, well, as I was saying, it seems to me that it doesn't matter how happy a relationship appears, or how well suited a couple, the truth is the two are very rarely in perfect equilibrium.*

She walked on, skirting a large sea-water puddle.

On the surface they may be a match. She likes sushi and fast cars. He drives a Mazda sports coupé. He's crazy about Mafia movies, she's got Joe Pesci's autograph. He has a thing about oral sex . . . she's an Ear, Nose and Throat consultant . . .

She hesitated at that, decided it was smart-arse and vulgar and not to include it when she typed up her notes, and then continued.

But that's just the packaging of their lives. It's the Eternal Seesaw that makes the rules. And emotionally you can be sure that at any given moment, one of them is soaring through the air having a terrific time and the most wonderful life, while the other is stuck, knees buckled on the ground. And if you're still not convinced, although you should be by now, just look in any mirror and ask yourself: at which end of the plank are you sitting?

She didn't see him, but Tim spotted her as he hurried down the cliff road to the town. A solitary figure on an empty beach, it occurred that she looked strangely romantic out there by the sea, like the traditional widow waiting hopelessly for her sailor to return. Then, overtaking her, he crossed over a short promenade and entered the town.

As a seaside resort it was tiny, a row of bathing huts behind the front, half a dozen defiant palm trees, a few white-fronted Regency houses, some shops, their windows boarded up for the winter, a tiny theatre still advertising last summer's attractions and, behind everything, a delta of pastel-coloured cottages bearing hopeful B&B signs.

The place he was looking for was close to the theatre, a short Victorian shopping arcade. The little electric and music shop Darrell had told him about was at its far end.

Quickly he found a new pair of headphones to replace the ones he'd broken, and he was heading back down the arcade when a bookshop a few doors along caught his attention. Some shops he just couldn't pass.

A green note had been stuck to the door of Madame Cora's Palmistry: *Closed—due to unforeseen circumstances.* So much for her predictive skills, Amy told herself, and, leaning on the first-floor balcony railing of the arcade, she looked around for a phone shop. She didn't see one. What she did see was a very large, black-and-white cut-out photograph. It was of her and it was in the mullioned window of a little bookshop across the arcade. She was surprised, flattered actually. Common sense suggested she ignore it. She was supposed to be in hiding. But she was an author and her books were obviously on sale in numbers here. One quick look couldn't hurt. And, with her short, khaki-coloured hair, she did look very different now.

Going down the spiral staircase she crossed the arcade and, pulling her hood closer round her head, she entered the bookshop. Inside there was another surprise. The cut-out was double-sided, so that it also gazed across the shop, right over a display of Amy Miller novels. You never got such promotion in London between books. The book-shop owner must either be an Amy Miller fan or had been made an offer of a job lot at some giveaway price.

Keeping her face turned down, she moved towards the neat stacks of her books. Had they been there in those exact positions since the previous summer? She was a realist. Probably. Quickly she began to do some calculations. Twelve copies of *Porcupine*, seven of *The Garden Bench*, nine of *Figure Skating in the Dark*, but only one of—

'Hello!'

She swung round, startled. The man with the bandage was smiling, a sale copy of a book about film music in his hand.

'Oh! Yes. Hello!'

'Small world.'

'Yes. Well, small town, anyway,' she replied. She edged in front of the cut-out photograph of herself, blocking his view.

'You know, for a second, I thought you were . . .'

'Yes?' He'd recognised her, she was sure. She'd have to move on.

'Well . . . counting.'

'Counting!' He hadn't recognised her?

'The books.'

Relief. 'Oh! Yes! Was I? That's a terrible old habit.' She thought quickly. 'I used to work in a bookshop. We had to count the stock every night to see how many had been stolen.' Actually, that wasn't true.

'Oh, I see.'

'*Teach Yourself Criminal Law* was favourite.' Nervous, and playing for time, she embossed the lie.

He smiled. 'Very useful, I'd have thought.'

'Yes?'

'For book thieves.'

'Absolutely!' She'd now begun to move him towards the door, but he stopped and looked at the display of her books. 'I can't imagine anyone wanting to steal Amy Miller books though, can you?'

That was a surprise. 'You don't think?' she said, trying not to sound indignant. Obviously the idiot had never read any.

'Would you?' he asked easily.

'Probably not,' she agreed, then led the way out into the arcade.

She was prettier than he'd realised: a bit younger, too, but her face was half hidden by her hood so it was difficult to tell. For some reason he wanted their conversation to continue. 'I saw you earlier,' he said. 'You were on the beach when I was passing.'

'Ah, yes! I was taking the scenic route to Madame Cora's. I thought she might be able to tell my future,' she said. 'But she's not there.' She indicated the palmist's booth on the balcony above them.

He shook his head. 'Isn't that always the way?'

'What way would that be?' They were walking slowly down the arcade.

'You know, the future never being around when you most need it.'

'Did I say I needed it?'

'Er, no. Do you?' He wasn't sure where this conversation was going.

She smiled now. 'Don't you?'

'I think I'd rather wait and see what happens.'

She dipped her head to one side as though accepting the point, but then said, 'If you'd been able to predict the future you might not have that bandage round your head.'

He was puzzled. She was teasing him and he was enjoying it. 'That's true. But think of all the nice surprises I've had that wouldn't have been surprises if I'd known about them in advance.'

They'd reached a phone shop. She stopped walking. 'But what about the disappointments?'

He shrugged. 'We need those, too. Don't you think? They make the good days so much more special.'

She seemed to think about that for a moment, as though it had some specific pertinence to her current mood. Then suddenly she became practical. 'Perhaps. Anyway, it's been nice meeting you. But I have some shopping to do.'

'And I should be working,' he replied. 'I'm Tim, by the way.'

'Tim, right.'

He waited for her to exchange her name. She didn't. Inwardly he shrugged. No matter. 'Well, anyway, I'd better be off. Bye.'

Strange woman, he thought, as he made his way back towards the sea. She'd been reserved then joky, chatty then not. Not that it mattered. Reaching the harbour he began walking back up the steep hill towards the hotel. Dark clouds had pushed in from the west, and now the first drops of a new squall began snapping at his face. All the same, the North Devon Riviera didn't seem quite so alien any more.

Michael and Eleanor saw him go by as they sat in the window of the Old Tea Rooms, which stood on an elevated pavement above the promenade. After breakfast, wearing wellingtons and anoraks, they'd set off for a walk around the town. They agreed it really was the prettiest of places, and the surrounding cliffs and hills much more wooded than they'd expected. In fact, they told each other, they couldn't imagine why this part of the world wasn't more famous. But then, as they'd settled into their tea and scones in the teashop and watched the occasional passer-by, their conversation had frozen.

'Isn't that the young man . . .?' Michael began, then stopped. Tim was so obviously their fellow guest it wasn't worth saying.

Eleanor nodded.

Neither spoke for a few more moments, so Michael refilled their cups. 'Perhaps if it clears up again we could try a walk up the gorge this afternoon,' he suggested.

'That would be nice.'

'Yes.' After that he couldn't think of anything to add.

It was Eleanor who finally broke the silence. 'I'm sorry that I'm spoiling your honeymoon, Michael,' she said.

Michael touched her hand. 'Don't be silly. You are my honeymoon. I'm having a lovely time just being with you.'

'You know what I mean,' she pursued.

He was embarrassed. 'Sex isn't everything, Eleanor,' he consoled.

She looked at him. 'How do you know?'

He gazed out at the rain again.

Amy bought a new mobile phone and chose a new number. Then, because it wasn't yet charged, she phoned Teddy from a payphone in the arcade, and left a message with her new number. She felt better after that. Now she need never miss a call when he wanted to talk. Yet a murmur inside her stirred: pathetic, it said.

He was halfway back up the hill when the people carrier drew alongside him. A window wound down.

'I thought it was you. Pneumonia next stop. Hop in.' It was the hotel manager, her round face beaming.

For just a moment Tim considered declining. But the rain was getting heavier. 'Thank you,' he said and climbed into the car.

Immediately the manager giggled. 'I'm sorry. My name's Jane, by the way, and you're squashing my darling pussy-face.'

He'd accidentally sat on something, of that he was certain. 'Sorry!' he said, pulling a brown paper bag from under him. A collection of red, satin-hearted Valentine decorations fell into his lap. *My darling pussy-face*, read one. He tried to smile.

'Don't worry. Just throw them in the back with the rest. They're gifts and decorations for our Valentine's Ball on Friday night. You're a musician, aren't you? A composer, yes?' She was probing now.

'Actually, I'm a music teacher mainly.'

'Don't be so modest. The room maid said she couldn't help but notice. Quavering crotchets all over the bed.' She giggled loudly. 'I don't think we've had a composer stay with us before. You must be a very quiet one. We haven't heard a single note.'

'Oh, no. You won't hear anything. The only sound is in my headphones.' And he opened his bag to show her the new set he'd bought.

'But we'd *love* to hear something!' Jane gushed. 'What about a little concert? Just to give us an idea of what you're working on up there.'

Tim pulled a face. 'I really don't think . . .'

But now she was coaxing. 'We have a beautiful piano in the Tiverton sitting room. It's Korean. With rosewood inlays. Shall we say teatime?'

Tim felt as though he'd missed a chapter. 'Today?'

'It needn't be very long.'

'I'm afraid I always work in the afternoons.'

Jane smiled triumphantly. 'Tonight it is, then. Splendid! A musical soirée at the North Devon Riviera Hotel. Thank you *very* much.'

Already they were pulling up by the front of the hotel. Tim stared unhappily at the new headphones in his hands. 'I really don't think your other guests will like my music,' he said finally.

Jane ignored that. 'They'll be bilious with envy at the Grand,' she murmured as they got out of the car.

Somehow Tim doubted that.

Jane went straight to her flat at the back of the hotel when she got in. She was regretting the sexy double entendre she'd used in the car. She'd behaved foolishly. He was nearly a generation too young for her, for heaven's sake, not to mention that he was a guest, and head office in Bristol had strict regulations that staff and guests did not mix socially.

Not that she would have had a chance with this chap, anyway, she reflected, as she re-touched her make-up. She knew that. She knew what she looked like. She'd known since school. 'Moon Face' some of the other children had called her. Big and bossy, that was her. When you were a plain and single woman of forty-nine-plus you'd accumulated enough scars and rejections, and regrets, too, to at least know that much about yourself. Though it didn't stop you wanting or hurting and sometimes making a fool of yourself.

Then, with her front restored, she set off for the kitchens. Domingos, the chef, had been complaining about a fault with the main oven again, and, typically, Bristol still hadn't sent anyone to take a look at it.

Will Abbott couldn't imagine why he hadn't realised it sooner. He'd spent the previous day researching and seeking a character as thin as a ghost. Amy Miller appeared to have had little past before she began writing. The biography offered by her publisher was skeletal. *Born in London . . . university in Edinburgh . . . Amy Miller wrote her first novel,* Porcupine, *while working in a London bookshop. She has since written four other novels.* That was more or less it, and now, since she'd disappeared, she had no present either. No one who knew her professionally would, or perhaps could, tell him where she'd gone. In fact, no one who knew her well was even prepared to talk to him about her, beyond demanding to know why his newspaper was hounding her.

Then his phone had gone. 'Have you found her yet, Will?' It was Polly, the schoolgirl snitch, calling in her lunch hour.

'Hi, Polly. How's school today?' He'd asked her to let him know if Amy Miller came home again, but she'd called three times yesterday and was becoming a pest. She was developing a crush on him, he suspected, or at least on the idea of the exciting life of the journalist.

'School is school,' Polly came back dismissively. 'But I was thinking about our friend Amy, wondering if she'd lived when George Eliot did whether she would have had to have a *nom de plume*, too.'

A *nom de plume*! Why hadn't he thought of that? Already he was reaching for another phone.

'Well, George Eliot was really a woman called Mary Ann Evans and she looked like a horse without a bridle and no one fancied her. Anyway, she had to change her name because . . .' Polly was continuing, and was well into the plot of *Silas Marner* before he could get her off the line.

'Amy Miller . . .' he said into his second phone to a young foot soldier trainee across the office. 'You wouldn't like to check with the latest electoral roll and find out if that's her real name, would you?'

As he put the phone down, a familiar scent drew close. Suzy leaned over his shoulder, her camera case sliding onto his desk. 'How are you today?' she murmured, the top of a thigh touching his shirtsleeve.

Was that by accident? he wondered. He knew it wasn't. She wasn't a bad photographer either.

Mommy, *what's adultery?*

As the television studio audience whooped with a hilarity the line didn't deserve, Amy's finger hesitated on the remote. She'd been lying on her hotel bed, devising races for raindrops, as huge, horizontally flying globules of water hit her window, when she'd finally given up and turned on the television. On her bedside table her shining new mobile phone, still charging, awaited its first call.

At home, watching television in the afternoon would have seemed degenerate. But she wasn't at home. Time lounged uselessly around her and only the prospect of door-stepping paparazzi had dissuaded her from catching the next train back to London.

She'd worked on her book, of course. Then she'd made herself some tea at four o'clock and casually begun flicking through the TV channels, past news and sport to a situation comedy. That was when she'd heard: *Mommy, what's adultery?*

The scene featured a girl of about ten having breakfast in a dazzling Hollywood kitchen while her mother prepared her lunch box.

Is it like Monopoly? the child persisted.

This brought a roar from the audience.

Her mouth open in comic surprise, the TV mother emerged from the fridge holding a carton of orange. *Actually, it's the exact opposite of Monopoly*, she answered.

But it is a game, isn't it? Is it a good game? asked the girl.

There was more laughter from the audience.

The mother snapped the lunch box closed on the table. *I guess that depends on who you play it with.*

The laughter turned to confirming applause at that. Amy wanted to change channels, but she didn't. For a second she wondered if Teddy's wife, Gillian, was watching. She hoped not.

Come on, eat! You'll miss the bus, the TV mother harried.

Can I play adultery? the girl now asked.

No, you can't.

Why not?

Why not! Because . . . it's for grown-ups only.

You mean it's an adults' game.

Well, sort of . . .

Is that why it's called Adult-ery?

The audience loved this. They hooted and clapped. Amy hated it. She hated the word.

Probably. I don't know. Come on, let's go.

But the script hadn't finished. There was more to be milked. *Does Daddy play Adultery?* the little girl persisted.

The mother's impossibly pretty face closed like a trap. *I would say . . . whenever he gets the chance*, she virtually spat.

Amy switched off the TV. She couldn't see anything funny about adultery. It might inspire plenty of jokes for those not involved—the cuckold's horns, the husband returning home unexpectedly with the lover hiding in the closet. But when you were on the wrong side of love, just waiting and hoping, feeling bad about yourself, blocking out thoughts of your lover having sex with his wife, living a secret, and feeling somehow left out of the world, it wasn't a game at all. It wasn't much of a life either.

Tim spent the afternoon distracted by thoughts of Amanda. Sitting at his keyboard, he found himself continually playing his way into dead ends, his mind veering off repeatedly as he pictured her, dressed as always in black, joking with the orchestra. She'd been excited, effervescent, when she got the late call as a replacement for the tour of America after the resident percussionist had sprained a wrist. She liked touring and she liked the camaraderie of an orchestra. Pretty girls often did.

He'd met her at a festival in Bamberg in Germany. She'd been involved in some modern workshop productions, while he'd been helping with a children's orchestra from South London. At first, he'd thought she was Italian or Spanish, so black and shiny was her hair, so vibrant her personality, so cherry red her lipstick. He'd also been unaware that she'd even noticed him, so surrounded was she by admirers. Then, on the penultimate night of the festival, he'd been sitting alone in the refectory when she'd asked if she might join him. He'd discovered later that the dashing conductor with whom he'd mostly seen her had publicly criticised her playing. She'd been devastated. He learned much later, because she told him, that they'd been sleeping together.

They'd got on immediately, Tim being a good listener. And on the next night, the last night of the festival, they'd become lovers, somewhat to his surprise, although sex and music were hardly strangers. He'd expected that they'd lose touch once back in London, his life and his music being quite unlike hers. Amanda had thought differently. They hadn't moved in together, but their relationship had taken root. She was social, vivacious, driven, and he was flattered that she found him such good company. 'You're like an old, blue-jeaned hippy, you know,' she would joke sometimes, looking around his cluttered flat, while running a hand through the waves of his almost shoulder-length hair. It was true. But, though he thanked her when she bought him a black velvet jacket for the smart events she liked to take him to, that was as far as his make-over went.

What puzzled her most about him, she would say, was his lack of ambition. That hurt, although he hid it. Success for Amanda would be red carpets and public, artistic and, most of all, avant-garde approval. She liked people on the edge. Tim wasn't so sure. Most of the people on the edge looked to him like poseurs who should be given a gentle shove. For him ambition fulfilled meant contentment in what he was doing. And it wasn't the same. They didn't argue about it, but little by little he'd felt the pressure to do things her way.

He'd always composed, or fiddled around with tunes, as he thought of it. Now he did it for her. She had plans for them both. Amanda said they made a pretty pair. She liked the idea of that, of being half of a good-looking, artistic couple. He went along with the notion. He didn't want to let her down.

But did she let him down, this beautiful social woman who enjoyed going on tour so much? She'd let other lovers down. She'd told him. He knew about her past and all her other lovers and he'd been jealous of them. How much of her present did he know about?

Outside, the rain hammered against his window.

'Get off, you pest! Get off!'

The voice was amused as much as angry, but it was enough for Darrell. He hurried into the dining room.

'Go away!' It was Shona, of course, trying to hold Giles the dog off, its front paws resting almost on her bosoms.'

Darrell grabbed hold of the dog under his front legs and pulled him away. He felt almost gallant, though, in truth, Giles was the softest guard dog. 'I'm sorry. He shouldn't be in here,' he apologised, grateful for their moment alone together. Shona had hardly spoken a word to him all day, and when she had it had only been to mock his country accent and unfortunate haircut. But in the day that she'd been at the hotel his entire waking life had been transfigured.

'He's a mad thing,' she said, brushing imaginary paw marks off her uniform. 'You didn't find him on the moors, did you? He isn't the Hound of the Baskervilles in disguise, is he?'

'He's just friendly. Pleased to see you. He must like you. I've never seen him like this with anyone else.'

'Ah! I see. That's nice.' Shona smiled. 'And what about you, Darrell?'

'Oh, he likes me, too,' he replied. 'Don't you, boy?' And holding the excited dog's collar he dragged him out of the dining room.

It was only later that it occurred to him he might have misinterpreted what Shona had been asking. But then, he really couldn't be sure. She came from Sussex.

Tim considered the Korean piano and its rosewood inlays, then played a few bars. The keys were stiff and a tuning was overdue, but it was better than many of the pianos he regularly played in lounges around London. He tried a little ragtime to warm up and then stopped.

Amanda had always been dismissive of his evening cash job. It wasn't her idea of being an artist. But he quite enjoyed being a bar pianist, wandering from tune to tune as the feeling took him, playing Stevie Wonder or George Gershwin in the style of Chopin or Liszt just for the fun of it, watching everyone while hardly anyone watched him.

Tonight would be different. Tonight the people would be coming just to hear him play, virtually a captive, probably a captured, audience.

He looked around the sitting room as the old lady wheeled her husband into the room. The two elderly sisters were already there along with the Scottish hiking couple, without their maps for once. From outside in the lobby he could hear Jane, the manager, trilling away, waylaying anyone who tried to escape to their rooms. 'This way for the concert. Starting soon. Musical treats for all!'

Tim grimaced to himself.

'Quiet down this way in February,' a conversation opened at his side. It was the chap with the brown suit, tonight wearing a pea-green shirt with it; he was leaning on the piano, viewing the guests as they entered. He was overweight, in his mid-forties, with thinning hair.

'That's what I came for,' Tim replied.

'You wouldn't like August then. The name's Barry, by the way, Barry Harrison.' And he put a half-full glass of beer down on the piano.

'Probably not,' Tim said, mildly irritated. He always resented it when a piano was used as a bar. It was a musical instrument, for God's sake. He would play soon and get the whole silly episode over.

'It's sex on tap in August,' Barry went on matter-of-factly.

Tim didn't need to know this. 'Really? Water shortage, is there?' he said quietly and drily to himself, and then watched as the honeymoon couple entered and found two places.

Barry hadn't registered Tim's sarcasm. 'A lobster isn't safe in her pot in August around here,' he went on, picking up his glass.

'But this is February!' Tim countered.

Barry's face now brightened for the punchline he was about to deliver. 'Well, if you don't tell her, I won't.' And he cackled loudly.

Tim smiled politely at the joke. Through the open door to the lobby he could see Jane stopping a final guest. It was the young woman he'd met that morning in the bookshop. With a look at best of bored surrender, the woman entered the sitting room and found a seat. Suddenly Tim realised that he was pleased to see her there.

Standing alongside the piano, Barry watched her closely. 'See this,' he bragged quietly. 'I'm on a promise here.'

It shouldn't have mattered to Tim, but for some reason it did. 'Really?'

'Gagging for it. Alone in a hotel! A woman like that! Why else would she be here?'

Tim looked back at the woman. She nodded at him, with just half a smile of recognition when she saw him looking. 'Probably the same reason as you and me,' he replied.

Which gave Barry the opening for another riposte. 'And why d'you think I'm here?' And this time he brayed so loudly that everyone in the room turned to look.

Tim smiled out of politeness then stared at his piano and waited as the last of the audience arrived, Darrell and Shona, followed by a young man and woman in chefs' outfits.

At last, satisfied that no one would miss this moment, Jane moved to the centre of the open space in front of the piano. 'Thank you so much for coming, everyone. It's so nice to see such an enthusiastic audience.' And she shone her smile around, as though she really hadn't had to twist any arms at all. 'As regular guests will know, the North Devon Riviera Hotel has long been recognised as a fortress of culture . . .'

'The Colditz of the arts . . .' sniggered Barry.

Jane shot him a glance of pure contempt, then continued, 'So tonight we're especially thrilled to be able to bring you our own composer in residence . . .' She beamed at Tim. 'Mr Timothy Fairweather . . . who will now play the opening movement for a composition he is still, I believe, working on. So, if all mobile phones could be switched off . . .'

In the audience a crease crossed the brow of the young woman from the bookshop as she complied. Tim noticed.

Jane turned to him again. 'Mr Fairweather . . .' The room was his.

Tim contemplated the piano. He was angry with this silly woman, but crosser with himself. He should have just refused. Well, this would give them something to think about. And he began to play.

A tumour had been the bait to draw Amy into the room. 'I'm sorry, I really don't feel in the mood—' she'd begun as Jane had stopped her.

But then that little extra moment of pressure. 'He's been told it's probably benign, but . . .' And Amy had followed Jane's eyes to Tim's bandage. Oh God! What had she said that morning?

Now she was totally perplexed. Notes were being played, but if there was a pattern she couldn't follow it, if there was a tune, she couldn't hear it. Yet the bandaged composer was concentrating hard on his handwritten manuscript. Singly, in clusters and in runs, what sounded to Amy like discordant chords and random notes followed one another.

She looked furtively around the room. Just behind the piano the horrible Barry was frozen, his pint glass halfway to his mouth. To the other side of the piano sat the manager, her expression going through the seasons of change, from expectation to confusion, impatience and now betrayal.

As though aware of the growing confusion around him, the pianist now began to increase the tempo. It still sounded awful, but suddenly a giggle erupted from the old man in his wheelchair. Behind him his wife, as though trying to keep time with the ever-changing rhythm, began to rock his wheelchair backwards and forwards.

This must have amused Shona, because, leaning against a wall, she, too, began to rock on her heels, as if imagining the rhythm that wasn't really there. Amy had to smile.

At that moment the pianist looked up and saw her. Immediately she was sorry. 'I'm not laughing at your music,' she wanted to shout out, little though she understood it. But surprisingly he smiled back, and then, without pausing, segued into 'Smoke Gets In Your Eyes'.

Immediately the mood changed. By the window the two elderly sisters soundlessly applauded in relief, while the old lady standing by her husband's wheelchair now began to move from one foot to the other in a slow foxtrot, quickly followed by Shona who, rocking slightly, showily, in front of Darrell, began a little shuffle display.

Amy relaxed as the weight of embarrassment in the room lifted.

'Come on, then, it's a party! Up you get,' a loud voice noisily announced. And, without warning, she found herself being pulled from her seat into a burp of beer fumes, as Barry took her in the arms of his brown suit, and began a slow smooch round the room. '*So I smile and say, when a lovely flame dies, smoke gets in your eyes,*' he crooned.

With great effort Amy attempted to hold her body away from his, but he pushed a knee between hers. She could feel a lot more of him than she wanted to. With her eyes fixed over his shoulder, she could see the expressions of astonishment in the eyes of the staff and other guests. That was when it got worse. Holding her ever tighter as they revolved slowly on the spot, a podgy, brown-suited thigh began to rub between her legs. In desperation she looked towards the piano.

The pianist saw the plea. Instantly the music changed again, the rhythm increasing to a fast, marching disco beat. *I'm so excited, and I just can't hide it . . .* The lyrics of the song, absolutely appropriate for her partner, bubbled into her mind. For a moment Harrison tried to hold on to his smooch, but already Amy was pushing him off, bobbing away, forcing him to do the same. Quickly she half danced her way to the sanctuary of the piano, leaving her partner stranded. Then, with a flourish, the pianist finished the recital-that-never-really-was.

The guests applauded, of course, it would have been impolite not to have done, and then quickly made for the door, as though half afraid that this was only an interval and there would be more terrible music to follow. Jane slipped silently, unhappily, from the room.

Amy turned to her rescuer. 'I owe you a drink,' she said.

He nodded. 'I need one.'

'But not here,' she said quickly.

He laughed. '*Anywhere* but here.'

They walked down the hill into the town, laughing with relief. It had stopped raining, and the lights of the promenade and jetty were mazily reflected in the shifting sea, which at high tide was now washing heavily along the beach. Near the beginning of the harbour wall was a former customs cottage turned into a pub. It was almost empty. Sitting in an old red banquette with a table between them, they dawdled over their drinks.

'You mean, you haven't got a tumour? Not even a benign one?' Her face was a query of amused indignation.

Tim laughed. 'Sorry. Concussion at the worst.'

'So, she lied to me to get me in?'

'She was selling tickets, or at least trying to give them away. In music circles that doesn't count as a lie. It can't be easy entertaining guests down here in the middle of winter.'

Amy shook her head. 'But you *are* a composer?'

Tim pretended to look hurt. 'It was that bad?'

'Oh, no. No. It was . . . it was the audience,' she stammered.

'You mean you liked it?'

'Oh . . . yes. Yes.'

'Ah, good.' He looked at her. She became prettier each time he saw her. He hadn't noticed before how small her nose was. 'Was it the melody you liked . . . or . . .?' he teased.

'Er . . . and the rhythm.' She was so anxious not to offend.

'Right,' he mused. 'You didn't think you'd perhaps heard it somewhere before? Because, you know, that's every composer's nightmare. That they accidentally rewrite or steal Beethoven's Fifth.'

She smiled now. 'Your tune is definitely not Beethoven's Fifth.'

'No? Good. What about Grieg's Piano Concerto?'

She was laughing at herself for having been taken in. 'That didn't spring to mind either.'

'Ravel, perhaps?' Tim continued. 'Or what about Gershwin, Stockhausen, the Blind Boys of Alabama . . .? I like them.'

'I don't think I know anything by Stockhausen,' she said.

'Well, that's a relief. He's a bugger to hum along to.'

Giggling, she pushed strands of hair behind her ears. He watched her, enjoying her company so much it amazed him.

'I know it isn't easy . . . musically,' he said at last, slightly more seriously now. Then, seeing that she didn't know what to say next, he joked, 'It isn't easy for me, either. No wonder I've had a headache.'

'I'm sure Beethoven had his off days,' she threw back. It was her turn.

'Probably. But he was deaf. So he didn't have to listen to what he was playing.'

Self-mockery came easily and she laughed out loud at that. This woman, who had looked quite sophisticated when he'd accidentally bumped into her with his keyboard, was suddenly so approachable. 'You haven't told me your name yet,' he said.

She hesitated for a moment. 'Er . . . Millie.'

'"*Er* . . . Millie"! Is that supposed to be with a hyphen, or was it just a dramatic hesitation?'

'Millie.'

'Well, thanks for your support tonight, Millie.'

For a moment they sat quietly together, one of those lay-bys in life when a new arrangement has just been made and time has to be taken to reflect on the situation and plot the way forward.

In the end she broke the silence. 'Perhaps I shouldn't ask this, but . . . if you really find your music so difficult, why do you write it?'

He winced inwardly, but didn't answer.

'I'm sorry. That was rude?'

He shook his head. 'No, not at all. It's just that there is a sense to it, you know, though perhaps I was being a bit spiteful trying it out on the hotel guests. Actually, very spiteful. I knew they'd hate it.'

'Oh, I don't think they hated—' she began.

He stopped her, mulling over her question. 'Why do I write it? Why do I do it?' Why *did* he do it? He tried to answer. 'Well, there is a sense of exploration going on, of finding out where music can go, what can be done with it—' He stopped. He was beginning to sound like one of Amanda's poseur pals. He shrugged and tried again. 'I mean, not *everyone* hates that sort of stuff. Some people quite like it.'

'Yes. I'm sure. Of course.' Then: 'Someone special?'

He was amused. She was intrepid. But he was flattered by her interest, too. 'Well, yes, I suppose . . .'

Now she smiled. 'Can I ask who it is? A girlfriend? Wife . . .? Or boyfriend, perhaps?'

He stopped her there. 'It isn't a boyfriend,' he said with a smile.

She was feeling guilty. No one had called her Millie since she'd been a little girl. It had been her grandmother's name for her, another diminutive of Amelia, her full name. Her mother had deemed Millie old-fashioned, so Amy she'd become. Now, although they were talking about his music, she was still half-worrying about the little lie she'd told. 'So the piece you played . . . the one you're working on . . . your girlfriend likes it?'

He looked dubious. 'I'm not sure yet. It's for a competition. Let's see how it goes. I hope she will, when it's finished.'

'I'm sure she will,' she encouraged. 'What's her name?'

'Amanda. She's on tour in America with an orchestra at the moment, while . . .'

'. . . you're here writing your great opus.'

He smiled. 'Until I got mugged, I was. It might help, you never know. Perhaps a creative clout was what I needed.'

'And Amanda, is she a pianist, too?'

'Actually, she's a percussionist.'

'Oh, right. You mean she likes banging things.'

He seemed not to see the joke. 'I think there may be a bit more to it than that,' he answered. 'And you haven't told me what you do yet.'

'Oh, nothing too exciting . . .' she said lamely, which was actually true on a day-to-day basis. She really didn't want to talk about herself.

'Such as?' he persisted.

She thought quickly. 'Well . . . paper,' she explained. 'I work in the paper distribution business.' Technically speaking, at least, that wasn't another lie.

But it *was* a dead end. 'Oh right . . . yes. And you're here for . . .?'

'Just taking a break. Time to think,' she said. Then, glancing out of the window and seeing squalls of rain blowing past, she added, 'And . . . right now, I think it's raining again. And I'm going to need some more wet-weather clothes if I'm to survive down here much longer.'

'**W**elcome to the Hotel Passion Killer, such a lousy place, such a lousy place,' sang Shona to the tune of 'Hotel California', as, balancing on a step-ladder, she pinned a pink *Welcome* heart to the lobby notice board.

Darrell considered her from behind a pile of decorations on the desk. Jane, in a huff, had dropped them there after the failed piano recital, demanded abruptly that he and Shona begin hanging them, and then disappeared to her flat. She could be a bossy, sharp-tongued woman, Darrell had thought as he'd watched her go, but she was fair with him. The hotel was her first as manager and she was desperate to make a success of it. Sometimes it was nearly possible to feel sorry for her.

How he felt about Shona he couldn't tell. One minute she wanted him to dance with her, the next she was ridiculing him and everything the North Devon Riviera stood for. He'd never been so confused. 'Our Valentine Ball's a big thing down these parts,' he said loyally. 'People come from miles around. Taunton, Bampton, Shillingford. All over.'

Shona raised her eyebrows wickedly, which Darrell now noticed were pencilled and arched like brackets. 'Get away!' she taunted. 'Not Shillingford, too. Well, whatever next!'

Again, Darrell felt the curdle of being a country bumpkin, and he looked at her, hurt into silence. Perhaps Shona noticed, too, because she was eyeing him carefully, but at that moment he became aware of one of the guests watching them from the hotel bar. It was Barry Harrison and he was signalling for another drink.

Darrell hurried through. 'Same again, Mr Harrison?'

Harrison nodded. He'd been very quiet since the dancing incident. He had, it was believed, a small company that laid floors and he was using the hotel as a base while he worked the entire North Devon coast looking for business. But the gossip was that his company wasn't doing very well. Darrell was under strict instructions from Jane not to let him run up a large bar bill.

Harrison took the new whisky and soda, then he indicated Shona. 'You want to get stuck in there, boy,' he said.

Darrell was embarrassed. 'She's not my type,' he replied quietly, afraid that Shona might have heard.

'Come on, it's winking at you.' Harrison smirked. 'Did you know that the heart-shape Valentine symbol isn't that shape because the ancient doctors thought a heart looked like that. It was meant to represent a woman's you know what. Did you know that?'

Darrell could feel himself blushing. No, he didn't know that. And he didn't want to hear it. It was embarrassing when someone as old as Mr Harrison got smutty.

Harrison was warming to his theme. 'Then there's the Cupid's arrow. Think about it, Darrell. There it goes all of a quiver right into the heart that isn't really a heart. God! When I was your age I was like a walking advert for the rampant sexual orgies of Sodom and Gomorrah . . .'

Darrell had heard enough. 'Well, if you don't mind . . .' he said, and went back into the hotel lobby. From her ladder Shona watched him, quiet now. He knew she'd been listening.

At that moment the front door opened with a slap of cold air, and the pianist and young woman from London hurried in out of the rain, laughing, their faces and shoulders soaked.

'I wonder, can you do me a very great favour?' The woman approached Darrell. 'Could you open the hotel shop and sell me a decent umbrella and cagoule?' She was in much brighter spirits than she'd been a couple of hours earlier.

'Of course.' Darrell was already halfway across the lobby to the little shop, noticing that she was deliberately ignoring Harrison's presence.

There actually wasn't much choice in the shop, burgundy or blue in cagoules and just one umbrella. The guest wasn't the fussy type. She chose the blue cagoule and pulled out a credit card.

Darrell swiped the card, and, as she signed, packed the cagoule into a bag. He was aware now that Mr Harrison was watching the couple through a mirror next to the fireplace, while Shona was observing everything from her stepladder.

Then, wishing everyone good night, even Harrison, who pretended not to hear, the guests went up the wide staircase together.

As soon as they were out of earshot, Harrison sprang to life. 'Did you see that?' he snorted. 'I pump up the tyres. He rides the bloody bike.'

On her stepladder, Shona giggled.

They reached Tim's door first. Amy stopped. 'Well, thank you for the drink. I really enjoyed it.'

'Thanks for being an audience,' Tim returned. He pulled out his key.

She moved along the landing a little and then stopped, with a sudden thought. 'Will you be calling Amanda tonight?'

'I'll probably email her. It's easier.' He hesitated. 'What about you?'

'Me?' She was surprised.

'Don't you have someone to call?'

'Did I say I had?'

Tim shrugged. 'No. But if you have, and you believed in surprises, there might be something good waiting for you on your voicemail if you call home. Good night.' And with a grin he opened his door.

Amy was already pulling her mobile phone from her pocket as she reached her door. She'd turned it off hours ago. How could she have forgotten? What had she been thinking of? Closing the door behind her she tapped into her voicemail. *You have no messages*, came the reply.

Tim stared at his laptop screen. *You have no email*, it read. He threw his coat onto the bed and sat down at his keyboard amid the litter of discarded manuscript. What had she said? 'Why do you do it?'

Why did he do it?

Eleanor listened to the regular breathing from the darkness across the bed. Neither of them had slept much the previous night, but this evening, a little light-headed from dinner when, in nervousness, he'd had more red wine than he was used to, Michael had dropped off quickly. She was relieved. He'd spent the day trying to convince them both that they were happy. It hadn't worked. Before they'd married they'd been unembarrassed to fall silent in each other's company, the sort of silence that comes from a mutual confidence. But now they were inventing conversations, commenting, in little blind alleys, on the ever more mundane. Only now, with Michael no longer awake and worried, could she recognise him again, the quiet man who liked his country walks and detective novels, his historical biographies and television football, the man with whom she'd fallen in love.

She peered through the blackness of the bed trying to make out his features. How easy it would have been for her to move across to him. But she couldn't. She thought about the nurses in the hospital and how she'd been shocked by the things she'd overheard them laughing about. Now she envied them their honesty.

She'd never been honest about her desires, but for so long her life had been lived more in her imagination than in reality. She'd liked her daydreams, reliving her childhood while she did her convent chores, remembering herself as a quiet, unremarkable girl from a village in Norfolk. What she hadn't known in the convent was whether she was really happy. It wasn't a prison. She wasn't in an enclosed order. She went out and saw the world. She could have left at any time. But for some reason she'd chosen not to. Occasionally, the spectre of an alternative life had occurred, and she'd wondered how things might have been if just one tiny circumstance in her history had been different. And then she'd met Michael, and, with her life consumed with thoughts of him, had found herself longing for the road not taken.

Chapter Three

JANE RAN HER HANDS like smoothing irons down her dark brown skirt, first across her stomach then her hips and thighs. She did it every morning, each day with the same mantra: 'No, no, no.' But already it was too late for the Valentine's Ball and for the new dress she'd bought specially for it at Monsoon in Exeter. She would be slimmer by the summer, she reassured herself. She would wear it then, at the Midsummer's Eve dinner dance. An unwelcome thought hovered as she chose her shoes for the day. Would she still be here in the summer? Would head office keep her on if this spring's figures didn't improve? 'Special events' had been the cry twenty months ago when she'd been sent to North Devon, but with a tiny budget and a wet summer in the South West it had been impossible to transubstantiate events into profits. And all the time self-doubt grew. Was she just not up to the job?

Turning away from the mirror, Jane pulled on her jacket, left her flat and went downstairs into the main part of the hotel to let the dog out. At the back of her mind the lyrics to 'Smoke Gets In Your Eyes' circulated as she watched him tear around the small closed garden. The humiliation of the previous evening still stung. She'd made a mistake with the pianist. He hadn't wanted to play, but she'd demanded an 'event', something special to put in her report to head office. She was embarrassed now, as she'd been jealous when it had been the pretty guest, and not her, who'd gone off for a drink with him. In a life of hotels, of watching and waiting, she hadn't often been the one chosen.

She let the dog in again and filled his bowl with water. There were two days to go before the Valentine's Ball, she mused as she watched him lapping thirstily. It would have to be the best ever or she might as well start looking for another job.

Tim was sitting alone by the window, deep in thought, when Amy reached the breakfast buffet. Collecting her coffee, melon, fruit juice and toast she hesitated for a moment, considered an empty table, then, making a decision, approached him. 'Is it all right if I join you?' she asked. It might have seemed rude to have sat elsewhere; on the other hand, was it presumptuous to assume he'd want to share a table with her?

Tim looked up. 'Oh, yes! Of course! Please!' he said, quickly clearing a space for her. His smile told her she'd made the right decision. 'No room service for us today, eh!' A note had been slipped under the guests' doors the previous night explaining that, as the staff were busy with preparations for the Valentine's Ball, it wouldn't be possible for breakfast to be served in the rooms for the rest of the week.

'How's the head this morning?' Amy said.

Tim tapped his bandage gently with a finger. 'Thick and empty.'

'But with new encouragement?'

He didn't follow. 'Sorry?'

'From Amanda,' she reminded.

'Oh, yes, right!' he said vaguely. 'Yes! Lots of encouragement. And you? A nice surprise?'

He's fibbing, she thought. But now it was her turn. 'Oh . . . yes!' And she wondered if she was as obvious in her lie as he'd been in his.

They went silent for a moment. Amy sipped her coffee and Tim watched Shona and Darrell unroll a long banner across one wall. 'So, it's official then,' he said, indicating the banner with his eyes.

Amy swivelled in her chair. 'Love makes the world go round' she read aloud, then, turning back to her breakfast, thoughtfully cut into her melon. 'Maybe. But I'm not sure it's necessarily true down here. It seems to me that this hotel has all the symptoms of a designated romance-free zone,' she said. 'Those two, for instance . . .' She indicated Darrell and Shona. 'He's infatuated.'

Tim nodded. 'I think so. And she doesn't realise?'

'Oh, she realises all right. She just doesn't know what to do about it. Then there's . . .' Amy's eyes now flicked to Michael and Eleanor, who, having just arrived, were standing at the breakfast buffet nervously making their choices.

'Don't tell me. Honeymoon hell?' Tim said softly.

'Purgatory at the very least.'

Now it was Tim's turn to look around, his eyes quickly passing the dancing crooner in the brown suit and Jane, the manager, who was pointedly ignoring him. Finally, he reached the elderly couple. 'They seem happy enough,' he offered as he watched the old lady buttering her husband's toast.

Amy examined them. It was true. This woman was contented. 'They must know the secret,' she said.

'Ah, there's a secret?' He was playful now. 'Well, if you find out what it is . . .'

'I'll let you know.'

He put his napkin on the table. 'So, what are your plans for today?'

Amy reached for the brochures in her bag. 'I was thinking of taking a look around when the rain stops,' she said. 'The forecast is better for this afternoon. Only occasional gales. What about you?'

'Oh . . . I . . .'

'You can come along, if you like.' The invitation just slipped out.

She could see that Tim was surprised. So was she. For a moment he looked uncertain. 'Well, I'd like to, but . . .'

She nodded, embarrassed now, backing off, wishing she hadn't made the suggestion. 'I know,' she said. 'Your music won't write itself.'

'I'm afraid not!' He laughed, getting up. 'Enjoy your day.'

She got on with her breakfast, opened a tourist pamphlet on local sea birds, then closed it, and wondered why she felt disappointed.

At the end of the room Darrell and Shona admired their banner. It had obviously been used several times before, but now in one corner it bore Shona's embellishments—a cartoon of a naked Eve standing half behind a tree, holding out an apple to a bearded little Adam who was scratching his bare bottom in a quandary.

'I hope Jane doesn't notice,' Darrell worried, though actually he was filled with admiration for Shona's skill with a felt-tip pen.

'We'll tell her it was on there when we opened the box. That some rude, horrible person must have done it last year,' Shona scoffed.

'You're a good drawer,' Darrell said. She was, too, though he half expected to be hurt again with some sharp riposte.

He wasn't. For the first time since she'd arrived at the hotel, Shona looked genuinely pleased. 'D'you think so? Thank you.'

At that second, time stopped for Darrell. Shona was really pretty when she smiled. Then, awkward again, he began searching for stick-on hearts for the hotel windows. 'Well, better be getting on . . .'

'Darrell'—Shona was loitering—'will you be sending any Valentines this year?'

Darrell didn't look up. 'I dunno. I haven't given it much thought,' he muttered. He'd never sent a Valentine card in his life.

'No?' Shona looked surprised. 'Well, you should. Girls like to get Valentine cards. It makes them feel . . . you know . . .' And she opened wide her big pale eyes.

Darrell looked at her. He thought he knew what she meant, but if he was right, he wasn't sure his mother would approve.

'Anyway, I'll see you later,' she said, and sauntered casually away.

Darrell watched her go. And then he calculated whether he would have time to go down to the card shop in town during his break.

Still at her table, Amy waited until the dining room was almost empty, certainly until everyone else was out of earshot, and then made her call. The message service answered yet again. This wasn't usual. Was it the Press that Teddy was trying to avoid, or her? No, she refused to believe that. She whispered a message. 'Hello, it's me, just to say "hello", wondering if you got my call about my new phone, and the number . . . Anyway that's all. Er . . . bye.' Then, as an afterthought, she repeated the number.

She felt wretched. Why ask, when you can beg?

Will Abbott scribbled rapidly on an envelope. 'Great! Terrific. Well done, Jerry. Thanks.' He put down the phone. 'Yes!' he exulted.

On his way to the morning conference across the floor, assistant editor McKenzie noticed. He changed direction. 'So?'

'We've found her. Amy Miller used a credit card to buy a mobile phone yesterday and again last night at a hotel, in Devon . . . under her full name Amelia Ann Millerton.'

McKenzie nodded wiithout expression. It wasn't like him to show enthusiasm. 'So, let's not frighten her off this time, all right!' he said brusquely, and strode on.

Abbott watched him go, murmured 'Prat!' to himself, and cast a brief but grateful thought towards Polly the snitch. Then, looking across the editorial floor at the picture desk, he considered Suzy. Sitting on an empty desk, she was leafing through a large book.

Casually he made his way over to her. 'What's that?' he asked, indicating the book.

'Oh, just some freebie the miseries on the women's page gave me.'

He took the book from her and read the jacket notes. *The Ladder of Sex. Climb the ladder of sexual fulfilment. Chapter by chapter, you, too, can learn the mysteries of perfect physical love.*

'It's a guidebook,' she said, her eyes never leaving his.

'So I see. Fancy a few days in Devon?'

She didn't answer for a moment, holding her head slightly back and to one side: a confident look. 'Work?'

'What else?'

She shrugged. 'OK.'

Abbott passed *The Ladder of Sex* back to her. 'You should bring this with you. It might be useful.'

She didn't even raise an eyebrow.

He tried working at first, but nothing he wrote satisfied him. It wasn't bad, he didn't think, but it wasn't good either. Getting up, he opened the book on film scores he'd bought in the town. Writing film music had been his dream when he'd been younger, using a theme in different ways to mirror and highlight different actions and emotions on the screen. A section on how Francis Lai wrote the theme music for the film *A Man and a Woman* caught his attention. Amanda thought it was sentimental and silly. He liked it because it was sentimental and silly. He liked the movie, too. He turned back to his keyboard. But once again he couldn't concentrate. The closing and locking of a door further down the corridor distracted him. He knew it wouldn't be Michael and Eleanor. They'd gone out already. Light footsteps passed in the corridor outside. He stared at his keyboard.

'Is it too late to have second thoughts?' he called as she climbed the path away from the hotel towards the cliffs.

She turned, surprised. 'What changed your mind?'

'Edward Elgar, probably,' he answered, catching up.

'Elgar?'

'Well, there he was writing all that wonderful music that we always associate with the beauty of England, and there I was cooped up inside when it was all around me waiting to be discovered.'

'And your own music?'

'For the time being . . . unfinished.'

'An unfinished symphony, you might say.'

Tim pulled a face. 'You might, I wouldn't. Unplugged at best.'

She laughed. Then threading their way through the pine grove on one side of the hotel, they set off through the gorse bushes along a muddy path, the beach of wet shingle and pebbles far below, above them the winter brown of the moors. Soon the sun grew clearer as they climbed, lighting up their faces, and it occurred to Tim that he felt comfortable. More than that, he felt happy. It puzzled him.

'Aren't you glad that I tempted you away from your work?' Amy asked. The cliff path had widened, and they'd stopped to enjoy the curving scallop cut of the bay below. With the light blinking off the sea, and the line of the South Wales hills clear across the Bristol Channel, the entire world seemed in sharper focus today.

Tim nodded. 'Actually, it wasn't very difficult to drag me away,' he owned up as they walked on. 'I was having trouble concentrating. When it's going well . . .'

'Nothing can drag you away, right?'

'Something like that. You know what it's like?'

She hesitated, and then said, 'I have friends who write.' She quickly changed the subject. 'This competition you've entered . . . what is it?'

'It was Amanda's idea. It's for what they call "new composers".'

'And is that good?'

He touched his bandage unhappily. It was, Amy noticed, beginning to become slack and slightly grubby. 'To be honest, I don't know. It's a sort of postmodern thing.'

'I see.' For Amy anything with the word 'postmodern' attached signalled time to talk about something else.

But Tim hadn't finished. 'Post-structural, too,' he suddenly added. 'Post-harmonic, even . . .' he conceded and smiled to himself.

'Ah.' She was amused, too, as he played with the thought.

'Post-rhythmic, as well, come to think of it. Post-tone . . . post-cadence . . . post-melody, post- . . .' He ran out of ideas.

'Early for Christmas?' she offered.

She was expecting him to laugh, but he didn't. 'Without the "Jingle Bells" bit. That would be too much like a tune for them.' He stared unhappily at the flashing light on a buoy. 'Sorry,' he said quietly.

'There's nothing to be sorry for.' She changed the subject. 'Amanda sounds very . . . forward looking.'

'She has ambitions for me.'

'That's good—to have someone who believes in you—right?' She meant that. For all his declarations of love, Teddy rarely talked about her books. She wasn't sure that he'd ever read one. She'd never made an issue of it, but it still hurt.

Tim didn't reply because as they rounded a large overhanging rock a painted sign came into view. 'Here you go! *Lovers' Leap*,' he read as they approached it. 'Isn't this where you get off?'

She was surprised. 'You think so?' she said carefully. 'I'm not a broken-hearted lover. Do I look like one?' Perhaps she did.

'No, but after hearing your breakdown on the nuclear freeze in the romantic life of the hotel this morning, I don't think you're in the paper business either.'

What was he saying? 'No?'

'No way. You're running a lonely hearts club, setting up a dating agency at the very least. Or you should be. You're a born romantic.'

She was relieved. 'All right! If wanting people not to be lonely or unhappy makes me a romantic, I'm a romantic. Isn't everyone? I bet Amanda is.'

'Actually, Amanda's a flirt more than a romantic,' he said.

'Men like that in a girl, don't they? Being flirty, I mean.'

'When she's someone else's girl they love it,' he said quickly, and set off down the path again.

She didn't mention Amanda for the rest of their walk. She'd touched a nerve. Instead, though she was usually disinclined to talk much about herself, she told him about her mother, whom she saw rarely, but who now lived virtually on a golf course in Connecticut. While for his part, Tim told her funny stories of playing in the bars, the observer who watched the nightly rituals of human mating, slyly adding an appropriate tune to his medley whenever he could think of one that might fit.

It was the prettiest of walks, but still very wet in places, especially when they dropped down from the moors and returned towards the hotel through the grey haze of a leafless birch forest in the fold of a gorge.

They were in sight of the roofs of the town when Amy's new mobile finally rang. She jumped, she was so surprised. 'I'm sorry, I'll just . . .'

'That's OK,' Tim said and walked on a little way to the edge of a waterfall.

She checked the caller's number. 'Hello? Hello, how are you?'

'Hi, Amy.' Teddy's voice was back to its usual confidence.

'How are *you*? I wasn't sure you'd got my messages.'

'I'm sorry. I just never got a moment alone to call, but I—'

She didn't need explanations. 'Teddy, d'you think if I came back now they'd still be on my doorstep?'

There was an intake of breath. 'Well, I don't know. Yes, probably. You know how the Press are. You're not enjoying it down there, right?'

He sounded so casual she was almost angry. 'Well, hiding from the tabloids wasn't exactly how I planned to spend my thirties.'

'Yes, I know . . . it must be a drag, but maybe in a couple of days . . . after the weekend—' He stopped abruptly. 'Oh Christ!'

She could sense that someone had entered the room he was in. She wept inwardly. 'Teddy . . .'

His voice was now very low. 'Look, I've got to go.' He stopped again. Then: 'I'll call you later, OK. Bye.' And he was gone.

'Goodbye,' she said to no one. She needed a moment to collect herself. She could feel her eyes brimming and wiped them on her sleeve. Ahead of her, Tim still waited by the waterfall.

'All right?' he asked kindly when at last she rejoined him.

She sniffed and tried a smile. 'He had to go.'

They began to meander on.

'He usually does,' she explained after a moment. And then, angry that she had to blink back tears, she added, 'I'm sorry.'

'Don't be.'

'It's just the Lovers' Law of the Eternal Seesaw. You know. Me on the ground . . .'

'Him in midair. Stephen Sondheim, "Send In The Clowns"?'

'Right. The seesaw's never in perfect equilibrium. Not when it comes to relationships. Do you know what I mean?'

He thought about that. 'Yes, I think I do.'

She smiled an acknowledgment of his empathy, and then together they turned to cross a small iron bridge that spanned the gorge, twenty feet or so above the fast-flowing river.

'Can I ask a favour?' she said quietly. 'You see, I've always wanted to play the piano. You couldn't give me a lesson, when you have a minute, could you?'

It had been an accidental discovery, but Michael felt almost furtive. The dead hour before dinner had driven them to the tiny hotel shop, and now, while Eleanor searched for a present for Sister Catherine, Michael was sifting through the postcards. He'd already chosen a couple showing impossibly sunny beaches, when he reached the saucy seaside selection. He would have been embarrassed to have been seen chuckling over illustrations of red-cheeked women, all bosoms and bottoms, when he became a priest. But he was a married man now.

A cartoon drawing of an unhappy shipwrecked mariner sitting on a desert island beside a beautiful mermaid, her blonde hair falling around D-cup breasts, made him smile. *I don't know what you mean when you say you still miss the better half*, the mermaid was saying, swishing her fish's tail coquettishly.

'What's the joke, Michael?' Eleanor was at his side.

Michael felt himself blushing. 'Oh, just a silly thing.'

Eleanor looked innocently at the cartoon. For a long moment it seemed that she didn't get the joke. Then she obviously did. Her mouth suddenly sagged as though she'd been insulted. Immediately she tried to hide it. 'Yes!' she said, faking amusement. 'Yes! Funny!'

Michael put the mermaid back in her rack.

The scream could have been heard in Taunton.

'What is it?' Shona demanded, rushing into the kitchen, Giles, the dog, bouncing after her.

But before there was any answer, sous chef Agnieszka had scrambled onto the kitchen stool and was pointing in horror into a corner. Giles didn't need any directions, immediately beginning to play football with something on the red-tiled floor, barking and yelping with excitement.

'What's he got?' Shona asked, as Darrell grabbed at the dog's collar and tried to pull him back. Then she saw it. A huge black spider, a truly vast one, was struggling to get away from the tormenting dog.

'My God! It's bigger than the Gdansk shipyards,' Agnieszka gasped.

'I'll get it!' Shona offered quickly.

'And get that dog out of here. This is a kitchen not a pet shop!' snapped Domingos the chef in defence of his territory.

Darrell pushed Giles out of the kitchen and closed the door.

Carefully Shona picked up the spider in a sheet of paper towel.

'Ugh!' Agnieszka moaned from the stool.

Domingos looked across at her, amused by her reaction. 'They don't have spiders in Poland? Come on! In Amazonia . . .' He held out his fingers and wiggled them at her. 'As big as your hand! Furry legs, too.'

Agnieszka looked sick and said something to him in Polish. It sounded very rude. Domingos just laughed.

Shona watched them. He enjoyed baiting her, it was obvious. Did she secretly like it? It was hard to tell. She folded the paper towel into a little pouch. 'I'll put it outside,' she said, and stepped out into the courtyard. 'Sorry about this, fella, but you should have kept out of sight,' she said as she hurried across to the staff accommodation.

'See what I've got for you today,' she said out loud as she entered her bedroom. Then kneeling by the bed she pulled out the large cardboard box. 'How about this for a treat, then?' And she tipped the spider into the box.

Romance.

Amy stared at the word on her laptop screen. Tim had called her a romantic. Of course she was. But what exactly was romance? She began to write.

Romance. Scientists explain it as a sudden flow of an endorphin called oxytocin to the brain; evolutionists consider it a trick by nature in order to persuade us to perpetuate our genes; teenagers think it's not noticing each other's pimples, and cynics call it sex through rose-tinted condoms.

She hesitated, running the sound of Teddy's voice through her mind as it had sounded on her mobile that afternoon. Had she dreamed it or had there really been a slight sigh of impatience?

Returning to her laptop she read her notes again and then added:

But something that hurts so much can't just be sex, can it?

Then, because she really needed to think, she went to run the water for a very long bath before dinner.

In the Exmoor Suite, Tim was waiting for the hotel operator in Denver.

'I'm sorry, sir. I'm getting no answer. She must have gone out. I'll put you through to her message box.'

'Thank you . . .' he said. Then he stopped. 'On second thoughts, don't bother. It doesn't matter. Goodbye.' And he hung up.

A few minutes later he slipped out of his room and pushed a sheet of the hotel stationery under the next door but one. On it he'd written: *I was wondering if instead of sitting at separate tables we might make it easier for the staff tonight and share one. Just a thought. Tim.*

'**N**ot a bad little hideaway as hideaways go.' Will Abbott sat at the wheel of his black, secondhand Porsche at the back of the car park and surveyed the North Devon Riviera Hotel. Above the car the pine trees swayed in the sea breeze. From the passenger seat Suzy stretched out a hand and ran a finger along the crease in his trousers at the top of his thigh. This was the fifth time she'd done that since they'd left London four hours earlier. He'd never known such a sensuous woman. Well, not recently. He glanced across at her. She was smiling at him. With difficulty now, because the car was small, she began to pull on her denim jacket over her T-shirt. It hardly fitted. Abbott looked back at the hotel. 'Not a bad little hideaway at all,' he repeated. From inside the hotel the sound of a gong reverberated across the car park.

'**T**hat's for the entire Valentine's weekend, I assume?' the hotel manager asked. Abbott nodded. 'Jolly good. I'm afraid our porter is helping to serve dinner at the moment, but . . .'

'We can manage quite easily, thank you,' Will Abbott responded, picking up his bag. Apart from Suzy's cameras and modem, hidden inside her case, they were travelling light. They weren't here to enjoy the sights.

'If you're quite sure. Your room is on the first floor . . .' A key slid across the desk. 'We take orders for dinner until nine.'

'Thank you.' Abbott was taking up the key when a peripheral movement on the stairs caught his eye. A man and an attractive woman were coming down. He looked casually away, waited until the couple had passed, and then followed Suzy up the stairs. Amy Miller's expression had never altered. Only when they were alone on the landing did he allow himself the smile of the triumphant. 'Got her!' he whispered.

'Who was the guy with her? It certainly wasn't Teddy Farrow.'

Abbott shrugged. 'Gay cover. That droopy bandanna said it all.' Then, finding their room, he opened the door for her and followed her in. 'We'd better get down quickly for dinner.'

Suzy flopped back on the bed. 'Are you sure? If we're going to do this right . . . not rouse suspicions like, shouldn't we take our time?'

Abbott looked at her. 'Well . . . I don't know . . .'

But already Suzy was pulling *The Ladder of Sex* from her bag. 'It starts getting really interesting in Chapter Nine,' she said. 'What d'you think?' And she smoothed out a crease on the patchwork counterpane alongside her with the palm of her hand.

Amy looked around the quiet of the dining room as Darrell reset a table for two. Tonight, the murmur was even more hushed than usual as eyes were on them. By the window the old lady said something to her husband and smiled, while the two elderly women in floral dresses carefully considered the new dining arrangement. 'You know, I have a sneaking feeling that we might just have become . . .' she began.

' . . . a talking point?' Tim finished. 'I hope so. After the music I made them endure they deserve some light entertainment.'

As Darrell lit a candle and stepped back from the table, they sat down together.

'What did you do with the spider?' Amy heard Darrell whisper as Shona passed with a tray.

'Just don't eat the boeuf bourguignon,' Shona hissed back, and, flouncing on, put a plate down with a flourish in front of Barry of the brown suit. 'One boeuf bourguignon!' she gushed. 'Enjoy!'

Amy looked up at Darrell. He was staring at Harrison with a mixture of awe and dismay as the guest stuck his fork into a piece of meat. 'I'll just get your water,' he said, and hurried after Shona.

Putting aside whatever little games might be being played by the staff, she turned to Tim. 'You never told me how long you intended staying here, but you'll be here for the Valentine's Ball tomorrow night?'

'It's beginning to look that way.'

She nodded to herself. 'Well, at least there'll be someone else in the hotel not involved.'

Tim smiled, then, in keeping with the other guests in the room, they both fell silent, watching as Michael and Eleanor entered the room and made their way to the next table. Even with an easy-going companion like Tim, Amy thought, dinner at the North Devon Riviera Hotel could still be a serious matter. A murmur close by soon caught their attention. It was Michael making the sign of the cross. 'In the name of the Father and of the Son and of the Holy Ghost,' he began.

'Do they say grace at your school?' Amy whispered.

'Actually, they're bigger on the last rites.'

Amy giggled.

'Bless us, Oh Lord, for these Thy—' Michael began.

Suddenly he stopped as a low, rhythmic, pumping sound interrupted the hush of the dining room.

'Can you hear that?' Amy asked. The rhythm faded.

Alongside, Michael continued his grace. 'These Thy gifts which—'

The thumping sound came again, but now louder and more urgent.

Oh, no, Amy thought, recognising the rhythm.

Facing her, Tim put a hand to his bandage, covering his face.

Michael hesitated in confusion. At the door to the kitchen, Darrell was looking up. Next to him, Shona was giggling. By the window, the old lady was nudging the old man, while Barry in brown had stopped eating. Only Eleanor looked puzzled.

Michael struggled to finish: ' . . . which we are about to receive—'

But at that moment a woman's distant cry interrupted.

'Was that a seagull, Michael?' Amy heard Eleanor ask.

Tim was now smiling. Amy bit her lip as the cry grew louder and more desperate. It was like one of those moments at school when she'd got the giggles. The more she tried to hide it the worse it got.

Michael, meanwhile, was still staring at his soup, his face reddening. At last Eleanor seemed to realise what was happening.

'Someone got lucky,' a woman's voice said behind Amy. It was the Polish sous chef talking to Shona at the door to the kitchen.

Hearing her, Barry grinned: 'That'll give them an appetite.' And he guffawed, eyeing Agnieszka.

She ignored him, as across the room the old lady's face twinkled with fun. Even her husband seemed to be smiling.

By now, Amy's face was in her napkin. Tears of laughter, which she was desperately trying to hide from Michael and Eleanor, were rolling down her cheeks.

Michael wasn't giving in. As the final sob of relief broke in the room above he made one last effort: 'Through Christ, Our Lord.'

'Amen,' murmured Eleanor.

At which point, Giles, the dog, began to howl, too.

In their bedroom above the dining room, Suzy languidly opened her eyes. Alongside her lay Abbott. He'd been around quite a bit, but nothing had prepared him for Suzy. 'Not bad, eh?' she said, and stroked his bottom. 'D'you think there's time for Chapter Ten before dinner?'

He was comfortable at a piano, confident. Just sitting at a keyboard made him feel empowered, his fingers finding the notes as though magnetically drawn to them. Here he could do anything, anything he wanted to, anyway. He was in control. As a boy he'd enjoyed his piano lessons, but best of all had been those evenings when he'd just sat and played, discovering new structures and where the notes might take him. When he'd been a little older he'd sometimes played at parties, late at night after most people had gone home. He'd read somewhere that Billy Joel had done that and it had been a good way to get off with girls. It might have worked for Billy Joel, but Tim had never noticed it working for him. He hadn't minded. He'd never minded, not even at college when he'd been keyboard player with a student grunge band and had his contribution completely hidden by howling guitars and drums. He just liked playing. Sometimes when they'd first got together, Amanda had watched and listened as he played. It was the most flattering thing she could have done. But then, she was a musician, too. She hadn't asked him to play for her for some time now. She'd been very busy.

Sharing the piano stool he could now feel the outline of his new pupil, the girl who liked to weigh everything before she answered, and who was having a tough time with some man she didn't want to talk about. She was a mystery to him, and probably he to her. But they got along in some carefree, indefinable way, both amused at the hotel, and both intrigued by its winter guests and the situation in which they'd found themselves. It was good to have a new, albeit temporary, friend when the foundations of so much else seemed uncertain.

She'd asked for a lesson, so, driven by the giddiness of dinner, they'd soon found themselves at the Korean piano in the sitting room. It hadn't taken Tim long, however, to realise that what his pupil really wanted was to play without learning, certainly without practising. It wasn't an unfamiliar wish. 'I think your best bet would be if we doubled up and played a duet,' he said after a few minutes' dancing her around middle C and some basic chords.

'Yes,' she said giggling; a bit drunk. 'Like Elton John and Jools Holland.'

'Exactly like them!' he agreed. 'Put your finger here.' And taking her forefinger, he placed it on a note. Her hand was cold and he felt a tingle of intimacy as he touched her. Once again his reaction came as a surprise. 'Now keep pressing on that note like this . . . like a pulse.' With his finger on hers he began a steady rhythm. 'Let's see how we get on.'

Concentrating hard, she now kept the rhythm going as he began to play around her, building the tune as he went, moving her one finger up and down the keyboard as she, delighted, accompanied him. Occasionally he glanced at her, noticing for the first time the slight vertical scar to one side of her eye. But when she caught him looking he glanced quickly back at the keyboard.

They played on, songs by Cole Porter, Aimee Mann and Smokey Robinson, until in ones and twos the other guests made their way from the dining room to listen while waiting for their coffee. Apart from watching television there wasn't an awful lot more to do after dinner in mid-February in the North Devon Riviera Hotel.

Eleanor didn't know what to say. Actually, she didn't know what to think. She couldn't really remember what she'd expected marriage to mean just a few days earlier, but now she felt as though she was sailing farther away from Michael as each day passed. She'd hardly eaten at dinner, longing for Michael to say something about what they'd both heard, to make a joke perhaps, because it had so evidently amused most of the other guests. But he hadn't been able to find the words.

Now they sat distantly together, aware of the fun being enjoyed at the piano across the room, but hardly listening. After a while, a still smiling Shona served them coffee and a couple of After Eights. Eleanor bit off a corner. Then she put it down again, no appetite for luxuries.

Michael noticed. 'Don't worry,' he said at last. 'It'll get better.'

It took her some moments to formulate an answer. 'I feel like a relic from another age,' she trembled. 'Like the Latin mass.'

'No,' he protested. 'Don't say that. That's just silly. Ridiculous.'

'Ridiculous?' she repeated softly. 'Two late-middle-aged virgins in a honeymoon suite, with a mirror over the bed and adult videos on Channel Thirteen! *That's* ridiculous, Michael.'

This time she saw the pain. Immediately she was sorry she'd spoken. That had been too unkind. He looked so defeated, so completely at a loss to know what to do. And for the first time she found herself hating her religion for mis-shaping their minds and needs, Michael's as well as hers, and for leaving them out of the real world for so long. But then, just as quickly, she made a short prayer asking for forgiveness for her momentary loss of faith. 'I'm sorry, Michael,' she said at last.

Michael watched the piano players.

Will Abbott was watching Amy Miller, wondering where the guy next to her fitted in. He might be a complication. It would have been easier if she'd been on her own. Mainly, however, at that moment he was telling lies. Standing in the semi-darkness in the doorway that linked the sitting room with the sun lounge, called the loggia in this hotel, he was feigning world-weary boredom into his mobile phone. 'No, it's a bit of a dump, really,' he was saying. Then to a question: 'I can't say really. I could be stuck down here all weekend. Anyway, I'd better go. Kiss the boys for me. I'll call tomorrow. Good night, God bless.' And hanging up he returned the phone to his jacket pocket.

Seeing that, Suzy moved towards him. 'All right?' she said.

He nodded.

Suzy smiled to herself, one of those satisfied little smiles of quiet triumph that some girls wore when they thought they'd won a tiny skirmish over a sexual rival. He didn't like it and turned away.

She moved closer. He did like that.

'Then there's Chapter Eleven, "The Wheelbarrow Position".'

Abbott looked back at Amy Miller. He'd wait, keep watch on her before he confronted her. There was no hurry. He had all weekend.

They stopped at Tim's door, lingering in the corridor. She was still giggly. 'Thank you *so* much. That was fantastic. I'm a pianist. My second greatest ambition fulfilled.'

'Only your *second* greatest ambition?'

'Well, yes, I mean, if I could one day play in a band! At school I used to dream about being a member of Fine Young Cannibals. Or The Smiths. That would be the ultimate. Can you imagine!'

'Well, they say nothing's impossible.'

They both hesitated. She looked towards her door.

Tim took the hint. 'Anyway . . .' he began.

'Yes . . .' she agreed, but didn't move. Then suddenly she leaned forward and tried to push a loose strand of his bandage, which was hanging down towards his right eye, back into place. It still didn't feel quite right. She tried again. 'No. It won't go. Look, can I return the favour?'

He didn't follow. 'I'm sorry?'

'Your bandage. Perhaps I could . . . you know. I was a Girl Guide when I was twelve. For five weeks. We did elementary first aid.'

'Oh!' He was surprised. 'I mean, yes, please. Actually, I have a new bandage in my room. In my bag. It's been difficult for me to put it on.'

She smiled. 'I can see.'

He was strangely embarrassed. Pulling his room key from his pocket, he opened the door for her to go in. 'Right,' he said, putting on the overhead lights, 'I'll just get the stuff they gave me in the hospital.' And he went into the bathroom, leaving her to look around the room.

When he returned she was toying soundlessly at the keyboard. Quickly leaving it, she switched on a desk lamp. Then, turning round the chair on which he worked, she patted it. 'Sit here,' she indicated, taking the bandage from him.

He sat down.

Standing behind him, she now very carefully unclipped the safety pin that was holding the bandage. 'Tell me if I hurt you,' she said, beginning to unwind the bandage from his head.

'Actually, I think I'm pretty well immune to—' he began. 'Ooh!' he gasped. The bandage had pulled the lint from the wound on the back of his skull.

'I'm sorry,' she apologised. 'There's a lump like Australia, well Tasmania, here. But the cut's healing. It's closed. Well, it was until I just opened it again. They could have killed you.'

He laughed at that. 'Not really. It was my fault. Playing them *Romeo and Juliet* without the gang fights and stabbings. They probably thought they had to improvise their version of *West Side Story*.' As she carefully began to re-dress the wound, he felt strangely contented.

'You must be a good healer,' she said as she worked her way through his hair.

'You're a good nurse.'

'Not really.'

He winced as she pulled the new bandage too tight. 'No, well, you might be with practice,' he added. The re-bandaging now progressed more slowly. For a few moments they didn't speak as she concentrated. Then: 'This afternoon . . .' he began. 'That chap who phoned you . . .?'

'Yes?'

'Is he in love with you?' Where the question came from he would never know.

'Yes.'

'Good. That's nice.'

He couldn't see her face, but he could feel the hesitation in her hands. 'Actually, to be honest, I'm not sure if he is.'

'Oh, he's bound to be.' He surprised himself with that, too.

Perhaps she didn't notice because she suddenly said, 'He's married.'

'Yes.' He'd assumed that.

'Yes,' she repeated, and went back to her task. 'And Amanda?'

He thought about Amanda, pictured her pretty face and dark hair. 'She's more than a flirt,' he said at last. 'She's away a lot. On tour.'

'Oh, come on. That doesn't mean anything. Lots of people hardly ever see each other—'

He had to interrupt. In Amanda's case it did mean something. She'd always been careless with the evidence. Perhaps she wanted him to know. 'It's someone in the strings,' he said. 'A cellist.'

The bandaging had finished. Now she came to face him, perplexed. 'But if you know that . . . why do you carry on?'

'Why?' It was a question he couldn't answer. Because he loved Amanda; because he didn't want to admit the failure of their relationship; because, despite everything, he didn't want it to end. People stayed with unfaithful partners all the time. Why? Because they were remembering when things were better, or because they were hoping for things to improve. Was it both or neither?

But then there was the music he was writing. *Why do you do it if it's so difficult?* That had been yesterday's question. He hadn't been able to give an answer then. But he knew now.

The new bandage was in place. He didn't want this conversation to go any further. 'Hey, that's pretty good!' he laughed. 'Thank you.'

She looked at her watch. 'Good. Well, I'd better go.' She went to the door. 'Thank you for the piano lesson.' She stopped as the door swung open. 'I'm very glad I met you,' she said. And with that she was gone.

Tim stroked his new bandage and stared at the door.

It was after midnight. The hotel was silent. Even the Shaggy Wallbangers, as Shona had immediately christened the newly arrived, seemed to have gone quiet for now. Darrell was still thinking about that. He'd never heard such a racket before. Shona, of course, had taken it in her stride, which just went to show what kind of world she lived in, but Domingos and Agnieszka in the kitchen had been giggling about it all night. And that was strange, too, because they rarely spoke to each other, not civilly, anyway. What was it he'd read about football and sex being the only true international languages?

Now the last chairs and tables had been cleared away in the dining room to turn it into a ballroom, and he and Shona had stuck the last of Jane's red hearts to the last window panes.

'Well, that's about it for tonight, I think,' he said, wishing he could think of something else for them to do together to prolong the moment.

Shona didn't appear to be listening. 'You know something, Darrell . . . I was thinking, seeing all those hearts we've stuck up, it makes me feel quite romantic. D'you know what I mean?'

Darrell looked at her, expecting some put-down to follow. There wasn't one. She was smiling, more friendly than he'd ever seen her. 'Well,' he said studiously, 'I imagine that's probably just the ozone.'

She frowned now, as though that wasn't the answer she'd expected. 'What ozone?' she asked.

'Don't you know? Sea ozone makes everyone feel a bit, you know, fruity. It's a normal chemical reaction. It's the same with chocolate.'

For a moment he thought she was going to laugh at him. But she didn't. 'Will you dance with me at the ball tomorrow night, Darrell?' she suddenly blurted. 'The last waltz, perhaps?'

He couldn't have been more surprised. 'Well, I dunno . . .' he began, looking away, awkward, rubbing his nose, although it wasn't itchy. 'I've never done a waltz.' In truth, he'd never done any sort of dance with a girl. The limit of his experience had been a limp, solo, robotic effort on the periphery of the school disco. 'A waltz is old-fashioned, isn't it?'

She was having none of it. 'A dead camel could manage the last waltz, Darrell. See, I'll show you.'

And stepping up to him she put his right hand on her waist and taking the left one began to turn him round slowly on the spot.

He couldn't think what to say. He just grinned like a madman and looked into those bright blue, magnified eyes as she moved him in tiny circles around the dining room, and felt her soft, round hip pressing into him when he was supposed to change direction.

'Not bad,' she said at last as they paused for a second. 'But we might have to rehearse a bit more if you're going to get the hang of it in time. Now, let's try again, one-two-three, one-two-three . . .'

She couldn't sleep. She was puzzled by a feeling she couldn't quite explain. She wanted to write, though she wasn't sure what or why. Reaching for her laptop, she sat up in bed and put down whatever came into her head.

> So, love, as we all agree, is an evolutionary mechanism. But it's also the decoration we give to our lives. It's a comedy, a tragedy, a sport and a farce. It's biological, psychological, chemical, olfactory and blind. It can be promiscuous and fleeting, or lifelong and exclusive. Love can be lonely and crippling, or euphoric and joyful. It can also be erotic or chaste, exotic or quixotic, both faithful and treacherous, platonic, heroic, shared, one-sided, addictive, hallucinatory, a game two can play, a three-in-a-marriage Princess Diana style, or a dream for one more vivid than reality. It can hurt, it can bite, and it can be cosy and warm; a fairy tale or a nightmare, sensible or irrational, idealised and unrealised. It can be all of these things. It can, they say, help heal people, and, if deaths from broken hearts are to be believed, kill people, too. It can be lustful or companionable, provide the will to live and the inspiration for great and not so great works of art, and when it really gets going it can instigate murder and suicide, even war—although, frankly, some of us find the Helen of Troy story a bit hard to believe, especially after seeing the film. All the same, most of the time it can cripple the lovelorn, and everyone has experienced those long, clammy, sleepless nights, with sheets soaked from worry and tears. But on the good days, when the seesaw is in balance, and adoration and desire are met and returned . . . is there any feeling better in the entire world?

She stopped wondering where she fitted into all this, and if Teddy had a place at all. And she thought about Tim and her piano lesson.

Laying her laptop down on the carpet beside her bed, she switched off the light. She would make sense of all this tomorrow. Then she remembered. Of course she would. Tomorrow was St Valentine's Day.

Tim noticed the light go off on the next balcony but one. He stroked his new bandage and wondered about the married man in her life. Something she'd said came back to him. 'I'm very glad I met you,' she'd said. Mentally he repeated it. *I'm very glad I met you.*

He returned to his keyboard. The ideas were coming tonight better than they'd ever done. He had to get them down before they dried up.

Chapter Four

JANE WATCHED the red Royal Mail van cross the wet car park towards the hotel. It would help to get good news, she thought; thanks from head office, for instance, or a ten-day trade-union convention booking for March. Failing that, a morning without worry would do.

She'd been awake since before six, making plans. There was still much to do before the ball. Valentine balls were major events in a hotel calendar, winter cash crops. Head office had high expectations.

'Morning,' the postman said, holding out a wedge of envelopes as he considered the red hearts that Shona had stuck around the walls.

'I hope we'll be seeing you tonight, Adrian,' Jane bloomed, taking the post. 'There's a free welcome glass of sparkling wine to all guests.'

The postman sniffed a wet nose. 'The wife won't let me out,' he said.

'It's a *Valentine's* Ball, Adrian. You're supposed to bring her with you.'

The postman looked at her with a vaguely mystified contempt. 'In that case, I might as well stay at home,' he jeered. And off he went.

Jane returned to the collection of trade brochures with their giveaway discounts, which made up most of the post. Business was thin right through the hotel trade in the two months after New Year, and all the ancillary trades had offers to make. The rest of the post was made up of invoices, legal documents to the guest in Room 24, Barry Harrison, and a large, white, spongy envelope. It bore a local postmark and it was addressed to Shona McWilliams.

'Oh God! Oh! Oh!' Will Abbott felt as though his head had been punctured as his face collapsed into the pillow.

Beneath him, Suzy sighed comfortably. 'Lovely,' she gurgled.

That was more than lovely, Abbott thought. But even as he did, a sliver of guilt began to unpeel. He should be at home now, with Jenny and the boys. Never mind, he'd make it up to them when he got back. Linking Amy Miller and Teddy Farrow would be page one. And Jenny would be interested in the story. She loved to read about celebrity adultery. She'd be proud of him for getting it.

Suzy turned to him. 'Hello, you,' she said, and put a hand to his face.

He didn't show it, but that bothered him. She sounded almost affectionate. That wasn't part of the deal. Removing her hand, he said, 'Is that bacon I can smell frying downstairs? Just what we need to start the day.'

Michael had made the tea as quietly as possible, then put the cups and saucers on the tray with a silent delicacy. Lastly he added an envelope. Only as he put the tray down on Eleanor's bedside table did she wake.

She smiled. 'Good morning.' Then she saw the envelope. 'What's this?'

Michael felt the sudden slam of colour to his cheeks. 'Happy Valentine's Day,' he said, his voice scarcely above a whisper.

'Oh, Michael.' Her eyes filled. Very carefully she opened it.

Already he was apologising. 'It was the best they had in the shop.'

'It's beautiful,' she said, gazing at a rustic watercolour of a couple of black and white goats. 'To my darling wife,' the billy goat was saying to his partner, 'the Valentine of my life.'

Now tears were tumbling. Michael offered a tissue.

'And I'm being so terrible to you . . .' She blew her nose.

'No, no, you aren't. Not at all.' Tears led to silences. He thought of a way out. 'Did you know there were at least two St Valentines? Or maybe even three. One was a third-century martyr in Rome.'

'I didn't know that.' She wiped her cheeks.

'Oh, yes, the legend was they cut the poor man's heart out while he was still alive and sent it to the emperor.'

'Good heavens. On St Valentine's Day!' A sudden new thought must have occurred because Eleanor's damp eyes brightened. 'I wonder, Michael, when they'd cut it out, his heart, did it fit into the envelope?'

Catching her expression, Michael began to giggle. You would never have thought it to look at her, but she had a very droll sense of humour.

'There's a ruin of an old church along the coast,' Eleanor said, between sips of tea. 'It might make a nice walk this afternoon.'

'I'd like that,' Michael said.

He heard the laptop *twing!* of the incoming email as he was shaving.

I'm sorry if I've been difficult to get hold of these last few days. But things have been tricky here. See you soon. Love you. Amanda xxx

He read the message several times, not because he didn't understand it or because he was wondering why Amanda had been impossible to reach for days, or even because he wanted to know why things might have been tricky for her. What puzzled him was that he didn't know what he was supposed to be feeling.

He was finishing shaving when his phone rang.

'The bandage wasn't too tight, was it?'

She didn't have to introduce herself. He was already smiling. 'It was fine. Still is.' And he checked it in the mirror.

'Good. Slightly amazing, but good. Look, it's a sunny morning and I wondered if you were free for breakfast. Somewhere out, I mean . . . if you're not working.'

He didn't know what he was supposed to be feeling about this invitation either, but it pleased him. 'I'm not working,' he said.

She was waiting for him in the garden, watching the sunshine on a pattern of gold and purple crocuses that stretched across a lawn. This place got prettier all the time, she thought, as together they strolled down the hill to the little town. It was a warm and clear day.

This being February there was, of course, nowhere for them to buy breakfast. They settled for some croissants from a tiny supermarket. After picking up a couple of coffees in polystyrene mugs from a van by the bus-stop, they strolled out along the stone quay, which, built like a battlement, guarded the entrance to the harbour.

She knew Tim wanted to know more about her, but having started out with a lie there was no way of going back. Besides, his life seemed so much more real than hers, his days fuller than any of the recent phoney, lonely hours she spent at her computer daydreaming imaginary situations for made-up people while waiting for Teddy to call.

When they'd talked in the bookshop she'd seen Tim as a diffident, uncertain man, who made a conversation out of half jokes. She'd misread him. Today he was excited, even though he said he'd been up working half the night. 'Does that mean the music's going well now?' she asked.

'For me. Yes. I think so. Last night was good. The best it's been. I don't know if it will work out, but *I'm* happy with it.'

'So the kids who crowned you did you a favour, really. They made it possible for you to come down here to work without any distractions.'

He reflected on that, then he said, 'Distractions aren't always bad, you know. The right ones can help. In fact, sometimes, they *do* help. Definitely.' He looked at her, then as though realising how pointed that had sounded turned quickly away again.

It was almost a declaration, and so unexpected she didn't know where that conversation might lead; or even if she wanted to know. So, carefully, she steered him towards safer ground. 'If you could afford to, would you give up teaching and write full time?'

He didn't have to think about it. 'No, I'm sure I wouldn't. There are bad days at school, I know, but there are great days, too, like when you see some boy or girl begin to make the musical connections. And you realise that, whatever he or she does, his or her life will never be quite the same again, that a whole new world is opening up to enjoy. It's a real thrill to see a life change like that.' He was smiling. Amy felt a twinge of envy for his enthusiasm.

They'd now come to the end of the quay. Across the harbour and up the hill she could make out a yellow van being unloaded at the hotel. Tim watched with her. 'Will you be going tonight, to the Valentine's Ball?' she asked.

Tim hesitated. 'To be honest, I hadn't intended to. But perhaps if I had someone to go with . . .'

She nodded. 'Just what I was thinking.'

And, not quite embarrassed, but uncertain, they laughed together as they finished their coffees and made their way back down the quay.

'**Y**es! Yes! That's it! To me now!' Peering into her viewfinder Suzy was willing her subject on, despite the fact that Amy Miller was fifty yards away. 'Will!' she said quickly. 'Pass me the other camera!'

Pulling a face because he didn't see himself as a photographer's assistant, Abbott reached for a second camera armed with an even longer lens. From the cover of a windbreak on the miniature golf course, they were watching Amy and her companion as they walked back along the quay towards the town. They'd followed them since they left the hotel.

'That's better!' Suzy's motor shutter ran a procession of snaps.

'Be careful she doesn't spot you.' Abbott was nervous, peering through a slat in the windbreak. Suzy's head was slightly above it.

'You know, Will . . .' Still staring into her viewfinder, Suzy was thoughtful. 'From where I'm looking, by the expressions on their faces, if that guy with her is gay, like you said he was, I'm Rock Hudson.'

'To many people, Valentine's Day is just a joke,' Jane began, 'a time for lovey-dovey cards. And here at the North Devon Riviera Hotel we like to enjoy Valentine's Day like everybody else. It can be fun. And we hope it is. But for us it isn't a joke.'

Shona looked around the kitchen as the hotel staff, including the two women from the town who did the bedrooms and who spoke only to each other, watched Jane without expression.

'Here,' Jane confided, 'Valentine's Day and with it the success of our Valentine's Ball is pivotal to the survival of this hotel during the off-season. Because if this hotel had to close during the winter, jobs would go. Perhaps mine, perhaps some of yours. So, tonight, I know I'm going to get sterling work from everyone.' She finished with a school-prize-day smile. 'Now, any questions?'

For a moment there was the usual English embarrassed silence when-ever questions are demanded. Then: 'Darrell said that it's a local custom on Valentine's night to spike the Devon cider with an aphrodisiac . . .' Shona was smiling wickedly.

By the dishwasher, Darrell's pleasant features contorted in a spasm of embarrassment. 'I never did,' he blurted.

Jane looked witheringly at the girl. 'Not a beverage you'll ever need, I dare say, Shona,' she jibed. But then, turning to Domingos and Agnieszka, she added, 'That being said, if Chef can manage any little culinary love potions, romantic treats from South America, I'm sure all our guests will be more than grateful . . .' She looked around at her staff. 'But now I think it might be a good idea if we got back to work.' And she marched out of the kitchen.

'Love potions,' Domingos said and wandered down the kitchen.

Darrell made his way across to Shona, who was surreptitiously retrieving half a sausage from a guest's plate. 'I dunno how you can tell such lies,' he murmured, still flushed.

But Shona was ready with her biggest smile. 'Sorry, Darrell. It was only a joke. And thanks for the Valentine card.'

As soon as she could, Shona hurried up to her room, clutching her card. It was the first Valentine she'd ever received, and she didn't mind at all that it seemed to be made of Dunlopillo covered in blood-soaked crimson velvet.

Inside her room, she re-examined the card for any sign of a signa-ture. There wasn't one. Of course not. Anyway, like a detective of romance, she'd already checked the handwriting on the envelope with Darrell's notes at the reception desk. It had matched.

Propping her card on her dressing table she smiled to herself, a little ripple of triumph. At home she'd sometimes been embarrassed by the absence of male interest in her, her sisters' universal popularity being applauded by everyone. But then, they never disappointed.

Now, though, she had a Valentine card! And it was beautiful.

Feeling in a plastic bag for the piece of sausage she'd purloined, she pulled her cardboard box out from under the bed. But as she slipped the top from the box her face buckled. It was empty.

'Oh crikey,' she gasped. Then lying on the floor she scanned the room. 'Come out, wherever you are,' she demanded. 'This isn't funny.'

Nothing moved. Then she noticed it. A large gap between the skirting board and the floorboards. She frowned. 'Oh, no!'

A brand-new and worrying thought. If love is the all-conquering, single-minded obsession that we know it to be, how do we explain the sudden, unexpected, uninvited, totally irrational, romantic yearning for someone other than the object of one's dreams?

Amy didn't write this then, but she thought it and she knew she would write it later, as she watched Tim make his way back up the hill to the hotel, a footloose piece of bandage beginning to flap from his wavy hair. It made him look slightly madcap, she thought.

Tim had left her to go back to his work and now she needed to do some shopping. Leaving London the way she had, she hadn't even packed a skirt, let alone a dress. But she was a conformist. If she was going to a Valentine's Ball she should be wearing something feminine. It vaguely occurred to her that she might have more choice if she took the bus to Exeter, but then that might have been making too much of what probably wouldn't be any more than a local hop. There was something else. Stuck like a fugitive down here in Devon, she was beginning to block out the reason she'd come. More than that, she was beginning to enjoy being the person she was pretending to be. To leave the little town, if only for a few hours, would be to risk breaking the spell. She'd surely find something she liked here.

So she set off for the shops, offering a friendly smile to the randy couple who'd arrived the previous night and who, as she changed direction, she suddenly found coming her way. She'd spotted them earlier mucking about on the miniature golf course, which had seemed an optimistic pastime for February. Now, when they saw her smiling at them, they looked slightly shamefaced. That amused her. If they were having a good time on a dirty weekend, good for them.

He kept wondering if he'd dreamed it, this theme that he seemed to know before he played it, before he wrote it. He'd made a joke about not wanting to subconsciously steal from Chopin or Schubert. Was he doing that now as he sat over his keyboard and copied down what he was hearing in his head? Even if he was, it didn't worry him. He was enjoying his work. He was flying. He was happy. And when he imagined the beautiful, brow-knitted Amanda looking over his shoulder reading the manuscript as it was shaped, always just about to make a suggestion, he quickly replaced her in the orchestra of his mind with a part for a pianist who only played with one finger.

High on a tor above a sheer cliff, it was one of those churches that looked as though it might have been built in the Middle Ages as a beacon for sailors returning home up the Bristol Channel.

'*Originally Saxon, then with Norman additions, but sacked in 1536 during the Reformation and later abandoned when the population declined . . .*' Eleanor was reading from her Devon guidebook as, resting at a stile on their climb up the hill, they considered the chapel ruins.

'It must have been quite a scramble for people to get to Mass,' Michael panted. He was fit but the narrow path had been steep and long. 'The sermons would have had to be good.'

'But, remember, when the congregation got here they'd have been that bit closer to God,' Eleanor offered wryly. 'A good fifteen hundred feet, anyway.'

Michael chuckled. 'As in the Tower of Babel.' It was good to see Eleanor making her little jokes again. With this pilgrimage, albeit to the now desanctified St Gytha's, they were doing something together they'd done all their separate lives; which had, in fact, *been* their lives.

He looked up at the crumbling arrangement of grey stones that lay between the thickets of gorse above them. There wasn't much left of the chapel, with barely three walls still standing, while the tower and the roof must have gone long ago. But it was still recognisably a church, a sanctuary where people had come for solace, for baptism, death and marriage.

Then Michael turned and gazed back at the empty moor they'd hiked across. Had any of the parish priests who'd once lived here faced the moral quandaries he and Eleanor had struggled over? Had they ever fallen in love and had to choose? Surely they must have done. Human nature never changes.

A stray black and white goat like the ones on the Valentine card he had bought for Eleanor had been trailing them across the moor. Now it lifted its head and watched them.

'Well, Michael, are you ready?' Eleanor broke into his musing. 'Last one in the church is a doubting Thomas.' And she set off stoutly uphill.

He watched her as she went, huddled in her anorak, this kind, grey woman whom he'd admired impossibly from afar in the hospital. Please let it work out soon, he prayed silently. Then he followed her.

The van arrived from the poultry farm just before lunch. Darrell was on reception checking Mr Harrison's bill. It was three weeks in arrears and his Visa payment had just been turned down. Jane would be facing a difficult encounter, though not as difficult as Mr Harrison's.

'Here you go, every quail's egg in Devon and then some,' the chicken farmer said, beaming, as he put the carton down on the desk.

Darrell looked at the box suspiciously. The North Devon Riviera Hotel wasn't the sort of hotel where quails' eggs were on the menu.

'For Mr Domingos,' the farmer explained, pulling out an invoice.

'Ah, at last! They come!' Domingos was already hurrying fussily from the kitchen to claim his eggs. 'It's nearly too late. Love potions, like love itself, take time to prepare.'

Leaving Harrison's account, Darrell followed Domingos into the kitchen. Already Agnieszka was arguing. 'Quails' eggs! What are quails? Pigeons? Sparrows? They're no good. Superstition! Give people vodka if you want aphrodisiac. That get anyone started.'

'And finished, too . . . too quickly,' Domingos said quietly, examining his eggs. 'In my country we do things more delicately . . .'

'With voodoo, mumbo-jumbo from Africa.'

Darrell smiled. At least Domingos and Agnieszka were arguing in English today, probably for the benefit of Shona who, drafted into the kitchen to help prepare the buffet for the ball, was laughing happily.

Domingos wasn't insulted. He never was. Reaching for a large bowl, he began to break the eggs into it. 'Brazil is the world capital of sex and love, as your country, Poland, is the capital of beetroot and cabbages. Tonight you will see. Now we must make enough choux pastries for everyone. We need at least three hundred heart-shaped profiteroles. Believe me. I will make magic. Now, for this I need peanuts and catuaba.'

'What's catuaba?' Shona enquired.

'He probably just made it up,' said Agnieszka.

Domingos was unperturbed. 'I don't know the English name, but it doesn't matter. We improvise. Crushed walnuts in quails' eggs to make the vanilla custard. But we must be quick. Love can't be kept waiting.'

Agnieszka snorted. 'Only a man could say that. Some of us wait for years and still don't get it.' But she went to get the flour just the same.

Darrell watched Shona. She was smiling, lopsided, comically, as she helped, her arched, pencilled eyebrows high on her forehead like those of a clown. She wasn't what his mother would call a 'nice Devon girl', but she was the most exciting girl he'd ever met by a country mile.

Then he looked back at Domingos. Did he really know some black-magic recipe for making people fall in love?

Amy wasn't sure. Was powder-blue really her colour now that her hair was khaki? And, more worryingly, was the dress cut too low at the front? The trouble was there wasn't another dress in Double Entendre that she liked, and there wasn't another dress shop in the town. And it *was* a pretty dress. *She* was the problem.

'It looks lovely, dear.'

She swung away from the mirror. The elderly lady from the hotel was standing watching her, smiling. Her husband was sitting in his wheel-chair by the door. 'Hello. Thank you. Do you really think it suits me?'

'Absolutely. And I'm sure your young man will think so, too.'

'Er, young man . . .?'

'Well . . . the young man at the hotel . . .'

'Ah!' Amy was suddenly embarrassed. 'Actually, he's just a friend.' Then, though she would have denied it, she was aware of a small glow of pleasure at the misunderstanding.

'I see.' And the elderly woman gave her one of those knowing smiles that older people wear when they suspect they're being fibbed to. 'He seems a very nice friend, anyway.' Now Amy noticed that the old lady had the slightest touch of a strawberry-blonde rinse in her white hair.

'Yes. Yes, he is.' She looked again at the dress. 'You don't think it's too low, do you?'

'For a girl of your age, never! You've got the rest of your life to cover up. When you get to my age they'll be *demanding* you cover up.'

Amy laughed. 'That's good enough for me. I'll buy it.' And she turned to catch the attention of the young sales assistant.

'Of course you will,' said the old lady. 'Now, where do you think I might find some North Devon razzle-dazzle for the rock-up tonight? I don't want to be underdressed.'

There were probably fifty years separating the two women, but there was something defiantly jolly about the old lady, and she and Amy got on perfectly as they now helped each other shop. Firstly, Double Entendre provided a turquoise trouser suit for the old lady, complete with a silver stole, as well as new tights for Amy. Then it was off down the street for shoes with just a hint of dancing glitter, while in a handi-crafts shop they went silly and emerged with all kinds of beads and bangles set with stones from the seashore.

As they shopped, gradually the old lady's situation unpeeled. Her name was Grace and her husband was George. George had had a bad stroke three years earlier. Until then they'd been one of those active old couples who were spending a well-off retirement seeing the world. It was trickier now, Grace said. But although George couldn't walk or talk properly any more, and needed help eating, 'and et cetera, et cetera', as she put it, he didn't want to be left out of anything. 'He might not be able to do it all himself any more, not physically, anyway, but in his mind he's as young as you are,' she explained as Amy took a turn in pushing George. 'Probably even younger, because he has a very dirty mind for someone so old and respectable. Isn't that right, George?'

Positioned behind the wheelchair, Amy couldn't see whether George reacted or not. She liked to think he smiled.

Engrossed in their shopping they'd missed lunch at the hotel, so instead they settled for a salad in a pub next to the maritime museum. Watching them together as they waited to be served, Grace the ever attentive carer, George not obviously grateful, Amy was intrigued.

'Do you mind if I ask you something?' she said at last.

'So long as you don't want to know what I was doing on the day Queen Victoria was crowned.'

'It's just that . . . well, I couldn't help noticing you both this week . . .'

Grace laughed. 'Haven't we all been watching each other?'

'Well, yes. And it seems to me that you and George are happier together than almost any couple I know. Certainly more so than my parents were before they divorced.' She was surprising herself to be even mentioning that. The years before their divorce, when she'd been at school, life at home had been fraught. When her father had later died her mother had shown little grief, which had been almost more upset-ting than the divorce.

'Yes, you could say we're happy,' Grace was saying.

'What I mean is . . .' Amy pursued, perhaps now a little too much the writer in search of a new chapter. 'You seem to know the secret.'

'There's a secret? We know a secret? Well, aren't we clever!'

'Well, you know, the secret to the stuff the Valentine cards tell us to dream about: lifelong love, romance, devotion, fidelity—'

Grace's smile had faded into a deep crease between her eyes. 'Don't you think you're being perhaps a little presumptuous there?'

Amy was instantly apologetic. 'I'm sorry, I didn't mean to pry.'

Grace was shushing her. She looked at George for a moment, hesitating. He'd now fallen asleep in the warmth of the pub. 'How do you know we've always been loving and faithful? Yes, we've loved each other all our lives. But things happen in a long life. I wasn't always eighty. And George had his moments, too, though he thought he'd made sure I'd never find out. He's always been very kind like that.'

Amy was ashamed, embarrassed. 'I'm really sorry . . .'

'Don't be. Just don't run off with the rose-tinted idea that just because you see us happy together now, the path was always straight. I don't think it's ever completely straight. Not for anyone. George and I were just lucky that we always seemed to find our way back onto it.'

Amy felt chastened. 'There goes the last of my romantic illusions. There's no great secret,' she said, and watched George's eyes open.

'No, I don't think so. To be honest, I've always thought that St Valentine is a bit like Father Christmas. He only works if you believe in him. Like fairies, the old-fashioned Tinkerbell sort, I mean. I think that's a big part of it.'

'Believing in the idea of love, you mean?'

'Or perhaps making a decision to work for it, to believe in it, even when things go wrong. That's it. Making a decision.'

'And the other part?'

George's soup had now arrived.

Grace had had enough. 'I don't know, ask me another time. Can't you see the poor man's starving?' And putting a spoon to the soup, she tasted it to make sure it wasn't too hot, and then held it to George's lips.

Tim would never know where the day went. The music stole the hours as he stayed at his keyboard. The competition that Amanda had insisted he enter, with its rules and expectations of content and form, was forgotten. He was writing for himself.

Midafternoon, having taken off his headphones for a break, he heard footsteps in the corridor outside, then the sound of the door next but one to his being unlocked, opened and closed. And for a moment he allowed his forefinger to play a solitary, rhythmic, silent note, over and over as a welcome ghost sat beside him.

Then he returned to his work, composing for the joy of it.

Inside the three standing walls the church was even more reduced than it had appeared as they'd pushed their way up the hill and across the little plateau of grass outside. Only one wall was still high enough to show the gaps where a couple of small stained-glass windows would once have stood, while at the far end, where they imagined there might have been a little altar, all that was left was a pile of lichen-covered stones. Yet to Michael and Eleanor, everything was of interest as they picked their way through the centuries of weed-covered rubble.

'I wonder would these be the remains of a baptismal font?' Michael said, pulling back a stone to reveal a smoother, rounder one beneath.

It was possible, Eleanor agreed. More certain was the outline of the ancient square cross roughly carved into one of the large stones close to where they decided the main door would once have stood.

At first they were busy pointing out various features to each other, surmising where, had there been one, the pulpit might have been, but there wasn't much to work on and after a while they went quiet. Then, stepping outside, they gazed across the sheer line of cliffs and down to the pebbled beaches and shining sea below.

It was already nearly four and, because it was a long walk back to the hotel, Michael knew they couldn't stay long. But there was a restful solitude here and with the afternoon sun coming from somewhere way out to sea towards Ireland, it was casting a rosy glow on Eleanor's pallid winter complexion. Michael smiled as he looked at her.

'What is it, Michael?'

'I was thinking how pretty you looked.'

'Don't be silly.' She was embarrassed, yet obviously pleased. Then, probably because she didn't know what else to do, and because he kept looking at her, she turned away and went back inside the little church.

He watched her go, seeing her foot just miss crushing a tiny patch of white crocuses flecked with a suitably ecclesiastical purple.

By the time he joined her, holding a posy of those crocuses, she was standing in front of the rubble that might have been an altar. He passed the flowers to her.

'I missed the Mass, Michael,' she whispered sadly as she took them. 'The Nuptial Mass.'

He understood. The Church had never acknowledged that a priest could abandon his order and marry, so a church wedding for them had always been out of the question. That Father Dermot had attended their ceremony in a register office must have been tantamount to condoning heresy in Dermot's eyes. So, yes, Michael understood.

'It was a lovely day and I love you, but . . .' She searched for her meaning. 'God makes marriages, not a civil servant from the town hall.'

'God and two people,' Michael corrected quietly.

'Yes, God and two people.'

After a while Michael said, 'You know, in America it's becoming fashionable for couples to sometimes reaffirm their vows, get married again, as it were . . . to go to a chapel and tell God and each other how much they still love each other.'

'So I've read,' Eleanor murmured.

He left the thought with her.

Slowly she turned to him with a smile of pure hope. 'Will you marry us, Michael? Marry us properly?'

For a moment he didn't follow.

Eleanor touched his arm. 'You could, Michael. Here. Now. In a church, as it should have been before. You're a priest. A priest is a priest for life. Yes? I know you know the words.'

He was so surprised he didn't answer for a moment. Then he said, 'I don't think Canon Law has made provision for this sort of situation.' But he was smiling. 'It's a very unusual request. In fact, it might be considered sacrilegious. I might have to ask a higher authority.'

Eleanor looked up at the gaping open sky above them. 'I'm sure He's listening. We're here in a church, at the altar. I think He'd understand, don't you?'

How could a merciful God who saw, understood and forgave every one of our foolish ways not understand? 'I think He might,' Michael agreed. 'But if we're going to do this properly, perhaps we should kneel down.'

Taking great care, they found a patch of soft soil among the broken stones. Then, kneeling down together, they bent forward to consecrate their lives to each other, but this time in the certain knowledge of God's presence and understanding.

'Do you take this woman to be your lawful wedded wife from this day forward until death do you part?' asked Michael the priest.

'I do,' replied Michael the groom.

'I do,' repeated Eleanor when the time for her response came. In the register office her expression had rarely been less than worried. Now her soft eyes brimmed with happiness.

It wasn't entirely a lonely wedding. There was one witness, the black and white goat who'd followed them up the hill and who watched and grazed as they prayed for a happy life together.

Ever since Tim had arrived he'd regretted not having the legs for his keyboard, the table he'd requisitioned never being completely satisfactory. Now, after hours of work, it was wobbling more than ever. Reaching across to the chest of drawers by the bed he pulled out a couple of telephone directories. They might help, he thought, and prepared to push them underneath. Then another idea. Would it work better without the complimentary newspaper he'd stuffed there on his first morning? Propping up the keyboard one-handed he began to withdraw the newspaper with the other hand.

It was her chin and mouth he saw first. Then the tiny nose. He stopped. Then, more slowly, he pulled again to reveal the eyes.

Quickly pulling out the rest of the paper he held it up to the bedside light. The hair was different. It was long and fair in the photograph, now shorter and darker. But it was her all right. The girl who'd told him her name was Millie.

SO WHERE IS AMY? read the headline above a caption.

Amy?

Amy Miller, best-selling romance author, was last night said to be in hiding after rumours about a mystery man in her life . . . Then came an instruction to turn to page 7. He turned on. Here there was a different, bigger photograph. And now there could be no doubt. There was also a short piece about Amy Miller's writing success.

Amy? Millie? Amy? A famous author?

For some minutes he stood confused. Millie or Amy? Someone who worked in the paper distribution business or a best-selling novelist? It was hardly even a white lie when you thought about it.

The newspaper referred to some unnamed lover as 'mystery man'. The previous day, when he'd waited by the waterfall as she'd taken a call, he'd imagined a stolid, rich, married businessman, possibly someone in paper production. But the famous Amy Miller would surely have someone more glamorous.

Second by second, his mind was retracing their moments together, every word she'd said. The collision in the hotel lobby when they'd arrived, the fit of giggles over dinner and the way she'd re-bandaged his broken head. 'I'm very glad I met you,' she'd said as they said good night. *I'm very glad I met you.*

But mostly he was thinking about the exchange in the bookshop, the display of Amy Miller books and the life-sized, cut-out photograph of the author. She'd stood in front of it, and still he hadn't noticed. He must have been blind. And what had he said? *I can't imagine anyone wanting to steal Amy Miller books though, can you?*

Probably not! she'd said and smiled. Of course she'd smiled. She'd been laughing at his ignorance, prejudice and arrogance. He knew nothing about Amy Miller books. She'd guessed that.

He looked again at the newspaper. Then, checking his watch, he got up and reached for his coat.

Mobile phone in hand, Will Abbott, wearing his shirt but no underpants yet, watched from his window as the tall guy with the hair and the bandanna left the hotel and set off towards the town. Abbott's room didn't have a sea view, but it was excellent for watching the comings and goings of the guests. A couple of hours earlier he'd seen Amy Miller return from shopping with the elderly couple.

Now, wearing just her knickers, Suzy was bending over her laptop, sending her selection of pictures back to the office. They were good: Amy Miller in the hotel grounds with a new hair colour and style, Amy Miller by the sea, and Amy Miller shopping in town. But as the photographs raced down the wire there was a tension at the other end of Abbott's phone that he didn't like. Why was it that every time he went away those bastards in the office started being difficult?

'So what's she doing down there then?' McKenzie was demanding.

'"What's she doing?" Nothing much. Hanging out with some humpty-dumpty of a pianist.' Abbott noticed Suzy smile at that.

'Who's he?' McKenzie asked.

'God knows. Some hotel guest she's got pally with, I think. This could take a while.'

'Unfortunately, we don't have a while, Will,' McKenzie suddenly said in a seen-it-all-before voice. 'You'd better front her up.'

'Yes. Obviously. But not yet.' He was watching Suzy again as she recovered her *Ladder of Sex* book from her bag. It was a stupid book, they'd both agreed, but in the right circumstances, such as these, not without its entertainment and instructional value.

'We want it for tonight, Will.'

'*Tonight?*' Abbott scoffed. 'It's too soon.'

'Very possibly. But the word is the *Sunday Times Magazine* has a cover story on "Teddy Farrow the devoted family man" going in this weekend and we want to spoil their day. So we need the Amy Miller tale tonight.'

'Jesus!' Abbott swore. 'There's a way of getting these things, you know.'

'Yes. I do know. That's why *you're* there.' McKenzie's voice suddenly lightened. 'Nice pictures, by the way. Very nice. You've got Suzy Tallis down there with you, I see.'

'Yes. She does a great job.'

From the bed Suzy beamed.

'So Ed Halliwell said when he worked with her in Spain,' came back McKenzie. 'Anyway, speak to you later.' And he rang off.

The phone was still at Abbott's ear.

'They want you to file tonight?' Suzy enquired. 'It's too soon.' Abbott didn't answer. 'Why?' Still no reply. 'Will?'

'You didn't tell me you'd been to Spain with Ed Halliwell,' he said at last.

'You didn't ask me. They liked the pictures, yes?'

'So you did?'

'Did what?'

'Go to Spain with Ed Halliwell.'

'Mmm,' she said casually, making herself comfortable on the bed. 'It was a footballers' wives story. A wild-goose chase. It never got in.'

'"It never got in!"' repeated Abbott.

'No.'

'And what about Ed Halliwell?'

'What?'

Abbott was now standing over the bed. 'Well, he's hardly known for living by a strict monastic code, is he? So what happened?'

'When?'

'You *know* when. In Spain. You and Ed Halliwell.'

Suzy peered up at him as though surprised she was having this conversation. 'What does it matter what happened?'

'It doesn't matter. I just don't know why you didn't tell me.'

She shrugged. 'It didn't seem important.'

There was a pause now as Abbott looked away from her. Ed Halliwell, for Christ's sake! He turned back. 'How long were you there?'

Suzy shrugged. 'About three days. Four, I think.'

'And what happened?'

'Nothing happened.' There was now a sullen defensiveness.

Abbott just about smirked. '*Nothing*? With Ed Halliwell? In Spain? For three, four nights? Come on!'

'Well, nothing much.'

'And what does "nothing much" mean?'

'Oh, come on, who cares!' Exasperation was turning to anger.

'No one cares. You're a grown girl. You can do whatever you want.'

'Thank you. I did.' Suzy was now off the bed.

From the window Abbott looked down at his Porsche. He'd parked it at the far side of the hotel car park, under the trees. It really was a car for a single man. He'd get rid of it soon. Behind him he could sense Suzy wondering if the interrogation was over. But, God, Ed Halliwell!

'What do you mean, "you did"?' he asked at last. 'Did what?'

'I thought you didn't care,' Suzy retorted. 'When are you going to front her up?'

'Soon. Soon. And I *don't* care.'

'That's all right then.' She pretended to smile, cheeky, like a young girl.

'Yes.' He hesitated. Then: 'What did you do?'

'Well, the usual, I imagine.'

Abbott's brow knitted. 'The usual? What's usual?'

'"What's *usual*?"' Suzy looked around her in despair. Her eyes fell on *The Ladder of Sex*. 'Well, Chapter Ten, I suppose.'

Abbott stared in astonishment. 'Chapter Ten is *usual*?'

One by one, the bookshop sales assistant ran the bar code of every book against the scanner on the cash register. 'That's nearly a complete set. You're an Amy Miller fan, too, are you?' she said.

Tim looked at the life-sized photograph of Amy across the shop. 'Her biggest,' he said.

Nursing her laptop at a chair by the window, Amy was fighting to concentrate, as the hotel sang with shouts and instructions as last-minute preparations for the ball were demanded.

So, what is it? What *is* love? Is it spiritual, psychological or biological? Too many pheromones up your nose, a chemical screw come loose on the Eternal Seesaw, or just some celestial marketing spin on the sexual necessity for reproduction?

Putting cotton wool in her ears, she tried hard to concentrate further, wondering about the fabled sense of smell, well-balanced features, wide hips, lustrous hair and the effect of the time of the month in choosing a sexual partner. But when the band arrived, and began setting up downstairs, with fragments of electronic music rolling up the staircase and along the landing, capitulation was close.

Again and again she cast glances at her new dress, liking it more all the time. Then the matter of deciding which of her new earrings to wear became a further distraction, until at six she closed her laptop and ran her bath. It was all very silly, just a Valentine's Ball in an out-of-the-way, unfashionable place, yet she was as excited as a teenager.

Back in his hotel room, Tim turned the books over and over, studying their uniformly similar jackets and spines, examining the identical photograph of Amy Miller on the backs of all of them. It made her look slightly misty, more whimsical than the woman he knew. Inside each book was a curt paragraph of biographical information about the author: *Amy Miller was born and lives in London. Educated in England and Scotland, she is the winner of several international awards for romantic fiction.*

That was it. She was as secret to her readers as she nearly was to him. And although when he looked her up on Google he found thousands of reviews, blogs and comments about her, and inducements to buy her books through eBay and Amazon, in French, German, Russian and numerous other languages, she remained an enigma.

He chose a recent book called *Drifting Without Guilt* to read. It was the story of a single woman in her thirties who couldn't settle down to a profession, a home or a regular partner. Whether the book was good or not, he had no way of knowing. It hadn't been written for someone like him. But he read on, laughing at the good jokes as the main character's life unravelled, while all the time seeking cryptic little clues to the personality of the author, though never knowing if he'd found any. Not that it mattered. True or otherwise, he could hear Amy talking on every page. And mainly, it seemed, she was talking to him.

Shona took one last look under her bed, taking great care not to get any dust or cobwebs on her white tights or the apple-green velvet mini-dress she'd bought at the charity shop in Midhurst for occasions such as this. A larger size might have been preferable but the colour was deliciously vivid, especially when worn with the bright crimson sash she'd rescued from the bottom of her eldest sister's cupboard. Natasha had worn it when she'd played Napoleon's beautiful, sexy wife Josephine—very successfully, as usual—in her second year at Oxford.

Finally giving up the search, she stood up. 'OK, suit yourself,' she said out loud. 'You can play hide-and-seek for ever if that's what you want. But I've got stuff to do. Tonight's the night on the North Devon Riviera and you're going to miss it.' Then she turned to the mirror and, for luck, applied a final lacquering of guillotine-red lipstick to a mouth that was already as shiny and swollen as a painted plum.

Satisfied that she was at least kissable, she considered her reflection for a moment. Somehow the Bo-Peep ribbon, the dangling Somali earrings and the liberally applied mousse that had made her hair fizz out hadn't quite produced the effect she'd hoped for. She wrinkled her nose. She would never be as glamorous, clever or as beautiful as her sisters, no matter how much she tried. But 'interesting' might be in with a chance.

At least she wasn't being forced to wear that French maid's uniform to the ball. 'A North Devon Riviera Hotel name tag will be quite sufficient to let nonresidents know who you are, should they be in need of assistance,' Jane had said as she'd passed the plastic tags around.

There was still an hour before the guests would begin to arrive, but she could hear the band testing their equipment. It was time to go and meet them. Goody-Goody-Darrell would already be down there. She smiled fondly as she pictured him waiting anxiously at the hotel door. Before she went, though, there was one further thing to do. She pulled a chair to the middle of the room, climbed onto it and carefully removed the light bulb.

It had been such a fine day that they'd scarcely noticed the bank of mist lolling off the coast. It was their wedding day, their real wedding day, why would they notice it? But now, as, arm in arm, they made their wedding march back along the cliffs, and across the edge of the moor, the mist was creeping off the sea and joining them in the heather. Now, though, they called it fog.

Perhaps Eleanor should have been afraid as, eyes focused on the path, they followed the coastal route home, but there was no fear in her. For the first time she felt like a proper married woman, and the grey clouds swirling around her were just the clouds of the new heaven she'd entered that afternoon in the ruins of St Gytha's. To one side there was a drop down to the sea, hundreds of feet, she imagined, while to the other was the danger of being lost on the moors and of wandering into a bog, as travellers so often did in Victorian books. But Michael was with her, his arm warm, pressing hers tightly against his body. No bride ever felt more protected.

They didn't say much, other than to agree on the route they were taking, or to periodically, optimistically observe that they thought the fog was lifting as the night drew in, and to reaassure each other that they would surely soon see the lights of the little town. And after a while they found themselves singing, not to keep their spirits up, because they were not at all afraid, but out of pure happiness. Michael began it, humming quietly, before Eleanor joined in with the words to tunes they both knew, hymns like 'Faith of Our Fathers' and 'Immaculate Mary Our Hearts are on Fire', which reminded Michael of a pilgrimage he'd once made to Lourdes.

But today they'd made a pilgrimage back into history and forward into married love. And Michael knew another song, one based on a Robert Browning poem he'd read at school, which someone, he didn't know who, had put to music. He sang that, too, in his croaky, middle-aged murmur:

> 'Grow old along with me
> The best is yet to be . . .'

'God bless our love,' murmured Eleanor, as they walked on through the fog and the night. 'God bless our love.'

Chapter Five

THEY'D COME FROM much farther afield than Taunton. There must have been people from Minehead and Tiverton, from Bridgwater and Bampton. There was even a coach party from Wiveliscombe. Darrell had never seen so many cars in front of the hotel, never known a jam like it. He was almost sorry he'd advised his mother not to come, but she wasn't really one for dances. Besides, by all accounts Valentine balls could get a bit lewd later on when the drink started working and the music got slower. His mum didn't like anything like that.

He had pinned his name tag to the lapel of his sports jacket. There would be people coming tonight who'd been at school with him. A name tag made him look more like an assistant manager than a porter, and to give Jane her due, she did give him all kinds of respon-sibilities above his station. Some people had suggested he was being exploited: he liked to think he was being trained up. It was some-times hard to tell.

Anyway, stationed tonight in the lobby it was his main job early on to greet the guests with a glass of sparkling wine and direct them to the bar, where Ernie Loxton with the one arm, and his son Gary from Shillingford, had been specially employed for the night to deal with the optimistically hoped-for crush. And as they wouldn't be having any heavies on the door, Jane had also stressed that he keep his eyes skinned for any undesirables. Frankly, Darrell thought the most unde-sirable elements likely tonight were the band, Lorna and the Doones, especially Lorna, but as they were to be the centrepiece of the evening it seemed unwise to express that opinion too loudly.

Not that anything he said could be too loud when the Doones were playing. They weren't a bad band, but they were very loud, especially when they went off on an AC/DC trip. They loved AC/DC, which just showed how narrow a mindset you could get if you grew up in North Devon. Darrell liked to think of himself as more of a Coldplay man. Hopefully Shona might be a Coldplay fan, too, he thought, but he hadn't dared confess his admiration for them yet, because people could go right off you if you followed a band they hated. And with Shona you could never tell in which direction she was going to go with anything.

'Hello, Darrell. I hope you're suitably armed tonight,' Barry Harrison, the floor coverings man, was standing behind him in the lobby.

'Armed?' Darrell was puzzled. 'I don't think we'll be having trouble.'

Harrison smirked. 'Armed in case you get lucky.' And taking a glass from the tray Darrell was holding, he indicated a troupe of young girls from the town arriving, all hens' legs, bare midriffs, a pierced navel or two and very high giggles.

Oh God! thought Darrell, hoping none of them had heard Harrison.

'They say they like the taste of the vanilla-flavoured ones best,' Harrison continued. 'Followed by the chocolate banana, if you get my meaning.' He guffawed. Darrell felt the beginning of a blush. Harrison hadn't finished. 'Did I ever tell you about that dance I went to in Swindon? I picked up some girl and when the interval came I took her outside and round the back for . . . you know . . . So, there we were going at it when suddenly she says, "Eh, can you hurry up? I think the band's coming back on".' And again Harrison rocked with laughter.

Darrell stared at the tray he was holding. 'I think the manager was looking for you, Mr Harrison,' he said. 'She asked me to tell you.'

Harrison's dirty smile crumpled. 'Oh, right, thank you,' he said. 'I wonder what that's about.' And then he hesitated. Darrell felt bad. Both he and Harrison knew very well why Jane wanted to see him. 'Well, perhaps I'll run into her later,' Harrison said, and, pushing through the excited girls, he made his way towards the bar.

Darrell crossed his fingers for him. Ernie Loxton was under instructions to only accept cash tonight. He hoped Harrison would have enough money in his pocket to at least buy himself one drink.

Crrrrrannnnnng!! The violent storm of an electric chord reverberated.

'Crikey, are they starting so soon?' It was Shona running up behind him. He'd heard she'd been helping Domingos and Agnieszka out with the experimental profiteroles in the kitchen but now here she was looking as he'd never seen her before. Part Sugar Plum Fairy, part vamp and wholly zany. His heart flipped. It did. He felt it. And it was wonderful.

Together they peered past the crowd into the dining room, now festooned as the ballroom. With the lights turned low and reflected through pink filters, it looked more romantic than should have been possible at the North Devon Riviera Hotel. Darrell stole a glance at Shona. For once she wasn't smirking, but laughing at the joy of it all, with her eyes drawn inevitably to the collection of six cadavers in black T-shirts on the low stage under the big red heart that she and Darrell had hung there—*Love Makes The World Go Round*.

'*They're* the Doones?' she asked. 'Where's the girl?'

'What girl?' asked Darrell.

'You know, Lorna. The lead singer.'

Was she being funny, or did she really not know? 'Lorna's a boy.'

Shona's face puckered. 'Lorna of the Doones is a boy? He wasn't in the version I saw on the telly.'

'No, well, that's the joke, you see. Lorna's that one at the front with the long hair. His real name's Craig. He'll start singing soon.'

Shona edged closer to the door to get a better view. 'You mean Lorna's the one who looks a bit like a young George Clooney? Wow!'

Now Darrell felt another lurch to his heart. But this one was quite different, more of a sag into his stomach. 'Yes, well, he . . . he was at my school,' Darrell stammered. 'His real job is working for the council. He drives one of those motorised hedge cutters in the summer. Actually, he's useless at it. The farmers all complain when he's been around.'

But Shona didn't appear to be listening. She stood just inside the ballroom, carefully watching Lorna as he began to wrestle the microphone and strut the tiny stage in the way they always did on television.

Darrell felt his mouth drying. If Shona fancied Lorna, what chance had he got against a star?

She had to admit it, she loved the dress. It was loose and flowing and girly. Altogether she liked the way she looked. Surprisingly, blue did work with her new brown hair. Actually, it was more golden, not khaki. The girl in Economy Cutz hadn't done too bad a job after all. It already seemed like weeks since she'd looked like Amy Miller, not just four days. She stared at herself in the long mirror. She liked her new shoes, too, dainty little dazzly things. She would never have worn them in London. In London she was more the bookish sophisticate; more sensible; earnest and snooty. A bit of a bore, really, she thought.

The music was roaring from downstairs now. She checked her watch. It was eight thirty. That was the time she'd agreed to meet Tim. She was surprised she hadn't heard from him since the morning. He must have become engrossed in his work and lost track of the time.

Twenty-five to nine. She was nervous. She added a touch more scent to her wrists. At twenty to nine she opened the door. At that moment her laptop pinged. *You have email*, said the AOL voice.

She considered ignoring it, but of course she didn't. Leaving the door ajar she crossed to the computer and opened the file. She was surprised. The message was an electronic Valentine's card, a simple screen showing just a bright pink heart and the lines:

Come live with me and be my love,
And we will some new pleasures prove . . .

John Donne, she said to herself. Teddy liked to quote John Donne. She'd quickly discovered that Donne was the only poet he could quote.

Happy Valentine, Amy.
I've managed to sneak a break. Will be driving down first thing tomorrow morning. I'm borrowing a pal's cottage near Honiton so we can have a couple of days together. Pick you up around ten.
Longing to see you. Love you, Teddy

PS Better be ready on the hotel steps so that we can be off before anyone spots me.

Sitting down on her bed, she re-read the message.

Her door was ajar. Tim knocked lightly.

'Yes? Oh, sorry. I'm coming,' she called as the door swung slightly open to his touch. She was sitting with her laptop, looking serious, but she smiled as she saw him. Quickly closing the computer, she hurried towards him. 'So, did you have a productive day?' she asked.

'A *great* day!' He was waiting on the landing, wearing the black velvet jacket that Amanda had bought him, and a clean pair of jeans. '*Wow!*' he said, as she locked her door and turned to face him.

'*Wow?*' She looked puzzled.

'As in "*wow*, you-look-sort-of-wonderful-wow"!'

She laughed. 'Well, it *is* a ball!' She was trying to be casual. 'And you look very smart, too. I didn't know you owned a jacket.'

He was still staring at her. He couldn't stop.

'What is it?' she asked. 'You're looking at me differently.'

'I am?' Tim shrugged. 'That's probably because you're looking different.' That was true, of course. But it wasn't the truth. She didn't just *look* different to him, she *was* different. Millie the anonymous girl in paper distribution was now Amy a famous writer. 'Shall we go?'

Abbott and Suzy watched through their partly open door as they passed their room.

'Right!' Abbott said, getting up from a chair. It was the first word he'd spoken in two hours. He'd been thinking about Jenny and the boys, wondering what he was doing down here on a Friday night. And why, whenever he got the opportunity, he just couldn't resist it.

Carefully, he patted the pocket of his jacket and felt the outline of his microphone. He wished Amy Miller had left her room earlier. It was getting bloody late if he was to catch even the London edition. But if he'd just knocked on her door and announced who he was she'd have slammed it in his face. Better to catch her off guard in a public place when there was nowhere to run. At least she'd have to say something.

Suzy was already waiting, a bag over her shoulder where she kept a lightweight camera. She'd liked him, he realised now. Quite a lot. But he hadn't asked her to like him a lot, just enough to go to bed with him. She looked hurt, as though he'd had no right to interrogate her about her sex life, especially as he was the one who was married and she was unattached. She was right, he hadn't the right. But *Ed Halliwell*! That bastard McKenzie would have made sure he was already the office joke.

'Ready?' he asked. She nodded. 'Just take your lead from me. No snaps until I give you the nod.'

It was a better turnout than Jane could have dreamed of. If the bar could keep up with demand, and this was an occasion when, prejudice against the handicapped aside, she rather wished there were four hands there instead of three, Bristol would have little to complain about.

What *always* surprised her at hotel functions, was how well the local women turned out, how pretty and glamorous the most dowdy, ordinary girls suddenly looked. Not many of the men seemed to try very hard, but the women were butterflies, almost every one. And, though, yes, she was jealous of the prettiest and the shapeliest and those accompanied by the most attractive and attentive men, she was also pleased with herself that she and her staff had made this night special, not just for the accounts people in Bristol, but for the guests and the people of the town. As she stood on the stairs, hoping she looked reasonably attractive, or at least magisterial, wincing at the music, and making a mental note to do something about that very soon, she felt proud, really proud of her hotel.

'I understand you need a word with me.' Barry Harrison was at her side. He sounded awkward. 'I know what it's about.'

Jane turned and considered Harrison. His eyes were watery.

When he'd first arrived some weeks earlier, he'd been full of himself, boasting of the new floor coverings company he'd started with what he'd described as solid City backing, thrilled to be finally divorced and 'free to roll'. But week by week she'd watched the cracks in his bluster spread. The investment hadn't materialised. She realised that when he asked for a deal on his room. And she could tell by his demeanour when he returned to the hotel in the evening after a day on the road that orders had been slow, if any. She'd known for weeks he was existing on a wallet full of credit cards. One day while he'd been out touring the north Cornish coast she'd taken a look in his room, not prying, just making sure the bedroom staff were doing their jobs. It seemed he'd brought just about everything he possessed with him, including a photograph of a hard-faced, silver-blonde woman and two serious-looking children in school uniform. That was when it had hit her. He was there because he had nowhere else to go. When you ran a hotel you got to know more about your guests than they ever realised.

He could, she knew, be crude and vulgar, and he liked to pretend to Darrell that he was a big hit with women. Everyone in the hotel, apart from Darrell, probably, knew that would never have been the case. The hard, scornful look in the eye of the blonde woman in the photograph · had confirmed it.

As the manager of the hotel, Jane ought to have demanded Harrison either settle his bill or leave at that moment and expect legal action. She almost did. But it was Valentine's night. Everybody was having a good time. She didn't want a scene. It could wait until tomorrow.

'Why don't we talk about this in the morning!' she said coolly. 'In the meantime, they seem a little short-staffed in the bar.' And with that thought lodged in his mind she replaced her smile and walked down the steps and into the ballroom to get that bloody band to play something the guests could actually dance to.

'Are you sure these things will be safe to eat?' Shona asked as she watched Domingos squirt a thick yellow paste-like substance from a piping bag to form a heart-shaped éclair.

'Of course,' said Domingos, mock offended.

Shona glanced around the kitchen. Just about every flat surface was now covered in baking trays covered in hearts. 'Well, I hope so, because we had a lecture at college on public health and the serious penalties they hand out these days to kitchen staff involved in widespread food poisoning. I think they said it falls under mass murder.'

Domingos shrugged his huge shoulders. 'You want aphrodisiac? Maybe you have to be a little adventurous. Different country, different recipe. If we only had catuaba from the rain forests of Amazonia . . . the bark of the tree of love. No more frigidity, no more impotence, no more boredom with long-time married love. Just romance. And everybody happy.' And he flicked a kiss to his fingertips.

'It's a pity the catuaba tree doesn't grow in North Devon then, isn't it?' Shona said. 'Crushed walnut in quail's egg custard sounds more like something your loopy great-aunt serves up for Sunday tea.'

'Pah!' At Domingos's side, Agnieszka wagged her head dismissively. She, too, had spent hours making pastry hearts. 'He make up as he go along. This phoney love potion never work. We need vodka.'

Shona shrugged. 'Whatever!' But she hoped it did work. Just a bit.

And collecting a tray of clean wineglasses from the dishwasher she headed back into the ballroom, where suddenly Lorna and the Doones were playing the Rolling Stones's 'Brown Sugar' and the entire floor was alive with some very uncool and over-energetic dancing. You didn't get that in Midhurst, not in the places Shona went to, anyway. Everyone there was too self-regarding. But this looked like fun. She'd hated all the crap rap and AC/DC stuff that the Doones had opened with. At least Jane, who was standing on the short steps to the stage like an overseer, knew what the people wanted to hear. Even the middle-aged Scottish couple of hikers she'd served with porridge at breakfast seemed to know the words.

'So what do you think of our Valentine Ball now, then?' Darrell asked, relieved from his duty on the door.

Shona smiled, mischievously. Darrell was so easy to tease. 'I think the band's great . . .'

'Hello, Darrell, you're looking fit tonight!'

Shona turned. A couple of young girls, bleached, leggy little dolls, prettier and sexier than she would ever be, were smiling at Darrell.

Darrell beamed towards them, obviously flattered, distracted for a moment. Then they were gone. He turned back to Shona.

For a moment she didn't speak. Then: 'Yes, I think the band's great,' she found herself repeating. 'Especially Lorna. He's just my type. Those lips. That tongue. I wonder if he'd like to taste my . . .' And she ran the tip of her tongue sexily across the underside of her top lip.

She regretted it instantly as she saw the sudden stab of pain in Darrell's eyes. She'd never done anything so vulgar in her life before. She hadn't meant it. Perhaps the song had suggested it. But, no, she knew it was just more stupid Shona bravado. More showing off. *You've always been a disappointment to us,* her father had said. But he'd only been half right. She was a perpetual disappointment to herself.

For a moment Darrell looked as if he was trying to reconcile two parts of something that were unfathomably opposed. Then he was gone, moving quickly away between the dancing couples, his pudding-basin head down, gathering up paper plates and abandoned glasses.

Shona watched him go in despair. Too late. She'd spoiled everything.

'*I said yeah, yeah, yeah, yeah,*' howled Lorna of the Doones.

The dope couldn't even sing.

They'd arrived late, for Devon, then sat out most of the rest of the first half of the evening, taking their drinks into the loggia. They hadn't been able to resist 'Brown Sugar', though, not even when it was the Doones's version.

A draggy Commodores song followed, a slow, sauntering-on-the-spot sort of dance, which gradually emptied the floor as it was almost the interval anyway. Tim and Amy stayed, however, dancing slowly, but not holding each other. They'd never touched hands since they'd met, apart from at the piano, though Tim constantly imagined he felt Amy's fingers rebinding his bandage.

'Hey, you're staring at me,' Amy pretended to chide.

'I know,' Tim agreed. 'Can I tell you a secret?'

'You're a man with a secret? I didn't know.'

'We all have secrets.'

Amy thought about that. 'That's true. What's yours?'

'That I think you're terrific!'

Amy blinked in surprise and what looked like pleasure. 'You're still concussed. You're forgetting someone. Her name's Amanda.'

'I haven't forgotten Amanda. I'm just not thinking about her. I'm thinking about you.'

Amy shook her head, and moved in a little semicircle around him. 'You don't know anything about me.'

'I know some of you, the part you've let me know. And I think that part's terrific. And, though I know it won't happen, because I'll never see you again after this weekend, if I got the chance to know any more of you, I'm sure I'd grow to like those parts just as much.' He grinned.

She looked at him. 'But . . .'

'Yes, I know. You're in love with some guy. Which is a shame. But I just wanted you to know how I felt about you. And now you do know.'

The band had stopped playing, just drizzling away to nothing halfway through the song, as all the other dancers had retaken their seats or made their way to the bar.

Tim and Amy stood looking at each other, as though stranded after the tide of the song had gone out. 'Tim . . .' she began, with a tone of voice that suggested she might have something nice but negative to say.

He wasn't ready for this yet. 'Actually, after all that I'm so dry. I've just got to get a drink. What would you like?'

Perhaps she wanted to delay the moment of rejection, too, because she said, 'Good idea. White wine. I'll be back in the bamboos. Waiting.' She indicated the loggia.

There was something about the way she said 'waiting' that gave him some small comfort, and he hurried towards the bar, almost stumbling over the couple who'd arrived by Porsche the previous night. He'd spotted them earlier, sitting glum-faced, not speaking, just watching the dancing. Obviously Valentine balls weren't for everyone.

The table they'd been sitting at was now taken, so Amy pushed on to the end of the loggia where on sunny days there would have been a pretty view of the beach. Tonight, though, all she could see was the swirl of mist around the hotel, and for a moment it struck her that she and Tim were in a cocoon, sheltered tonight from their problems. She liked the feeling. Teddy was for tomorrow and another world.

'Good to see you again . . . Amy.'

The name 'Amy' punctured the air. She stopped dead.

'I'm a great fan of yours . . .'

She turned. It was the couple with the Porsche she'd seen in town that morning. Had she ever met them before? She knew she hadn't.

The man stepped closer to her, smiling all the time. 'I love the make-over, by the way. I hardly recognised you with the new hair colour. You look quite different from the other night . . . on the roof.'

She'd guessed anyway. Casually, the man pulled a business card from his newspaper and pushed it into her hand. 'The name's Will Abbott. And we hear you're having an affair with Teddy Farrow.' It was said with the subtlety of a thumb under the eye.

'I'm sorry, I . . .' She was trying to turn away, looking for deliverance.

Abbott pushed his advantage. 'We know all about it. Those television researchers can't help gossiping. The word is Teddy won't leave his wife. And you've given him an ultimatum. That's right, isn't it?'

'I'm sorry. I don't do interviews. Now, please . . .' She tried to get between Abbott and the wall but he remained blocking the way.

'Or is it perhaps his image as the nation's most popular television performer that's the problem? I can see why he'd be afraid to lose that.'

'Would you, *please*, excuse me?' Her voice was rising.

Now her tormentor tried sympathy. 'Look, it's nothing to do with me. But we'll be running this story tomorrow whatever you or I think. People at the office have already written it. But I'm with you, I don't want them to get it anything less than a hundred per cent accurate. So why don't we just sit down and have a drink and you can put your side of things before it all comes out wrong?'

By now she was physically pushing him. 'I want to get past.'

'So, I'd be right in saying you're not denying you're having an affair with Teddy Farrow?'

'*Please!*'

There was a sudden flash, and Amy looked up into the lens of a small camera being held by the reporter's moll. Flash! Flash! Another and another. Other guests were looking at them.

On his way to the bar he'd run across Darrell carrying a tray of glasses.

Back almost immediately with the wine, he'd seen it all unfold. As the hunters had closed in he'd heard the name 'Teddy Farrow', and caught the word 'affair'. Teddy Farrow was the mystery lover? Of course. It was bound to be someone rich and famous.

By now he'd reached Amy. She wasn't quite cowering but she was cornered. He'd no experience of these things, but suddenly he knew what to do. 'So, what affair's this then?' He laughed, clumsily elbowing the girl photographer to one side and passing Amy her wine.

'Actually, this doesn't concern you,' Abbott spat at him.

'Well, I think it might,' Tim replied. Then he smiled at Amy as he tasted his wine. 'Sorry, it's a bit warm.'

'Tim!' Her expression warned him not to get involved.

He ignored it and turned back to Abbott. 'I mean, if you're suggesting that my fiancée is seeing another man I'd say it very much concerns me, wouldn't you?'

He looked back at Amy. Her eyes were bright in astonishment. At last she said, 'It's all right, Tim.'

'Well, it isn't all right really, is it?' he said. He turned bluntly on Abbott. 'I think I'd have been aware if she was seeing someone else, don't you? Especially as she spends virtually all her time round at my place writing. Or with me at her place. Isn't that right, Amy?' And he looked back at her. *Amy!* He'd said her real name! Had she noticed? She blinked. Yes. Tim smiled. He was almost enjoying this.

Abbott was smirking. 'Listen, mate, we checked you out. You met each other here. Arrived separately, signed in separately . . .'

Tim laughed in his face. 'That's right. Absolutely! Well spotted. Separate rooms, separate beds, pretending not to know each other. Then one day . . . bingo! We meet. Perhaps not quite by accident, and it's like love with a stranger. Have you ever tried it? You should. It makes for a *very* sexy weekend.' He smiled cheekily at Suzy. '*You'd* love it. I'm Tim Fairweather, by the way.'

Suzy looked confused. Amy watched the performance in wonder.

'I don't believe you,' Abbott said at last, but now with the demeanour of a man who'd lost his bearings.

'Oh, yes, honestly. I'll show you my passport, if you like.' Tim was mocking now. 'But later, because now, if you'll excuse us, Amy and I have something rather important we have to do.'

And grasping Amy's hand he positioned himself as a wedge between Abbott and the wall and drew her very firmly away from the reporter.

'I told you he wasn't gay,' he heard the photographer say as they moved back to the dance floor.

'**H**ow long have you known?' Amy asked as Tim pulled her towards the stage.

'That you were Amy Miller in disguise? Long enough to be glad I didn't know sooner. I'd probably have been too shy to talk to you.' Then he turned to the Doones's shaven-headed keyboard player who was drinking from a bottle of beer and talking to a couple of local dads. 'Any chance of borrowing your keyboard for a couple of minutes?'

'Can you play?'

'A bit.'

The player shrugged. 'It's yours then.' And he moved aside.

Climbing up onto the stage, Tim pulled Amy up after him. 'OK, you said you wanted to be in a band. This is your chance. Imagine you're a Fine Young Cannibal. Big finger on that note there and off we go again. It's called "Green Onions", by the way, and you have to play it with a lot of Memphis soul.'

And, standing together at the keyboard, off they did go, Amy keeping that one finger going as Tim weaved rhythm and tune around her. Soon some of the Doones came back from their break to support him, first the drummer, then the bass player, then the two guitarists. And once again the dancers took to the floor. Alongside Tim at the keyboard with the spotlight playing on them, for Amy it seemed the most natural thing in the world.

'**W**hat d'you mean "it's a good story"? It's bollocks. The bastard just made it up. She's screwing Teddy Farrow.' Standing hunched outside the front door, Will Abbott was explaining the failure of his venture.

'Well, she's not screwing him tonight, is she?' McKenzie's voice was indifferent. 'You'd better put over what you've got. We'll go on that. It's a thin night. "*Romantic Amy's secret sex games in hideaway love nest with rock-star fiancé*". That sort of thing.'

'But he was lying. And he's not a bloody rock star.'

'Well, he's playing "Green Onions", isn't he? I can hear it from here. We'll reveal him as a fraud next week, and Amy Miller as a fickle, two-timing bitch who's been shagging both him and Teddy Farrow.

You'll enjoy writing that one. I'm putting you over to copy now.'

There was a click on the line, a pause, and then the voice of a copy-taker. 'For the newsdesk, right? Ready when you are, Mr Abbott . . .'

Footsteps suddenly approaching through the fog prompted Abbott to look round. 'Good evening!' Two middle-aged figures, a man and a woman in anoraks, were emerging, arm in arm, out of the grey mist, their faces bright with happiness. 'We've been for a walk along the coast and got a bit lost in the fog,' the man said jovially. 'Hope we haven't missed too much.' And, still smiling, the couple walked on past Abbott into the hotel.

'Mr Abbott?' the copytaker reminded as she waited for him to begin.

'Jesus Christ!' snarled Abbott.

'Er . . . is this a religious story then, Mr Abbott?'

Shona couldn't join in. She watched as Darrell moved around the floor, dutifully clearing up the mess. He looked so broken, scrupulously avoiding her eyes, trying to smile as the guests spoke to him, but distracted by hurt. It was all going wrong. While everyone else was enjoying the music, the Doones's regular keyboard player being not at all put out to have been replaced and now beating a tambourine instead, Shona's mind was a tumbril of regret.

Even the oafish Lorna, who actually looked nothing like a young George Clooney when you saw him properly, was getting in on the fun, especially as the guest artists were now playing, and he was singing, the Village People's song 'Y.M.C.A.'. God! how he loved himself! Up there in front of a posse of local girls, their arms above their heads as they made out the letters *Y,M,C* and *A.*

'Are you all right, Shona?' It was Grace, the old lady. She'd been standing by George's wheelchair, like a physiotherapist trying to get him to do the arm movements, and getting it hopelessly wrong.

'Yes. I'm fine!' Shona's voice was breaking.

'*Y-M-C-A,*' roared the dancers in front of the stage.

'You don't look very happy. I thought you might be crying.'

Shona hadn't been crying. Not quite. But she was now. As sympathy was offered she couldn't stop herself. Tears welled; she sobbed.

'*Y-M-C-A . . . It's fun to stay at the Y-M-C-A.*'

Grace put a hand out. 'What is it? Do you want to talk about it?'

'No.' Shona shook her head. She wiped away her tears with her sleeve, though not as quickly as new ones arrived.

'Right then.' Grace just smiled. And waited.

'*Y-M-C-A . . . You'll find it at the Y-M-C-A.*' Now everyone on the North Devon Riviera seemed to be joining in.

She'd said she didn't want to talk about it, but she did. 'It's just me. I spoil everything. I always let everyone down. I'm not clever or pretty. I'm just a big, stupid, odd-looking lump who shows off, always saying the wrong thing, and I never know why. I don't mean to. But I always do. I just disappoint everyone and get everything wrong.'

Her tears were now flash floods, her body shaking and gasping. Even George looked up from his wheelchair.

Grace's hand tightened on her. 'You're wrong, you know, Shona. People *do* like you. You're not an odd-looking lump and you aren't stupid. You're witty and clever and you make us laugh. And you have eyes to die for. But I'm sure you already know that.'

But Shona carried on sobbing, shaking her head, the make-up she'd so carefully applied to give her her sisters' cheekbones that she'd always wanted melting into two dirty smears.

Grace wasn't giving up. 'You know, when I was young I always thought I wasn't pretty enough or clever enough. But at some point we all realise that there are always going to be more beautiful people in the world than we are, better athletes, more brilliant people. But, Shona, you can be something much better than any of them. You can be the nicest person in the world. Because you are nice, not in a dull, negative way, but in an extraordinarily exotic and individual way. You're wonderfully different. And, you know, there's nothing as attractive as being nice. In fact, I was just saying to George yesterday how lucky we were to get you serving us this week. They call it charisma, and God showered you with it. You might not realise it, but you're a very lucky girl.'

Shona's breathing was beginning to come under control. She found a handkerchief. She suddenly felt foolish to have been seen crying in public. She hoped not too many people had noticed.

Grace hadn't finished. 'But you don't have to believe me, because there's a boy across the room who knows all this better than anyone.' She was looking at Darrell. 'And I think if you just gave him a chance, because he's young like you and shy, like you again, I suspect, I think you might both remember this Valentine's Ball for a very long time.'

'But I upset him. I was jealous and said something stupid and crude and . . . I really upset him, because he's not like that . . .'

'Which is why he'll be so much happier when he understands that you didn't mean to upset him, and that it was just a mistake. We all say silly things sometimes, things that come out wrong and upset people. Why don't you wipe your eyes now and then go over and talk to him again? I bet you a million pounds he's wishing you would.'

'Now press C to the count of eight, then E for eight more, G . . .' Tim was laughing, holding Amy's hand over the notes, but now his hands were resting on hers for longer. He looked at her. She was flushed with excitement as all the band now joined in with them. She looked so pretty, Tim thought, and so happy to be silly. He knew she was over thirty and famous, but tonight she was seventeen again and anonymous. And whatever age she was she was certainly a good generation too young for Teddy Farrow. Yes, he was a real star. But Amy deserved better than that. Much better. Something she'd told him was nagging at the corner of his mind, something about being on the downside of the seesaw? As bright and vivacious as she was, she was certainly on the wrong side of Teddy Farrow's seesaw.

Then almost at his shoulder he felt Amanda's presence. 'Presenting Devon's own Lorna and the Doones, featuring brilliant modern com-poser Tim Fairweather . . . on rock-and-roll keyboard,' she was mocking, that touch of spite behind the pretty, over-intelligent smile. They were both, he and Amy, on the downsides of separate seesaws. He could see it now. Could she? And as her body leaned comfortably into his as she reached for a higher note, he was aware of a stray thought slipping under his guard: This is what it should always be like.

He looked up at that moment and caught sight of Michael and Eleanor, doing their own, polite, respectful approximation of a dance, smiling at each other as he'd never seen them smile before.

What a night this was. Such a night.

'So, how go our love potions?' Jane looked down the rows of baked, golden-brown éclairs just out of the oven, as Domingos, Agnieszka and the newly recruited Darrell went about splitting each one.

Darrell really didn't mind missing the dance. He felt as though he'd been kicked in the heart. He could actually feel it, the physical pain.

'I thought they'd make nice good-night presents for our guests,' Jane said, quickly checking her watch. 'They will all be ready? Yes?'

Domingos nodded. 'And the proof will be in the pudding.'

Out of their lines of vision Agnieszka shook her head silently.

'So, if there's a North Devon population explosion at Christmas we'll know who to blame, ha-ha,' Jane trilled. She was a little bit drunk but quickly re-assumed her managerial dignity. 'Anyway, jolly good. And especially well done to you, too, Darrell. You'll go far in this business.' And she returned to the ball.

Darrell had barely noticed the compliment. He couldn't get an image of Shona and Lorna out of his mind, Shona and Lorna doing things together in the Doones's black van with the black windows, where all kinds of things were said to go on.

'So, all we need to do now is add the filling and . . . population boom!' And Domingos tapped the large pan of cream filling, before peering inside the oven to check the last batch of love éclairs.

'Boom nothing!' Agnieszka muttered to herself, surreptitiously tasting the cream filling she was stirring. 'This never work. Quails' eggs! We need vodka.'

Now Darrell rather hoped it wouldn't work.

From the oven there was a sudden outburst: 'No!' Domingos's head withdrew. 'The power's gone. The oven don't bake no more.' And, muttering in Portuguese, he withdrew the last batch of éclairs and went down the kitchen to the trusty old Aga.

Then it happened, so quickly that Darrell could hardly believe what he'd seen. He saw Agnieszka empty the bottle of vodka she kept in the kitchen for small celebrations into the pan of cream filling. In a second, the bottle had disappeared and she continued stirring. She didn't even know Darrell had seen her. For a moment he wondered whether he should say something. But Domingos would find out soon enough, and tonight Darrell really didn't care about anything.

She couldn't keep up her one-finger recital for ever, and, her ambition achieved, after a storming version of Stevie Wonder's 'Superstition', in which Tim managed to make the keyboard sound like the quacking of a very tuneful duck, the guest artists left the stage to merry applause, leaving the Doones to play out the rest of the evening.

Now Tim and Amy did touch as they danced, as the Valentine's mood demanded that the music slow and the lights dim further, his hands on her waist, hers at his shoulders. Nor was she embarrassed to be staring so closely at him. It struck her that she'd never actually seen his face without the bandage. That white band across his forehead was a part of how he looked, like the colour of his eyes or the size of his wide, curly nose.

All around them couples were beginning to smooch, but not them. This wasn't the start of an affair, she told herself, as she spotted a scowling Abbott and his photographer at the back of the crowd still watching them. They were just two friends who'd seen off a dirty newspaper reporter with a small lie. Tomorrow she'd be seeing Teddy again.

Eighteen inches from her eyes Tim was smiling. She smiled back and rested the side of her face on his shoulder. But only because it had been a busy day and she was tired. Nothing more.

'So you work here, do you?' Lorna was squatting down between songs, leaning from the stage, as Shona, her face washed and make-up re-applied, filled a tray with empty glasses.

She nodded, getting on with her work.

'Bit of a dump, isn't it?'

Shona continued collecting the glasses. 'Actually, I like it here,' she heard herself say, noticing that the singer had some side teeth missing.

'Yes, well, maybe, but there's a party in Taunton when we finish. I bet you'd enjoy that more. You could come with us in the van. You'd like that. There's plenty of room. What's your name?'

For the first time, Shona noticed that Darrell was standing close by, overhearing the conversation, though pretending not to. 'Shona.'

'Shona! That's an exciting name. Shona! Very sexy!' And smiling right at her he handed her his empty glass.

Taking it, she was about to turn away, but at the last moment she just couldn't resist it. 'Do you think so? Do you really think so? Thank you. That's nice. But you can call me B, if you like.'

Lorna smirked victoriously. *Pulled!* his eyes said. 'B? Ah! A second name. Mysterious, eh! Better and better. What's B short for, then?'

Shona smiled sweetly. 'Hepatitis. Enjoy your party, dickhead!' And, picking up her tray, she strutted away towards the kitchen.

Thank you, God, Darrell said to himself. Thank you, thank you!

On the stage, Lorna, seeing him watching, laughed, not at all offended. Then, standing up, he looked around for another girl who might fancy a drive in the Doones's black van. There were always a couple to choose from, even at the North Devon Riviera Hotel.

'And so the reclusive, romantic Amy Miller and her new fiancé, danced the Valentine's night away, lost in each other's arms . . .' Will Abbott, a hand over one ear, added additional, late detail to the story he'd filed earlier, his eyes never leaving Amy and Tim. 'Ends,' he snapped.

'Just putting it through to the newsdesk basket,' the copytaker said. 'It's lovely, isn't it? Just like one of her books. A nice happy ending.'

'I bloody well hope not,' Abbott stabbed back, and hung up.

Suzy was waiting, watching the dancers and looking hopefully towards the dance floor. Surely she didn't want to dance? For God's sake.

So was this it? Amy thought, as the evening slow-danced towards bed-time. Was this the ritual face of romantic love in its various guises? Love the addiction, love the physical tyrant, lips on lips, hands on bottoms, and thighs scissoring? Or even love the fairy tale, leaving some couples dreamy and coy, and others caught in the euphoria before the delusion? Perhaps, for some, there would be no delusion. Could love have a happy ending? And she looked across at Grace moving slowly around George's wheelchair, murmuring along to what everyone knew as the Robin Hood song that Bryan Adams had sung, 'Everything I do, I do it for you'; carer and cared for, lover and loved. Was this what love looked like? Or was love just the selfish gene in all of us endlessly re-inventing ways to continue the species?

She knew which she preferred. Again she nestled her head into Tim's shoulder. I must remember this moment, she told herself. When I write again tomorrow I must remember what I've been thinking.

Tim felt her breath on his neck. And exulted in the moment.

Embarrassed, and still avoiding each other's eyes, they nearly missed it. Recalled to the kitchen to be ready with the éclairs, the song was halfway through before Shona realised. Dare she? 'Darrell, you promised me!'

He hesitated.

'It's the last waltz . . . you did promise me. Didn't you?'

For a moment, she thought he was going to turn away, not want her and make an excuse about what Jane would say. Then suddenly he was pulling her through the swing doors into the ballroom, bossing his way to the middle of the floor. 'Thank you,' she whispered.

But he just smiled and smiled, as holding each other they made their tiny circles, more shuffle-shuffle than one-two-three. Nothing could spoil their moment.

'D'you ever think about leaving here, Darrell?' Shona ventured at last.

'Where would I go?'

She shrugged. 'Anywhere. I thought about going around Hungary after Easter. We could go together. The hotels are really cheap there. I'm sure you'd like it.'

'Hotels?' Darrell's round face was dimpling in amusement.

Shona was puzzled. 'Did I say something funny?'

'Well, the idea of me in a hotel!'

'What do you mean?'

He was in difficulties. 'Well, hotels are places to work. I've never *stayed* in one. Not as a guest. I wouldn't know what to do.'

For a moment, Shona stared at him. Then she hugged him very tightly. 'Oh, Darrell, you are lovely.'

The balloons had been Jane's idea, so naturally it was she who released them. As the Doones struck their final chord, Barry Harrison handed her the kitchen scissors and she cut the string. Now the nets opened and down and around the balloons floated. 'Very nice,' smiled Barry.

'Thank you, Mr Harrison,' she replied graciously. Now there was just one more thing to do, and before the final applause had begun to fade, she'd launched herself onto the stage, and taken the microphone from its stand. 'Well, that's about it for this year,' she said. 'We at the North Devon Riviera Hotel would like to thank you all for coming and hope you've all enjoyed a wonderful, romantic evening—' A startle of applause from the Wiveliscombe coach party momentarily interrupted her. Jane acknowledged their support, then continued a little spicily. 'And I imagine that for some of you the romance of Valentine's Day might not be quite over yet—' The interruption this time came in the form of a beery guffaw from some lads close to the now-closed bar.

She'd intended to finish there, but suddenly her tone changed. 'And I hope that will apply even to those who are no longer young and beautiful. I hope that the romance of tonight, whether real or illusionary, will stay with you . . . because there are leftovers in love, too, you know, those who can't find a chair when the music stops and always seem to be left standing.'

The guests who'd been thinking about collecting their coats stopped. A murmur of embarrassment moved across the room and fell to silence.

'You see, being unloved doesn't mean that one doesn't yearn for love. In fact, I'm sure the unloved yearn for it more than anyone else.'

Across the room, Amy was concentrating. Michael and Eleanor were holding hands. Barry Harrison looked uncomfortable. Even the Doones were listening.

'So, for all those here tonight, who sometimes feel like the forgotten in love, let me just say, never give up hope, because, though you may not know it, somebody always loves you.'

From the lobby came the rude bang of a balloon being burst.

Finally, Jane remembered the purpose of her speech and raised her hand towards the kitchen. 'Anyway, to round off the evening we thought we'd present you all with a little going-home love potion that Domingos, our wonderful Brazilian chef, has concocted for us.'

And at that moment the kitchen doors opened and Domingos, Agnieszka, Shona and Darrell emerged bearing trays of éclairs above their heads.

You don't taste anything quite like this every day,' Tim mused as he savoured his éclair.

Amy was licking the cream, which was escaping from the two halves of her pastry. 'It must be eighty per cent proof. God knows what's in it. Some kind of nuts, Devon clotted cream, maybe . . . and is it vodka? D'you think we're allowed another?' And without waiting for an answer, she reached out and took two more from Darrell's plate.

Tim looked around the room. Everywhere perplexed-looking guests were considering what it was they were eating, because the éclairs really did have a quite peculiar taste. Close by them, Michael and Eleanor were eating theirs delicately, as though trying to guess what ingredients had been used, Grace was feeding George his before eating her own and Jane, the manager, was giggling over a third helping with Barry, who seemed to have been recruited as a temporary member of the staff. And finally, having served everyone else, Darrell was cautiously nibbling at his, while Shona gulped hers down in almost one bite. Certainly everyone was smiling about these love potions, with the exception of the reporter who, having refused his, was now sulking at the back of the room, his eyes still on Amy.

But it was late and, quickly, as the éclairs went, the room began to empty. Now Shona and Darrell began again, clearing glasses and plates, while by the kitchen door the chef and his assistant seemed to be having some sort of friendly argument in a mixture of Polish and Portuguese.

'I suppose that's it then . . .' Amy said, almost sadly, as she and Tim left the ballroom.

'Glad you came now?' asked Tim.

Amy looked over her shoulder at the reporter who was still watching her. 'Glad I came,' she agreed. 'And thank you. For everything. I was struggling. Out of my depth. Thank you for the white lie.'

'Thank *you*,' Tim said. They'd reached the landing and began making their way towards their rooms.

'You know, you've really helped these last few days—'

'Snap!' he interrupted. 'You've helped me write. I was stuck, blocked. Going the wrong way. Blind. Not now.'

'That's nice,' she said. 'It's been . . .'

'A special time. For me, anyway.'

'More than special,' she blurted. Then she stopped, looking as though she'd said more than she intended. They'd reached Tim's door.

'Oh-oh!' Tim was glancing back down the landing.

From the stairs came the sound of Abbott and the photographer. 'If bloody Rambo hadn't been stuck to her side like a barnacle on a barge's arse all night . . .' His voice carried up the stairs.

'Sounds like your pals are coming.' Tim unlocked his door. 'Maybe you'd better come in here or they won't believe we're really engaged.'

Amy hesitated. 'Er . . . I'm not sure that's a very good idea. I'm being picked up tomorrow morning and—'

Abbott and Suzy rounded the corner.

'Oh God!' Amy said and walked quickly into Tim's room.

He closed the door after her. 'Did you hear that?' he whispered, mock indignant. 'Do I look like a barnacle to you?'

She giggled. 'Better a barnacle than a barge's arse.'

'I promise you, you're nothing like a barge's arse.'

'Thank you.'

'Well, perhaps a very small one.'

They were both smiling, Amy with her back to the door. 'I think you ought to know I don't do this sort of thing,' she said. 'I mean, I don't go into hotel bedrooms with strange men.'

'Nor me,' Tim said. 'But I'm not really that strange, am I?'

'Not strange at all. But I think you know what I mean.'

He knew very well what she meant. They stood and looked at each other. Dare I, thought Tim. If I don't, I'll spend the rest of my life regretting it. But what if she looks pained and turns away?

She was still looking at him.

He dared. Leaning forward, he kissed her neck.

She tilted her head sideways and craned her neck slightly. She didn't look pained at all. Or even long-suffering. So he kissed her again.

She began talking again: 'I mean, I know lots of friends might think, "Oh, what the hell, Teddy's been messing me around. Now it's my turn to have some fun" . . .' Was she trying to pretend he wasn't kissing her?

'I can't believe that,' he teased. And he kissed her once more.

'Oh, yes,' she went on matter-of-factly. 'But not me. I don't think like that. I'm one of those pathetic, clinging, boring, faithful creatures.'

'Good.' His lips had now found the side of her cheek.

'I mean. I've never had a one-night stand in my life.' Now the side of her mouth.

'No?' He didn't mean to, but he must have sounded surprised.

She looked slightly guilty. 'Well, almost never.'

He'd reached her lips fully. A small kiss. 'Everybody has some youthful indiscretions.'

'But what I'm trying to say is that whatever you're expecting, don't. Because it isn't going to happen.'

'I know.' Another kiss. Longer.

'You know?' This time she stopped him. 'How?' she demanded.

'I've made my mind up. What kind of pushover do you take me for?'

'**W**hat d'you mean, "we're going"? It's after midnight.' Suzy was sitting on the bed watching as Abbott packed.

'Well, there's nothing to stay here for now, is there?' He knew that was a brutal thing to say, but he wasn't sorry.

Suzy's eyes creased as she registered the insult. Then she began to pack, too. They'd brought so little it hardly took more than a few moments. The last item to be pushed into her shoulder bag was her book, *The Ladder of Sex*. She didn't bother to close the bag.

Abbott was ready. 'OK, let's go!' And he opened the door and walked on ahead of her down the landing right into Michael and Eleanor as they came round the corner, laughing together.

A pace behind him Suzy had to stop suddenly, her bag toppling from her shoulder onto the fold of her elbow.

'Excuse me! I'm terribly sorry,' Michael apologised earnestly, although his face was pink and amused. Eleanor was beaming.

Abbott ignored them, and, pushing past, continued angrily on his way. Hitching her bag back up Suzy followed him down the stairs.

'Oh dear!' Eleanor said, and pulled a funny face. 'Perhaps she should have had that éclair after all.'

Michael didn't follow.

'The young lady said she was slimming when they offered her one.'

'Ah, well, that's their loss.' Michael laughed and continued on his way.

It was at that moment that Eleanor saw the book lying on the floor. She picked it up. *The Ladder of Sex*, she read silently to herself. Then she opened it. She gazed in astonishment and wonder rather than shock at the first full-page photograph, then turned the page. There was another erotic picture there and then another and another. So much sex. She'd never realised there was so much to it.

Michael had already opened the door.

Had the young couple dropped their book? she wondered. She should give it back to them. Then another thought occurred. Might they be embarrassed if she suddenly pursued them with it? Perhaps finders keepers might be the most delicate way of resolving the problem.

She looked inside the book again. On the very last page was a photo-graph of a naked man and woman on a white bed, the man lying back staring happily above him, the woman curled up comfortably inside the protection of his outstretched arm, her eyes closed.

'Eleanor!' she heard Michael call from their room.

She moved to the door of the Passion of the West Country honeymoon suite clutching the book. There was so much to learn. 'Michael!' she said. 'Do you still believe in miracles?'

And smiling happily, she went inside and closed the door.

Amy watched as Tim poured the boiling water onto the instant coffee in the two mugs. First he kissed her, *then* he made some coffee. That was back to front. She was embarrassed. 'I'm sorry if I misread the situation, but you're putting out some very confusing signals.'

'I don't see what's confusing. Milk? You don't take sugar, do you?'

'Yes, milk. Thank you.' He'd noticed about the sugar. That was nice. Teddy could never remember. He passed her the coffee.

'Look, when you said you'd made up your mind that it wasn't going to happen, were you sort of saying that you just don't fancy me?'

He nodded. 'That's right. I just don't fancy you.'

'Ah! I see. That's all right then. Good.' She sipped her coffee, trying not to show her disappointment.

'No. Bad,' he said. 'I don't just fancy you. I'm in love with you. It isn't the same.'

Abbott and Suzy left without paying, the manager being deep in conversation on a sofa in the bar with a guy in a brown suit. The hotel had Abbott's credit card details. They could send the invoice on.

By the time they reached the Porsche, the car park was empty. 'We shouldn't be driving in this fog,' Suzy fretted. 'It isn't safe.'

'It's only a local sea mist. We'll be out of it in five minutes,' Abbott said, unlocking the car doors and climbing in.

Suzy slid in and slammed her door.

He put the key in the ignition and turned on the engine. The engine was cold. He revved it for a few moments.

'It's a pity we never got this far,' Suzy said suddenly as they waited.

'What?'

'In the book. "Chapter Seventeen. Spice Things Up with a Different Location." There's a whole section on sex in cars. It looked interesting.'

He looked at her. She was a very, very sexy woman. Then he thought about Ed Halliwell. 'This car's too small for that.'

'I thought the seats went back,' she said, 'like recliners.'

'You know about sex in cars, too, do you?' he snapped unkindly.

'Thank you.' Again she looked hurt. Then she bit back. 'Doesn't everyone? Don't you?'

It was true, he thought. Nearly everyone had had sex in a car at some time in their life. 'We couldn't do it here, anyway. Someone might see.'

'In the fog?'

He hesitated. 'Did you read it . . . the bit about sex in cars?'

'Yes. But it doesn't matter. Let's just go.'

He looked around at the fog. It really was quite thick. He turned off the Porsche's engine. 'Do you want to try?'

'The car's too small. You said it yourself.'

'No, it isn't. Not really. I'm sure we could manage.'

'It would be very awkward.'

'More fun then.'

'You're a real bastard, you know,' she said. 'I really liked you.'

'Yes. I am a bastard. I do know,' he replied honestly. And putting his hand to her belt he undid the top metal button of her jeans.

She looked at him and it occurred to him that her pretty pug-like face was smiling as though she'd won a final little victory. She had.

With the absence of a sofa in the Exmoor Suite, Amy made herself comfortable on the bed, propping her back against the headboard. 'I think you're just imagining you're in love with me because Amanda's away and you're lonely,' she said. 'It's a well-known fact. Abstinence makes the fond heart wander.'

'Not in my case,' Tim said. 'I really am in love with you.' And he joined her on the bed.

She made space for him, puzzled for a moment, and then said, 'Or perhaps it's because it's Valentine's night and you want to feel romantic.'

'Wrong again,' Tim came back, watching her closely.

A sudden look of triumph appeared. 'I know. It's the Brazilian love potion they gave us. It must have worked.'

'I doubt it. That was just a profiterole soaked in alcohol.'

Finally she sighed. 'Well, there must be some explanation.'

Tim nodded. 'Yes. There is. I keep telling you. But you just don't want to hear it.'

The guests were long gone. Only the staff remained, Jane having reopened the bar, sharing a last drink with Barry Harrison, Shona taking down the decorations, Darrell filling plastic bags with party refuse, and Domingos and Agnieszka tidying the kitchen. There'd nearly been a row earlier when Domingos had tasted one of the éclairs. Catching Agnieszka watching him to see his reaction, he'd suddenly burst into laughter and said something in Portuguese, which had made her laugh and reply in Polish. How much they each understood of what the other was saying was hard to tell, but probably more than Shona had initially realised. Their relationship was a puzzle, but, in its off-hand, sniping, duo-lingual way, it seemed to work.

'Oh dear, are you all still up? I think you can leave the rest until tomorrow, don't you?' Jane was standing in the door to the bar holding a glass. Shona had never seen her so friendly. Behind her Barry Harrison, now in his shirtsleeves, was watching.

'Thank you,' Shona said. 'Good night.'

Darrell put down his plastic bag as Jane returned with Harrison to the bar. 'Well!' he said, watching them together.

Shona didn't care about Jane and Harrison. Grabbing hold of a streamer made of red plastic hearts she put it round Darrell's neck like a Hawaiian garland. 'That's my Valentine to you.'

Darrell shone. 'Thank you,' he said and glanced towards the kitchen to see if Domingos and Agnieskza had noticed. They'd already left.

'I suppose we might as well go to bed then,' Shona said. Picking up a stray balloon and a bottle of red wine that wasn't quite finished, she led the way across the ballroom.

Turning out the lights, Darrell followed her to the staff quarters. She didn't look back, not even when she sensed him hesitate at his door.

Shona was already unlocking hers. 'You've never seen my room, have you, Darrell?' she said. 'It's really nice.' She stepped inside leaving the door ajar. There was a second hesitation from the corridor. Then Darrell followed her in.

She tried the light switch. As expected, the room remained in darkness. 'Oh, no! The bulb seems to have gone,' she said, hoping she sounded convincingly surprised.

'Not to worry, I'll just pop down to the storeroom and get another,' Darrell offered quickly, ever helpful.

She leaped between Darrell and the door and closed it. 'Oh, no! No. It doesn't matter. Honestly. It will do tomorrow.'

Darrell looked at her. Standing there, her balloon hovering at her shoulder, in the yellow glow sieving through the fog from the courtyard lights, she was beautiful.

Jane looked at Harrison. For weeks she'd known and slightly despised him, as a boastful, vulgar, pathetic loser. He'd lost his wife and children to another man. His business hadn't worked. He had no home and no real hopes. All this had spilled out between the drinks, not in bitterness or anger, not even in self-pity. He was just puzzled by life. He couldn't understand how it had happened. She could. But she no longer despised him, any more than she despised herself. Loneliness can make even the best of people behave foolishly.

He must have been five or six years younger than she was. He still had time to make a difference to his life. If she reported him to head office, they would, she was sure, pursue him for the hotel bill he couldn't pay. But there were ways and means of hiding a bad debt.

'Look, you can forget the hotel bill,' she said. 'When you leave tomorrow, and you must leave tomorrow, just consider it paid. But you must never come back again.'

'Thank you,' he said simply.

Then, very deliberately, she put a hand on his and left it there. Perhaps, for once, if only for a night, two leftovers in love could find a place together now that the music had stopped.

She hadn't really been lying to him, she protested softly as she finished her coffee. Withholding her real name and profession were only minor sins forced on her by the circumstances. All the same, she was sorry she'd done it. He wasn't the sort of person who should be lied to.

Tim just smiled. 'That's all right. I think I've been misleading myself for a lot longer.' And he considered his keyboard. All his life music had been a companion. Only when he'd betrayed it by trying to make it do something he didn't believe in had that friendship faltered. Little wonder he hadn't been able to write.

Now, looking back at Amy, he played in his mind his new music, the music he'd been writing all day. He was happy.

'I thought you wouldn't like me.'

Darrell was puzzled. 'Why's that?' They were sitting next to each other on the edge of Shona's bed, drinking the wine.

'I don't know. I think I frighten boys. I put them off. I liked you straight away but I really thought I'd put you off tonight. Sometimes I say things I don't really mean. It's a medical syndrome.'

'We just call it silly talk down these parts.'

'Yes. That's probably it. That's what I've got. The silly-talk syndrome. Aren't you going to kiss me?'

Darrell smiled to himself. He couldn't believe how confident and handsome he suddenly felt. 'Is that the syndrome talking?' he asked. 'Or do you mean it?' Shona giggled in the darkness. That was nice, too. He didn't usually make people laugh: not on purpose, anyway.

Shona helped herself to some more wine and then lay down on the bed. 'You can lie down, too, if you want to,' she said. 'There's room. You must be dead tired. You've been on your feet all day.'

Darrell did want to lie down. As she moved closer to the wall he stretched out awkwardly alongside her at the edge of the narrow divan.

For a few moments neither of them spoke. Darrell wondered what Barry Harrison would say he should do next.

'Shall I tell you something?' Shona said at last, then, without waiting for an answer, did anyway. 'I've never had a boyfriend.'

'Never?' Darrell found this hard to believe. A glamorous, exotic girl like Shona must have had stacks of boyfriends.

'Not a proper one. Not one I was crazy about who was crazy about me. Actually, nobody's ever been crazy about me.'

'I am,' Darrell said. He was now leaning on his side, trying to see her features in the darkness.

'Honestly? Well, you *have* to kiss me now,' she said. 'At the very least!'

Very carefully, he rested his weight on his arm, leaned over and lowered his face to hers. Her eyes were closed.

Suddenly he stopped.

After a moment her eyes opened. 'What's the matter?'

He was staring at something to the side of her right ear. 'Don't move! By your head,' he gasped. Lying on the pillow in the glow from the outside lights was the head and part of the trunk of a long narrow snake.

Shona swivelled her head to look. 'Oh, that's just Monty!' she said.

Darrell kept on staring, rigid in fear. 'Monty?'

'As in python. But he's not really a python. He's just a pet. I've been wondering where he's been all day. I'll put him back in his box.'

But the snake had already slipped back down the side of the wall and under the bed. Carefully Darrell sank down again alongside Shona.

'I knew you didn't really have Hitler's missing testicle in that box,' he said at last.

He felt Shona's lips smile as he bent to kiss her. 'Actually, I did,' she said. 'But Monty ate it.'

She was sleepy now. Stifling a yawn, she looked around the room at Tim's computer and scattered sheets of music manuscript. How similar his life must be to mine, she thought, and she remembered the first book she'd written, not for the fame or the money, but because she wanted to. And she wondered whether Amanda understood that emotion. Instinctively she knew she wouldn't, any more than Teddy understood why she sometimes cried when she invented setbacks for her characters. 'How can you cry about characters and events you've invented and which exist only in your imagination?' he would tease. She didn't know how. She just knew she did.

She didn't tell Tim any of this. She said, 'You can't fall in love with me, anyway. This is a designated romance-free zone. Remember?'

'That was your description, not mine. And you were wrong.'

Sleep was hovering now, but something was still bothering her. 'Don't think I'm being provocative, because I'm not. But you didn't actually say why you don't want to make love to me.'

'No, I didn't.'

'Well, why not? I'm just wondering, mind you, not encouraging you.'

At her side, Tim became thoughtful. 'Shall we just say, I don't want to make love to you while you're thinking about somebody else?'

Amy smiled to herself. What had she been writing when Teddy had phoned her to say she was being watched by the reporter?

Given the choice, which would you prefer: that the person you love is making love to you and thinking about someone else, or that he, or she, is making love to someone else and thinking about you?

She closed her eyes.

Chapter Six

OVERNIGHT THE FOG had dissolved and now the sky was a wispy seaside blue as Darrell made his way across the enclosed garden to the hotel building. It really did feel like spring, he thought: a wondrous day.

But how did *he* feel? Like he could never have imagined. Different. Happy, yes, but strangely more adult. He even felt taller.

He hadn't wanted to leave Shona. She'd looked so peaceful, seemingly amused by something in her sleep. He should have woken her and insisted she come to work. But he'd let her sleep on. She'd talked half the night, and the other half . . . well . . . she hadn't.

It didn't matter if she was late for work. She was only temporary staff, on a college placement, being paid hardly anything. The hotel could manage without her for another hour. He, however, had a responsible job. It was a Saturday. Saturdays were busy days in hotels.

As he let himself into the hotel through the back door, Giles bounded up to him affectionately. He didn't grumpily try to push the dog off, as he usually did. He didn't mind anything this morning. And he left the back door open for Giles to run outside.

Reaching the lobby he was surprised to find it still deserted. Usually Jane was already there, ready to chivvy everyone along. Not today. And though there was the smell of breakfast from the kitchen, there was none of the usual arguing. Peeping in, he found Domingos with a friendly arm round Agnieszka as she stirred a bowl of scrambled eggs. The day had begun far more happily than any other he'd known in his time in the hotel.

Going through into the loggia, he smiled as he began pulling down the decorations. Last night had been the best night of his life. Torquay United's draw with Manchester United didn't even come close.

So engrossed was he in his reverie he didn't hear the taxi until it was at the front door. Going to the window he looked out. A tall woman with crow-black hair was climbing from the cab.

He was puzzled. New guests shouldn't arrive until two at the earliest, and he hurried through to the lobby to unlock the front door as the bell rang twice.

A smiling, slightly cocky, metropolitan sort of woman in a black suit stepped inside. In her thirties, she was pretty, but a bit terrifying. 'Good morning. Sorry if I got you up,' she said sarcastically.

'Oh no, I was just—'

She cut him off. 'It's just that I'm looking for one of your guests . . . a Mr Fairweather? Tim Fairweather. He told me he was staying here.'

Sensing the newcomer's arrival, Giles padded into the lobby.

'Oh, yes. Mr Fairweather . . . that's room seven, the Exmoor Suite. But he'll probably be asleep. We had a dance here last night. I'll just . . . Shut up, Giles!' The dog had begun to bark excitedly. 'I'll just give Mr Fairweather a ring to tell him you're here. Giles! Stop it!'

The woman's exaggerated expression of patience suggested that she was neither used to being kept waiting nor a dog lover.

'You're going out!' Darrell said, pulling the dog towards the front door. 'I'm sorry about this. I won't be a minute. What name shall I say?'

But a minute would clearly have been too long. 'I'll find my own way. Room seven?' The woman said and began to climb the stairs.

At the front door Darrell was stranded as he tried to push the dog outside. 'Actually, nonresidents aren't allowed up to the bedrooms,' he shouted. But, although she must surely have heard him, the woman made no attempt to stop.

Tim was awake when the phone rang. He had been for an hour, lying alongside Amy, both still dressed but covered by a blanket he'd pulled over them in the middle of the night. He'd been wondering about the person he'd fallen in love with who'd told him her name was Millie. Did it matter that she was actually somebody else, someone far richer and more successful than anyone he knew? And that her name was Amy Miller? Only that it put her out of his league. Soon she would be returning to her old life and her married lover who didn't deserve her, and that would be that. These moments with her sleeping alongside him he would remember for the rest of his life.

Amy stirred with a slightly bewildered look as she heard the phone. He picked it up. 'Hello?'

'Sorry to wake you, Mr Fairweather. Front desk here. There's a lady on her way up to see you.' Darrell sounded embarrassed.

For a second, Tim couldn't quite make sense of this. 'What lady?'

'She didn't give her name. I'm sorry, I couldn't stop her.'

At his side he could feel the mattress give as Amy began to move. She'd heard what he said. Almost simultaneously there was a knock on the door. He clambered off the bed. Then came another knock.

Within a moment Amy was standing by the French windows. Sadly, she tried to smile. Was this the way he would remember her? he thought. As she was at this very second, her hair tousled, eyes bleary, the dress she'd bought for the ball crumpled, holding her party shoes in her hands?

The knocking grew louder. 'Tim! Tim!'

Amy unlocked the French windows.

'Mr Fairweather . . .?' Darrell was prompting down the phone.

'It's all right, Darrell. I'll deal with this.' And, hanging up, he crossed to the door.

Swinging her leg over the balcony rail, Amy dropped down onto the narrow ornamental ledge with the low wrought-iron rail that connected all the balconies along the side of the hotel. Then she began to edge along it towards her own room. Five days ago she'd never had to escape from anywhere in her life, now she was doing it for a second time. What was happening to her? She only hoped she'd left the door to her own balcony unlocked.

She didn't look down but kept her eyes on the wall as she reached the window of the suite between Tim's room and her own. At least the curtains would be drawn, she thought, remembering the teenagers she'd accidentally seen petting as she'd climbed down the side of her apartment building. She was only half right. As she passed the window she found herself looking through a small gap in the curtains into the honeymoon suite. Lying curled happily together in the centre of the white-laced four-poster were Michael and Eleanor.

Quickly averting her eyes, she hurried on, clambering over the rail to her own balcony, and her mercifully unlocked French windows.

Tim stood back as Amanda entered the room.

'God, I thought you must have a girl in here at the very least!' She laughed. 'You aren't even undressed. Don't tell me you worked all night.'

'No, I didn't work. I had a lot of thinking to do.'

She put her arms round his neck. 'Aren't you going to kiss me?'

Tentatively he kissed her lips. He'd forgotten how she smelt. Her perfume, once so familiar and welcome, now seemed too sharp.

'Well, I've had more enthusiastic welcomes!'

'I'm surprised to see you. I thought you were still in Denver.'

'I came back. How's the head?' She was staring at his bandage.

'Fine. I told you it was nothing. Did the tour finish early? How did you get here?' He looked at his watch. It was hardly eight thirty.

'I quit. There were problems. You know how these big tours are. It got messy. So I flew home yesterday. I tried to get here last night. Got to Taunton but the taxi driver said it was too foggy on the moors. Didn't want to bring me. So I stayed there. And here I am, up with the badgers, to enjoy the weekend with the man I love.' She hesitated. 'It seems I missed the big dance.'

He nodded. And, yes, he did know how these tours were. Everyone in music did. He knew Amanda, too, and it occurred to him that he was looking at a woman he'd thought he loved. But now he couldn't remember why.

Amanda was still talking. 'Your messages sounded so bleak . . . stuck here by yourself. So, I thought, I know, I'll give him a nice surprise!' And then she added, like an afterthought, 'Besides, I missed you.'

Amy was already in the shower. I'm not crying, she told herself. I've nothing to cry about. How could I be crying?

Perhaps a fleeting shadow at the window had disturbed Michael, but he'd woken to a new world. At his side he felt the warm, white skin of Eleanor pressed against his. So *this* was what married life meant. Closeness and contentment. In the night he'd been amazed at how perfectly their bodies had fitted together. But this morning, this waking moment, made him happier. This was their future together, as naked as babies and almost as innocent.

Lying at the bottom of the bed was the book Eleanor had found, *The Ladder of Sex*. They'd laughed about it the previous night, and wondered whether they truly had been served love potions. He knew they hadn't. Their private ceremony among the ruins of St Gytha's had been all the love potion they needed . . . and, all right, perhaps a little encouragement from the Holy Ghost.

Shona hadn't stayed in bed long. She wanted to be with Darrell. Just to be near him, helping him, accidentally on purpose touching his arm as they passed, and sharing little knowing smiles with him was a thrill. Life was suddenly dazzling.

'A degree in hotel management?' Her father had laughed when she'd told him what she was going to study at university. 'Whatever will these new places think of next? Oh, well, if that's what you want to do with your life . . .' She'd been hurt at the time, having half thought that for once she might be congratulated for her enterprise. Last night she'd told Darrell about the course she was on. He'd been very impressed. 'That sounds really good. Your parents must be proud of you.'

'Mmm . . . well,' she'd said vaguely. She hadn't had the heart to tell him that hotel management was not the academic course her parents would think a daughter of theirs should be taking.

'I'm proud of you, too,' he'd then said.

'Really?' she'd asked. And she'd found herself disguising her tears of happiness by pushing her face into her pillow.

Now she was busily helping set out the breakfast display in the loggia, with the Scottish hiking couple already down, while Darrell had been asked to take some coffee and toast up to the Exmoor Suite. Outside in the car park Giles was barking repeatedly at something, which was irritating, but at least he wasn't jumping up and frightening Monty.

Quickly she went into the kitchen to give Agnieszka the Scottish couple's order. By the Aga, Jane was going through a list of requirements with Domingos. With her hair dishevelled and her make-up apparently hurriedly applied, she looked, thought Shona, as though she'd been slept in.

'And, Shona, when you have a minute could you see what Giles is so excited about?' Jane said as Shona passed on the order.

'Of course.'

Jane smiled. 'Good girl.'

Good girl! What had come over the woman?

Room service had been Amanda's idea. Tim had been about to tell her that it wasn't fair on the staff to make demands after such a busy night, but, on reflection, he had no desire to parade Amanda before the entire hotel either. Besides, she only wanted a round of brown toast.

Since she'd arrived she'd been edgy, and over-casually bored when he'd asked her how the tour had gone. He hadn't pursued the subject. He didn't care how it had gone. Actually, that wasn't quite true. He was pretty sure he knew exactly how it had gone.

'Anyway,' she said at last, 'how's the piece coming?'

'It's coming,' Tim replied without expression.

'Great! Actually, I thought I might be able to help you with it . . .' Passing him, she ran a hand flintily across his shoulders then sat down at the keyboard and picked up some sheets of manuscript. 'Is this it?' Quickly she read the music, then shook her head. 'Oh, no, it can't be.'

'Actually, it is,' Tim said.

She laughed. 'No, seriously. Can I see it?'

'*Seriously*. You're looking at it. That's what I've been working on.'

She looked at him as though half believing he must be teasing her. She turned back to the manuscript. 'Tim . . .' she said at last, running her forefinger along the lines of notes. 'This is pure romantic melody.'

Tim nodded. 'Yes. Quite a nice little tune, I think, don't you?'

Amanda was becoming impatient. 'Well, nice it may be. But you'll be laughed out of the competition with a "nice little tune".'

Keeping his eyes on her Tim smiled to himself. 'I'm sure I will be.'

When her new mobile rang there could only be one caller.

'Amy. I'll be with you in about ten minutes.' Teddy was in bouncing form. 'I got away early. See you at the front door of the hotel. OK?'

'Er . . . yes.' Amy had been sitting, dressed, watching the sea.

'Fantastic. Can't wait to see you.' And he hung up.

Amy pulled out her bags, collected her belongings and began to pack. Taking a sheet of hotel stationery from the desk she wrote a note for the room maid and placed it with her party dress, shoes and earrings on the un-slept-in bed: *I won't need these any more, so if you would like them for yourself, or anybody else you know, please take them.*

Signing the note *Amy Miller*, she made for the door.

'**G**iles! Giles! Come here, boy!' Shona yelled. The dog ignored her, tearing round the car in the corner of the car park, barking repeatedly and jumping up at the window. Shona continued towards it. She was too happy to be cross. 'Come on, boy! Here, Giles!'

When she was almost at the car, Giles turned to her, as if wishing to show her something. That was her chance. Reaching down she grabbed the dog by his collar. Then, just as she was about to return to the hotel, she happened to glance inside the car.

At first she didn't quite understand what she was seeing. Puzzled, she looked again to make sure.

'You're behaving very strangely. Are you sure your brain wasn't buckled when you fell off your chair?' Amanda's voice had turned brittle.

Tim didn't reply immediately. 'Actually, I think it might have been straightened,' he said at last. 'I'm seeing things more clearly than I was.'

Amanda was still by the keyboard. 'And?'

'Well, I think I've been trying to be something I'm not.'

'Your brain has definitely been buckled.' There was just a touch of derision there.

'No. I don't think so. You've got me wrong, Amanda. Dead wrong! You want me to be someone else. And I can't be. I can't write the music you'd like me to. I thought I wanted to. For you. For us. But I can only do what I can do. I'd never have a hope in the competition. You know that. I don't even like that stuff.'

'But I *love* what you do, Tim.' Amanda's voice suddenly softened. 'Forget the competition. What do those judges know, anyway? All I want is for you to expand your horizons. Can't you see? You could be so much more than you are, Tim . . . if you could just . . .'

Tim suddenly wasn't listening. His mind's eye was filled with Amy. 'I'm sorry, there's someone I have to talk to . . .' And walking past her, he hurried from the room and down the corridor.

'Yes . . . police and ambulance. This is urgent!' Jane was pink, as though she'd been running, shouting into the phone. At her side, Shona was nodding her head vigorously.

In front of the desk, Amy took her bill from a distracted Darrell and keyed in the PIN of her credit card as Domingos and Agnieszka hurried through the lobby and out into the car park. Shona followed them. 'Thank you,' said Amy as Darrell gave her a receipt.

'Thank you,' murmured Darrell, glancing through the window.

Picking up her bag and laptop, Amy crossed the lobby and stepped outside, almost colliding with the newsagent and his stack of papers.

'Morning,' he smiled. 'Seems like something's going on over there.'

Amy looked across the car park. 'Yes. I don't know what it is.' The Scottish hikers were now approaching the car, too.

Normally she would have gone to investigate, but at that moment she saw Teddy's black BMW coming swiftly up the drive. He smiled as he drew up beside her. 'Amy, love.'

She climbed in and the car accelerated away.

Tim watched the BMW leave, scarcely aware of the drama developing across the car park. Had he been a second earlier . . .? No. What could he have said? It wouldn't have made any difference. She was gone, out of his life. He stared down the empty drive.

Suddenly he became aware of a squeal of delight behind him. 'Congratulations! I'd no idea. Amy Miller! Here! This is wonderful publicity. Bristol will be delighted. Thank you *so* much.' It was Jane, blushing with excitement, holding a newspaper out to him. Tim looked at it. At the bottom of the front page was a large photograph of Amy walking along the quay with him the previous morning, seemingly sharing a joke. **ROMANTIC AMY IN DISGUISE—KINKY WEEKENDS WITH SECRET FIANCÉ**, ran the headline.

'You naughty things!' teased Jane. 'And now she's gone again! It's like hide-and-seek. Such fun!' Then she was off again, back across the car park. Tim didn't care about the car. He was staring at the newspaper.

So was Amy. It had been waiting for her on the passenger seat of the BMW, Teddy having spotted it when he'd stopped for petrol on the way down. 'But it isn't true!' she gasped. 'None of it.'

At the wheel, Teddy was laughing in triumph as he drove quickly up towards the moors. 'How about that for a pick-up? No one even saw me. Well done! And you're looking wonderful. Truly wonderful! The sea air's done you good. I love the hair, too. Like burnished gold! You're nothing like a platypus, even if you are engaged.' He chortled.

Amy was shaking her head. 'But I'm not engaged. You know I'm not. He just said that to put them off the scent.'

'So? Who cares? The papers get it wrong again. It happens every day. My, have I been looking forward to seeing you!' And suddenly putting a hand out, he stroked the top of her thigh.

She didn't like that. It wasn't affectionate. It was proprietorial. She studied the newspaper, turning to an inside page to read the main story and the suggestion of sexy games she was supposed to have played. 'This is terrible,' she murmured.

Teddy was still breezy. 'Come on, it doesn't matter.'

'What? *Doesn't matter!*' She stared at him. As usual, not a hair was displaced, his smooth face was tanned and healthy-looking, and his clothes looked as though he was wearing them for the first time. Everything about him suggested success and wealth. And self-satisfaction. An image of the shaggy Tim, his long hair and his bandage coming loose again, peeped at her from the previous night.

The siren of a police car travelling quickly in the opposite direction across the moor made her look at the road. A couple of hundred yards behind it an ambulance was following, its light flashing.

'What did you do back there before you left? Murder someone? Was it that boring?' Teddy joked.

Amy put the newspaper on her knee. 'Teddy . . .'

He sighed. 'Amy, OK! You had a holiday fling! You're entitled. It happens. You're a single girl. Pity the papers got to know, but—'

'But it didn't happen. I didn't have a fling.'

Teddy gave her a sideways, old-fashioned look. 'Amy! Come on!'

'I *mean* it.' She was almost shouting.

Teddy shrugged. 'OK! I really don't mind. It doesn't matter.'

'"*Don't mind*"?' Amy could feel herself going red with anger.

'It's worked. The papers are off our backs. We're in the clear. In some ways this guy . . . whatever his name is . . . he's perfect.'

That was it. 'Stop the car!' Amy snapped.

'What? We're in the middle of the moor!'

'Just stop this bloody car!'

The dash across the car park had now become a gentle stampede as Barry Harrison put his two suitcases down on the hotel steps and hurried over, passing the elderly ladies on the way. Even Michael and Eleanor, who was dressed today in an almost daring plum-coloured jacket, couldn't resist the temptation. Only Tim had no interest.

'Tim!' He looked round. Amanda was holding a newspaper she must have picked up at reception. 'Why didn't you tell me?'

He didn't answer.

'This is sick!' She began to read. '*According to her fiancé, Tim Fairweather, the couple meet regularly in out-of-the-way hotels for sex, pretending to be strangers. Is this true? No. Don't try to lie. Why else would you be in this godforsaken dump? Christ! Amy Miller! There's an overpaid, over-rated, chick-lit tart if ever there was one!'*

Tim had never hated anyone. He rarely actually disliked anyone. But at this moment Amanda was coming very close to being the first.

She hadn't finished. 'How long has it being going on? How long have I been wasting my life on you . . . doing everything I could to help your career . . . introducing you to new music . . . new ideas . . . new people·

. . . when all you want to do is write mushy, trite little melodies to match Amy Miller's pathetic little stories.' The sound of a police car and ambulance entering the car park interrupted her venom. 'Well? Can't you say *anything?*'

Tim could have said so much, mainly that for the life of him he couldn't imagine why they'd ever got together in the first place. He didn't. There was no point. 'I think it's time we both tried other see-saws,' he said.

Amanda pulled a face, her beautiful, classical, clever features twisting into a sharp slice of bitter derision. She looked almost ugly. 'If that's some kind of cryptic riddle . . .' she spat.

But he wasn't listening. Turning away, he walked across the car park to the crowd and watched as the police conferred, the ambulance waited and a fire engine arrived. Everyone was there. Jane was supervising, while telling the police officers that Amy Miller had just been a guest; George and Grace were watching, bemused, and Darrell was standing gallantly alongside Shona, who appeared to be feeding something under her shirt. Beyond them, Michael and Eleanor were hand in hand; the white-clad kitchen staff had their arms round each other, and Barry Harrison was leering fruitily.

Peering over Harrison's shoulder, Tim looked at the car. It was the reporter's Porsche. Inside he could make out the bare cheeks of Abbott's bottom, framed by the two jackknifed thighs and knees of his pretty photographer wedged under him. With one foot stuck in the spokes of the steering wheel, she wasn't looking quite so cute today.

Harrison was smiling. 'It's St Valentine's Revenge,' he whispered overloudly. 'They must have been there all night. Looks like he's been clamped.' And he chuckled smuttily to himself.

A sudden flash made them both glance round. And then another. No one had noticed a local photographer appear on his motorcycle. Some newspaper would pay handsomely for photographs like this.

Tim had seen enough. Backing away, he ignored the hotel, where Amanda was still waiting, and set off down the path towards the town. There was only one person he wanted in his thoughts, and she wasn't here. Everything else was just getting in the way.

For some reason, though numb with cramp, Abbott was thinking about Polly, who'd got him into Amy Miller's apartment block. She'd got a crush on him, believing his profession to be glamorous and exciting. Would she still have a crush on him when she saw the photographs of his backside on news-stands across the country tomorrow morning?

Would she still want a tour of the newsroom? And would Jenny, his wife, be thrilled? And the boys?

If he could have sighed he would have done. What was it, he puzzled, that drove reasonably sensible, intelligent men and women to mate as promiscuously as bonobos whenever the opportunity presented itself? Were some people like him built with a design flaw, something that dictated that no matter how happily married they were—and he and Jenny were very happily married—they just couldn't turn down the opportunity of a quick extra-marital adventure?

From the angle at which he was stuck he couldn't see Suzy's face, just her ear and the dark roots in her thick, bleached hair. They'd stopped talking hours earlier when they'd given up trying to move. They'd never had much to say to each other at the best of times. But now, as indignity was added to the hours of cramp and pain, he felt ashamed. She'd been affectionate and kind. She didn't deserve this.

Out of the corner of his eye he now saw the sparkle of a fireman's acetylene cutting equipment approaching. It looked like a firework, but it was hardly the best way to celebrate the end of a dirty weekend.

Teddy had pulled the BMW off the road into an Exmoor picnic area.

'Amy?' He waited.

She was hunched up against the passenger door. 'It just won't work any more,' she said. Perhaps she should have had tears in her eyes, but she couldn't feel any.

Teddy was confused. 'What? Why, Amy? What are you saying?'

She shook her head. She couldn't explain.

He took the newspaper from her. 'Don't worry about this. It means we can still see each other. In secret. And if you want to, you know . . . continue with . . .' He indicated the newspaper and the photograph of Tim. 'Well, you know, I'm married, I'm not the possessive type.'

'That's the point,' Amy burst out. 'What's wrong with the possessive type? I am the possessive type, and I want the possessive type.'

Carefully he put a coaxing arm on the back of her seat. 'I'm sorry. I didn't mean that. Look, just come and see the cottage. We'll talk about it later. You've had a tricky time. You'll feel different tomorrow.' The smooth talk spilled out of him like honey from a broken jar.

Amy watched as a small pack of ragged-coated Exmoor ponies made their way slowly across the picnic area. 'I can't,' she said.

With the skill of the interviewer, Teddy suddenly changed tack. 'This music teacher guy . . .?' He was about to probe.

She stopped him. 'He's been reclaimed.'

'Ah!' He watched her. He was, she knew, hoping she would break down so that he could comfort her.

She didn't. In the distance a bus had appeared over a hill. That decided it. 'Look, thanks for coming down all this way,' she said. Then with a sudden deft kiss on his cheek, which he wasn't expecting, she opened the car door, pulling her bag and laptop after her.

'Amy! Amy, wait! Where are you going?'

'There's someone I need to see,' she said, then added, 'I'll still watch your show.'

Slamming the car door she hurried back to the road, waving to the approaching bus to stop. The last she saw of Teddy Farrow was as she clambered along the inside of the bus. He was standing by his car, gazing in astonishment after her.

'Isn't that Teddy Farrow?' a fat lady in a yellow raincoat remarked to her thin friend as the bus pulled away.

'No. Nothing like him. He's much taller than that,' the friend replied. 'What would he be doing here, anyway?'

Only now, sitting alone on the back seat as she watched the ponies make their lugubrious way across the moor, did Amy's tears begin to leak. Exactly what or who the tears were for, she wasn't certain.

As the firemen put away their equipment, ending the tragi-comedy of the now roofless Porsche and its driver and girlfriend, the audience of guests and staff began to disperse. Jane was the last to leave the scene, watching until the hotel car park was free of outsiders. Waiting for her in front of the hotel was Barry Harrison.

'I just wanted to say thank you. I'll pay you back when I get straight.'

Jane shook her head. 'No. It's dealt with. The account is clear.'

He nodded, then shook her hand. So formal now.

She watched him as he loaded his bags into his Toyota. He wasn't a lover she would have chosen if she'd had any choice. He wasn't a looker, or a great conversationalist. But he wasn't a bad man, and a lover he had become: a lover she'd enjoyed. Sometimes a girl just had to take her pleasures where she could get them. It had happened before. Hopefully it would happen again. And he seemed to have been quite grateful, too. His car pulled away. He waved from the window. She waved back. It had been a good night.

Had it had anything to do with Domingos's love potions? She doubted it very much. But they were a token. And if Bristol allowed her to stay on at the North Devon Riviera Hotel she'd make jolly sure she served them again at next year's Valentine's Ball.

'The answer is yes, by the way,' Darrell whispered as he and Shona reached the hotel to return to their chores. 'Yes, I would like to go around Hungary with you after Easter and stay in hotels.'

She touched his hand fondly, bright with pride. 'That'll be just brilliant, Darrell. Boyfriend and girlfriend. You won't be disappointed.'

Tim only noticed the taxi after it had passed him. He didn't see the passenger's face, but he recognised the angular scythe of black hair in the back seat. Amanda didn't turn to look at him, though she must have seen him. He was glad.

He walked on. It was a pleasant day. On a whim he suddenly climbed down to the beach and made tracks along the wet sand. This was where he'd seen Amy walking that first morning. Just being here, he felt closer to her. For a couple of brief days he'd lived a little fantasy, away from the uproar of school, the rattle of the bars where he played so anonymously and the dampness of his flat. But now it was over. And finding a large rounded boulder, he climbed onto it and thought of what had just been.

They'd taken a stroll along the front every day, so Amy knew where to find them, Grace and George, sitting on the otherwise deserted promenade.

Grace laughed when she saw her get down from the bus. 'We thought you'd left,' she said. 'You missed all the excitement.'

'I remembered there was something I needed to ask you.'

Grace chuckled. 'It's over-rated, you know, this wisdom-of-the-elderly thing. We've forgotten anything useful we ever knew. We've all got galloping Alzheimer's. You'd get as much sense out of that seagull.' And she pointed to a very large gull sitting on the iron railings.

Amy shook her head. 'I don't believe you. Yesterday you said that love only worked if you believed in it, like Tinkerbell in *Peter Pan*. That love was a decision. That that was half of it, anyway.'

Grace became mischievous. 'I said that? It must have been one of my better days. Usually I just moan on about my rheumatism and what it was like during the war.'

'Yes, you did. But you also said that there was something else, another half, which I should ask you about some other time. I was wondering if now might be the time.'

'Well, George,' Grace teased merrily, 'shall we tell her? What d'you think? Can she be trusted?'

Amy was sure the old man would have smiled.

Tim wasn't aware of her approach, so quietly did she tread across the sand, so muffling the sound of the sea. He was thinking about her.

'Do you mind if I share your rock?' She looked so casually pleased to see him and he was so surprised that words left him. 'I mean, it's the only dry one around here. Could you budge up a bit?'

He moved over. She scrambled up and joined him, and for a long moment they sat together, exchanging smiles.

At last she said, 'You remember how we thought Grace and George must know some secret because they seemed to be so happy?'

He nodded. His bandage was coming undone again.

'Well, according to her, the secret is to make your friend your lover and your lover your friend. If you can.'

'It's that easy?'

'Seems like it. You and me . . . we're pretty good friends, aren't we?'

'I hope so.'

'I know we are. And well . . . I was thinking, after what you said last night about being in love with me, which I didn't believe then, though I wanted to, and I really want to believe now . . .'

'It was true then and it's true now. Even truer.'

She dimpled with pleasure. 'Good. Because that's how I feel about you, too.'

'No!' That he couldn't believe.

'Yes. I'm afraid so. So perhaps we should, you know, see if we can balance the equation.'

'Balance the seesaw, you mean.'

'Exactly! The Lovers' Law of the Eternal Seesaw. In balance . . .'

'By being lovers and friends, friends and lovers.'

'And never thinking of anybody else when we're making love.'

He pretended to frown. 'Why would we ever want to do that?'

'We won't.'

They looked at each other. 'Are you by any chance trying to get off with me?' he teased.

She giggled. 'I'm trying very hard to get off with you.'

'Good,' he said, and put his arm round her.

Suddenly she pulled away. 'Just a minute. If you're going to kiss me, and I hope you are, there's something I have to do first.' Then very carefully she began to undo the bandage from round his head. 'It seems to me,' she mused as she parted his hair and examined his scalp, 'the wound has healed now. You won't need this any more.'

There really ought to have been music to accompany them, Tim thought, as he held her, and they kissed, and as, for the first time in days, he felt the draught round his forehead and ears where his bandage had been. Something by Francis Lai or one of those other famous film composers was what was needed.

But as there wasn't, he'd just have to write it himself.

They could have gone back to London, but where was the hurry? A double suite at the North Devon Riviera Hotel for a few days more seemed a better idea; somewhere that Tim could work at his keyboard and Amy at her laptop. Sometimes she would watch him as he worked, and sometimes he'd watch her. Then sometimes they'd break off and not work at all. And afterwards they'd just lie there and plan a future together. There would be a future together, they never doubted that. Lovers and friends. Together their worlds would be reconfigured.

But Amy still had her book to write. And now as Tim played in the background the ideas flowed.

Whatever it is, or why ever it is, young love, old love, shared love or unrequited love, half-remembered love or never forgotten love, first love or secondhand love, a chaste afternoon of still wet-behind-the-ears, walk-in-the-park love or raunchy, nine-times-a-night, deep-down-dirty love; a night's love or a lifetime's love, the truth is no part of romantic love is really essential to life.

But when we feel it, somehow everything we do becomes more worth the doing. And life itself seems to become more alive. We know that biologically human beings could go on reproducing for eternity without love. We could. We really could.

But who wants to live in a loveless eternity?

Ray Connolly

After reading social anthropology at the London School of Economics, Ray Connolly became a journalist, writing a weekly interview column for the *London Evening Standard*. The era was the late Sixties and Ray concentrated mainly on people in popular music—among them the Beatles—and popular culture. 'Since I interviewed the Fab Four so many times, I became known as a chronicler of their careers,' Ray told me. He was, in fact, due to meet John Lennon on the day the pop legend was shot.

'Just about everybody who is old enough remembers where they were when they heard that John Lennon had been murdered. For the millions around the world the shock of his killing by a mad fan called Mark Chapman was almost impossible to comprehend. But for me, it was more than shocking. Following a phone call from Yoko Ono earlier that day I'd been about to fly to New York to interview John when I heard the news of his death.' Later Ray was to write a biography of Lennon and a radio play about the much-loved star, entitled *Unimaginable*.

Having known and been a lifelong fan of the Beatles music, I asked Ray to name his favourite song. 'That's really difficult because I love so many of them.

Eleanor Rigby is just about perfect,' he mused. 'And *Let It Be*, maybe because Paul took me into a spare room one night at Abbey Road studios when he was writing it and played it on the piano—though he hadn't yet got all the lyrics. He just la-la-la'd the bits he hadn't written! Plus, *Penny Lane*. All three are Paul McCartney songs. Sorry, John.'

A love of music and film led Ray to write the original screenplays for *That'll Be the Day* and *Stardust*. '*That'll Be the Day* was David Puttnam's idea and began one Saturday afternoon in 1972 when I went to his house to borrow a book. We had a cup of tea and got talking about films and by the end of the day I'd been commissioned to write my first screenplay. Basically it was a dark story about growing up and dropping out in the Fifties, and becoming obsessed with rock music. The film turned the singer David Essex into a star.'

Ray now works freelance writing features mainly for the *Daily Mail*. He frequently receives a call at 2 p.m. to write and deliver a piece by 6 p.m. He has also been commissioned to write for television, most notably the two series *Lytton's Diary* and *Perfect Scoundrels*, as well as for radio. His first novel, *A Girl Who Came To Stay*, was published in 1973, followed by several other novels and the biography of John Lennon. *Love out of Season* is his latest book and is, as Ray puts it, 'quite unashamedly romantic. I've always liked the idea of a romantic comedy with a Shakespearian construction, in the style of *As You Like It*, where several different love stories are worked out simultaneously. And I wanted to write a love story not just for teenagers or twenty- or thirty-year-olds, but for all age groups, because it seems to me that love doesn't start at seventeen and stop at thirty. And then the idea for *Love out of Season* popped up, complete with a romantic writer at the centre, and I was off. Some people say that men can't write about romance, but that's just a silly sexist prejudice. Men feel as strongly when they're in love as women do. I've been ripped apart when I've been in love. And I've enjoyed the incredible highs too.'

> 'My philosophy for a happy life is: marry your best friend and make your hobby your job. It's certainly worked for me.'

Among the highs have been Ray's forty-year marriage to Plum and his three children and two grandchildren. 'I love spending time with my grandchildren. I adore being a grandfather because grandfathers can just be silly. They can get away with anything and the children love them unequivocally. My philosophy for a happy life is: marry your best friend and make your hobby your job. It's certainly worked for me.'

Jane Eastgate

The Matchmaker
of Périgord
Julia Stuart

'Not everyone falls instantly head over heels,' said the matchmaker. 'Love is like a good cassoulet, it needs time and determination. Some bits are delicious, while others might be a bit rancid and make you wince. You may even come across the odd surprise like a little green button, but you have to consider the whole dish.'

Chapter One

GUILLAUME LADOUCETTE WIPED his delicate fingers on his trouser leg before squeezing them into the glass jar. As he wiggled them around the cold, slippery fat he recognised what he felt was an ankle and his tongue moistened. He tugged it out and dropped the preserved duck leg into the cassoulet made by his mother thirty-one years ago and which had been on the go ever since. The ghostly white limb lay for several seconds suspended on haricot bean and sausage flotsam before disappearing from sight following a swift prod with a wooden spoon.

Custodian of the cassoulet ever since his mother had gone cuckoo following the death of her husband, the barber gave the dish a respectfully slow stir and watched as a goose bone appeared through the oregano and thyme vapours. The flesh had long since dropped off, his mother having first added it to the pot nineteen years ago in celebration of his opening a barber shop in the village.

From among the beans emerged an onion dating from March 1999, several carrots added only the previous week, a new thumb of garlic which he failed to recognise and a small green button still waiting to be reclaimed by its owner. With the care of an archaeologist, he drew the spoon around the bottom and sides of the iron pot to loosen some of the blackened crust, which, along with an original piece of now calcified Toulouse sausage, were, the barber insisted, the secret of the dish's unsurpassable taste. There were those, however, who blamed the antique sausage for turning the pharmacist Patrice Baudin, who had never previously shown any sign of lunacy, into a vegetarian, a scandal from which the village had never recovered.

Keeping the cassoulet going was more than just the duty of an only son, but something upon which the family's name rested. For the cassoulet war had been long and ugly and there was still no sign of a truce. All those fortunate enough to have witnessed the historic spectacle agreed that the first cannon was launched by Madame Ladoucette when she spotted Madame Moreau buying some tomatoes in the Place du Marché and casually asked what she was making. When the woman replied, Madame Ladoucette recoiled two paces in horror.

'Tomatoes have no place in a cassoulet!' Madame Ladoucette cried.

'Yes, they do. I've always used tomatoes,' Madame Moreau replied.

'The next thing you'll be telling me is that you put lamb in it as well.'

'Don't be so ridiculous, I would never commit such a perversion!' Madame Moreau retorted.

'Ridiculous? Madame, it is not me who puts tomatoes in a cassoulet, it is you. What does your husband have to say about this?'

'He wouldn't want it any other way,' came the terse reply.

Moments later, several onlookers witnessed Madame Ladoucette striding up to Madame Moreau's husband, who was sitting on the wooden bench by the fountain said to cure gout. Monsieur Moreau looked up to see a pair of crane legs, whose owner was carrying a straw basket.

'Monsieur Moreau,' she began. 'Forgive me, but it is a matter of utmost importance. Should a cassoulet have tomatoes in it or not?'

Monsieur Moreau was so startled that he could think of nothing but the truth. 'The correct method of making a cassoulet is always a source of contention. Personally, I prefer it without tomatoes, as my mother made it, but for God's sake don't tell the wife.'

According to Henri Rousseau, who happened to be standing next to Madame Moreau as she was paying for her tomatoes, Madame Ladoucette walked straight back up to her and repeated the entire conversation, adding that it was her civic duty to cook a cassoulet correctly. Precisely what Madame Moreau called her in return Henri Rousseau failed to catch. In no doubt, however, were the events that happened next. Madame Ladoucette reached into her basket, pulled out what was unmistakably an eel and slapped Madame Moreau across the nose with it before leaving its head wedged down her cleavage and stalking off. She had made it halfway down the Rue du Château, when, much to the delight of the villagers, Madame Moreau put her hand into the paper bag she was holding and hurled a tomato at Madame Ladoucette. It landed with such force, her victim momentarily staggered.

While the pair never spoke again, the salvos continued. From that day, Madame Moreau insisted on keeping a large bowl of overripe tomatoes near her kitchen window, which she used as ammunition from behind her white lace panels whenever her enemy passed. Madame Ladoucette retaliated by always doing her eel impression whenever she caught her adversary's eye in the street.

Guillaume Ladoucette had always been embarrassed by his mother's prolonged and public war with Madame Moreau. Recently, when he had returned from taking yet another of her tomato-splattered coats to the dry-cleaner's, he had invited Monsieur Moreau round for an apéritif in the hope that he might persuade his wife to desist, or to at least cut back on her ammunition given his mother's frailty. After apologising profusely for his wife's behaviour, Monsieur Moreau explained that in all his years of marriage he had never once managed to change his wife's mind over anything. The only consolation he could offer his host was that such was the advancement of her years, his wife could now only hit her target in one throw out of every five.

Leaving the duck leg to heat up, the barber decided to fetch a lettuce from his *potager*. By the time he reached the back door the soles of his bare feet had collected a small sharp black stone, a ginger-coloured feather, two dried lentils and a little sticky label from an apple bearing the words 'Pomme du Limousin'. Resting his right foot on his left knee, he first removed the stone, lentils and label. Then, with a muttered blasphemy, he picked off the feather.

Crawling his hairy toes into a pair of brown sandals by a sack of walnuts from the tree in the garden, Guillaume Ladoucette opened the back door just wide enough to poke his head round. After scanning the tops of the walls, still warm in the evening sun, he bent down to look underneath the lacy pink hydrangea. Satisfied that the coast was clear, he ventured out, quickly locking the door behind him. Filled with the anticipation of supper, he headed past the well with its pointed stone roof and the old white sink with its jolly red geraniums. The only sound was the thwack of cheap supermarket leather shoes against dry heels and the cuckoos' incessant two-pitched mating call, which showed a spectacular lack of imagination.

Legs wide apart over his oak-leaf lettuces, he picked enough of the burgundy-blushed leaves for a good serving. As he collected a couple of tomatoes, he congratulated himself on their aroma, then glanced at his tiny potato plants.

Silently unlocking the kitchen door, he peered inside. After casting his eyes along the tops of the cupboards, he bent down to check underneath the table. Relieved that he was still alone, he rinsed the salad and tomatoes. Arranging them in a bowl, he placed it on a tray along with a fork, a small blue jug of dressing and a white napkin with his initials embroidered in red in the corner. He then added a glass of disappointing Bergerac that he vowed never to buy again, but which he decided he might as well finish. Next to it he placed a packet of his favourite Cabécou goat's cheese, despite the fact that he had already reached his self-imposed weekly ration. After a final stir, he spooned out a bowlful of cassoulet, making sure that it included the duck leg, then headed towards the back door with the tray.

In the garden, Guillaume Ladoucette settled himself at the warped wooden table on his chair speckled with lichen underneath the walnut tree. Picking up the fork, the barber selected a piece of plump sausage for his first mouthful. But, as he went to spear it, he suddenly stopped and, very slowly, put down the empty fork. He sat back, as a warm, fat tear slid down his crow's-feet, rattled over his stubble and came to an abrupt halt at the bottom of his chin.

It was not the realisation that he had tweaked his moustache while cooking and that his world would forever smell of duck fat that had upset him. Nor was it the view of Lisette Robert's underwear pegged out on the washing line in the distance, a sight said to have broken at least seventeen bachelors' hearts. Neither was it the tiny pair of black eyes he'd just spotted bearing down on him from his neighbour's roof. The reason for his sudden despair was the memory of Gilbert Dubuisson's head when he walked into the barber shop that afternoon and sat down in the chair with the words 'Same as usual, please'. For, when the postman took off his cap, Guillaume Ladoucette looked down and saw to his horror that the man was almost completely bald.

Hairless customers were not a problem Guillaume Ladoucette had foreseen when, at the age of fifteen, he left school and entered the Périgord Academy of Master Barbers. Initially, his father had had other ideas for his only child, who had taken so long to be conceived. A worker in the disused stone quarry that had been turned over to the cultivation of button mushrooms, Monsieur Ladoucette had spent many an afternoon bent over piles of horse manure, his back in as much distress as his nostrils, imagining the baby his wife was carrying sitting comfortably on a plump chair in a bank. But when the child was born, there was no doubt as to his future employment. For the boy's fluttering fingers were the most sublime things he had ever seen. As soon as he was able to crawl, his mother was obliged to hide all the scissors in the house after returning from the garden one day to find the sitting-room curtains fashioned into the shape of a walnut tree.

The obsession followed him into school. When asked for an essay on the Revolution, the boy handed in a cut-out working model of the Bastille, complete with miniature guillotine. He discovered the joy of cutting hair, and its life-changing effects, when his schoolmate Émilie Fraisse asked him to shorten her butter-coloured tresses, which she found a source of great vexation when climbing trees. Guillaume Ladoucette never regretted accepting the request, even when forced to stay in his room for the remainder of the holidays after Madame Fraisse appeared on his doorstep demanding an explanation for her only daughter's sudden resemblance to her cockerel.

Guillaume Ladoucette, who had never previously applied himself to learning, was the most studious of his year's intake at the Périgord Academy of Master Barbers. With ferocious concentration he watched as his teacher performed the cornerstone of gentlemen's hairdressing, the short back and sides. He looked in wonder at how the two sides of the model's head were perfectly symmetrical, how the line on the back of the neck was as straight as his schoolteacher had always wanted his margins, and how a dab of gentleman's pomade, applied with a movement so fast it resembled sleight of hand, sealed the work of art.

He studied the *Périgord Academy of Master Barbers' Revised Guide to the Art of Barbering*, Second Edition, with such intensity that his mother feared he would go blind. So nervous was he before the final exam that for four days he refused to eat. By the time he entered the examination room, the colour of an oyster, he had checked that his pen was still in his pocket thirteen times out of fear that it might vanish into thin air. When he read the first question—How Should A Barber Comport Himself?—his appetite instantly returned. Triumphantly he wrote: *A barber must combine nobility and honour with trustworthiness and cleanliness. It is most necessary to avoid stagnant breath and obnoxious body odours. The partaking of daily bathing is vital. In order to retain his customers' patronage, the successful barber must avoid at all costs quarrels, loss of temper, boisterous attire, blasphemy or the spreading of gossip.*

By the time the boy read the second question—How Should A Facial Hairpiece Be Applied?—he felt nauseous with hunger as he answered verbatim: *In the case of a moustache, apply spirit gum to the upper lip, wait until tacky, position moustache and gently press down with a suitable cloth. For a beard, repeat, but apply spirit gum to the chin area.*

By the third—What Should You Remember When Tapering?—he started to nibble his question paper as he recalled: *That it is better to taper with caution and clarity of mind. One must remember that after the hair is cut it cannot be replaced.*

At the end of the practical examination, Guillaume Ladoucette left the Périgord Academy of Master Barbers with a distinction. The following day, his mother put the certificate into a frame, which caused the boy considerable embarrassment as he carried it from village to village searching for a position. But his shame soon came to an end when Pierre Rouzeau agreed to take him on at his shop in the town of Nontron. For the first week the hour-and-forty-three-minute cycle ride made him walk as if he had a *pain de campagne* wedged between his thighs.

Initially, the apprentice was charged with sweeping up the trimmings, but after several months, the boy was given his first client, chosen by his boss for the man's habit of never leaving the house without a hat. But his caution was unnecessary, for Guillaume Ladoucette, whose fingers were by now fluttering with such a desire to get started that he could barely control his bicycle, did such a wondrous job that the customer forswore his malodorous beret.

The barber shop was a happy place to work and the boy even had enough wages left over each week to start saving for a moped. Two years later, he finally had enough coins. On his next day off, he got a lift into Périgueux, the nearest city. He rode the journey back home half-terrified, half-thrilled by his new machine. When he arrived, the first person he took out on it was Émilie Fraisse. The pair swayed hesitantly down the Rue du Château, both pairs of feet reaching for the comfort of the ground. Then, tucking in their legs, they picked up speed as they flew out of the village.

Guillaume Ladoucette's only disappointment as they shot past the maize fields was not being able to concentrate fully on the fact that Émilie Fraisse's thighs were finally around him. The hair her mother had forced her to grow back streamed behind them like a butter-coloured magic carpet, until she turned to look at the retreating village and her hair blew across Guillaume Ladoucette's face, obliterating all view of the road. They mounted a small bank, both emitting the sort of wail that follows the sudden realisation that something painful is about to happen. In the end, Émilie Fraisse only suffered toothache, having landed on top of her friend with her mouth still open. Guillaume Ladoucette's biggest injury was to his pride. Not only did he have to explain the limp, but that the nearest thing he got to a kiss was the bite mark on his cheekbone.

No one had expected the death of Madame Ladoucette's father. Guillaume Ladoucette had been at his grandfather's house the day before he died, wondering why, at the age of twenty-four, he still wasn't allowed to go anywhere near his fig tree. Madame Ladoucette explained that it was because he still hadn't forgiven his grandson for the time when, at the age of five, he had discovered a pair of hidden scissors, climbed up a stepladder and snipped off all the tree's branches which took seven years to bear fruit again.

The house was left to Madame Ladoucette, who, despite adoring her son even more than her precious husband, immediately suggested that he moved there. For the young man's snores would float down from his gaping mouth onto the floor, tumble across his bedroom, roll underneath the door, skate across the hall, bump down a steep flight of wooden stairs, turn two corners and penetrate the thick stone wall of her bedroom and its painting of the Virgin Mary. Monsieur Ladoucette insisted that his son's ability to sleep peacefully while manufacturing such a monstrous sound was a result of his mother having continually disturbed him when slumbering as a baby to check that he was still alive. However, her perturbation was far from over after he sailed through infancy without a single illness. For, at the age of six years and three months, she suddenly noticed to her horror that he had developed a habit of sleeping on his back with his arms straight down the side of his body. 'He looks as though he's already dead in his coffin,' she would wail to her husband.

Guillaume Ladoucette happily moved into his grandfather's house, suddenly discovering a freedom he hadn't even known existed. He left the dishes until the next day and ate entire packets of Cabécou in one sitting. When Pierre Rouzeau noticed that he was unusually quiet, he assumed he was still grieving for his grandfather. But what was actually weighing on Guillaume Ladoucette's mind was the fact that he had decided to set up his own barber shop and was wondering how to break the news to his boss. In the end, Pierre Rouzeau's response was immediate: 'You must open your own barber's, of course. It's what every barber aspires to. That and to never have a customer in his chair with more hair on the tops of his ears than on his head.'

The sum Guillaume Ladoucette's grandfather had left him was in no way sufficient to buy premises in the village, equip it with a chair and basin and pay him a salary while it was getting on its feet. But he soon came up with a solution.

With the help of his best friend Stéphane Jollis, the baker, who was used to humping around large sacks of flour, it didn't take long to convert his grandfather's kitchen into a barber shop. First they built a small kitchen at the back of the house and then pulled out the existing one. Guillaume Ladoucette ordered just one sink for the shop to begin with, as expansion was something to consider in the future, and a black leather chair, the same make as those used by Pierre Rouzeau. Didier Lapierre, the carpenter, put in a bench along the wall facing the mirror. A set of shelves was built and mounted next to the window to hold the products the barber hoped to sell to boost his profits: the combs, pots of pomade, shampoos, boxes of razors, false sideburns, lather brushes, hair tonics and pencils to colour greying moustaches.

If Émilie Fraisse was Guillaume Ladoucette's first love, the shop came a very close second. Business picked up within weeks of opening and, after two months, there was an average of three people waiting at any one time on the bench on a Saturday. Not all, admittedly, were customers. Some villagers came simply to warm up, but they continued the habit of sitting around the place well into spring claiming that the showers drove them in. In the summer, they would complain about the heat, shouting at everyone to close the door behind them to keep out the hot air. When the shop was particularly busy, the barber would shoo them off the bench and they would scatter like wild goats.

Guillaume Ladoucette never forgot his training. Every morning, before coming downstairs, he made absolutely certain that he was A Living Example. He wouldn't leave the bathroom until his hair and moustache were of sufficient splendour to arouse his customers' interest in similar services. He took particular pride in his finger wave. Twice a week, after washing his hair and applying styling lotion, he would carefully position a finger on the front section of his hair, form a ridge with the help of a comb and then continue the procedure round the rest of the head. He named his three variations The Troubadour, The Pompadour and The Ambassador. And while there was not much call for any of them, Guillaume Ladoucette took great satisfaction from simply knowing that the service was available should anyone request it.

As the years passed, the barber gradually built up a small, yet curious collection of old barbering utensils which he found in the numerous antique fairs held in the streets of neighbouring towns and villages. He discovered several shaving bowls with a semicircle cut out of one side to enable them to hug the neck. He also purchased a number of wooden balls which would be placed inside the cheek to facilitate shaving. Then there were the little brass moustache tongs which, after being heated, created the most magnificent of curls, and the numerous cutthroat razors, his favourite of which had a mother-of-pearl handle. He displayed the collection on a table in the front corner of the shop.

Despite his passion for his profession, the barber eventually grew tired of living in the same place as his work, so when, three years ago, his widowed mother could no longer cope alone in the family house and moved to a one-bedroom place in the village, Guillaume Ladoucette returned to his childhood home with its splendid walnut tree in the garden and took over the custody of the family cassoulet.

The barber had never heard of Jean-Baptiste Rigaudie until he saw his neighbour Yves Lévèque up a ladder attending to the curved, salmon-coloured tiles on his roof. Guillaume Ladoucette, who had just started on a pigeon braised in half a bottle of Pécharmant, while sitting on the chair speckled with lichen beside the warped wooden table, stood up. Slipping his hairy toes back into his sandals, he thwacked his way across the garden. 'Hey, Yves! What's happened?'

Yves Lévèque glanced down to see his neighbour looking up at him.

'Some of the tiles are loose and they're keeping me awake at night,' he explained.

'Not that,' called the barber. 'I mean you . . . your hair.'

Yves Lévèque slowly climbed down to the last but one rung, looked at his neighbour and then at the ground.

'I'm sorry, Guillaume, it's just that I haven't been with a woman for such a long time. It's hard on a man. Surely it's not too much to ask to have the soft mounds of a woman's breasts against your back at night.'

'I'm not with you,' said Guillaume Ladoucette.

'A man has to do what he can to make the most of himself and I'm not getting any younger. As you know, I've tried The Troubadour. And The Pompadour and The Ambassador just aren't me. Someone told me about this new barber in Brantôme called Jean-Baptiste Rigaudie. He was trained in Paris. What do you think? It's called The Pine Cone.'

'It wouldn't be right for me to comment on another artisan's work. Good luck with the roof,' Guillaume Ladoucette replied, returning to his pigeon. But its succulent breast had lost its appeal.

Four days later, the barber was walking home from his shop when Didier Lapierre rounded the corner. From the sideburns up, the carpenter looked as though he had been caught in a cataclysmic typhoon. Guillaume Ladoucette, who had been wondering why he hadn't seen him in his chair recently, knew where the perfidious wretch had been. As soon as he saw him, the carpenter looked down and hurried off. The barber watched him disappear down the Rue du Château, the first time he had ever seen him doing anything at speed. 'Turncoat!' he muttered.

The following week, as the barber was waiting to be served in the village's Bar Saint-Jus, his eyes travelled up to its owner's hair, which looked suspiciously like a pine cone.

'Ah, Guillaume!' said Fabrice Ribou. 'What can I get you?'

'A glass of red, please, Fabrice,' Guillaume Ladoucette replied evenly.

The bar owner poured out a glass, and pushed it towards him across the wooden counter. Realising that the barber was studying his hair, his eyes dropped. 'Oh, by the way, Guillaume, I was meaning to tell you. The reason why I've stopped coming to the shop is that my mother's started to cut my hair.'

The barber, who was just about to take a sip, held his glass below his lips. He had heard Fabrice Ribou tell more convincing lies to his ex-wife.

'Is that so?' he asked.

'Absolutely! I was at her house the other day and she said she'd always wanted to take up hairdressing and was thinking of doing a course. She asked whether she could practise on me.'

'Fabrice,' said Guillaume Ladoucette, resting an elbow on the bar. 'We both know that your mother is ninety-two and is registered blind.'

'That's the whole point, she's got a great sense of touch!' Fabrice Ribou replied.

Over the following few weeks, Guillaume Ladoucette began to notice a sharp drop in the number of people waiting on the bench on Saturdays, despite the ferocious sun which had baked the lizards as hard as biscuits. If the barber was already troubled, it was nothing compared to how he felt when he spotted Henri Rousseau coming out of the grocer's. As soon as he saw the barber, Henri Rousseau, who had never shown any interest in his appearance, immediately started running up the Rue du Château. Guillaume Ladoucette tore after his customer as Henri Rousseau sprinted in the direction of the Bar Saint-Jus. Just as he made it past the church he found himself cornered by a tractor.

'Forgive me, Guillaume,' he called out as the barber approached, panting. 'Blame my wife. She said that everyone was trying out this new barber in Brantôme who knew all the latest styles. I was quite happy with the way you always cut it, but she said I had to go as it was she who had to look at me all the time.'

'What's it called?' asked the barber.

'The Forelock,' replied the fifty-eight-year-old, looking at him with his right eye, his left covered by a flop of hair stretching from his crown.

Now, as Guillaume Ladoucette sat in front of his bowl of cassoulet, remembering the sight of Gilbert Dubuisson's freckled scalp earlier that day, he thought of all his other regulars who had deserted him on account of having gone bald owing to their advancing years. Despite employing his best salesman's techniques, he had only managed to convince four of them to wear a hairpiece. The barber then counted up how many regulars he had left and thought of the letters from the bank asking him to come in for a talk, which he had ignored. As Guillaume Ladoucette realised that his days as a barber were over, the tear on his chin dropped to the floor.

Chapter Two

A BREEZE SNIFFED ROUND the adjustable sign at the entrance to the village which read: SLOW DOWN! THERE ARE ONLY 33 OF US. A day never passed without a wind blowing. None of the myopic meteorologists from Paris who made regular visits to the tiny community in the northwestern tip of the Périgord Vert could agree on a cause for the curious microclimate. Some pointed to the gusts as an explanation for the reputation of the place, for wind was widely accepted as a cause of madness.

There were numerous explanations as to how the village came to be called Amour-sur-Belle, only one of which was true. Belle, as everyone correctly pointed out, was the name of the river which lolloped its way through. It wasn't much of a river, no wider in places than Stéphane Jollis was tall, a fact noted by those who happened to see the baker fall in while picking wild mint one afternoon. He lay for several minutes unable to move, his giant stomach sticking out of the clear water like a half-moon. The sight was so arresting it took a while for those on the bridge to stop staring and help the man get back up.

Lisette Robert the midwife had insisted that the name referred to the love that permeated generations of her family, one of the oldest in the village, until it was pointed out that her great-great-grandmother had pushed her great-great-grandfather down a well; and that Lisette Robert herself, who was a widow, hadn't even come close to finding love again despite her unrivalled beauty.

Gilbert Dubuisson claimed that the village was named after St Amour. According to the postman, the fifteenth-century former heretic converted to Christianity on seeing the beauty of the place, which he insisted could only be God-given, and went on to found a monastery in the nearby woods. He stuck by the story even when it was pointed out to him that the village had never been anything to look at; and that the only remains of a construction in the woods was a battered old hunters' shack where the frantic throes of adulterous affairs took place.

The truth was that Amour-sur-Belle was named after Marcus Damour, a Roman soldier who left the army in order to fight for the Gauls as he had heard that their food supplies were better. After fathering six ugly children, he went on to cultivate a mysterious new crop in the fields around the village, which his compatriots had brought with them from Italy. It produced bunches of red or green berries which, when crushed, fermented and drunk proved to have an ability to improve the inhabitants' mood.

The village was frequented by Romans marching between Angoulême and Périgueux. Intolerable numbers would stop, lured by its fountain which was widely believed to cure gout. When the area succumbed to Christianity, the miraculous fountain was dedicated to St Pierre, and once a year the place was overrun by pilgrims.

There was one brief moment of glory in the village's ignoble history. Before Napoleon left for his Russian campaign, he asked the owners of the local forges, including that of Amour-sur-Belle, to produce his cannons, an honour so great it made the inhabitants who worked there tremble with pride. They trembled once more, this time with fear, when men arrived in 1936 with their horses and carts to install the first electricity pylons. And they trembled again, with excitement, when they returned in their vans in 1967 to lay the pipes for running water.

Amour-sur-Belle's questionable looks worsened with time. A community with four times its current population a generation ago, eleven deserted houses had since slumped to their knees in despair. Several stone barns, their doors long rotted away, stood throttled by an infestation of weeds. However, its humble appearance worked in its favour. For the English considered the place far too ugly to colonise. As a result, Amour-sur-Belle enjoyed the distinction of being the only place for miles inhabited solely by natives. Tourists who happened to come across its forlorn château, whose ramparts were too scandalous to warrant a mention in the guidebooks, simply carried on driving.

There was a time when the residents of Amour-sur-Belle tried to pass the place off as a town in the hope of securing more amenities from the local authority. Yves Lévèque, who had always fancied a municipal swimming pool, wrote a letter to the council stating that following a particularly cold winter the village had experienced a population explosion. Not only that, but many outsiders had suddenly noticed the unrivalled charms of Amour-sur-Belle and had made it their home. Within weeks the dentist received a reply stating that the first stage of any alteration to the status of the village would be a population head-count, for which a date had been set for two months' time. Letters were hastily sent to relatives across the country, who hadn't received a Christmas card for years, inviting them for a visit and indicating the precise date when the offer was open.

When the day of the headcount arrived, however, the population had swelled by just two people. His plans in tatters, Yves Lévèque rushed to the barber shop and asked Guillaume Ladoucette for all the wigs, false beards, moustaches and sideburns that he possessed. The dentist struggled out with a large cardboard box and distributed its contents among the villagers. When the man from the council arrived, he discovered a surprisingly hirsute population. As he walked around the village with his clipboard, he came across a resident standing on the church steps, panting. He had exactly the same features and attire as the man who had just been sitting outside the Bar Saint-Jus. But what astonished the official most was that some of the gentlemen with the longest beards undeniably had breasts. By the time he had finished his count, the population of Amour-sur-Belle, many of whom, he noted, were desperately short of breath and suffered from chronic perspira-tion, stood at eight hundred and ninety-seven. That evening, a victori-ous Yves Lévèque started asking around the bar for volunteer lifeguards.

The following Tuesday, however, a second inspector arrived unan-nounced. Yves Lévèque, who happened to be attending to his roof at the time, was the first to spot him stalking around the village with his clipboard. Horrified, the dentist shot down his ladder. But in his panic he was unable to remember who had the box of hairpieces. By the end of the week, a letter arrived at the dentist's house stating that after two official audits of the population of Amour-sur-Belle, its status would remain unchanged.

The barber swung his legs out of bed, settled his feet on the floor and peered cautiously between his ankles. Satisfied that he was alone, he stood up and made his way to the bathroom. Pressing an eye up against the crack between the door and the frame, he surveyed the room. Above the bath taps was a set of shelves bearing a collection of exquisite gentlemen's soaps. Lined up on top of the small, marble-topped table by the basin was a razor in its box, a blue shaving mug that had belonged to his father and a shaving brush with an ivory handle.

Seeing nothing untoward, he poked his head round the door as an extra precaution. Satisfied that she wasn't there, he walked in, rested both hands on the basin and raised his eyes to the mirror. The reflection was far from that of A Living Example. The right side of his moustache was thirty degrees higher than the left and urgently needed re-waxing into position. His finger wave had taken on the appearance of a rolling tempest as a result of a night of eternal tossing.

But Guillaume Ladoucette did not pick up the tiny spirit level he used to line up his moustache every morning. Neither did he open the jar of wax, or indeed his pomade the colour of figs. Instead, he put his fingers under the tap, ran them through his hair and wasn't in the least bit concerned about the lamentable results. He shuffled back into the bedroom and sat on the edge of the bed. Eventually, he looked around for his clothes, but his trousers hanging in the wardrobe seemed too far away. So too did the pile of white cotton underpants next to the rows of neatly paired socks in the top drawer of the dresser. An hour passed before he summoned sufficient will to clamber into a fresh pair of underwear. But once they were in position, his motivation abandoned him again, and he pulled on the rest of the clothes he had worn the previous day.

In his bare feet, the barber walked slowly down the creaking wooden stairs, and stopped on the last one. Craning his head forward, he surveyed the sitting room. On top of the back of the brown settee was a plump green velvet cushion against which he rested his head while watching television. The pale stone mantelpiece bore a wooden framed clock whose ticking had driven one relative to suicide, above which was mounted his father's shotgun that had claimed three wild boars.

Grabbing the handrail, Guillaume Ladoucette slowly crouched down, tipped over to one side and looked underneath the table. Satisfied that he was still alone, he walked through to the kitchen. He scanned the tops of the cupboards bearing the casserole dishes and the pale stone mantelpiece with its row of old Peugeot coffee grinders. Crouching down again, he leaned to one side, peered underneath the table and saw nothing other than a fallen walnut kernel.

He pulled out a chair from under the table and sat down. Immediately the barber felt something collapse underneath him. He shot to his feet and inspected the red cushion. There, crushed into the fabric, were pieces of shell, and smears of egg yolk were rapidly seeping into it. It was then that Guillaume Ladoucette felt something wet against his buttocks. 'That infernal chicken!' he cried.

Violette, the infernal chicken, who belonged to Fabrice Ribou, the bar owner, had never dared set a scaly toe in the house while Madame Ladoucette had been living there. But since the old woman had moved to a smaller home, the bird had taken to entering the house as if she owned the place. Guillaume Ladoucette had tried everything he could think of to get rid of her, short of blasting the bird off his garden wall, where she would sit warming her fluffy undercarriage while staring at him. He had even tried locking all the doors and windows whenever he went out, but it was no use. He would return home to find peck marks in his butter and black-and-white droppings on his freshly washed cotton underpants airing in the cupboard.

After scraping egg off the cushion and changing his trousers, the barber left the house taking care to double-lock the front door behind him. He had no idea where he was going. All he knew was that he had to escape the fog of panic swirling around his ankles.

As usual Madame Serre, hair the colour of pigeon down and fingers crooked with age, was sitting on a picnic chair in the morning sun out-side her front door. But the barber, engulfed in doom, failed to notice his next-door neighbour and walked on by without his usual greeting. Eventually he came to the Rue du Château, one of four in the village. Only one, however, led to the castle. The peculiarity had come about following a complaint by Gilbert Dubuisson, the postman, that some of the street signs had become illegible with age. An administrative blun-der resulted in a job lot of 'Rue du Château' signs being sent to Amour-sur-Belle. Well aware that it would take years for the mistake to be admitted and rectified, the residents simply took down the faded old ones and replaced them with the new delivery.

As Guillaume Ladoucette continued on his walk, his hands deep in his pockets and his moustache an alarming thirty degrees out, his mind was buffeted in one direction after another as he sought a solution to the catastrophe. He would have to find new employment and fast. But what could he do?

Turning a corner, he headed past the church which had been stripped of all traces of beauty during the Revolution.

'Morning, Guillaume. Everything all right with you?' called Marcel Coussy, the old farmer, shuffling up the road in his work slippers.

'Fine, thanks,' the barber lied.

'Have you heard about the shower?' he asked.

'No,' Guillaume Ladoucette replied and carried on his way.

As he passed the empty pharmacy the barber's heart suddenly sprang. 'That's it!' he said out loud, cupping his hands against his temples as he peered into the window at the shelves of exotic-looking bottles covered in a silent shroud of dust. 'I'll become a pharmacist!'

The business had remained closed ever since the mini-tornado of 1999. At first, the villagers had assumed that the persistent breeze was just blowing a little stronger that morning. By the afternoon, Guillaume Ladoucette had telephoned his customers who wore hairpieces warning them not to venture outdoors. When evening fell, the curved, salmon-coloured roof tiles rattled up and down like pan lids and the wind screeched so loudly that the villagers could no longer hear their neighbours' arguments over what to do. Not expecting to live to see the morning, they descended into their cellars and brought out their best wines, jars of foie gras, wild boar terrines, bottled truffles and preserved duck legs and confessed their sins between mouthfuls.

No one realised that Patrice Baudin, the pharmacist, was still out in the worst of it. What was certain was that he never made it further than the grocer's. For, suddenly, the skinny vegetarian was swept clean off his feet into the air, never to be seen again.

The following day, when the sound of retching eventually subsided, and the wood pigeons could be heard again, shutters started to open and pale faces appeared. Several barn roofs were missing, two uprooted oak trees had been thrown against the front door of Yves Lévèque's house preventing him from getting out, and the château had lost yet another section of its crenellations.

Patrice Baudin's absence was noticed by Lisette Robert when she came to the pharmacy seeking the morning-after pill. When she found the shop shut, she went to the one in Brantôme but was so caught up in her own predicament that she failed to mention his absence. Two days later, when numerous villagers went to the pharmacy in search of relief from chronic constipation, word spread that Patrice Baudin was missing. At the end of the week, by which time several were in need of prescriptions, a search party was mounted. The surrounding fields were combed and the woods were scoured, and only then were the police called. But all the officers found were the pharmacist's cracked, gold-rimmed spectacles hanging from the church guttering.

Not long after the mini-tornado, Henri Rousseau's wife, who had a mania for order, demanded that the number of residents on the village sign be reduced to thirty-two. However, it was decided that the sign be left as it was out of respect for the pharmacist who had always resisted gossiping about the ailments of his customers, no matter how many drinks he was bought in the Bar Saint-Jus. Modeste Simon, who never spoke again after witnessing his unfortunate disappearance from her bathroom window, kept his broken spectacles in the drawer by her bed, along with a photograph she had secretly taken of him.

But almost as soon as the idea to take over the pharmacy came to Guillaume Ladoucette, as he stared inside the darkened shop he quickly dismissed it. He knew only too well that he could never comprehend the subjects the pharmacist had had to study, despite having left the Périgord Academy of Master Barbers with a distinction.

Turning away from the window, he returned his hands to his pockets and continued up the street. Suddenly, he heard a voice from behind.

'Hello, Guillaume! Dawdling a bit today, aren't we?' asked Sandrine Fournier, the assistant ambulant fishmonger.

The barber turned and stopped. 'Hello, Sandrine,' he replied.

'Have you heard about the shower?'

'No,' he said, forgetting to say goodbye as he turned the corner. There must surely be something that he could do, Guillaume Ladoucette told himself. But he could think of nothing. Amour-sur-Belle already had all the tradespeople it could sustain. There was no role for a man of forty-three who had dedicated his life to conquering the cowlick, the double crown and dandruff.

By the time he turned into the Rue du Château, the barber's trousers began to feel loose round his waist as he thought of all the luxuries he would no longer be able to afford. As he imagined the gentlemen's soaps he would no longer be able to buy from his favourite shop in Périgueux, Guillaume Ladoucette was certain his armpits had begun to reek.

Shuffling along the banks of the Belle through the patches of wild mint, he thought of the repugnant beard he would have to grow to keep him warm. He spent the next hour trailing around the village staring at the ditches in which he would undoubtedly end, wondering how long he had left to live. By the time he reached the Bar Saint-Jus he had barely enough energy to hoist his skeletal frame onto a stool at the bar.

'Hello, Guillaume!' said Fabrice Ribou, the bar owner. 'You're looking well. Nice trousers by the way. Are they new? What can I get you?'

'A glass of red, please,' said the barber, who still hadn't forgiven him for his treachery, despite the fact that he hadn't charged him for a single drink since his new haircut.

'On the house,' said the barman, pushing the glass towards him.

The barber picked it up and took it to a table by the window.

'Hey, Guillaume! Have you heard about the shower?' asked Denise Vigier, the grocer, standing at his table.

No,' replied the barber, suddenly remembering his manners and getting up to kiss her on both cheeks.

'You haven't?' she asked, sitting down opposite him. 'The whole village's talking about it. Where have you been all day? Someone said you didn't open the shop today.'

'Oh, I've been busy.'

'You'll never guess what the council has decided to do,' she said.

'What?' he asked out of politeness.

'Well, you know how it hasn't rained for ages?'

'Yes.'

'From next month they're banning everyone from taking a bath and installing a communal shower in the village!' she said triumphantly.

'We'll all have to take a shower together?' Guillaume Ladoucette asked, horrified.

'No! One at a time, but they'll fine anyone who takes a bath.'

'How on earth are they going to regulate that?'

'God only knows. Apparently they want to see how it works before introducing it elsewhere. Everyone's saying they picked Amour-sur-Belle because of that headcount business. Apparently they were furious and that first inspector got suspended.'

'If Yves Lévèque had given me back those wigs and beards immediately after the first headcount, as I'd asked him to, none of this would have happened,' replied the barber. 'When he eventually returned them, they were all twisted into funny shapes. I couldn't sell them.'

'Where do you think they'll put it?' asked the grocer.

But the barber didn't want to speculate about the location of a municipal shower. He drained his glass, forgot to kiss Denise Vigier, the grocer, goodbye and left. When he returned home, he retired to bed without eating or bathing and remained there for six days, four hours and nineteen seconds. At that point, he raised his head from his pillow, looked out of the window and caught sight of his mother in the distance, recognisable by the tomato splat on the back of her pale green dress. It was then that Guillaume Ladoucette had his Brilliant Idea.

Chapter Three

As HE SAT WAITING in his car, Guillaume Ladoucette pulled down the sun visor to kill time. Turning his head to the right, and then to the left, he critically surveyed his morning's handiwork in the mirror. It was indeed a splendid creation, he noted with immense satisfaction. He admired how it stretched out beyond the edges of his mouth, rising at both ends with an elegant lift that he'd fashioned fifteen degrees higher than usual on account of his ebullient mood. A number of white hairs had been camouflaged with the aid of a black moustache crayon, and the ends twisted skilfully to such a fine point they looked as if they could spear cockroaches.

After snapping the visor back up, he looked around the car for something else to do. Leaning over, he opened the glove compartment and peered inside. Instantly bored by the sight of its contents, he shut it again. After staring blankly in front of him for several minutes, he sighed and looked at his watch for the fifth time.

Despite the time, Guillaume Ladoucette forgave Stéphane Jollis for keeping him waiting. It was a habit the baker had never broken even though the pick-up time for their fishing trips hadn't changed for more than twenty years. But the barber's compassion had nothing to do with tolerance. The reason for Guillaume Ladoucette's ability to pardon his best friend's abominable timekeeping was sitting on the back seat underneath a white tea towel. For while the two men were fiercely competitive when it came to fishing, their unspoken rivalry was not over what one another caught, but the contents of their picnic baskets. And the barber, who had been labouring in the kitchen since five that morning, was convinced that victory would be his.

The passenger door suddenly opened and a strong, hairy arm reached in and placed an equally large basket made from sweet chestnut on the back seat. The limb momentarily disappeared and returned with a red tea towel that was carefully placed over it. The car suddenly tilted towards the right as the baker held on to the roof with one hand and manoeuvred his substantial frame inside, followed by his head.

'Hello. Sorry I'm late,' he said.

Guillaume Ladoucette looked at the baker. Having showered as usual on a Sunday lunchtime after shutting the shop, his friend appeared a decade younger owing to the absence of flour in his thick, black curls. The barber had been cutting them for years in exchange for a daily loaf. It was a system that worked more in his favour since Stéphane Jollis only bothered to surrender his scalp every few months.

'Not to worry,' he said, starting the car. 'Got everything?'

'Yep,' replied the baker, winding down the window.

The pair drove out of the village and turned right at the field with the ginger Limousin cows that winked. After passing a series of maize fields, they slowed down to a precise 49 kph as they trundled through the village of Beauséjour, where the traffic police waited for their prey in collapsible chairs in the sun. Each time the barber changed gear, his knuckles rubbed against Stéphane Jollis's thigh, which bloomed over the passenger seat as if it was baked with too much yeast.

'Bring any lunch with you?' Guillaume Ladoucette enquired, trying to sound as casual as possible.

'Just a snack,' the baker replied, staring straight ahead of him. 'You?'

'Just a snack,' said the barber, wrinkling up his nose dismissively.

When they arrived at Brantôme, the two men, each carrying a family-sized picnic basket, made their way along the bank of the Dronne. They passed the metal steps where swimmers clambered out of the water and continued until they reached the NO FISHING sign. They then put down their baskets at their usual spot, both filled with the comforting knowledge that a splendid afternoon lay ahead of them.

After Stéphane Jollis had wiped his sweating forehead on both shoulders, he joined the barber on the edge of the bank in the shade of the tree which neither could name. The baker then took out a baguette from his basket, broke off an end, pulled out some of the soft, white innards, rolled it into a ball with his artisan fingers and pierced it with his hook. Once the barber had impaled a worm on his, they both took off their shoes and tied their lines round their right ankles. Carefully rolling up both trouser legs to the knee, they plunged their feet into the cool water.

'That's better!' said Guillaume Ladoucette, wriggling his hairy toes.

'Bliss!' agreed Stéphane Jollis, raising his right trouser leg slightly higher. 'Hot, isn't it?'

'Scorching,' replied Guillaume Ladoucette. He peered down between his legs. 'Plenty down there.'

'It's definitely the best spot,' replied the baker.

They sat in contented silence, freckles of sunlight warming their knees through the leaves, watching the turquoise dragonflies land on the dusty water that slowly creaked by.

'Remember that trout Yves Lévèque caught?' asked the baker.

'I've never seen anything that size before.'

'I couldn't believe it,' the baker said. 'It was huge.'

'Massive,' agreed Guillaume Ladoucette. 'It was so big he said he couldn't eat it all in one go. Where did he say he caught it?'

'Somewhere near Ribérac.'

There was a pause.

'I bet he bought it from the assistant ambulant fishmonger,' said Guillaume Ladoucette.

Silence fell again as both men leaned back on their hands. Occasionally, one would lift a foot to change his bait or to pick out a piece of green weed that had slithered between his toes.

'I suddenly feel a bit peckish,' Guillaume Ladoucette announced, as he watched a male duck start chasing a female across the water.

'So do I,' said Stéphane Jollis, who, unbeknown to the barber, had spent the whole of the previous evening cooking. They shuffled backwards along the grass on their bottoms towards their respective baskets. Stalling for time, Guillaume Ladoucette pretended to look for his penknife as he waited to see what would appear from the rival basket. He watched as a bunch of tomatoes-on-the-vine surfaced and were placed on the red tea towel. Next came a jar of *cornichons*, followed by a bunch of pink radish and another baguette. Then, with what was unmistakably the hint of a sly smile, a large earthenware container was brought out and placed on the grass.

'Bit of pâté from the grocer's?' Guillaume Ladoucette enquired.

'No, actually,' replied the baker, tearing off a piece of bread and loading it up. 'I made it myself. I had a few minutes to spare and already had the duck foie gras, so thought why not? The recipe says to add two soupspoons of cognac, but I always use four. I find you get a much richer taste. But fifty grams of truffle juice is about right.'

Guillaume Ladoucette watched as Stéphane Jollis opened his mouth and crammed it in. 'Oh, delicious,' came the verdict. 'Fancy any?'

'No, thanks, otherwise I won't manage this!' he replied, drawing out a large flask from his basket and unscrewing the lid. 'I tell you, nothing beats a bit of vichyssoise glacé soup on a hot day. It's the leeks from the garden that really makes it, I think. Want to try some?'

'No, thanks, otherwise I won't manage this!' replied the baker, carefully lifting out a bowl from his basket with two hands. 'What I really love about this particular salad is the way you cook the potatoes in their skins. Delicious. Then, of course, ham, red peppers and lobster tail are always such a great combination. It makes all the difference, of course, if you picked the lobster yourself while it was still alive so that you knew you were getting a good one. Let me give you a little taste,' he said.

'No, thanks, or I won't be able to manage this!' cried Guillaume Ladoucette triumphantly, holding up a goat's cheese tart. Stéphane Jollis glanced at it unconcerned and plunged a fork into his salad.

'Can't wait to try it,' continued the barber, cutting a slice with his penknife. He paused for dramatic effect and then added before taking a mouthful: 'I milked the goat myself.' Stéphane Jollis made what was undeniably a choking sound.

'I was round at Marcel Coussy's farm and we got milking the goats, and then I thought I may as well help him make the cheese,' continued the barber before taking another bite. 'Mmm, really goaty! Fancy some?'

'No, thanks, otherwise I won't manage this!' the baker announced, lifting a walnut and apple cake out of his basket with a flourish. But they both knew it was useless: nothing could have beaten Guillaume Ladoucette's caprine masterstroke.

Emboldened by his victory, Guillaume Ladoucette decided to broach the subject that had been curling around in his mind ever since he lifted his head from the pillow after his six-day repose.

'Stéphane . . .' he began.

'Yes,' the baker said, biting into a tomato and squirting his white T-shirt with seeds.

'You know I've closed the barber shop . . .'

'Yes,' he replied, flicking at his chest. 'I haven't mentioned it in case you didn't want to talk about it.'

'I've decided to set myself up as a matchmaker.'

'A matchmaker?'

'Yes.'

'Why a matchmaker?'

'Well, how many people do you know in the village who are in love?'

Stéphane Jollis stopped chewing as he considered the question. His friend did indeed have a point. For, despite its name, love was something that Amour-sur-Belle was sorely lacking. The majority of the inhabitants were single, not helped by the number of divorces which had taken place following the famous mini-tornado of 1999, during which infidelities, crimes and other depravities were drunkenly confessed on the assumption that no one would live to see the morning.

A number of residents weren't even speaking to each other. Stéphane Jollis himself and Lisette Robert hadn't passed the time of day since the episode of extreme weather, during which Patrice Baudin wasn't the only thing to disappear. The tornado also elevated the contents of Lisette Robert's pond and the resulting shower of frogs landed in the baker's garden. It was widely believed that the baker, who smelt fiercely of garlic the next day, and who was spotted buying quantities of butter in the grocer's, had eaten the lot. This was despite the man's protests to the contrary, which included the fact that only tourists ate frogs' legs having fallen for a joke, started in 1832 by a mischievous French merchant while in London, who claimed that they were a national delicacy.

Then there were those who said as little as possible to Denise Vigier, the grocer, having never forgotten that her grandmother had been found guilty of horizontal collaboration at a tribunal in 1944 and given a 'Number 44' haircut in front of a spitting crowd in Périgueux.

Fabrice Ribou had refused to serve Sandrine Fournier at the Bar

Saint-Jus ever since the death of his father. The old man had pestered the assistant ambulant fishmonger so often to tell him where in the woods she found such marvellous ceps that she eventually blurted out 'by the hunters' shack'. While the remains of the omelette were rushed to the hospital, it was not fast enough to identify which poisonous mushroom the old man had mistakenly consumed.

Stéphane Jollis swallowed his mouthful. 'Brilliant idea, Guillaume,' he said, pausing before adding, 'Please don't take this the wrong way, but you're not exactly married yourself. And never have been. Some might question what you know about love.'

Guillaume Ladoucette looked at his knees. The pair had grown up together and the boys' friendship had been sealed through afternoons spent by the Belle trying to see whose pee could reach the far bank first. But despite their bond, the baker knew nothing of the tumultuous state of Guillaume Ladoucette's heart. The affliction was such that his doctor had taken one look down his ears and gasped at the decades' worth of unwept tears. He baulked at the hormones that had cascaded down his legs and collected at his toes where they produced dense hairs.

'Monsieur Ladoucette,' he began after his patient had dressed again. 'I think we both know what your problem is. You may recover. You may not. I'm afraid that there is no medical intervention that can ease your suffering. If it gets any worse—and it may well do—you are, of course, welcome to come back, but there is nothing that I can do. I'm sorry.'

The barber picked up his coat and shuffled towards the door. Just as he was about to shut it behind him, the doctor called out, 'Whoever she is, I hope she's worth it.'

There were many in Amour-sur-Belle who would have thought that Émilie Fraisse was indeed not worth it. It would have been a different matter, of course, during her youth. While not the prettiest in the village—Lisette Robert carried that particular burden—there was certainly no limit to the approving glances she received as she was growing up. When she was ten, she started charging a stream of schoolboy admirers fifty centimes to stroke the butter-coloured hair that so annoyed her, the proceeds of which she spent on gunpowder for her father's rifle which he lent to her when his wife wasn't looking. When she got older, and requests came to touch other parts of her, they were smartly rebuffed. The only boy she let anywhere near her was Guillaume Ladoucette, who never asked.

When, at the age of seventeen, Émilie Fraisse left Amour-sur-Belle, she gave Guillaume Ladoucette her Nontron hunting knife with its boxwood handle and ancient pokerwork motifs and asked him to look after it while she was away. He never got to say goodbye because he was help-ing his father collect firewood, and was too embarrassed to explain why he wanted to suddenly leave. When he came back to the village, Émilie Fraisse had gone. Several weeks later, a letter arrived from Bordeaux in which she recounted how much she was enjoying working in her uncle's butcher's, but Guillaume Ladoucette, whose mind was already afflicted, couldn't think of how to reply. After he read and re-read the letter, he folded it up, put it inside an empty tin of Docteur L. Guyot throat pastilles and buried it underneath a flowering hellebore in the garden.

It wasn't long before Émilie Fraisse attracted the attention of Serge Pompignac, a local landowner who came into the shop to buy a brace of pheasant. When, as she was wrapping them, he asked, as a joke, whether she had shot them herself, the girl replied, 'Of course', as if he had just asked the most foolish question imaginable.

Unable to get the thought of the girl with the long plait out of his mind, he returned to the butcher's three days later, caught sight of her thin frame between the coils of black pudding and was inside before he realised he had moved. He hung around the shelves of preserves and mustards, avoiding the other staff until she was free to serve him and then asked for another brace of pheasant.

The following week, he walked straight up to the counter and ordered everything that was for sale, including all the jars of mustard and preserves. Once all his purchases were eventually loaded into the van waiting outside, he turned to Frédéric Fraisse and said, 'I presume your niece's work is over for the day. Do I have your permission to take her out for an afternoon walk?'

Six months later, exhausted from the disappointment of coming downstairs every morning to find letters only from her mother, Émilie Fraisse agreed to marry Serge Pompignac.

It wasn't long after she had left her aunt's house and moved into her marital home that her husband suggested that she stopped working in the butcher's. Émilie Fraisse, who had refused to change her name, at first ignored her husband's repeated requests, but she finally gave in on the tenth day of him not speaking to her.

She spent her early days wandering around the vast house staring at the ugly oil paintings and grotesquely carved furniture, thinking about Amour-sur-Belle. When, a year later, her mother asked why she still didn't have any grandchildren, Émilie Fraisse counted the number of times she and her husband had made love and found that she didn't need more than one hand. She had suspected something was wrong when it took almost three months to consummate the marriage. But the problem was never discussed, and the more it continued, the more Serge Pompignac held it against the woman he had thought would cure him.

With no children to look after, Émilie Fraisse spent her days cleaning the house, locking herself in each room so as not to be disturbed by the maids who had already done them. When she had exhausted herself cleaning and polishing one room, she would set upon another until she had finished the whole house. The maids started complaining that there was never enough polish, so Émilie Fraisse began to buy her own and burned the holey dusters in secret. At the dinner table, Serge Pompignac would look at his wife, with her hair that had turned prematurely grey, and try to remember the girl in the butcher's shop.

It came as a relief when, twenty-six years later, Serge Pompignac handed her more money than the butcher's shop could have made in a decade. 'I'm sorry,' he said. 'I thought it would be different. Forgive me.'

'I do,' she replied.

'What will you do?' he asked.

She thought for a moment and then replied, 'I'm going to buy the château in Amour-sur-Belle. It's filthy.'

During the years she was away, Guillaume Ladoucette had had a number of romantic liaisons, but nothing had come close to what he felt for Émilie Fraisse. He would catch glimpses of her on the rare occasions she would return to the village to see her parents. But he never spoke to her, lacking the courage to approach.

When, the previous week, she returned permanently to Amour-sur-Belle and brought up the château's drawbridge behind her, whispers started about her long grey hair and lack of children. Versions of how she came to afford the mournful building with its scandalous ramparts were buffeted around Amour-sur-Belle on the perpetual breeze.

Guillaume Ladoucette simply tried to think of what he would say to his first and only love when he eventually bumped into her.

'I may still be a bachelor, Stéphane,' conceded Guillaume Ladoucette, 'but that doesn't disqualify me from being a matchmaker.'

'Yes, you're right. You'll be marvellous,' replied the baker. 'Any help you need, just ask. Where will the business be?'

'Where the barber shop is.'

'Splendid.'

They sat in silence as the fish refused to bite and Guillaume Ladoucette wondered what to call his new venture. After a while Stéphane Jollis, so convinced that his friend's lunatic plan was doomed for failure, asked for a piece of goat's cheese tart as a gesture of solidarity.

Chapter Four

IT WAS MONSIEUR MOREAU who first spotted the stranger walking around Amour-sur-Belle one Wednesday morning. The villager was in his usual position on the wooden bench by the fountain said to cure gout absorbed by a procession of ants, whose progress he had followed on numerous occasions. When not staring intently at the ground by his feet, Monsieur Moreau, who many used as a local landmark when giving directions, could be found slumped on the bench, the back of his head resting against the stone wall behind him. The old man's closed eyelids, open mouth and faintly malodorous air caused many to assume that he had died, which resulted in the widespread habit of people poking him as they passed.

On this occasion he didn't see the stranger's face, just his highly polished left shoe that was threatening to crush an ant he had named Arabella, which already that morning had survived being flattened by two tractors, a bicycle, three cats and a pigeon as it rattled across the street with an outsized piece of twig.

'Watch where you're stepping!' Monsieur Moreau yelped, sticking an arm out in front of him to prevent the carnage. The man quickly stepped aside, turning back several paces later to look at the ground, still unsure of what he had almost stepped on.

The next person who saw him was Denise Vigier, the grocer, who was outside her shop arranging some oak-leaf lettuces, her colossal bosom poking out either side of her white apron. 'Half-price lettuces,' she lied, when she spotted him approaching. But the offer failed to detain him and the opportunity to find out what he wanted was gone.

Yves Lévèque had just settled himself at a table in the Bar Saint-Jus, rejoicing that a patient had just cancelled, when he looked up from his newspaper across the Place du Marché.

'Good God!' the dentist exclaimed. 'It's the man from the council who carried out the first headcount!'

There was a painful sound of scraping of chairs as the customers abandoned their seats and walked over to the window, where they stood as close as their stomachs would permit.

'You're right!' declared Fabrice Ribou. 'He's put on a bit of weight, hasn't he?'

'Are you sure that's him?' asked Marcel Coussy, the farmer.

'Positive,' replied Yves Lévèque. 'He's still got the same pair of trousers on. I used to have a pair. I'd recognise them anywhere.'

'I wonder what he's doing here,' said Didier Lapierre, the carpenter.

'Whatever it is, he hasn't come to measure up for a swimming pool, that's for certain,' said the dentist. 'Watch out, he's coming over!'

By the time the door opened, all that could be heard was a hideous ensemble of exaggerated slurping.

The man walked straight up to the bar and introduced himself as Jean-François Lafforest from the council, and informed Fabrice Ribou that he had come on official business. Clutching his soft leather brief-case to his stomach, he announced what had taken him three weeks to memorise on account of the nervous breakdown he had suffered following the taunts of his colleagues over his preposterous headcount.

'Ladies and gentlemen,' he announced, facing the room. 'You will all receive the following information in the post within the next few days, but I am here to inform you myself in the event that there may be some immediate questions. I'd like to make it clear that the following announcement is a council matter and decided by a committee.'

With a raised hand, Fabrice Ribou, whose mind was never far from his takings, interrupted the man, telling him that if he was about to make a public announcement it was only fair to round up the other villagers. To his immense satisfaction, after a series of phone calls, his clientele had doubled.

On seeing by how much his audience had swelled, Jean-François Lafforest hugged his briefcase closer to him. 'As you are no doubt aware, it has not rained for some considerable time, before which the reservoir was already at a worryingly low level,' he continued. 'It is my duty to inform you that a municipal shower will shortly be installed in the Place du Marché. From that time no baths will be permitted in Amour-sur-Belle and anyone caught infringing the regulation will be fined.'

'How much is the fine?' asked Gilbert Dubuisson, the postman.

Jean-François Lafforest rubbed his upper lip as he muttered a figure.

'How much did you say?' asked Lisette Robert.

'One hundred euros,' repeated the man from the council.

'One hundred euros!' exclaimed Marcel Coussy, the farmer.

'For having a bath in our own homes?' said Madame Moreau.

'If you would like to take the matter further, I have a list of names of people you could get in touch with,' said Jean-François Lafforest, wiping a trickle of sweat from the side of his face.

'How will you know if anyone's had a bath?' asked Lisette Robert.

'Spot checks will be carried out,' replied Jean-François Lafforest, 'the details of which will be determined. By others. Not me.'

Quite what happened next, Jean-François Lafforest was never certain. All the man from the council knew was that one moment he was in the bar and the next he had been deposited back at the far end of the square, his soft leather briefcase arriving seconds afterwards.

Guillaume Ladoucette didn't attend the meeting, having resisted Fabrice Ribou's sales tactics with the insistence that he was busy. After putting down the phone, he took the key to the barber shop from its nail by the kitchen mantelpiece, dropped it into his trouser pocket and locked the front door behind him.

It was warm inside the barber shop. As he pushed open the door, a pile of letters skidded across the floor. He stood looking around, noticing the dust that had flourished on the mirror in just over a week. The grey nylon cape, which had slipped from its peg on the wall, lay slumped on the floor.

Reminding himself that today was the start of his new life, Guillaume Ladoucette set to work. As he picked up the post and put it in a neat pile by the door to take home, he thought 'no more dandruff'. As he folded up the cape, he muttered: 'No more pretending to customers that they're not going bald.' Cheered at the thought, he dropped all the products that had been for sale into a bag, including the combs in three different colours, the pots of pomade and the bottles of hair tonic.

Into a box he packed his small, yet curious collection of old barbering utensils, including the shaving bowls, the sets of brass moustache tongs and the assortment of cutthroat razors. He went to the other side of the room and looked up at his certificate from the Périgord Academy of Master Barbers, but something stopped him from taking it down.

When Stéphane Jollis arrived to remove the barber's chair and basin, Guillaume Ladoucette disappeared into the back garden, unable to watch. Once the task was done, the two men then stood back and contemplated the empty room.

'Why don't you just whitewash it?' suggested the baker.

'It's been white for nineteen years. What about pale pink?'

'Pale pink? They use that in hospices.'

'What would you have, then?'

'White.'

'I don't want white,' said Guillaume. 'What about cream?'

'If you're going to have cream you may as well have white.'

'What about red, then?'

'It would look like a bordello. That's a point, why don't you open a bordello?'

'Stéphane, would you mind concentrating on the issue at hand?'

'White,' he replied before leaving to return to the bakery.

The morning Guillaume Ladoucette opened his new business, the sun was firing with such ferocity the pigeons had gone mad. Unable to remember how to fly, they tottered after Madame Ladoucette in a feathery grey shadow recognising in her a similar suffering. A number of them, a spark having suddenly fired in a prehistoric part of their brain, thought that they were fish again. Monsieur Moreau found six drowned in the fountain said to cure gout.

As Guillaume Ladoucette approached the shop, he admired once again the fancy lettering of the words 'Heart's Desire' above the door. It had cost him more than he expected, but he was delighted with the result. After unlocking the door, he turned the sign hanging on the inside so that the word *Open* in swirling red letters faced the street. After hanging his new navy suit jacket on the peg where the nylon grey cape used to hang, he gave it an affectionate brush with his hand. Savouring the moment, he then slowly sat down at the oak desk, which he had bought in Brantôme, facing the window. Slightly battered, with a prominent ink stain, which had secured its free delivery, an afternoon of polishing and buffing had vastly improved the desk's appearance.

After lacing his fingers behind a clean sheet of white paper, he bared his most welcoming of smiles and waited. A few moments later, when nothing had happened, he slowly moved his pen from the right hand side of the piece of paper to a horizontal position above it. He re-laced his fingers and smiled again.

Not long after jaw-ache had set in, he looked down and, feeling a twist of excitement, slowly slid open the narrow drawer that sat just above his stomach. There, each in its own little compartment, was a rubber, a pencil, a stapler, a selection of pens and the contents of a large packet of multicoloured rubber bands which had been split into two sections, according to colour. After moving the stapler to a different compartment, he slowly closed the drawer again.

Guillaume Ladoucette resumed his original position of unfettered expectation. When, several minutes later, he was still alone, he glanced around the newly painted walls, silently congratulating himself for having opted for pale pink after all. He then got up, walked round to the other side of the desk and sat on the chair with the peeling marquetry, which he had also bought in Brantôme, seduced by its cushion bearing a hand-embroidered radish. 'Most comfortable,' he concluded, rubbing the ends of the armrests, before returning to his swivel chair.

Two hours later, Guillaume Ladoucette had made the gratifying discovery that if he put one hand on the edge of the desk and spun himself round, he could, on average, achieve three revolutions before the chair came to a standstill.

When midday finally came, he took his new navy jacket off the peg, put it on and went home for lunch. Returning after his pig's head soup, medallions of pork, green beans fried in garlic and a round of Cabécou, the matchmaker looked around for a sign that a customer had dropped by—a little note on the door, perhaps—but everything was just as he had left it. After hanging up his jacket, he returned to his seat. He lifted the receiver of the phone, which he had placed over the ink stain to hide it, and found that, despite the absence of calls, it was indeed working. Sliding open the narrow drawer above his stomach, he surveyed the contents again with equal satisfaction and slowly slid it shut. Chin in his left hand, he then gazed across the road to the home of Gilbert Dubuisson and looked at the man's meticulous window boxes. Two hours later, telling himself it was still early days, he straightened the cushion with the hand-embroidered radish and returned home.

By the third day, the matchmaker had decided to leave his jacket at home, twirling around on his new chair had lost all its allure and the most significant event that had taken place in Heart's Desire was that the stapler was now back in its original position. By the afternoon he started to wonder where all his customers were. Everyone knew he had opened for business, surely? The previous week he had called the *Sud Ouest* and a charming young reporter came to see him expressing considerable interest in his new venture. His picture had even appeared alongside the article, which the photographer had taken from a crouching position south of his chin, resulting in a shot which gave the impression that a giant fruit bat had just landed on his top lip. But, despite the publicity, the only person who had opened the door since was a workman who asked the way to the Place du Marché.

By the seventh day, Guillaume Ladoucette was back in his short-sleeved checked shirts and comfortable trousers that he had worn for barbering. Instead of being shod in a pair of new, hard, black lace-ups, his feet were now stark naked having been slipped out of his supermarket leather sandals, and were enjoying the cool of the red-tiled floor.

The contents of the narrow drawer hadn't been inspected for days, as the thrill had long since worn off, and the stack of plain white paper in the top right-hand drawer had gone down by half, having been snipped into a variety of creations with a pair of scissors he'd retrieved from his cardboard box of barbering utensils in the cellar.

By the thirteenth day, the matchmaker had come to detest the colour of the walls. As he sat with his elbows on the desk, his eyes turned to the framed certificate from the Périgord Academy of Master Barbers that he had been unable to take down, and he thought of his life's passion that had come to an end because of his stubborn refusal to change.

He looked down at the desk with the ink stain that stood in mockery of the venture that had failed before it had started. But most of all he thought of the woman he had lost, his idiocy in not replying to her letter and the twenty-six years they could have spent together, now gone and dusty.

Just then the door opened.

Guillaume Ladoucette led his first customer to the chair with the peeling marquetry and made sure he was comfortably settled on the cushion with the hand-embroidered radish. He then padded round to the other side of the desk with the ink stain where he sat down on the swivel chair, his oil-drop eyes not leaving his new arrival for a second.

'Welcome to Heart's Desire!' he announced with a smile of such breadth his moustache swept even closer to each ear. 'A little coffee?'

'Yes, please.'

Guillaume Ladoucette trotted off to the back of the shop and poured a couple of cups from the percolator on the small table with the antique lace tablecloth. He placed one in front of his customer, settled himself back on the swivel chair, pulled off his pen top and declared, 'Now, just a few formalities to go through before we get down to business.' Pointing his nib towards the paper, he raised his eyes and asked, 'Name?'

'You know very well what my name is,' the man replied. 'We've known each other all our lives.'

'Name?' Guillaume Ladoucette enquired again.

Silence ballooned between them.

'Yves Lévèque,' came the eventual reply.

'Address?'

'I'm your next-door neighbour!'

'Address?'

'Amour-sur-Belle. And that's in the Périgord Vert in southwest France, in case you've forgotten that too.'

'Age?' Guillaume Ladoucette asked, his head still lowered.

'Thirty-five,' the dentist replied.

'Age?' the matchmaker repeated with the weariness of a courtroom judge who had heard one too many deceits during his career.

'All right, forty-four.'

'So, how can I help you?' asked Guillaume Ladoucette, lacing his fingers in front of him and resting them on the desk.

'Well,' the dentist said. 'I heard you'd set yourself up as a matchmaker and I just thought I'd come and see what it was all about.'

'Splendid! Heart's Desire offers three levels of service,' Guillaume Ladoucette explained, 'all uniquely tailored to suit your individual needs. We have the Unrivalled Bronze Service, the Unrivalled Silver Service and then, of course, the Unrivalled Gold Service.'

'And what do they involve?'

'The Unrivalled Bronze Service enables you to help yourself in your quest to find love. We offer tips on where you might be going wrong, suggesting ways in which you could improve your appearance, perhaps, and point out any unfavourable personal habits that need to be confronted. The rest is then up to you. Customers who choose the Unrivalled Silver Service are matched up with the utmost thought, care and consideration to someone of unparalleled suitability on our books. And finally, those who opt for the Unrivalled Gold Service can stipulate the person to whom they wish to be introduced, providing that he or she lives within a certain radius and that the object of their affection is single. Those who opt for the Unrivalled Silver or Unrivalled Gold Services automatically get the benefits of the Unrivalled Bronze Service free of charge.'

Yves Lévèque adjusted his spectacles with his long, pale instruments of torture. 'So, how many people have you got on your books?'

The truth bolted before Guillaume Ladoucette had a chance to rein it back in. 'None,' he replied, already smelling defeat.

'I see,' said Yves Lévèque frowning. 'And how much are you charging for all this?'

His hopes rising again and his fingers fluttering, Guillaume Ladoucette pulled the brass handle of the top left-hand drawer of the desk with the ink stain. He took out a price list printed on cream card and slid it across the surface of the desk with his index finger. Yves Lévèque looked at it, then looked at it again to make sure he had not misread it.

'So let me get this right,' said Yves Lévèque, sitting back in the chair with the peeling marquetry, the price list in his hand. 'I could pay you a small fortune and opt for the Unrivalled Bronze Service to be advised on such matters as clipping my nails regularly. Or I could pay you an even bigger fortune and choose the Unrivalled Silver Service and you'll match me up with myself, as things stand. Or, thirdly, I could plump for the Unrivalled Gold Service and pay you an unsightly fortune for you to sidle up to someone and tell them that I fancy them.'

'Come, come, Monsieur Lévèque.'

'You can call me Yves, Guillaume, as you have done all your life.'

'Yves. The fact that there is currently no one else on the books is a mere formality. It is only a matter of time before things pick up. And, as my first customer, you would, of course, be eligible for a ten per cent discount. Now, I must point out that the Unrivalled Bronze Service is not designed for a man of the world such as yourself. Heavens, no. Your problem, as I see it, is simply lack of opportunity, although there must be many suitable women who come into the surgery. You're the only dentist for miles.'

'Well, yes,' said Yves Lévèque, looking beyond the matchmaker as he thought. 'But the problem with getting romantically involved with a patient, of course, is that when you eventually split up and they come back for treatment, they assume that whenever you tell them that they need a filling you're just trying to cause them more pain.'

'I see,' said the matchmaker. 'Is there anything you might have done recently to improve your chances that hasn't perhaps worked?'

As Yves Lévèque shook his head, the spikes of his pine cone rattled.

'Nothing I can think of,' he replied.

'Something to do with your appearance, perhaps?'

The dentist looked blankly at the matchmaker for several minutes.

'Well, maybe that's a little something to think about,' said Guillaume Ladoucette quickly. 'So, well, I suppose you could always carry on as you are, but what you've tried so far clearly hasn't worked, which is a shame because there's nothing quite like the soft mounds of a woman's breasts against your back at night, is there?'

Yves Lévèque remained silent.

'There's a woman out there waiting to find you, as you are waiting to find her,' Guillaume Ladoucette continued. 'My job is to unite the pair of you before she finds someone else. So, which service will it be?'

'I'm still not convinced about any of this,' protested the dentist, but he felt again the sharp edges of loneliness that had been rattling around inside his stomach for half a decade. As he sat rubbing his palms on the stained wooden arms of the chair, slowly the loneliness rose and became wedged in his throat. The more he tried to speak the more it strangled him and his cheeks lit up with the struggle. He shut his eyes and with one final gulp he swallowed the obstruction back down. When he finally opened his mouth, he let out a squeak like a rusty weathervane, coughed, and whispered, 'The Unrivalled Silver Service.'

Over an hour later, having divulged more about his ill-fated love life than he even realised he knew, Yves Lévèque got up. Before leaving, he poked his head out of the door to check that no one was around to witness his exit. Once the dentist had gone, Guillaume Ladoucette turned over the sign on the door, locked up and headed home.

The matchmaker failed to take in anything of the short journey home. Such was the extent of his jubilation at finally having a customer on his books, a sudden onset of delirium had blanked out the curved salmon-coloured roof tiles and the ancient stone walls on top of which wild irises grew. In their place was the image of Yves Lévèque sitting on the terrace of one of the exquisite riverside restaurants in Brantôme holding the hand of a woman opposite him with perfect teeth. By the time he had reached halfway home, the woman had fallen for the dentist's hitherto disguised charms. When the matchmaker had turned into his street, the couple were standing before the priest in the Romanesque church, he was best man and the groom had finally apologised for returning his box of hairpieces in such a state of turmoil.

Arriving at his front door, the matchmaker slid his key silently into the lock and gently turned it. Slowly pushing the door ajar, he then took a small hand mirror from behind the flower box on the windowsill, slid it inside the door and tilted it in various directions as he tried to see every angle of the kitchen.

'Good evening, Guillaume! What on earth are you doing?' came a voice. The matchmaker jumped and turned his head to see Madame Serre holding a watering can with fingers twisted with age.

'Ah! Good evening, Madame Serre. Err, nothing. That's what I'm doing, absolutely nothing. Nothing at all. Not a single thing. I'd better go, actually, because I'm not doing anything and it's about time that I was. Bye!' replied the matchmaker and closed the door behind him.

Once inside, he poured himself a glass of still mineral water from a bottle in the fridge, and sat down at the kitchen table with a nectarine. As he cut into it, he wondered what to have for his victory supper. When he had finished it, he dabbed his mouth with his favourite white napkin with his initials embroidered in red in the corner, let the nectarine stone slide off the plate into the bin and put the plate into the sink. He then walked over to the cellar door, turned the handle on which hung a necklace of dried red chillies, and slowly descended the stairs.

At the bottom, he pulled a cord which lit up a naked bulb furred with dust. One of his favourite places as a boy, the cellar still held its allure. While the majority of the fruit and vegetable conserves were now his own, there were still a few at the back of the shelves which had been made by his mother.

There were other treasures down there too, including a large collection of his ancestors' clogs, their soles shod with what appeared to be tiny horseshoes. His favourite was the ornately carved pair made of poplar which had belonged to his grandfather.

But they were not the only delights. Ignoring the bite of his grandfather's Sunday clogs, which he still put on when in the cellar despite the aggression of their nip, the matchmaker moved along the shelves of jars and inspected the contents of his bottles of *pineau*. The previous year he had crushed the grapes in a food mixer and then sieved the results through a pair of tights, the purchase of which had caused numerous smirks in the grocer's. He had then added enough cognac to create a concoction of forty per cent alcohol and sixty per cent grape must. He looked with satisfaction at the clarity of the liquid in the top three-quarters of several of the bottles, and calculated that it would only be a matter of weeks before he would try it.

Passing the pickled tomatoes, their flushed cheeks pressed up against the glass, he then turned his attention to the bottles of walnut wine that he had made the previous August. He had spent a happy afternoon picking the green nuts from the tree in the garden, breaking them up, mixing them with eau de vie, sugar, the zest of an orange and a cinnamon stick. The murky liquid had all been filtered with a pair of tights, purchased this time from Brantôme.

But the biggest change to the cellar since Guillaume Ladoucette had returned to his childhood home were the astrological maps and planetary charts which now covered the walls above the wooden shelves. For, as his years advanced, he had followed the inevitable steps of a man who had discovered a white hair in his moustache and embraced his *potager* with the enthusiasm of a new lover, intoxicated by its alluring yields and tormented by its capricious failures.

The colour maps and charts were the cornerstone of his seduction technique. For Guillaume Ladoucette was of the utter conviction that plants were as responsive to the cycles of the moon as the tides. A high priest in the cult of lunar gardening, no task in the *potager*, no matter how small, was undertaken unless the moon was passing in front of the correct zodiacal constellation. Preparation of the soil, sowing, thinning out and hoeing, for example, were only performed while the moon was passing in front of Capricorn, Taurus and Virgo. The optimum time to concern oneself with leaf crops such as lettuce and spinach was when it was passing in front of Cancer, Pisces or Scorpio. And if the moon was in Gemini, Libra or Aquarius, it was the turn of artichokes, Brussels sprouts and broccoli.

Having checked the position of the moon, the matchmaker struggled out of his grandfather's clogs and found relief in his supermarket leather sandals. After clicking off the light, he creaked back upstairs and headed towards the back door.

Thwacking his way across the grass towards his *potager*, he passed the well with its pointed stone roof and the old white sink with its jolly red geraniums. First he admired his row of garlic, which he had planted four days before a full moon. He decided not to dwell on his artichokes, which, instead of standing straight as soldiers had more the air of a group of conscientious objectors about them, despite having been planted when the moon was in Gemini. But their mournful sight, and the nagging regret of not having added more cinnamon sticks to his walnut wine, suddenly reminded the matchmaker of his capacity for failure and his mind turned to Yves Lévèque. As he reached for a weed and tossed it into a basket, he wondered whether he really would be able to find a woman who would overlook the dentist's much-discussed parsimony, his annoying habit of looking at people's teeth when spoken to, and his unspeakable efforts at growing *cornichons*.

Bending over to pick some large, floppy leaves of spinach, though, his heart suddenly began to soar. 'I know that woman exists and I shall find her,' he told himself, marching back to the house with his pickings to prepare his celebratory supper.

Chapter Five

THE ONE PERSON in Amour-sur-Belle who welcomed the fact that the pigeons had suddenly forgotten how to fly was Émilie Fraisse. A number of residents, infuriated by repeatedly tripping over them when they scuttled out of nowhere like feathered rats, had resorted to kicking them with rage. Yet the châtelaine, for the first time in a week, was now able to sleep past five in the morning without being woken by the tapping of dry, horny beaks on the ancient château windows by grey crowds jostling on the enormous stone sills, a sound which had driven one fifteenth-century owner over the ramparts in despair.

Émilie Fraisse slept on the right-hand side of the four-poster Renaissance bed, the position she had assumed throughout her marriage. She had picked the side nearest the door on her wedding night to enable a swift exit should the worst of her fears come to pass. But instead of the pain she was expecting, her groom simply kissed her on the forehead and went to sleep, leaving her blinking in bewilderment. It was not until almost three months later that Émilie Fraisse finally lost her virginity after several attempts. A year later, when still not pregnant, she attempted to increase the frequency of their lovemaking, but her efforts were rebuffed and Serge Pompignac began to turn his back on his wife in a bog of self-hating frustration. The more the matter remained unspoken, the more the pair felt unable to talk of other matters, and, eventually, the stitches binding them together came undone.

It was during her first night in the château of Amour-sur-Belle that she rediscovered the joy of sleeping alone. Instead of lying on her side facing away from her husband, she lay on her back, her arms stretched out either side of her as if she had been dropped from a great height. And when, in the middle of the night, the unfamiliarity of her surroundings woke her, she experienced the delight of getting up, going downstairs and returning with a steak sandwich. And on opening her eyes the next morning, she realised that for the first time in over two decades she was not disappointed to be awake.

Eager to explore her new home, Émilie Fraisse covered her slender nakedness with a white cotton dressing gown with dark blue embroidered flowers. She hadn't bothered to inspect the château before purchasing it, relying on her memory from the last time she had visited it on one of her rare visits home to see her parents. The sale had come after almost five years of the building being on the market, during which time it had crumpled into a pitiful state. André Lizard, the previous owner, had been determined to repair the scandalous ramparts, which were missing so many sections of their crenellations, raze the nettles in the dry moat and coax the Belle back into it. There were plans to drive out the bats from the bell tower; to replace the junk-shop furniture, which had been bought to fill in the gaps left by the ancient treasures sold by previous owners to feed a variety of disturbing addictions; and to prevent the rain from leaking through the roof into the King's Bedroom, which had been kept permanently ready for a royal visit that had never come.

It wasn't long before André Lizard discovered the folly of his dream. As the years grated painfully by, bringing only a handful of visitors a week during the summer months, there was no income to fund the restorations. When news finally came of a cash buyer for the château and its contents, André Lizard immediately handed over the enormous iron key to his solicitor and left within the hour, his threadbare slippers crunching over the crisp pigeon droppings covering the drawbridge. He left behind him a large quantity of rare wine hidden in the dungeon from the Nazis and a colourful colony of moulds that the scientific world had long thought extinct.

In her bare feet, Émilie Fraisse walked slowly down the corridor, stopping to touch the rough stitches of the faded tapestries lining the walls. Pushing open the heavy wooden door to one of the bedrooms, the châtelaine was heartened to see that nothing had changed since her previous visit. Running her hand along the top of the dressing table, she was instantly comforted by the sight of the grey powdery residue on her fingers. Shutting the door behind her so as not to disturb the dust, she visited every room, opening the heavy wooden shutters. By the time she had inspected every room, Émilie Fraisse knew she had made the right decision to buy the place: it was just as filthy as she had remembered it.

Without stopping to get dressed, she opened the vast front door, which had been bleached fossil-grey by the sun and padded across the courtyard to the splendid late fifteenth-century chapel, where she cut armfuls of ivy that was growing up its stone walls. Inside the château, she filled vases with twists of the evergreen, and placed a single apricot rose, which had been rambling for centuries, in a glass next to her bed.

Finally daring to enter the bathroom, she inspected with curiosity the insect carcasses lying in the bottom of the stained tub. Taking a bar of soap from her solitary suitcase, she then went outside, took off her white cotton dressing gown with the dark blue embroidered flowers and happily showered under the cold water of the garden hose. As she strolled naked around the château to dry off, she came across a leather chest studded with brass in one of the upper bedrooms. Her curiosity stoked, she knelt on the floor, heaved up the lid with both hands and discovered a nest of antique dresses. Standing up, she pulled them out one by one and inspected them. After selecting one in iris mauve with lacework covering the bodice, she stepped into it and, to her surprise, found that it fitted. Looking into the mirror dappled with age, she twisted her long, grey hair into a pile at the back of her head and secured it with one of the jewelled pins she found in a tortoiseshell box on the dressing table. She rustled her way back along the corridor and descended the stone spiral staircase, the bottom of the gown rippling down the cold steps with their lamentable repairs. In a pot by the kitchen sink she found a large pair of scissors and hacked off the bottom of the dress from the knees down. She then set about looking for dusters.

When, within an hour, she had exhausted them, the châtelaine climbed into her car and drove to the nearest supermarket where people glanced in confusion at the woman in the antique shorn-off dress, whom many failed to recognise, purchasing an enormous quantity of cleaning materials, along with a week's supply of food. Arriving back at the château, she stuck a note over the opening times saying 'CLOSED FOR THE WEEK' and pulled up the drawbridge behind her.

Her treat for the day, which had filled her mind as she drove back, was the llama skeleton that stood in the hallway and had developed the pallor of ash. Working on each of its seventy-nine bones, after several hours she had returned it to its natural colour of unripe Brie.

Over the course of the week, the châtelaine navigated steadily through the rooms with her warship of dusters, brushes and scented polishes, sustained by the comfort of knowing that as soon as she had finished she would immediately have to start again. As she wiped and rubbed she found beauty in the decay of the place, which she had no intention of restoring, and looked in awe at the vast palette of the moulds. When her back and neck could take no more, she would climb to the roof and sit by the scandalous ramparts admiring the curves of the Belle, the bright yellow irises in the dry moat below, and the flight of the buzzards, their big floppy feet hanging below them.

On her final day before opening, Émilie Fraisse looked inside the *grand salon*. There, stretching towards the enormous stone fireplace was the reversible floor, one side oak, the other walnut. According to the visitors' guide, the floorboards, originally installed in 1657, were turned every 200 years. Émilie Fraisse took a bucket and first lightly washed down the oak boards that were uppermost. When the sun's fingers had dried them, she got back down on her hands and knees and polished each one until the floor reflected her shadow. Then, ignoring the fact that the boards weren't due to be changed for another ninety-four years, she turned them all over as she had been longing to do. By the end of the day the rippling walnut was so dazzling that the house martins that flew in couldn't find their way back out.

Rising early the following morning, Émilie Fraisse lowered the drawbridge and removed her note from the board. Halfway through the afternoon, while picking quince from the overgrown orchard, a

German tourist in becoming shorts appeared at her side asking for a tour of the château. After offering him a quince, she put down her basket and led him to the hall.

When she and her guest arrived at the llama skeleton, and he enquired where it had come from, Émilie Fraisse said nothing of the fact that, according to the visitors' guide, its body had been found in the moat seventy-two years ago after it had escaped from a travelling circus. Instead, she found herself telling him how the animal had been ridden back from Persia by a fourteenth-century troubadour as a gift for his beloved after she had rejected both him and his previous offerings. The llama, a species that wasn't even known to exist at the time, appeared to do the trick. For a period the three lived in harmony in the château, with the animal enjoying a bedroom all to itself with views of the garden and a place at the dining-room table despite its unsavoury habit of spitting. But after a while, the woman began to pay more attention to the llama, which wasn't afflicted by a need to recite atrocious poetry. Twisted with envy, one night the ungrateful poet killed his winning mode of transport. It was never known what happened to the man, but his headless ghost still haunted the place.

When Émilie Fraisse had finished her story, the enraptured German, who was slightly confused because he thought that llamas came from South America, immediately asked her to take his photograph standing next to the skeleton.

Arriving at the *grand salon*, the tourist naturally enquired about the splendid reversible floor. The châtelaine then found herself recounting how it had been copied from a similar one at the nearby château of Bourdeilles in an escalating seventeenth-century war of neighbourly one-upmanship. It developed into such a vicious feud between the two owners that they each kidnapped the other's daughter, and locked her in one of the towers to increase the other's misery. When, after a week, neither could bear their prisoner's incessant wails, they both unlocked the tower door hoping the girls would flee. But it took several months for the captives to realise that they were no longer imprisoned, by which time they had become attached to their surroundings and refused their freedom. Each father was then stuck with a daughter he found more infuriating than his own. Such was the pity the men developed for each other's plight, they took up falconing together, during which they spent most of the time bemoaning the curse of fatherhood.

The German, who couldn't disguise his delight, immediately bent down and stroked the lustrous wooden floor.

And so it was for every room, every piece of furniture or detail whose history Émilie Fraisse either didn't know or found too pedestrian, and each embellishment was countered with phrases such as 'it is believed', 'so the legend goes' or 'some say'. Her motives were in no way pecuniary. She had enough money to sustain her for the rest of her life without a single visitor. Neither was it mischief, nor, indeed, was it boredom, for she couldn't remember when she had felt so engaged with the world. She simply didn't want to disappoint the German tourist.

When he left, as charmed by the decrepit château as he was by its owner, he handed her four euros, which, according to the notice board outside, was the entrance fee. But she waved it away, grateful for the longest conversation she had had in years. Later that day, she found the coins in an envelope in her letterbox along with a thankyou note and a recipe for quince jelly handed down from his father.

Inspired by her visitor's letter, Émilie Fraisse slipped her feet into a pair of vast gentlemen's Wellington boots to protect her legs from scratches, and slopped over to the garden knitted with weeds. Near the wall, topped with bearded irises, she discovered a plot of heirloom vegetables and marvelled at the ancient varieties, long-forgotten—the blue potatoes, the hyacinth beans with their startling purple-red pods, the strawberry spinach and the round black radish. She spent the evening in a state of utter contentment, her bare feet padding back and forth across the kitchen, making jams, jellies and chutneys in the enormous copper pans. The most exquisite was the black radish jam made with honey and a whisper of fresh ginger. When they had cooled, on each of the jars she stuck a handwritten label stating the contents, the date and the words 'From the Ancient Gardens of the Château at Amour-sur-Belle'. After filling the larder with half of them, she tied around each of the others a piece of antique lace from the bottom of the dresses she had cut off, then put them for sale in the window of the wooden hut at the entrance to the château, erected years ago to house the ticket seller for the crowds who never came.

The following morning Émilie Fraisse explored the contents of the armoury, which she had cleaned but not lingered over. Slowly, she drew a finger along the mother-of-pearl inlay on the crossbows and noticed how the tiny flowers glinted lavender in the light. She then chose a small engraved musket, grabbed a handful of shot and closed the door.

After changing into a pair of britches, a long-sleeved shirt, which she found hanging in a wardrobe, and some gentleman's buckled leather boots, she crunched her way over the drawbridge and headed for the woods. Slipping between the branches, she recognised the trees of her childhood, and stood disbelieving the height they had reached.

Curiosity set her following the wild-boar track to see whether it still passed the old hunters' shack. After a while, to her surprise, she saw in the distance the outline of the hut that she was expecting to have tumbled down long ago. As she got closer, she was struck by the fact that it was no longer as desolate as she remembered. Indeed, it appeared that someone had set about transforming it, for the hut no longer tilted perilously to the left. There also seemed to have been repairs made to the roof, and, as she approached further, she noticed that someone had replaced the glass in the tiny window which had always been broken.

As she continued on her way, she glanced inside the hut. There, on the floor, were two villagers whom she instantly recognised. But what perplexed her more than their nakedness was the fact that as far as she knew, one of them was very much married to someone else. The couple were so engrossed in their physical pursuit that they failed to notice the woman standing dumbfounded at the window.

The châtelaine made her way as quickly and as quietly out of the clearing as possible, and headed for the far reaches of the woods. The spectacle turned her thoughts to the corrosion of her own marriage. Wounded by envy, she stopped and leaned against a tree felled by the famous mini-tornado of 1999, and for the first time since she had returned to Amour-sur-Belle felt the familiar drizzle of melancholy. She stood getting wet until she spotted a fallen leaf whose colour reminded her of her newly lustrous walnut floor, and she put it in her pocket. Her mind then slid to the other pleasures the château had given her, including the llama skeleton. Before she knew it, the smell of rain had passed and she was aiming at a large hare, which she felled with one shot.

As she carried it back to the château, she thought of the two terrines she would make from it, one of which she would put for sale with the other jars in the disused ticket hut. Stepping over a fallen branch, she suddenly wondered what had happened to her Nontron hunting knife with its boxwood handle and ancient pokerwork motifs. Then she remembered the last afternoon she had spent in the woods with Guillaume Ladoucette before leaving Amour-sur-Belle. She had tried to pretend that the occasion was of no importance, but had not been able to sustain her indifference. Handing him her knife for safekeeping, she had hoped that he would recognise the significance. But the teenager took it without a word and slid it into his pocket. For an instant she wondered whether he was going to kiss her, and she remained still. But the moment never came. She then thought of the following morning and how she had put her suitcase in her father's car early and waited for Guillaume Ladoucette to come and say goodbye. But he never came.

Eleven months later she learned from a neighbour on her first visit back to the village that he had been cutting firewood with his father and had arrived running shortly after the car had pulled away. He then sat on the garden wall, head bowed, hands in his pockets, for hours.

Her mind then turned to the countless mornings she had come downstairs in her aunt's house in Bordeaux to find that there was still no reply waiting at her place at the table. She wondered again as she had all those years ago, why he had never written back. Squeezing through the branches, she came to the same conclusion as she always had—that he didn't feel the same way that she did. And, as she had learned to do as a teenager, Émilie Fraisse put all thoughts of Guillaume Ladoucette out of her mind and headed back towards the château.

Chapter Six

THE INSTALLATION of the municipal shower turned out to be a far more wretched procedure than Jean-François Lafforest had predicted. When he arrived at Amour-sur-Belle to inspect the work, he saw to his surprise that the shower had been sited in the correct spot next to a wall on the far side of the Place du Marché. But he discovered that instead of the door facing the wall, which would have afforded the villagers a degree of modesty, it was in fact facing the square. And, as the drainage work had already started, the mistake could not be rectified.

As the plumbing work continued, it soon became clear by the amount of water billowing up from the trench and crawling across the square towards the Bar Saint-Jus that the wrong size pipe had been ordered. When, three days later, he returned to the site and asked the two labourers, whom he eventually tracked down to the bar, why the work had not progressed, he was told that the new part had still not arrived. He then went in person to the council's purchasing department where he was informed that the pipe would have to be ordered from Spain, which could take up to four weeks. He nodded in silence, knowing full well that no parts were ever ordered from outside France out of national pride, and that any mention of Spain was simply an indication of yet another colleague having been infected with inertia.

Aware that there was no cure, Jean-François Lafforest noted down the precise measurements of the pipe that was needed, drove to a large DIY store on the outskirts of Périgueux and bought one. He then took it to the purchasing department and explained that one of his friends had just been to Spain and managed to pick one up. Knowing that the man in front of him would now claim that the pipe would have to be vetted before being deemed acceptable, Jean-François Lafforest silently placed on his desk a large Serrano ham and bottle of Rioja which he had bought in a supermarket to help alleviate his colleague's frightful symptoms. They worked in an instant and the pipe was approved.

Returning to Amour-sur-Belle, the man from the council handed the part to the two disappointed workers who were in the same place as he had left them. When, the following day, he made a surprise visit, he found them yet again sitting at Fabrice Ribou's highly polished counter. Correctly suspecting that the bar owner with the curious haircut which resembled a pine cone was giving them free drinks in order to disrupt the work, Jean-François Lafforest made the decision to stay every day at the site, sitting on the collapsable picnic chair he kept in the boot of his car while clutching his soft leather briefcase to his fleshy stomach.

When the installation was finally complete, notices were sent to each household informing the occupant that baths were forbidden from midnight onwards, and that the shower would be ready for use the following morning. That night, Guillaume Ladoucette filled up his bath, stepped in and remained recumbent for several hours.

Yves Lévèque, who had a pressing reason to smell his best that day, had set his alarm for 5.30 a.m. hoping to beat the early-rising baker to the shower. When it went off, the dentist immediately bolted out of bed, pulled his green-and-white striped dressing gown on over his navy pyjamas and slid his feet into his shiny, maroon backless slippers. Grabbing his drawstring washbag, he checked to see that his bottle of shampoo was inside, then slipped out of the front door.

As he strode down the road with a white towel over his shoulder, he thought how marvellous it was to be the first to crack open the day. But on reaching the Rue du Château, he suddenly heard footsteps. He turned round to see the undeniable bulk of Stéphane Jollis in a voluminous white T-shirt and tartan boxer shorts coming up behind him. The baker was clutching a blue towel and moving at a much faster rate than normal, stirred from his bed by the thought of catching a glimpse of Lisette Robert in a state of undress.

Several paces later, the dentist looked over his shoulder again and coming up behind Stéphane Jollis was Lisette Robert in a short red satin nightdress with a towel tucked under her arm, who had been driven from her sheets by the fear of having to shower after the early-rising postman, Gilbert Dubuisson, who was known for his despicable habit of urinating behind trees whenever caught short on his rounds.

Not far behind Lisette Robert, Yves Lévèque spotted the postman, naked apart from his blue towelling dressing gown that was flapping open indiscreetly. Scurrying along with a turquoise towel hanging round his neck, he had decided to take a shower before work. On his tail was Guillaume Ladoucette in an elegant burgundy silk dressing gown, with two towels and a fiercely guarded piece of soap from his favourite shop in Périgueux in his pocket. He had been roused from his sleep by the torturous sound of a chicken egg slowly rolling across the wooden landing floor. Driven to a state of fury and unable to get back to sleep, he could think of nothing else to do at that hour than to try out the new shower. But sprinting past them all was Sandrine Fournier, the mushroom poisoner, who had been woken by the shuffling of slippers underneath her window. Looking out, she noticed all the towels and washbags and, while she couldn't understand why there was such an urgent need to get to the shower so early, decided to try to beat them all just in case.

When Yves Lévèque finally returned home, he lay on top of his bed, still wrapped in his green-and-white-striped dressing gown, fuming at the indignity of being seen by his neighbours in his nightclothes. As he tugged the pillow under his head, his eyes fell to his feet and he saw to his horror a cigarette butt stuck to the bottom of his shiny maroon backless slippers. He immediately suspected Didier Lapierre, who had insisted on smoking in the queue.

The dentist kicked off his slippers in disgust. He had told the carpenter countless times that smoking restricted blood flow to the gums, but like his customers who indulged in the pernicious habit, the stained results of which he was obliged to remove, the man never listened. He removed his glasses, carefully folded them, and put them on the bedside table. But, despite the fact that it was still almost two hours before the time he usually woke, he was unable to drift off again. As he lay, looking at the ceiling and thinking about the day ahead, he remembered when, two days earlier, Guillaume Ladoucette had telephoned him, despite having just greeted him over the garden wall, and asked if the dentist could come and see him at Heart's Desire.

The man with the formidable moustache had taken a file from his desk, which struck Yves Lévèque as rather thin, and announced with a

384 | Julia Stuart

degree of fanfare that he now had a number of clients on his books, and that he had found him a most suitable match. She was a woman in her late thirties with splendid teeth and an array of other notable attractive features. She had a love for nature and was financially solvent having worked in retail ever since leaving school. 'So she won't be after your money,' the matchmaker had remarked, raising his eyes from his notes. 'Nor are there any children to support.' Yves Lévèque had immediately suggested that they went for lunch.

As he continued to look up at the ceiling, the dentist wondered what he was going to wear. He soon decided on a white shirt and a pair of jeans, which he hoped would give him a youthful, casual air. But what worried him most was not his appearance, but what he was going to say to his match. There was, after all, only so much conversation to be had about the many benefits of flossing.

Having previously cancelled his morning patients in order to prepare for his lunchtime appointment, the dentist got up and moved slowly round the house so as not to generate a sweat. He cooked himself a breakfast of two soft-boiled eggs and six plump asparagus spears, then spent the rest of the morning sitting on the bottom stair trying to conceive inspiring conversation. Defeated, he picked up a book and started to read, but was unable to take in the meaning of the words. When, eventually, it was time to get ready, he ironed his jeans and white shirt, put them on and inspected himself in the mirror on the front of his wardrobe. But instead of the young, casual reflection he was hoping for, he saw instead a forty-four-year-old bespectacled dentist with a haircut that still gave him a start whenever he caught sight of it.

Aware that there was nothing more he could do with his appearance, he dribbled some aftershave onto his long, pale instruments of torture and patted his neck in the hope that he would at least appeal to one of his match's senses. Pulling the front door behind him, he got into his car and, as he drove through the village, told himself that the date would go splendidly. Turning right at the field with the ginger Limousin cows that winked, his thoughts turned to the advice that Guillaume Ladoucette had given him. He was not to talk about himself incessantly, a male trait which women apparently found particularly irksome. He should demonstrate interest in his match not only by asking her questions, but also by listening to the answers. And at the end of the meal he was expressly forbidden to ask her to split the bill. And while the dentist couldn't understand how vegetable counsel came into the remit of the Unrivalled Silver Service, as he got up to leave, the matchmaker had put his hand on his shoulder and informed him gravely that of all vegetables, *cornichons* were the most sensitive to the cycles of the moon, and that if he really wanted to get anywhere with them he ought to sow them when it was passing in front of the constellation of Aries.

As he turned off the road to Périgueux and pulled into the restaurant car park alongside a field of green, stubby maize, Yves Lévèque remembered the disagreement they had had over his choice of venue. The matchmaker had insisted that Le Moulin de la Forge was far too modest a place for a first date. But Yves Lévèque had been adamant. Why, he argued, would he want to invest a lot of money in a woman when there was no guarantee that he would like her?

Choosing a table in the far left-hand corner, he pulled back a chair and sat down facing the diners. The room was full of labourers and artisans in their jeans and short-sleeved shirts, resting their enormous hands on the white paper tablecloths. While it couldn't be described as elegant, there was undoubtedly a degree of charm about the place, he thought. And while the choice of decor wasn't to everybody's taste, you had to admire the owner's courage. Marie Poupeau had selected a wallpaper depicting the interior of a wood which engulfed diners in a perpetual state of autumn. Whenever newcomers asked where the lavatory was, she would always reply 'up the path', while pointing to a section of the back wall which showed a leaf-strewn track disappearing into a boisterous orange horizon. It wasn't until they approached that they noticed a handle and then a door. The proprietress had advanced the motif further by hanging the mounted heads of deer and a wild boar on the walls, which had been caught by regulars.

Yves Lévèque watched as Marie Poupeau in her straight black skirt and tiny pink blouse darted around the room like an erratic breeze never forgetting at which stage of the six courses her customers were.

As he poured himself a glass of water, Yves Lévèque noticed Sandrine Fournier, the mushroom poisoner, come in and start talking to Marie Poupeau who was on her way back to the kitchen with an empty wine carafe. He remembered the sight of the woman speeding past him in the early hours with a white cotton nightdress hitched up to the knees and a pair of towelling slippers, which she had stopped to take off as they were impeding her trajectory. The assistant ambulant fishmonger had beaten him to the shower, despite his last-minute sprint. He was then inconvenienced further by the seventeen minutes and twenty-three seconds she had spent under the water.

After counting all the leaves on the wall to his left, the dentist then looked at his watch and saw that his match was eleven minutes late. He started to count the leaves on the wall to his right to distract himself from his unease. When he had finished, he surveyed the room with a short sigh. The only women there were Marie Poupeau, who was bringing in a platter of quiche, and the assistant ambulant fishmonger, who was sitting alone at the table in the adjacent corner looking directly at him. It was then that Yves Lévèque realised to his horror that Sandrine Fournier was the woman he was waiting for.

The dentist tried to avoid her eye, but within seconds she was standing at the side of his table and he could think of nothing else to do other than get up, kiss her on both cheeks and gesture to the chair opposite him. The pair spent the first few minutes talking about the man they couldn't get out of their minds, such was their desire to throttle him, who at that very moment was sitting underneath his walnut tree with a large bowl of cassoulet, silently congratulating himself on his brilliance. They praised his enterprising spirit and the colour of his walls. And when they had run out of things to say, they remembered the comfort of the cushion with the hand-embroidered radish.

Much to their relief, Marie Poupeau then arrived with a large steel bowl of communal soup which was passed from table to table. Putting it down in front of them, she complimented Sandrine Fournier on her hairstyle, telling her that she should pin it up more often as it suited her. And when she asked whether her sleeveless blue dress was new, Sandrine Fournier, who had bought it only the day before, replied firmly that it wasn't.

After they had helped themselves to a bowlful of the clear liquid steeped with tiny pasta stars, they immediately started eating. It was then that Yves Lévèque noticed that his match had a tendency to slurp.

'Guillaume Ladoucette said that you loved animals,' said Sandrine Fournier after several minutes of silence.

'I fish,' the dentist replied, presuming it was what the matchmaker had been referring to.

'I like fish too,' replied Sandrine Fournier. 'But admittedly they're dead ones.'

'So how long have you been working on the fish van now?' he asked.

'Twenty-two years. As we travel around so much I tend not to get bored. I'm allergic to shellfish, so it keeps me on my toes.'

When the second course arrived, the dentist was unable to enjoy his quiche, which was widely exalted, such was the strength of the noxious waves of perfume lapping his nostrils. Instead, he spent the time explaining the do's and don'ts of fishing, during which Sandrine Fournier noted his habit of pointing at her with his fork.

'Quite a few of our customers are fishermen, actually. I'm sure some of them try to pass off our fish as their own. Not, of course, that I'm suggesting that you would, even though you do always ask for the biggest trout we've got,' she replied evenly.

By the third course, fat slices of moist roast pork with haricot beans, Sandrine Fournier found that she was no longer hungry as her stomach had clamped shut at the overpowering stench of aftershave. The dentist noticed her picking her teeth with her thumbnail, and suddenly found himself asking her whether she was still remembering to floss.

During the fourth course, the only sound from the table in the far left-hand corner of the restaurant was the furious crunching of walnuts and lettuce as both tried to bring the misery to a swift end.

When the communal cheese board arrived, passed from the table behind them by Marie Poupeau, Sandrine Fournier watched the dentist's long, pale instruments of torture gripping the knife as he cut himself a piece of Brebis. She then imagined them tracing the length of her bare thigh and was so overcome by repulsion that Yves Lévèque felt obliged to ask her whether she was feeling all right.

When Marie Poupeau finally brought the sixth course, a basket bearing two tubs of ice cream, they simultaneously reached for the chocolate one. Yves Lévèque felt Sandrine Fournier's nails, which he was convinced still harboured traces of smoked haddock from her morning's work, lodge themselves into the back of his hand. And such was his feeling of nausea, he immediately gave up his claim to the dessert.

As soon as the mushroom poisoner had finished it, the dentist asked for the bill, insisting that he had to get back to work. When it arrived, he suggested that they went 'halvies-halves'.

Once in the car park, they turned to face each other. 'I've had such a marvellous time,' lied Yves Lévèque.

'Me too,' lied Sandrine Fournier.

'We really ought to do it again,' lied the dentist.

'Can't wait,' lied the assistant ambulant fishmonger.

As they drove off in different directions, they both vowed that it would never happen.

When Lisette Robert answered her door to find Guillaume Ladoucette clutching a bouquet of artichoke stems, she immediately assumed that he had come to discuss one of his little matters. He always arrived on her doorstep unannounced on such occasions, armed with meticulously clean root vegetables in the winter and thoroughly rinsed frilly lettuces in the summer, which he would hand to her at the door insisting that he grew far too much for a bachelor.

Guillaume Ladoucette's visits to Lisette Robert, which had been going on for years, rarely varied. Depending on the weather, the pair would sit either at her kitchen table or outside on the old faded red sofa against the back of the house underneath the vine trellis. They would chat for several hours, for, after so many years as a barber, not only was Guillaume Ladoucette as accomplished at small talk as he was at levelling sideburns, he was also highly experienced in the art of listening. Over the years Lisette Robert had learned to accept his reluctance to pass on the gossip served up by his customers and satisfied herself with the odd titbit that happened to tumble from his plate.

As they talked, he would gallantly try to resist glancing at the midwife's underwear in such tantalising proximity either on the washing line or airing in front of the fire. Then, during a pause in the conversation, he would announce, as if the thought had suddenly struck him: 'Oh, by the way, Lisette, I was meaning to ask you something . . .' and offload whatever medical anxiety was troubling him.

Guillaume Ladoucette had been suffering from a mild form of hypochondria since childhood. His mother, convinced that he had caught the disease at school, refused to allow him to return to the classroom for a month to avoid further contamination. She insisted that her husband planted a medicinal herb garden next to the *potager* to provide the boy with the necessary compounds to cure him.

Usually, after raising his medical perturbation, Guillaume Ladoucette would be satisfied with Lisette Robert's insistence that he was still a considerable distance from death. Only once had she suggested that he visited his doctor, which was the time when she secretly suspected that he was suffering from an acute form of lovesickness. For several months after his visit to the doctor, who confirmed the midwife's fears, Guillaume Ladoucette avoided coming round to see her, in the fear that she would ask him the object of his affections.

Now, Lisette Robert welcomed the matchmaker in and stood back to let him pass with his bouquet of artichokes. The midwife immediately got out a glass for his customary *pineau*. Guillaume Ladoucette, who had suffered the indignity of the shop-bought confection made in the neighbouring department of the Charente for so many years, felt it far too late to admit to his loathing of it and took the glass with a smile that he hoped concealed his secret dread. Both agreeing that it was too hot to sit outside, the matchmaker rested the vegetables on the table, pulled out a wooden chair and sat down.

'You're lucky to catch me in, actually,' said Lisette Robert, sitting down opposite him with a glass of red. 'I've only just got back.'

'Where from?' he asked, squinting as he tried to read the label on the back of a jar of purple mustard on the table made from grape must.

'I've been to see Émilie Fraisse at the château.'

Guillaume Ladoucette was so taken aback at hearing the name, he immediately forgot his sudden concern about his eyesight. Despite his frequent strolls around the village, he had seen Émilie Fraisse only once since her return. She had been making her way slowly up the Rue du Château—the one that did actually lead to the castle—carrying a basket of groceries and wearing a curious emerald taffeta dress which appeared to have been shorn off at the knees. As he watched her walk away, he noticed that something pinning up her quicksilver hair sparkled. It was an image that had pawed at him ever since, winding round his legs whenever he walked, almost tripping him up.

'I think she looks great, I don't know why everybody's going on about her having gone grey,' said Lisette Robert. 'She's done a great job of that château. Remember how filthy it was? It's spotless.' Lisette Robert then got up from the table and fetched a jar of hare terrine from the counter. 'Look! She even sells little pots of things she's made, although she wouldn't let me pay for this one.'

The matchmaker took the glass jar and looked at the handwriting on the label, which he instantly recognised, having dug up her letter only the day before. It had been easy enough to find, several feet under the flowering hellebore. When the spade tapped the metal, he reached in and pulled out the old red tin. Bringing it back to the kitchen, he covered the end of the table with an old copy of the *Sud Ouest* newspaper and sat down to clean it with a damp tea towel. After wiping off the soil, he saw again the words *Doctor L. Guyot Throat Pastilles, First-Class Pharmacist, Containing Tar, Terpene and Menthol Benzene*. It was stiff at first, but eventually the tin opened to reveal Émilie Fraisse's letter just as it was the day he had put it there twenty-six years ago.

Guillaume Ladoucette summoned up the courage to take it out, then he carefully unfolded and read it again. And when he reached the final line—'Hope to hear from you soon'—he felt the familiar ache of regret.

As he sat at the kitchen table, with more years behind him than there were in front, he thought of the day Émilie Fraisse had left Amour-sur-Belle and the hours he had spent sitting on the stone wall in front of her house having arrived too late to say goodbye. He thought of the tiny bunches of lily of the valley that he had secretly left there every May Day since to bring her good luck, according to the custom. He thought of his joy on the day when her letter arrived, and the unbearable fear of having nothing of interest to say, which had prevented him from replying.

When the matchmaker finished scolding himself for not having replied, he folded the letter and put it back in the tin. Slowly, he went upstairs, sat on his bed and pulled open the drawer of his bedside table. He placed the tin inside next to the only other thing the drawer contained—an oiled Nontron hunting knife with a boxwood handle and ancient pokerwork motifs, which hadn't been used for twenty-six years.

'It looks delicious, doesn't it?' asked Lisette Robert. 'I was just about to have some. Would you like to join me?'

'That would be lovely, thank you,' Guillaume Ladoucette replied, his mind elsewhere.

'Can't wait to try it. She said she caught the hare herself.'

And with that, Lisette Robert placed a baguette and a jar of *cornichons* on the table, followed by two plates and two knives. She then reached inside the fridge for the Cabécou and placed it near to her guest, knowing its capacity for acting like salt in the cement of his resistance against passing on tittle-tattle. Sitting back down again, she opened the terrine, smelt it, declared it delicious and offered it to her guest. His manners prevented him from refusing it. After helping himself, Guillaume Ladoucette gave the jar back to his hostess. He watched as she pressed a dark, coarse corner onto a piece of bread and put it in her mouth. 'Marvellous!' she declared. 'Do tuck in.'

The matchmaker silently loaded up a piece of bread and reluctantly brought it to his lips. He hesitated for a moment before tasting the musky meat fused with garlic, thyme, red wine and onions, all touched by the hand he had wanted to hold for almost three decades.

As they ate, Lisette Robert talked about the wretched municipal shower and how she had mistakenly left her new bottle of shampoo in the cubicle, only to find it empty when she had returned to fetch it. It had such a distinct smell of apples, she added, it wouldn't be long until she had sniffed out all the culprits. Guillaume Ladoucette was relieved that the bottle had been empty by the time he had squeezed it.

'I expect you've had some successes at work?' the midwife then asked, sliding the Cabécou closer to her visitor. It was only then that the matchmaker remembered why he had come. Suddenly he stood up, picked up the bouquet of artichokes and presented them to her with as much fanfare as he could muster. 'These,' he announced, pausing for effect, 'are for you.'

'Thanks very much, Guillaume, that's very kind of you,' the midwife replied, taking them. 'They look splendid. I thought you were having trouble with yours this year?'

'They're not mine,' said the matchmaker as he sat down, annoyed that someone had been talking about his artichokes behind his back. 'Someone else grew them. Your secret admirer, in fact.'

'Secret admirer?'

'Lisette, I have to confess that I am here in an official capacity. A gentleman came into my office and signed up for our Unrivalled Gold Service. Now, that means that he has someone very specific in mind that he would like to be introduced to. And that, my friend, is you.'

'Why would anyone want to be introduced to me?' she asked.

From the day that Lisette was born, her mother had recognised that this daughter, unlike the rest of her shrew-like children, would carry the colossal burden that beauty brought for the rest of her life. Every night she included in her prayers the supplication that her daughter's looks would fade, while her husband, who knew nothing of the problems that lay ahead, kissed the top of the baby's head so often she was left with a permanent hollow. The girl's many siblings, whose looks at kindest could be described as theatrical, had been far too young to know that their sister's allure was anything but a blessing and instantly started calling her 'ugly' out of spite.

It was easy, at first, to hide the affliction. When the baby was in the pram, her mother simply covered her face with one of her husband's white cotton handkerchiefs. But as she got older, the child would pull it off and the secret was out. On hearing of her unrivalled beauty, people came from the surrounding hamlets to marvel at the infant, until her mother could take no more. 'She's not a circus freak!' she cried.

Her prayers were not answered. And to make matters worse, her daughter's physical charms appeared to increase the older she became. The moment her mother realised, she refused to set foot in church again, not even for the funeral of her great-aunt, which she had been looking forward to for decades. She started dressing her youngest in the most gruesome of clothes, mixing her older sisters' worst fashion mistakes with her brothers' most hideous hand-me-downs. But it was no good. They simply highlighted the girl's beauty and afforded her her own unique style.

When boys—and men—started showing an interest in her from an early age, Lisette Pauillac, who grew up believing her siblings' insistence that she resembled a truffling pig, assumed they were being ironic and ignored them. But one of the younger ones was more persistent than the rest and, by the time she was eighteen, Lisette Pauillac, exhausted from refusing him, finally married Pierre-Albert Robert. While the bride assumed that the wedding would signal the end of her troubles, for neither he—nor anyone else—would now pursue her, her mother correctly suspected that it was only the beginning of them.

For more than two years, Pierre-Albert Robert couldn't believe his luck. At times when the couple were eating, the mobile butcher was unable to hear what his wife was saying so struck was he by the dark curls that tumbled to her shoulders. She only had to look up at him, her eyes shining like freshly opened horse chestnuts, for him to lose his appetite. When she got up to clear the table, he would look at the silhouette of her body through her frightful dresses and he would see more graceful curves than those of the Belle flowing outside.

It was her husband who taught her how to dress, buying her ecstasies of silk and lace in fantastical colours to wear underneath her new frocks, which delighted her as much as him. But when he pushed his lips through her waterfall of curls and whispered into her ear the extent of her beauty, she never believed him.

However, the attraction of a new possession never lasts and Pierre-Albert Robert eventually came to the realisation that his mother-in-law had been dreading ever since the day her daughter was born: Lisette Robert was just like everybody else. He first suspected that his wife was imperfect when he noticed that the fatter of the two chocolate *religieuses* she had bought for them that morning had disappeared. Up until then she had always offered him the biggest of everything. Putting it down to a woman's natural craving for *pâtisserie*, he was further surprised to note a few weeks later that she had also beaten him to the lamb cutlet in the fridge which he had been really looking forward to. Having settled into her marriage, Lisette Robert had simply resorted to her natural familial instinct of getting to everything before the others.

Not only could his wife not be trusted to share things fairly, but her piano-playing irritated him beyond measure. The musical instrument, the only one of its kind in the village, had been her family's only treasure and was given to the couple on their marriage, so relieved was her father at finally getting rid of the last of his enormous brood. But as time wore on, Pierre-Albert Robert soon realised that his wife, like a cuckoo, knew only one tune. What had seemed so charming at first, eventually became a source of utmost annoyance.

Pierre-Albert Robert rode swiftly through the reality phase of his marriage until he arrived at the inevitable staging post of disappointment. While most eventually moved on to acceptance, the mobile butcher lingered for so long that he lost all sense of direction. He would suddenly find himself in the naked arms of customers who instantly recognised the bitter taste of disillusionment on his tongue. But they didn't complain, happy in the knowledge that for the next eight minutes and forty-three seconds he had chosen them over Lisette Robert, and grateful for the *gigot* of lamb he would leave on their kitchen table.

His wife never suspected a thing, her only confusion being why her husband's takings were down. But she never thought to question it. His dalliances continued until the day that one of Pierre-Albert Robert's special customers came to the conclusion that Lisette Robert had too many blessings in life and, in her desire for a greater share, slipped a stocking into the mobile butcher's pocket.

But the woman had overestimated her rival's concern for domesticity and it was Pierre-Albert Robert who found the stocking. He recognised it instantly and when he challenged its owner he realised he was dealing with a woman who would stop at little to destroy what he had. Unable to bear the look in his wife's eyes if she ever found out, he went to the Bar Saint-Jus to decide what to do. When he could drink no more, he drove to the customer's house hoping to persuade her to keep their secret. His van was found the next morning by Gilbert Dubuisson while the postman was on his rounds. It took the firemen more than forty minutes to get it upright and pull it out of the ditch. And it took them less time than one of Pierre-Albert Robert's liaisons to conclude that his neck was broken in two places.

His death spared Lisette Robert the realisation of his shortcomings and she buried her husband with the natural pain of a widow. It didn't take long, however, before the mourners became suitors, and she was back to where she started.

The matchmaker looked at the midwife and replied, 'Lisette, you have a wealth of charms that you don't even know about, which only adds to them. That you are in demand comes as no surprise to me.'

'Who is it?' she asked, nudging the Cabécou even closer.

'I'm afraid customer confidentiality forbids me to say.'

'Well, what's he like?'

'He's a solvent bachelor with a love for the outdoors.'

'He might not like me.'

'Lisette, he likes you very much, which is why he wants me to introduce you to him.'

She licked her finger, stabbed some crumbs on her plate, and sucked them off as she considered his proposal.

'Why not?' she replied.

Shortly afterwards, Guillaume Ladoucette stood up, kissed Lisette Robert goodbye and left. On his way home, he waved to Modeste

Simon tying up her white hollyhocks, who still hadn't uttered a word since the unfortunate disappearance of Patrice Baudin, the pharmacist.

Of all the villagers to bump into he was grateful that it was she, for he had no time to chat. The reason for his haste was the sudden appearance of Stéphane Jollis's head round the door of Heart's Desire the day before. It wasn't the sight of the baker that had unsettled him, for he regularly dropped by. It was Stéphane Jollis's suggestion that they go fishing the following afternoon that had confounded him.

As their next scheduled trip had not been until two Sundays' time, and the baker never took time off on a Wednesday afternoon, Guillaume Ladoucette smelt a rat. Suspecting that the baker had something of unrivalled succulence up his sleeve, as soon as his friend had left, the matchmaker had closed Heart's Desire and hurried home, despite the fact that it was only three in the afternoon. He flung open all his cupboards, fought his way to the back of the fridge, then shot down into the cellar where he clattered around in his grandfather's Sunday clogs that nipped, trying to find something extraordinary among the preserves. He then stood in the middle of the kitchen in despair, engulfed by the thunderous ticking of the clock on the sitting-room mantelpiece that had driven one relative to suicide.

Suddenly he grabbed his keys, fled to his car and drove for two hours to Bordeaux. On his return, he set to work and didn't retire to bed until after three, by which time his snores were so monstrous they woke the birds in the woods and set off the dawn chorus several hours too early.

Arriving home from Lisette Robert's house, the matchmaker put a bowl and flask inside the picnic basket. Carefully carrying the basket to the car, he placed it on the back seat and covered it with a white tea towel. He then drove to the baker's house, turned off the ignition and immediately pulled down the sun visor to kill time. But before he had time to critically assess the elevation of the tips of his moustache, or to bore himself by looking at the contents of the glove compartment, the passenger door suddenly opened and a strong, hairy arm reached in and placed a basket made from sweet chestnut on the back seat. The arm momentarily disappeared and then returned with a red tea towel that was thrown over it. The car suddenly tilted towards the right as the baker held on to the roof with one hand and manoeuvred his substantial frame inside, followed by his head.

'Hello, Stéphane,' said Guillaume Ladoucette evenly, his suspicions raised even further by the fact that his friend hadn't kept him waiting.

'Hello, Guillaume,' replied the baker.

'Got everything?'

'Yep.'

The pair sat in silence as they drove out of the village and turned right at the field with the ginger Limousin cows that winked. As they slowed down to pass through Beauséjour, the matchmaker decided to test the water.

'Bring any lunch with you?' he asked, sliding his eyes towards his passenger.

'Just a snack,' came the reply. 'You?'

'Just a snack,' said Guillaume Ladoucette, wrinkling up his nose.

Silence slipped between them again as they continued their journey to Brantôme. Once they arrived, the two men made their way along the bank of the Dronne to the NO FISHING sign. They put down their baskets in their usual spot and loaded up their hooks. A pair of supermarket leather sandals was then slipped off, followed by a ridiculously small pair of floury shoes. After each tying their line to an ankle, they rolled up their trouser legs and plunged their feet into the river.

'That's better!' said Guillaume Ladoucette, momentarily distracted by the unsurpassable pleasure of cool water seeping between his hairy toes. But Stéphane Jollis, who was mopping his forehead on his shoulder, didn't reply.

As he watched the turquoise dragonflies hitching a ride on the dusty surface of the shifting water, the matchmaker decided to leave the suggestion of lunch as long as possible, hoping to lull the baker into a false sense of security. But three minutes later, like a torture victim unable to take the agony any more, Guillaume Ladoucette suddenly squealed, 'I feel a bit peckish!'

'So do I,' replied Stéphane Jollis.

They shuffled back on their bottoms until they reached their baskets, pieces of emerald-green weed dripping with water hanging from the fishing lines. The matchmaker pretended to hunt for his penknife as he waited to see what would come out of the rival basket first. He watched as a loaf of six-cereal bread appeared.

'Baked that this morning, did you?' asked the matchmaker, impressed by his friend's subterfuge with such a pitiful start.

'No, actually, I sold out. I had to buy it,' came the reply. 'Want some?'

'No, thanks, otherwise I won't manage this!' said Guillaume Ladoucette, reaching inside his basket and pulling out a flask of chilled sorrel soup. He slowly poured a serving into a bowl, raised a spoonful to his lips, swallowed loudly and declared, 'Marvellous! I think it's always better when you thicken it with an egg yolk. But what really makes the difference, of course, is when you've grown the sorrel yourself. Want some?'

'No, thanks,' replied Stéphane Jollis.

The matchmaker waited for the rest of his usual reply, but it never came. Just then, the baker reached a hand inside the basket made from sweet chestnut and brought out a packet of cheese still in its plastic supermarket wrapping.

'Emmenthal?' exclaimed the confounded matchmaker, wondering what ruse Stéphane Jollis was up to.

'Want some?' asked the baker.

'No, thanks,' replied Guillaume Ladoucette, unable to disguise his horror. 'They make that in Switzerland. Anyway, I can't, otherwise I won't manage this!' As he spoke he carefully lifted out of his basket a plate on which was spread a dozen open oysters, followed by a dish containing four spicy chipolatas and a bottle of Bordeaux. After pouring himself a glass of wine, he bit into a sausage, then speared an oyster with a fork and slowly brought it to his mouth. After swallowing loudly he let out a sigh of immense satisfaction.

'Bordeaux oysters, what a sublime dish!' he concluded. 'Whoever thought of that combination was a genius. But, you know, what I find is that it's never quite the same as actually going to Bordeaux to choose the oysters yourself, picking up the ingredients for the sausages and popping into a vineyard to select the best vintage to go with it. I sent you a postcard while I was there, actually. Fancy any?'

'No, thanks,' replied Stéphane Jollis, biting into his bread and cheese.

Guillaume Ladoucette waited for his customary reply, but nothing else came from the baker's basket. Unsure of how to proceed, the matchmaker put a hand into his own, pulled out a jar and put it on the grass between them.

'Fruits in kirsch,' he said meekly, looking at his friend. 'I picked the fruit from the garden two years ago and it's been fermenting ever since. Should blow our heads off. Fancy any?'

'No, thanks,' replied the baker.

Guillaume Ladoucette could take it no more.

'What's wrong, Stéphane?' he asked.

'Nothing,' replied the baker, staring ahead of him.

'Come off it. You're not your usual self. You can't turn up with some Swiss cheese and pretend there's nothing wrong, Stéphane.'

The baker carried on staring at the opposite bank.

'Is it something to do with work?' the matchmaker asked.

'No.'

Guillaume Ladoucette took a mouthful of soup as he thought.

'Fed up of not having caught anything in the last thirty-odd years?'

'Nope.'

The matchmaker put down his bowl of soup and joined the baker staring at the bank opposite.

After a while, Stéphane Jollis swallowed.

'I was wondering . . .' he started.

'Yes?'

'If I might . . . have a go.'

'Of course you can,' the matchmaker replied. 'What with?'

'The gold one.'

'What gold one?'

'The unrivalled one.'

'I'm not with you.'

'The Unrivalled Gold Service. I'd like to sign up,' said the baker, keeping his eyes firmly ahead of him.

'What a splendid idea!' exclaimed Guillaume Ladoucette, turning towards the baker. 'Who have you got in mind?'

'Lisette Robert.'

'Lisette Robert? But you don't even talk to each other. What about the business with the frogs?'

'I didn't eat them,' said Stéphane Jollis.

The matchmaker paused, looked at his friend and narrowed his eyes to accusatory slits.

'Not even sautéed with garlic and butter?'

'No! It wasn't me! I've never eaten frogs in my life. Nobody in their right mind would. Have you?'

'Of course not! Only tourists do.'

'There we are then.'

There was a pause.

'So, can I sign up?' the baker asked.

Guillaume Ladoucette studied the Dronne as he considered the ethics of introducing two Unrivalled Gold Service clients to the same woman. It certainly didn't feel right, he thought. Just as he was about to turn his friend down, his eyes fell on the baker's ridiculously small floury shoes sitting on the bank next to them, and the baguette he had broken in two in search of the soft white innards for his bait. The matchmaker then thought of the pitiful lunch the baker had brought, and his worrying descent into the dubious world of Swiss cheese.

'Stop by tomorrow, there are procedures to go through,' said the matchmaker, helping himself to another oyster. 'And expect a haircut.'

Chapter Seven

'DID YOU OR DID YOU NOT suggest going halvies-halves?' asked Guillaume Ladoucette, studying the dentist closely from behind the desk with the ink stain.

Yves Lévèque moved uncomfortably on the cushion with the hand-embroidered radish, but remained silent.

'Well?' demanded the matchmaker, folding his arms across his chest as he waited for an explanation.

'There might have been a mutual agreement that the bill was split,' muttered the dentist, looking at the red-tiled floor.

'A mutual agreement? Yves, I have three eyewitness accounts stating that you very much put it to Sandrine Fournier that she paid half.'

'I just didn't like her.' The dentist shrugged. 'She's not the sort of woman I'm looking for.'

'Not everyone falls instantly head over heels,' said the matchmaker. 'Love is like a good cassoulet, it needs time and determination. Some bits are delicious, while others might be a bit rancid and make you wince. You may even come across the odd surprise like a little green button, but you have to consider the whole dish.'

'I don't even like cassoulet.'

'How can you not like cassoulet? You've obviously never had a good one. Have you ever tried mine?'

'No, but Patrice Baudin did and look what happened to him.'

'Patrice Baudin's unfortunate conversion to vegetarianism was a result of dark forces at play. Anyway, that's beside the point. I think you should give it another go with Sandrine Fournier.'

'Can't I just have my money back?' asked the dentist.

'I'm sorry, it's not possible.'

Suddenly the dentist felt the sharp edges of loneliness shift around his stomach.

'You must have other people on your books,' insisted Yves Lévèque.

The matchmaker tugged at the brass handle of the top left-hand drawer, pulled out a file, which struck Yves Lévèque as rather slim, waggled it in front of the dentist and put it back inside again.

'Of course I have other clients, but I don't think you have made enough effort with Sandrine Fournier,' he argued.

'But I told you, there's just something about her I don't like. She gives me the creeps. What has she said about it?'

'Much the same as you. But as I explained earlier, time and determination—that's what you need. Whenever you feel hopeless, just think of a Toulouse sausage and some haricot beans.'

As the dentist got up to leave he asked: 'What were you saying about a green button?'

'Never mind.'

Just before he opened the door for his customer, the matchmaker put his hand on his shoulder and added, 'Remember: A man is only as good as his last meal.'

Once Yves Lévèque had left, Guillaume Ladoucette made his way back to his desk. Just before he sat down, he noticed a flaked almond on the floor and his thoughts turned to his first customer that morning. Stéphane Jollis had arrived with a brown paper bag containing two almond croissants fresh from the oven which, in view of the landslide on the brow of his white T-shirt, would not be his first this morning.

'I don't wish to be rude, Stéphane, but would you mind giving yourself a bit of a shake before you come in,' the matchmaker had called.

'I see what you mean,' said the baker, looking down at himself. He took a step back and gave a cursory sway of the hips.

'Think dog, rather than hula-hula,' suggested the matchmaker.

After the baker had shed his gastronomic fallout, Guillaume Ladoucette gestured to the chair with the peeling marquetry. Once the baker was comfortably installed, the pair immediately got down to business. From his bottom drawer, the matchmaker took out two plates and two paper serviettes. They then helped themselves to a plump almond croissant each, which they savoured with a cup of freshly brewed coffee from the percolator on the small table with the antique lace cloth at the back of the shop. After they had finished, they dusted their mouths and the matchmaker returned the plates to the bottom drawer. They both sat as still as basking lizards in the warmth of their contentment. Eventually, Stéphane Jollis remembered what he had come in for. After checking that his client hadn't changed his name or address overnight, the matchmaker filled in his particulars and then disappeared down into the basement. He re-emerged with a grey nylon cape in which he swiftly captured the baker.

'But I don't want my hair cut!' protested Stéphane Jollis.

'I'm not introducing any client of mine who has signed up for the

Unrivalled Gold Service looking as though an otter has constructed a dam on his head. Really, Stéphane.'

Within seconds, Guillaume Ladoucette's fingers were fluttering and long black tendrils coated in flour were dropping to the floor.

'Right,' said the matchmaker, after sweeping them up and walking his friend to the door. 'I'll make the necessary arrangements and keep you posted.'

The baker left, enjoying the sensation of the perpetual breeze on his newly shorn head as he walked down the road, and bracing himself for the outrage from the queue of customers waiting outside his shop door.

Guillaume Ladoucette dropped the flaked almond into the bin, sat down on the swivel chair and stared blankly in front of him. Putting his elbows on the desk, he rested his chin on the palms of his hands and wondered what on earth would become of him. Heart's Desire had been open for several weeks now and what did he have to show for it? A parsimonious dentist and an ambulant fishmonger with an allergy to shellfish who couldn't stand the sight of one another. Then there was the business with Lisette Robert. While the midwife deserved a chance at love just like everyone else, was it really fair to encourage two Unrivalled Gold Service customers to take up arms in the battle for her affections, and did either of them stand a chance anyway?

The matchmaker reflected on the handful of clients who had come in the previous week, and the one who concerned him the most, Gilbert Dubuisson. The postman had needed little persuasion to forget about the Unrivalled Bronze Service and proceed to the considerably more expensive Unrivalled Silver Service. But what woman would ever want a man with despicable urinary habits? Ever since Heart's Desire opened, the man had been driving him into an almost daily state of irritation by his frequent visits from his house opposite 'to see how things are going'. The matchmaker was certain that Gilbert Dubuisson's presence was putting off potential customers.

Maybe my Brilliant Idea wasn't so brilliant after all and I've made an awful mistake, thought Guillaume Ladoucette, staring in front of him. What happens if I don't find my customers anyone to love? I'll get driven out of the village. Who will look after my *potager*?

He continued to stare ahead of him, seeing nothing. Who am I to give advice on matters of the heart, anyway? he wondered, remembering the letter he had dug up the day before, to which he had never replied. Guillaume Ladoucette sighed and was just about to get up to make himself another cup of coffee, when something on his left supermarket leather sandal caught his eye. He picked it up and held it under his nose. Just as he was inspecting with increasing fury what was a constellation of peck marks, the door opened. It was Émilie Fraisse.

Guillaume Ladoucette looked at her for several minutes, his open wound of mortification preventing him from moving. Eventually, he bent down, dropped his supermarket leather sandal on the floor and crawled his toes back inside. He stood up and must have made his way to the door, but when he tried to replay the moment in bed that night he couldn't remember how. The next thing he remembered was holding the door open in silence. He must have just stood there because Émilie Fraisse asked, 'Can I come in?'

'Yes, yes, of course, come in, come in,' he replied and watched as she walked past him, stood in the middle of Heart's Desire and turned to face him. Suddenly remembering his manners, the matchmaker approached her and kissed her on both cheeks. As he did so, he breathed in the scent of her skin which, after twenty-six years, was instantly familiar.

After showing the châtelaine to the chair with the peeling marquetry, and offering her coffee, he went to the small table at the back of the shop to make it. But as he stood in front of the percolator with his back to her, he found that he had forgotten what to do. And when he finally remembered, and had been standing waiting for the water to pass through the filter for several minutes, he suddenly realised that he had unplugged the percolator at the wall, a habit learned from his mother in case of an electrical storm. As he waited again, he imagined Émilie Fraisse sitting on the cushion with the hand-embroidered radish and hating the pink walls, and he wished that he had repainted them.

Finally, he brought the cups over and put them down on the desk with the ink stain, which he quickly covered with the telephone. He then sat down on his swivel chair and looked again at Émilie Fraisse, who looked back at him with eyes the colour of fresh sage, and smiled.

'It's lovely to see you,' he said, smiling back.

'It's lovely to see you, too, Guillaume,' she replied.

'You're just as I remembered.'

'I've gone grey,' she said, embarrassed, her hand instinctively reaching for the back of her head.

'It suits you very well.'

'Thanks.'

The pair held each other's gaze.

'Lisette Robert said you've stopped barbering and set yourself up as a matchmaker.'

'That's right. And you've bought the château, I hear.'

'Yes, yes, I have.'

'How's that going?'

'I adore it.'

Silence bloomed again.

'Actually, I was wondering whether you might be able to help me,' Émilie Fraisse said.

'Of course. I'm sure you need all the help you can get sorting that place out. What is it you'd like me to do?'

'Oh, it's nothing to do with the château. I was wondering whether you could possibly help me to find love?'

Half an hour later, in an antique saffron dress that appeared to have been shorn off at the knees, and with a white dahlia tucked into the back of her hair, which was pinned up with something that sparkled, Émilie Fraisse left Heart's Desire having signed up for the Unrivalled Silver Service.

After crunching her way back over the pigeon droppings covering the drawbridge, the châtelaine pushed open the wooden front door bleached fossil-grey by the sun. She removed her ridiculous seventeenth-century shoes and padded past the llama skeleton along a corridor with a patch of florid yellow mould thought by scientists to be long extinct. In the cool of the vaulted kitchen, she surveyed the splendid collection of copper pots, pans and utensils now sitting on, or hanging from, freshly painted pale blue shelves on three sides of the room. Looking forward to an agreeable afternoon cleaning the few pieces still left to be done, Émilie Fraisse took down the largest brioche mould and settled herself on the seat with wild boars carved on its feet. In and out of the curves she rubbed until she could see her head distorted to hideous proportions. Returning the mould to its place on the shelf, she then took down the diamond-shaped turbot pan. Just as she was about to start on the flat lid, the bell rang. She padded back down the corridor in her bare feet and opened the door. There, squinting in the sun, was a man with a clip-board in one hand and a soft leather briefcase in the other.

'Forgive me for disturbing you, Madame. My name is Jean-François Lafforest and I work for the council,' the man said.

'Lovely to see you,' said Émilie Fraisse. 'You'd like a tour, I presume?'

'I'm afraid I'm here in an official capacity, Madame.'

'Oh, I see. Well, come in, come in. Excuse the state of my hands, I've been cleaning the copper. Follow me to the kitchen so I can wash them and I'll be all yours.'

The châtelaine led Jean-François Lafforest along the corridor with its patches of rare yellow mould to the vaulted kitchen, where he stood in his unfortunate trousers which didn't fit, his hands on his hips as he marvelled at the glowing pots and pans.

'I must congratulate you on your efforts, Madame, it really is a beautiful collection. I visited the château many years ago and one wouldn't even have known they were made of copper.'

'Please, sit down,' she said, offering him the ancient wooden seat which slid open to hide the salt from the tax collector. While she was washing her hands, the man from the council apologised again for disturbing her.

'Not at all. It's nice to have some company,' said Émilie Fraisse. 'Very few people stop here as they're too horrified by the scandalous ramparts. Now, what can I get you to drink? A glass of rosé, perhaps?'

'Water would be fine,' replied Jean-François Lafforest.

After handing him a glass, Émilie Fraisse sat down and asked, 'Now, what can I help you with?'

The man from the council looked at the floor and then at the châtelaine. 'As you will know, Madame, we have been obliged to install a municipal shower in the Place du Marché because there is hardly any water in the reservoir and it hasn't rained for so long. It has been brought to my attention that according to the ledger outside the cubicle that villagers are obliged to fill in, so far you have failed to use it. It is not for me to pry into people's washing habits, but as you will be aware from the letter sent to all the inhabitants of Amour-sur-Belle, the taking of baths is forbidden.' He paused. 'It embarrasses me to say this, Madame, but I will have to inspect your bath.'

For several seconds Émilie Fraisse considered the request and then said, 'Of course. Of course. Oh dear me, come this way, you might not like what you see.'

Jean-François Lafforest followed the châtelaine up the stone spiral staircase, her bare feet silent on the steps with the lamentable repairs. They passed along a corridor hung with faded tapestries until they reached a door with an iron handle which she turned then stood to one side. The man from the council walked up to the bath, peered inside and started with such violence that he dropped his soft leather briefcase.

'I didn't know where else to put it,' Émilie Fraisse explained. 'I found it in the garden pond while I was clearing it out. I couldn't resist it. It was a bit of a job getting it out. The pond was filthy, as you would imagine, so I thought if I kept it in some clean water for a while it would lose its brackishness.'

When the man from the council had recovered from his surprise, he congratulated the châtelaine on her beautiful eel and asked her how she was planning to cook it. Émilie Fraisse replied that she hadn't yet made up her mind, though she tended to prefer them stewed rather than roasted. As they walked back down the stone spiral staircase, she added: 'You must be wondering how I keep clean. I use the garden hose outside.'

Once back in the vaulted kitchen, Jean-François Lafforest sat down immediately. His hateful task over, he suddenly felt a fog of fatigue swirl up around him and snuff out his senses.

'It's almost five, you must have finished for the day. I expect you're ready for an apéritif?' asked Émilie Fraisse.

Jean-François Lafforest happily accepted. And it wasn't long before he felt the first fern of happiness unfurl inside him while in Amour-sur-Belle. His senses restored, he looked at the woman in a curious saffron antique dress, whose hair was pinned up with something which sparkled, and asked whether it was possible to have a tour after all.

The châtelaine happily agreed and took her guest into the dining room where she proudly showed him the original *pisé* floor. He marvelled at the smooth stones in various shades of white and brown, the size and shape of potatoes, which were intricately laid out in rose-window patterns. When Jean-François Lafforest asked whether she knew anything of its history, Émilie Fraisse found herself telling him a story of how, during the sixteenth century, one of the château owners had fallen in love with a young villager, having watched her bathing in the Belle from the magnificent ramparts. In an effort to win her heart, he sent her love letters in the form of paper boats which he launched from the moat. The clandestine correspondence continued for several months until his wife discovered what he was up to and ordered that the river be diverted around Amour-sur-Belle. Not only was his hope of love thwarted, but the villagers had nowhere to bathe or wash their dishes and an abominable disease broke out. Many died a frightful death, including the young girl. The stones had been collected from the bottom of the river where the young woman used to bathe, and made into a floor so that he could walk over them in bare feet every day in order to be close to her.

When she had finished the story, Jean-François Lafforest smiled at his hostess, enchanted.

As they entered one of the bedrooms with its original ceiling made of sweet chestnut, the man from the council questioned the provenance of a little footstool the like of which could only be found in the most dispiriting of junk shops. Émilie Fraisse suddenly found herself telling him that it was stuffed with the hair of a famous horse, whose master had one day discovered its remarkable ability to predict the weather. He took the animal from fair to fair and stood it inside a little tent where people queued to witness its forecasts. Rain was signalled by a nod of its head, winds by a swoosh of its tail, hail by a pawing of its left hoof and sun by a bearing of its colossal yellow teeth. The horse, which was always accurate, soon earned the man a fortune. One week, a terrible storm was on its way, the arrival of which the horse was all too aware. However, its master misinterpreted its whinnying, during which it bared substantially more of its colossal yellow teeth than usual, as a month of uninterrupted sunshine. Instead of quickly harvesting their crops, the farmers left them to enjoy the forthcoming good weather. But their corn and wheat were ruined. They immediately blamed the horse, even though it had been right all along. Having nothing left to eat, one night the farmers captured the animal and made it into sausages. Its master was so upset he decided to keep some of its hair as a memento.

'It's said that whenever there's a storm on its way the room suddenly fills up with the smell of damp horse,' added Émilie Fraisse, closing the door behind them. Jean-François Lafforest, who had never heard that story either, was enraptured.

When Émilie Fraisse had finished peddling her fiddlesticks, she picked up a basket and the pair left the cool of the château for the garden. They walked alongside the warm stone wall on top of which bearded irises grew, until they reached a clump of knitted brambles and determined grasses. She pulled them apart revealing the rows of heirloom vegetables. 'You'll be staying for supper, I hope?' she said, picking some of the long-forgotten ancient varieties, including black tomatoes, square-podded peas and violet sweet potato.

When they returned to the vaulted kitchen, Émilie Fraisse refilled their glasses. 'Now, where's the pig's bladder?' she asked out loud as she looked inside the fridge. Eventually it was found, cleaned and stuffed with a plump duck which had been swiftly and expertly plucked. She lowered it into one of the copper pans on the stove containing veal stock to cook until it was tender. The man from the council sat watching her from the ancient seat which slid open to hide the salt from the tax collector, another fern of happiness uncurling inside him.

'Let's eat in the dining room,' said the châtelaine. 'Every guest is a special occasion.' At her suggestion, he went to open the lattice windows to let the velvety evening in. While he struggled with the stiff handles, she descended the death-cold steps of the dungeon to fetch a bottle of red wine which had been hidden from the Nazis. They brought through their plates and sat opposite each other in the middle of the long oak table which had been stolen from a monastery.

As the sun slithered away, and they finished their first bottle, they were seduced by the confidence of strangers. It wasn't long before Jean-François Lafforest told his hostess about the first time he had come to Amour-sur-Belle to carry out a headcount when the village was trying to pass itself off as a town. He told of the dastardly tricks the residents had played on him, and the subsequent trouble he had got into at work. He told of the merciless ribbing he had received at the hands of his colleagues, who had all taken to wearing wigs and false beards in the office. He told of the nervous breakdown he had suffered and how he had been determined to return to work, because without it, what was he? He told of how he was saving for a house with a garden where he could erect a greenhouse like the English had, so that he could cultivate orchids in impossible colours because he wanted something beautiful to look after. And when Émilie Fraisse asked was his wife not beautiful? he replied that he had never married. He added hastily that he was perfectly happy on his own and that he wasn't looking for anyone in his life.

Émilie Fraisse then told of how she had recently returned from Bordeaux to the village where she had grown up and of how she had bought the château with no intention of restoring it, and that she liked the scandalous ramparts with their missing sections of crenellations just as they were. She then told him how she could well believe the dastardly tricks that the villagers had played on him, and that, knowing them as well as she did, he had got off lightly.

The bats had taken up their circular swooping over the fifteenth-century chapel by the time that Jean-François Lafforest asked Émilie Fraisse whether she had ever known love. She told him she had once been married, and that although her former husband hadn't been a bad man, they had failed to make each other happy.

'Was that the only time?' the man from the council asked.

Émilie Fraisse watched the night pouring in through the open lattice windows. 'There was another time, many years ago,' she replied.

'Would you like to have someone in your life now?' he asked.

'Oh, yes,' she said, turning to him. 'Without love we are just shadows.'

At the end of the evening, Jean-François Lafforest thanked his hostess for a wonderful dinner, and Émilie Fraisse thanked him for being a wonderful guest. They said goodbye at the front door which glowed like mercury in the moonlight. When, eventually, he arrived home and opened his soft leather briefcase, the man from the council found inside a jar of black radish jam tied with a piece of antique lace.

Guillaume Ladoucette was already in bed with just a sheet over him, trying to remember every word that he and Émilie Fraisse had spoken. He thought of how captivating she had looked with her sage-green eyes, curious dress, and hair pinned up with something which sparkled. He thought of how ridiculous he must have seemed peering at his supermarket leather sandals when she walked in, and he wished that he had been wearing a different shirt. He thought what a fool he had been for taking her on as a customer and not telling her there and then of his years of undiminished love.

In the early hours, when sleep still hadn't sniffed at him, he finally came to the conclusion that there was nothing he could have done except agree to take her on. The only question that remained was who would he match her with? Two hours, fourteen minutes and thirty-three seconds later, just as he heard the first hurried scuff of slippers as a villager headed for the municipal shower, the perfect solution came to him.

Yves Lévêque stood in his garden contemplating the unspeakable state of his *cornichons*. As he studied the deformed green fruit, no bigger than peanuts, he wondered whether his neighbour had actually been right about something. Maybe he should have sown them when the moon was passing in front of the constellation of Aries after all. Certainly, they were a catastrophe, he thought, moving aside the leaves in the hope of finding something worth pickling. Unable to bear the humiliation any longer, particularly as Guillaume Ladoucette's upstairs shutters opened onto an uninterrupted view of his garden, he wrapped his long, pale instruments of torture round the base of the stems, tugged them out of the ground and threw them onto the compost heap.

Maybe the matchmaker was right about Sandrine Fournier, the mushroom poisoner, as well, he thought, wandering back inside and slumping onto his brown leather sofa, inherited from a late uncle. She hadn't looked that bad in her sleeveless blue dress with her hair up, he reasoned. And if a relationship did develop, there was always the tantalising prospect of getting a discount on his purchases from her fish van. But with the alacrity of a cut poppy shedding its petals, the dentist abandoned his delusions. The woman was an abomination, he concluded. Her new sleeveless dress had cut into her over-sunned flesh, sending it cascading over the top like burnt brioche. Her hair should have been left down for its ability to camouflage what should never have been on public display. And as for a discount on his purchases at her van, he had always managed to confuse her sufficiently with his orders so that she gave him too much change anyway.

The dentist looked at his watch. There was still half an hour before he would have to leave the house to meet her. Maybe he would just not turn up, he thought, suddenly filled with the fire generated by a good idea. Yes, he would make up an excuse that would silence both her and the matchmaker. He would say that a customer had appeared at his door tormented by toothache and that he had no option but to take him in and tend to him. And such a story would also serve as a warning to Sandrine Fournier about the horrendous consequences of not flossing, he thought, sunning himself in the warmth of his ingenuity.

Two days later, Émilie Fraisse sat on the curiously unworn steps of the church in Amour-sur-Belle fiddling with a lizard baked like a biscuit in the sun that she had picked up from the ground. The châtelaine had no idea who she was waiting for. She had received a phone call from Guillaume Ladoucette, who sounded in a particularly gleeful mood, telling her that he had found her the most perfect match. The gentleman was an outstanding communicator, with a particular interest in trees, who had suggested that they go to the *floralies* at Saint-Jean-de-Côle.

Émilie Fraisse happily accepted the suggestion, immediately remembering the village as a rival to Brantôme on account of its beauty. As soon as she put down the phone, she raced up the stone spiral staircase, her bare feet slapping on the lamentable repairs. Opening her wardrobe, she scanned the row of antique dresses she had found in the leather chest studded with brass, which now hung from hangers like captured butterflies, and suddenly came across a cream organza gown that she had never worn. When she tried it on, to her surprise it fitted. She hurried back downstairs, found the kitchen scissors and hacked off the bottom third, as well as the arms that had been ravaged by moths. She then ran upstairs again, looked into the mirror dappled with age, put up her hair and secured it with a jewelled pin from the tortoiseshell box on the dressing table. Before leaving, she rubbed the llama's tailbone for good luck and crunched her way across the drawbridge.

As she waited on the church steps, the châtelaine noticed Madame Ladoucette approaching on the other side of the street, whom she had not seen since her return. But the old woman failed to hear her greeting and Émilie Fraisse watched her slow crane-legged procession, wondering what the red splat marks were on the back of her green dress, and why she was being followed by a shuffling crowd of obese pigeons.

Soon after Madame Ladoucette came Fabrice Ribou, sporting an unfathomable haircut, and, for a moment, Émilie Fraisse thought that it was him she was waiting for. But the bar owner simply returned her greeting. She then spotted Denise Vigier coming from the other direction wearing a pink dressing gown and matching slippers, a white towel slung over one shoulder. Several minutes later, Didier Lapierre drove up and parked underneath one of the lime trees. Émilie Fraisse couldn't help but notice that his haircut was equally as baffling as that of the bar owner, and wondered whether Guillaume Ladoucette had been forced to give up his job because he had lost his barber's eye.

Bored of tracing designs in the ground with the stiffened lizard, Émilie Fraisse got to her feet to look round the twelfth-century church. She pushed against the studded wizened door and immediately inhaled incense laced with mould spores. Descending the stone steps into the crypt, she was surprised to see that the bones of priests who had once served in the church, which had been desecrated during the Revolution, were still scattered on the floor. Back upstairs, where all traces of beauty had been plundered during the same raids, she contented herself with admiring the flourishing emerald wall fungus.

Startled by the viciousness of the sun when she re-emerged, the châtelaine didn't immediately recognise the person who was standing with his back to her on the steps. It was not until he turned round that she saw that it was Gilbert Dubuisson, the postman. Seizing the chance to ask him about a package she was expecting, she approached him. It was then that she noticed his unusually smart trousers and suddenly realised that the man she had been waiting for was him. The postman, who looked momentarily taken aback, then kissed her on both cheeks. They then worked out that during the time that she had lived away from Amour-sur-Belle, they had seen each other at three weddings, one cancelled funeral and two annual fêtes in honour of the village patron saint, whose name no one could remember.

'Don't worry, I'll fill you in on what's been going on,' said Gilbert Dubuisson, walking towards his car underneath one of the lime trees and opening the passenger door.

'Do you remember the mobile butcher?' asked the postman, as he drove out of the village.

'Didn't he die in a car accident?' asked Émilie Fraisse.

'Yes, he did, poor soul. It was me who found his car in the ditch at the side of the road. Shocking business. Anyway, watch out for his replacement. They took his licence away for two months because he was putting *trompettes-de-la-mort* mushrooms in his pâté and trying to pass them off as truffles.'

As they passed along the flat-bottomed valley below Brantôme, the postman asked, 'Remember where we were standing on the church steps?'

'Yes,' said Émilie Fraisse.

'They found Patrice Baudin's spectacles in the guttering above,' continued Gilbert Dubuisson. 'Remember him, the pharmacist? He became a vegetarian after eating Guillaume Ladoucette's cassoulet. Anyway, Patrice Baudin blew away during the mini-tornado and Modeste Simon hasn't spoken since. Fancied him rotten.'

They reached Saint-Jean-de-Côle and, surprisingly, found a parking space on the side of the road. They walked up the narrow lane that led to the château, across which were strung garlands of tangerine and red paper flowers made by locals. When they stopped at the table to pay, Émilie Fraisse got out her purse, but Gilbert Dubuisson politely told her to put it away. After the back of their hands were stamped with a dark blue tulip, they continued up the narrow lane and stopped to look at the first flower stall. They gazed at the battalion of geraniums and pelargoniums in astonishing colours, and the postman admitted to taking considerable pride in his window boxes. He then pointed out a variety with burgundy stained leaves and yellow edges, and said that he found them most pleasing. Émilie Fraisse, who said she also found them charming, then pointed to some pelargoniums with star-shaped leaves, which Gilbert Dubuisson correctly identified as *Distinction*. They then both agreed that you should never buy anything from the first stall you come across. Then they considered the prospect of the stallholder selling out and within moments there were two bags of plants behind the counter already paid for to be picked up on their way out.

Bonded by the warmth of an early purchase, they turned right at the end of the narrow lane. Émilie Fraisse headed towards the stall selling laurels, as Guillaume Ladoucette had told her that her match had a particular liking for trees, but when she mentioned this to the postman, he was at an utter loss as to what he could have been meaning.

They strolled on into the open market hall with its wooden pillars and tiled roof, but quickly came out agreeing that the striped petunias were too vulgar. As they approached the main street, the postman pointed towards the roofs of the pastel-coloured houses and asked whether they were the ones referred to as 'the finest in the Périgord Vert'. And when the châtelaine replied that she thought they had been called 'the finest in France', the postman said, 'I'm sure you're right.'

Wandering along the stalls, they came across a collection of tiny-flowered geraniums beneath a vast umbrella, with a small, handwritten sign saying: *Touch and Smell!*

Émilie Fraisse stretched out a hand, rubbed one of the leaves and brought her fingers to her nose. 'It smells of walnuts!' she exclaimed.

The postman then rubbed the leaves of another plant. 'This one smells of eucalyptus!' he said.

Émilie Fraisse rubbed the leaves of a third plant. 'And this smells of carrots! How funny!' she remarked.

As they crossed the Gothic hump-back bridge over the River Côle, with its bulbous cobbles, the postman took the châtelaine's arm lest she tripped. But there was nothing to see since the succulents failed to interest either of them, and they made their way back over the bridge.

'Shall we have something to drink?' suggested the postman.

'What a good idea,' replied the châtelaine, and they sat down at the bar opposite the rose-seller with her butterscotch, vanilla, raspberry ripple, marmalade and cassis blooms.

Gilbert Dubuisson returned with a bottle of red Saint-Jean-de-Côle, and filled their glasses.

Émilie Fraisse asked Gilbert Dubuisson about his job, and he told her how much pleasure it gave him. While it meant having to get up early, it left him the rest of the day to please himself. His vines took up a fair bit of his time, he explained, and then, of course, he felt morally obliged to pop in to see Guillaume Ladoucette in his shop opposite as he seemed so lonely.

'He's lonely?' Émilie Fraisse asked.

'Well, sometimes I look in the window and he's staring into space and I know he's just willing me to come in for a chat.'

'And is he lonely in his personal life?' she asked.

'He's had his share of interest, but he just hasn't met the right one, which is a bit ironic considering he's set himself up as a matchmaker.'

'And what about you, Gilbert? Have you ever found love?'

'Once,' he said. 'But it was a long time ago.'

The postman refilled their glasses and, for the first time ever, found himself recounting the true story of Sandrine Fournier, the mushroom poisoner. He had loved her throughout school, he explained, and had thought she was keeping herself for him. It was when she took him to the old hunters' shack one afternoon some years later that he discovered that she hadn't kept herself for him at all. But he was so grateful he didn't care. She taught him things that he didn't even know existed.

But Gilbert Dubuisson feared Sandrine Fournier's carnal appetite was too much for one man to satisfy and he let her go, afraid she would venture elsewhere. He managed to capture the attention of Fabrice Ribou's younger sister, Yvette, but such was Sandrine's jealousy that when Yvette Ribou's father next begged her to tell him the best place in the woods to find ceps, she told him that it was by the hunters' shack, for she knew that he would find his daughter there with Gilbert Dubuisson in a state of undress and put a stop to the relationship. But when the young couple heard him coming, they hid underneath the blanket which had covered generations of illicit lovers.

As it was, Monsieur Ribou was far too taken with what he thought were fungal delights to bother looking inside the hunters' shack. After a while, Gilbert Dubuisson looked out of the broken window to see who was outside, and saw Yvette Ribou's father picking the mushrooms that he recognised as being poisonous. Fearful of being discovered with the man's daughter, he pulled the blanket back over his head. When the postman heard that Monsieur Ribou had been taken ill, it was he who rushed the offending omelette to the hospital. But it was too late.

Fabrice Ribou blamed Sandrine Fournier for his father's death and banned her from his bar. Despite his pleas, the assistant ambulant fishmonger never took Gilbert Dubuisson back. Nor, indeed, would she serve him from the fish van again whenever he came for his weekly prawns, claiming that she had developed an allergy to shellfish.

'Oh, Gilbert, I am sorry,' said Émilie Fraisse when he had finished.

'And now, from what I understand, she's seeing the dentist.' The postman carried on looking ahead of him, then patted the châtelaine's arm. 'But that's all in the past. I must say, I've had a marvellous time.'

'So have I,' agreed Émilie Fraisse.

When they had finished the bottle, they both agreed that it was time to go. 'I'll just be a minute,' said the postman, getting up. When he returned, he was carrying a bag, which he presented to Émilie Fraisse.

She looked inside and, recognising the plant, rubbed the leaves and brought her fingers to her nose, breathing in the aroma of carrot.

Chapter Eight

IT WAS MADAME LADOUCETTE who first noticed that there was no hot water in the municipal shower. She came across the contraption during one of her daily meanders, the arrival of which her son had never bothered to explain because of her sudden and obstinate preference for washing in a cauldron. Her curiosity tweaked, she tried the door then

stepped inside and invited her feathered shadow to join her. Once satisfied that everyone was aboard, Madame Ladoucette looked around her
and decided to turn what appeared to be a handle. Much to her hilarity,
she suddenly found herself drenched in water. Her companions, however, were not so amused. Such was the violence of the commotion, the
door burst open and the expelled participants left the scene.

When the old woman was subsequently spotted wandering around
the village, her sopping blue dress clinging to her crane's legs and still-
commanding bosom, a crew of soggy birds trailing in her wake, several
people popped their heads round the door of Heart's Desire and said,
'Your mother's been in the Belle again.'

When Guillaume Ladoucette found her behind the nectarine display
at the grocer's, he took her home to get dry. After pouring out the water
from her black shoes, he questioned again his decision to move her into
the small house in the village centre, in the hope that it would provide
fewer opportunities for mischief. But whenever he dared to mention
the retirement home in Brantôme, with its cheery staff and benches in
the sun, she regained all lucidity and squawked, 'Not on your nelly.'

Once dry and on the streets again, everyone naturally assumed that
Madame Ladoucette's repeated comments about the temperature of the
water referred to that of the river. It was not until several hours later,
when Lisette Robert turned on the shower, that news of the absence of
hot water spread.

As soon as Guillaume Ladoucette had made sure that his mother was
safe and dry, he hurried back to Heart's Desire as fast as a pair of supermarket leather sandals would permit, anxious to hear how Émilie
Fraisse and Gilbert Dubuisson had fared. Once back at work, the
matchmaker found that he was unable to sit still on the swivel chair
and set about cleaning the place. As he dusted his framed certificate
from the Périgord Academy of Master Barbers, he imagined Gilbert
Dubuisson's unremitting conversation that would have surely driven
Émilie Fraisse to distraction. And then he thought of the man's obsession with his window boxes, which would surely have bored her as
rigid as a week-old corpse. He then plumped up the cushion with the
hand-embroidered radish, and thought of the man's despicable habit of
urinating behind the nearest tree when caught short on his rounds, and
was convinced that his bladder would have failed him at some stage.
Once the floor was swept, he made himself a cup of coffee, sat down at
his desk and picked up the phone to take down the messages left while
he was out. But there were none.

In an effort to cheer himself up, Guillaume Ladoucette slowly pulled open the narrow drawer above his stomach. Peering down, he admired the selection of pens all neatly lined up in their own little compartment, as well as his fine collection of multicoloured rubber bands split into two according to colour—red and green on the right, and yellow and blue on the left. Just as he was about to move the stapler to another compartment the door opened. It was Émilie Fraisse.

Sunset-pink, he closed the drawers, got up to greet the châtelaine and then ushered her towards the chair with the peeling marquetry. As he was pouring her a cup of coffee, his embarrassment left him as he began to smell the delicious news upon which he was about to feast.

'So!' he said, passing her the cup and getting himself comfortable on the swivel chair. 'How did it go? Gilbert Dubuisson is such a charming fellow, I expect you had a marvellous time.'

'We did indeed,' replied Émilie Fraisse, smiling.

'You did?' asked the matchmaker, horrified.

'Yes, I can't thank you enough. He was exactly as you described him—really chatty—and we caught up on old times and he told me all about what's been going on.'

'Not too talkative?'

'No! Between you and me, my husband and I didn't talk very much, so it's refreshing to be with someone who has something to say.'

'I expect he told you at considerable length about his window boxes?' Guillaume Ladoucette enquired.

'Oh, yes!' Émilie Fraisse then turned and pointed to the postman's house. 'See those geraniums with the burgundy ring on their leaves and the yellow tips? We bought them together at Saint-Jean-de-Côle.'

Panic rising, the matchmaker slowly followed the sage-green gaze.

'He didn't happen to dash off suddenly at any time, did he?' he asked. 'Because if he did I can explain precisely what he was doing.'

The châtelaine stopped for a moment to think. 'Yes, now that you come to mention it he did,' she said. 'We were sitting having a drink—'

'There's just no hope for the man—' started Guillaume Ladoucette.

'—and he nipped off and came back with a geranium with leaves that smelt of carrots because it had made me laugh. Wasn't that lovely!'

'Well, I expect it's too early to say whether you'll be seeing each other again,' said the matchmaker, reaching into his top left-hand drawer for his file of customers. 'Maybe we should set you up with someone else in the meantime?'

'Oh, we've already arranged something. Gilbert's coming round to the château for dinner. He wants to see my heirloom vegetables.'

'I didn't know you grew heirloom vegetables,' whispered Guillaume

Ladoucette from underneath the stone that had rolled onto him and crushed him.

'Oh, yes, I've got quite a collection. Gilbert's particularly interested in the white carrots. Anyway, I'd better go. I wouldn't want to take up any more of your time. I just wanted you to know that everything went splendidly, and to thank you.'

Émilie Fraisse, who appeared to be wearing an antique gown of deep nutmeg shorn off at the knees, with a pale pink rose in the back of her hair, where something sparkled, got up to leave.

'What a lovely rose,' was all that Guillaume Ladoucette could think of to say to delay her.

'Thank you. Gilbert left it for me on the drawbridge this morning, with a little note explaining that it was from his garden. Do smell it. I've never known anything like it.'

Guillaume Ladoucette slowly got up and approached Émilie Fraisse. He stood behind her and leaned in on the pretext of smelling the rose, hoping instead to draw in the exotic scent of her bare neck. But the flower's spicy aroma was too overpowering. And it was as she walked out that he remembered the flower's name, and his horror was complete: Bride's Bouquet.

After closing the door, the matchmaker returned to the swivel chair. He sat with his chin in his hands, staring out onto the street, but whenever he tried to look elsewhere, his eyes kept returning to the six new geraniums in the window boxes opposite. Reaching down to his briefcase, he took out a bag of mini-*saucissons* and tore it open. By the time they were finished he hadn't tasted one.

Unable to bear the torturous sight of the postman's geraniums any longer, the matchmaker decided that his day's work was over, despite the fact that it was not yet even lunchtime. Not bothering to lock the shop, he walked home, oblivious to the full force of the sun's arsenal.

Jean-François Lafforest arrived at Amour-sur-Belle that afternoon. For the first time he had taken pleasure in the journey, remembering the châtelaine who had slipped a jar of black radish jam into his briefcase.

He was spotted as soon as he parked and, within moments, an uppity crowd had formed. It followed him to the Place du Marché, and as he walked, he drew his soft leather briefcase closer. Once at the shower cubicle, he circled it several times inspecting it from every angle. He then went inside and turned on the shower, putting his hand in the spray. When he came out and asked to speak to the villager who had discovered the problem, Lisette Robert was called for.

But the midwife was attending a delivery and it was another two hours before she was seen parking outside her house and received her immediate summons. By the time she arrived, Fabrice Ribou had brought over some of his bar chairs, arranged them in a grandstand formation around the cubicle, and was selling drinks to the crowd. Lisette Robert, whose figure, both the men and women noticed, curved more gracefully than the Belle, was then asked to explain to the man from the council what had happened. She recounted the fact that the water had been cold from the moment she had turned it on.

'So, what's wrong with the shower?' asked Yves Lévèque.

'There appears to be no hot water,' said the man from the council.

'We know that, that's why we called you out,' he replied.

'There's nothing I can do, I'll have to get someone onto it.'

'Why did you bother coming out if there's nothing you can do?' asked Denise Vigier.

'I had to first check that there was no hot water,' replied Jean-François Lafforest, fiddling with one of the buckles on his briefcase.

'So what are you going to do about it?' asked Didier Lapierre.

'I'm going to get someone to sort it out,' said Jean-François Lafforest. 'You'll just have to put up with it for the moment, I'm afraid.'

'Put up with it?' exclaimed the dentist. 'We're not going to endure cold showers while you try to sort it out. It could take months at the rate you lot move. We'll have to go back to having baths.'

'I'm sorry. That's not an option. The fine will still stand,' said the man from the council uneasily.

'The fine will still stand?' repeated Yves Lévèque, dumbfounded. But by then the man from the council with the trousers which didn't quite fit had already backed away and made for his car.

It took considerable time for the crowd to dispel as Fabrice Ribou prolonged the post mortem by coming up with as many theorems, postulations and untruths as possible to increase his takings.

As the discussions continued, Lisette Robert returned to the municipal shower. She flinched under the stream of cold water, and when she left, checked twice that she hadn't left her new bottle of shampoo behind. Walking home, she was grateful for the continued assault from the sun and, as she passed Monsieur Moreau, who was back on the bench, poked him to see whether he was dead or asleep.

Standing in front of her wardrobe, she tugged at the door handles which always stuck and set the glass bottles on her dressing table trembling when they finally opened. Reaching in, she took down her new periwinkle-blue frock. Stepping into it, she wondered whether the man she was going to meet would like it. She then combed her rivulets of damp hair and went downstairs. After pouring herself a glass of *pineau*, which she kept in the house for Guillaume Ladoucette, she took it outside and sat on the faded red sofa against the back of the house underneath the vine-strangled trellis. Taking a sip, she wondered how on earth the matchmaker could like the sweet ruby liquid so much. She persevered nonetheless and, as she watched the day finally lose its bloody battle with the evening, she thought of the man she hoped he had set her up with. When, at last, it was time to meet her mystery suitor, Lisette Robert brought her glass back inside and shut the door. And on her way out, she looked in the mirror in the hallway and saw the reflection of a truffling pig.

Arriving at the Bar Saint-Jus, the midwife was surprised to find that no one was waiting outside. Unsure of what to do, she opened the door and looked around. Walking up to the bar, she ordered a kir and sat down with her glass at an empty table in the window. She pulled towards her a copy of the *Sud Ouest* and looked at the front page. As she turned the page, she heard the sound of the chair opposite her being pulled back, and looked up to see Marcel Coussy, the farmer.

'Hello, Marcel, how are you?' she asked.

'Fine, thanks, how are you?'

'Well, thanks. I hope you don't mind, but I'm waiting for someone.'

'I know,' he replied.

'You know?'

'Yes. It's me.'

Lisette Robert tried to match the image the matchmaker had painted of the solvent bachelor with his own transport and a love for the outdoors, with the man who was sitting in front of her. While it was true that he was solvent, it was clear that the reason the farmer had reached his eighty-second year without having married was because no woman would have tolerated his reluctance to bathe. And as for his own transport, the only vehicles Marcel Coussy ever bought were tractors.

As she took a sip, Lisette Robert noticed that the elderly farmer had brushed himself up to a state of refinement normally witnessed only on Christmas Day. Unsure of what to say, she asked after his ginger Limousin cows and why they winked when people passed.

'Because they're happy,' he replied. 'Like me.'

She then asked after his dog, which was skilled in the art of rounding up geese and had won numerous trophies. Next she complimented him on his artichokes, which not only looked beautiful but tasted outstanding. The farmer answered distractedly, so taken was he by the vision before him. Then, for several moments, they stared at each other.

'Would you like a drink?' Lisette Robert asked, to rebuff the silence.

'I'll get them. Same again?' asked Marcel Coussy.

'Yes, please,' replied the midwife. But by the time the farmer returned from the bar, Lisette Robert was nowhere to be found.

When Lisette Robert returned home, she phoned the matchmaker. Guillaume Ladoucette was already in bed asleep. Defenceless from having been pulled so violently from his dreams, he agreed to meet her at once at Heart's Desire. As he dressed, he tried to think what on earth could be wrong, then suddenly realised.

The midwife was already waiting for him by the time he arrived. She said nothing as he opened the door, but as soon as they were inside, and the door was closed behind them again, she demanded, 'Guillaume, how could you?'

'Please, take a seat,' he said, ushering her towards the chair with the peeling marquetry. 'Glass of wine? Or perhaps a little something to eat?'

'Guillaume, stop trying to divert my attention.'

The matchmaker walked round the desk with the ink stain, sat down on his swivel chair and held up his hands. 'What was I supposed to do?' he asked. 'Marcel Coussy came in here, signed up for our Unrivalled Gold Service and then asked to be introduced to you. I could hardly say "No, you're too old and too malodorous, you don't stand a chance." Anyway, he doesn't know how ugly he is and *you* don't know how beautiful you are. You have that in common. It could have worked.'

Lisette Robert continued looking at him in silence.

'I did my best with him,' insisted the matchmaker. 'As you've probably noticed, he hasn't used the municipal shower. A friend of mine in Nontron lent me his bath. We soaked him for three days.'

'He didn't have anything to talk about!'

'That shouldn't have happened,' said the matchmaker frowning. 'I told him plenty of interesting things to say. He must have forgotten.'

'I can't understand why we had to have a drink in the Bar Saint-Jus, either. I thought we were going to meet outside and then go elsewhere?'

'Well, that was the plan . . . Look, everyone deserves a chance at love, Lisette,' said the matchmaker. 'You can't blame him for trying.'

'I'd bought a new dress and everything.'

'Well, the good news is that it won't go to waste. I have another Unrivalled Gold Service customer who wishes to be introduced to you.'

'I'm not going through that again.'

'Come on, Lisette, it wasn't that bad. Well, it wouldn't have been if Marcel Coussy had stuck to the game plan.'

'Who is it?'

'I can't tell you that. I'm bound by customer confidentiality.'

'What's he like?'

'I'd described him as a well-built gentleman. He's got a lovely haircut by the way—not like the horrors some people have got round here—and a refined palate.'

'I don't know. I've already fallen victim to your powers of exaggeration once.'

'Lisette, you won't have to meet this gentleman in the Bar Saint-Jus. It'll be out of Amour-sur-Belle, I promise you. I'll make sure it's one of your favourite places. How's about that?'

'All right. But this is the last one I'm agreeing to, Guillaume Ladoucette,' said the midwife, getting up from the cushion with the hand-embroidered radish.

After the matchmaker had walked her home, he returned to bed, where he lay for several minutes in his usual position on his back, his arms down the side of his body as if already dead in his coffin. He then switched on his bedside light and took a headache tablet, lest the postman elbowed himself back inside his dreams.

Much to his dismay, the matchmaker arrived at work early the next morning. The ruthless temperature of the water meant that he hadn't delayed in the municipal shower, despite the heavenly scented purchase from Périgueux that he'd slipped into the pocket of his burgundy silk dressing gown before leaving the house. Such was his brevity under the water, he even had time to sit down on the wooden bench in the changing area just inside the door and dry between each of his hairy toes, a luxury he had not enjoyed since the shower's installation.

Heart's Desire was the last place he wanted to be, and it wasn't just because of his deafening headache. It was only a matter of time before the postman would breeze in and tell him in torturous detail about his time with Émilie Fraisse at Saint-Jean-de-Côle. Bending down to pick up a letter on the doormat, the matchmaker put what was clearly the electricity bill in the top right-hand drawer of the desk with the ink stain, and made himself a cup of coffee. After moving the chair with the peeling marquetry so that it obscured the view of the recently planted window box opposite, he sat down on his swivel chair, dreading the unmissable sound of the door opening.

Several hours later, just as the matchmaker had decided that the red and green rubber bands would look better on the left-hand side of the narrow drawer with the compartments, and that the blue and yellow ones would look better on the right, he looked up to see Lisette Robert driving past. Not long afterwards, having changed his mind and returned all the bands to their original compartments, he noticed Stéphane Jollis driving past in what was undeniably a new white T-shirt. He got up and stood in the doorway watching the car disappear.

As he returned to his desk, the postman opened the door.

'Guillaume, my old friend! I'm so glad I caught you. I've prepared a little lunch to thank you for you know what.'

'That's very kind of you, Gilbert, but I've already got plans.'

'Nonsense! It's all prepared. Come on, shut the door! That's it. I've got so much to tell you. You won't believe how well we got on. I admit I had my doubts when you first set yourself up as a matchmaker—as the whole village did—but it seems you really have a talent for it. Have you seen these? Just look at those leaves. Aren't they beautiful? They're called *purkulettes jaunes*. I bought them at the *floralies* with Émilie Fraisse.'

If the over-sautéed veal in cep sauce and the potatoes under-fried in goose fat weren't painful enough, Guillaume Ladoucette had to endure them while listening to the many virtues of Émilie Fraisse, of which he was all too aware. When that was over, the postman then asked him whether he had heard the rumour that the council had discovered that the municipal shower's hot-water pipe had been sabotaged. Displaying not the least bit of interest, his guest replied that he had indeed. The postman then asked Guillaume Ladoucette what he had heard, but the matchmaker wiped his moustache, placed his serviette on the table and insisted that he really had to get back to work.

As he got up to leave, he was swiftly headed off and ushered out to the back garden, where he was subjected to a guided tour of his host's horticultural triumphs, followed by an even more protracted contemplation of the man's window boxes at the front of the house. Then the postman disappeared and returned with a deep pink flowering plant that he presented to him saying that he had grown it from seed. Guillaume Ladoucette, who insisted that it was all part of the service and there was really no need, reluctantly accepted the plant and returned to Heart's Desire, where he placed the gift in a corner.

When Lisette Robert arrived in the small dusty car park outside the town hall in Bourdeilles, she turned off the engine and looked around. Unable to see anyone fitting the matchmaker's description, she stayed put. But the heat soon drove her out and she headed for the grass and sat down on a bench on the river bank, where she watched the Dronne sloping by. After a while she felt the weight of someone sitting down next to her. Much to her surprise, she turned to see Stéphane Jollis without his black tendrils and wearing a new white T-shirt.

'Hello, Lisette,' he said.

'Hello, Stéphane,' she replied.

They kissed each other on each cheek.

'Guillaume said that—' started the baker, but stopped.

'That we'd be spending the afternoon together?' asked Lisette Robert.

'Yes, if that's OK with you?'

'Yes, of course.'

'Lisette, I just want to say . . . about the frogs. It wasn't me.'

'I know,' she replied.

'*You know?*'

'I never thought it was. It wasn't me who started the rumours.'

The baker looked confused. 'So why haven't we been speaking for all these years?' he asked, his eyes hunting the grass in front of him for the answer. But he failed to find it and nor did Lisette Robert provide one. Eventually he smiled, his eyebrows soaring like two startled blackbirds. 'Well, it seems like it was all just a misunderstanding,' he concluded. 'Never mind. These things happen. Now, I thought we would go to Les Tilleuls for lunch and then visit the château. How does that suit you?'

'I'd love to, I haven't been here for ages,' she replied. But Stéphane Jollis was only half listening, as he was trying to work out which of the midwife's curls had brushed his cheek when they kissed.

As they walked over the Gothic bridge, they stopped to admire the seventeenth-century ivy-clad mill house in the shape of a boat in the middle of the river, with its painted staircase leading to an elegant garden. After taking a moment to watch the shaggy green river weeds being combed flat by the current, they continued up the road.

Arriving at Les Tilleuls with its awnings and shutters a fresh shade of lichen, they were immediately shown to a table under the lime trees.

It wasn't long before the waitress brought a basket of bread and took Stéphane Jollis's order for a bottle of rosé, which he chose because he had been studying the colour of Lisette Robert's lips. The waitress then returned with the menus, but the baker took so long to decide, such was his befuddlement, that she had to come back three times.

When Lisette Robert's *périgourdine* salad arrived, the baker complimented her on her choice. And when Stéphane Jollis's salad of three warmed Cabécous arrived, the midwife complimented him on his choice. After offering her the breadbasket, Stéphane Jollis helped himself to a piece, tore it in half and put it into his mouth. But so caught up was he with the sight of a duck's gizzard slipping into Lisette Robert's mouth, that for the first time in his career he failed to evaluate the work of a fellow artisan. He then brought a mouthful of goat's cheese to his lips, but they were still echoing with the touch of Lisette Robert's cheek, and he put down his fork to prolong the heavenly sensation.

When Lisette Robert's pot-roasted pigeon stuffed with figs arrived, the baker complimented her on her choice. And when Stéphane Jollis's perch in Pécharmant sauce arrived, the midwife complimented him on his choice. As they continued chatting, so taken was the baker with the sound of her voice, that he was unable to hear a tourist sitting behind him ordering frog's legs.

After being offered the dessert menu, the baker was in such a state of delirium that he kept forgetting to choose. Lisette Robert, who could wait no longer, had to tap the menu to get him to concentrate.

When Lisette Robert's warm chocolate pudding with vanilla ice cream arrived, the baker complimented her on her choice. And when Stéphane Jollis's pear sorbet arrived, the midwife complimented him on his choice. But so struck was he by the fit of her periwinkle blue dress, that he forgot a woman's wholly natural desire to try all the desserts on the table, and when she asked, 'Can I have a lick of yours?' he turned a shade of burgundy. When, finally, he understood her true meaning, his hand was trembling to such an extent that he didn't think himself capable of the task. He loaded up the spoon and started its journey towards her mouth. But when the spoon was finally between her lips, the baker was in such a state of rhapsody that he forgot to pull it out again and the midwife had to recoil her head to disengage it. When Lisette Robert eventually swallowed, her face was such a picture of ecstasy that the overcome baker summoned the waitress and, when he eventually found his voice again, ordered another bowlful.

Once Stéphane Jollis had recovered from the spectacle, he asked for coffee. But when it arrived, so lost was he in Lisette Robert's eyes, which shone like freshly opened chestnuts above the rim of her cup, that he forgot to give her the little chocolate that the waitress had placed in his saucer. After having unwrapped and eaten hers, Lisette Robert waited patiently for what was the duty of a gentleman. But it never came. When she finally asked him whether he wanted his chocolate, the baker berated himself and immediately offered it to her. And when she returned from the lavatory, she found a further fifty-seven on her place mat as a result of the bribe he had slipped the waitress.

After Stéphane Jollis had paid the bill, they heaved themselves up from their seats, and eased their way slowly up the hill towards the château. At the ticket office, the midwife insisted on paying the entrance fees, in gratitude for the fifty-seven tiny chocolates that she had scooped into her bag. When the ticket-seller handed the baker a guide, he passed it to Lisette Robert to hide the fact that he had suddenly lost his ability to read. After admiring the ginkgo tree, they made their way up the path to the medieval fortress.

As they entered the cobbled courtyard, Lisette Robert read out the history of the thirteenth-century château, including its flits between French and English owners during the Hundred Years' War. But Stéphane Jollis wasn't listening, such was the racket of his thundering loins. Clueless of his surroundings, he followed Lisette Robert up the wooden steps to the splendid banqueting hall with its vast inglenook fireplaces. When the midwife went to sit on one of the stone window seats and peered down at the Dronne below, the baker followed her, his knees no longer his own. And when she remarked that the room still smelt of musty old hearths, Stéphane Jollis couldn't reply as flames of desire had singed his voice box.

As the midwife headed to the stone staircase which spiralled up the magnificent octagonal keep over 100 feet high, the baker trotted after her. Pointing to the round wooden trap door on the ground, she remarked that the dungeon underneath was thought to have once held members of the Order of the Knights Templars when it was destroyed by the King of France. But Stéphane Jollis didn't look, so imprisoned was he now by the sight of the periwinkle blue bottom swaying up the stone steps in front of him. And when they got up to the roof, with its wondrous view of the town and surrounding fields, and Lisette Robert leaned up against the crenellations to take it in, the baker had to stop himself throwing himself over them such was the grip of his mania.

After climbing back down again, they walked the short distance to the Renaissance château, and before they went inside, Lisette Robert read out loud its history, but such was the commotion of the baker's heart, he had turned stone deaf. They then walked down the hallway admiring the ancient oak chests. And when Lisette Robert pointed out that they were marriage chests, the baker suddenly regained his hearing, which was even more acute than when he had lost it.

After climbing the elegant steps to the first floor, the baker gazed at the bizarre wooden cupboards on the landing, which were used to store food that was waiting to be checked for poisons by the taster before it was served. But Lisette Robert had disappeared into the Golden Drawing Room. Here he found her marvelling at the beams lavishly painted with intoxicating bouquets, sphinxes, family initials and fantastical animals, which continued along the edge of the room. She pointed out the splendorous panels on all four walls painted with landscapes, ruins, parks and châteaux and she led him to the oil paintings hanging above the fireplaces at either end of the room. But Stéphane Jollis saw none of it as her beauty had distorted his vision.

When they reached the second floor, the baker guided by the musical sound of Lisette Robert's footsteps up the elegant stone staircase, they both turned right into the first room. But neither of them saw the exotic seventeenth-century Spanish strongboxes with their multitude of locked drawers intricately inlaid with ivory, gold leaf and tortoiseshell. Nor did they see the Parisian seventeenth-century tapestry of Renaud and Armide. Instead they both stared, the baker's vision instantly restored, at Charles V's bed on the left-hand side of the room. It wasn't its sumptuous gilding that held their gaze, nor indeed that it was called the Bed of Paradise. The reason for their arrest was that they were both suddenly confronted with the memory of the tumultuous night they had spent in bed together during the mini-tornado, which Lisette Robert had hoped would evaporate, but in which Stéphane Jollis had bathed every night since.

Later that afternoon, Guillaume Ladoucette was still staring at his gift from the postman, which hadn't been moved from the corner of the room, when the door opened. It was Lisette Robert.

'Lisette! Come in, come in. Sit down. Glass of wine?' asked the matchmaker, hoping for some good news to raise his spirits.

'That would be lovely, thank you,' she replied, sitting on the cushion with the hand-embroidered radish. The matchmaker opened his bottom left-hand drawer, poured out a couple of glasses and handed one to the midwife.

'Walnut?' he asked, offering her a bowlful.

'No, thanks,' replied the midwife, who had her own to get through.

'Now, tell me, Lisette. How did it go in Bourdeilles?'

Lisette Robert told him about their most enjoyable lunch at Les Tilleuls, including the fifty-seven chocolates she had left with in her handbag. She told him about the impressive ginkgo tree near the kiosk where they bought the tickets. She told him about the tour they had taken of the medieval fortress, including their climb up the magnificent octagonal keep over 100 feet high. She told him about the wondrous treasures they had marvelled at in the Renaissance château, including some marriage chests and the tapestries. She told him of the ravishing Golden Drawing Room that had thrilled them both with its sumptuous ceiling. She told him how they had stopped on the Gothic bridge on the way back to admire yet again the little mill house in the shape of a boat. And she told him how they had said goodbye to each other in the car park outside the town hall, both agreeing that they were delighted to be talking to one another once again.

But what Lisette Robert didn't tell Guillaume Ladoucette about was the tumultuous night they had spent together during the mini-tornado, brought back with such alacrity when they had been confronted by the gilded Charles V bed in a room on the second floor of the château.

The residents of Amour-sur-Belle had grown so used to the perpetual breeze that few noticed when the wind was up that afternoon in 1999, and by the time it was remarked upon it was blowing with considerable force. Marcel Coussy noticed that instead of lying down as they did when rain threatened, his cows had suddenly started to walk backwards. It frightened the farmer to such an extent that, not trusting his decrepit barn, he locked himself in his house with all his cows.

When the crops became uprooted and turnips started to come crashing through their windows, the horrified residents tried to close their shutters. But the gusts simply got hold of them, wrenched them from their brackets and hurled them into the air like playing cards.

Lisette Robert had opened her windows hoping that the wind would blow round the house and spare her the job of dusting. It wasn't until she tried to shut them that she realised something much stronger than her was pushing in the opposite direction. Her immediate thought was for her son, and she thanked God that he had gone away for the weekend. Her second thought was for the only possession that meant something to her: the family piano. At first she sat on top of it, keeping the lid down with her feet. When she travelled with it down the side of the sitting room, and the curved salmon roof tiles started rattling, Lisette Robert decided she couldn't possibly die having mastered only one tune.

It was her elephantine attempts at learning another that alerted Stéphane Jollis to her plight. He had just closed his shutters, called his parents to bid them farewell, and was sitting in his kitchen drinking a bottle of champagne. The baker recognised the poisonous sound the minute it came down the chimney accompanied by a roar of wind that was perfectly in tune. He had suffered the bothersome noise often enough, but it was an irritation too far in his final hours.

Getting to his feet, he put on his jacket and opened the front door. Gripping the window ledges and drainpipes, he followed the snatches of music transported by the murderous wind. When he saw Lisette Robert through the open window of her sitting room squinting at a musical score, he climbed in, put her over his shoulder and carried her back to his house. After standing her up in his kitchen, he started on the monumental task of heaving the front door shut. Once it was closed, he disappeared into the sitting room, returned dragging the sofa, and pushed it up against the front door as an extra precaution. He then calmly got out another glass, filled it with champagne, offered it to Lisette Robert and sat down.

By the time they had finished the second bottle, the baker had decided it was much more pleasant to die in company, and, grateful for his guest, suggested that they had their final meal together. He emptied the fridge and cupboards and spread his delicacies on the kitchen table, including a *confit* of goose, several game and rabbit pâtés, and a partridge terrine. They picnicked on the sofa with a couple of baguettes.

While they were on their seventh bottle of champagne the baker suddenly remembered his manners and announced, 'A woman cannot die without pudding!' Lisette Robert followed him through the adjoining door into the bakery and stood next to him by the counter filled with little cakes. Given first choice, and fearing that time was short, she automatically picked her favourite, a chocolate *religieuse*. Once the nun was dispatched, she then turned her attention to a coffee *religieuse*. Meanwhile, Stéphane Jollis was enjoying a couple of apricot tarts.

It was while they were on their ninth bottle of champagne that they both noticed that only one little cake remained. The baker naturally offered the *Paris-Brest* to Lisette Robert, who suggested they share it. She scooped up some cream with her finger, held it to the baker's lips and watched as he licked it off. He then scooped some up with his finger, held it up to her lips and watched as she licked it off. Within minutes Stéphane Jollis had lifted Lisette Robert onto the counter next to the till. Her legs still wrapped around him, he then carried her upstairs and continued to knead her for the rest of the night and such was the height of their ecstasy they thought they had reached heaven.

Lisette Robert slipped away the following morning and discovered that, despite her suspicions, she was not in the land of the living dead. On discovering that the pharmacy in Amour-sur-Belle was shut, she drove over to Brantôme and purchased the morning-after pill. Such was the depth of her embarrassment, she was unable to speak to the baker. He assumed her silence was as a result of the rumours circulating that he had eaten her frogs and refused to speak to her because his gastronomic honour had been slighted. But whenever the villagers shuddered at the memory of the night of that mini-tornado, Stéphane Jollis shuddered with delight.

It was then that Lisette Robert told Guillaume Ladoucette the reason why, despite having had such a marvellous time with the baker, she was unable to pursue a romance with him.

'I love another,' she said.

'Another? So why did you agree to go on these dates?' the matchmaker asked.

'Because I kept hoping it would be him,' she replied meekly.

'Who is it?'

'The man from the council.'

After insisting on signing up there and then for the Unrivalled Gold Service, the midwife then got up from the cushion with the hand-embroidered radish and left. But this new customer gave the matchmaker no pleasure, for all he could think of during his walk home was how he was going to break the news to his best friend.

Chapter Nine

ÉMILIE FRAISSE WOKE UP in her four-poster Renaissance bed feeling the natural joy of having slept alone and immediately remembered her excitement over Gilbert Dubuisson coming to dinner. Lying in the middle of the ancient white sheet, her hair coursing over the pillow like molten silver, she recalled the pleasure it had been to spend time with a man who actually liked to talk, and the marvellous time they had had at the *floralies*.

While his baldness had at first surprised her, she reasoned that if he could accept the fact that despair had turned her hair prematurely grey, then she could accept that age had stolen most of his. And she then considered his job as a postman, which was an entirely suitable profession for a future husband because not only did it serve as a vital community function, but it also kept him moving and less likely to cultivate a stomach the shape of a pumpkin.

It wasn't long, however, before the châtelaine left her sheets and padded down the stone spiral steps with the lamentable repairs in her bare feet to the front door. Peering round it hoping not to be caught in a state of undress by an early-morning tourist, she shot across the courtyard. As she showered with the hosepipe, she debated again whether to stew or bake the eel. And, as she washed her hair, she thought of the poor man from the council who had admired her find, and hoped that he had enjoyed his jar of black radish jam.

Once dressed, she stripped the thick white monogrammed sheets from her bed and replaced them with fresh ones. While she had no intention of allowing Gilbert Dubuisson to slip between them at this early stage, he would undoubtedly want a tour of the château and she wanted everything to look its best.

After flinging open the heavy shutters on the inside of the windows, normally kept closed to protect the few genuine antiques from the bloodsucking sun, she prepared a battalion of cleaning materials and advanced her way with determination through the rooms. First scrubbing what didn't need scrubbing, she then polished what didn't need polishing and dusted what didn't need dusting. When she stood back to survey her efforts, what already shone, shone and what already gleamed, gleamed.

When her slender arms ached as if they had been punched, and her knees were the shade of an obstinate raspberry stain, she untied the cord that the previous owner had put across a Regency tapestry armchair to prevent visitors from sitting on it. As she rested, Émilie Fraisse wondered whether she should go and speak to the matchmaker to calm her nerves, which had taken her by surprise. She then thought how ironic it was that Guillaume Ladoucette, whom she had grown up assuming she would marry, but who hadn't replied to her letter, had introduced her to a man who had spent his life delivering them. Her mind then turned to the last day they had seen each other before she moved away, and she remembered giving him her precious Nontron hunting knife with its boxwood handle and ancient pokerwork motifs. And she wondered whether he had kept it.

When her energy returned, she sank her bare feet into her Wellington boots, which were several sizes too big, to protect her legs from the brambles, and slopped her way across the courtyard to the garden. After filling her basket with apricot roses which had been rambling for centuries, she went back inside and arranged them in vases, which she carried into the dining room.

After consulting her recipe book, she returned to the garden to pick the herbs she would need and, before closing the door bleached fossilgrey by the sun, bent down to rub the leaves of a geranium. She then smelt her fingers and inhaled the scent of carrots.

On her way to the vaulted kitchen, she stopped to admire the florid yellow mould in the corridor, long thought extinct, which was slowly turning violet. Like the other patches around the château, its incredible beauty had prevented her cleaning it off. She then sat down on the ancient seat which slid open to hide the salt from the tax collector and thought about how she was going to dispatch her eel.

When Guillaume Ladoucette's alarm went off, it wasn't the insufferable noise that brought him to his senses, but the shock that he was still alive. Hauling himself out of bed, he made his way to the bathroom, looked at his reflection in the mirror above the sink and failed to see the slightest hint of a Living Example of either a former barber or a match-maker. He hoisted the tips of his moustache to a cursory 180 degrees and, when they immediately returned to their crumpled position, he left them as they were as he no longer cared.

Lacking the will to brave the torturous temperature of the municipal shower, which still wasn't fixed, he went to get dressed. As he sat on his bed aiming his arm into a shirt already limp from wear, he remembered the last time he had lost the spirit to put on fresh clothes: the day he realised he would have to shut his beloved barber shop. And what had he achieved since? Yes, he had set up the matchmaking business and even had some clients. But the only match that had worked so far involved the one woman he wanted for himself.

Guillaume Ladoucette went to work that morning simply because it was easier than having to explain why he hadn't opened. He brought a coffee to his desk with the ink stain, and, after drinking it, picked up the plant with the tiny pink heart-shaped flowers that the postman had given him and put it out of sight on the table at the back of the room next to the percolator. Just as he returned to his swivel chair, the door opened. It was Yves Lévêque.

Fortunately for the dentist, the matchmaker didn't have the will to upbraid him for cancelling his date with Sandrine Fournier. Instead, he had reluctantly agreed that Yves Lévêque could come into Heart's Desire in order to discuss a new date.

'Are you all right?' enquired the dentist, sitting down. 'You look a little . . . how can I put it? Shipwrecked . . .'

'I'm just feeling a little off colour,' Guillaume Ladoucette replied.

'Don't I get offered a cup of coffee this time?'

'Sorry, do excuse me. Actually, what time is it? I've forgotten my watch.'

'Twenty-seven minutes past nine,' replied the dentist, wondering what on earth had befallen Guillaume Ladoucette's moustache.

'Bugger coffee,' said the matchmaker, pulling open the bottom left-hand drawer of the desk with the ink stain and taking out a bottle of Pécharmant and two glasses. He filled them both and handed one to his customer. 'Walnut?' he asked.

'No, thanks,' replied the dentist, who had his own to get rid of.

'That's better,' said the matchmaker after taking a sip. 'Now, listen carefully. Which two words are not to come from your lips today?'

'Halvies-halves,' replied the dentist.

'Correct. What are the other two words you are not permitted to say this afternoon?'

'Dental floss.'

'Correct. Now, why do you compliment a woman on her dress?'

'Because you're more likely to get it off?'

'No! No! No! Because she has spent hours shopping for it and then hours wishing she'd bought the other one.'

'I see.'

'Now, can you think of anything that I could do to help your appearance before you go?'

'No.

'Nothing at all?'

'Can't think of anything.'

'Sure?'

'Yes.'

'Right, then. She'll be waiting in the square in front of the château in Jumilhac-le-Grand at ten forty-five. You'd better get a move on. I've told her you plan to take her gold-panning and she said she'd always wanted a man with a sense of adventure, so you're well ahead already. Now, remember to treat her as you would a good cassoulet: ignore the rancid parts, delight in the duck leg and shrug your shoulders at the little green button. Good luck.'

Yves Lévèque emptied his glass, shook the matchmaker's hand and got up from the chair with the peeling marquetry. He walked home as quickly as he could without breaking into a sweat so as not to spoil his freshly ironed shirt. Before starting the car, he checked his reflection in the mirror, and, after failing to find the slightest trace of allure, comforted himself by baring his teeth. As he turned right at the field with the ginger Limousin cows that winked, he tried to imagine the woman he was about to meet.

The dentist enjoyed the drive to Jumilhac-le-Grand as he wound through the mottled shadows of oaks and pines, which offered a moment's relief from the sun's vicious assault. He hadn't been entirely truthful when he explained to Guillaume Ladoucette why he wanted to take his new match gold-panning. While it would indeed demonstrate that he had initiative, a characteristic he knew to be greatly admired by women, the real reason was that if she turned out to be as abhorrent as the mushroom poisoner, there was always a chance of recovering the sixteen euros the activity would cost him if he happened upon a little gold nugget.

Arriving at the square in front of the wondrous château, he parked underneath a plane tree and got out to admire the fairy-tale skyline of pointed roofs and watchtowers surmounted by bizarre figurines, and sensed someone standing behind him. He turned round to find that it was Denise Vigier, the grocer.

The dentist had put up with a lot from the matchmaker over the years. There was the time when Guillaume Ladoucette convinced him that false sideburns were all the rage and sold him a pair that he had never worn, having come to his senses as soon as he left the shop. There were the complaints he had made about the state of his box of hairpieces after the community headcount; there was his unwanted advice about his *cornichons*; and then, of course, there was the business matching him up with the assistant ambulant fishmonger. And if all that wasn't enough, he had now set him up with the abhorrent grocer.

After greeting Denise Vigier, who appeared equally taken aback, Yves Lévèque complimented her on her blue-and-purple-patterned dress that made him shudder.

'It's so much nicer than the other one,' he added.

'Which other one?' asked Denise Vigier.

'The one you wished you'd bought instead.'

'There wasn't one I wished I'd bought instead,' she replied, confused.

Silently cursing Guillaume Ladoucette, and wanting to get the agony over as quickly as possible, Yves Lévèque suggested that they made their way immediately to the nearby village of Le Chalard where the gold-panning was to take place. When the grocer suggested going in one car instead of two, the dentist strongly opposed the idea as he was hoping to lose her along the country lanes. But each time he looked in his mirror, he was tormented by the sight of the abhorrent woman crouched over her steering wheel.

When they arrived at the village, Denise Vigier disappeared inside the café to use the lavatory, and the dentist, who was waiting on the terrace, cursed when he came face to face with the instructor holding his cash box. The dentist's long, pale instruments of torture reluctantly found their way into his pocket and pulled out enough money for both of them.

After the instructor's demonstration in the dancing waters of the River Isle, Yves Lévèque grabbed a sieve and pan and waded away from the group. After a spurt of furious panning he cast a look at Denise Vigier, described by Guillaume Ladoucette as an 'astute business-woman with a zest for life', who was still on the river bank tucking the sides of her blue-and-purple-patterned frock under her knicker elastic to make it shorter. Her dress was an abomination, he thought again, and did nothing to help disguise her colossal bosom, the weight of which made her stand as if pitched against permanently driving rain.

As Yves Lévèque clambered across the rocks, he thought about the unspeakable prices Denise Vigier charged in her shop. Shovelling a new load of sediment into his sieve, he hoped that the grocer wouldn't approach, but much to the dentist's fury, Denise Vigier came splashing towards him, yelping that she had got something. After wiping the river water from his spectacles, the dentist took a look at the object in the palm of her hand that had fleeced him on so many occasions. And when the grocer insisted that he kept the sizable nugget, all Yves Lévèque could think about was her treacherous grandmother who had been found guilty of horizontal collaboration at a tribunal in 1944 and given a 'Number 44' haircut in front of a spitting crowd in Périgueux.

Guillaume Ladoucette turned the sign on the door round to 'Closed' and headed home after a day that had never progressed beyond wretched. For over two hours Stéphane Jollis had sat inconsolable on the cushion with the hand-embroidered radish.

'But I can't understand it, we had such a wonderful time,' he had wailed, running his fingers through his hair. 'And I'd cleaned my shoes.' All the matchmaker could do was agree that his shoes were certainly unrecognisable, and that the fifty-seven tiny chocolates had been a masterstroke. In an effort to cheer up his friend, he even suggested that they both closed for the day and went fishing, despite the fact that he had nothing remotely victorious in his fridge. But the only thing that the baker wanted was Lisette Robert.

Eventually a search party made up of incandescent customers had arrived to escort Stéphane Jollis back to the bakery.

When he arrived home, Guillaume Ladoucette found a bunch of borage hanging from the front-door handle. He recognised it instantly as a gift from his mother, as the tiny blue flowers and leaves put into wine were believed to cure sadness. After untying it, he brought it inside and put it in a vase of water. Gazing out of the back window, he couldn't bring himself to mow the lawn, even though it was the last favourable day in the month to do so. Nor could he face anything to eat, as the thought of the eel Gilbert Dubuisson had told him Émilie Fraisse was preparing for them that night had driven away his appetite. Drawn to the sound of the clock on the vast stone mantelpiece, whose ticking had driven one of his relatives to suicide, he sat down on the sofa, and imagined what the pair might be up to.

When the châtelaine opened the door of the château, Gilbert Dubuisson immediately offered her a posy of flowers picked from his garden, which surprised Émilie Fraisse as it had been so many years since a man had made such an effort to please her. As they walked past the llama skeleton and along the corridor with the mould that was turning violet, he complimented her on her cinnamon-coloured antique dress which appeared to have been shorn off at the knees. And once they reached the vaulted kitchen, he stood and admired the splendid collection of copper pans and utensils on three of the walls.

After offering her guest the seat which slid open to hide the salt from the tax collector, Émilie Fraisse poured them both a glass of wine. But as she sat down, she found that nerves had made off with her voice. Fortunately, Gilbert Dubuisson was as talkative as ever, so she leaned back on the seat with wild boars carved on its feet and listened. By the time she had finished her wine, her voice had returned and she chatted back, feeling as content in the postman's company as she had at the *floralies*. And when he asked whether he could have a tour of the château, as he hadn't been round it for years, she was delighted.

Wishing she was barefoot as she clattered her way down the corridor in her ridiculous seventeenth-century shoes, the châtelaine passed a modern wooden chest poorly encrusted with mother-of-pearl, bought by the previous owner on a visit to Turkey to avoid getting into a fight. When Gilbert Dubuisson stopped to ask her about it, Émilie Fraisse found herself saying that it was the bottom half of a Renaissance armoire that had been in the château for centuries. She then told the story of a man who had spent so many years travelling the Pacific islands that he eventually cast aside his britches, ruffled shirt and plume-topped velvet hat, and went native. He spent his days fishing with the locals and learned to hold his breath underwater so that he could dive for pretty shells to please his fifty-six wives, who found him exotic beyond measure. One day, a local with only thirty-two wives decided to dive even deeper than usual to find a highly prized shell to increase his standing in the village, which had sunk since the newcomer's arrival. But the water was far too deep for any human to bear and the man started to drown. The Frenchman, who was the only one still in the ocean, noticed that the local was in difficulty and managed to rescue him. The man was so grateful that he gave him the beautiful shell that was still clasped in his hand. Such was the enormity of his gratitude, he also insisted that his rescuer took all his wives, who were only too happy for a change. But before long, the Frenchman was dead with exhaustion. On his deathbed he sent the beautiful shell to his brother, who lived in the château at Amour-sur-Belle, along with a letter asking that it be made into a piece of furniture to serve as a warning about doing people favours.

When Émilie Fraisse finished, the postman pulled open one of the doors and said that he couldn't understand why the previous owner hadn't told him the fascinating story when he had showed him around.

After taking him up the stone spiral staircase with the lamentable repairs, the châtelaine opened one of the bedroom doors and invited Gilbert Dubuisson in. He looked around and then strode to the window where he stood admiring a Louis XV marble-topped chest of drawers. Explaining that it was, in fact, a vanity trunk, Émilie Fraisse pulled out the second drawer, lifted up the hinged mirror, and showed him the compartments on either side used to store perfume bottles. Once she had closed it again, she then pulled the left-hand handle of the fourth drawer which swivelled open to the right to reveal a white bidet. When Gilbert Dubuisson exclaimed how marvellous it was and asked whether she knew anything of its history, Émilie Fraisse found herself telling him that it once belonged to a woman of exceptional charm who took it with her as she travelled all over the Périgord Vert visiting her numerous lovers. One day, a former owner of the château discovered that he was not the sole object of her affections. Scandalised, despite having numerous lovers himself, the next time they had exhausted their passions, he smothered her with a pillow. It was then that the man realised that he had not only killed the only woman he had ever loved, but also the only person willing to fulfil the more extreme of his carnal pleasures. Knowing that he would never reach such heights of ecstasy again, the man became a eunuch and set about destroying every vanity trunk in the country. However, he was unable to bring himself to destroy the one that had belonged to his accommodating mistress and it was the only one that survived.

When she had finished the story, Émilie Fraisse suddenly realised its sexual nature and blushed. The postman, who failed to notice the fire in her cheeks, said that the story was remarkable and ran his hand along the marble top in wonder.

On entering the *grand salon*, Gilbert Dubuisson admired the reversible floor and the tapestries at length, then asked if he might see the châtelaine's heirloom vegetables. In the battle-weary, bloody evening sun, they followed the ancient stone wall on top of which bearded irises grew. Pulling apart the overgrown brambles and wild grasses, she first showed the postman the strawberry spinach, with its tiny red fruit which she made into jam and put out for sale in the ticket seller's hut built for the tourists who never came. The leaves, she added, tasted like hazelnuts and should be cooked like spinach.

The châtelaine then walked over to the rows of asparagus lettuce, and pointed out that instead of a heart they had a central stalk which was sufficient for one person. It was eaten raw in salad, she added, or steamed like asparagus, and its frilly leaves were to be ignored.

And finally, she showed him her slender perpetual leeks, with tiny new vegetables already growing out of them. The transfixed postman showed so much rapture that Émilie Fraisse immediately picked some of everything for supper.

The châtelaine and her guest then returned to the kitchen, where she completed her dish of eel stewed in Burgundy. However, she forgot to warn Gilbert Dubuisson that she was going to ignite the dash of cognac she had added after bringing the dish to the boil with cubes of bacon, which made him jump. Once the postman had regained his composure, she then showed him into the dining room with its *pisé* floor, where candlelight fluttered across the vases of rambling apricot roses.

Eventually stirred from the sofa by the cacophony of his empty stomach, Guillaume Ladoucette got up and wandered upstairs. After taking a regretful look at the dry bath, he made his way to his bedroom and slid open the drawer of the nightstand. He then sat with his back against the bed head, his legs out in front of him, and carefully oiled Émilie Fraisse's Nontron hunting knife with its boxwood handle and ancient pokerwork motifs. Forgetting to take off his two-day-old clothes, he then turned off the bedside light and braced himself for another terrifying night on the high seas. Less than an hour later, such was the height of the waves of anxiety lashing around the house, Violette, the infernal chicken, came out from her hiding place, climbed up onto the bed and spent the night on his pillow lest she drowned.

After dinner, Émilie Fraisse accompanied Gilbert Dubuisson to the door glowing like mercury in the moonlight. As the bats performed loops of the courtyard, Gilbert Dubuisson gently took the châtelaine's hand and kissed the backs of her fingers. Again he complimented her on her cinnamon-coloured antique dress, the unsurpassable dinner, the vigour of her heirloom vegetables and her efforts with the château. And he added that if she needed any help scrubbing the moulds off the walls, he would be more than happy to oblige.

It was then that Émilie Fraisse went off Gilbert Dubuisson.

Heart's Desire was closed the following morning. Guillaume Ladoucette had only managed bouts of sleep between the frantic gasps for breath of a man overboard. Buffeted all night, it wasn't until the sun had already gone into battle that he collapsed, marooned on his back, into the deepest of slumbers, arms and legs outstretched with exhaustion. The clamour of his monstrous snores prevented him from hearing the alarm, which eventually gave up. It wasn't until he slowly opened his eyes to search for the horizon, and came face to face with the unfortunate features of Violette, the infernal chicken, that he fully woke. Such were his screams of terror that the bird instantly laid an egg.

Hoisting himself to his feet, he cast off his sodden clothes and made his way to the bathroom. He refused to look into the mirror above the basin, fearing that his reflection would only disorientate him further. After putting on his burgundy silk dressing gown, he walked his feet into his slippers, collected his washbag and towel, and left for the municipal shower. At first, he was unable to feel the ruthless temperature of the water collapsing his moustache into a soggy horseshoe. But it quickly brought him to his senses.

Once home, the torment of his stomach from having eaten nothing the previous night drove him to the fridge, and he cooked himself a breakfast of scrambled eggs in which he tossed a handful of *lardons*. But the salt in the bacon reminded him of his tempestuous night, and, falling into despair again, he found himself unable to get up from the table. When he next looked over at the clock on the oven it was almost lunchtime. Convincing himself that it wasn't worth opening Heart's Desire for such a short period, the matchmaker stayed where he was while his mind forced upon him images he didn't want to see.

When he stirred several hours later, Guillaume Ladoucette immediately felt shamed by his behaviour for it wasn't respectable for a grown man to still be in his dressing gown—no matter how elegant—while the rest of the world was working. By the time he arrived at the shop, he had managed to put on a clean set of clothes, and his moustache was waxed so as not to hang down to his chin. He turned round the sign on the inside of the door and made himself a cup of coffee. As he slipped into his swivel chair, he told himself that the most important thing was that Émilie Fraisse was happy. But part of him wouldn't listen.

Just as he had got out his file of customers, which was rather slim, a head appeared around the door. It was Stéphane Jollis wanting to know whether everything was all right as a number of his customers had noticed that Heart's Desire had been closed all morning. When the matchmaker replied that he was just feeling a little under the weather, the baker came in.

'Would you like a drink?' the matchmaker enquired.

'Yes, please,' said the baker.

Guillaume Ladoucette brought out a bottle of Bergerac from the bottom left-hand drawer of the oak desk and poured two glasses. He then reached back inside and brought out a bowl of cracked walnuts, which he put in front of the baker.

'Walnut?'

'No, thanks,' replied Stéphane Jollis, who had his own to get through. 'So what's wrong?'

'I just didn't get much sleep last night.'

'Nor did I,' admitted the baker.

While Guillaume Ladoucette had been cleaning Émilie Fraisse's hunting knife, Stéphane Jollis had been sitting up in bed inspecting the hair clip he had kept in his bedside drawer ever since finding it on the bakery table the morning after the mini-tornado. Despite knowing every detail of it already, he gazed at the swirl of diamanté, several specks of which were missing, then at the little clasp on the back, and then at the swirl of diamanté again. Eventually, he returned it to the drawer, shuffled down the sheet and lay on his back.

Over two hours later, he was still lingering over the memory of that night. As always, he found it hard to believe that a man such as himself could have had the great fortune to share his bed with Lisette Robert, and at times he had had to get out her hair clip just to prove to himself that it was true. And while he was well aware that bakers, along with fire-fighters, held the highest place in the nation's affections, and that the job carried such prestige that for years the family bakery was the only place in the village with a telephone, he had never imagined that such a gift from heaven would come his way. It was then that Stéphane Jollis finally came to the conclusion that it was time to see it for what it was: a miracle the like of which only happened once for a man such as himself. The baker then fell into a peaceful sleep, and, for the first time since that unforgettable night, wasn't disturbed by the haunting memory of poisonous piano-playing coming down the chimney.

After pouring them both another glass, Stéphane Jollis announced that he wanted to sign up for the Unrivalled Silver Service.

'What a marvellous idea!' replied Guillaume Ladoucette. 'Nothing like getting back on that horse, eh? And don't worry about Lisette Robert. Everyone wants to go out with her. That's the way of the world.'

The matchmaker opened the file of customers on his desk. 'Now, let's see,' he muttered. 'Who have we got? Not her. Not her. Can't see you two together. Not her. Her! There we are, Stéphane! Oh, maybe not.'

'What's wrong?'

'She's looking for someone tall and slim.'

'I'm not that short,' protested the baker.

'No, but there's the other matter.'

'Guillaume, a baker of distinction cannot be skinny. As you always said when you were a barber, you have to be a Living Example. What would it say about my bread and cakes if I were able to resist them?'

'You're quite right, of course. But I'm not prepared to take the risk.'

The matchmaker carried on looking through his file. 'No. Too old. No. Now what about her? Let's see . . . Yes, that's a very good match indeed. You two should get on splendidly. Now, I expect you want to get moving right away. Would you like me to call her now?'

Stéphane Jollis nodded enthusiastically. The matchmaker dialled the number and indicated that the woman had picked up the phone by pointing at the receiver and raising his eyebrows at the baker who was watching him closely. Guillaume Ladoucette introduced himself, exchanged several pleasantries and then announced that he had found her a most favourable match. The man in question, he said, was a dark-haired artisan who liked to seize the day by rising early, and then went into considerable detail about his splendid haircut. And when the woman enquired as to whether he was athletic, the matchmaker replied that he was a very keen fisherman, and that he enjoyed swimming.

Guillaume Ladoucette put down the receiver.

'She's very keen to meet you,' he said triumphantly. 'However, there's one minor problem. She's going away after the weekend for a short holiday and the only time she can meet you is Sunday morning.'

'I'll be at work,' replied the baker. 'As you know, it's one of the busiest days of the week. And I've got problems this Sunday as it is. There's no one coming in to help serve.'

'I see your point.'

The two men sat in silence.

'I know!' said Guillaume Ladoucette. 'I'll look after the bakery while you're gone. You could get up really early and prepare everything.'

'But, Guillaume. You can't add up.'

'I can.'

The baker raised his eyebrows.

'OK, so maybe I can't,' said the matchmaker. 'But I could work it out on the till. It can't be that hard. I had one in the barber's, remember? Come on, Stéphane! She sounds right up your street.'

With great reluctance, the baker finally agreed, but not before laying down certain conditions. Guillaume Ladoucette was not to do any sums in his head, nor was he to take advantage of the trays of little cakes. There were a number of customers who came in at the same time every week for the same order and he had to make sure that he didn't sell out before they came in. 'Whatever you do, make sure there are enough little cakes left for the women,' he added. 'Oh, yes, and Émilie Fraisse always comes in on a Sunday morning for a *millefeuille*.'

'Émilie Fraisse always comes in on a Sunday morning for a *mille-feuille*?' repeated the matchmaker.

'Yes.' The baker then left, muttering something about being hunted down if he didn't get back to his shop.

In no mood to face Émilie Fraisse coming in to tell him about her splendid evening with Gilbert Dubuisson, the matchmaker stood up, turned the sign over behind the shop door, and went to look for the man from the council.

He found Jean-François Lafforest at the municipal shower in his unfortunate trousers which were now starting to fit, talking to two workmen. When the matchmaker approached and asked whether he could buy him a drink at the Bar Saint-Jus, the man from the council immediately became suspicious and politely refused. Undeterred, Guillaume Ladoucette suggested that they went for a little walk together instead, and took him along the river bank. They walked through the patches of wild mint until they came to the old public washing place.

After inviting the man from the council to sit next to him on a stone slab underneath the pitched roof, Guillaume Ladoucette then told him all about Heart's Desire, the Unrivalled Gold Service and the special woman who wanted to be introduced to him.

Clutching his briefcase to his stomach, his eyes on the shallow square of green water, Jean-François Lafforest listened to what the matchmaker had to say. When he had finished, the man from the council told him that while it was very nice to know that a woman held him in such high regard, he couldn't entertain the idea of meeting her.

Guillaume Ladoucette was taken aback. 'Monsieur Lafforest, I must impress upon you that the woman in question is no ordinary woman. I am talking about a woman of exceptional beauty.'

'I'm certain she's extraordinary.'

'I don't wish to give away her identity, but I would wager she's the most beautiful woman you've ever seen.'

'No doubt, Monsieur Ladoucette. But I'm afraid I am not interested.'

The matchmaker then plundered the depths of his considerable sales skills. He first tried to appeal to the man's nobility, describing the woman's caring nature, generosity and discretion. When that failed to work he talked of the woman's figure that was widely known to curve more graciously than the Belle, her eyes that shone like two freshly opened horse chestnuts, and her hair that coursed down her shoulders like a waterfall. But the man from the council simply thanked Guillaume Ladoucette for his interest, bade him good day and left.

The matchmaker walked back along the bank of the Belle alone and dumbfounded. As the scent of wild mint threaded through his ankles, he ran through his sales pitch and couldn't for the life of him see where he had gone wrong. How could a man refuse such a woman? And how on earth was he going to break the news to poor Lisette Robert?

Over an hour later, back on his swivel chair, the matchmaker was still trying to work out how he was going to tell the midwife when the door opened.

It was Émilie Fraisse wearing an almond antique silk dress which appeared to have been shorn off at the knees. The matchmaker got up to greet her and ushered her to the cushion with the hand-embroidered radish, then quickly sat down again. Just as he was preparing himself for the torment of listening to the details he couldn't bear to hear, he took a closer look at Émilie Fraisse and asked whether she was all right.

'I didn't get much sleep last night,' she replied. Guillaume Ladoucette tried to catch his heart as it sank, but missed.

After the postman had wished her good night and started across the courtyard, Émilie Fraisse immediately closed the door. Slipping off her ridiculous seventeenth-century shoes, she sat on the bottom step of the stone spiral staircase with the lamentable repairs, her cheeks resting on her fists. How could she possibly love a man who was unable to see the beauty of the moulds that decorated the château walls like priceless works of art? And as she thought about her wasted efforts—the roses she had picked, the eel she had cooked—the familiar flints of disappointment thudded down on her.

When, finally, she found the will to stand up, she climbed the cold stairs, walked along the corridor with the rough, faded tapestries and turned the enormous handle on her bedroom door. In front of the mirror dappled with age, she slipped off her cinnamon-coloured dress. She then took out the pin that was holding up her hair, which dropped like cinders down her naked back. And as she looked at her body which hadn't been touched for years, she scolded herself for having thought that she had finally found the man who would love her until her body caught up with her aged hair.

After pulling back the heavy cotton sheet on her four-poster Renaissance bed, she lay on her back and, as she looked up at the tapestry canopy, she thought how foolish she had been to think that one day Gilbert Dubuisson might have joined her in it as her husband. And when her mind returned to the man she should have married, but who had never replied to her letter, so many flints of disappointment dropped onto her she was unable to move for the weight of them.

She soon lost consciousness, but woke again in the early hours when the pain returned. Down the stone spiral steps with the lamentable repairs she descended and made her way straight to the vaulted kitchen. The copper pans, lit up by the moonlight, flickered like flames. She opened the fridge door, made herself a steak sandwich and brought it back to her desolate sheets.

When Émilie Fraisse woke the following morning, she immediately had an urge to feel the sun on her skin. After showering with the garden hosepipe, she went into the dining room and looked in dismay at the remains of the eel, before running back and forth to the vaulted kitchen until the table was cleared. After washing up, she went to wipe the table that had been stolen from a monastery. But before long, she found that she had got out her beeswax and was rubbing it furiously. She then turned her attention to the side table. Once the dining room was completed, she opened the door to the *grand salon* with its huge stone fireplace and gleaming reversible floor. Onto her knees she descended and started polishing the walnut boards which were uppermost. And even though they were not due to be turned for another 200 years, once she had finished, she heaved them over and started again.

When Émilie Fraisse eventually went to see Guillaume Ladoucette and sat down on the cushion with the hand-embroidered radish, her knees were so red they appeared to have been scalded.

'So you had a good time with Gilbert Dubuisson last night?' the matchmaker forced himself to ask.

'Very,' replied the châtelaine.

'Excellent. Did he bring you flowers?'

'Yes. From his garden.'

'Thought he might. Did you give him a tour of the château?'

'Yes. He liked it very much.'

'And you showed him your heirloom vegetables?'

'Yes, he was enchanted.'

'And the eel. How was that?'

'A triumph.'.

Just as Guillaume Ladoucette could feel his feet touching the ocean bed, Émilie Fraisse added, 'But I couldn't possibly see him again.'

'Why ever not?' he asked. But he never fully understood her reply. He caught something about moulds, and there being a lovely blue one, and there was also a concern about the postman wanting to restore the scandalous ramparts next. But the matchmaker had no idea what she was talking about as his mind was elsewhere. For it was then that Guillaume Ladoucette decided to reply to Émilie Fraisse's letter.

Chapter Ten

THE MATCHMAKER HAD INTENDED to write his letter to Émilie Fraisse immediately after his Saturday lie-in, which turned out to be such an unusually protracted affair that when he eventually rose after eleven hours on his back, arms down the side of his body as if already dead in his coffin, his immediate concern was for bedsores. After showering in the ruthless waters of the municipal shower, which still hadn't been fixed, and treating himself to some award-winning black pudding from the splendid butcher's in Brantôme, he sat down at the kitchen table in front of a piece of writing paper. But he found that his stomach was writhing like a bag of snakes and he was unable to sit still. After having only written the date, he was up on his feet again to make himself another cup of coffee, despite the fact that the cube of sugar in his first hadn't yet dissolved. Returning to his seat, he wrote the words 'Chère Émilie', but then found himself by the back door with his hand in the sack of the previous year's walnuts, though he was far from hungry. After cracking them open, he installed himself back in front of his letter, scratched out '*Chère Émilie*' and replaced it with '*Ma chère Émilie*'. But the snakes continued to writhe and he reached for his copy of *Antiquité et Braconte* magazine. As he flicked through it, he noticed a listing for a little antiques fair in the streets of Villars, and before he knew it he was in his car hoping to find another Peugeot coffee grinder to add to his collection on the pale stone kitchen mantelpiece.

After parking next to a front door either side of which hung a small three-legged cauldron filled with pink geraniums, he wandered up the lane alongside the locked church with its splendid carved scallop shell over the door. He stopped by the first stall to inspect the handmade lace tablecloths and, as he ran his fingers over the bundles of white monogrammed napkins, he found himself beside a customer from his barbering days who asked how the matchmaking business was going.

'It's a bit like the dozen oysters you buy on a Saturday morning from the stall in the Place du Marché. There are always one or two that are a bugger to open,' he replied, left the stall and turned into the square. By the time he had visited each stall, he realised that he had completely forgotten to look for a Peugeot coffee grinder.

While pulling the car door shut, his mind flashed him the blank letter waiting for him on the kitchen table, and the snakes twisted again. The matchmaker immediately decided that as he was in Villars, he may as well visit the famous grottoes with their glistening calcite formations. Climbing down the steep staircase into the caves, he felt the chilled, damp air rise deliciously up his trouser legs. Making his way slowly through the vast chambers, he stood and admired the strangely thin stalactites that hung like spaghetti from the roof. As he passed deeper inside, he marvelled at the strange black drawings of beasts by prehistoric man. But when he saw the semi-translucent yellow and ochre draperies that hung from the ceiling like bed sheets, all he could think about was the woman he wanted to go to sleep holding.

Returning to his car, the matchmaker decided that the writing paper on the kitchen table was not in the least bit suitable, and he started driving in the opposite direction to Amour-sur-Belle. Forty-two minutes later, he arrived in Périgueux and immediately headed for the best *papeterie* in the city. He spent over an hour drawing in the wondrous aroma as he chose between the colours and weights. Afterwards, as all he had had to eat at midday was a sausage in a piece of baguette at the antiques fair, he headed off for supper in one of the squares.

By the time he arrived home, Guillaume Ladoucette was too tired to embark on any more delaying tactics. As the night squeezed in through the gaps either side of the shutters, he installed himself at the kitchen table again. He untied the ribbon on his new set of cream writing paper, took out one of the tiny sheets and launched into the letter without stopping to write her name in case it stalled him again. By the time he signed the letter, he had finally told Émilie Fraisse how much he had loved her at school, how much he had loved her when she left, how much he had loved her while she was away, how much he had loved her when she came back, how much he loved her now and how much he would always love her. He then added that his biggest regret in life was not having had the courage to tell her sooner, but that his feelings for her were so overpowering they had weakened him. After finishing his *pineau*, the matchmaker put his glass in the sink, went up to bed and remained on dry land for the entire night.

Descending the stairs the following morning, he was struck by the ghastly image of a black and white dropping on his smooth, cream paper. But when he entered the kitchen the letter was just as he had left it. Knowing no corner of the house was safe from the infernal chicken, he picked it up, folded it carefully and slipped it into his pocket.

Stéphane Jollis had got up before some of the birds had retired to their nests in order to get everything done before leaving the bakery in the hands of Guillaume Ladoucette. Sunday was always the most tiresome morning of the week, not only because he wanted to remain under his bedcovers until after Mass like everybody else, but also because the demand for his cakes was at its highest as people needed something sweet to ease the suffering of having to eat lunch with their relatives.

When he opened the connecting door to the bakery, wearing his voluminous checked blue shorts and white T-shirt, he immediately turned on the radio to take his mind off the fact that he was awake at such a heinous hour. With his surprisingly small hands, which his schoolteacher had remarked would rule him out of ever becoming a concert pianist, he made his pastry for the *millefeuilles* and the strawberry and raspberry tartlets. He then opened the oven door and slid them inside, along with the apple tarts he had prepared the day before.

Opening his plastic box of prepared choux pastries, he loaded up his piping bags and filled half the heads and bodies of the *religieuses* with chocolate *crème pâtissière* and half with coffee. After heating up their chocolate and coffee icing, he then dipped each cake into its corresponding pan, smoothing the icing over with his finger as he went.

Once the oven was empty again, he opened the door to the cold room and fought his way round the sacks of flour he was obliged to keep in there as the insufferable heat was making his dough over-inflate. He wheeled out the racks of trays lined with lengths of dough that had bloated overnight and positioned them near the oven. Placing one of the raw baguettes on the head of a long-handled, wooden shovel, he slashed it five times with a razor blade kept between his lips, lifted up the shovel and then fed it into the far reaches of the oven. He continued slashing and shovelling until all the baguettes were inside.

Once the oven door was shut, he made his first cup of coffee. He then returned to the cold room for the loaves.

Having filled and glazed the strawberry and raspberry tartlets, he cut the *millefeuille* pastry into three long strips, slathered two with rum-laced *crème pâtissière*, stacked them all up and painted the top with white icing. But when he cut them into portions, and found, as always, a delicious little slice at the end which was too small to sell, his mind was still so unbalanced from the early shriek of his alarm clock that he simply threw it out.

Once all the bread was cooked, Stéphane Jollis went in search of the trays of *viennoiserie* which had been blooming overnight in the cold room. Out came the croissants—rolled-up triangles of pastry layered with butter; the *chocolatines*, which Parisians called *pains au chocolat*; and the *pains aux raisins*. He loaded them into the oven, along with the brioches.

But just as one mountain was scaled, another peak appeared, and he went in search of some flour to prepare the following day's bread. As he was waiting for the machine to finish rolling and stretching the baguette dough, he sat down for a moment on his battered white stool. It was then that his floury feet started tapping to the music on the radio, a habit that didn't usually start until he had had his fourth cup of coffee. But by then Stéphane Jollis had finally come to his senses, stirred from his somnolence by thoughts of the woman he was about to meet at the annual Donkey Festival in Brantôme.

By the time Guillaume Ladoucette arrived with his empty stomach, all the breads were standing up on end in their correct baskets along the back wall of the shop, and the little cakes lined up in neat rows behind the glass counter. All he had to do, the baker explained, was to serve. He pointed out that everything was clearly priced, and then carefully showed him how the till worked.

But the matchmaker wasn't listening because he had his eye on the oven which he could see through the door. 'If there's a lull, can I have a go at making a loaf?' he asked.

'The day I allow you near my oven with some dough is the day you allow me near your hair with a pair of scissors,' replied Stéphane Jollis, who was in no mood to humour his friend. 'I don't think you're taking this very seriously,' admonished the baker.

Guillaume Ladoucette protested, insisting that he took the task very seriously indeed, and that if there was anyone the baker could trust with his shop it was him. The baker then ran through the orders again and reminded him to make sure that there were enough little cakes left for everyone, particularly the women. As he went next door to get ready, he instructed the matchmaker to acquaint himself with the till while he was gone. But Guillaume Ladoucette immediately wandered into the kitchen, where he noticed a bowl of dough into which he sank a finger and tasted the raw brioche flavoured with aniseed and filled with raisins fat with rum.

When the baker returned to ask whether he looked all right, he was alarmed to see something hanging from his friend's whiskers. Noticing his expression, the matchmaker quickly congratulated his friend on the state of his shoes, admired the fit of his new white T-shirt and declared his hair a triumph. Reminding him not to pick his teeth with his fork if he and his match had lunch together, he then swiftly opened the door, insisting that it was always better to arrive early.

But Stéphane Jollis stood his ground and reminded Guillaume Ladoucette that he was not to do any sums in his head or eat any of the little cakes. He then added that it was imperative that the bakery closed for the day at 12.30, after which he was to shut the blinds and ignore any subsequent hammerings on the door, no matter how desperate.

'Will do,' the matchmaker replied, ushering the baker out. He stood by the door watching his friend drive off and, as soon as the coast was clear, Guillaume Ladoucette went in search of breakfast.

Sitting in the back grounded by the weight of the largest warm almond croissant he could find, the matchmaker wondered how he was going to deliver his letter to Émilie Fraisse. He certainly didn't trust the clot of a postman. Nor did he have any intention of handing it to her when she came into the bakery. At a loss as to what to do, he decided to to have just one little cake to help him think.

It was while he was finishing off his third tart, and eyeing up the other delights among the racks of little cakes, that the thought struck him. He picked up a pair of tongs, went over to the rows of *millefeuilles*, lifted one up and carried it carefully to the steel work counter. After inspecting it for size, he reached inside his pocket, brought out the letter and folded it several more times. Selecting one of the baker's sharpest knives, he then prised the cake apart and slid the letter between its pastry leaves. After closing it again, he inspected it from every angle, and, satisfied that it was barely visible, put it on a plate and carried it to the front of the shop. He then added it to the row of *mille-feuilles* already on display, positioning it nearest to him.

Standing and admiring his own genius, Guillaume Ladoucette was suddenly brought out of his reverie by a thunderous rap at the door. The matchmaker looked at his watch and noticed to his horror that he was already thirteen minutes late in opening the shop. It was another four before he had worked out how to raise the blinds, located the bunch of keys, and discovered which one opened the door.

By then there was little he could say to appease the infuriated crowd waiting outside. With the agility elderly ladies muster when confronted with a queue, Madame Moreau darted to the front and demanded an explanation as to why Guillaume Ladoucette was there. When the matchmaker replied that the baker had urgent business to attend to and that he was just helping out for the morning, she requested a *gros pain* and five mixed fruit tarts. After packing the tarts and handing her the bread, the matchmaker discovered that he had no idea how to work the till as it was nothing like the one he had used in the barber's. He proceeded to calculate the sum in his head, but his total was immediately corrected by the old woman who had the backing of the crowd. Unable to open the till, he was then obliged to furnish her with an IOU for her change. By his fourth customer, the stress was such that he was no longer capable of even attempting mental arithmetic, and as he worked his way through the crowd, a number left with startling bargains.

Taking advantage of the shop being momentarily empty, Guillaume Ladoucette wandered into the back to recover on Stéphane Jollis's battered white stool. But just as he sat down, the bell went. Heaving himself off the stool again, he sloped back into the shop, hoping that whoever it was had the correct change so he wouldn't have to hand out yet another IOU. Standing at the counter was no ordinary customer, but Émilie Fraisse wearing an antique amber dress which appeared to have been shorn off at the knees and something pinning up her hair which sparkled. The jubilant matchmaker immediately marched up to the counter, explained that Stéphane Jollis had left the bakery in his capable hands for the morning, and asked what he could get for her.

'A *millefeuille*, please,' she replied.

Leaning over the counter, Guillaume Ladoucette saw to his relief that the pastry was still there, instantly recognisable by its unusual bulk.

'Certainly! Stéphane Jollis said you'd be in and asked me to save one for you specially,' he replied, picking up the slice with his tongs and placing it inside a box. So elated was he that his plan had worked, he then added another three, announcing that they were on the house.

As he was tying the string, Émilie Fraisse asked whether he remembered the haircut he had once given her, which had made her look like a cockerel, much to the fury of her mother. Guillaume Ladoucette replied that he did indeed, and asked whether she remembered the mushrooms they used to pick together in the woods and cook over a fire in the caves where the Resistance hid during the war. When Émilie Fraisse replied that she did, the matchmaker then started another box and lowered several coffee *religieuses* inside to keep her there longer. As he was tucking in the lid, the châtelaine asked whether he remembered the accident they had had on his new moped when she fell on top of him. Guillaume Ladoucette replied that he did indeed and leaned over the counter to show her that he still had the scar from her teeth. When Émilie Fraisse apologised again, Guillaume Ladoucette then opened another box and placed inside four *babas au rhum* to show that there were no hard feelings.

By the time Émilie Fraisse walked out of the bakery, not only had Guillaume Ladoucette boxed up all the little cakes for her, but he had waved away any attempts at payment as he didn't want the châtelaine to know that he couldn't fathom out how to work the till. She ended up with so much to carry she was obliged to fetch her car to take all the *pâtisserie* home with her.

The fury of Stéphane Jollis's customers at finding that there were no little cakes left did nothing to dampen Guillaume Ladoucette's elation that his plan had worked. Such was his newfound ebullience, the matchmaker even shut the bakery half an hour early when he could no longer face writing another IOU.

Walking home, he imagined Émilie Fraisse biting into her *mille-feuille* while sitting at the dining-room table, her pretty feet resting on the *pisé* floor. He saw her discovering his letter secreted between the pastry leaves and reading it enraptured. After having admired the beauty of his hand, as well as the letter's ingenious and unsurpassably romantic mode of delivery, she would look no further than the poet who wrote it in her search for love. So enchanted was he by the image, that when Guillaume Ladoucette stopped outside his house he found that he was so happy his appetite had been crushed. He decided to have lunch anyway, though, as it went against nature not to. After several slices of cow's muzzle, followed by a salad of oak-leaf lettuce and two rounds of Cabécou, he went upstairs for a siesta. As he passed the spare bedroom, he went inside to close the shutters against the sun, which was in direct firing range. As he did so, he looked outside and noticed that Yves Lévêque's unspeakable *cornichons* had vanished. Magnanimous following his victory with the letter, upon waking the matchmaker decided to pop next door to offer the dentist his condolences. He was also keen to discover how his date with Denise Vigier had gone, as the man hadn't been to see him since their gold-panning expedition.

Reluctantly, Yves Lévêque let him in. They went into the garden to the bed where the *cornichons* had once been, and as they looked at their withered bodies lying on the compost heap, Guillaume Ladoucette resisted the urge to point out that they should have been sown when the moon was passing in front of the constellation of Aries.

Sitting at the garden table, Yves Lévêque described his morning with the abhorrent grocer. Nonetheless, the matchmaker commended him on having paid for Denise Vigier, as well as for complimenting her on her dress. He even praised his skill at accepting gifts from others on learning that he had swiftly pocketed the golden nugget. Such was his joyful mood, he didn't even scold him for dismissing her out of turn because of what her grandmother had done during the war. He simply reminded him that he would get nowhere in his quest for love if he didn't concentrate on the duck leg, ignore the rancid parts and shrug his shoulders at the little green button.

'How did she say it had gone?' the dentist asked.

'Denise Vigier is blessed with optimism and said she would give it another go. I would suggest that you do.'

Eager to change the subject, Yves Lévêque went inside and returned with a tray upon which were two almond *tartelettes*, one of which he put in front of his neighbour. The matchmaker was taken aback because he hadn't seen the dentist in the bakery that morning.

'Where did you get these from?' the matchmaker asked, picking his up and taking a bite. 'Delicious!' he declared, his mouth still full.

'The château.'

'The château?' he asked, confused.

'Apparently you sold all the little cakes to Émilie Fraisse. She wasn't sure what do with them so she started giving them away. Word soon got around. All you had to do was go up there and she would give you a boxful.'

It was then that Guillaume Ladoucette realised that any one of the residents of Amour-sur-Belle could at that moment be reading his love letter to Émilie Fraisse, which had taken him twenty-six years to find the courage to write. He instantly put down the almond *tartelette* as all he could taste was horror.

Chapter Eleven

UNFORTUNATELY FOR THE RESIDENTS of Amour-sur-Belle it was Madame Ladoucette who discovered that the hot water was back on in the municipal shower. She returned to the cubicle in the early hours of the morning, woken from her dreams by a troop of edible dormice clattering their way between the rafters in the bathroom ceiling. But when Madame Ladoucette got up to look for her husband, having forgotten that he was long since dead, she found that she was not in the family home with its perpetual cassoulet on the stove and magnificent walnut tree in the garden, but a tiny house in the centre of the village.

Suspecting that her husband was out somewhere picking apples, Madame Ladoucette quickly put on her pale blue frock, shoes and stockings and stepped outside into the aromatic night. She wandered round the empty streets, poking her head over garden walls searching for him in the darkness. But there was not a trace.

It was when she was making her way out of the Place du Marché that Madame Ladoucette spotted the hilarious contraption next to the wall. Remembering its potential for amusement, she abandoned her search for her husband and pulled open the door. Refusing to allow her feathered shadow to join her, because of their previous shameful behaviour, she stepped in alone. The birds stood outside, tapping their horny beaks mournfully against the plastic door as Madame Ladoucette stood under the warm water in a state of delight while her shoes overfilled. It wasn't until over two hours later, when the water had started to run cold, that they were finally reunited.

The second person to open the door of the municipal shower was Stéphane Jollis, who enjoyed two minutes and twenty-three seconds of tepid water before it reverted to its previous ruthless temperature for the rest of the day. The brief respite only infuriated the baker further, having had to get up earlier than usual to sort out the catastrophe caused by Guillaume Ladoucette. He had never felt entirely comfortable leaving the bakery in the hands of the matchmaker, particularly when he arrived at Brantôme two hours early for the Donkey Festival, having been ushered out of his own premises by the man. But as he sat sipping his fourth coffee and having to eat another man's croissants in the *salon de thé* to kill time, he decided that it was a risk worth taking for a chance at love.

When the time eventually came, Stéphane Jollis paid his considerable bill and made his way to the curious sixteenth-century bridge, which, rather than straddling the Dronne in a straight line, was bent at an angle like a dog's leg. Unable to see anyone who fitted the matchmaker's description, he busied himself reading the information panel on the wall, then walked to the middle of the bridge and stood looking at the ducks swimming in the reflection of the splendid abbey. And, as the abominable sound of braying rose from the Monks' Garden, the baker wondered again why it was that out of all his eight siblings only he was still unmarried.

After watching the tantalising trout sashay their way down the Dronne, he looked up again to see if anyone else had arrived, and noticed a small, dark-haired woman in shorts standing on her own near the information panel. When he approached and asked whether her name was Vivienne, she replied that it was indeed. She then said that he must be Stéphane and that she had seen him on the bridge, but hadn't approached because he seemed so unlike the description the matchmaker had given. And when Stéphane Jollis asked her whether she was disappointed, she replied 'not in the least'.

As they walked across the bridge towards the sound of the abominable braying in the Monks' Garden, the baker asked the cashier where she was from. Vivienne Chaume replied 'St Felix of Mareuil or of Bourdeilles', and explained that the row over the name had been going on for several centuries and that the council had settled for both. When she asked where he was from, the baker replied 'Amour-sur-Belle' and pointed out that its ugliness worked to its advantage in that no English lived there. And he added that while, despite its name, there wasn't much love there either, the village matchmaker was doing his best.

After finding a spot on the grass in the shade of a large magnolia tree, they sat down to watch the contestants ride round in a circle in home-made chariots pulled by their pet donkeys, while the commentator admired the beauty of the beasts' legs, the sturdiness of their necks and the angle at which their colossal ears hung.

The cashier and baker chatted while they waited for the obstacle course to be set up, and clapped with glee with the rest of the crowd when the commentator announced that the competition was about to begin. They watched as the first contestant wearing a black felt hat and waistcoat walked his donkey, without its chariot, in and out of a line of barrels. But when man and beast approached a green plastic sheet stretched across the grass, instead of walking over it, the animal sunk in its front legs and refused to budge. And no amount of tugging on its reins would shift it, because by now his pet had lowered its shaggy bottom to increase its resistance. After having to walk round the sheet, the pair then proceeded between the planks of wood without any trouble. Nor did the animal make any fuss when it was walked to the centre of the ring for each of its feet to be lifted. It was when they reached the low, wooden seesaw that it revealed the true depth of its delinquency. After refusing to walk over it, the donkey marked its objection further by raising its tail and releasing a volley of undigested hay in undigested chunks.

When the commentator announced the beginning of the final round during which the contestants had to drive their chariots around the obstacle course, Stéphane Jollis and Vivienne Chaume, who were thoroughly enjoying themselves, shuffled forward on the grass to make sure of an uninterrupted view. They watched in admiration as a woman in a floor-length skirt made her way round with only minor glitches, and then nudged each other when it was the turn of the man with the black felt hat and waistcoat. They clapped as he wound in and out of the barrels, despite his being docked a point for missing one out. They clapped as he drove his pet over the green plastic sheet of which it showed not the slightest hint of fear. And they cheered when the donkey bolted over the finishing line, much to the terror of its owner rattling in the homemade chariot behind.

While the prizes were being given out, Stéphane Jollis suggested to Vivienne Chaume that they went to look round the cheese and wine fair in the park. When they approached the first stand, the baker was so thrilled by the man's Rosée des Prés that he bought four bottles. They then visited the stand of the woman from Berry who was selling pieces of *casse-museau*, a non-sweetened cake made with goat *fromage frais* according to an ancient recipe, which was eaten either as a salad or an hors d'oeuvre. Stéphane Jollis was so intrigued he bought a whole one for each of them to take home. And when they reached Michel Fallet's champagne stall, the baker could see no reason why not to buy a bottle and drink it right there and then with the delectable Vivienne Chaume, who not only appreciated a good-looking donkey when she saw one, but was splendid company.

As he handed his match a glass, the baker invited her to come to the bakery one day the following week for a *dégustation* of his little cakes. Vivienne Chaume then horrified Stéphane Jollis by thanking him, but refusing all the same on the grounds of her being on a diet. The baker, who could see no possible future with a woman who would deny herself the pleasure of choux pastry expertly filled with *crème pâtissière* by his award-winning fingers, felt instantly that it was time to go home.

Guillaume Ladoucette sat at the desk with the ink stain, dreading the door opening. While he knew he would be in deep trouble with the baker, his was the only arrival he didn't fear as he was one of the few people who couldn't have received his love letter intended for Émilie Fraisse. Having omitted to write her name at the top of it in case it stalled him in his outpour, there was no doubt that its recipient would naturally assume that they were the subject of his amorous declaration. As a result, he had risen early in an attempt to avoid bumping into anyone at the municipal shower, but had been caught out by Gilbert Dubuisson who, when the matchmaker opened the door, immediately asked whether there was anything he could do to make Émilie Fraisse change her mind and see him again. Guillaume Ladoucette assured him that as far as he knew he had acted like the perfect gentleman throughout, but that she had made up her mind. He added that there were several women on his books who would find his company a delight, and that he should come by the shop when he had a moment.

The matchmaker had just retreated to the back, where he hoped to be less conspicuous, when the door opened. It was Lisette Robert.

'Are you all right?' she asked, sitting down on the cushion with the hand-embroidered radish.

'Fine, thanks. Why?' he replied, approaching the desk and trying not to show the least flicker of emotion.

'You're looking at me in a funny way.'

'You didn't happen to see Émilie Fraisse yesterday, by any chance?' he asked.

'Yes, I did, actually.'

'At the château?'

'Yes, why?'

'Just wondered. She didn't give you any little cakes, did she?'

'Well, yes, that's what I went up there for. Apparently you sold her the lot and she called me to see if I wanted any. I got a boxful.'

Guillaume Ladoucette paused. 'There didn't happen to be any *mille-feuilles* in there, did there?'

'Two custard tarts and two *choux Chantilly*. Why?'

'Just wondered! Now, Lisette, glass of red?'

After offering her a walnut, which was refused as she had her own to get through, Guillaume Ladoucette then had the unfortunate task of breaking the news to Lisette Robert that, as incomprehensible as it may seem, the man from the council wasn't interested. The matchmaker told her about their long talk at the washing place and that while he hadn't revealed who she was, he had gone to great lengths detailing her considerable charms, but Jean-François Lafforest was having none of it.

Lisette Robert listened carefully, blinked several times and then asked dolefully, 'Is there nothing more you can do?'

'I'm afraid not, Lisette. The man is resolute.'

The midwife stared at the floor, and the matchmaker looked at the pen next to the blank piece of paper in front of him. In a moment, he raised his eyes and said, 'While there is nothing more I can do in my professional capacity, let me ask you this, Lisette: what would any right-minded person do if they went to the woods to pick mushrooms and came across a sign that said "The Picking of Mushrooms is Forbidden"?'

'Carry on regardless,' she replied without hesitation.

'Exactly!' he said.

Guillaume Ladoucette was correct in his suspicion that Lisette Robert was responsible for the sudden lack of hot water in the shower. She had fallen quite unexpectedly for the man from the council. She had noticed him the first time he came into the Bar Saint-Jus with his soft leather briefcase, which he had clutched to his stomach, and his unfortunate trousers that didn't quite fit. There was a gentleness in his being that attracted her, as well as the weight of a past pain that he carried. When, to her delight, he returned to oversee the installation of the municipal shower, she would sit at the window of the bar, glancing at him over a copy of the *Sud Ouest*. At night, as the perpetual breeze rode up and down her curves, which were more graceful than those of the Belle, she would lie awake, her mind stirred to its sediments with thoughts of him. One dawn, unable to bear the agitation any longer, she got up to compose him a melody. Instead of the villagers being roused from their dreams by the poisonous sound of her elephantine attempts at piano-playing, the most angelic strains rose from the keys and fluttered around Amour-sur-Belle.

Such was her devastation that Jean-François Lafforest no longer had any reason to come to the village once the shower was completed, she slipped out one night with her spanner to provide him with one. When, the following day, she was summoned to the cubicle by the villagers to explain to him how she had discovered that there was no longer any hot water, she was delighted for the opportunity to stand as close to him as possible.

After the midwife left Heart's Desire to start running her first of five baths that day, Guillaume Ladoucette looked at his watch hoping it was lunchtime, but it was only twenty to eleven.

Reaching into the top left-hand drawer, he took out his slim file of customers and started to read through them hoping to be struck by an inspiring match, but his mind kept parading him ghastly images of his amorous declaration in the most inappropriate of hands.

Just as he was checking his watch again, only to be disappointed a second time, the door opened. It was Stéphane Jollis looking more floury than usual.

'I can explain everything!' said the matchmaker as soon as he saw him.

'I was hoping you could,' replied the baker, heading for the chair with the peeling marquetry and sitting down.

'Émilie Fraisse came in and we got talking about the old days and before I knew it I'd sold her the lot. I got carried away.'

'But you didn't exactly *sell* them to her, did you, Guillaume?' replied Stéphane Jollis. 'I've counted up the money you left by the till, which for some reason you didn't open, and it certainly doesn't account for the two hundred and forty-six little cakes I left in your custody. And on top of that, people have been coming in waving IOUs at me all morning.'

'Forgive me, Stéphane. I'll make it up to you, I promise,' insisted Guillaume Ladoucette. 'And, of course, I'll pay for all the little cakes.'

'Not only were there no *babas au rhum* left for Madame Serre so she had to go and hunt one down at the château,' the baker continued, 'but you were unable to correctly add up a croissant and a six-cereal loaf.'

'I'll waive the fee for the Unrivalled Silver Service as well. How's about that?'

'It's a start,' replied the baker.

'Anyway,' said the matchmaker. 'On to more exciting things—how did it go with the charming Vivienne Chaume?'

'She's on a diet.'

'How extraordinary!' replied the horrified matchmaker. 'No, no, that will never do. You want someone who will revel in your talent, not recoil in terror each time you whip out your piping bag. Do accept my apologies, Stéphane. I had no idea. It just goes to show that you shouldn't judge people by their appearance. She seemed perfectly sane when she walked in here. I'll mark it on her file. Now, let's see who else we can find for you . . .'

But Stéphane Jollis said he had to return to work and that he would leave it for a few weeks until things had calmed down. When the door closed, the matchmaker watched his friend walk past the window in his blue-and-white checked shorts, his ample calves finishing in a pair of ridiculously small feet. Guillaume looked at his watch. It was a perfectly reasonable time to close, he concluded, as it was only half an hour before midday and matters of the heart shouldn't be discussed on an empty stomach. He packed his things up as quickly as he could, and congratulated himself on having shut the door behind him before anyone could sit down on the cushion with the hand-embroidered radish and thank him for such a wondrous declaration of devotion.

Having walked home the long way round in the hope of avoiding bumping into anyone, the matchmaker arrived at his house, opened his front door and locked it behind him. In an effort to remind himself that life still had its pleasures, he descended the creaking wooden steps of the cellar, clattered around for a while in his grandfather's Sunday clogs which nipped, and emerged triumphantly with a jar of potted goose. But just as he took his first mouthful at the kitchen table, it occurred to him that Madame Serre hadn't been sitting outside her front door like a sentinel on his return, and he imagined the reason why she was no longer at her post was because she was hiding from him in horror of his amorous outpourings.

Hoping to take his mind off his troubles, he went into the garden to begin the first of his walnut wines, which he would make according to the leaf method, because tradition stated that the green nuts shouldn't be used until after July 14. But as he climbed his ladder, he thought of what a fool he had been to have given Émilie Fraisse all the little cakes. As he put the leaves to steep in four parts of wine to one of brandy, and added the sugar and orange peel, he thought how ridiculous he had been to ever imagine he could win her back. And as he poured the mixture into bottles and carried them down to the cellar to stand for a year, he wondered what she was doing.

Émilie Fraisse was in the vaulted kitchen looking for a little something to quell her appetite, when she came across the last of the boxes from the bakery. The châtelaine still couldn't understand how she had managed to come away with quite so many, particularly when all she had asked for was a solitary *millefeuille*. She hadn't been home long before she realised she couldn't possibly get through all of their contents on her own and started calling people in the hope of offloading them. Not, of course, that she had minded the embarrassment of *pâtisserie* because each time Guillaume Ladoucette had filled up and tied another box with string she had gained a few more moments in his company.

She carried the box to the kitchen table, along with her glass of sweet white Château Marie Plaisance Bergerac. Lifting up the cardboard lid, she took out the first *millefeuille* that Guillaume Ladoucette had chosen for her, which she had naturally kept for herself because of its size. It wasn't until several chews and swallows later that it struck Émilie Fraisse that Stéphane Jollis's baking was far from its usual glorious standard. Inspecting it to determine what had gone wrong, she suddenly noticed something wedged inside. Pulling the cake apart, she retrieved a lump sodden with rum-laced *crème pâtissière*. When, eventually, she managed to unfold it, she found before her what appeared to be a letter. While the ink had bled, and parts, including the signature, had been swallowed, she could just about make out the words. And as she read, she realised that she had received her very first love letter which was of such rapturous sentiment her heart soared higher than the buzzards above the scandalous ramparts. But what Émilie Fraisse couldn't understand was how the baker could have loved her all these years and not given her the slightest inkling.

It was when Guillaume Ladoucette walked slowly downstairs in his burgundy silk dressing gown and spotted Violette, the infernal chicken, sitting on the rim of his pot of cassoulet, her tail lifted over its contents in readiness, that he finally snapped. The bird matched his shriek of outrage with a squawk of similar volume and immediately took to the air, flapping round the kitchen in frantic circles that sent the pans clattering into each other on their hooks and the row of Peugeot coffee grinders on the pale stone mantelpiece crashing to the floor.

Ducking down, the matchmaker ran to open the back door, through which the bird fled for the safety of the garden wall. After locking the door again, the horrified matchmaker rushed to the stove fearing that the family's perpetual cassoulet, which had outlasted seven presidents, had been ruined in the flick of a tail feather. After examining the surface, he took a wooden spoon and poked through the contents, scrutinising the pieces of Toulouse sausage, sifting through the haricot beans and lifting out the grey goose bone for closer inspection.

Yet the relief at finding the dish unsullied was not enough to calm Guillaume Ladoucette. Neither was the novelty of warm water in the municipal shower able to improve his mood. After returning home to dress, he headed immediately to the Bar Saint-Jus with as much determination as he could muster in a pair of supermarket leather sandals. Ignoring Sandrine Fournier, the mushroom poisoner, who approached him wanting to know whether he had found her another match, he walked straight up to Fabrice Ribou, who was cleaning the coffee machine, and announced, 'Your chicken's stalking me.'

On seeing his fury, the bar owner immediately offered him a seat and a drink on the house. He sat and listened as the matchmaker related how for the last six months he had suffered the indignity of peck marks in his butter, feathers in his *pineau* and eggs in the most unacceptable of places. When he told him that the final straw had been the sight of Violette, the infernal chicken, about to defile his cassoulet, Fabrice Ribou immediately leapt to the bird's defence claiming that a creature of her nature couldn't possibly be responsible for the man's torment and that it was probably someone else's. But the matchmaker told him that Violette's unfortunate features were quite unmistakable.

'She must be very fond of you,' concluded the bar owner, leaning back in his chair. 'She never comes anywhere near us.'

'But I don't want the affections of a chicken! I assure you her feelings are totally unrequited,' replied the exasperated matchmaker.

When Fabrice Ribou suggested that he kept his back door shut so she couldn't wander in, Guillaume Ladoucette leaned towards him. Not only did he keep his back door shut at all times, he insisted with quiet rage, but for the last six months he had locked it again every time he had come through it. Neither was she getting in through the windows as he tied them in such a fashion that there was only the narrowest of openings through which a bird of her figure would be unable to squeeze. How she was getting in was an utter mystery.

Fabrice Ribou sighed and brushed off an invisible crumb from the table. While he couldn't lock up the bird, as she deserved her freedom, he reasoned, and nor was he responsible for whom she fell in love with, he would be willing to come round at some stage to shore up Guillaume Ladoucette's defences. But the matchmaker, who rarely put his foot down, insisted that he came that instant.

Leaving the bar in the hands of his wife, Fabrice Ribou accompanied Guillaume Ladoucette home. After checking the locks on the front and back doors, he then asked the matchmaker to show him how he tied the windows and agreed that a chicken of Violette's girth couldn't possibly squeeze through the gap.

As they trooped up to the attic, Guillaume Ladoucette pointed out the path the eggs took when rolling across the landing at night when he was trying to sleep. He then opened the airing cupboard in the bathroom and showed him a fresh black-and-white dropping on a pile of otherwise clean cotton underpants. As they turned the corner on the stairs, he picked up a ginger feather from the floor and held it silently underneath the bar owner's nose. Once in the attic, Fabrice Ribou inspected the three tiny arch-shaped holes under the eaves which once served as entrances for pigeons at the time when they were kept for food. But the bar owner found that like all the others in the village, the holes had been blocked off with a pane of glass decades ago.

'That only leaves the chimneys,' he concluded. The two men then headed back down to the kitchen. After Guillaume Ladoucette had picked up the coffee grinders from the floor, two of which had cracked, they peered up inside the blackened opening above the fireplace and Fabrice Ribou announced that he would go and pick up some wire meshing and cover the tops of the stacks so that not even Father Christmas with his wily ways could get down them.

Showing him out, the matchmaker thanked the bar owner for his help, unaware that it was rooted solely in his fear that Guillaume Ladoucette would put Violette in a pot before he did. The matchmaker had intended to spend the rest of the weekend behind closed doors, but Stéphane Jollis was insistent that he helped him at the *Fête de la Saint-Jean* celebrations that evening, reminding him that he still owed him a favour.

To take his mind off the misery that lay ahead of him, Guillaume Ladoucette went outside to lose himself in the cultivation of vegetables. As he started to prepare the earth next to a row of round courgettes, he heard the clattering of Fabrice Ribou's ladder. And, for the first time upon spotting Violette, the infernal chicken, warming her fluffy under-carriage on the garden wall, Guillaume Ladoucette smiled.

Finding a spot in the shade on the scandalous ramparts, Émilie Fraisse sat down, her back against the stone wall. In her hand was the partly eaten letter, which, after having carefully wiped off from it as much of the *crème pâtissière* as possible, she had left out in the sun to dry. As she read it yet again, it spoke of such rapturous affection that her heart blossomed. It was only upon remembering that it wasn't from the man she had always loved that the petals dropped. As she sat looking at the discarded walnut shells left by squirrels, she wondered whether she could ever feel the same ardour for the baker as he did for her. But while his letter was such bewitching poetry, and she had the utmost admiration for his work as an artisan, she knew that his were not the arms in which she longed to shelter.

More aware than most that letters had to be answered, Émilie Fraisse decided to go and speak to Stéphane Jollis. When she arrived at the bakery, she found a long queue and asked the woman standing at the rear why so many people were waiting. The woman replied that a love note had been found in one of the baker's cakes and, while the sender's identity was uncertain, they were all hoping to find one of their own. The shocked châtelaine, who had told only two people of her discovery, both of whom had sworn to keep the matter to themselves, decided to return later.

It wasn't Lisette Robert who had let slip about the curious piece of correspondence in Émilie Fraisse's *millefeuille*. When the châtelaine knocked at her door asking for help in deciphering the words blurred by *crème pâtissière*, the midwife had taken one look and recognised the hand of Guillaume Ladoucette. However, her cursed inability to gossip prevented her from pointing out the sender's true identity.

The person responsible for the enormous queue at the bakery was in fact Sandrine Fournier. When news spread that Émilie Fraisse had made off with all the bakery's little cakes, the assistant ambulant fishmonger had knocked at the château door in the hope of wresting a coffee éclair from her. When Émilie Fraisse explained that they had all gone, such was the woman's disappointment that she immediately invited her in for an apéritif to console her. It was when Sandrine Fournier got up from the seat which slid open to hide the salt from the tax collector that she noticed the letter on the table. Despite the châtelaine's bountiful imagination, she was unable to come up with an explanation for the soggy missive other than the truth, that she had found it in her *millefeuille*. The assistant ambulant fishmonger told Madame Serre of the discovery while wrapping up her trout, and advised her to inspect her *babas au rhum* carefully. Madame Serre, who had failed to catch the name of the recipient, changed it each time she repeated the tale.

As Émilie Fraisse was making her way back up the Rue du Château that did lead to the castle, Yves Lévèque pulled over to thank her again for the almond tarts. It wasn't courtesy that had made him stop, but a desire to put off as long as possible his rendezvous with Denise Vigier. He was obliged to move, however, as Marcel Coussy had come up behind him with two bales of hay impaled on the front of his tractor. Driving out of the village, the dentist turned right at the field with the ginger Limousin cows that winked and headed for Sorges. As he entered the flat green valley, he tried to remember how on earth the matchmaker had talked him into meeting the repugnant grocer again.

After parking outside the church, Yves Lévèque was disappointed to see a sign indicating the way to the Truffle Museum as it meant he would be unable to go home on the pretext that it was impossible to find. The stone in his heart plummeted even further when he saw Denise Vigier, the grocer, already standing in the shade of a plane tree outside the museum mopping herself with a handkerchief. Kissing her on each cheek from as far a distance as possible, he then complimented her on her atrocious dress, which was completely devoid of allure.

Once inside, the pair stood together at the kiosk until Denise Vigier could no longer resist the lure of the gift shop and darted off. When the woman behind the counter handed him two tickets, Yves Lévèque knew he was cornered and reluctantly his long, pale instruments of torture found their way into his pocket. Wanting to get the ordeal over as quickly as possible, he entered the exhibition devoted to the prized Périgord truffle, known as the Black Diamond, and walked up to the first panel. As he was reading that truffles had no roots, shoots, leaves or true fruits, which had often baffled scientists as to whether they belonged to the animal or vegetable kingdom, he looked at Denise Vigier who had just come in holding a tiny paper bag and was studying a panel out of sequence. As she stood learning about how the celebrated fungus could be found in the circular bare patch of earth that surrounded certain trees, pitched forward by her colossal chest as if battling against driving rain, the dentist wondered again what in heaven's name the matchmaker had been thinking of.

When the grocer disappeared to look at the exhibits round the corner, Yves Lévèque hung back and approached a cabinet of what appeared to be scorched brains in specimen jars. But as he peered at the *570 gram Truffe du Périgord* found in Sorges on December 19, 1995, by Monsieur Jean-Noël Combeau, all he could think about was the monstrous price Denise Vigier charged for her mushrooms compared to those in the supermarket.

The dentist was just about to suggest to the grocer that it was time to leave, when suddenly one of the panels caught his eye. He retraced his steps and started to read about how Venus, when mourning the death of Adonis, was consoled by Amour telling her that a new fruit had been created in her garden that would cause eagerness in couples, and that it would be attributed with Adonis's virility. Amour then buried Adonis's body in a field where it germinated and converted into black truffles. Once harvested, he served them for supper at Venus's house when Mars was invited. While Venus refused to eat them, Mars finished the lot. The blonde Venus was never so beautiful the following morning and Mars beamed with utter satisfaction.

The dentist immediately went in search of Denise Vigier and asked her whether she fancied a spot of lunch in the village's Auberge de la Truffe. The grocer, who had found the museum fascinating, and was thrilled with her purchase of a truffle-shaped nailbrush from the gift shop, thought it a splendid idea. Despite the restaurant's reputation, the pair managed to get a table with a yellow tablecloth in the conservatory overlooking the terrace. When the gracious waiter arrived to take their orders, Yves Lévèque suggested that they both tried the special four-course truffle menu at 100 euros per head, and that she wasn't to worry at the staggering cost because it was all on him.

It wasn't long before the truffle consommés arrived. As they marvelled at the forest flavour and found to their delight slices of truffle lurking in the bottom of the oaky water, the dentist discovered that Denise Vigier had the most exceptional sense of humour. And as they joyfully savoured their scrambled eggs flecked with truffles, served with a magnificent foie gras resting on a bed of apple in a succulent truffle sauce, the grocer noticed the intense blue of the dentist's eyes.

As the waiter appeared with their cod stuffed with slices of truffle, and wished them 'bonne continuation' before turning silently on his heels, Yves Lévèque found himself patting the grocer's knee as he asked her whether she wanted some more bread.

When the fourth course arrived in the form of two large ovals of puff pastry, the gracious waiter carefully cut a circle in the top of the one he had placed in front of Denise Vigier, and with the words 'Voilà la merveille!', lifted it up to reveal an enormous truffle inside sliced with a potato. And when Yves Lévèque started to cut open his, he thought to himself that he had already found his marvel.

After the truffle ice cream arrived, and the dentist declared that he couldn't eat any more, Denise Vigier found herself resting a hand on his arm as she told him it was too rapturous to miss. As she held up a spoonful to his lips, and the fungal ecstasy slipped down his throat, it was then that the dentist realised that a colossal bosom was nothing other than a triumphant asset. And when, later that afternoon, he felt the soft mounds against his naked back, Yves Lévèque sent up a silent prayer of thanks to St Anthony, the patron saint of truffle-growers.

After receiving a second call from the baker asking where he was, Guillaume Ladoucette reluctantly made his way to the field on the edge of the village where the fête was taking place. Already, the enormous bonfire was stacked up with a young oak propped up in the centre.

Just as the matchmaker had feared, people were already arriving, though it was only five o'clock. He found Stéphane Jollis behind the bar serving villagers pitchers of rosé. Guillaume Ladoucette hovered, hoping that everything was in hand and that he could slip away, but the baker spotted him and told him that help was needed with the food.

As Guillaume Ladoucette approached the trestle table covered with bowls of salad and grated carrot, Monsieur Moreau, who had, for the moment, vacated the bench by the fountain said to cure gout, informed the matchmaker that he was needed to baste the mutton that was already turning on the spit. Guillaume Ladoucette picked up the paint-brush, dunked it into the marinade and started dabbing at the sheep's carcass. Despite keeping his head down so as not to be recognised, it wasn't long before he heard someone calling his name. He looked up to see Madame Serre approaching. Within minutes he had learned that it was Didier Lapierre who had received his letter.

The matchmaker continued prodding with his brush wondering what he should do. Should he wait for the carpenter to bring it up, or should he go and tell him that it had all been a terrible mistake? He worked through the various options as the meat hissed over the fire. But before he had made up his mind, the man appeared before him. However, Didier Lapierre didn't want to thump him at all. Instead, the man with the pine-cone haircut wanted to know whether it was true that Madame Moreau had received a love letter from a secret admirer.

It wasn't long before the villagers were demanding to be fed and Monsieur Moreau informed Guillaume Ladoucette that he was needed to carve. First in line was Fabrice Ribou, who not only asked for a big slice in view of having blocked up the matchmaker's chimneys for him, but couldn't resist telling him that Denise Vigier had found a love letter in a little cake from a mystery admirer.

'I thought it was Madame Moreau,' hissed the matchmaker.

'It wasn't either of them,' interrupted Madame Ribou who was stand-ing behind her husband listening with the attentive ear of a woman who had worked in a bar for three decades. 'It was Modeste Simon.'

After carving them each a slice, Guillaume Ladoucette noticed to his horror that Modeste Simon had just joined the end of the queue. Slowly, she moved up the line towards him and eventually held out her plate, maintaining the silence she had kept since the unfortunate disap-pearance of Patrice Baudin, the skinny vegetarian pharmacist. After he had served her, keeping his eyes lowered, Guillaume Ladoucette then watched as she found herself a seat at one of the trestle tables under-neath the lime trees. As he was still wondering what to do, since it was unlikely that she would reply if he spoke to her, one of the inhabitants from a neighbouring hamlet called his name, held out his plate and asked, 'Did you hear about the love letter Marcel Coussy received inside an éclair? Apparently it was a work of unparalleled poetry.'

As night squeezed out the day, and the accordion player struck up, Guillaume Ladoucette started to leave. But Stéphane Jollis insisted that he had something to eat for his efforts. Though his appetite was

464 | Julia Stuart

nowhere to be found, the matchmaker reluctantly helped himself and found a seat underneath the lime trees next to the postman.

He stayed put as people left the benches, joined hands and started dancing round the fire and singing in outrageous disharmony to the old tunes played by the accordionist. As the singing became more monstrous, the postman turned to the matchmaker and said: 'I now understand why things didn't work out with me and Émilie Fraisse.'

'Why?' asked Guillaume Ladoucette, wiping his moustache on a paper serviette.

'It's Stéphane Jollis she's after. She's been hanging around the bakery all day. The last time I went past he had locked the door and was taking her into the back. He probably gave her a *dégustation* of his little cakes. I bet it works every time. If only it could be that easy for the rest of us.' The postman then turned back to face the fire and added, 'It's still chucking out some heat, isn't it?'

But Guillaume Ladoucette was unable to feel the warmth of the flames because his heart had suddenly turned cold.

Chapter Twelve

GUILLAUME LADOUCETTE ARRIVED outside the bakery to pick up Stéphane Jollis for their scheduled fishing expedition and switched off the engine. He didn't bother pulling down the sun visor to critically assess the splendour of his moustache in the mirror. Nor did he open the glove compartment to kill time. He didn't even curse the baker's abominable timekeeping. Instead, he sat staring straight ahead of him wondering what his friend and Émilie Fraisse had been up to. If only he had tried harder to convince Lisette Robert of the baker's many virtues, instead of accepting that she loved another, then Stéphane Jollis wouldn't have needed to look elsewhere, he concluded.

Suddenly, the passenger door opened and a strong, hairy arm reached in and placed a large basket made from sweet chestnut on the back seat. The limb momentarily disappeared and returned with a red-and-white checked tea towel that was carefully placed over it. The car tilted towards the right as the baker held on to the roof with one hand

and manoeuvred his substantial frame inside, followed by his head.

'Hello. Sorry I'm late,' said Stéphane Jollis.

'Not to worry,' replied Guillaume Ladoucette, starting the car. 'Got everything?'

'Yep,' replied the baker, winding down the window.

The pair then drove out of the village and turned right at the field with the ginger Limousin cows that winked. As they headed towards Brantôme past acres of maize fields lashed by flicking water cannons, each time the matchmaker changed gear, his knuckles rubbed against the baker's thigh blooming over the passenger seat. And, for the first time, Guillaume Ladoucette felt uncomfortable.

'Bring any lunch with you?' the matchmaker eventually enquired.

'Just a snack,' replied the baker, staring straight ahead of him. 'You?'

'Just a snack,' said Guillaume Ladoucette, wrinkling up his nose.

As they arrived in Brantôme, they turned left away from the infestation of tourists and parked by the river. The two men, both holding family-sized baskets, then made their way along the Dronne into which children hurled themselves much to the outrage of the ducks.

Once they reached the NO FISHING sign, they put down their baskets in their usual spot. Settled at the water's edge, they both took a piece of weighted fishing line from their pocket. The baker then searched in his basket for a baguette, broke off an end and foraged inside for the soft, white innards. Once he had sufficient, he rolled it up into a ball and speared it with his hook, while Guillaume Ladoucette opened a tin and selected a worm. After the matchmaker had taken off his supermarket leather sandals, and the baker his floury shoes, they tied their lines around their right ankles. Carefully rolling up both trouser legs to the knee, they then sank their feet into the dusky water and felt the lines pirouetting down towards the bottom of the river.

'That's better!' said Guillaume Ladoucette, waggling his hairy toes, feeling the cool river slipping between them.

'Bliss!' agreed the baker.

The pair sat in silence for a while as they watched the leaves spinning on the surface of the water which sauntered slowly by. But Guillaume Ladoucette couldn't enjoy his favourite spot along the Dronne, where the ducks tipped themselves over headfirst to reveal their feathered bottoms. For he kept imagining the baker slipping off Émilie Fraisse's ridiculous seventeenth-century shoes, tying a fishing line around her ankle and then offering her the most delectable contents of his basket.

'I feel a bit peckish,' the matchmaker suddenly announced, determined to get the better of him.

'So do I,' replied Stéphane Jollis.

As they shuffled backwards towards their baskets, their lines emerged out of the water festooned with lurid green weed. Stalling for time as he waited to see what would appear from the rival basket, Guillaume Ladoucette pretended to look for his penknife. He watched from the corner of his eye as a jar of *cornichons* appeared, followed by another baguette. Then, with a sly smile that Guillaume Ladoucette instantly recognised, the baker brought out an earthenware bowl.

'A little green salad with diced hard-boiled egg to begin with? Lovely,' said the matchmaker with relief.

'There's nothing more satisfying than eating a fresh egg from one of your own chickens,' remarked the baker through a mouthful of salad. 'Marcel Coussy does a great job of looking after my birds at his farm. And he's always very grateful for the walnut oil I press myself which I give him in return. He says he's never tasted anything like it. I've used some in the salad dressing, actually. Fancy any?'

'No, thanks, otherwise I won't manage this!' said Guillaume Ladoucette, reaching into his basket with both hands and taking out a shallow earthenware dish. 'Tomato salad marinated in eau de vie on a hot summer's day. My favourite! Of course, the tomatoes always taste better if you've grown them yourself. But what really makes this dish unsurpassable is if the eau de vie is made from your own plums. I took them to the man with the travelling still last year and watched it being made. Fancy any?'

'No, thanks, otherwise I won't manage this!' replied Stéphane Jollis, needing both hands to lift out an enormous dish from his basket. He whipped off the lid with considerable flourish.

'Bit of pie?' asked Guillaume Ladoucette. 'Lovely. I think I've seen that one in the supermarket.'

'It's actually boned stuffed duck baked in a pastry crust. After I boned the duck, I sliced off layers of the breast and thigh, diced them up and placed them back inside having sprinkled them with cognac and port.' The baker paused before adding, 'The recipe says that adding a truffle is optional, but I thought I might as well use that whopper I found last winter. Shame, really, because apparently it's the biggest that's been found in the Périgord in the last ten years. I must say the oil preserved it perfectly. Now, where's my carving knife?'

Stéphane Jollis then cut off a large slice which he speared with a fork and offered to Guillaume Ladoucette. 'Fancy some?'

'No, thanks,' replied the matchmaker bringing out a dish covered in foil. But he failed to mention that the quails had been cooked in the leaves of the vine that grew over his door. Nor did he bother bringing out his walnut tart made with honey he had collected himself, because he knew he had been defeated by the baker's fungal masterstroke.

'I must say, I really can't think of anything I'd rather be doing now. Isn't this marvellous?' declared the baker, his mouth full.

'Yes,' replied Guillaume Ladoucette, without conviction.

Stéphane Jollis then poured them both a glass of Bergerac, handed one to the matchmaker and said, 'There's something I have to tell you.'

'Oh, yes?'

'I've met someone.'

'Thought so,' replied Guillaume Ladoucette, his despair complete.

'She kept coming in buying little cakes because of a rumour going round that a love note had been discovered inside one of them. God knows how on earth that one started, but I can't tell you how good it's been for business . . . Anyway, she kept coming in, so naturally we had a little chat each time. I assumed she was only interested in my *mille-feuilles*, but then guess what happened?'

'I couldn't possibly.'

'Well, I'd just locked the door one evening after work and was on my way to the municipal shower, when I heard a voice behind me.'

The baker paused, waiting for Guillaume Ladoucette to ask him who it was. When no reply came, he continued with his story.

'I looked round and there she was! It was a bit embarrassing, actually, because all I had on was my dressing gown. I thought she was after some more little cakes, but she didn't mention them. There wasn't a queue when we got to the cubicle, so I went straight in and she was still there when I came out. We then went over to the Bar Saint-Jus for a drink, though Fabrice Ribou sent me home to get dressed first because I'd forgotten I was still in my dressing gown and slippers. We've been seeing each other ever since.'

'Fantastic,' said Guillaume Ladoucette, his eyes not moving from the far bank.

'You don't sound very interested,' said the baker, hurt.

'Sorry,' said the matchmaker. 'I am, honestly.'

'It's strange that I've never bumped into her before. She only lives in Léguillac. Mind you, she hasn't been there long.'

'Léguillac?'

'Yes. It's Sylvette Beau. Do you know her?'

'I've heard her name,' said Guillaume Ladoucette. For the first time since the baker had begun his story, the matchmaker looked at his friend as his mind adjusted to the fact that it wasn't the châtelaine.

'I must say, that Émilie Fraisse is a bit of a weird one, isn't she? She came in to see me the other day and was going on about how she'd never read such unsurpassable poetry, but that we didn't have a future together as she'd always loved someone else, who hadn't replied to some letter she sent him. God knows what all that was about. I took her round the back and gave her a *millefeuille*, which calmed her down a bit. I think she's been spending too much time alone in that château.'

It was then that Guillaume Ladoucette untied the fishing line from round his ankle and handed it to the baker with the words 'Sorry, Stéphane, I've got to go.' He didn't stop to pick up his tomatoes marinated in eau de vie made from the plums he'd grown in his garden and taken to the man with the travelling still. Nor did he collect his quails cooked in the leaves of the vine growing above his door, or indeed the walnut tart made with honey he'd collected himself. Instead, he started running down the bank of the Dronne as fast as was humanly possible in a pair of supermarket leather sandals.

If the authorities had known that another mini-tornado was going to strike Amour-sur-Belle, certainly no one had informed its inhabitants. The first time that the matchmaker noticed that the wind was up was when he turned left at the field towards Amour-sur-Belle and saw to his horror that the ginger Limousin cows had started to walk backwards. As he approached the village, the green-eared maize was lurching grotesquely from side to side as if riding a murderous sea. And by the time he parked outside his house, sunflowers wrenched from the earth were battering the windows.

Lisette Robert had just run yet another bath when she heard the curved, salmon-coloured tiles rattling on the roof like pan lids. Instantly recognising the sound, she rushed round the house closing the windows and bolting the shutters, remembering what trouble she got into last time. Once everything was secured, the midwife decided to take advantage of the sunflowers that had sailed in through the sitting-room window. After snipping off their roots, she put them in a vase on the kitchen table to embellish her final hours. She then looked inside the fridge, wondering what to have for her last meal, and regretted not having been to the supermarket earlier. It was while she was standing on a kitchen chair hunting through the cupboards for something befitting such a momentous occasion as her approaching death that the midwife heard a sound at her door. Assuming it was just the thuds of maize stalks, which had started to take to the air like tribal spears, she ignored it. When she heard the noise again, she opened the door in the hope that it was someone with a better-stocked fridge than she inviting her round to share their dying moments.

When the midwife saw that it was the man from the council, she immediately forgot her disappointment about not having gone food shopping and invited him in. But such was the force of the wind that Jean-François Lafforest, who was holding on to the door frame with only one hand, as he refused to let go of his soft leather briefcase with the other, disappeared, and it took several long minutes before he staggered back into view again. As soon as he re-emerged, Lisette Robert shot out an arm, grabbed him by the shirt and hauled him in.

Once he had straightened his hair, tucked his shirt back in and apologised for disturbing her, Jean-François Lafforest announced that he had come on official business. Clutching his briefcase to his stomach, he went on to explain that he had received a large number of reports that she had taken to having baths.

Lisette Robert, who had informed as many people as possible of her lawlessness, owned up at once. She then took the official upstairs and showed him her most recent transgression. And, as she stood by the edge of the bath, a pink sponge brazenly skimming across the water, she asked for other similar offences to be taken into consideration.

Once back downstairs, Jean-François Lafforest sat down at the kitchen table. Taking a form from his soft leather briefcase, he studiously filled it in in block capitals. Once the form was safely back inside his briefcase, Jean-François Lafforest sat back and took a sip of the *pineau* the midwife had poured for him. And, after they had shared two tins of wild boar terrine and half a baguette, accompanied by the best red wine she could find in the cellar, the man from the council accepted Lisette Robert's offer of joining her in the bath.

Guillaume Ladoucette immediately went to check on his mother. He found Madame Ladoucette in her kitchen, happily milking a goat that had happened to blow in through the window. When finally convinced of her safety, he started down the Rue du Château, which did lead to the castle, heaving against the wind that pummelled his chest.

Keeping his head down as he attempted to cross the courtyard, the wind grabbed him by the legs and spat him against the door bleached fossil-grey by the sun which had fled. Once back on his feet, he thumped on it with his fists, but there was no reply. Feeling the gale tugging at his thighs again, he let himself in, and, once inside, backed up against the door in order to close it. The matchmaker called out, but there was no reply. He entered the vaulted kitchen where the collection of copper pans and utensils rattled on their hooks as if possessed. But when he looked around, the seat which slid open to hide the salt from the tax collector was empty.

Retracing his steps, he found himself in the dining room with the *pisé* floor, but neither was there anyone hiding under the table stolen from a monastery. When he tugged open the door to the *grand salon*, all that could be found were the bodies of three dead house martins.

Pounding up the stone spiral staircase with its lamentable repairs, he headed along the corridor hung with faded tapestries. It was as he knelt down to look underneath Émilie Fraisse's bed that the matchmaker spotted his love letter, which had stiffened in the sun, lying on her night table next to a glass of quivering water. He saw the bite mark where his signature had been and reread what he could of his writing which had bled because of the succulence of the rum-laced *crème pâtissière*. And as his eyes moved over the outpouring of adoration, the unwept tears of longing that had been trapped inside him for twenty-six years made him wince with pain. Grabbing the pen next to the bedside lamp, he signed the letter for a second time and left it to search the tower.

Once he had been through the entire château calling her name until he was hoarse, he staggered like a drunkard back across the courtyard as the wind tormented him and sections of the crenellations thudded to the ground around him. When he reached the drawbridge, an agonising roar made him turn round and he saw to his horror the chapel roof opening up like a can lid. For several seconds it hung in the air, as competing gusts tried to snatch it right and left. Suddenly they both let go and it plummeted from the sky in haunting silence and crashed to the ground several feet behind him. It was then that Guillaume Ladoucette fled.

When the matchmaker pounded on the door of the Bar Saint-Jus to be let in, there was already a considerable crowd inside trying to forget the lives they had wasted, and were about to lose for ever. When his knocking was eventually heard, the door was opened and he was pushed inside by the maniacal wind. As several villagers wrestled it shut again, Guillaume Ladoucette immediately asked whether anyone had seen Émilie Fraisse. There was a moment's silence before Sandrine Fournier and Monsieur Moreau both said that they remembered seeing her heading towards the woods. The matchmaker ordered a drink and sat by the window. And as the wind coming in underneath the door clawed at his legs, Guillaume Ladoucette knew that the châtelaine didn't stand a chance.

Just as the villagers were about to start the lengthy process of confessing their sins, there was a furious pounding at the door. His heart tightening, the matchmaker immediately got up to unlock it. However, it wasn't Émilie Fraisse who staggered inside, but a man with a beard like Spanish moss drifting down to his umbilicus.

'It's Patrice Baudin the pharmacist!' cried Modeste Simon, suddenly finding her voice for the first time in seven years. 'He's recovered!'

It wasn't until midday that those slumped on the floor of the Bar Saint-Jus began to rouse, stirred by the shrill call from their stomachs alerting them to the fact that it was lunchtime. The first to wake was Fabrice Ribou who had escaped the confusion of legs and arms on the floor by sleeping on top of the bar, as was his privilege as owner. Assuming he was in bed, he immediately rolled over to reach for the glass of water on his nightstand, and instantly dropped onto Yves Lévèque causing the only fracture of the last twenty-four hours. Once the villagers had settled their arguments over whose limbs were whose, they got to their knees and it wasn't long before they were able to stand. Eventually, they found that they could focus, and even remembered their own names. When they staggered out of the bar, and saw the frightful state that the village was in, their hearts immediately soared knowing that the chances of the English buying homes in Amour-sur-Belle were now even more remote.

Guillaume Ladoucette, who was not in the least hung over, stepped out into the new day and hurried off in search of his mother. Once he had got past the goat in the hallway which was scattering droppings across the floorboards like marbles, he found Madame Ladoucette sitting at the kitchen table next to a tiny pile of duck feathers happily making an eiderdown, with a foie gras on the stove.

Satisfied that she was unharmed, the matchmaker immediately fled to the château and discovered its courtyard pitted with crenellations. Picking his way through the remains of the chapel roof, he pushed open the door bleached fossil-grey by the sun and called for Émilie Fraisse. But the only reply was silence. His stomach writhing, he then searched the woods, calling her name as he clambered over crippled trees, their intimate roots exposed to the world. Not knowing what to do next, the matchmaker returned to Heart's Desire. As he was lifting Gilbert Dubuisson's window box out of the shop, Didier Lapierre, the carpenter, walked past and told him that all the villagers apart from Émilie Fraisse had now been accounted for.

The matchmaker, who hadn't eaten all day as despair had flooded his appetite, returned to the château. After searching every room, he combed the fields and then set out into the woods again with a torch. When he returned home in the pale early hours defeated, Guillaume Ladoucette took out Émilie Fraisse's Nontron hunting knife with its boxwood handle and ancient pokerwork motifs, placed it in the dip of his chest which his grandfather had said was an ideal place to keep salt when eating a boiled egg, and tried to sleep. But sleep never touched him.

The following morning, the *Comité des Fêtes* announced that the celebrations to mark Patrice Baudin's recovery from vegetarianism would be held that afternoon. Many of the villagers hoped that the fact that now that the lunacy was finally over Amour-sur-Belle's miserable standing in the Périgord Vert would improve. But it was not the only reason why the residents were grateful for the man's return. Not only would they no longer have to travel to Brantôme with their prescriptions, but the pharmacist's surprise arrival in the Bar Saint-Jus had distracted the drinkers from confessing their abominable sins.

For once, there were no arguments about the menu. The bodies of fourteen chickens had been found among the church gravestones, five dead cows had been picked up in three of the Rues du Château, seven lifeless pigs had been dragged down from rooftops, numerous deceased ducks had been scooped out of the dry moat and seven sheep carcasses had been found dotted around the balding maize fields.

When word got round that help was needed for a feast, the villagers started hunting out their spits and barbecues. They brought their apparatus to the field where members of the fête committee were decorating the fences with uprooted sunflowers.

Guillaume Ladoucette, his brain furred from lack of sleep and his stomach rolling with anxiety, had not the slightest intention of attending. After thanking the glazier for coming so promptly, he picked up the cushion with the hand-embroidered radish, took it outside, and shook off some soil he had just spotted. Returning inside, he decided to give the floor yet another sweep. As he was putting the broom away, the door opened. It was Stéphane Jollis.

After the two men embraced, the baker then headed for the chair with the peeling marquetry, his shoes more floury than usual as he had been at work since just after dawn baking for the festivities. Guillaume Ladoucette, his bare feet hunting for a cool patch underneath the desk with the ink stain, apologised for suddenly dashing off during the fishing expedition. After pouring them both a glass of Bergerac, the matchmaker offered his friend a walnut, which was refused as he had his own to get through. He then told Stéphane Jollis of his love for Émilie Fraisse; how he had eventually replied to her letter twenty-six years later; how, in the most romantic of gestures, he had slipped it inside one of the baker's *millefeuilles*; and how she hadn't realised that it was from him because the succulence of the rum-laced *crème pâtissière* had made the letter go soggy and she had swallowed his signature. The worst of it, the matchmaker added, the weight of his heart reducing his words to almost a whisper, was that she was still missing.

As the baker poured the matchmaker another glass, he assured him that Émilie Fraisse would be found at some stage, adding that even Patrice Baudin had turned up eventually. He then offered to make a search of people's gardens and the woods.

'I've already looked,' said the matchmaker flatly.

Announcing that he had to get back to work, Stéphane Jollis stood up. But before he left, he thanked the matchmaker for the part he had played in helping him to find the delectable Sylvette Beau, who would never have come into the bakery if it wasn't for the rumour that a love letter had been discovered in one of his cakes. He then added, while heading for the door, that if he didn't see the matchmaker at the fête that afternoon he would come to find him and carry him there himself.

Guillaume Ladoucette remained sitting on the swivel chair and, just as he was wondering whether to search the fields again, the door opened. It was Yves Lévèque with his arm in plaster. The matchmaker got up immediately to help him with the door. The dentist thanked him, walked to the cushion with the hand-embroidered radish and sat down.

As the dentist started to recount how he hadn't enjoyed his time at the Truffle Museum, Guillaume Ladoucette, who felt he had exhausted his cassoulet simile, immediately started searching for other culinary words of wisdom. But it hadn't mattered, the dentist continued, because they had had such a rapturous time at the Auberge de la Truffe that it had more than made up for it. Denise Vigier had been the most sublime company, he said, adding that he felt such a fool for not having recognised her countless virtues before. And when the matchmaker asked whether he wanted him to arrange another date with her, the dentist replied that he did indeed, and the sooner the better. It was then that Yves Lévèque reached his long, pale instruments of torture inside his sling, drew out a gold nugget and placed it on the desk in front of the matchmaker with the words, 'I'd like you to have it.' Guillaume Ladoucette replied that he couldn't possibly, but the dentist, who had clutched it throughout the night of the mini-tornado praying to St Anthony that the grocer would survive, was insistent.

Stéphane Jollis kept his word. As soon as he saw that the matchmaker hadn't turned up to the fête to celebrate Patrice Baudin's recovery from vegetarianism, he went in search of him. Finding Heart's Desire empty, he went to Guillaume Ladoucette's home and discovered him in the back garden checking his potatoes. It wasn't until the baker threatened to sit on the crop if he didn't come with him that the matchmaker reluctantly followed.

As they arrived at the trestle tables decorated with sunflowers in the shade of the lime trees, an unsavoury argument about the seating arrangements was taking place. Gilbert Dubuisson was trying to encourage Sandrine Fournier to sit next to him, but the assistant ambulant fishmonger was refusing. Modeste Simon, who hadn't stopped talking since regaining her power of speech, following the unexpected return of Patrice Baudin, was trying to persuade Lisette Robert to swap places with her so that she could sit next to the pharmacist. But the midwife was refusing to move because she was saving the place next to her for the man from the council. Madame Moreau was demanding to be moved as Madame Ladoucette was making eel impressions at her. And Didier Lapierre, the carpenter, didn't want to sit next to Denise Vigier on account of what her grandmother had done during the war.

The villagers were suddenly distracted from their squabbles by the arrival of the man from the council, whose trousers now fitted. Not only did they fail to understand how he had been invited, but neither could they fathom how he managed to get a place next to Lisette Robert. But what they were even more insistent upon knowing was when he was going to take away the municipal shower. Jean-François Lafforest replied that the decision wasn't up to him and they would probably have to wait until the end of the summer. He was spared further questioning by the announcement that the food was ready.

Several villagers sat praying for a mini-tornado every year as platters of blushing beef; pork infused with white wine, garlic and thyme; spit-roasted ducks wrapped in bacon; whole golden plump chickens and chunks of mutton coated in garlic, rosemary and ginger mustard were placed on the tables. As the villagers picked up their knives and forks and started to eat, a rare moment of tranquillity fluttered through Amour-sur-Belle.

Guillaume Ladoucette, however, was far from at ease. As he sat with his bare feet cooling on the grass, he failed to enjoy the succulence of the pork. Neither did he take delight in the mustard crust on the mutton. He didn't even ask for someone to pass him the Cabécou when the cheeses were served. Instead, he just thought of the châtelaine and the terrible death that had befallen her and how he was to blame for not having found her in time.

It was after everyone had been served one of Stéphane Jollis's *puits d'amour*, a choux pastry love-well engorged with rum-laced *crème pâtissière*, that the baker nudged the matchmaker and said, 'There she is.'

Guillaume Ladoucette turned round and saw to his astonishment Émilie Fraisse walking barefoot towards them in an antique emerald dress that not only appeared to have been shorn off at the knees, but was ripped in several places. Her hair, which was usually pinned up with something that sparkled, trickled over her shoulders festooned with leaves. And her knees were no longer the colour of raspberry stain, but smeared with mud.

Silence fell as the villagers put down their spoons and listened as the châtelaine explained herself. When the mini-tornado struck, she had been in the woods looking for summer truffles. As the trees let out their dreadful moans as they fell to their deaths, and the birds were too terrified to call, she became disorientated and was unable to find her way back to the château. Fearful that she may go the way of Patrice Baudin, she sought refuge under the still-warm body of a wild boar, which had died in shock. Upon waking the following morning, she returned home and was just crossing the courtyard when part of the crenellations plunged to the floor in front of her. Terrified, she fled back to the woods where she spent a second night, hiding underneath the door of the old hunters' shack. She had only just summoned the courage to return to the château, and, seeing how badly damaged the village was from her bedroom window, came at once to see whether anyone had survived.

But the villagers had stopped listening by then. Their curiosity sated, as soon as the châtelaine drew breath again, they picked up their spoons and lowered their heads. Guillaume Ladoucette then gave the baker an elbow in his considerable flank. Instantly recognising its meaning, Stéphane Jollis shuffled up and Émilie Fraisse sat down between them. The matchmaker pushed his *puit d'amour* with its caramelised top in front of her and passed her his spoon. Émilie Fraisse then turned towards Guillaume Ladoucette with eyes the colour of fresh sage and whispered, 'Thank you for the letter.' But the matchmaker was unable to reply.

When everything had been eaten, and Guillaume Ladoucette had recovered his power of speech, he offered to accompany Émilie Fraisse back to the château. Once there, they stood on the drawbridge looking in despair at the courtyard pitted with enormous crenellation stones. The matchmaker, sensing the depth to which the châtelaine's heart had spiralled at the sight of such devastation, immediately strode inside and announced that he would hoist them back up himself and if the rope snapped he would simply try again. Worried about her heirloom vegetables, Émilie Fraisse then led him to the garden through the scattered bones of the chapel roof. Despite the volley of roof tiles that had landed among them, the ancient varieties were largely unscathed. Émilie Fraisse picked up a couple of baskets that had been blown against the garden wall, and handed one to Guillaume Ladoucette. As they picked some of the round black radishes, Émilie Fraisse asked the matchmaker whether he remembered the summer when the château was between owners and a group of them slipped in, dressed up in dented breastplates and ran round playing hide-and-seek among the antiques and junk-shop furniture. And Guillaume Ladoucette replied with a smile that he did. As they helped themselves to the square podded peas, the matchmaker asked whether she remembered how their gang, the Wet Rats, so called because they lived near the Belle, attacked the Bog Weeds every Thursday afternoon with catapults. And the châtelaine replied with a smile that she did. And, as they filled their baskets with strawberry spinach, Émilie Fraisse asked him whether he remembered when they used to go out and steal apples and bake them in the ashes of a fire outside the den they made in the woods. And Guillaume Ladoucette replied with a smile that he did.

As they walked back to the château, Émilie Fraisse fell silent and when the matchmaker asked her what was wrong, she admitted that she was still too frightened to stay there. Guillaume Ladoucette then said that she was welcome as his guest while it was being made safe, and she dashed in to collect a couple of antique dresses which had been shorn off at the knees.

When they arrived at the matchmaker's home, he put the bag of heirloom vegetables on the kitchen table and carried her case up to one of the spare bedrooms. As she was washing her hands and knees in the bathroom, he went outside and picked a white dahlia from the edge of his *potager* which he put in a vase by her bed. When he came back down, Émilie Fraisse was looking at the handbell which Madame Ladoucette rang in the street during the war whenever De Gaulle had been on the radio from London. 'The house is just as I remember it,' she said, turning to gaze at his father's shotgun mounted over the fireplace. The matchmaker then took out the old water bottle filled with homemade *pineau*, and a couple of glasses, and they spent the rest of the evening at the kitchen table recounting the years they had lost. When, in the early hours, they both started to feel hungry again, Guillaume Ladoucette served them both a bowl of cassoulet. And it was then that Émilie Fraisse found her little green button.

Both too weary to stay up any longer, Guillaume Ladoucette decided to risk the wrath of the council and ran Émilie Fraisse a bath, leaving out for her the most exquisite bar of soap from the bottom shelf. Once she had finished, and disappeared into her room in her white cotton dressing gown with the dark blue flowers, the matchmaker ran another for himself and experienced the unparalleled joy that he had been denied for too long. Again he saw the wondrous sight of the islands of his knees rising out of the water, and his hairy toes lined up underneath the taps. And he stayed lapped by the sweet-smelling water until he found himself asleep in it, his moustache afloat.

Quietly shutting his door so as not to disturb his guest, he then got into bed, pulled the sheet over him and turned out the light. As the perpetual breeze fluttered in from the window, he relived the moment when he turned round at the fête and saw Émilie Fraisse in her torn antique emerald dress.

Just as he was wondering what delectable delight he would make her for breakfast, the door opened. He then heard the sound of a pair of small bare feet crossing the wooden floor, and felt the châtelaine, who was unable to bear being apart from him any longer, slip in next to him, her quicksilver hair caressing his arm as it fell. Pulling Émilie Fraisse towards him, Guillaume Ladoucette told her everything he had written in the letter, and when he had finished his outpouring of love, he started again. And by the time he had got to the bit about always loving her, he heard the rhythmic rise and fall of her sleeping, and he turned on his back into his usual position, his arms straight down his sides as if already dead in his coffin.

As he wondered what he would do if he ever lost her again, a tear suddenly ran down the side of his face into his ear. Promising himself that he would never let her go, he turned onto his side and tucked into the warm contours of her body. Sheltered in the harbour of Émilie Fraisse, he fell asleep and was lost in the production of his monstrous snores. And it was only Émilie Fraisse, woken by the uproar, who heard the sound of a freshly laid egg rolling across the landing.

Julia Stuart

Can you tell me a little about yourself? Where do you live now? Are you married? Family? Pets—golden retriever or goldfish?

I live in southeast London, but would much rather be in southwest France. While I don't own any pets, I do have a fiancé, Digby, whose tail wags when I arrive home. I used to have a budgie, long since dropped off her perch, some of whose feathers I keep in a wooden box on my mantelpiece. I'm due to marry in September, unless, of course, Digby discovers the dead budgie feathers and heads for the hills.

What sparked your imagination to write a novel set in Périgord?

I fell in love with the beauty and character of the place while visiting on holiday. This is a region that dedicates itself to the high arts of eating and drinking. Even the churches shut for lunch. Some residents were still washing their laundry in river water when I was born, and it wasn't that long ago that they stopped ironing their ducks before plucking them to enable the feathers to come out more easily. I couldn't resist.

Did you sample the five-course speciality truffle meal at the Auberge de la Truffe?

I did indeed sample the special truffle menu so that I could describe it in the novel. It was an absolute joy. And the waiter did actually wish me '*bonne continuation*' as I soldiered through the numerous courses. While it was the most expensive meal I've ever bought, it was worth every Euro. In fact you save money in the end because it takes at least four days for your appetite to return.

I love the way you repeat phrases such as 'the scandalous ramparts', the dentist's 'instruments of torture' as well as the 'fishing/picnic' scenes involving Guillaume Ladoucette and his friend Stéphane Jollis. How did you develop this style?

I think the repetition may have been influenced by Alexander McCall Smith's *The No. 1 Ladies' Detective Agency*. I found it reassuring that Precious Ramotswe could always be found sipping bush tea or rattling around in her tiny white van. I wanted to give my readers some comforting familiarity along the way, which hopefully heightens the surprises. I hadn't intended to repeat the competitive picnics, but, after the second one had taken place, I felt it was only fair to allow both gentlemen a deciding best of three.

Do you enjoy cooking and have you got a favourite cassoulet recipe?

I don't enjoy cooking at all. It brings on a bout of performance anxiety. While I admit I'm capable of grotesque creeping as far as my publishers are concerned, the following is absolutely true: the best cassoulet I've ever tasted was cooked by my publisher Transworld's head of sales. He served it at his home to trade buyers in an effort to seduce them into taking vast quantities of my book. The recipe was from *Goose Fat and Garlic* by Jeanne Strang.

How did you research how Stéphane Jollis does his Sunday morning baking?

I spent three months in Périgord Vert writing and researching the novel. During that period I interviewed a baker in Brantôme, and watched him slash the loaves with a razor blade that he kept in his mouth before shovelling them into an ancient oven. I also interviewed one in Mareuil and returned twice at 7 a.m. to watch him make his *pâtisserie* and *viennoiserie*. I was in heaven. He even let me roll up a croissant. His wife pointed out that if a love note had been hidden inside a *millefeuille* it would go soggy. She was right, of course, so I made it part of the plot. We still write to each other.

Do you envisage a sequel?

I do indeed. After all, finding love is only the first hurdle.

How do you set aside time to write alongside a very busy life as a journalist?

Something had to give and it was my social life and cleaning my flat. I wrote almost half of the novel in about six months during weekends and in the evenings. I then took three months off work and completed it in France within ten weeks. It was one of the happiest periods of my life.

Do you have any burning ambitions to fulfil?

I would like to write more novels and travel in style on the Orient Express. I have promised Digby that if ever we could afford such luxury, I would resist the urge to provide our fellow passengers with an entertaining whodunit by poisoning him.

Jane Eastgate

PICTURE CREDITS: COVER: © Getty/Photographer's Choice. Louise Bagshawe photograph and page 198 © Mads Perch. Ray Connolly photograph and page 334 © Mads Perch. Julia Stuart photograph and page 478 © Mads Perch. Back jacket © Mads Perch. GLAMOUR: pages 6 & 7: © Getty/Altrendo Images. LOVE OUT OF SEASON: pages 200 & 201 © Rachel Ross. THE MATCHMAKER OF PÉRIGORD: pages 336 & 337 © Annie Boberg @ The Organisation.
ACKNOWLEDGMENTS: LOVE OUT OF SEASON: *I Can See Clearly Now*, written by Johnny Nash, is published by Warner Chappell Music Ltd. *YMCA*, written by Jack Morali, Henry Bololo and Victor Edward Willis, is published by EMI Music Publishing Ltd. *Smoke Gets In Your Eyes*, written by J. Kern and O. Harbach, is published by Warner/Chappell Music Ltd in association with Universal Music Publishing Ltd. *Brown Sugar*, written by Mick Jagger and Keith Richards, is published by ABCKO Music Ltd., Onward Music Ltd and Westminster Music Ltd. *I'm So Excited*, written by Anita Pointer, June Pointer, Ruth Pointer and Trevor Lawrence is published by EMI Songs Ltd. *You're So Vain*, written by Carly Simon, is published by Campbell Connelly and Co Ltd.

Printed and bound by GGP Media GmbH, Pössneck, Germany

601-041 UP0000-1